# THE
# WOODBENDER

Tripp Berry

THE WOODBENDER
Book one of: War of the Nephilim.

Three Strands Publishing, LLC
Livermore Falls, Maine 04254

Cover art by www.100covers.com.
Cover layout and chapter graphic designs by Kim Couture, K&J Couture
Designs, Jay, Maine. www.behance.net/kjcdesignsme.
Map by Edward Snyder, www.fiverr.com/rogue451.

Ebook: ASIN B0B5PKKLTQ
Paperback: ISBN 978-1-7345735-6-5
Hardcover: ISBN 9798879599312
Edition: 1.13 2024.11.28

# Also by author Tripp Berry

**War of the Nephilim Series**
Book 1:    *The Woodbender*
Book 2:    *The Storming of Blackstone Castle*
Book 3:    *Crimson River Yard*, A Side Adventure
Book 4:    *Windward on the Sea of Fire*
Book 5:    *Hero of Ulneer*
Book 6:    TBD

**Business Books**, as Bob Berry
*Buying Bacon:* Practical Finances for Small Business Owners
*Pipe Wrench to Payroll:* Grow Your Business from Self-Employed to CEO

*For my Granddad, Robert L. Berry Sr.*
*A better man I've never known.*

*To my wife, Lisa-Anne Berry,*
*my sweetness revealed,*
*always without end.*

# Parental / Trigger Warning

DINOSAURS. You heard there were dinosaurs in this book. Well, there are! Tyrannosaurs, Triceratops, Brachiosaurs, Stegosaurs, Allosaurs, Ankylosaurs, Velociraptors, and lots of Scelidosaurs stomping all through the pages of this book. More, too. Dinosaurs are cool.

Dinosaurs will probably attract younger readers. Parents, I want to talk to you about that.

I love kids. I've raised three of my own. I work with kids in youth group and Sunday school at our church. I'm a big kid myself. The very last thing I want to do is say something to negatively impact a child.

In this book, violence happens. There's quite a lot of it, medieval style, so sensitive readers should be careful. There's an intense scene where someone is strapped down and beaten with a stick, similar to a modern-day caning still practiced in places today. In this book, sex is implied but never described. If someone loses an article of clothing, it isn't described. People's desire for each other is discussed. Trigger warning: slavery and cruelty are used to show the evil in men's hearts. There's lots of foul language, but no modern swear words. Dragonscrape. I'd call it PG-13. By young adult standards as a genre, this book is, I think, moderate to heavy. But I can be old-fashioned in this regard. I'd let my teens read this, but not my pre-teens.

If you let your child watch Jurassic Park, Star Wars, James Bond, and Marvel, there's really nothing here they haven't seen on screen. If not, I encourage you to find a different book for your younger kids. I recommend Alcatraz and the Evil Librarians, by Brandon Sanderson. It's a delight and not just for kids.

I am, thankfully, in no position to tell you how to raise your kids. That's your job, not mine. If you have a concern, read this book before deciding whether to let them. And I urge you to ask for wisdom from the source of all wisdom. Kids are a challenge. Us parents need all the help we can get.

# Table of Contents

# MAP

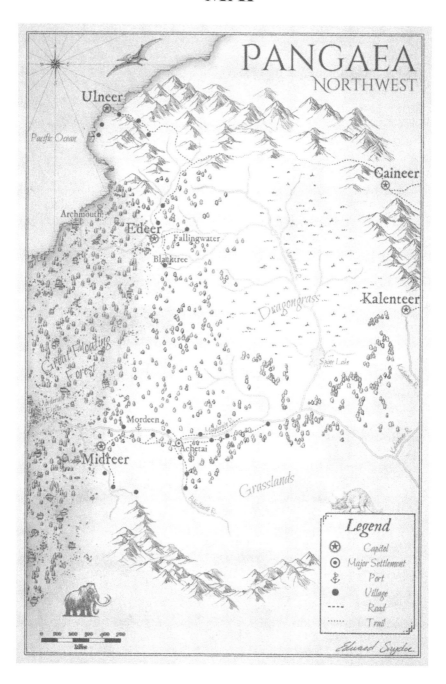

# Prologue
## Black in the Moonlight

KENAN froze in place, one hand on his walking stick, the other holding up a bundle of firewood. An enormous tree rose nearby, and a small flock of bluebirds flew a curve around the trunk. "What was that?"

"What was what?" Nehamane asked, curling his lip. "You're always hearing things."

"Well, I heard something. I thought someone yelled." Kenan dropped his bundle of wood on a root big enough to serve as a table.

His older brother frowned at the bundle and kicked the root with a booted foot. He turned his perpetual grimace back on Kenan. "Pick that up. Our mother will..."

They both heard the yell this time.

Nehamane dropped his own bundle into the forest duff. "What're you waiting for? Let's go!"

Kenan followed his running brother through the forest of gigantic trees, massive ferns twice their height, and tall bushes covered in flowers. A pair of darterdragons burst out of a thicket, chasing a chipmunk. The sun slanted beams of warm light in the late afternoon.

They soon reached the dragonring, the defensive barrier surrounding their village to keep wild animals out. Sharpened stakes of varying diameters and heights pointed upward at an angle to deter wild animals, like a stalkdragon or, worse, a mawdragon. They slipped between the big poles while tiptoeing through knee-high stakes to avoid getting poked. Both men jumped a narrow but deep ditch and continued through the village gardens towards Blacktree.

Nehamane skidded to a stop, leaving a furrow in a patch of carrots. "I just heard it!"

Kenan stopped next to him. "Another yell?"

"No, someone playing a reed flute. Of course, a yell. A woman!"

"Which way did it come from?"

Nehamane glowered at him. "That's what I'm..."

A female shriek again echoed amongst the massive tree trunks. The voice sounded familiar. Perhaps some young women were playing a game? He heard another shriek, then several more in fear.

Kenan pointed. "That way!"

They took off in the direction of the cries. Kenan's hand-axe handle slapped his thigh as he ran, passing through gardens and below fruit trees between the giant, black-barked trees of his village.

Kenan, now in the lead, took one trail, then angled off on another, vaulting over some yellowberry bushes. He heard another cry up ahead. Images of a marauding hissdragon filled his mind. But he remembered the games he played as a child, too. There'd been much screaming and yelling. Could this simply be a game amongst teenagers?

He skidded to a halt at the orange-dyed marker. It read, "Women's bathing area. Steer clear or face our wrath." He knew it well. He hadn't been beyond this marker since he'd been a teenager, when he'd been caught in the tree over the pool where the women bathed and chatted. Wrath indeed. His instincts said the sign didn't matter if someone was hurt. His community's culture stopped him short. What if one of his sisters caught him? Or his mother? Or, worse, his seventhmother? That woman could peel a man with a glance.

Nehamane caught up, running into him from behind. "What're you doing, you dragonstool? Oh, yeah. We can't go there. We need to go back to..."

"No, Nehamane," Kenan objected. "If someone's in real trouble, we should go help."

"Listen to me, boy. We'll do what I..."

Another yell came from not far past the sign. Was that a man's voice? Then he heard a noise quelling all hesitation: the guttural choking of someone in physical distress.

Kenan charged forward, sprinting down the unfamiliar trail, Nehamane's steps thumping behind. They didn't go far and reached the open area by the pool of water, contained by a short stone wall and fed by a gushing spring.

He stopped in his tracks again, his brain not capable of understanding his eyes. Nehamane thudded to a stop next to him.

A huge, green and brown fandragon lay on its stomach at the far end of the clearing. It stretched nearly thirty feet long, which was twice the size of any he'd seen in the nearby swamps. Its large fan, turning red near the top, stood at least twice his height off the ground. Large baskets had been lashed to its back with rough rope, several on each side of the fan.

Next to one of the baskets stood a man in leather armor, wearing a short sword on his hip and a shield on his back. He wrestled an unconscious woman up and over the lip of the basket. She was almost bare. Other baskets were already crowded with unconscious women, legs and arms sticking out haphazardly. A couple of baskets contained girls in their preteen years. One girl, no more than eight years old, stared at him with wide eyes.

Beside the creature stood dozens of other women in various states of dress or lack thereof. Their hands were bound high behind their backs. A cord connected each one by the neck in two rough columns. Most of them had fat lips or bloody noses. He knew all of them and was related to many. Three were sisters.

Older women or small children lay around the area on the ground or floating face down in the pool. None moved. Blood splatter on the ground shone wet and bright against the forest floor.

Thirty rough men worked in the area. They had varying armor of wood, leather, brass, or bronze. Each had a weapon and shield to hand, surrounding and threatening the last of the women to be tied into the column. A few were leering and jeering at the women, but most were quietly performing their tasks with brusque efficiency.

"You!" came a shout from the closest man. He stood short, bulging with muscles, and in his middle years. Massive hairy arms, painted red from shoulder to knuckle, flexed out the sides of a wide, leather vest covered in brass discs. A shield on one arm covered his side. His bald head dripped in sweat and dark, beady eyes glinted at him. He was the ugliest man Kenan had ever seen. His exposed red skin puckered everywhere, crisscrossed with random scars.

The ugly man pointed a notched shortsword at Kenan. The bronze blade had been bloodied and bent, but the man twirled it once with practiced ease, as an extension of his arm. "Don't you move, tree rat," the man growled. Other men were looking at him, now. Several drew their own weapons.

Kenan stood, jaw agape. He turned to Nehamane, but his brother was gone. Women cried. Bodies oozed blood. All the men looked at him. A man in shiny metal armor squared his body towards him, his face shadowed inside a steel helm. Even the fandragon turned its massive head and eyed him. An older sister, gagged and standing naked in the column with her arms tied high between her shoulders, plead to him with her eyes. Run!

Time to go. Kenan sidled back.

"Stand right there, tree rat!" The man growled at him in a strange accent.

Kenan took another step back.

The man growled again and quick-walked towards Kenan, shield up. A menacing, white spider painted on the shield made Kenan's knees go weak.

An arrow arced over the approaching man's shoulder and ripped past Kenan's left ear. He felt a tug and a sharp pain. The archer yelled, "Cols, get out of the way, man!"

Cols kept charging towards Kenan.

The arrow and his bloody ear did what Kenan's mind and heart could not. Kenan spun and ran for his life, away from the look of glee in Cols' scarred face as he charged.

Kenan sprinted. His legs pumped fast, leaping logs and stones, ducking underbrush, and dodging vegetation. He didn't know where he was going. He ran away from the thumps of booted feet and grunts of exertion of the man behind. Cols kept pace, shield and bronze sword at the ready, always smiling his battle hunger at him.

Kenan saw a massive black trunk straight ahead. He sprinted up the root, leapt, and grabbed the bark. Cols ran right behind. Kenan pulled himself up by arms alone and picked up his legs. He heard the metal of Col's bronze sword bite into the bark just below him. Frantically, he pulled himself higher. He tried, failed, and finally found foot purchase, his roughened boot soles gripping. He climbed higher.

"Come down 'ere!" Cols shouted. His voice was not only raspy but high for such a wide-chested man.

Kenan climbed higher.

Cols changed tack. "Listen, I just want to talk, see?"

Kenan reached the first branch but continued past, up along the massive trunk.

"Fine," said Cols.

Kenan glanced down to see Cols rooting around in the duff. He came up with a fist-sized nut. Kenan climbed higher.

A brief grunt was followed by a thud and pain in Kenan's leg. But he continued to climb.

A man with a bow trotted up to the tree.

Cols bounced on his feet. "E's right there! Stick 'im with an arrow!"

"I see 'im, 'old on," came the reply from the archer.

Kenan hauled himself up on a wide branch just as an arrow thudded into the bark next to his thigh.

Cols yelled, "You missed! 'Ow could you miss? We 'ave 'im treed!"

"'E moves fast, Cols. 'E's like a big squirrel."

"Shut up, you useless dragonscrape. Give me that thing. I'll shoot 'im myself."

The archer didn't give his weapon to Cols.

Kenan ran down the branch, angled left at a fork, then leapt a good fifteen feet to a branch leading him higher into the tree.

"Woah," Cols said. "Look at 'im go."

Out of the corner of his eye, Kenan saw the archer nock smoothly and draw. Kenan ran quickly up the branch, exchanging a little vulnerability for elevation.

The arrow ripped by his stomach so close he felt its passing. He'd had no idea arrows didn't glide through the air. They didn't fly or float. They *ripped* through the air, as if tearing the wind open for itself. He'd never been downrange of an archer. He kept moving.

"Silt! I don't see 'im anymore," said the archer.

"My old blood-mother can shoot better than you, you muddy eel!"

As Kenan reached another, yet higher, branch, a third man trotted up to the tree.

"What's going on?" he asked.

"That tree rat," Cols responded. "'E's up in this 'ere tree."

"So, 'oo's going to climb it?" the archer asked.

The three men just looked at each other.

After a pause, Cols said to the archer, "You missed 'im. Go get 'im. 'Ere, take a sword."

"I'm no squirrel, Cols. I'm not going up there."

"Fine. 'Immons, you go up there and ..."

The third man, Himmons, said, "Sorry, Cols. We should get back. Everyone's leaving. What's 'e going to do up there, anyways? 'E's not much more than a kid. We'll be gone before 'e can do much."

The archer offered, "You can use my firepole."

Himmons wavered. "You sure? We're not supposed to unless..."

Cols sneered. "Shut up, 'immons. You always follow the rules?"

Himmons shrugged. "'Is rules, yeah."

The archer dropped his bow and pulled something off his back next to his quiver. Cols rasped out a chuckle of anticipation, looking up eagerly into the tree branches.

Kenan wiped his brow. What to do now? If a firepole was like a thumper, then trouble was coming. He climbed a little higher, finding a spot screened from below by wide leaves. He could make his way to the edge and jump to the next tree if he had to, but not easily. It was a long way. Besides, what was the point? The next tree looked no safer than this one. They'd just follow him to the next trunk on the ground.

After some effort, the archer finally lit a little wick and held up the firepole. Peering between the big leaves, Kenan could see it was a small thumper. The wooden tube, about the length of his arm, had been tightly wrapped in cord for strength. The hole in the business end threatened black death.

The archer held the thumper out to Cols and looked up. "You know where 'e is?"

"I think so," said Cols, and pointed. "The branches keep wiggling over there. 'Ow many you got loaded?"

The archer answered, "Four. Lean into it. Should 'ave a pretty good spread."

Cols took the device and raised the tube to his shoulder, sighting down the wood barrel. He leaned into it and flicked the catch with his thumb.

The device didn't thump, like the town's thumpers. It *banged!* A gout of flame, smoke, and noise bellowed out the end.

Kenan rolled over on the branch to minimize his exposure, but too late. One of the balls exploded through a small nearby limb, sending splinters everywhere. Kenan felt a burning pain in his shoulder and the side of his face.

"Does it 'ave another go?" asked Cols.

"I'm checking," the archer responded, inspecting the wood barrel. "It's not looking good, but it 'as maybe one more shot left."

"What is going on over there?" The deep voice boomed from the direction of the pool. "Return and rally!"

"Muddy muck," muttered Cols. "Don't look at me like that, 'immons. Let's go."

The three men trotted off, but not before Cols gave the tree branches a final glare.

Kenan waited in his spot. He heard the booming voice dressing down the three men on their return. Then, amidst whimpering female voices and a few snaps of a whip, he heard the party move away. The fandragon tread lightly but still cracked branches in the forest duff and broke brush.

Kenan moved to come down but hesitated with a thought. What if this was a ruse? What if the three men were just waiting for him to come down? But some of those women were his sisters, aunts, and cousins. What if any who would follow from the village lost the trail because he waited? No, the huge fandragon would leave a clear trail. Unless, of course, they detoured up or down one of the many brooks and streams in the area. Babelwind Brook stood only a few miles to the east. Or maybe other dragons in the area would obscure the track. Then again, Kenan was a good tracker in the woods. But they might take pains to obscure their trail. When it got dark, it might be hard to follow. And where was Nehamane?

Kenan argued with himself for a quarter hour, all the while listening carefully for the White Spiders or Nehamane. Finally, he slowly descended and sprinted for Blacktree Flat.

He didn't make it. Before he could get there, he heard a man shouting at him. "Kenan! Hold up!"

Kenan almost ran by a group of twenty men and a few teenage boys. He fell in relief when he saw them.

Three of the men were older switchbrothers. He spotted two uncles. One of the boys was a nephew. The others were all from other houses of the village.

"Catch your breath, lad," one of the older men said. Kenan was 26, hardly a lad any longer. But he probably looked it to Haghal, who was 438 years old, grizzled but still solid.

"Sorry," Kenan gasped.

After a moment, Haghal continued, "Okay, now. What's going on? We heard that noise."

"A kind of thumper. The women," Kenan breathed, bent over and holding his knees. "They have them. A group of men." Another deep breath. "Took them. From their bathing pool."

The party of men all looked at one another. The teen boys went pale. Tales of other village raids were discussed from time to time at hearths and in the temple to the Almighty. But Blacktree was safe. They hadn't been attacked by anyone but a wayward bear for a hundred years or more. Yet, a few of the men had knowing and fearful looks. They remembered something from long ago.

"What happened?" Haghal demanded. "Are those splinters? Tell me, lad. How many men? Mounted or on foot? Are they still there? What happened?"

Before Kenan could answer, Nehamane ran up to the group. "Raiders! At the bathing pool! Don't listen to him. We need to go there, now!"

As soon as Nehamane finished, the party sprinted back to the pool. Kenan followed, wishing for the seventy-seventh time that Nehamane didn't resent him. It was an old pattern with him.

They each stumbled to a stop upon entering the clearing by the pool. A few of the younger men retched where they stood. Several men recognized an older woman or young child left where they lay and ran to them. Nehamane bent over their seventhmother, skinny, frail, and now with only one arm. She'd never glare at a man again.

They checked each body where they reposed. They were all dead. Some were marred by grotesque sword or axe wounds. One had a broken arrow in her back. Several were drowned in the pool, lying face down over the short stone wall around it. Each woman was over 400 years old with at least some gray in their hair. Every child was under six years old.

"They only took the younger women," one of the teens mumbled to himself. "Why? Why did they kill the others?"

Once the shock had passed, several of the men cut huge leaves from nearby bushes to lay over the bodies. The men placed the children's bodies with the old women. One leaf covered each woman and her charges from head to calf. Eighteen leaves lay unmoving in the quickening dusk.

With that done, they gathered in the center of the clearing.

"What should we do?" asked Nehamane. He frowned around at the men, his eyes always challenging.

"Go after them. Right now." Haghal's words seemed final.

Kenan stood at the back of the group, picking splinters out of his face and wiping away blood. But at this, he looked up.

"Wait," Kenan said, stopping them before they could all run off in pursuit. The fandragon trail beckoned.

"What?" Nehamane clipped out. Kenan almost stepped back from his brother.

"Easy, Nehamane." Haghal stared him down. "No reason to treat your own brother like that."

Nehamane scowled but stepped back. No one wanted to challenge Haghal.

Kenan spoke once Haghal raised an eyebrow at him. "Well, we should send the teenagers back to the village."

One of the men agreed. "Yes. They're too young to fight."

Kenan nodded. "That, and the elders need to know. We here are not enough to take them. They're at least thirty strong. We need more men."

Haghal regarded Kenan in thought. "Yes. You're right, of course." Turning to the boys, "You three, run back to the village. It's dusk now, but the moon's full and it'll be clear tonight. They'll be able to see and make their way. Gather the village elders. Tell them what happened. Get them all moving. They'll have to catch up."

"There's a few more of us unarmed," said one of Kenan's uncles who had a little gray at his temples. "We'll go with them and come back with more men and weapons."

They turned to go.

"Wait." Kenan stopped them again.

They all turned back. Nehamane glared at him.

Kenan ignored his brother as he worked at another splinter. "Shouldn't we tell them to only send half the men? We don't know if the raiders will circle back." He and the younger villagers flinched as he pulled a long splinter from his cheek. "And we should tell them we'll mark trees with axe blazes. They can run to catch up in the dark by following the blazes easier than following this trail. Wait, wait. And tell them to come with shields. They have archers."

Nehamane said, "Listen, if you think..."

Haghal interrupted Nehamane with a finger. "The lad's making sense. Do it." He nodded in approval. The boys and three of the unarmed men sped off towards Blacktree Village. "The rest of you, follow me." Kenan and the other armed villagers followed Haghal after the raiders.

The trail was clear. Broken branches and bushes showed the fandragon path. The beast often dragged its heavy tail. Booted feet marked the sides of the raider's trail. Smaller bare feet marked where some of the women marching in roped columns.

The villager's weaponry seemed paltry. Five men carried dragonpikes: long, blackwood poles with bronze heads used to defend against aggressive dragons. Three, including Kenan, held bronze hand-axes. The rest had a motley assortment of long knives, hammers, and one wooden shovel. There wasn't a single shield or sword among them.

Almost immediately, they crossed out of the dragonring. In one location, the small and medium stakes had been pulled. Two of the big outer stakes showed claw marks where they'd been pushed aside by the big paws of the massive fandragon. Where had they found one so large? Do they grow larger outside of Edeer? For Kenan was sure these men weren't from Edeer.

The men moved on, and Haghal set pace at a fast walk. The women would not move quickly. Kenan knew the fandragon could move very fast but only for a few seconds. Otherwise, its walking pace was no more than theirs. The Blacktree men should be able to catch up to the raiders quickly. Kenan used his hand-axe to mark trees every thirty paces, choosing understory trees with dark bark and white wood. He marked twice if the trail turned.

No one suggested a break.

Kenan trotted forward to Haghal, who glanced at Kenan in the rising moonlight. He kept moving forward with a quick, determined stride and an equally determined look on his lined face.

"Haghal, these men are dangerous. They're better armed, better armored, and more aggressive."

"I know," he replied. "But I'm feeling pretty aggressive myself." One of Haghal's mothers lay back by the pool under a leaf.

"Then what's your plan?" asked Kenan.

"What do you think we should do?"

It was always a test with Haghal. He was well-known as the best fighter Blacktree could offer. He'd spent much of his life training with old Medahal in the art of Jempo.

Haghal waited patiently as he walked. After a moment of thought, Kenan said, "I think we should just locate them, then trail them, leaving blazes. When they hit Babelwind Brook, if they don't just cross, we'll know whether they took it upstream or down."

Haghal grunted, nodding. "Good plan, lad. You're probably right. And fandragons are great swimmers. You'll be a town elder someday."

"Maybe. In five hundred years."

Haghal grunted again. "It happens quick. Now, spread the word."

Kenan did so. He added a reminder to be cautious of the fandragon's head and tail. Also, there were women and girls in the baskets. Nehamane glowered at him.

Nehamane's dislike of Kenan wasn't new. Nehamane was the youngest of his siblings by his father, who passed when he was young. Kenan came along as the only child of a different father, and their mother doted on Kenan when he was young. The battlefield had been clearly marked ever since.

Soon, the sky faded to full dark. Kenan stopped to mark another blaze, then ran to catch up.

They heard the distant crack of a large branch broken in the forest. Every man stopped in his tracks to listen. The fandragon was perhaps a few hundred paces ahead. They all listened carefully, their breath loud in the dark.

One of the men asked, "Was that the fandragon?"

Nehamane said, "Had to be. I think they're just up ahead,"

"You're right. They are," came a deep voice from the dark in front of them.

All the men stiffened. A few gasped.

Three arrows flew out of the night, striking three of the unarmored men of the Blacktree party full in the chest. Two of them gurgled and coughed as they went down. The third turned and sprinted right into an understory tree. The impact drove the arrow out his back, and he fell bonelessly sideways.

The entire party crouched and twisted this way and that, weapons raised. Several dodged away, looking for cover.

Three more arrows followed. One Blacktree man gasped, clutching the arrow piercing his arm. The other two arrows missed their targets.

Six men stepped forward into the moonlight, three of them dropping bows and pulling swords, hammers, and shields painted with the White Spider, which glowed white in the moonlight. Many had pieces of brass or bronze plate on their chest and forearms. The man in the center was covered in real steel armor on his head, chest, arms, and thighs. He carried what could only be a steel sword.

Fifteen against six.

"Attack!" screamed Haghal.

"Yes, do!" came the deep reply from within the steel helm. Kenan thought he saw the eyes flash orange from the deep dark of the open-faced helm.

The Blacktree men surged forward, screaming to bolster their courage. The raiders charged forward as well, silently, led by the deep-voiced man and his steel sword.

Kenan, having been behind due to his task of blazing the trees, followed at the rear of the group. He had his axe now in both hands. He paused, looking for an opening to attack in the moonlit chaos.

The groups collided with metallic clangs, grunts, and screams. Haghal lost his head immediately to the steel sword, briefly spouting blood into the air. Nehamane took a spear butt to the side of his head and dropped like a full sack of long nuts.

All six of the raiders moved forward. Almighty help him, the raiders moved so quickly. They slid to the side avoiding one blow while stabbing at a different opponent. They blocked with a shield and slipped sideways around it to stab at the ribs. They stepped back only to thrust forward with spears and swords at the onrushing villagers. These men were not just raiders. These were warriors.

The steel-clad man moved with liquid grace and ferocity. He glided around attacks, deflecting blows with an armored forearm while simultaneously slicing open thighs and stomachs. As an axe was about to bite deep into his helmet, he twisted his hips and the axe whistled past, missing by a finger. He used the twist to attack a different Blacktree man. His deep voice boomed out laughter as he fought, counting his cuts.

"Three!" Innards spilled onto dead leaves. His eyes flashed with orange light again. "Four!" Blood gushed from a deep thigh gash, black in the moonlight. His eyes shone supernaturally bright again, and a glowing orange vapor rose off his steel helm. "Five!"

A villager fell in front of Kenan. A raider with a bronze sword, mismatched armor, and shield stepped over the body. Kenan raised his axe, not sure what to do.

The man growled softly and stepped closer. Kenan stepped back, but not far enough. The man swung his sword.

Kenan deflected the blade with a wild swipe. The man moved with Kenan's parry, twisting his sword around and along Kenan's forearm. It must have missed. He didn't feel a cut. The tip of the blade flicked towards Kenan's face, and he jumped back desperately.

Something caught his heel and he fell backwards. His breath left him on impact.

"Easy, boy. You 'ave nothing more to worry you." The man brought the edge of his shield down to Kenan's face. He turned his head at the last moment. The moonlight winked out, and he knew no more.

KENAN awoke to water being poured into his mouth. He gagged and coughed. Rolling to the side, he grasped the side of his head and groaned. His head was splitting with pain.

"Quiet now, lad. Your head's split."

"Yeah," Kenan hissed through gritted teeth. "I felt that."

Wait. Where was he? When was he?

Kenan cracked his eyes. The gloom of early morning filtered in through his lashes. He laid in the forest, but most of what he could see were boots and spear shafts. Men stood all around him.

Kenan squeezed his eyes shut. The pre-dawn light hurt his head fiercely. He felt worse than after a night drinking maple beer at his secondfather's table. His switchfather's father had a liver like a chimney stone.

"Don't worry, lad. We'll leave someone here with you. We're moving on to catch those dragonscrape raiders."

Wait. "Is that you, Haghal?" Kenan creaked out.

"No, lad. It's Medahal."

Medahal. Right. Kenan groaned again as he remembered. Haghal no longer had a head.

"How am I alive?"

"The Almighty's own grace, I'd say. We thought you dead."

The large force moved off. Eventually, the forest grew quiet. With some time and coaxing from the two teen boys left with him, Kenan was able to sit up. They tied a cloth around his head and pulled him over to a root to recline. He could see better, though half his sight was still red. Somehow, he also had a deep gash down his left forearm, from elbow to wrist. Wait, no, he remembered the sword. He hadn't felt the cut at the time, but it throbbed now.

Men lay strewn through the forest, reposing quietly. The insects were not so quiet. Where had all the flies come from? There was Haghal's head, looking away from him, Kenan was relieved to see. He felt guilty for being relieved. He searched. Two of his brothers lay dead. His uncles were dead as well. Blood was spattered everywhere, drying on the forest duff. Congealed blood oozed down slanting leaves and ferns. Kenan's hair was matted with it, his overshirt crusty.

But there weren't enough men here. Kenan started a count through squinted eyes. Thirteen men lay dead. One was not from Blacktree. Twelve Blacktree men lay dead and only one of the raiders. Only one!

A teen boy said, "We lost twelve, here. Are any missing?"

Kenan winced at the too-loud words. "Yes. Five."

"Where'd they go?"

Kenan groaned at his pain. "I don't know."

"Oh."

The other boy shrugged. "Probably took them with the women."

Kenan looked again. Nehamane was missing. Where was he? But instead, he asked, "How many?"

"How many what?"

"How many of the women and girls were taken?"

"Oh. Not sure, but about forty."

Forty. God Almighty, why? Why did you allow this? Weren't you a god? What kind of god were you? Did you even exist?

Kenan lost hope, laid his head back against the thick root, and slept.

# Chapter One
# Saving Face

*56 Years Later.*

KENAN Blacktree looked up at the pair of little wrens flitting past him overhead. He listened to their song and smiled to himself. It was 1602 AC, summertime, and the earth teamed with life. Kenan took it all in, enjoying creation while he could. He knew it wouldn't last.

He carried a blackwood walking staff as tall as his shoulder, absently flicking twigs and large bugs from underfoot. His belt axe, hand knife, and a small pouch hung at his waist. His leather pack hung empty on his back. He would fill it later today.

He stood at average height, somewhat lithe and strong. His forest green overshirt covered him down to his bare knees. He carried a hand-axe at his belt and a long knife tucked in a boot.

The forest buzzed with noise. Insects of every kind flew in all directions, and birds swooped and looped to catch them. A brown bat flew higher in the canopy. Above, far beyond the tops of the massive black trees, he saw a single glidedragon against the blue sky, soaring on the wind, its long neck and longer head pointing its path forward. Birds called. Bugs buzzed. Spiders wove. Squirrels scampered. A large snake coiled nearby and watched him as he passed.

He continued walking past one of the many spring-fed pools in the area, whistling a little tune to himself. He loved the forest and the massive trees dominating the flat land west of Blacktree village. Giant black trunks, each thirty or more feet in diameter, towered up through the understory. Huge branches and copious greenery blotted out much of the sky. Not to be outdone, the early morning sun streaked through with bars of light, illuminating fluff seeds floating on air currents.

A dragonfly, bigger than a dinner tray, sped in and stopped, hovering in place just out of arm's reach ahead. They regarded each other, both inquisitive.

Kenan liked dragonflies. He'd once seen one eating a spider. Dragonflies were good. "Well, hey there, my friend."

The dragonfly dipped down, and back up.

"Careful. There's a big snake just over there. He'd probably find you tasty." Kenan pointed with a thumb.

The big dragonfly dipped again, its wings creating a downdraft and stirring up more fluff seeds. The four translucent wings, each an arm's length long, buzzed loudly.

"Are you going to let me pass? I've got work to do, you know."

The dragonfly hesitated a moment, bobbed to the side, then sped off. Did it go to find food or maybe to pester someone else? He couldn't know.

Kenan smiled to himself and wiped his dark brown hair out of his eyes, tucking it away. He'd taken to holding it back with a leather cord while he worked. He preferred his hair cut short, but Anna liked it a little longer.

Anna would soon be his betrothed. Betrothed! Just last week, his mothers had gathered, held a small feast, and made their wishes known. It was time for Kenan to take a bride, and a local woman at that.

Kenan was generally pleased with the match. Anna was beautiful and kind, though young. She was only 44. He was 82, just into his prime. His fourthmother told him he was late in taking a bride, but he wasn't so sure. Plenty of the patriarchs hadn't taken this step of life until after they were a hundred years old.

He smiled at the thought of Anna. Her beauty jumped into his mind. He thought of her as he walked, continuing down the trail. But he shook his head and picked up his pace. He had woodbending to do out in the gopher tree grove. It was a four-hour walk from Blacktree.

As he walked along, he heard voices ahead, raised in anger. One voice sounded like Johlick, one of Anna's many little brothers. Kenan hurried forward.

He came into view of a small group of teenage boys standing on the trail near a stompdragon.

The stompdragon stood impassively, chewing a flower it had found beside the trail. The animal was relatively small, as dragons go, at twelve feet long and only waist high. Gray and green, its lumpy, scaly skin held oval bone plates in lines down its back. This one was harnessed to a cart containing several empty baskets.

Johlick stood next to the beast, his hands balled into fists at his sides. His fifteen-year-old face sported a scuff like he'd been struck, and his eyes shone in defiance. His nose bled down over his lip, and his overshirt had mud on it.

Another boy, Lian, stood facing him, stance aggressive. Several others gathered around, laughing and jeering at Johlick.

Kenan's mood darkened as he stalked forward at a quick pace.

The stompdragon craned its head around to look at Kenan as he approached. One of the boys noticed and turned to see Kenan coming. The boy's eye looked puffy and red. He slapped Lian on the shoulder to get his attention. Everyone turned to face Kenan as he approached. Most were in their late teens. Lian was nearly twenty.

Kenan came to a stop before them, eyeing them all over. "Hey there, boys."

The other boys sidled back, but Lian held his ground. "Kenan."

Kenan regarded Lian. Fully grown, he stood at Kenan's height. His shoulders and chest flexed under his overshirt. The boy worked the saw pits.

Kenan met Lian's eyes. "Do I need to ask what's going on here?"

Lian answered. "No, Kenan. Just a disagreement among friends."

"Uh huh."

Two more men came through a patch of nearby ferns. The lumbermen carried axes on their shoulders. They stopped in their tracks when they saw the group.

"Kenan. We heard some shouting."

Kenan responded, "Me too."

The second lumberman said, "Want some help?" Both men scowled at the boys. They knew this group. These boys often caused trouble in the village.

"No. Thank you. I can handle this."

The men grinned at each other. They nodded and settled in to watch.

Kenan regarded Lian. The boy had an audience. He wasn't backing down now. Kenan shook his head. "You don't have to do this, Lian."

"Do what?"

"Attempt to save face. You'll lose more than your pride and position."

"Is that a threat? You don't scare me!"

"I should hope not. There's four of you. Just me and Johlick to send you away. Not good odds for us."

Lian pointed at the lumbermen. "Those two will help you."

Kenan tossed his walking staff to the side. "No, they won't. This is between you and me."

"Only because you interfered."

"Of course, I did. You're a bully, and you struck my friend."

Lian's scowl deepened. "I didn't. He tripped and fell on his own."

"Right."

"Ask him."

Kenan looked at Johlick, careful to keep Lian in view. Anna's little brother wiped his nose on his forearm, smearing blood across his face. Kenan looked back at Lian. "Don't need to. The truth is literally all over his face."

Lian subtly adjusted his body stance. "Yeah? So, what are you going to do?"

"Challenge you."

"Challenge me?" Lian turned to his friends. "He's going to challenge me!"

"Yes."

"Challenge me to do what?"

"Challenge you to apologize and walk away."

"What?"

"You heard me."

Lian sneered. "Why would I do that?"

"Because you're in the wrong. Because you made a stupid mistake. Because it's the only way you're getting out of here without harm."

"Is that so? And you're the one to give it to me?"

"No. You'll trip and fall." He nodded his head at Johlick. "Just like he did."

Lian glared at Kenan. The boy's eyes glinted with anger, fear, and finally, decision. His back big toe pressed down into his boot sole, wiggling a little twig lying in the trail.

Kenan leaned imperceptibly to one side and let his arm hang, giving Lian an open target to his face.

Lian drew his arm back and lunged with a vicious cross punch towards Kenan's head. But Kenan had already moved. The punch passed Kenan's ear, and he stepped slightly to the side, turning in towards Lian.

The boy's punch carried him forward and his back foot stepped, only to be interrupted by Kenan's instep.

Lian's momentum brought him angling down. The boy thudded off the packed earth and roots of the trail.

No one moved. Everyone watched Lian struggle, roll over, and touch his bloody lip. His eyes widened, and he spit out a piece of tooth.

Kenan looked down at the boy, keeping his body turned so he could see the other three boys from the side. "This is your moment, Lian. You can change your ways. Do what is right. Apologize now and grow."

Lian rose carefully to his feet. He glared at Kenan, at Johlick, and at the two men who could barely contain their amusement. Finally, he turned and stalked off.

Kenan sighed, then turned his full attention to the other three.

The boy with the puffy eye looked at Kenan out of his good eye. He made his own decision. The boy turned to Johlick. "I'm sorry, Johlick. I was wrong and stupid. I'll make it up to you."

The other two boys hurriedly repeated the sentiment.

The two lumbermen rose and hefted their axes. "Right then," one said. "If you three have nothing better to do, you're with us. There's nothing like good, hard work to set the mind right."

"Yes. And we'll pay wages," the other man said.

The three boys brightened.

The man continued, "To the lad's father, of course. Let's go, boys."

The boys all looked at each other, nodded to Kenan, and trotted off after the lumbermen, leaving Kenan alone with Johlick and the stompdragon.

Kenan watched as Johlick brushed the mud off his overshirt. He nodded, appreciating the boy's courage. "You okay?"

Johlick nodded. "Yeah. Thanks. I thought I was in for a beating."

"Not too bad. They didn't want to really hurt you. They wanted to feel strong."

"Lian is already strong."

"In body, yes. But that's not what bullying is about. He's not strong in his heart, and he knows it."

Johlick looked up at Kenan. "I don't understand."

"You will. And someday, so will he. Looks like you put up a fight."

"It was four to one. I had to do something."

"Yes. Of course."

Johlick sighed. "Lian will come for me."

"Maybe, but I doubt it. He now knows you'll strike back. He'll find someone else to pester. But I'd advise you to head the other way today and against spending time out here alone tomorrow. Besides, if he's going to come after anyone, it'll probably be me."

"I bet you can handle it."

"Maybe."

"Anna said you train with Medahal. You can do Jempo."

Kenan smiled at him. "Perhaps you should as well. I'll speak to your father."

Johlick brightened. "Really?"

"Yes. But Medahal doesn't take many students any longer, and you're young, yet. Whether or not he trains you will be up to him."

"Can you train me? All my friends are bigger than me."

"Maybe someday." Kenan put his hand on the boy's shoulder. "You're small for your age, but you won't always be so. Your mother and father are tall. Your brother is massive! Heh. You'll get there." Kenan stooped for his staff. "Now, what are you gathering today?"

"Brown nuts and firewood."

"Right. Head that way and gather over there. You'll find some. Stay close to the village today. I'll see you tonight."

"Okay. And Kenan, thank you. I'm glad you and Anna will be married."

Kenan smiled at the boy. "Me too."

Johlick took up the lead rope to the stompdragon and moved off into the trees. He had to pull on the lead to make the stompdragon, who'd found another flower, follow.

Kenan backtracked to make sure Lian had truly left. Seeing he had, Kenan trotted back to the west. He had a date with a gopher grove.

# Chapter Two
# The Sway of a Limb

KENAN left the trails far behind and moved west through the untamed forest. In the morning, he enjoyed rays of sun slanting through the trees. The mid-day gloom came when the leafy canopy of massive trees above all but blocked the sun.

He moved along a game trail and saw a rabbit scampering away. He checked where it went. The little side trail was heavily and recently used by game, so he used a couple of sticks, a cord, and a bent branch to set a snare. He moved on.

Kenan planned to walk straight to the gopher tree grove, but he stopped at a particular tree he recognized. Dropping his pack and walking stick in a cradle of large roots, he pulled a stray lock of hair out of his hazel eyes and inspected the giant black tree. He rubbed his hands together, spit on them, and rubbed them some more until they were dry. He climbed up on a huge, sloping root, its diameter easily as wide as he was tall, picking up speed until the trunk became a nearly vertical wall. Using his momentum, he leapt, catching the rough black bark in his hands with practiced ease. His leather boots with roughened soles found purchase in the hollows of the bark pattern as he began to climb.

About eighty feet up, he reached the branch he needed, hoisted himself up to it, and sauntered down the limb. His impeccable balance and natural grace shifted his weight in tune with the wide branch as he walked. He took a left branch. Then he took a right. The branches became thinner, no wider than his waist. He paid it little mind. Stopping, he turned, and leapt through the air to land on another limb. He continued walking down the branch, ever further from the trunk, until he found his work.

A group of branches were twisted and turned into a woven pattern. The places where they rubbed were already starting to grow into one another. Kenan eyed it closely. It was about two feet wide and four feet long. Was it ready to be cut? No, not quite yet. It would make a valuable decorative window lattice to sell in the market, but it needed another two years to finish. He made a small adjustment to the branch ends. Maybe the pattern could be a little longer. Six feet would do nicely.

He continued down the main branch, ducked under a limb, and hopped to a new branch. He ducked again as a large green beetle, shell up and wings out, thundered past his head. He gave it a frown. The insect was the size of both his fists together and would have hurt if it'd made contact. The beetle flew on, not noticing Kenan or apparently even caring.

Kenan heard a chirping far below. He looked down the long drop to see a group of darterdragons scampering past. They didn't notice him, and he smiled at the little omnivores. They were only dangerous if you were immobilized. Like, from a fall, he thought wryly. Kenan didn't mind heights, of course, but he raised his head and kept it on what he was doing.

He inspected several other bendings, making adjustments in their growth, until he nodded in satisfaction. Re-sheathing his tools, Kenan trotted down the branch, taking ever smaller limbs until he reached a much thinner branch. He eased his way out towards the end. The limb creaked and dipped under his weight. As the limb drooped and the angle steepened, he jumped, caught a branch near the edge of the tree canopy with one hand, and descended safely to within an easy drop to the forest floor. The thick duff cushioned his landing.

He collected his pack and walking stick. The little flock of darterdragons observed him from the top of a mossy log. They chirped at him, and he chirped back in perfect mimicry. Whatever he said must have irritated them because they turned and darted off through the brush. Kenan chuckled and continued westward. He whistled as he walked to ward off any nearby dragons or bears.

His thoughts turned to Anna again. Once, many years ago, they'd had a moment. They'd shared a look, a smile, that perhaps held promise. He usually kept to himself. She was so sociable, so admired by the boys of the village. Instead of pursuing her, he'd retreated.

More recently, they'd spent time together. He'd come to admire her optimism, her quick wit, and her love of life. As she grew into full womanhood, he appreciated everything about her.

He thought about her smile and the way her cheeks dimpled. He thought about the way she'd reached up and fingered the scar on his ear. He thought about her wavy blond hair and the swish of her long dress hem. He thought about the way she moved. She never just turned, she twirled. She never just walked, she almost skipped.

Kenan stopped whistling as he walked, but he didn't notice.

He felt grateful to his mothers. Now, he just needed Anna's father, Jaret, to accept the bride-price he had saved. It wasn't much. Jaret would do better to follow the Elder's teaching and send Anna to another village. He wouldn't do that, would he? The man must be in an untenable position: defy the Elders or defy the women of the village. Well, Kenan knew what he would do in Jaret's place. One didn't toy with the women of Blacktree.

Something moved, just ahead. Kenan stopped mid stride, his front foot hovering over a little clump of mushrooms. All thoughts of Anna and her family flew from his mind, and his senses went on high alert. This far from Blacktree, stumbling on an aggressive dragon held a real threat.

A narrow dragon snout poked through the sapling leaves, not ten paces in front of Kenan. He caught the motion immediately. It was indeed a big dragon. Its head was easily two feet long, with droopy nostrils. But it wasn't an aggressive dragon.

It moved again, taking a step forward. It shifted its head side to side, trying to gauge the distance between them. As it stepped, the bulk of the animal became known as it pushed aside saplings and tall ferns.

Ah, it was just a slabdragon.

This was an average specimen, female by the look, with a body more than twice his height and twenty-five feet long from nose to spiked tail. A double row of large bony slabs stood along her back, swaying back and forth as the slabdragon took another step. Its back muscles bunched and rippled as it moved.

Slabdragons typically weren't aggressive. Many of the poorer farmers used them to pull plows and thresh grain. They were only dangerous when protecting a nest.

The slabdragon took another step forward, shaking its head. It snorted loudly. Behind it, a small understory tree with a trunk a palm wide broke and fell over from the thrashing tail.

"Woah, there, girl," Kenan placated, taking a step backwards, then another. "Easy, now. I'm no threat. Your eggs taste like dragonstool. I'm not here for you."

The slabdragon's muscles bunched. The animal loomed over him.

"I'm not here for you!" Kenan shouted again as he turned and ran to the side.

Most of the larger quadruped dragons could charge quickly over a short distance but couldn't turn worth a dragonscrape. This proved true as Kenan sprinted to the side, then turned again to run on his original course. He saw the nest, half a dozen eggs cradled in a hollow made of sticks and leaves. He gave it little mind as he sprinted past. The slabdragon turned. He needed to reach the swamp quickly in case it followed.

Follow it did. He could hear the small understory trees and branches snapping as they both ran.

He gauged the distance. Could he reach the first swamp pool before the slabdragon caught up? If not, he'd have to circle around again, taking sharp corners. He could feel the ground thump as the slabdragon closed the gap.

He increased to a sprint, branches snagging and leaves slapping his face as he skirted a spring and sped towards the swamp.

Out of his periphery vision, concealed in the green ferns and leaves, he caught the outline of a toedragon's upper body, not five feet away as he sprinted past. Great. Just great. This was turning into a wonderful day.

Toedragons were carnivorous and aggressive, though somewhat skittish around humans. Each stood about thigh high, bipedal, and roughly six feet long, give or take a foot or two. Their feet each had a toe claw that jutted up and curved forward, long and sharp. One was no match for a man with a stick, let alone real weapons. But where there was one, there were a dozen, hunting together in a pack.

The toedragons screeched their aggression. He heard them to his left and right as he continued his dash towards the swamp. He heard no screech ahead. But then again, if it heard him coming – and how could it not – it wouldn't make a sound as it lay in ambush. They hunted together and were too smart for Kenan's taste. He raised his blackwood walking stick as a bar in front of him just in case.

Kenan probably couldn't outrun a pack of toedragons. But then, neither could a slabdragon.

Kenan broke out of the ferns to see the first pool of the swampy forest. A little flock of darterdragons scurried away from the opposite bank. He knew the pool, part of an old oxbow brook. The mud channel in the forest stretched to either side. A log, covered in moss and dead branches, spanned the muddy pool. He had better places to cross, but this would have to do.

Especially when the slabdragon, half covered in toedragons, erupted out of the ferns behind him.

Kenan darted across the log, deftly picking his way on the moss and through the branches. Any of the dragons could cross or wade the pool, but not quickly.

The slabdragon bugled. The high pitch noise irritated human ears. The toedragons didn't seem to mind. They did, however, mind the thagomizer.

Foot-long bone spikes tipped the slabdragon tail, which, well-muscled and flexible, swept about with abandon. Toedragons were impaled, swept aside, and crushed by the mighty tail and sharp spikes. Three died in moments. One was knocked unconscious. Two more writhed on the ground, trying to regain their feet. The rest fled into the lush forest vegetation.

Kenan watched the slabdragon regard him from across the pool, its nostrils flaring and great ribs heaving. Spittle dripped from its mouth, splattering the tall grass growing on the edge of the little pond. A few red scratches showed on its dark gray hide. The beast's wild eyes regarded him for a moment. Finally, it turned its bulk back into the ferns between the trees and pushed its way back towards its nest.

Kenan suspected a toedragon had already cleaned out the eggs. That's how they worked. But he smiled at the great beast lumbering away, admiring the design of the creature.

He wanted some of those toedragon claws, but the rest of the pack wasn't far. So, turning, he slid deeper into the watery forest, away from danger and towards his work as a woodbender.

DEEPER in the swampy forest, Kenan had to pick his way from dry spot to dry spot, sometimes climbing trees to cross brackish water via branches. Each time he stopped, he pulled a cord with loops woven into each end, slipped them over the ends of his staff, and hung it on his back. If a particularly narrow branch gave him pause, he would take the staff off and use it to help balance.

A small gaggle of noisy monkeys pestered him at one such crossing, throwing nuts at him. He caught one and threw it back. It hit the monkey square between the eyes. The funny creature looked back at him in shock. The gaggle moved off, carrying their young and screeching in outraged consternation.

He skirted a beaver bog along the dam. Fish jumped and darted around in the water while the enormous beaver regarded him warily from on top of his stick-and-mud house. Eventually, it dropped to its belly and slid into the pond, slapping a tail the size of a small tabletop on the water and diving below the surface. The splash sent all the fish scattering. A small flock of tall wading birds took flight, long tail feathers trailing behind in a dazzling display. On the far side of the bog, two giant stalkdragons lounged in the water, incredibly long necks reaching up to chew on leaves from nearby trees. A younger stalkdragon rolled in the mud on the edge of the bog. Kenan smiled and continued onward.

He finally reached the first grove of giant gopher trees. Though not quite as tall as the black trees near his village, they made up for it in girth. He approached the wall of tree trunk, shouldering his staff and picking his spot. Gripping the stringy bark, Kenan began to climb.

On the lower branches, he found small puddles of oily gopher sap. Raw, it was only good for torches. But mix a little with a small barrel of squeezed round nut oil, it made excellent, smokeless lamp oil that burned with a bright yellow light. Refined and mixed with several other extracts, it could be used as propellant in thumpers. Kenan reached into his pack and filled a jar from a dozen puddles.

He climbed higher and found his work. Numerous branches were already twisted and shaped for a myriad of uses. He favored gopherwood for its strength, flexibility, and resistance to rot. People used it in structures, ship building, cogs, and other mechanical works, as well as many other human applications.

Kenan prized it primarily for tool handles and really everything else.

Kenan moved from branch to branch of the giant trees, collecting a sampling of the long leathery leaves as he moved from spot to spot, tucking them under his belt. He twisted branches together, holding some in place with splints and twine. Making small cuts, he split branches or grafted shoots to form shapes suitable for one tool or another. It would take years to heal and grow into what was needed. But Kenan had the time. Many centuries lay in front of him and Anna.

He kept one eye on a swampdragon squishing past in the mud below. Usually, he found them sitting quietly in still pools, like submerged logs, waiting for dinner to come to the edge for a drink. When walking on land, its short stubby legs held the twenty-foot body as high off the ground as it could, dragging its heavy tail behind. Its long snout sprouted with pointed teeth.

He finished the last branch modification before climbing higher still. He found a nest of fresh bird eggs. He took two but left the rest.

Near the top of the largest gopher tree in the grove, the sky opened to him. He paused to bask in the warm sunshine. A pair of glidedragons soared in the distance, swooping around each other. Looking east, he could see the towering black trees of Edeer standing sentinel over the wild land. Far to the north, the distant hills of Ulneer roughened the horizon.

He looked for the sea to the west. He knew he wasn't far from the shore, but a great floating forest stretched for hundreds of miles out of sight.

Looking around, he found a single cluster of gopher nuts ripe for the picking.

Kenan pulled the clump of leaves he'd collected from under his belt and deftly wove himself a neat, pear-shaped basket with a single hole at the top sized to pass a gopher nut. The gopher leaves fit together so well the basket was watertight. He threaded a small vine around the mouth of the basket and hung it around his shoulder. Then he picked the fist-sized nuts and dropped them in his basket. They all fit.

Wary of the swampdragon, which was now nowhere to be seen, he descended the trees. He went to the edge of the grove, found a spot, and planted one of the nuts. With luck, this would grow and enlarge the grove. A small nearby tree showed where he had done this in the past. In a hundred years, it would be a mature gopher tree. He would climb it and remember.

Kenan finished his work with this grove, marking a tree trunk by carving in his name and the date. He considered going further out into the swamp to another grove he knew. Gopher trees did well in wet conditions. He had the time. But maybe he could be home a bit early and check on Johlick. Perhaps the boy would be with his sister, gathering in the forest around Blacktree. He could carry her pack basket for her. It only made sense to spend more time with her. Of course.

Kenan started for home, stopping for a lunch of purple fruit he picked and some cheese from his pack. He took a route well around the slabdragon nest and found a fresh deer carcass. It looked like the toedragons had more than slabdragon eggs for lunch.

He only had to backtrack once when he heard a bear in the forest ahead snapping its jaw in warning. Bears were skittish with people, but not when their cubs were nearby. He wasn't about to mess with a bear. He might as well take on the pack of toedragons.

As Kenan got closer to Blacktree, he collected up a rabbit for dinner from the snare he'd set earlier. He stuffed the little carcass in his pack and continued towards home.

He checked the angle of the sun. He was even earlier than he thought. A couple other blacktrees had branches he should tend. He headed towards the nearest one.

A man hopped over one of the huge tree roots sloping down from the tree trunk. He continued to walk but stopped when he saw Kenan. The man said, "Oh. Hello there."

Kenan didn't recognize the man. He knew everyone from Blacktree, but not this man. He was tall, with light brown hair, brown eyes, and a trimmed beard. His uncolored overshirt hung to his knees, but unlike everyone Kenan knew, he wore leggings underneath tucked into his boots. The man carried a pack and hand knife, but no weapons.

Kenan looked at the man. "Hello. I'm Kenan Blacktree. You are?"

The man stared at Kenan for a long moment, then said, "Where are my manners? Sorry. I haven't talked to anyone in a bit of time. Nice to meet you, Kenan."

"Um, you're not from around here. Are you from Shallowbrook?"

"No. Farther. Do you happen to know where I can find a dragonfly? I love dragonflies."

Kenan regarded the man. "Dragonflies?"

"Yeah. You know, four wings, long tail. They fly about. Dragonflies."

"Why are you looking for dragonflies?"

"I want one."

"Really? What for?"

"To take with me."

"Don't you think it'll just fly off?"

"I don't know." The man looked thoughtful. "Do you think it will?"

"If it's alive, then yeah. I think it will. They're fast, you know."

"Well, that's not great. I'll think on it. Maybe I can make a little leash. I could fly it along, a little like a kite, right? So, have you seen one?"

Kenan grinned at the thought. "Yes. I saw one this morning."

The man's face brightened. "Really? Where?"

Kenan didn't know what to think of this man. He appeared friendly, but who wanders the forest in search of a dragonfly? Kenan pointed. "That way."

"Fantastic!" The man moved to go in the direction Kenan had pointed.

Kenan said, "Uh, there's a village nearby."

"Oh?"

"Yes. Over there." Kenan pointed again. "Not much more than an hour's walk. There's a place to sleep there tonight. If you want."

"Oh, thank you."

"Blacktree."

"Yes, they're massive, aren't they? Majestic, really. I've never seen so many in one place."

"Yes, but no. Blacktree is the name of the village."

"Well, that makes sense."

Kenan scratched at his own short beard. "I suppose it does."

The man smiled and turned to go.

Kenan raised his finger. "Oh, one more thing. There's a pack of toedragons to the west. They've eaten today, but I wouldn't spend the night nearby. They've been bloodied, and they're likely to be in a bad mood."

The man barked a laugh. "Ha! They're never really in a good mood, are they?"

Kenan couldn't help but grin. "No. I guess they're not."

The man looked thoughtfully at Kenan. "Well, thank you, Kenan Blacktree. I'll return the favor. There's four men over that way, the direction you're going. I heard them talking. I don't think they like you."

Men talking this close to Blacktree wasn't a surprise. That they were talking about him was a surprise. "Me?"

"Are there many Kenan's in Blacktree?"

"Well, no."

"There you have it."

"What did they say?"

"Something about making you pay. One had a puffy lip. Looked like he'd been struck in a fight today."

Lian. "Right. Thank you."

"You're most welcome. And Kenan? Be careful." With that, the strange man trotted off.

Kenan just stood there as the dragonfly man disappeared into the undergrowth. What had he just seen? Kenan called out to the man. Hearing no response, he followed to talk more with him, but quickly lost sight of him. The tracks disappeared in the duff. Kenan stood a long time, looking around for the Dragonfly Man, but saw no sign of him. Finally, he gave up and turned back towards Blacktree.

Apparently, Lian didn't wait long to plan retribution. Four men meant he'd gone to get help. Help meant Asher. He'd seen them hanging around.

Several days back, Kenan had embarrassed Asher in the sparring ring. The big man had cornered Kenan's sister, so in the ring Kenan had taken the man down, bloodying him in the process. Asher and Lian apparently found two of their friends to help. Four to one. He had a feeling this was about more than bullying.

Kenan continued towards home. Though he should have circled around to avoid the men, he moved towards them. He needed to teach these men the cost of causing trouble. Maybe it wasn't the smart move, but he could handle himself. So, he walked on, watchfully.

He came to a massive black tree he knew, slung his staff onto his back, and climbed the tree. He grabbed the rough bark with strong fingers. His woodbender boots dug into the tree. He moved from tree to tree, often stepping casually between their overlapping branches. Sometimes he leapt to catch a branch which bent to his weight and slowed his fall to land on another branch.

He saw one of the men. Lian crouched down below on the ground, watching westward where Kenan should have been returning to the village. The others were probably nearby.

Kenan moved along a branch to change his angle, looking for Asher and the other men. He passed a thin branch bent in a uniform spiral coil. He'd been tending this tree. This would be a platform spring, mostly used in tree structures and mountain wagons where a longer leaf spring could be difficult. The way the black trees grew made coil springs easy to shape. The white wood fibers were resilient and would work for many years, especially if kept wet. This one should be ready in less than a year. Kenan couldn't help but pause there. He felt safe in the tree.

He made a small adjustment in the twine holding the branch in shape. Kenan planned to use it to steady the new addition he was building in his home. When the trees swayed in the wind, the springs eased the stress on the house structure. Anna would want more space. Marriage meant children, lots of them. He smiled at the thought of little Kenan-spawn scampering all over the house.

They'd probably destroy everything. Kenan paused in thought. What would life be like in a house full of his own children? He saw the toll on his switch-father, his mother's husband, who escaped into the forest on a regular basis.

Did he even want children? Well, they were coming, like it or not. What kind of mother would Anna be? Carefree and spirited, would Anna be happy washing diapers and...

The limb under his feet quivered from an impact.

Kenan looked over and saw Asher crouched, regaining his balance on the branch between him and the wall of the tree trunk.

"Asher," Kenan said, his tone even.

"My friend! I knew you'd take to the trees." Asher straightened to his full height and held his muscled arms out with palms up. The big man showed his teeth in a broad smile. A bronze sword hung on his right hip, a long knife at his left. Kenan knew he kept a hand knife in the small of his back and another in his boot. But his feet were bare, so no boot knife. Asher came to the village alone three years ago, staying to work. He'd been causing trouble ever since.

Kenan asked, "What can I do for you?"

"Do for me? Why, friend, I just wanted to congratulate you. Quite a display the other day."

"Sorry."

"Sorry? Don't be sorry. Not for taking me down in the practice ring."

"I used more force than I strictly should have," admitted Kenan. Asher's nose was still an angry red.

Asher shrugged. "Is this about Lidai? She and I were just having a chat." Asher stepped closer. His arms hung loose, and he seemed relaxed. But he stiffened his torso as he walked. Asher still hadn't learned to sway with the branch.

Kenan took a step back by feel, watching Asher. "She didn't seem thrilled."

"Oh, that scamper rat!" Asher said, too loud. "She can take care of herself."

"She can. But she's my sister."

"Hands off the sister. I get that," Asher admitted, nodding thoughtfully. "Totally understand. If she were my sister, I'd feel the same way. But then, my sister is a mawdragon with a sore tooth. She'd eat you alive before you could wink at her. Seriously, that woman will look you over, deciding whether to take off your arm or take you into her..."

"Asher. I think we're done here. I'm sorry I humiliated you. And please leave Lidai alone. She's only 34."

"Humiliated? Yes, you did that. Dragonspit, but I was overconfident. I shouldn't have been so. That's on me."

"I'm glad you see it that way."

"It's only polite." Asher didn't look like he was being polite.

"What do you want, Asher?"

"I want to see the real you." Asher stepped closer, now only ten paces away. "I thought you were a stompdragon: hard working but otherwise useless, except perhaps as prey. Then you go and show me you're actually a hissdragon, all teeth and claws." Asher's smile looked predatory, now. "You've been holding out on me, Kenan. You played me for a fool."

Kenan edged back another step, his heel contacting an obstruction. He didn't look back, but glanced down and to the side, his mind spinning fast.

Asher stepped closer. "Is this the real you? You back off. All the while, you know you can handle yourself?"

"I can." Kenan glanced to the side again.

"The survivor of Babelwind Brook, and yet you back off. You won't even stand up to me." Asher's eyes glinted. It wasn't the flash of orange light Kenan remembered from nearly sixty years ago, but he could see the intent there. Asher stepped forward again, his right hand on the pommel of his shortsword.

Kenan quietly said, "I stood up to you in the ring. How'd that turn out?"

"Stand up to me here, Kenan," challenged Asher, hopefully. Hungrily. "Tell me no. Tell me to leave your little sister alone. Tell me to back off."

"Listen, you have a grievance. I understand. Let's take it to the elders. They'll..."

"Those old fools won't help me. And they can't help you. Your Almighty himself can't help you."

"I've got no use for a god. And I've got no use for you. Back off."

"There it is." Asher smiled. His right hand closed on the sword hilt, yanked it from the sheath, and let it fly overhead. He caught it and pointed it at Kenan with a grin on his face, anticipating. Wanting. There would be blood, and Asher wanted it.

Kenan knew this look. He had seen it before, decades earlier, at Babelwind Brook.

"I've had about enough," Asher continued. "My time is short. I don't like the way you figure things out. You're thinking, even now. So, your time is over. Have a nice afterlife, Woodbender."

Kenan had no sword. His blackwood staff was strapped to his back, out of the way. A leather case at his hip secured his hand axe. It would be slow to draw. His hand knife was quick to draw, but a fight on a branch would be linear. In a linear fight, the longer reach had the advantage. And Asher had the longer reach, in arm and weapon.

The footing was Kenan's, but this was a fight Kenan would lose.

Asher lifted the bronze sword up and over this right shoulder, quickly, with little effort. The weight of the bronze meant nothing to a man so large. Then he brought the sword diagonally down in a powerful blow, aimed at Kenan's collarbone.

But Kenan shifted his weight with hips and legs. The branch swayed and Kenan shifted to the side. Asher's sword sliced just over his head and shoulder, barely missing.

Kenan didn't stop. He used his momentum and the branch's rebound movement to leap. As he fell forward, he heard another whoosh from Asher's backhand swing. But Kenan was already away, falling to another branch below.

Kenan landed roughly but pulled himself together and turned to look back at Asher.

The large man clung to the branch on his belly, both arms and legs wrapped around the swaying limb. The sword was nowhere to be seen. Asher had both hatred and fear in his eyes.

Kenan saluted him with a couple of fingers to his eyebrow and moved towards the canopy edge for a quick descent. He heard Asher swear and struggle to his feet as the branch continued to sway.

Kenan quickly made his way out to the canopy edge, jumped, grabbed a limb in one hand, and descended smoothly to the ground. There he saw Asher's boots. Kenan dropped a small stone in one and started off into the underbrush. He needed to find one of the others and take him down. He would take them each down one at time on his own terms. If he could surprise the first one, he would...

A thud behind him made him look back. Asher had jumped and landed in a bed of giant mushrooms and spore balls. Through the swirling spores, Kenan saw him rise and brush himself off. Then he looked up, made eye contact, and smiled with predatory bloodlust.

Asher had no sword. His belt scabbard hung empty. But with a quick flip of the leather binding cord, his long knife appeared in his hand. The three palms of blade length caught a ray of sunlight and flashed bronze along the sharpened edge.

A second man rushed into view. He shouted, "Over here!"

Well, that was just fantastic. Kenan turned and sprinted away. He couldn't outrun Asher, he knew. And he wouldn't make Blacktree before being cut down from behind. But he would face him, and it would be on ground of his choosing. He picked a tree and hoped he could scramble out of reach in time.

He should have listened to the Dragonfly Man.

# Chapter Three
# It Will Be Okay

LIDAI Blacktree stalked beside the tower of muscley man leading a harnessed shielddragon down a wide forest trail. She wanted to punch him hard enough to leave a bruise. Well, a little bruise, maybe, where she couldn't see it.

The man was too tall at six feet and a couple of palms. Lidai, a woman grown now, was only a little over five feet. He was too muscled, with arms like gopher branches. She held herself straight, even if she was slight. He was too fair, blond of hair and blue of eyes. Her hair was dark brown and her eyes hazel, like all her siblings she'd met. He was too old at 84. She was only 34, and still a child, so her mother thought, even though she'd lowered her dress hem four years ago.

Wren was big, smart, and a total pain in the dragonsphincter. He had a stupid name. He treated her like a child. And he wasn't even listening to her.

"Are you listening to me?"

"Of course, I am." Wren clucked his mouth at the shielddragon, who ignored him and plodded on.

"Then what did I just say?" Lidai demanded.

"You were just saying how Maren thinks I'm cute," he answered with a glance down towards her. She caught it and saw the twinkle in his eye.

"That's not what I said at all! Arggh! You totally missed the point."

"Well, little one, what was your point?"

Little one? Little one? She swooshed the bow she carried angrily through the air. Oh, the game was on, you big oaf.

"Listen here, you, you... stalkdragon! I am not..."

"Stalkdragon?" Wren interrupted, a mock look of horror on his face. He looked over his shoulder, then spun around, craning his neck in a vain attempt to see his own rear end.

"What are you doing?"

"Looking for a tail. Stalkdragon tails are rather long. They look like the trunks of cedar trees, you know."

She rolled her eyes. "Not funny. Maren thinks you're cute. Bethany thinks you're cute. Rachel and her sister Allanniel both think you're cute. My ninthmother thinks you're cute and she's over 800 years old."

"Really? I thought she was blind."

"She is."

"Then she can't think I'm cute."

"She, um, likes your voice."

"My voice?"

"Yeah. I caught her fanning her face after you left the pavilion the other day."

"What? That's gross."

"It's not gross. It's cute."

"I thought I was cute."

"Cute," she deadpanned. Lidai rolled her eyes for the seventy-seventh time. "Wren, you're not cute. You're intolerable."

"All those other women think I'm cute. You just said so."

"Yes. Glad to see you listened. Now do you see my point?"

"You have a point?"

She punched him on the arm, except he saw it coming and flexed. Her hand rolled under, and it hurt her wrist. "Ow!"

He stopped to look down at her. "Did you hurt yourself?"

"No." She worked her wrist to loosen it.

"Want me to look at that?" He reached for her arm.

"No." She, of course, let him take it. Her skin almost burned at his touch.

She'd grown up with Wren and Kenan. As a child, she'd followed them around. But he hadn't touched her since she'd turned thirty, until now.

He gently rolled her wrist in his strong fingers. "Is that better?"

"Yes, thank you."

"Sorry I hurt you."

"I'm fine."

His brow furrowed as he let her go.

Dragonscrape. "What?"

"A female 'fine' is usually followed by crossed arms and a scowl."

Lidai stopped herself from crossing her arms just in time. "You think you're smart."

32

He smiled directly at her, and it nearly took her breath away. "Cute and smart. I'm a real catch."

"Right. Now you see my point."

He turned and got his shielddragon moving again. "Nope. Spell it out for me."

She tapped her lips. Instead of spelling it out, she asked, "Why aren't you already married?"

He tripped on something imperceptibly small and almost fell onto the trail. "Um," he choked out. "I don't know."

"Uh huh. I'm waiting."

"For an answer?"

"Yes."

He quirked his lips. "Well, I guess I don't want to get married."

"Really?"

"Well, not right this moment." Wren smiled to himself and walked on next to his shielddragon. Intolerable, even if they'd almost had a moment there.

The dragon was mostly gray and dark green, twenty-five feet long, nearly as tall as Wren at the back, and walked on all fours. It had a beak for a mouth, a short horn above that, and two brow horns sticking straight out over its nose. They weren't very long yet, and the sharp tips had been blunted with little balls of hardened resin. The dragon wasn't yet fully grown. From the back of its head spread a tabletop-sized shield of bone and tough, scaly skin edged in knobs that would develop into spikes. The animal would grow into that shield, she knew. A sturdy leather harness was strapped to its shoulders and up around the shield to the brow horns.

Wren reached and patted the beak of the animal affectionately. "Why are you stomping?"

Before she could stop herself, Lidai asked, "Me?"

"Well, I wasn't talking to my shielddragon, Lidai."

"I'm not stomping," she replied, changing her gait. "I'm trying to take bigger steps. You walk too fast."

"I do not."

"Of course, you do. You have crazy long legs."

Wren looked down at his legs. They were proportionate to the rest of him, muscled and hairy, what you could see of them between the hem of his overshirt and tops of his boots.

The oaf started taking overlong steps.

"Ugh! Stop that! I'll have to run." With her bow, Lidai slapped him on the skin just above the boot. She should have done that before. She hoped the sting would at least slow him down enough for her to catch up.

It evidently did sting because Wren skipped a step. "Ow! You've grown more violent than I remember." He bent to rub the back of his leg while he walked and put on a frown of disapproval.

He was not her father. "Stop it."

"Stop what?"

"What you're doing," she demanded.

"What am I doing?"

"You're the one doing it. Why should I have to point it out?"

"Because I don't know what I'm doing."

"I knew that," she said, grinning now with satisfaction. Maybe men weren't as hard to deal with as she'd heard.

Wren frowned down at her. "Now hold on." He raised a finger at her.

She looked at it. Her father used to raise a finger at her like that when she was young. Ugh. This wasn't getting better.

"I'm not a child, you know," she said, putting her hands on her hips and arching her back a little to look up at him.

"I noticed."

Her heart skipped a beat. He noticed. She mulled that over for moment and had to run to catch up once more. He'd noticed.

Wren looked down out of the corner of his eye at her. "Why are you here, again?"

"Because I wanted to be."

"Very independent."

She bristled. "Women are independent. Well, some are."

"Right."

Lidai huffed a little, just to show her displeasure, and trotted to catch up.

He smiled as he glanced at her again. "If you can't keep up, you could always ride my shielddragon," he said.

Right. That sounded condescending. She didn't like the way this conversation was going. But she was still glowing inside. He'd noticed.

Time to change the subject. Her ninthmother said that with men, redirection was better than butting heads. But she was old, and not quite right in the high balcony any longer. Turned on by a voice? At her age? Well, still, redirection seemed worth a try.

"Don't you think it's time you named your shielddragon?"

"Why does he need a name? He pulls logs. He eats my grain and sleeps in my shed. He doesn't deserve a name."

"Anna must have named him by now."

"Yes," he confirmed.

"Well?"

"Well, what?"

"Dragonstool. What did Anna name him?" She let a little too much frustration into her voice. It slipped into her words. Sometimes. Well, not all the time.

Wren glanced down. She caught it, again. He was having fun with her!

34

Intolerable. He said, "She called him Jumper."

Lidai looked over at the shielddragon. "I doubt that thing could jump more than a palm high. She did not name it Jumper."

Wren smiled again. "No, not Jumper. Though he'd surprise you. He's young, yet. Spinner?"

Lidai snorted. "Doubtful. Your sister is far better at poetry than she is at teaching her brother how to talk to a woman."

"Woman?"

Lidai bristled. "Yes! I am not a child." She barely controlled the urge to stomp her foot.

"And I said I noticed. No, its name is Woman."

"It's male."

"I noticed."

She could hear his smile. Drat him. Lidai growled deep in her throat. She thought it wasn't a bad mixture of irritation and adorability.

"Okay, why don't you name it," offered Wren.

"Me?" Lidai asked.

"Why not?"

"Okay..."

"That's a silly name."

She growled again. This time it had more adorableness, less irritation. Perfect.

"Okay," said Wren. Trying the word. "Okay. Okay. That might work."

Okay looked at him, eyes placid.

"Okay? That's not what I meant." Lidai looked dubiously at the lumbering shielddragon. Okay looked back at her. "That's not a silly name. That's a stupid name."

"Okay, but you're the one who named him." Okay looked back at him. "Look! He likes it," Wren declared.

"Wren, you can't name a shielddragon Okay. Okay?"

Okay looked back at her and blew out his nostrils. A little snot flew.

Wren put his hand on a brow horn and gave a little downward push. The shielddragon stopped walking.

"Let's try something," he mused. Wren took a few steps forward and turned to face his animal.

"Okay, come," Wren commanded.

Okay took a step forward.

"Okay, stop."

Okay stopped.

Lidai snorted again, rather prettily, she thought. "Look, that doesn't mean anything, okay? You already taught him the words stop and come."

Okay looked at her and started to turn.

"No, no!" She put her hands on his big jaw, but his massive head just pushed her back with no apparent effort. Stupid beast! Her feet skidded through the duff. It was like trying to hold back a boulder that had decided to roll.

"Push the brow horn, okay?"

Okay turned back to Wren.

"Well, now you've done it. He knows his name. I'm harnessed to a shielddragon named Okay. You understand, don't you, I'll have to live with it for decades? A century, maybe. Almighty, what will my sister say?"

Was he playing or really upset? Wren never knew when to stop, so how could she know? Either way, though, it served him right. Lidai grinned at him and picked up her bow.

His hands were on his hips, showing off his biceps. He didn't mean to. He wasn't like that. But she saw it, anyway. My, he cut a figure.

Before he caught her looking, she said, "You know, worse things can..."

"Shhhh!"

"What?" Lidai whispered, holding in place. Okay belched and it smelled like sour mash and squished bugs. Gross. She picked her way over the dead leaves and twigs to Wren. She was nearly silent. Her dress swished softly about her ankles.

"I heard something, like someone talking." Wren faced to the side of the trail. He shielded his eyes from the setting sun with his huge hand.

"I didn't hear anything. Besides, there are people about. We're not exactly far from home."

"Shhhh!"

"I'm whispering," whined Lidai. Hearing the whine in her voice, she clamped her teeth shut. She didn't need him to hear *that*.

They both looked into the forest, listening silently, side by side. Someone was talking, but far enough away to be hard to discern.

Wren turned to her. "Did someone just say, 'scamper rat'?"

"I think so," she said. "What's a 'scamper rat'?"

"I don't know," he replied. "Rats scamper, right? Something like a squirrel?"

"Maybe. Who do you think it is?"

"I don't know."

"Neither do I. Let's go find out." Lidai stepped forward.

"Lid, wait."

Lid. Lid. She mulled that over in her mind, trying to decide if she liked him shortening her name. It meant familiarity, which seemed good. But when her younger brothers called her that, she usually made them pay.

Wren moved over to Okay and pulled a big axe off the harness under the dragon's neck shield. The axe head glinted silver, the only steel axe in Blacktree. It had a long gopherwood handle her brother Kenan had made him years ago. The wood had been polished on delivery, of course, but a decade of use made it shine.

He turned to look at her.

She looked back, raising her eyebrows and shuffling her hands as if to say, "What are you waiting for? That way." She put a foot tap in it for good measure. It made her hip move in a way she'd seen Bethany use on boys. That girl had a rump to make men notice. But Lidai wasn't jealous or anything. No, no. Just observant.

His yellow eyebrows frowned slightly, and he quirked that ridiculous smile at her.

Seventy-seven eye rolls. How was he absolutely gorgeous and annoyingly goofy at the same exact time?

Lidai gathered her dress up in one hand, bow in the other, and turned to move into the underbrush. It exposed a smooth calf. She glanced at Wren and caught him looking. A little thrill exploded through her chest. Finally!

He caught her catching him look. He winked and turned back towards the forest. Drat the man. Intolerable!

They turned together into the vegetation. She nocked an arrow, moving quietly with eyes ahead.

# Chapter Four
# A Game of Murder

KENAN sprinted through the forest as fast as he could.

He hurdled a bumbling porcupine. Maybe Asher would stumble into it, but he wasn't holding his breath. He needed his breath to run.

The first blacktree had no sloping roots on this side, no place to make a running start up the trunk. Black bark made a vertical wall into the soil. He could climb it, but not in time. He changed course and sprinted on to another tree. Asher ran not far behind, and he could hear others coming on fast behind him.

A butterfly the size of a white wood platter slapped right into his face. He wrenched it off, coughing from the wing dust, running still. That's not helping. Not helping!

He ran on.

Two patedragons looked up as he ran, standing right in his path. The animals were each about fifteen feet long and nearly his height. They mostly walked on two legs, though they used their front legs when charging. The top of the round heads exposed a thick cap of bone wreathed in a spiked fringe, reminding him of a knit cap his mother sometimes wore in cold weather. Also like his mother, they were temperamental beasts at best and downright ornery all the time. Kenan considered them the bane of the forest.

He could hear Asher crashing through brush not far behind him.

Kenan dodged to the side, never slowing. Both patedragons gave chase, croaking out challenges.

Kenan sprinted through the lush forest. Just wonderful. He had Asher,

Lian, two other men, and two patedragons trying to run him down. He put on a burst of speed. Then he had an idea.

He plunged through a screen of ferns and flowers, instantly falling forward on his chest, arms forming a triangle and turning his head to the side to spare his face.

The two patedragons pounded past his prone form, first one then the next. They were close. Flying forest duff covered his side as their feet cleared his elbow by a finger span.

As soon as they were past, he jumped back up and whistled to get their attention. The patedragons skidded to a stop. One slipped and fell on its side, twisting wildly to get back up. Duff flew everywhere.

Kenan didn't wait. He immediately turned and sprinted back the way he came, right towards Asher and the other men.

He saw Asher almost immediately, long knife in hand. The man seemed pleasantly surprised his prey had returned to him. His surprise turned to shock as Kenan turned to the side and said, "Good luck," to Asher, never slowing his run.

The two patedragons burst through the ferns and flowers, croaking, and charged right at Asher. Yelling wordlessly, Asher spun and ran the other way. The patedragons followed hot on his heels.

Kenan stopped to catch his breath for a moment. That was almost too easy. But he didn't feel sorry for Asher or the others, not even a little. He heard another yell and a solid crack of bone on wood. Well, maybe a little.

Kenan trotted away, angling back. Two more men rushed by towards the tussle of Asher and the patedragons. Kenan waited a moment and was rewarded as Lian trotted past. Kenan stepped out behind him.

Lian skidded to a stop and spun back towards Kenan, just in time to catch the blackwood staff across his temple. The young man stiffened before falling backwards onto the forest floor.

Kenan checked him. He was unconscious but breathing strong. He would wake in a short time. Kenan flipped Lian, bound his hands behind his back with a cord, and left him there.

He moved with stealth towards the sound of men shouting and patedragons croaking. He wanted to see this. He should head back to Blacktree to inform the elders of Asher's actions. Asher would deny it, if he survived the patedragons, but the elder's wives were always watchful. They knew Asher's reputation with their daughters. He would be banished for sure, this time. Good riddance.

He heard another yell from the battle and a cry of pain. Asher shouted in rage. Maybe he'd survive after all.

Kenan heard a croaky cry of pain, then silence.

An owl hooted nearby and fell quiet.

Kenan listened closely. He heard a faint grunt. A dry branch broke. Two men muttered to each other for a moment. Silence returned.

Kenan considered his situation. Was someone hurt? Should he go help? No, they wouldn't give up their purpose, even if someone was hurt. That chance passed when Asher drew his sword. Should he return to Blacktree? Probably. But he wanted to end Asher's time here and send a message to any others.

He stood on a narrow forest trail between two thickets. They would have to come through here. Using his knife, he pared away some branches of a sapling, creating a stave taller than him. He wedged it between a couple of understory trees and, using cord, set a simple trap.

He heard men moving, not far away. Then a voice muttered, "Eghh. That's a *big* spider!"

Kenan moved to the edge of a little clearing along the trail. He pushed a foot-long millipede out of the way and crawled in under a fern. He settled in to watch.

Asher and one of the men burst into the clearing. The first man hit the trip wire, and the trap sprung. The supple stave was released, whistled through the air, and cracked against the man's kneecap. He cried out and fell.

Asher looked the trap over as the last man hobbled up, limping. One of the patedragons must have gotten him.

The first man lay on the ground, crying like a child.

Asher muttered, "Sneaky woodbender. And you, shut up. You'll live." He held a long knife in his hand, covered in thick dragon blood. The other man held an axe, also covered in blood. He used it as a cane as he fished something out of his shirt pocket and popped it in his mouth.

They took two steps more. Asher stopped, squatted, and studied the forest duff. Asher could track? Kenan had no idea the man had any wood lore at all. There he went again, assuming things.

At his lower position under the fern, Kenan could see Asher's eyes as he sat on his heels. The man studied the dead leaves and twigs. He twisted around, looking where Kenan had walked. Then he raised his eyes and looked right at Kenan's ferns.

Uh oh.

Kenan scrambled to his feet and bolted. He was headed away from Blacktree now, but there was no help for it. Asher was close, keeping pace again. Kenan put everything he had into speed.

He dodged to the left of a particularly lush pod of ferns twice his height, then around the other side of a bush with big fat leaves of dark green and purple, topped with open pink flowers. He slapped a broad leaf on the way by, and the bush exploded with small biting insects. Maybe that would slow them down.

Just up ahead, Kenan saw the pillar of a particular black trunk rising from the understory. That was the one. The tree had a great sloping root to make a quick climb. He might not outrun them, but he could certainly out climb them. He could keep them climbing around on branches all night if he had to.

Kenan burst through the underbrush at the base of the tree and skidded to a halt, nearly falling.

There, on the root, stood Wren.

His friend had planted his booted feet solidly on the broad root. His hands were folded over the butt of the axe handle, the gleaming silver axe head resting on the bark between his feet. The handle stood long enough that his hands were in front of his chest, forcing his elbows down and his forearms to bulge. The big man looked imposing.

"What're you doing, Kenan?" Wren asked lightly, raising an inquisitive eyebrow. He grinned, but that was almost normal on the man.

"Wren! They're right behind..."

Asher burst through the underbrush, swatting at his own face with his free hand. He saw Wren and slid to a stop. The long bloody knife went behind his back, out of sight.

"Hello, Wren," Asher said, panting a little.

Wren's face changed. The grin faded and the blond brows lowered. "Asher."

"What're you doing up there?" asked Asher as he sidled forward. His face smiled but the effect was ruined when he turned, closed one nostril with a finger, and blew a biter fly out of his nose.

Kenan moved to the side. He held his staff at the ready.

Wren said, "Following good sense. It always nose." He tapped his nose.

Kenan rolled his eyes. This was not the time for puns.

Wren grinned. One hand came off the axe handle and moved to rest on his hip, next to the hand knife in a belt sheath. Kenan saw it. It was a simple move, like the axe handle was too high so he would just move his hand down on his hip. But it was somehow dangerous, too. Asher saw it and stopped moving forward.

"I'm... I'm just playing a little game with Kenan, here."

Kenan stared at him. Yeah. A game of murder.

Wren quirked an eyebrow at him. "A game? Aren't we a little old for games?"

"Life is a game," said Asher, stepping forward once more. He seemed to be ignoring Kenan now. Asher smiled up at Wren.

Wren was big, almost as big as Asher. Wren was strong, maybe stronger than Asher. Wren even had the high ground and weapon reach. But Asher was a fighter. While Wren was handy with that axe, he only grappled for sport. Asher would cut him down in a moment.

"So you say," retorted Wren. "Game or not, life is dangerous." He left off, "and so am I," but they heard it all the same.

"Truer words never spoken," Asher said with a smile. His stance shifted slightly, indicating he would back off. But Kenan knew better. He'd seen Asher do this very thing in the martial yard before throwing a knife with deadly accuracy and strength.

Kenan turned to warn Wren, but he heard one of Asher's other men pushing through the underbrush towards them. Kenan spun towards the sound.

The man didn't notice Wren up on the root. The limping man emerged from the vegetation, and, with a wild look, came right at Kenan with an axe over his head.

Kenan deflected the blow and spun the staff to strike the man's elbow. The joint cracked and the man cried out. A snap roundhouse kick to the temple flopped the man over. Kenan stepped on his back. It was over in an instant.

"Smooth," said Wren.

Asher gaped at Kenan. His long knife was back in his hand, and he held a hand knife in the other, but he hadn't done anything with either, yet.

A motion above and behind Asher caught Kenan's attention. Up on a broad, black branch stood a girl with a bow. The sun was behind her, and he couldn't make out her face. But when she spoke, he knew instantly.

"Hey there, boys!" Lidai called down.

Asher spun.

An arrow ripped through the air, passing between Asher's knees and thudding into the ground. The arrow fletching vibrated just below his spread legs. He instinctively jumped back.

Before anyone could look up again, Lidai had another arrow drawn.

"Well, I guess you're not as endowed as you told me the other night. Why don't I adjust my aim up a foot or so?"

"No, wait! 'Ere, we can work this out. Okay?" Asher placated, palms out. Both knives fell to the ground. His plea came out high pitched and loud. Wren laughed.

Kenan looked sharply at Asher. He wasn't laughing with Wren. He was thinking about accents.

"Don't worry, *darling*," Lidai sneered, distorting her beauty. "I'll just tickle you a bit, like you promised to do to me." The second arrow ripped the air and poked a clean hole through the lower part of Asher's overshirt, high between his legs, front and back. The arrow stuck in the base of the giant root.

Asher jumped high and shoved his hand under his overshirt, pawing at his groin. He panted as he frantically searched. His hands came away without blood, and he wheezed in relief. When he looked back up, another arrow was nocked and drawn.

Wren snorted as his laughter subsided.

Lidai smiled. "Looks like you're not endowed at all, Asher. What exactly did you plan to do with me, anyway?"

She pulled further back, tucking her string-hand thumb behind her ear. She was anchored and ready to loose. Kenan knew she could hit Asher wherever she wanted. She regularly skewered flushing partridge out of the air.

"Okay, I give up," Asher declared. "I'll leave, right now."

Wren spoke, all mirth gone. "Blacktree."

"What?" Asher asked, turning sideways and looking at Wren. Asher was regaining his composure. Wren had already recovered his.

"Blacktree," Wren said. "You'll not just leave here. You'll leave Blacktree. You've plagued us long enough."

Asher tried to compose himself visibly, tugging on his overshirt collar. "Okay, Wren. Lidai. I was planning to go soon, anyway. I'll head out at first light tomorrow. Promise."

Kenan didn't think so. He'd have Asher at his house before mid-dark. He'd seen the look on his face. He had no doubt Asher was already making plans. "No," Kenan said. "You'll leave right now."

Asher turned again and looked at Kenan.

"So, you'll stand up to me, when you're with your friends."

"I'm standing right now. Try me," Kenan retorted.

Asher didn't move.

Kenan said, "Leave. Don't come back."

"Ever," reinforced Wren.

"If I lay eyes on your face again," added Lidai, "I'll put an arrow through it. You'll never see it coming. Darling."

Asher bowed his head. He was beaten. He stooped to pick up his knife.

"No, no, darling," said Lidai. "Leave that right there where it lay. Off you go. Shoo. Now."

Asher stood, shot Kenan a glare, and trotted off into the woods, heading north.

They all breathed a sigh of relief, and Lidai relaxed her bow. She watched as Asher jogged out of sight.

Wren beamed at her. "That. Was. Amazing!"

"Well, you big dragonstool," she said with a smile and leaned jauntily on her bow, "did you expect anything less? I'm not a child, you know."

"Oh, I noticed," Wren beamed back.

Kenan missed it all. He was busy binding the fallen man's wrists behind him. The man would be fine, but it would take a long time to heal the elbow, and he'd probably always have trouble with it. He found narcotic seeds in the man's shirt pocket. He must have been drugged out of his mind to attack him like that. The man had always been a fool.

Kenan straightened, satisfied at the way this turned out and thankful for his friends. But his mind turned on how he could have handled this himself.

He should probably thank them. Instead, he said, "There's one more. I think he's got a split kneecap."

"Your handiwork?"

Kenan shrugged.

Wren asked, "Where?"

Kenan pointed.

Wren nodded. "It's on the way home. Let's check."

"Home sounds good. I've got a basket of gopher nuts and a deep need to eat."

"Selah to that, my friend," Wren boomed. "Let's go!"

"Okay!" Lidai agreed as she reached the ground.

And just then, Okay trotted into the clearing, munching on a big, juicy leaf.

# Chapter Five
## That Kind of Friendly

AGLIRANNA opened her eyes and stretched in her hammock. Her first thought was about how to ditch Marjie today.

The polished pale boards of her ceiling showed a sliver of sunshine reflecting off her water stand. By the angle, she knew she'd slept in. Mother would not be pleased. Her fifthmother would surely have a few cutting words for her.

Anna flipped her blanket aside and rolled out of her hammock, pushing aside the bug netting and putting bare feet on the burnished yellow plank floor. Her fireplace sat cold, but it wasn't a problem. The air in her room already warmed with the day.

She put on a new undershift, then an overshift. She slipped her feet into her soft leather shoes while brushing her long, blond hair. The locks waved and bounced, sometimes unruly. Her sisters all had straight hair, but hers always waved and curled at the ends. It took extra brushing, and she didn't mind. Kenan had once remarked he liked her hair.

She strode over to her water basin and washed her face, neck, and forearms with a cloth. She was quick about it. She needed to join her mother as soon as possible, and she knew she'd be going to the women's bathing pool later today.

Mostly, she hurried to get into the common room before her mother came out of the kitchen. She was supposed to be tending her baby sister this morning.

She went to her small looking glass sitting on the whitewood mantle shaped like the graceful arch of a stalkdragon's neck, complete with a carved head looking at the firewood box. She checked her eyes and rubbed out a few small sleep grains the water had missed. She smiled. No wrinkles yet. One eyebrow had a lick of yellow hair angling up. She fixed it.

Her pale green dress draped over the back of her reading chair, right where she'd left it. With a deft toss, the dress settled over her head. After finding the sleeves, she laced up the bodice and straightened the knot into a neat bow. The hem moved about her ankles as she moved. She cinched her narrow waist with her thin, leather belt and adjusted her hand knife to the small of her back.

After a quick trip to the sluice privy, Anna trotted into the common room. Her father, Jaret, frowned at her but said nothing before turning back to his scroll. Her mother, Alannoon, sat at the table and frowned as well, but turned it on one of Anna's teenage brothers, Shathan. He was always in trouble. He sat on a pillow and ate unbuttered nutmash with a sour expression. He must have been belted. He usually deserved it.

Her fifth-mother, Jezeera, sat in her rocker by the fireplace. She had her gray hair pulled up behind her head as usual and concentrated on weaving a small basket with her gnarled hands. She spared a glance for Anna, however, and pursed her wrinkled lips. There it was. The cutting words would have been better. Anna smiled an apology.

Jezeera ignored the smile, turning back to her work. When the old woman thought no one was looking, Anna saw her slip a small seed into her mouth. Great. Where had she found those? Anna thought they'd all been cleared from the home.

The common room had been constructed of wood, except for the stone fireplace. Wood of many colors, curves, and grains decorated floor, walls, and ceiling. The massive rafters were woodbent to support the domed room. All the wood was polished and gleaming in the sun coming through the glass of the bentwood lattice window.

A long table and benches dominated the room. It could sit all thirty-three of them at the same time, but it was mostly empty now. The older adult children were out at their work. The younger children were out at play. A baby, her youngest sister Abidoon, crawled uncertainly across the floor towards a raccoon sitting on a chair.

The raccoon, a family pet for some time now, sat on its haunches, fat, irascible, and munching down a large slice of butternut squash at the moment, ignoring them all. Someone had named him Quick, and it'd stuck. Silly name for a fat raccoon.

Anna scooped up the baby. She had a fresh diaper. Anna had missed her chores. Oops.

One of her younger sisters, 36-year-old Haley, came into the room. She carried a tray of fried eggs and buttered nutmash. Haley smiled at the look of longing on Anna's face. Anna was famished.

"This is mine, Anna. You can go make your own."

Anna yawned while bouncing the baby. She pleaded at Haley with wide blue eyes.

"That won't work on me, and you know it. You were up all night talking with Kenan out on the balcony. I heard you. Kept me up, too." Haley pulled her thick and straight blond hair over shoulder as she sat down at the huge table.

"Come on, Hale. Just a little?"

"A little. You'll need to fit into the wedding dress I'm making."

Her mother quirked a grin at Haley's words as she came to take Abidoon, who was fussing. Anna was relieved to see the smile. An upcoming wedding can apparently melt a mother's heart.

"Thank you!" Anna cried. She moved to take Haley's tray.

"Go get your own tray. I'll save some of this for you. Some of it. Probably."

Anna sighed and made for the kitchen. Three of her other sisters were there, as well as two of the hired women. Clean-up duty frothed in full swing. Wood tubs of hot soapy water were filled with bronze baking sheets, copper pots, and floating wooden utensils. A table held a leaning stack of dirty cast iron pans. The women's backs bent to the scrubbing.

Her sister, nineteen-year-old Atarra, glowered at her over her shoulder as she scraped a pan. Anna gave her a commiserating look. Next week was her turn again.

But not for much longer. She and Kenan were to be wed next spring. She'd be moving out to a tree of her own.

She grabbed a whitewood tray off the stack by the door and dressed it with a wooden bowl and the pewter fork and spoon she was due as the oldest sibling in the house. She found some blueberries and filled a wood cup with them. A horn mug had already been filled with hot tea and sat on the sideboard. Bless you, Hales.

Next to the sideboard loomed a massive stone fireplace which housed hot coals, iron stands, and a big bronze pot hanging over the heat, half full of steaming water. One of her preteen brothers idly tended the coals, pleading at her with his face.

"Oh, come now. You have only two days left on kitchen duty." Anna smiled to encourage him. It didn't look like it worked.

On her return to the common room, Haley pushed her tray to the middle of the table so Anna could help herself to some breakfast. Haley snatched back the tray before Anna could take too much. Anna poured some blueberries onto the nutmash and set to work.

"What did you two talk about last night?" asked her mother, sitting nearby and feeding a suckling Abidoon.

"Oh, nothing," Anna said, holding a hand in front of her full mouth.

"Right," said Haley. "You two talked about *everything*."

"Not everything. Just... stuff."

Her father, Jaret, glanced at her over his scroll. After a moment, he looked back down at the paper. He probably wasn't even reading.

"He says," Haley offered, "that he's not sure Asher's gone. He said he thought he saw someone in the forest to the east."

Her father hmphed softly, the sound coming from low in his throat. He cleared his throat, then, and squinted at his scroll. His short blond hair bristled over the top. At 313, he had some creases on his face. He looked relatively young still, but his eyes looked older and sharp. He didn't like Asher. Her father had words with him after Asher had gotten too friendly with Atarra, though she didn't seem to mind his attentions. This latest report from Wren a week ago didn't improve her father's opinion of Asher a whit.

Her mother's brow creased. She did look her 245 years, still in her prime, but with older eyes.

"That splintered tower of ..." she paused, catching the next word in her throat. "Jaret, what? Well, that man hadn't better come back. If he does, you better hope your sons get to him before I do." She flipped her long blond hair over her shoulder so she could see her baby.

Jaret smiled fondly at his wife and youngest daughter.

Anna thought of Kenan. He had only smiled at her that way once. They were much younger then, she barely out of her teens, still a child really, with her dress hem at her calves. But it had lit her world and she never forgot it. She hoped to make him smile so again. He'd been, well, reserved. He smiled, but not quite like that. Not to her. Not to anyone. How could she make him smile at her like that again?

Anna ate fast, gulping the eggs and buttered nutmash. Haley looked at her with a quirked eyebrow and a little frown. Then she put her hands over her hips and made a bloating gesture.

Anna frowned back. She washed the food down with her tea, now cool enough to drain in one go.

Her mother watched and opened her mouth to say something. But just then, the balcony erupted with laughter, squeals, and the thrumming of many small feet.

The oval door to the balcony burst open, followed immediately by a half dozen children, all blond, ranging from five to fourteen. The youngest, a boy, had a three-foot-long green snake. It was harmless unless you happened to be a berry. The oldest, a girl with dress hems up at her knees, chased the group into the room.

"Mother, look what I found!" The boy squealed in excitement, showing the snake proudly. It tried to find purchase around his chubby arm.

"Put it back, Jared! It's grooooooss!"

"Father, can I go over to Kale's to..."

48

"Mother, what am I to do with..."

The teen girl made for the kitchen. "I think I left my tea in there."

All the voices erupted at once, all the while Jared swung his frightened prize around over his head. The snake writhed vainly.

Quick jumped up on the table and made for Haley's platter.

Her mother started answering her children. The baby cried for more milk. The young boys ran laps around the room. Her father mumbled an excuse about getting to his workshop and made for the oval door.

Anna saw her chance, pocketed a few blueberries, and followed him. As Jared passed, she snagged the hapless snake out of the air and took it with her.

Jared cried, "Hey!"

While Haley was turned to deal with an upset Jared, Quick had his face in her nutmash bowl.

OUTSIDE, her father stopped and stretched his back, looking out over the forest village. Anna unconsciously mimicked him. She fed the snake a blueberry before releasing the creature onto the balcony rail. It took the berry and made good its escape.

Though familiar, the view from the balcony still mesmerized her. Blacktree homes perched against the great black trunks of the village, using the massive branches for supports. The structures were made of wood, but the woodbent boards made fanciful shapes. Wood planks, bent and woven into each other to form a waterproof barrier when it rained, formed the roofs. No wall stood straight. Every home curved, with smaller rooms built at different elevations and sticking out the sides of the main structures in bulbous protrusions. Balconies surrounded the homes and connected with each other by hanging bridges made of rope and wide, whitewood planks. Smaller homes perched further out on the branches. Boardwalks lined many of the branches.

Further up, giant leaves sown into wide tarps formed rain pans. Vine tubes ran the water into clay cisterns strapped to branches. Resin-lined pipes channeled the water down into homes for washing, sluice privies, and power to turn woodworks when it rained.

About eighty feet down, on the first level, larger buildings secured to the massive trees provided workshops and storage buildings. Many structures wrapped the great trunks. She saw Kenan's woodbending shop. Over there, the temple to the Almighty rose tall and pointed towards glory, rubbed with nut oil and gleaming in the morning sun. She found it sad that nobody really used it anymore. Nearby, the great meeting hall could seat over a hundred people and spanned between two black trees. It once seated more, she knew, but part of it had been turned into an elevated granary decades ago.

She could also see one of the village's two defensive platforms. Each boasted two big thumpers mounted on the rails. Large, woodbent branches wove around the edge, offering shelter from archers on the ground, broken only where a rope bridge provided access. Woven rain shields hovered above, suspended by ropes. Two men now manned the platform, sitting on the rail and smoking pipes. Each wore wood armor and had bows and full quivers. A nearby brazier smoked. The platform usually remained unmanned except in times of imminent danger. Why were the guards posted now?

The ground sat another eighty feet down. The village center held an open and flat area, the ground packed solid. Surrounding the Flat were several large barns, then smaller barns. Beyond that, sheds and gardens nestled between the trees. The gardens grew smaller as one approached the dragonring. The large trees dominated everything.

Livestock moved about on the ground. Sheep, goats, stompdragon, geese, shielddragon, ducks in little pools, hairy pigs, and a pen of bovine made a cacophony. A lone slabdragon led by a skinny man pulled a log. Chickens ran everywhere, pecking at anything that moved and much that did not. People moved among them, feeding the animals, shearing them, slaughtering them, and gathering their eggs. A group of small boys chased down a black rooster who squawked his displeasure. In a flash, it turned around and charged back at the boys, sending them scattering and squealing.

She looked over and saw Lidai walking across her father's balcony and up a railed branch. She saw her looking and waved with a friendly smile. Anna waved back at her future sister-in-law.

She loved the view of her village. Her father's house had been situated well to see most of it.

"Anna?"

"Yes, father."

He paused, gathering his thoughts. She waited, wondering if a lecture was coming.

"Anna, how many sisters do you have?"

What an odd question. "Thirty-one."

"How many are here?"

"In Blacktree? Nineteen."

"How many are not?"

"Twelve. Eleven gone to husbands, and one was taken in the raid at the pool before I was born." She knew this family information, and he knew she knew. "Father, what's going on?"

Her father looked at her and she read the request for patience in his eyes. She waited.

Jaret looked out over the village, watching the people and animals move about. Finally, he said, "Where are your sisters that have husbands?"

Oh. Got it. "Four, no five, are in Edeer. Two in Embden. Three more in Bigrock, and Clover is over in Longbranch."

"Right you are," he confirmed.

"Father, is this about Kenan?"

"Yes. And no."

Anna watched him. Patience was a trial.

His eyes sparkled at her. "You'll soon be married and out of our house. Your brothers are here in Blacktree, but your older sisters are not. This is our way."

"Yes, but I will stay in Blacktree," she said. "Right over there." She pointed to a small house, beautifully made, with a curved frame for an addition. The roof had just been finished, though she could see inside through the wall posts.

"Yes. Right over there." He breathed in silence for a moment, then continued. "I wept like a young boy every time one of your sisters left. We see them from time to time, but not often enough." After a moment, he added, "I miss them."

"Me too," Anna whispered.

Her father looked at her.

"There're good reasons to send daughters away. It's not about bride prices and trade. Well, not only. It's about husbandry. Genetics. You understand. The patriarchs married their sisters, nieces and such, but we don't any longer. The elders spoke it long ago."

Thinking of a time not long past when he ignored the elders, she asked, "Do you always do what the elders say, father?"

"Obedience is not subservience..." he started.

"...obedience is respect and appreciation," she finished. She smiled at him, and he grinned back. They both let an identical little laugh escape.

Anna turned back to watch the bustling village. She felt uncomfortable and thankful for these village rules. A cousin? Sure. A secondnephew? Maybe, if her options were limited. But a brother? She thought of her big brother Wren. Her stomach soured.

"You may not know this, Anna, but the rule is not steadfast. I may choose whether or not I send a daughter to another village."

Anna turned to her father. The mothers had made the match, but it was her father who decided. If he rejected the bride price, her mothers would find a new match, and she would leave Blacktree.

The idea of leaving Kenan made her slump.

He smiled at her. "Easy, daughter. You and Kenan have my blessing. I will announce it at a feast."

She reached out and hugged him tight.

They released, and she looked deeply into his eyes. "I'll be here, father. Nothing could take me away."

"Let's make sure of it. It's only been a week and already people are disobeying the elders and venturing into the forest alone. That won't do. Not for you."

"I understand," she said, wondering if he knew that was exactly what she'd planned today.

"Do you? You don't disobey commands or shirk duties? You know, like being up at first light to take care of your littlest sister so your mother can take some much-needed ease?"

Ah. The lecture. Well, no surprise there. She supposed she'd earned it. "I'm sorry, father. It won't happen again."

"This isn't about your baby sister or your mother. It's not about Kenan. I want you here. I want you safe in Blacktree. You'll not stray alone. Agreed?"

"Agreed," she affirmed, smiling.

"Speak nothing of these things. When the time is right, Kenan will choose which daughters to send and which to keep close. Help him choose wisely, like your mother has done for me."

Mother advised this? Just when she thought she knew the woman, she discovered another layer.

"Okay," he said. "Now, go on. Gathering won't happen without hands and feet. I've a word for your mother. Sounds like those little monsters were all sent to the bunkrooms to pick up."

Anna kissed her father on the cheek before turning to go.

She walked to the edge of the balcony. There, a rope was stretched vertically, tied off with a loop on a rail post. She put her foot in a stirrup, pulled the safety loop off the rail, pushed on a little wooden lever, and stepped off the balcony. As she descended on the footlift, she saw her father still standing there, smiling at her.

THE footlift descended slowly at first, then picked up speed as the braking mechanism released the rope. Soon she descended at a rapid pace. With practiced ease, she hooked her dress with her free foot to keep it from billowing. She wouldn't want to give the men around here a reason to gawk.

Two young men watched her anyway, smiling with what could only be appreciation. The nerve! She was no pretty creature for them to admire. She scowled at them, and they moved off, side by side across a rope bridge, leading a little flock of goats by rope tethers.

She passed the counterweight as it rose nearby. She heard the rushing water refilling the clay cistern powering the mechanism controlling the footlift. She had no idea how it worked, with its cogwheels, grease, and springs. Wren knew of such things. She didn't need to understand it to use it.

The mechanism brakes caught again. The footlift slowed gracefully and shuddered to a stop at the first level, her free foot right at a small platform next to a potter's shop. She was still eighty feet off the ground.

She hung the loop onto the rail post and flipped the lever there, readying the footlift for whomever wanted to go up. As she did so, she smiled and said hello to Hallalah, the potter's wife, who busily kneaded a bucket of clay. The woman spared an endearing, "Oh, hello, dear," as she worked the material. She had wet, red clay up to her elbows. Anna smiled at her.

Anna almost skipped down the boardwalk. Almost. She didn't because she was too old to be skipping.

She knew she'd missed Kenan this morning. He always left early. However, she also knew just where to find him on his return this afternoon. She'd have to find a way to ditch Marjie, promise to her father or no.

She passed other villagers going about their morning work. Some carried baskets of vegetables or nuts, others rope or wood. One man used a hatchet to cut away a balcony rail that needed replacing. When he saw her coming, he almost lost a finger. She smiled at them all, and her hair bounced behind her. Many smiled back and watched her pass.

She crossed two rope bridges, easily swaying with their movement.

She stopped at her father's carving shop to say hello to a couple of her brothers, including Johlick, and three young nephews. She admired some of the intricate carvings they produced. She gave the rest of her blueberries to the youngest boy. One of her brothers congratulated her on her upcoming nuptials, which only she knew her father had approved. That made her think once again of Kenan.

She thanked her brother with a smile. Grabbing her pack basket, she left with a friendly wave to everyone there.

Does Kenan have any idea how she felt? Their conversations always danced around things like feelings. Kenan seemed so very... practical. Patient. Logical, yes definitely logical.

And he was so independent! He was now the oldest male child in his close-family. He had responsibilities. And he did it all himself, accepting no help from anyone. She worried he wouldn't see her as a partner in life. She was to be his helper. Would he see her that way, or was she to just make his babies?

Babies. The thought made her flush. A young man carrying a length of bent wood tripped and nearly fell over a rail. That one seemed to always be tripping. He'd fallen on his face just last week as she passed him on a rope bridge. He'll fall to the ground someday if he didn't watch where he walked.

Babies would wait. First things first. The wedding date approached. Anna certainly appreciated the attention the wedding would bring to her family. Not to her. No. But this would be a great gathering of her large family and Kenan's smaller family. What an event it would be!

Anna continued around the shop balcony, crossed a rope bridge, and came to the steptree. A smaller blacktree had been woodbent and carved into a spiral staircase hundreds of years ago. She stepped over the pin securing it to the balcony and lightly treaded her way down. Nine complete circles then seven more steps. She didn't want to count her way down, but she did. Thinking about Kenan while descending the steptree might get her neck broken.

At the bottom, the staircase spine was cut through for defensive purposes, she knew. A man was there, on his back checking the stones holding up the steptree.

She entered the Flat. The wide-open space, brown and packed flat from animals and people alike into a mat of soil, roots, and stones, bustled with activity. The village towered over her. All around the Flat, ropes raised and lowered footlifts and wooden platform lifts. People and supplies moved about: up, down, and around.

A stompdragon passed, pulling a cart full of fresh dragonhide, tended by a boy with a long slender pole. She covered her nose. The stompdragon didn't stink much, but the hides sure did. Its rear feet stomped as it walked, jostling cart, boy, and hides alike with every step.

Two crescentdragons, saddled and ridden by men with dragonpikes, passed nearby, headed north. These crescentdragons were quite large, thirty feet long and more than twice her height. They trotted by on two legs, the men in saddles riding smoothly. The backs of the crescentdragon heads held long, curved skulls. One of them trumpeted out a warning to the stompdragon.

Inside the Flat, market stalls formed neat, curved lanes. Today was trading day. Hawkers cried their supplies and merchants from away sold metalwork, glass, and wine. A grain merchant offered to fill her basket with corn. The wiry woman lifted a handful from a barrel for her to see. Each dry, yellow kernel the size of her thumb-joint fell with a click into the barrel. Anna smiled, shook her head, and moved on through the market.

A wine vendor called to her. "The best wine from Master Noah's own vineyard! Aged twelve years!" She smiled at him, too, and his mouth fell open as he stared at her.

She found a chipmunk sneaking from a vendor's bowl of cherries. Anna scooped the animal up with a darting hand. The creature froze in fear. Anna put the ball of fur in an empty belt sack, cinched the mouth closed, and continued through the Flat.

On the other side, she found Marjie, sitting on a bench carved out of a massive root, looking wistfully at the noisy market.

"Hi Marjie!" Anna called.

Marjie scowled back. "A little late, aren't you, deary?"

The plump little woman with curly, brown hair sticking out around a cloth cap shook her head at her. Anna could tell she was only trying to be irritable. It wasn't really in her.

"Don't be cross, Marjie. It's a beautiful day!"

Marjie snorted and rose, one hand on her ample hip, the other holding her pack basket. But she was already smiling. Well, a little. "Let's go, then. My cousin is watching my babe, but I'll need to be back in a few hours. These things start to ache if I go too long between feedings." She waved her hand across her chest.

Perfect. This will be easier than Anna had thought. "Really? Ache?"

"I'm just as surprised as anyone. The things they don't tell you! A babe takes more work than I thought, don't you know."

What would Kenan's babes be like? Would they have dark hair or blond? Hazel eyed or blue? Would they colic or rest sweetly? Would her chest ache, too? What would that be like?

The pair shouldered their baskets and moved away from the Flat, following broad paths between the trees. Marjie continued on about suckling babes, impatient husbands, and washing out nappies. Anna only lent her half an ear. She watched as butterflies, big and sparkling blue, swirled in the air above her, between the black tree trunks.

The village trails teemed with people. Women called to children, and children called to each other, playing chase games around the black trunks and large roots. Three stompdragons pulled a wagon full of nuts towards the Flat, passing under an enormous, arching tree root. A young boy napped on the broad shield of a tethered shielddragon. She saw Wren with his shielddragon, coming into the village with a big pine log. What a silly name for a shielddragon. What had possessed her brother? He probably thought the name funny.

A group of passing men holding tools or carrying baskets smiled at Anna and Marjie. Anna smiled back.

"Why do you do that?" Marjie asked. They stopped for a passing shielddragon pulling a wagon full of slat wood away from a nearby saw pit.

"Do what?"

"You know."

"I don't."

"Smile at them."

"Well, what am I supposed to do? Scowl?"

Marjie lowered her brows at her in consternation. "It wouldn't hurt."

"I'm just being friendly."

"Yeah, uh huh. Sure. They think you're friendly, all right."

A small beetle landed on Anna's shoulder. She picked it up and let it crawl around on her fingers, smiling at it. It was the size of her thumbnail and shined bright red in the morning light.

"Not *that* kind of friendly," Anna retorted.

Marjie chortled. "You may think they know the difference, but they don't. Men think of one thing and one thing only, all the time."

"Not all of them," Anna said as they continued on their way. She carefully dropped the beetle on a leaf to continue its business.

"All of them." Marjie sounded definitive. She always sounded that way.

Anna rolled her eyes. "My father doesn't. Not all the time."

"Well, no, not towards you," Marjie conceded. "That's different. But you just ask him. Ask him if I'm right. Better yet, ask your mother. I bet she'll tell you."

Thinking of her father made her feel guilty about her plans this afternoon to ditch Marjie and find Kenan. With easy effort, she pushed the guilt from her mind.

"Kenan's not like that."

"Ha!" Marjie barked. "He's a man just into his prime. He thinks about it all the time, I'm betting."

Anna frowned at her.

"Oh, there. I meant no offense. Kenan's a good man, he is. He'll make a great husband, surely, if you like them dark and a little broody, mind you. Many women do, don't you know. There was this one hussy I met over in Shallowbrook who..."

Anna let Marjie's torrent of words wash over her. They'd moved out of the village proper and past the bigger gardens. They approached the gate in the dragonring.

"...and she said he was very generous in the hammock..."

"Marjie," Anna interrupted.

"Oh! Yes. Sorry, deary. I'll help you."

Together they crossed the little wooden bridge over the deep ditch, navigated the diagonal path through the small stakes of the inner ring and opened the middle ring gate. It was heavy. Why did men build it so heavy? The gate bristled with fire-hardened stakes, the sharp ends pointing out. It took both of them to swing the gate open and shut again. Marjie didn't move out of the way fast enough and one of the stakes poked her in the hip.

"Ouch!" Marjie rubbed at the spot.

Anna smiled at her, seeing she wasn't really hurt. Anna usually went around the gate and squeezed between the middle ring stakes. Marjie probably wouldn't fit, not with her large chest and wide hips.

They walked side by side between two of the massive outer ring stakes. Anna paused, fished out the chipmunk, and let it go on the big stake.

"Almighty, Anna! Where did you get that thing? Have you had that all this time?" Marjie didn't like little furry creatures.

Anna just grinned at the little animal. It chirped, ran down the big stake, and scampered off. The women moved off into the forest.

Marjie picked up where she left off, or so Anna thought. She hadn't really been listening. "My mother told me the men down in Midreer can take any woman they want, any time they want."

"What?" Anna looked over at Marjie. "Why would she say such a thing?"

"'Cause it's true, don't you know? Midreer women never know whose babe they carry."

"You can't seriously believe that."

"You bet those cute little dimples you've got right there on your face." Marjie nodded and pointed to reinforce her certainty.

"Why, the streets would be chaos."

"The streets? Oh no, they've got buildings for it. Places, you understand, where you just go in and get yourself done up. You know how it goes. Then nine months later out pops a cute little one with no idea who its pap is."

"Marjie, that's ridiculous."

"Is it? Well, my second auntie... no, wait. She's my thirdaunt. Anyway, she said there's harems of women there. Girls, really. Their shaman, or priest, or whatever he is can bed any one he wants, any time he wants it."

Anna rolled her eyes and watched a stalkdragon's neck in the distance between the trees. She liked stalkdragons. They were gentle giants and kept the more problematic dragons away.

"Yes," Marjie continued, as if answering a question Anna didn't ask. "There's something living in him. Something evil. Something of Beelzebub, or something. Anyway, that's not important." Marjie paused for a quick breath, then rushed on with her juicy news.

"I hear Bethany is thinking of going there," Marjie announced, nearly giggling at the gossip.

Anna squinted at Marjie, a little mortified at the thought, even though it couldn't be true.

"Truly. She told my cousin who told Allaniel who told me that she wants to go. She wants to see their white tower and the hissdragon riders."

"Marjie, no one can ride a hissdragon."

"Really? How do you know? You probably haven't even seen a hissdragon in a dozen years." Marjie didn't like being countered.

Well, that was true. Anna hadn't seen a hissdragon in sixteen years. Happily. The only one she'd seen, far to the south, had looked at her too long. Its eyes held anger and intelligent hunger.

Marjie went on without skipping a beat. "The hissdragon riders live to chase down fleeing women. They put spears through the poor soul's calves as they run and then take them where they lay in the grass. They do it for sport."

Anna rolled her eyes. Again. She usually went out gathering alone. For the last week she'd gone with someone else, but last night Marjie had run into her on a rope bridge and asked her to go. Her new husband said if she didn't find someone to gather with then he was going to forbid her to go outside Blacktree. Anna felt it impolite to turn her down. Now, she wracked her brain, so she'd have an excuse ready next time.

As they walked, a thicket of vegetation close by presented an ambush point. Toedragons sometimes used thickets like this. Both women naturally skirted it with plenty of room, as they'd done their whole lives.

Marjie kept on talking as they walked. Anna kept half an eye on the thicket. She'd been ambushed by a group of toedragons, decades earlier as a child. She had a long scar on her back, thin but stark white. Sometimes it itched, to remind her of the danger. Wren had slaughtered three of the beasts with an axe before the rest ran away.

One of the toe claws rested in her belt pouch right now. She used it to scrape out tubers and truffles from the rich soil in the forest.

Just as they passed the thicket and she was about to look forward, she thought she saw something in it. Just there. Was that a... a face? Was someone there?

She stopped in her tracks, looking back at the thicket.

Marjie continued forward, still talking and oblivious to her surroundings.

Anna took a slow step back towards the thicket, peering into the green and shadows. The breeze made the leaves sway and the shadows dance. Sun dapple swirled in frantic circles on the thicket vegetation. A hummingbird zipped past, squeaking out a little chirp.

She heard another rustle in the thicket. Was it a rodent? An insect? A dragon? She hoped not a dragon. But she kept peering into the vegetation.

Nothing moved.

Margie finally ended her story and looked back at her. "Did you hear something?"

"Shhhh!"

"What is it? Agliranna?"

"Only my mothers call me that. Now, shhhh!"

"Did you see something?" Marjie persisted.

"I don't know. I thought I saw..."

"What? What did you see?"

Anna didn't answer. She continued to peer into the bushes. Her right hand reached behind her back to rest on the handle of her hand knife. Her fingertips deftly untied the leather binding cord. But she didn't draw it.

Anna watched in silence. It felt like a long time. Birds chirped. Insects buzzed. A solitary darterdragon ran into the thicket. She heard it scamper out the back.

A squirrel dropped a small nut on her head. The little seed bounced into her pack basket, rattling around in the bottom. The squirrel scolded them both before running off on small branches.

Marjie giggled.

"I guess it's nothing." Anna rubbed her scalp and grinned at the squirrel, the little rascal. She rebound her hand knife and turned to Marjie, who was resheathing her own hand knife. She did it with practiced ease, very matter-of-factly, as if she were in her kitchen. Anna suspected Marjie spent quite a lot of time in the kitchen.

"Let's go," said Marjie, then heeded her own command and walked away. Anna trotted to catch up.

Marjie said, "And then, they have a giant. He has a spear thirty feet long, so I hear. He uses it to..."

Oh, Almighty, would she ever stop?

They walked deeper into the forest and into a prime area for roundnuts, brownnuts, and yellowpetals.

"Marjie," Anna interrupted her in mid-sentence. She had been talking about some kind of room in Midreer where mawdragons were fed. "Is that a clump of yellowpetals? Right over there?"

"Sure enough, Anna, deary. Yes, there is. For sure. I'll go get them."

Marjie moved over to collect the petals of the bright, yellow flowers. They were used to sweeten a stew and to dye cloth.

Anna went the other way but stayed close enough to keep an eye on Marjie. Perhaps she should heed her father's order after all. She'd catch Kenan later, after her bath. She started to lay out a plan to bring up her feelings and concerns to Kenan. She was 44. Time to act like a grown woman and tell him how she felt. Her mother said young men were thick. A woman just had to tell them. The clods.

She looked up and saw a cluster of roundnuts, each three palms in diameter. Not that Kenan was a clod. He was quite sharp. She liked that about him.

She hiked up her dress to her thighs and set to climbing the tree.

THE man peered through the thicket vegetation and watched her and her long, strong legs wrapped around the tree.

# Chapter Six
# A Good Fight

CHAR Roughrock crept through the woods in the early afternoon warmth stalking his favorite quarry. He was sweating through his shirts. The leather armor kept it all against his skin. The brass plate on his chest gave it weight. At least the green smock covering it all remained dry.

His sword caught on a small bush, and he absently freed it with his left hand. In his right, he used an impromptu stick he'd found to lift a big leaf. Sure enough, the legs of a large spider withdrew into a hole. Its bite would have laid him up for a week. He shoved the stick into the hole with a satisfying squish. The end came out with globs of pale amber goop. Pleased, he moved on, slinking through the forest and making very little noise.

He didn't mind spiders. A white spider had been painted on the light shield he had slung over his back. He just had a job to do. Tonight. No need to take unnecessary chances now.

And yet here he was, taking a chance. He had no need to go to the women's pool. He might be spotted, though he was quite good at forest craft. He'd impressed his men with his skill at it.

His men. He'd earned the promotion, and he was good at it.

He scratched at a scar on his right hand. He had many scars on his hands. Everyone did. All people carried hand scars, but especially so among warriors. This one always itched. He didn't know why, but he took comfort knowing how the dragonscrape who did it suffered long before he died. Gut wounds did that.

He crept a little closer, then deftly climbed a big, black tree. This one, he knew, would give him a view of the pool.

Women bathed in the heat of the day, at least thirty of them. Some were old women with wrinkled, sagging skin and gray hair. His eyes flicked past them. Others were young. Too young. Some of his men liked them that way, but not him. He liked them twenty to fifty, just coming into their prime, before childbearing. And, most importantly, those fetched the best price.

He saw several at just the right age. He stirred as they swam in the water or dried their hair in the sun. He pushed the feeling back even as he drank in the sight. He had a job to do.

He saw one woman in particular. He flinched away and looked at others.

A blond woman in a pale green dress and another short, plump woman in brown came into the clearing. The creases in their dresses spoke to him of pack baskets and gathering. The tall blond in green almost flounced as the two women trotted up to the pool.

Sure enough, they immediately stripped and hopped in the water. The plump one did nothing for him as her body spoke of marriage and young children. The blond, though. She was something else.

He watched her. He had eyes for no other. Her proportions were perfect. Her hair darkened as it got wet, glistening in the sun. Yes. That one would be taken. He would make sure of it.

He had studied the village, mostly at night as the villagers moved about by lamplight. He knew which houses produced blond children. He might need to make an adjustment to the plan to make sure she was among those taken. He would find out where she lived. She would be his. He'd earned her.

With one last look, he moved back along the branch upon which he perched, moving quietly and slowly, until he could get back to a more solid limb. He didn't want any of them to see the tree leaves move. They might grow suspicious.

As he descended, he heard a sentry coming. The women's pool always had sentries now, he was told. They learned, these people, but they lacked experience. He hid under a fat bush and the woman walked right by. Of course, she did. She was looking up, not down. Edeerites always learn slowly. The people of Blacktree were no different. Most of them.

CHAR made his way back through the dragon ring, through the forest, and to his camp situated several hours from the village. One of his own sentries saw him, but too late. Char slapped him with the stick in the bronze helm before the man could call a warning. The stick snapped in two. Then he stuck the man in the stomach with the broken end. It didn't penetrate, but he'd be sore. The soldier should be more watchful. Char dropped the stick and moved into camp, ignoring the sentry rasping out an apology.

The camp was rough but tactically sound. A temporary dragonring surrounded the area. A round cooking pit had been dug near the edge with a dozen small cookfires burning and men tending tin buckets with heating water. Someone had felled several birds and... was that a porcupine? They were being skinned for the pots. Char mentally shrugged. Meat was meat.

Rough, wooden lean-tos lay scattered throughout the camp. Several circles of dragonpikes stood sentry inside the dragonring with a man next to each, facing out, ready in case something big came sniffing.

A very large fandragon lay on the far side of camp, sleeping. Two hissdragons lifted snouts and sniffed towards the cooking pit. They were securely tied and pulling at their ropes. Each stretched thirty feet long and stood fifteen feet at the hip. They stood on hind legs, but one used its strong arms to claw at the dirt as it strained. The other turned, looked at him, and hissed. Char smiled at it.

One brown tent stood in the center. He wished the tent were his. It should be his. He was in charge. But they had someone with them, someone due honor even if he was only an observer. The man's steel helmet sat on the top of a thin pole driven into the ground just outside the tent.

Rough men loitered around, sharpening bronze swords and axes. They thought they'd see action tonight. Their weapons should already have been sharp. He would speak to Cols.

Char marched into camp. He wasn't overly tall. He was strong but not bulky like Cols. His dark, brown hair hung thick. His eyes took in the camp and judged.

A yell sounded. Two men, far enough away to have missed Char's return, broke out into a fight over a cup of dice. They pulled knives and circled.

His force needed to attack tonight. They'd lost five men this past week, two to fighting and three to an ugly encounter with a pack of flashdragons. They had 56 men remaining. If they delayed any longer, their numbers would dwindle to an unacceptable level to launch the attack planned. This was no raid on a women's bathing pool. They were going into the village proper, right onto the Flat. They needed the men.

Char strode up to the pair with the knives. The one facing him saw his commander and dropped the knife. The one with his back to Char saw an opportunity and slashed wildly at his opponent.

The unarmed man dodged back. The wild swing came around. Char saw the danger in time to raise his hand and block the backhand slash at the wrist, but not in time to avoiding being cut on the cheek. A line of red formed. Blood ran down into his cropped brown beard.

Turning, the man with the knife saw what he had done. The knife dropped from his hand as his face grew pale.

"Ch... Char," the man stuttered. "Commander, I mean. I didn't see you there."

Char touched his face. His fingertips came away with drops of bright red blood.

The man's eyes grew wide.

"Pick it up," Char said quietly.

"N, no, Char. Commander. I wouldn't. I couldn't... "

"Do it," Char said. "Fail to obey and I'll string you up as a coward."

The man stooped to pick up the blade. Char knew the man was a good knife fighter with a strong heart. Sure enough, the man's eyes set in resolve. His body relaxed. He breathed deeply and his hands didn't shake.

Char knew the outcome remained uncertain. He raised to the balls of his feet, limbs loose, ready.

The man feinted to the left, then the right.

Char parried with the backs of his hands.

The man kicked a tin bucket at Char's shins and slashed at the same time.

Char was not fooled. He took a small nick on the left hand with a parry but was otherwise unharmed.

The knife fighter had patience. He knew a knife fight with only one knife was a game of patience. He slashed, stabbed, and backhanded, darting in and out.

Char dodged and backed away. He did not draw his sword, long knife, or shield. He had to make a point. The entire camp now watched.

If the man had offered up one of his slaves to Char, he would have shown mercy. One finger only, perhaps. If the man had slashed his own cheek, to remind everyone of the commander's power and position, he would have spared him, and perhaps given him a promotion. But the man had offered nothing, only an apology. An apology is only air without repayment.

The blade flashed again. And again. Char dodged and ducked.

Then, in an instant, Char blocked, stepped forward, and punched all at the same time. The man's nostrils spurted blood.

"One last chance, fool," Char offered.

The man's eyes became wild. Life or death. He lunged at Char, quick as a striking snake, knife first.

The man chose death, but Char wasn't a wasteful man. He shifted his weight on a heel, redirecting the man's lunge with a subtle hand just enough to cause the strike to miss. Both Char's hands clamped down on the man's wrist. Char then twisted around and fell backward, driving the man down to the ground. As they landed, the man's elbow dislocated with an audible pop. He screamed.

Char rolled the knife out of the man's spasming hands, catching it by the back of the blade. He rolled back down the arm, and away, smoothly gaining his feet.

The grunting man rolled over. His forearm and hand flopped

unnaturally, and he groaned.

"Squad leader!" Char shouted.

Himmons stepped up. He was in charge of this squad of eight men. Scratch that. Seven now. "Yes, sir."

"What do you think should be done here?"

"Sir. 'E'll be useless for a couple of moons. But 'e'll be a big 'elp when we go out in the spring. I suggest we string 'im up over by the fandragon. If you're not feeling merciful today, then we feed 'im to it. She'll be 'ungry soon."

Char looked down at the writhing man. It'd been a good fight.

"String him up against the post, lad. But have the bone doctor look at him, first. See if we can't speed the healing. We'll need him strong enough to walk soon."

Between grunts, the man looked up at Char. Actual appreciation shined in his eyes. "Thank you, sir," he breathed between the pain. "Good fight."

"Yes, it was, warrior. Yes. It was."

Char turned to leave the squad. He noted men all around camp watched, some nodding respect to their commander. Others stood sentry, watching the forest despite the show. Good men.

As he approached his shelter, the Nephilim came out of his tent. He put a hand on his steel helm and watched Char approach.

"I thought I smelled blood," the man said. His baritone voice grated out the words. Char knew its boom could carry. The man stood at average height, well-muscled, and had donned his steel armor. His black hair swept back. Sharp blue eyes watched everything. A white spider had been etched on the steel breastplate.

Char dropped to a knee and waited.

"Rise," came the command.

Char stood. "It was nothing, Prince Gharan. Just a camp squabble and a lucky cut."

"Our numbers?" Gharan asked.

"Fifty-five. The man survived but won't fight tonight."

"Excellent. Fifty-five is enough."

"Yes, my prince. I will get stitched and then we will meet with the squad leaders to finalize the plan."

"As you wish, commander. I will be in my tent, preparing for the evening activities."

"Yes, my prince." Praying, he meant. He'd stay in his tent and pray to his father while Char and his leaders planned. Then, Char knew he would have to explain it all to him just before they moved on Blacktree.

Such was Midreerian politics. Char knew he wasn't ready for that dangerous game. Not yet.

HOURS later, the commander had summoned the leaders to a planning session. One last time, Cols hoped.

He bounced on his heels, waiting for everyone to arrive. The bloodlust was already pounding through his veins. Old fashioned lust, too. Almost two moons had passed without a woman. He knew he'd have his choice tonight.

Cols had almost snuck off to the woman's pool for a peek. He knew where it was. He'd been there before. Maybe he could have pulled one of them away, just for a few minutes. After all this time, it wouldn't take long. But Char had forbidden anyone to go to the woman's pool. The report said security was heightened there. Well, he supposed that made sense.

Cols looked over the model of Blacktree village on the ground in front of him. He'd not been in the village proper. They'd only been to the women's pool last time. And this time, he hadn't been allowed. He wasn't a scout. He was a warrior.

Still, he studied it. He was captain around here, second only to Char and, of course, the man in the tent. He didn't want to think about the man in the tent.

The model showed a three-dimensional map of the village. Stakes driven into the ground indicated where the trees stood. Their front man had glued mushrooms to the sides of the stakes where the buildings were. He'd even used string to denote bridges and lifts, mapping travel routes through the village. Useful, that.

Asher was an arrogant dragonstool. Cols didn't like him. He was too tall. He looked down his nose at Cols. Cols didn't like that, either.

Asher had blade grass in his backside, too. Cols suspected his problem was about the delay. Asher was only supposed to be here a year. Didn't he have his fill of these tree girls while he was there? Three years. Cols would have had each and every one of them in three years.

Well, serves him right. Someone needed to cut Asher down to size. Soon. Maybe tonight.

Asher sauntered up just then, admiring his own work. Well, it *was* a pretty good model.

"Not bad, right Cols?"

Cols looked at him and nodded. Just you wait, he thought.

Himmons showed up next. Soon, the entire leadership corps was there.

The commander stalked up last. He had a bandage around his face, diagonally, covering the cut cheek and his nose. He also had a cloth over his head. He looked at each of them in turn from between the cloth.

"Tonight's the night, lads."

Cols felt a thrill run through his chest and down his arms at the Commander's words. He knew it!

"But," the commander raised a finger, "first, we need to go over the plan again. I have a few last-minute adjustments based on the latest scouting reports."

They all listened closely as the commander explained the changes.

Tonight was the eve of the village resting day. All the villagers would feast tonight and drink heavily, making them slow to respond. At dusk, the White Spiders would get into position and await the signal.

"These houses will be taken. This one," the commander touched the mushroom on the stake. "This one, and if there's time, this one on the way out. Squads A and D will have the task. Use this house," he pointed, "for cover. There's an old couple there. Eliminate them first." Himmons nodded to his commander. "At the whistle, retreat due east towards the wide part of Babelwind Brook. You know what to do. Cols will be ready for you."

Cols rubbed his hands in glee.

"Squads B and C, wait here," The commander continued. "You'll see me when it's time to strike. I want this house, this one, and this one. Especially this one. It had better be looted and every female taken. Unspoiled, mind. Then, if you have time, hit this one."

"Squad E, you're reserve. If B and C have no opposition, sweep in and hit this one and this one. Only if there's time. Otherwise, get some stompdragons or something and protect B and C. We want their haul. It should be good."

"Sir," inquired a man. "Is my squad to stick to the original plan?"

"Yes, squad F has no changes. You know what to do.

"One more thing. No one is to touch this house," said the commander. Cols looked at him sharply, listening carefully. "This one right here. Got it? Mark it well. I saw something there and we're not to mess with it. Do not go there."

The rest of the men nodded, but Cols frowned to himself. Asher also looked disappointed. What did that dragonspitter know?

"If all goes well," the commander continued, "squads B, C, E and F will head south. Load up the cargo and make for Babelwind Brook, at the narrow end. Location One. Form a rear guard, as usual. Retreat across the brook and take up position there as planned. The fandragon will be there, waiting for you. Defend until Cols gets to you with A and D squads.

"If it doesn't go well, we meet southeast at Location Two for a quick retreat.

"Under no circumstances do we come back here to this camp. We couldn't retreat fast enough if we have cargo with us."

"Sir, they've started to man the defensive platforms."

"I know," came the commanders reply. "Squad F knows, too. Okay, then. A few guards should make no difference. Take out the sentries. You know where they are. Watch their firepoles. They may not be like ours, but they will still mess you up. Got me?"

They all nodded.

"Squad leaders, keep your men in line." The commander was speaking to the others, but he looked at Cols when he said it. Typical.

The commander went on, looking around at them all. "This is in and out. These men are not warriors, but they will protect their women. They outnumber us seven to one."

"I like those odds, sir." Cols couldn't help but say it.

"Don't be so sure. They've got some sharp people. Listen, they're very skilled, even unarmed. Some of them make a sport of it. But their weapons are mostly just tools. They have dragonpikes but use them only against dragons. They don't know how to wield them properly against men, nor do they know how to work together. They have archers. Really good archers. Keep your shields forward. Look, they'll be mostly unarmored and half drunk. Hit them hard. Get the cargo. Get out. No dallying over a quick rut. I won't wait for you, but I won't hold you back later, either. Do you understand?"

Nods all around.

"Make sure your men know. No mistakes. That's it. Cols, with me."

The commander turned to leave, but Asher called to him. Cols rolled his eyes at the man's impertinence.

"What is it?" The commander responded.

"Why can't we 'it that 'ouse? I was looking forward to that one."

"Because I said so. I had better not see you there."

"Yes sir. 'Ow about this one?"

"Which one?" The commander was losing his patience, Cols saw. He would later have a word with Asher he wouldn't like.

"This 'ouse. Right 'ere."

"What of it? I don't think there's any women there."

"No sir. But I 'ave a score to settle."

"Settle it later, on your own time. Do what your squad leader says. You're with A?"

"Yes sir."

The commander hesitated. "I understand a score. I understand you were told one year but spent three. You did a good job. You have our thanks, and you'll get first pick of the slaves, after the leaders. But this is business and battle. There's no room for a personal grievance. Or disobedience. I'd better see you nod."

Asher nodded.

"Good. Get to it, lad."

Asher turned five shades of red, Cols was pleased to see. Asher was actually older than the commander. Lad, heh.

Come to think of it, Cols was older than the commander as well, old enough to be his fourthfather. But then, he didn't call Cols lad. Must be all the scars.

Cols followed the commander through the camp. The squads were gathering in their areas, being briefed and getting ready. Camp would be broken in short order.

"Is it ready, Cols?"

"Yes sir. It's ready. It's pretty 'ot, too."

"Good. You know what to do."

Cols nodded and moved off. He wasn't going into the village, but he was going to have a lot of fun just the same. He'd get a woman later. A good one. He got third pick, if any of those louts at Location One could contain themselves until he got there. They'd better, or there'd be blood.

THE men moved out. Char watched them march from the back of his hissdragon. The beast tugged at the reins and hissed at him.

"Soon, you dragonspit. Soon."

The men all had some armor and ready weapons. Well-equipped men were hard to come by in this business. Equipment was expensive. But they all knew how to fight. They were each raised in a blood family. Any one of them was worth three of the villagers, he knew.

He'd donned his brass helmet. He pulled his sword a palm out of the scabbard, just to make sure nothing bound the blade. He admired the shine of steel. It was a gift from his prince. He wished it were a few fingers longer, but he didn't complain. It was steel, after all.

His hissdragon shifted over a few steps and turned. Char whipped it with the reins. It hissed again, showing rows of sharp teeth between a set of jaws that could swallow a goat whole. After another smack of the reins, it got back in place. Char patted it on the neck hump. It was a good beast, mostly.

After the column passed, his prince approached on the back of the other hissdragon. The animal strode calmly forward on two legs, front arms held ready at the sides. It had hungry eyes full of malice, and it hissed at Char, baring teeth. But its body obeyed the lightest touch of his prince's knees. How did he do that?

"Are you ready?" The Nephilim asked through the open front of his steel helmet.

"Yes, my Prince."

"Good," Gharan said. "Tell me your plan."

Char suppressed a sigh and started talking, leaving only one detail out of his description.

# Chapter Seven
# Business and Battle

PLATES of meat, cheese, nuts, and berries covered the table. Kenan smiled at it. He hadn't eaten like this in weeks.

He was a guest in Jaret's house tonight, before rest day. He sat at the long table in the common room, opposite Anna. She caught him looking at her and gave him a bright smile.

He thought he'd felt a flutter in his chest last night as he sat talking with her on the balcony outside. She'd touched his arm. He wasn't sure, then. He was now. It came back with a vengeance. If he opened his mouth, giant butterflies would burst forth, surely.

He thought he knew what the feeling meant. He wasn't sure he wanted it or what to do about it, and he even feared it a little.

He looked down at his plate. He wouldn't be able to eat if she kept smiling at him like that. He wouldn't be able to do anything but slink out and hide. She wasn't just pretty. In the light of the late afternoon sun streaming through the lattice window, she looked absolutely stunning. Gorgeous. Radiant.

He looked down again. He had to keep his mind on the food. And her father sat right next to them. It wouldn't do to be caught leering at her.

Blond people surrounded the large table, all talking and laughing. Food on whitewood platters passed from person to person, each one helping themselves. A berry shot from the far end of the table and struck Johlick in the ear. He yelled in pain.

"None of that, now," Jaret said it quietly. Yet, they somehow all heard him through the din of the room. The guilty boy near the other end of the table scooched down on the bench to avoid his father's disapproving gaze.

Wren boomed out a laugh at something Lidai said. Anna had invited Kenan and his younger sister. Another young woman of the family made sure Lidai sat opposite Wren. Anna's mother eyed the pair in thought. Anna eyed them in glee. Kenan grinned to himself. Whatever these women wanted, they got. It was some kind of magic.

"It's some kind of magic, isn't it?"

Kenan started. Jaret grinned at him.

"Sir?"

"The women here. We men sit at the heads of our tables, judging and making pronouncements. All the while, they make everything happen as they wish. It makes a man think."

Dragonscrape. Jaret was no fool.

"Father," Anna chided. "We're not like that."

"Of course, you aren't, my dear." But he looked at Kenan with wryness in his eyes.

Kenan didn't know what to say, so he said nothing. To his relief, a platter of brownnut bread landed in front of him. He used the wooden tongs to drop a thick slice on his plate.

Thankfully, the whitewood platters kept coming. Next was buttered nutmash. Then came a pork loin smothered in a brown gravy, followed by a bowl of sweet redberries on clotted cream. Soon, another platter appeared with a trout, skin peeled and pink flesh steaming, surrounded by a bed of greens. How much more was there?

Jaret had hired several women to serve the feast so all of Jaret's family could sit at the table. A woman placed a horn cup on Kenan's tray and filled it with red wine from a clay pitcher. Jaret had bought a barrel of wine for tonight?

Kenan's attention shifted to Jaret as he stood, holding his pewter cup. Pewter, an entire cup of it! Jaret cleared his throat, putting force into it. The table quieted.

Just as Jaret opened his mouth, Wren called out, "Speech, father! Let's hear what you have to say!"

The family burst into laughter. Some young ones at the far end of the table clapped, but their mother shushed them.

"Wren," Jaret said with a twinkle in his eye. "You pipe down, son. You're a guest at this house, now."

Everyone cheered the pronouncement. Wren had just finished a beautiful house near the edge of the village, large enough for a big family. His mother looked at him from the far end of the table with one eyebrow up. Kenan could tell she wanted more second-babies. Then she turned her gaze on Lidai. Lidai? She was too young, surely. Wasn't she?

Jaret cleared his throat. "Alright. Calm down, all of you."

He caught a preteen at the other end of the table by surprise at the sudden quiet. Her last word hung in the air for all to hear. "Dragonpoop!"

Mother Alannoon's jaw dropped open. Jezeera snorted from her rocker by the fireplace. Everyone else laughed again, Wren loudest of all. He had to wipe a tear away before he could look up at his father.

Jaret waited patiently. He held up a hand as if irritated, but Kenan could see his amused expression. Finally, they achieved a tentative silence poised to flee from the boisterous house.

"It's not every day I approve a match with a daughter. The words have been said. The vows were spoken, before God and men."

More cheering.

Jaret turned to Kenan, who looked back. His face felt hot from the attention.

"Kenan Blacktree. Woodbender and friend. Stand and take my daughter's hand."

Kenan turned to look at Anna. Her face was flushed, too. Somehow the blush made her even more beautiful. She also stood and reached out to him, and Kenan clasped her hand. It was the first time he'd held it. She was warm.

"Before this family, before your friends, I pronounce you, Kenan, and you, Agliranna," he paused to fill his lungs. "Betrothed!"

The family jumped to their feet, yelling, clapping, and whistling. Wren slapped Johlick's back so hard the young man spit up some wine.

No one noticed Quick dragging away half the pork, trailing gravy in a streak across the floor.

BACK in his house, Kenan lay in his hammock alone in the dark, stomach full. He hadn't bothered to undress. He lay with his legs crossed, boots in the air. One arm he'd tucked under his head, the other rested loosely on his chest. He smiled to himself.

Well, that went rather well.

Anna's mother didn't seem to like him much. The woman never spoke to him. He expected this, of course. Jaret would be the one to converse with a man betrothed to their daughter. Still, she watched and never spoke to him. She never smiled either.

He'd always liked Jaret. They were colleagues of a sort, Kenan delivering bentwood to him routinely for Jaret's woodcarving business. The quiet man generally only spoke when needed. He was industrious, artistic, and friendly. The people of the village liked him. He possessed wisdom, too, it seemed. He could never live up to that. Could he?

A mosquito buzzed over his head. He couldn't see it in the dark, so he idly located it by ear as he mulled the evening over.

What was up with Wren and Lidai? The three of them had always been close. Friends. But was there something more?

Lidai was his sister. When she was younger, she made a total pest of herself, following him and Wren everywhere. He'd made her first bow. As she aged, he'd come to understand her and love her as his full sister, even though they didn't share a father. She was a woman grown, now, he supposed. The hem of her dress was down to her ankles and everything. She was eligible, tradition said. She had been for a few years now. But he couldn't imagine her married. His other sisters, yes, they were easy to picture married, a gaggle of children around them. Some of his older sisters already had secondbabies. But Lidai?

His free hand shot into the air, catching the invisible mosquito mid-buzz. He squeezed, then wiped it off his palm and onto the floor.

He thought of his brother, Nehamane, gone now pushing sixty years. He'd been his closest brother in age, but they'd never been close. Now, Kenan would have a different brother, one he respected and liked.

Wren had always been his close friend, ever since he could remember. They'd grown up together. They'd explored the forest together. Wren once climbed a stalkdragon's tail just because Kenan had dared him. He'd laughed the whole time, even as the beast charged through the forest, toppling understory trees and scattering everyone and everything in its path.

When they were younger, Wren and Kenan got drunk together and made mischief together. Today, they worked together in his shop. Wren was his best friend and brother without blood. Did he now have eyes for his sister? What would that mean? Was it some kind of betrayal? Should he talk to him about it? What would he say?

Kenan's thoughts tumbled in his head. He knew he was trying not to think about Anna. He had months to wait. He would wait. Almighty, it seemed like a long time just now. Best to think on other things.

With time, sleep came.

KENAN awoke with a jerk and fell to the floor. Had he really just fallen out of his hammock? Were those shouts?

An angry red light flickered through his lattice window. What was going on?

It came to him all at once. Someone shouted it from a distance. Fire!

Kenan leapt to his feet and towards the door. He tripped on something and fell forward. He broke his fall with head turned from long muscle memory, then scrambled back to his feet. He found his door and opened it. A house a couple trees over roared with flame!

Wait, should he bring something? Where was his bucket? Dragonstool! Whenever he needed it, it was missing. When he didn't, he was tripping over the dragonspitting thing.

Tripping! He took two long steps back, stooped, and felt along the floor blindly. Yes, there it was. He grabbed the wooden bucket and sprinted for his balcony.

Two houses burned. Men ran towards them from all directions. Some had buckets, others ropes and axes. Should he have grabbed his axe? No, the fire lines were already forming at the cistern. He needed his bucket.

How did two houses catch on fire at the same time? Kenan sprinted across one rope bridge and then another, joining a line of men running towards the fires.

He heard a scream. There! A man fell from a balcony. In the firelight, he could see the footlift rope play out above him, writhing like a snake in the air. The man's feet hit a branch and he tumbled the last part of the way. The scream ended abruptly.

What was going on?

Kenan continued his run towards the nearest fire, bucket in hand.

A woman screamed. She was falling, too. Her overshift fluttered up over her head as she fell. A footlift rope fell with her.

"Stay away from the lifts! Stay away from the lifts!" A man yelled it, over and over.

Kenan ran on. He closed in on a clay cistern where water was kept for many uses, including fire control. A crowd pushed against the cistern, everyone struggling forward to get to the water. The man continued to yell his warning about the lifts. A mother shouted her child's name in the dark.

An arrow ripped up through the air, striking the yelling man. It penetrated his stomach and stopped with the arrowhead protruding upwards from between his shoulder blades.

No. No, not a raid. It couldn't be. They'd posted sentries.

A man shrieked and fell from a dark platform two trees over. In the firelight, Kenan saw his arm fall separate from his body.

He looked higher. There, on the balcony around a darkened house, stood two armed men. They both had shields.

He could see the white spider painted on them.

No. No, not again. Not now.

"No!"

Kenan gripped his bucket handle and sprinted towards the dark balcony and the two men.

An arrow ripped past him. He didn't care.

Two other villagers joined him, but he outpaced them.

Not again. Not again!

He got close. Another arrow ripped by him, loud in the night. That one came close. Real close. He ignored it and made for the white spiders on their shields, snarling as he ran.

A whistle sounded out of the dark below. It called shrill and pierced the night.

The two raiders instantly started to back away. They did so blindly, feeling with their rear foot. They faced his charge, shields forward, dark swords pointed towards him.

Kenan didn't slow until he was on them.

The one nearest the rail lunged forward, sword first, right arm thrusting and left leg leading. Kenan didn't think. He acted.

Kenan deflected the blade to the side with the palm of his left hand, getting cut for the effort. Then he spun, the bucket arcing in the dark. He stepped in a front stance, placing his back foot carefully behind him.

The second man held his shield low. He probably had no armor there. The sturdy bucket swung high, catching him in the head with a dull, wooden thump, right below his leather half-helm. The man nose crushed, sending a spurt of blood down his beard. He fell backwards.

The first man pulled his sword back for another cut. Kenan slapped him with his free hand, hard across his bare face to distract him. The man wore pieces of metal armor on his chest, but it wouldn't protect him from what was coming.

Kenan already had his back foot hooked around his opponent's boot heel. The man had no idea. Kenan twisted, using the motion to push his knee against the man's knee, hooking the man's heel with the side of his boot. The man's forward leg straightened in an instant. Kenan's opponent lost his balance, falling back hard against the railing. The wood railing had been built to keep children from falling and give the elderly something to hold if they tripped. It had never been intended to hold against a very large, armored man falling on it with all his weight. The railing cracked and the man's eyes widened, but it held.

No matter. The bucket swung high and back down on the man's head. The railing broke and the man disappeared into the night without another sound.

Kenan turned back to the second man, who was just starting to lift his head up.

A spear flew in from behind Kenan, thrown by a villager. The tip caught the second man in the white skin below the jaw. His leather-covered helmet shot off the top of his head and over the side of the balcony, the body twitching violently against the spear haft.

More village men ran towards the scene.

Kenan heard a muffled yell further along the dark balcony, which curved around the home of an elderly couple. In the dark, he continued forward, bucket in hand. The home cast the area in deep shadows, but Kenan could make out a man standing at the railing, lowering a rope under strain.

The man looked at him, then let the rope go. The rope sped up over the rail and down towards the ground. A muffled female scream faded downward, into the night below.

The man's axe leaned against the rail. He grabbed it in both hands.

Kenan's chest heaved, but not from exertion. He would kill this man. He would kill them all. He leapt forward, swinging his bucket over his head in a downward arc.

The raider caught it on his horizontal axe handle. The bucket rebounded upwards with a clack. Then the man twisted to make a horizontal cut at Kenan's stomach with the axe head. Kenan stepped back a half step, out of harm's way, while he used the momentum of the rebound to swing the bucket all the way around, behind, then up and forward in an arc.

It caught the man under the jaw. The man's eyes rolled back as he stepped back once. Then twice. He teetered for a moment, eyes rolling. He took one more step back, one too many. He tottered against the rail before his body fell over backwards, followed by his legs and boots.

Kenan stood in the dark, still clutching his bucket and struggling to get his mind under control. He had to think. He could kill them all if he could just think clearly.

A group of village men ran up, some with spears. The man in front, a potter, had a torch and looked shocked. "A bucket, lad?"

"Quick," Kenan snapped. "Put out the torch!"

Too late. An arrow ripped up through the air and through the potter's head. The man's eyes bulged as he fell straight down into a heap on the planks.

Kenan and the rest of the men scattered out of the light.

Kenan moved to the edge of the balcony, hidden in the shadow of the dark house. He looked over the edge but saw nothing but blackness.

He could, however, hear men shouting down below. Suddenly he heard a whip crack and a female cry.

No!

He looked around. There! A thin branch hung close enough. He backed up two steps, dropped his bucket as he took two fast strides forward and leapt over the rail. He heard a man shout a warning behind him.

Kenan's hand closed on the limb as he continued to fall. He knew the thin branch wouldn't hold his weight. He used it to slow his fall and guide him to where he aimed. He thought he might bob to a stop, until he heard the snap of wood above him.

He fell again, quickly. Then he slowed once more. The branch split but had not completely broken. It dangled there with Kenan hanging on with one hand. He started to climb.

The limb split some more, and he fell further down before stopping. He gripped the limb tightly.

The limb continued to split and peel away. Finally, the strain was too much, and it broke free.

Kenan held it tightly as he fell into the darkness below.

WREN awoke to the sound of a woman screaming. He sat up in his hammock, breathing hard. Who was screaming? Was someone giving birth? What was going on?

He rose, ducked his head under a clothesline, and pushed through a damp overshirt. He heard another yell. Someone screamed something about the lift lines.

He reached the room's window opening. The frame sat empty and had no lattice or glass. He smelled smoke, but not the smoke of cookfires and hearths, which was ever present in the evenings. This smelled strong and acrid. Something big burned. His heart started to race.

He stuck his upper body out the window and craned his corded neck. He could see fire between the branches on the far side of the village. Fire!

He tossed the damp overshirt over his body and stepped into his boots. He couldn't find his belt in the dark, so he skipped it. He ran to his small kitchen and found the floor hatch, berating himself for not yet getting a rope bridge built to connect his house to the village. Ripping the hatch open, he grabbed the rope dangling there and dropped through the floor.

He slowed his descent with one hand, feeling some heat through thick calluses. He reached the ground sooner than he thought and hit hard, falling to the side. He jumped back to his feet and raced towards the Flat.

Passing a saw pit, he saw an axe in the end of a log. He snatched it on his way by. He might need it if he had to cut his way through a door or wall. He stored his own steel axe in the shed by Okay's pen. He'd be sure to keep it in his house in the future.

People raced throughout the village above. Many carried buckets. Some had spears. Spears? What good were spears against a fire?

He heard another scream, and someone fell to the ground nearby. He changed direction. He'd been going to sprint up the steptree. But if someone fell, they would need help, if they'd survived the drop.

He saw a man standing by a big tree root. The man held a bow with arrow nocked. Wren skidded to a stop as the man released the arrow upwards, into the people on a balcony above. His people. An old woman screamed and fell down through the air.

He knew what this was.

With a snarl, Wren charged the man.

As the archer nocked another arrow, he swiveled towards Wren, turning the bow on him. He didn't get time to draw. Wren swung the axe. It struck the man on the collarbone, sinking deep into the chest. The man's breath huffed out of him, and he dropped to his knees. The bow and arrow clattered to the ground. Wren put a boot on the man's chest and wrenched the axe free. Then he swung again. And, again, once more.

KENAN hit something hard. He hadn't fallen very far. Yes! The roof of the meeting hall stood right where he thought it should be. It sloped here, though. He started to slide towards the edge. It got steeper towards the eve. He slid faster.

This hadn't been part of the plan.

His fingers grabbed at the woven bentwood planks. His feet scrambled against the edges of the pattern. Panic took hold as he clawed at the roof, frantically reaching for some way to stop his slide to a deadly fall.

His boot caught an edge. It slipped but he had his fingers on another edge. He stopped, motionless, taking a moment to breathe. He looked down but couldn't see anything in the dark. Looking up, he started to climb.

Finally, at the flat top along the ridge line of the structure, he jumped up on the center plank and ran towards the far tree. He knew of a hatch there for maintenance.

He dropped into the structure and directly into the granary. It made for a soft landing. Scattering kernels of wheat, he made his way in the pitch blackness. He felt along for a hatch in the granary wall. He looked around in the black, starting to panic that he'd just trapped himself. But then he somehow saw the dark, bronze latch. In a moment, he fell out into the meeting hall amid a rush of grain.

Three villagers ran through the hall, all holding bows. They stopped and looked at him as he rose.

"Kenan!" One shouted to him. "What're you doing in there?"

"You're going the wrong way!" Kenan shouted back. "This way!" He sprinted down the long hall, and they followed.

The big wooden doors at the end opened out onto another balcony and a branch walkway. Kenan stopped to get his bearings.

Yes. There. The raiders had lit torches to run with their prizes through the night. He also found the coil of rope he knew was kept nearby for emergencies. He checked it and saw it had been properly tied to a strong rail post. He tossed the rope into the dark and lowered himself over the rail. He started to slide down.

"Over here!" One of the archers shouted. "We can see them!"

"Shut up!" Kenan hissed upwards.

Another arrow ripped through the dark and embedded itself in the man's chest. He looked down at Kenan and then at the arrow, confusion on his face.

Kenan relaxed his feet a little and dropped faster. His callused hands felt the heat, but he paid it no mind. Kenan landed smoothly on the ground. He shook the rope and heard the next man ease himself over the rail above.

Kenan didn't wait. He couldn't wait. He'd need to do this alone. He had to know where they went. He had to stop them. He couldn't stand failing again. He raced into the night after the raiders. He couldn't see their torches through the dark vegetation, but he could see the light on the underside of the big leaves above them. They were moving away.

Suddenly a man stepped into his path, holding hammer and shield. The white spider showed bright in the dark. "Where are you going in such a... 'ey!"

Kenan never slowed. He plowed right into the man.

The raider stood bigger by far but hadn't set himself. Kenan had momentum, lots of it. They both fell, the larger man losing his air on impact. Kenan heard the breath whoosh from him.

Kenan leapt back up and sprinted away. The big man wheezed behind him.

Kenan ran through the forest. He would catch them. He would free the women.

An arrow ripped out of the dark, catching Kenan in the thigh.

That did it.

Kenan spun around and fell out of control. He hit hard, lost his wind, and lay there for a moment, writhing in pain on the ground, mouth gasping for air.

A man walked up, wearing a dark green cloak, face expressionless. He carried a bow, and arrows poked out from a quiver at his belt. He looked down at Kenan, studying him. He bent down and pulled a knife out of his boot.

Kenan kept trying to catch his breath. The pain in his leg consumed most of his mind, but a small part of him screamed at himself to get up. He was going to die. He couldn't die. Not yet. They couldn't get away!

The man came close, squatting down, and tested the edge of his blade against his fingertips. "Nice work with that bucket, boy. I'm going to go get that bucket. Must be a magic bucket." The man's monotone voice hissed at him, the strange accent underlying the threatening words. "Don't worry, lad. Your run is all done."

Another arrow ripped through the night, piercing the man through one arm and into his middle, rib to rib. The man tried to stand, but fell back, kicked a leg, and lay still.

A village archer, one of Kenan's thirduncles, ran up to him. "Kenan! Thank the Almighty! I found you!"

"Yes," Kenan wheezed.

"Here, let me help you back. You're not going to catch them with that arrow in you."

"Nope," Kenan agreed. He tested the leg and found he could put weight on it. Barely. It hurt like dragonspit every time he stepped.

"Why didn't you wait for me? For any of us?"

Kenan grunted in pain. "Never occurred to me." He reached down to pull the arrow out.

"No, lad. Leave it alone. Let's get you back."

They stumbled back to the village, making slow progress. They had to stop once so Kenan could up-end the entire feast from Jaret's house, and maybe some from meals as far back as last week. It took a few minutes.

More light flickered ahead now. The fires continued burning. The village danced with torches, lamps, and people running everywhere.

They approached the village Flat. Kenan leaned heavily on his thirduncle, who was in turn breathing hard. Men slid down ropes. Weapons rained down on the south side of the Flat. People were emptying the small armory above. Pikes and spears quilled the ground.

Wren ran up out of the dark without a torch. Something dark and liquid covered his friend's front from face to boots. He grabbed Kenan. It took the big man little effort to take a lot of the pressure off the arrow in his leg. His thirduncle ran away with Kenan's thanks.

"Anna?" Kenan asked.

"Safe," Wren replied.

"What's happening?"

"No, you fool!" Wren shouted at a running man. "Stay away from there! You'll get skewered! Give them a minute!" He looked ahead again, half carrying, half dragging Kenan across the Flat.

Kenan repeated, "What's happening?"

"There was an attack."

"No kidding," Kenan said, looking down at the arrow in his leg.

"Right. We're going after them. Getting ready."

"No kidding," Kenan said again, looking at all the weapons being dropped from the armory.

"Right. Okay. Medahal has the men gathering. Torches. Shields. Spears." Another spear thudded into the dirt not far away.

"Hey!" Wren bellowed up. "We're walking, here! Drop them, don't hurl them!"

A pale face looked over the rail before pulling back into the night. Men with torches and lamps ran everywhere. Some had axes and shields. Some had wood armor or old copper helms rusted green.

A crescentdragon with a red head frill thudded up with Jaret on its back carrying a dragonpike. "Wren! Medahal is looking for you!"

"I bet," Wren muttered under his breath. To his father, he said, "I'll be right there." The crescentdragon trotted away with Jaret slapping its side for more speed.

"Hey. Was that your father?"

"What?" Wren pulled Kenan onward without pause. The big man wasn't even winded. Kenan was still having trouble finding his breath.

"Never mind." It occurred to Kenan he was mumbling. His tongue didn't want to work right.

The steptree stood right ahead, ringed by lamppost light. The two house fires seemed under control and fading. The women had formed a bucket brigade.

Kenan focused on pronunciation. "You pulling me all the way up the steptree? I'm not sure I can do it."

"Always complaining," grunted Wren.

"No, I'm not."

"Yes, you are. You croak like a stuck patedragon."

Kenan grinned despite himself. He felt lightheaded. Had he been drinking? Yes, earlier.

Wren saw the smile. "That's better. You'll be alright."

They detoured past the steptree and to a platform lift.

"We can't use the lifts," Kenan said softly. He was getting tired. Sleepy.

"Stay with me, Kenan. Yes, we can. Only a few were cut. This one's just fine."

Wren laid Kenan down on the platform. Kenan immediately reached for the arrow, but Wren stopped him with a meaty hand.

"No. Leave it alone."

"I knew that."

"Of course, you did."

"Where am I going?" Kenan's words were definitely slurring now, but he couldn't think what to do about it.

"Up. To my parents."

"Your parents? What's wrong with my mother's house?"

"What, getting picky, just because you have a splinter?"

"No."

"Yes. My parents are just above this lift. They're closer. My mother can help you. Now shut up and lie there. My sister told me that's what you do best."

Kenan used a little sign language.

Wren smiled wide, teeth gleaming in the dark. "There you go. That's better. Now hold on. You'll go up fast. You don't weigh enough to slow this thing down."

"Wha..."

"Coming up!" Wren bellowed. Then he pulled the lever.

Kenan shot into the air. He lost consciousness instantly.

# Chapter Eight
# Leave the Thinking to Me

WHEN Kenan awoke, Anna hovered over him. He didn't believe in angels, but if he did, they'd look like her. He smiled up at her.

"There it is," she said, smiling back at him. "I've been waiting for that."

"Waiting for what?" he croaked. Dragonstool! He *did* sound like a dying patedragon.

"Never you mind. Relax. It's been a couple hours and it's after middark now. The arrow's out."

Kenan looked. Anna stood next to him, her hand on his shoulder to keep him from sitting up. Sure enough, his bare leg was arrow free and wrapped in a neat white cloth, stained red near the puncture. He tested the limb. It ached fiercely when he moved it. Where were his boots?

"Where are my boots?" Kenan croaked.

"Oh, you don't want those anymore," Anna replied. "We couldn't get them off due to all the blood. We had to cut them off."

Dragonscrape. He liked those boots. "Where am I?" Kenan asked.

"You're..." Anna started.

"... bleeding all over my table, young man." Her mother, Alannoon, finished as she walked by.

Great. These were her first words to him since that unfortunate incident above the women's bathing pool when he'd been a teenager.

Kenan looked around. Yes, he was in Jaret's common room, lying on the same table right where he'd eaten only hours before.

The arrow lay broken in half on the floor nearby. Quick busily licked it clean of his blood.

Kenan scowled at it. "How'd I get here?"

"By lift," Anna answered.

Kenan remembered the lift, but nothing after. He looked at Anna smiling down at him. She was so beautiful.

She started to say something, then stopped herself.

"What were you going to say?" he asked.

"I'm not sure I..."

"Say it. Please."

She breathed it out. "I think I love you."

"Better leave the thinking to me."

Her eyes went wide, white showing around the bright blue irises. "What did you just say?"

Kenan started laughing. He couldn't help it. What was wrong with him? He didn't know, but he struggled to quell his mirth.

Anna hit him on the shoulder. It only made him laugh again. She hit him again, but she laughed, too.

Alannoon came back into the room, carrying a bundle of cloth. "Stop beating the patient, dear. You might break open his wound." Then she bustled on into the kitchen.

Kenan caught Anna's wrists. He pulled her down to him. She didn't resist much. He pulled her closer, taking her by the shoulders. Then he pulled her down for a kiss, their first. She wasn't resisting any longer.

A clatter came from the kitchen with a sharp word from Alannoon. Anna pulled back.

Kenan lost himself in those eyes. "I think I love you, too." He ruined the moment by giggling again. He tried to turn it into a manly chortle, but only managed to bite his tongue. "Ow!" For some reason, this made him giggle yet again.

Alannoon bustled back into the common room. "No kissing the patient, dear. That will definitely break open his wound."

Anna straightened and giggled a little as well. "Mother, he seems lightheaded. He can't stop laughing, and he's saying stupid things."

Alannoon sniffed. "It is the blood loss and the seed we gave him, my dear. But they all say stupid things. I cannot cure him of that."

Anna touched the bandage. "Should this be tighter?"

"No, dear. It is fine as is. You did good work."

Anna looked back to Kenan. "We broke the arrow and pulled it out. Mother says nothing vital was cut. You'll limp for weeks, but she says you'll heal nicely."

Kenan looked down at his leg. Then he saw himself, too much of himself. His overshirt and undershirt were hiked up to his groin to allow full access to his leg wound. Some of the older men wore loin girdles, but most men didn't. Blood rushed to his face, and he pulled the fabric down to cover himself.

Anna smiled at him and said, "Well, that's out of the way." She beamed at him, eyes sparkling.

Kenan sputtered and giggled again, but his face burned like a bonfire. Wonderful. Not exactly a wedding night.

Alannoon shook her head in disgust and stalked back into the kitchen.

"My family?" he asked.

"All fine," Anna answered. "Your switch-father's house wasn't touched. Earlier, I heard your mother barking orders. I think everything's fine over there."

Atarra trailed blond hair as she ran through the room with two buckets of water. She winked at Kenan and Anna. A younger girl followed sullenly with an armful of wooden cups.

Anna fingered his bandage. "My mother's been teaching me some medicine. Field dressings. Splints. Salves and teas."

"That's great," Kenan offered.

"Never thought it would be for you."

"He is exactly the reason I thought you needed to learn medicine." Alannoon strode quickly back into the room with a big wood bowl of hot water. Or was it wine? The older woman continued, "The man jumps around in trees all day. Sparks! What would you expect? Now, go in there and wash those cloth strips we cut up. Boiled water, now. We will need them soon, probably even before those rock-headed men run out into the forest to get all cut up and poked with holes. I will bet one of them is already bleeding, right now, out on the Flat."

Anna grinned at Kenan and ran for the kitchen.

A blond teen boy came in with a bunch of sticks and twine.

Alannoon called to him. "Joolin, no, Jarin. Wait, who are you? Johlick. Yes. Put that over there." She snapped her fingers and pointed.

Johlick gave his mother a droll look, then hurried to comply. Splints. Those must be splints. He gave Kenan a wink before sprinting from the room. Why did everyone in this house wink?

Kenan sat up and edged to the head of the table, leaving a smear in the drying blood.

Quick kept licking, noisily. Kenan scowled again at the hairy little beast as he tested his leg. It held.

Alannoon came over with a horn of hot wine. "Drink this."

Kenan took it and sniffed. His nose wrinkled. The horn held more than just wine.

Her frown deepened. "Drink it. You will need it, I suspect, before morning."

"What's in it?"

"I do not ask a third time, boy. For anything. From anyone."

That was asking? The woman stood there, hands on hips, daring him to speak. He drained it in one go and scowled into the cup, his body involuntarily shuddering.

She nodded. "Better. It will dull the pain in your leg without affecting your wits, what wits you have, boy."

Kenan just looked at her.

Her expression softened. "I saw what you did."

"I didn't mean to kiss her. It just sort of happened."

"Right. Not that. Did you lose more blood than I thought?"

"What'd I do?"

"You used a bucket. Two armed men. One bucket. It was quick, too. Very clean. Brash. Stupid. But clean."

"Three," he corrected.

"Three?"

"Three. There were three men. One was on the other side of the house."

"Now you are just showing off. I cannot abide that in a son."

Son. Huh. "Wren shows off all the time."

"Yes. The scoundrel." But she smiled. Well, a little. "You will do fine, Kenan. Now, off with you. You can walk, just no more running. Take a stick. There are a few over there by the door."

"Yes ma'am." He turned to go.

"And Kenan?"

"Yes?"

"No more buckets." She winked at him, smiling broadly. Ah. That's where Anna got it.

"Yes ma'am." He limped out the door, leaving the walking sticks where they leaned against the wall. He'd rather die than let his future wife's mother see him use a walking stick.

OUTSIDE on the balcony, he breathed deeply of cool, fresh air. Kenan hobbled up to the rail, gripping it for balance. He still felt light-headed, and his limbs felt heavy. At least the mirth had subsided.

Torches and lamps lit the village. Every available light source burned. Women walked briskly on both levels, carrying supplies and towing young children. He could see some men gathered on the Flat.

He needed to see what they were doing. And he needed to see his family.

Kenan limped carefully. It wouldn't do to lose his balance and topple over the rail. No more falling tonight. He crossed a bridge, which swayed, and he had to stop in the middle for a moment, just to hold on as his head swam.

Once out of sight of Jaret's house, he found a spear laying on a balcony where it had rolled up against the building. He collected it up. The narrow bronze head, chipped and green with age, topped a shaft taller than him. It made a good walking stick.

He came to a balcony with a view of the entire Flat. He stopped in the dark, leaning heavily on the spear, and started counting.

Three hundred and fifty men, give or take a few – it was hard to tell as they moved around – had gathered on the Flat. Pole torches burned everywhere. Men carried more torches and lamps.

They all had weapons. Most had a spear or dragonpike. Some hefted shields and axes or hammers. Many wore wooden armor, blackwood slats built into whitewood frames to cover breast and back with leather straps over shoulders and around ribs. A few wore old bronze helms of varying designs.

Eight crescentdragons shifted around in a group, dwarfing the riders standing together beside them. They had dragonpikes and were talking and gesturing.

Blacktree had assembled a small army down there. They'd conscript everything they'd need.

He picked out Wren, stalking back and forth near a group of men, impatient to go. Most of the men were fully grown, from perhaps 30 to 500 years of age. A sprinkling of older men filled the ranks, too. A bunch of teen boys handled twenty or more stompdragons being loaded down with baskets, water skins, and tools.

Were all the men leaving?

Medahal stood in the center, wrapped in a warm robe and leaning on a little stick. He gave orders and sent runners. The village elders congregated nearby, conferring. No one paid them any attention.

Men began shouting orders to other groups of men.

"Form up!"

"Stand to!"

"Line up!"

The men milled about, looking around. With agonizing slowness, they began to form uneven lines.

With more shouting, one of the lines moved east. They marched towards Babelwind Brook, just like last time, when he'd failed. Kenan's stomach fell. They hadn't found his brother or any of the women all those decades ago. Would they do better this time? They needed him to scout, but he wasn't going anywhere, not with this dragonspitting leg.

In truth, the men were better armed this time. Every man wielded an actual weapon of some kind. The wood shields and armor were new. Many of the men carried bows and were good with them.

None of the woodbenders or nutcutters were there. They must be already out, scouting ahead. Good. He could trust those men in the deep forest.

Kenan was no military man. But shouldn't there be a strong guard element out front? If it were him, he'd put out a force to the sides, too. He wondered if they'd do so. He wished he could ask, but the main body already moved off. Crescentdragons rode on each side of the force. The teenagers and stompdragons brought up the rear.

A force of fifty men lingered. They took a position at the base of the steptree and waited there. That seemed good. They weren't all leaving.

As the Flat quieted and darkened, he limped off to his switchfather's house, snagging a lamp along the way.

AT Kenan's knock, Lidai answered the door. Her dress was splotched with yellow nutmash and something green.

"Kenan!" She shouted and leaped to embrace him.

They stumbled out onto the balcony. He almost lost his lamp.

"Easy, there, girl. I've got a gimp leg."

"Oh! I heard. Sorry. But serves you right, calling me a girl."

"You're not a girl?" Kenan asked.

"You know full well what I meant, you clod."

Kenan smiled at her.

She led him into the house. "Mother! It's Kenan!"

In the common room, his mother looked up from slicing brownnut. "Kenan!"

They embraced as well. Then his mother, Mardai, held him at arm's length, looking him up and down for wounds. She stood the same height, frame, and coloring as his sister. In fact, the most noticeable difference between the two were the eyes. Lidai's eyes were hazel whereas Mardai's eyes were blue. His mother looked young for her 289 years. She and Lidai could be sisters and were often mistaken so by merchants from away.

"How's your leg, son?"

"Oh, it'll do. Alannoon fixed me up pretty good."

Lidai asked, "And Anna?"

"Fine. *Very* fine."

Mardai scowled at him. "None of that talk in my house, or I'll have you sitting on a stool in the kitchen, dicing onions."

"Apologies, mother." Yet a little giggle escaped his lips. He clamped a hand over his mouth.

Lidai scowled at him as well. "Did Wren go with the men? He must have."

"He did. I saw them all go. They're giving chase."

Mardai continued to frown at him. They looked nearly like twins, both scowling up at him. He never really understood why he was in trouble.

Mardai all but hissed, "Those animals. I hope they truss each one up."

Kenan knew his mother was not the kind of woman you crossed twice, small in size or no. It's good the men were in pursuit. If it had been Mardai leading the defense of Blacktree, the raiders would all now be in the kitchen with their arms up to the elbows in hot, soapy water.

"Kenan," Lidai inquired. "Did you really take down those men with a bucket?"

Kenan frowned. Did everyone know? "I suppose I did. Seemed like a good idea at the time."

Mardai eyed him again, her expression part exasperation for the danger he put himself in and part pride in his actions.

Kenan asked, "Where's your husband?"

Mardai tsked. "He's going out with them. I told him he was too old to be running around in the woods with an axe, but he wouldn't listen."

Lidai turned serious. "Father will be okay, right? I mean, it won't be like last time, will it?"

Mardai looked at her daughter. "Last time? What do you mean?"

"Well, when they took some of my older switchsisters, and when they killed your first husband."

Mardai opened her mouth, then closed it, pained by memories. Kenan came to the rescue. "I lost sisters, yes, and a brother, last time. But my father died before I was born, Lidai. He didn't die when they attacked the pool."

Mardai opened her mouth again, then again closed it.

Kenan noticed. "Mother, what is it?"

"My dear son, it's past time I tell you this. Lidai, this is private, but I want you to hear this, for your own good. Kenan, my first husband was not your father, as you know. I'm sorry I didn't tell you before, and now isn't really the time, either. It was..."

A gaggle of young brown-haired children of varying ages burst into the room, followed by a young woman, another switchsister with a gourd under each arm. The children saw him and charged over, yelling, "Kenan Bucket Brigade! Bucket Brigade! Bucket Brigade!"

His mind whirled like the children around him. What had his mother been about to say? He tried to scowl at them but couldn't maintain it in light of their enthusiasm. As they swirled about him, he used one arm to protect his leg from their energy. He shared a look with his mother before smiling at the children. They would talk later.

They cried, "Kenan Bucket Brigade!" over and over.

Mardai smiled at them fondly. Lidai looked sheepish.

Kenan eyed his sister. "You taught them this, didn't you?"

Lidai squared her shoulders to him. "I don't know what you're talking about."

Kenan raised an eyebrow and snorted.

A preteen boy struggled by with a huge pork hock over his shoulder. Another young teen girl followed with her apron full of fist-sized nuts.

"It's late. What's going on?" Kenan asked over the children's bobbing heads.

"Well, my dear," Mardai answered. "Those men will come back with a mighty need to eat."

The kitchen bustled with activity. Commotion and heat poured through the open doorway. Women and girls were talking, slicing, boiling, and kneading. It was late, but the women of Blacktree gave it no mind. They would be ready for their men when they returned.

His mother continued, "Alannoon is preparing medical works. She's mighty good at it, as you know. Freena, Johalla, and I have food. Toonah and her girls are all over there cleaning up the burned houses and salvaging what they can. She breeds those girls strong! How she does it with such a skinny husband is a mystery to me. Dinella and her girls are, well," she paused. "They're taking care of the fallen."

It *was* some kind of magic. The men had looked like a lost flock of ducks waddling through a brush pile compared to this organized and effective effort.

Kenan pushed the women of Blacktree aside. He had a worry on his mind. "How many fell?"

His mother fell silent for a moment. She looked at her milling brood. "Children! Kenan will tell you a story, but you must go to your bunkrooms, brush your teeth, drink your water, and get blankets." The children raced off in excitement. What were they even doing up at this hour?

His mother turned back to him. "Thirty-nine. The two houses were attacked – the savages! – and the men and boys killed. Five sentries have been found. None survived."

"How many... taken?"

"Kenan, there's nothing you can..."

"How many?" His voice held aged blackwood. She gave him a sharp look at his tone but submitted with a sniff. He was, after all, a man grown.

"Twenty-eight. Jennah and every one of her girls in the house old enough to walk are gone. Mary was killed, but they took all of her daughters as well. They found one of them bound on the ground, still alive but back broken. She fell from a balcony, apparently, and we're told she won't survive the night. Alannoon gave her something, and the poor girl is sleeping down below."

Kenan's face blanked as he remembered her muffled scream as she dropped into the dark. He'd killed the man who killed her, but he hadn't been quick enough to save her.

They were all silent for a time.

"Kenan, we'll talk more later. For now, enough," Mardai said with a clap of her hands. She was still his mother. "Look forward. If God had made us with our heads on backwards, we'd be bumping into every tree."

Indeed. The tension broke.

The preteen boy, a brother named Kental, came back through the common room. "Kenan? Did you really kill a man with a bucket?"

"Three men," Kenan said with a quirked grin.

"Woah."

"Kental, go for a second hock, please, my dear," Mardai ordered, then rolled her eyes at Kenan. She was an expert at it.

"Yes, mother," Kental said, trotting away towards a storage room. To himself, the boy said, "Three. Incredible."

Lidai pulled over a chair for Kenan. "Why don't you sit? You look ready to fall down."

"Go get him a cup of mulled yellowberry, Lidai. From the copper kettle, mind, not the bronze. He's looking mighty pale." Lidai moved to comply. "And then back to your mashing, if you please."

Lidai's scowl said she didn't please. As she moved to the hot, noisy room, he saw her gaze linger on her bow, propped up with a full quiver in the corner. She would want to go. She would want to be with the men, loosing shafts of revenge into evil men's hearts. Literally.

Kenan sat for some time in his childhood common room. The yellowberry tea warmed him from the inside and cleared his head. Lidai refilled it twice more for him as he told his story of bucket glory for the group of his young brothers and sisters gathered in blankets and pillows. He wanted to keep them out of their mother's way. Their rapt faces oohed and aahed at all the right places. He'd fight no more this night, but he could do this for his mother.

The common room warmed from the heat of the adjacent kitchen. One of his young sisters came by and opened the outside door a palm span. Kenan's bare feet felt the cool night air wafting along the floor. It felt good.

With his story of water-carrying weaponry done, the children pleaded for another. He pretended to object, saying he was too sleepy. But they grabbed at him and begged with large brown and hazel eyes.

One accidentally leaned on his leg. Oh, that smarted. Whatever Anna's mother had given him was wearing off. He eased the child away. "Okay, Okay!" he yielded, bringing his hands up. "What story do you want to hear?"

"Tell us about Wren riding the stalkdragon!" said one.

"I want to hear about Enoch and the Almighty!" said a young girl.

"No, tell us about the battle of fire at the well!" demanded another.

"Woah, there! Easy! How about I tell the story of the rabbit and the arrowhead?"

The children all cheered.

"Okay. Well, let's see. We'll start with the rabbit's mother, who was busy collecting up all the little berries she could find..."

Within minutes, half the children were fast asleep. He continued, voice softer, for the others.

Two stories later, he had three holdouts, their big eyes drooping but stubbornly still listening. He stopped speaking mid-word. What was that?

"Go on, Kenan," demanded little Leera, all of five years old. "Don't stop."

"Hold on, just a minute. I'll be right back."

He was serious. They sensed it and sat back in their blankets.

Kenan struggled to stand, grabbing the old spear he'd left leaning against the mantle. His leg had stiffened during the storytelling. He padded on his bare feet to the door standing ajar.

The noise from the kitchen overpowered his hearing. He opened the door all the way and stepped through, closing it behind him. He watched and listened on the dark balcony.

Many of the other houses shone with lamps, torches, and women moving about busily. It was well after middark, yet they bustled as if it were the heat of midday.

Through the muted clamor of busy houses, he heard two men walking on the first level below. Bows tapped on the boardwalks as they strolled along and chatted quietly to themselves. Sentries. Good. And clearly they hadn't heard anything.

He could see one defensive platform below his view from up on the second level balcony. A sentry with a bow stood by the iron brazier, illuminated in its red light. He could see the fire rod, one end on the floor of the platform, the other end with the wick in the coals of the brazier. Two thumpers rested on rail posts, ready for action. He could see the woven canopy suspended over the platform by ropes to keep man, brazier, and thumper alike dry when it rained.

From a nearby torch, he could see the outline of a man sliding down one of the canopy's suspension ropes, headfirst, silently easing towards the thumper platform.

Kenan stiffened and sucked in breath to yell a warning.

Then he exhaled the breath as an arrow ripped up from below and took the platform sentry under the jaw. He folded like a yellowpetal.

Kenan's heart sank. This nightmare wasn't over.

# Chapter Nine
# Improvisation

COLS sat in the dark on the big tree branch, legs dangling, and wished he were smarter. He knew he was smart. But Commander Char was smarter. The commander was really smart.

The business end of a dragonpike dangled down between his knees into the dark below. He rolled it in his hands.

He sat up high and scanned the area well east of the tree rat's village. He seriously doubted *anything* would come near this spot. He was about as safe as he could ever be. Far safer than a babe at his bloodmother's breast, he thought. Being around that woman had never been safe.

In all fairness, he was safe from her, too. He'd killed her decades ago. It'd been a necessary part of a promotion ceremony, held in a coliseum and everything. Plus, she'd had it coming. What a dragonspitter she'd been.

He idly poked down below with the dragonpike. The whole branch shook with the responding thump. His body swayed, and he felt a little precarious, so he grabbed one of the big, vertical logs lashed to the branch. The upper end of the log had been axe cut and rough under his hand. He smiled downward at the log wall disappearing into the darkness below. Good. Muddy good.

According to the commander's plan, he would see no action tonight. He caressed the sword hilt on his hip. He had two more on his back. They sang to him in yearning. He wanted to give them blood. Lots of blood.

The commander had given him only one job. He was to pull on a rope. A rope! Cols groaned to himself. A silty, mucky rope.

A deep groan emanated from below, echoing him. He poked again with the dragonpike. The groan became a low rumble. Good.

Cols scanned around again. There. Was that a flash of light? Sure enough, another flash of light pierced the dark forest, not close but on the right path. He waited and chortled a little with the anticipation.

The plan was solid. It had been muddy silt to prepare, which was to be expected when 55 men were taking on 400 or more, regardless of training and weaponry. Being prepared was half the battle. More than half, usually. He hadn't thought so at the time, but now he saw getting this ready was worth the effort.

The lights were closer. He could see the glow on the undersides of leaves. He held the pike in one hand, his other resting on the top end of the nearest vertical log. The rope he had to pull was tied to the vertical log on his other side, in easy reach. He swung his feet back and forth, back and forth.

Cols thought about his commander. Why exclude one of the houses? Asher had mumbled about a pretty girl and a pretty mother there. Why shouldn't they hit it? When Cols had asked, the commander had mumbled, in much the same tone as Asher, the single word, "Improvisation." Cols didn't know about that, being a little unsure what it even meant. He didn't understand the order, but he had a suspicion. He was blood hungry, not stupid.

Soon, a party of about ten men with torches and cargo passed by, not far away. Cols could see a few of the torches directly and outlines of men towing lines of women tied together at the neck. Nice. They had a good haul! At this point, those men were free and clear with the cargo. They should have no trouble. Himmons was a solid soldier. He knew what to do and would follow orders.

If the commander could make changes, so could Cols. He was a captain now, wasn't he? And so, yes, he'd use a little improvisation. Did it mean an attack? No. Probably it meant defense. Right? His swords called to him for blood. Improvisation must mean the best way to do something, like kill as many of the tree rats as possible. Or better yet, take as many of the women as possible. Why be exclusive? He'd do both.

Cols stabbed downward again with the dragonpike and was rewarded with another solid thump and another deep rumble. The vertical logs jumped in their lashings as something thrashed against them for a moment. Hot and muddy good.

Cols thought for quite some time, sitting up high on his branch. He thought about the women they would gather, imagining his time later tonight. It wouldn't be long. The women were goods to be transported and handled carefully. Don't want to damage the goods. But they could be used along the way, as well. It'd been too long. He was more than ready. All the men were.

Wait. How long had it been since squads A and D passed? An hour? Two? Cols sometimes lost track of time when thinking about women, especially with a sweet haul like this. Best to think on something else.

Improvisation meant to attack. Yes. What should he do? He wanted to use his bronze swords. He *needed* to use them.

The villager's response force would scatter in the night. Muddy hole, he would scatter, too. He would run for his life and not look back. But where would they run? Some would run north and away. Some might run south, right past him. Some might run back to the village. No, many would run back home. Silt, no one had thought of that. Can't have them running back to Blacktree. If enough of them reached the village at the wrong moment, well, it could be bad.

It seemed to him like a little chaos back to the west, along the back trail to the village, would be just the thing. Himmons would get the men over to Location One. Himmons was solid.

Cols eased his swords in each scabbard, then almost fell backwards when the branch shook again. Well, *that* would end it all right quick. He jabbed with the dragonpike again in retribution, with quick, repeated stabs. More rumbles from below, and a sharp growl, deep and metallic. Not too loud now. Not quite time yet, but almost.

More lights? Cols checked the moon. Yes, it'd been a couple hours. Maybe more. The response force from Blacktree was due.

Sure enough, more torches appeared. Then more. Some were pole torches held high above. Even more torches appeared. Black mud, did they muster the whole silting village?

Well, no worries there. More was better. That's what his mother used to tell him, usually just before she hit him.

Cols scanned the forest all around. The stupid tree rats didn't have a lead force, or even have flanking forces out, not that he could see. He looked back at the villagers moving quickly through the forest. The whole area was lit by torches and pole torches. They were all in one big mass pushing their way forward along the trail left by squads A and D. Safety in numbers, so they say. Just what you wanted to do to scare wild animals, but a poor tactic against a prepared enemy.

Well, in this case, more really would be better. He smiled to himself in anticipation.

Cols slashed with the pike a few more times, getting everything at just the right temperature down below. The branch jostled. He then dropped the pike and slipped the rope off the log end. He gripped it hard, waiting until just the right moment. Yes, he was about even with the front of the mass of men, and torches, and... wait. Oh good. They had crescentdragons, too. This would be fun.

Cols yanked the rope upwards sharply. The catch below released smoothly. The cross beam swung away, creaking invisibly in the night. The forest duff below rattled. Another growl, deep and guttural, followed. Then thumps sounded on the ground and the large vertical logs all twisted in their lashings, pushed outward by something below.

This would be very fun.

As soon as it cleared the area, Cols would drop off this cursed branch and circle west to harry villagers fleeing in that direction. How many kills would be good improvisation, he wondered? Ten? Twenty?

He wasn't exactly sure what improvisation was, but he thought for sure it was good.

WREN squinted his eyes against his torch, peering into the darkness to the side as he walked through the forest. One of the crescentdragons kept getting in his way. He couldn't see anything but men, spears, dragonhide, and lots of torches reflecting light off the huge leaves above.

He had no idea if this little army still followed the raider's trail. He'd have to trust the men up front and the scouts. He saw some of the woodbenders and hunters run from the dark into the torchlight. He had no idea what they told Medahal, who rode a stompdragon near the front.

Wren walked further to the back, bringing up the rear of the armed men but in front of all the teenage boys leading stompdragons carrying gear.

He yearned to be at the front. He wanted to be the first to see the men who must die. He would do it himself, with the steel axe hanging on his back. He would help free the women. He wouldn't stop until he had them back.

He cradled the torch in his left arm to keep his strong arm fresh.

"Hey Wren," said the man next to him. He struggled with a tall pole torch. "You think we're gaining on them?"

"I'm not sure, Joneth," Wren answered. "I doubt the women could move this fast. Most are barefoot. How fast could they go?"

Joneth shrugged. "Not fast. They'd probably fight, too. I bet they're slowing them down, right good."

"Hah! Probably have them all lined up, volunteering to scrub pots."

"Probably! If Meredeena hasn't already thumped one on the head, she... she would..." Joneth trailed off. Meredeena was Joneth's daughter.

"Joneth, she'll be okay. They'll all be okay. We're going to catch up. They're all coming back with us. They'll probably make us cook breakfast for them and clean up, too."

Joneth snorted and smiled.

Wren walked on. He would find those animals, and he would end them. He wouldn't sneak about, killing one at a time like Kenan might. No, he'd wade through the mass of them, chopping them down like so much brush. He peered into the darkness to the side, again shielding his eyes from the torch.

"Wren," inquired Joneth, again.

"Yeah?"

"You always know what to say, how to answer someone. How do you do it?"

Wren thought for a moment. "I'm not sure. Since I can, I guess it's my response ability."

Joneth turned to gape at him, tripped on a root, and almost fell. His pole torch cracked the man in front of him on the head. The man groaned but turned to shoot a scowl at Wren.

"Response ability?" the man asked. "Seriously?"

Wren grinned at him.

Just then, a heavy branch broke ahead, to the right. Wren stopped in mid-stride. So did the entire Blacktree army. What in creation was that? He saw movement, and the ground thumped. He could feel it through his boots. It thumped again. And again.

Men screamed. They pointed to the right, up into the trees. Some scrambled away, fighting through other men to escape. A few stood their ground, stepping on the butt end of their dragonpikes and pointing them at a high angle, set for an attack. What was happening?

A deep, metallic roar shattered the night. The sound hurt everyone's ears and lingered long. It couldn't be. No! Almighty!

The crescentdragons bolted, running away from the roar, trumpeting warnings and adding to the cacophony. Those on the right charged through the body of men, crushing many, their riders holding on for their lives. The stompdragons behind hooted in panic.

A large mawdragon head emerged from the dark, illuminated by torchlight. It roared again at the men holding dragonpikes, then charged right into them. Its dark gray body, mottled with brown and black, stretched fifty feet long and stood three times Wren's height. Its little arms deftly deflected several dragonpikes. Two dragonpikes caught the mawdragon as it charged, penetrating before snapping clean. If anything, the wounds only angered the creature.

The mawdragon continued forward into the midst of the scrambling men. It chomped down on men with its massive jaws. It chewed one man briefly. The bottom half fell to the ground while it swallowed the top half whole. As it stepped down, it crushed men where they stood, frozen in fear.

The beast twisted, sweeping both head and tail. Men flew through the air, smashing into trees, rocks, or other men.

Arrows zipped into the men from the front. Half a dozen arrows arced in from the trees, dropping men all around. Then another half dozen. Then another. Men fell to arrows and to the mawdragon. Chaos and carnage reigned.

Wren still stood beside Joneth. Both men stared in awe and confusion. Their army was disintegrating before their very eyes.

Suddenly, an arrow ripped in and took Joneth in his chest. He spluttered up blood, touched his lips, and looked at his red fingertips. He turned with eyes wide in shock to look at Wren. Joneth showed him his bloody fingers as he fell backwards, his open eyes glazing to blindness before he hit the ground.

Wren didn't know what to do. A mawdragon! And it was tromping his way. Men rushed by him, fleeing the giant dragon. More men fell to arrows as they ran to escape the carnage.

Wren didn't know what he should do, but he knew what he wanted to do, so he did that. He spun and fled the mawdragon. Getting stuck with an arrow was one thing. Dragonscrape, Kenan got stuck and he'd be just fine. But he had no desire to face a mawdragon. He ran for all he was worth.

He dodged through the stompdragons, who milled about in panic. The teenage boys had already fled. He vaulted the last stompdragon and ran into the night. A heavy thump and a stomach-churning popping noise told him the mawdragon had stepped on a stompdragon. Almighty! The beast was right behind him!

Wren ran on, his torch trailing flame.

One more thumping step came from behind. The mawdragon loomed right there, above him!

Wren hurled the torch to the side and dove into the underbrush in the opposite direction.

The mawdragon followed the torchlight with its enormous head. It stared at the flames burning up against a pile of bulbous mushrooms. Finally, it turned back to Wren where he hid, panting in the duff under a large fern.

The beast looked down at him, its maw slightly agape with bloody saliva running to the ground in slimy rivulets. Glops of it ran across Wren's legs.

Wren smiled up at the beast, gathering his courage. If he was to die, he would do it laughing in its face! His sanity quavered as the laughter started to bubble up.

Just then a group of men ran by, not far away, all holding torches aloft. The mawdragon's gaze snapped up to follow them with its glinting eyes. With a roar, it thundered after them, barely missing Wren with a giant, clawed foot. The tail swept above, flattening the ferns.

Almighty! That thing could have swallowed him whole.

Wren sat up in the duff, breathing hard in the moonlight. Men yelled and ran in all directions. Torches moved about. Arrows zipped by here and there. One ripped by, too close. Could they see him in the dark? Wren didn't think so. Still, he instinctively began to move away. He crawled behind some ferns before getting up and trotting westerly. The mawdragon roared again, more to the northwest. He angled southwest and made his way by moonlight.

He needed to head back to Blacktree. That's what most of the survivors would do. Blacktree meant safety, where they could reassemble. They could bolster their defenses. They could... well, he didn't know what they would do, but they'd do something. Almighty, what a catastrophe.

Wren trotted alone through the forest, moving by faint moonlight. He listened carefully for other survivors. He needed to find a group to join. He was too vulnerable out here alone.

A shape stepped in front of him. It looked like a short man. Was this a friend or one of the raiders?

"'Ello," the man rasped.

Wren took a step back. "Who are you?"

"I'm Cols," came the reply. The voice was relatively high and raspy.

"Why are you here?" Wren took another step back.

"I'm in my glory, 'ere in the dark."

"What?" Wren took one last step back, reached behind him, and freed the binding cord on his axe. The weapon dropped free, and he caught the long haft in his hand.

"What you got there behind your back, big man? Something for me?"

Wren didn't know who the short man was. But the man held shield and sword, was well muscled, and had an unfamiliar accent. Something white was painted on the shield.

"Yep. Something for you." With a quick jerk of his arm, Wren swung the axe around. He caught it in both hands, stepped forward, and continued the swing in one smooth motion.

Cols dropped to one knee, covering his head with his shield. The axe passed harmlessly over his head, ticking the shield on the way by. Cols jumped back, smile gleaming in the dark.

"That the best you 'ave, big man?" Cols asked.

Wren swung the axe, light in his big hands. "Not even close."

"Well, I 'ope not. Big men are boring."

Wren attacked. He swung the axe from the left, the right, and straight up. Cols ducked, stepped back, and dodged. Wren continued his attack. He wouldn't stop for anything.

Cols hadn't counterattacked. While giving ground, he asked, "Is that thing steel?"

"You want it? Come and get it!" Wren snarled at him.

"Okay, sure thing," Cols rasped lightly. He stepped over one sweep of the axe and ducked a higher return swing. As he ducked, his bronze sword flicked out and slashed the outside of Wren's thigh.

It didn't hurt at all, he thought. He'd worry about it later.

Wren brought the axe down with his bodyweight behind it. Cols rolled smoothly to the side. The ax buried itself in the soil, cutting roots as it went and biting deep.

"Oops," Cols cooed. Then slashed the side of Wren's arm across the bicep and triceps. The blade grated across the bone.

That one hurt.

Wren let go of the axe and punched Cols in the face. Except his face wasn't there any longer. The man could move! Wren overextended his reach and felt a line burn down his ribs as Cols sliced him from armpit to hip.

Wren fell. His leg wouldn't hold him any longer for some reason. Everything felt warm and wet. He lay in the duff, panting, with dead leaves stuck to him. His head spun.

Cols stood over him, grinning. He stepped to the axe and tried to pull it free. It was stuck fast.

"You've got a great muddy swing, big man. That's for sure. Steel. Where'd you get steel?"

"I found it under your mother's hammock."

"'Ah 'ah! I like you, big man!" Cols turned back to the axe. With several grunts and heaves, the axe finally came free. This Cols man was strong! Not many men could have pulled it out. Wren watched, willing his body to move but unable to act, as Cols tied a cord to the axe and slung it over his back.

Cols turned back to Wren. "I won't kill you tonight. I should. Muddy good improvisation." Cols said the word carefully, as though he wasn't sure he was saying it right. "But you'll live. Probably, if someone finds you soon enough. 'Ere." Cols tossed him a small waterskin.

"Thanks, you dragonscrape."

Cols laughed at him, grinned, and winked before he turned to go.

"Hey, Cols," Wren called. His voice sounded weaker than he wished.

Cols turned back and grinned down at him in the night. "Yeah?"

"Be good," Wren said.

"It ain't in me, big man. I'm going to wreak a little more 'avoc. Not sure 'ow. I'm making this silting stuff up as I go."

"Improvisation."

"Muck, yeah!" Cols pointed at Wren with his sword covered in Wren's own blood. "That's it, ain't it?" With that, Cols ran into the night.

Wren felt at his wounds. The deep arm wound hampered his movements. The cut along the ribs burned like dragonspit! But the thigh wound was bleeding freely. It didn't gush, so nothing major was cut. But it bled a lot. That one was his immediate problem.

Wren worked with one hand to pull his overshirt sleeve off. Pain flared on his cut arm. He took a moment to breathe through the pain, panting and squeezing his eyes shut. With long effort, fighting through dizziness, he finally got it ripped to a strip and tied around his thigh. Dragonscrape. Did it even slow the blood at all?

He lay there, focused on his breathing. His stomach hurt, too, like he was going to be sick. Why did his stomach hurt?

He was getting tired. A nap sounded mighty fine.

Two men ran by, close. Friend or foe? Wren no longer cared. "Hey! Come back!" His voice was soft, light.

The man in front heard and stopped. The second man piled into him, and they both nearly fell. The front man called, "Who's there?"

"It's me, Wren! I'm in trouble."

About half a mile to the north, the mawdragon roared again. Several men screamed faintly in that direction.

The two men approached slowly and found Wren sitting in blood.

"Almighty, Wren! What happened to you?"

"Help me up. There's a man in the woods. He's not one of us. Be careful."

Wren got to his feet with their help. He was far weaker than he ever remembered.

"Wren, you're dead weight, like a sack of longnuts. And dragonspit, boy! You're heavy."

The other man grunted. "Really heavy."

"I'm always heavy. Help me back or leave me here to sleep."

"We're not leaving you, Wren. Hold on." They struggled to get under both his shoulders. Wren hissed in pain as the slice on his ribs pulled further open.

"Listen. If you see a man with sword and a shield with a white spider, you drop me and run. Hear? Drop me and run."

"Sure, Wren. While we're at it, we'll just leave you for the mawdragon." The two men shared a wry look with a healthy dose of worry included.

"What, that little beasty?" Wren slurred his words as he spoke. "We shared a moment. We traded smiles and stared deep into each other's eyes. Almighty, we're practically betrothed now. The wedding is going to be unforgettable."

The men rolled their eyes in unison as they struggled west through the dark forest with their heavy load.

# Chapter Ten
# Darterdragons and Chipmunks

KENAN shouted into the house to his mother. She came rushing out of the kitchen.

"What's all the racket? You'll wake the children!" Indeed, the children stirred in their blankets on the common room floor. One sat up, rubbing an eye.

"They're back! We're under attack," he shouted at his mother. "Bar the door!"

Mardai stood, looking poleaxed. Lidai rushed in behind and dropped a bowl of nutmash all over the floor. The bowl skittered up to the hearth, clacking against an iron poker.

"Bar the door! Right now!" Kenan yelled, then hobbled back outside. His bare feet slipped a little on the planks. He wrenched his leg, and pain flared up his thigh. Gritting his teeth, he kept moving.

The door closed behind him. He heard the solid thunk of the bar being dropped and female voices shouting inside. It sounded like they were yelling at each other. Dragonscrape, he'd rather be out here, wounded with the White Spiders.

Using the spear to lean on, he limped quickly towards the nearest footlift.

Arrows ripped down through the air from above. Enemy archers perched unseen, high in the trees. One arrow nearly skewered him, but he moved on in the dark. Other arrows zipped up from below, and a sentry down on the first level screamed.

Kenan saw no raiders on the balconies or down on the ground. But they were coming. Were the village men down on the Flat enough to repel an attack? Kenan wasn't sure. What to do?

The only way from the lower village level to the upper house level was by lift or by climbing the blacktree bark. If the White Spiders came back for the women of Blacktree, he had to isolate the upper house level.

He reached the first footlift. Yanking his hand knife free, he sawed through the thick fibers and cut the lift rope. It snapped audibly. One end of the rope flew away in the night as he heard the counterweight spinning the nearby mechanism freely. It made a loud whirring noise. He limped towards the next footlift. Another arrow ripped by, but not close. The darkness protected him.

He cut the next footlift. He moved on, working his way across a rope bridge in the night, steadying himself with the spear.

When he reached the other side of the bridge, a man with a sword stood waiting for him. "No more of that, now. We want those lifts," the man growled in a familiar foreign accent.

Without pause, Kenan set his weight and hurled the spear.

The man ducked, but not quickly enough. The spear caught him just below the collarbone, and he went down on his backside, then fell over on his back, spear wobbling vertically above him.

Kenan hobbled up to him. The man wasn't dead and coughed blood into the air, splattering his face and the wood planks beneath him. The man's hand searched the dark boardwalk for his sword. Kenan pulled the spear out, then plunged it into the man's neck. The man's hand stopped searching, and he gurgled his last breath. A spray of blood coated Kenan's leg, warm and wet in the cool of the night.

Kenan snatched up the man's sword in one hand, spear in the other, and limped on. He found the next pair of footlifts and cut them both. The sharp sword cut the rope faster than his hand knife.

An arrow ripped through the night, piercing Kenan's bicep. It went clean through and stuck in the wood wall behind him. Kenan jumped in pain, too surprised to cry out. He backed into the shadows, gritting his teeth. His arm bled freely but wasn't spurting. He decided to ignore it. He had no time to do anything about it anyway. He had to get to the next lift to protect the village women and children. Then he had to get to the steptree. He had to pull the steptree pin to drop the entire structure.

A woman ran up to him. Though she moved fast, her face seemed calm. She clutched a hand knife in a fist. "What can I do?"

"Get inside. Stay out of sight."

"I can help you."

"No. I've got this. Get to your children. Now."

The woman frowned but sped off into the night.

He passed a rope bridge. This bridge led to several trees with houses lit by lamplights and torches. The sound of women talking drifted across the cool night air. No foot lifts from those trees connected down to the village level. He paused to cut the bridge, then paused again. He had an idea.

He sprinted across the bridge, adrenaline helping him forget his wounded leg and arm. A rope dyed red hung from the post. He strung the rope across the railing gap that opened to the bridge. Anyone from Blacktree would know it meant it wasn't safe to cross. Then he sprinted back and started to cut at the bridge ropes. The ropes hung thick and strong, meant to resist exactly what he attempted. He wished he had his axe, but the sword worked. Finally, he cut through all four ropes just enough so the bridge still hung but would probably snap under a load of men. He strung up the red rope on this side as well, hoping the raiders wouldn't know what it meant, and moved on to find more footlifts.

A short distance later, he found another two lifts. He cut them both. Another arrow ripped in, thunking into the rail post next to his head. Kenan hurried to finish his cutting before he backed into the darkness on the balcony.

He hobbled on, leaning on his spear.

CHAR sat on his hissdragon. Arrows zipped around the village, visible streaks as they passed through light from windows and lamps. A few shouts and cries echoed through the night. It wouldn't be long now. He would hear it when it was time.

His prince sat on his own hissdragon next to him.

Char said, "Not much longer, my Prince."

"We are ready."

"Yes, my Prince." Char adjusted the cloth across his face. The thing rode up to cover an eye if he talked, even with his brass helm seated firmly on his head holding the cloth in place.

A deep *thump* rolled out of the village, near the Flat. Many men screamed in pain and confusion. That was the signal. He kicked his hissdragon and urged it forward.

His prince did the same. Orange flashed out of the Nephilim's steel helm. Char noticed but said nothing. He'd seen it before. Both raised their steel swords and charged into the Flat.

LIDAI stood in her father's common room. Her mother and sisters had whisked the children away. She was alone with her nutmash all over the floor.

Alone with her bow and a quiver full of arrows.

She made her decision. She scooped up the quiver, slung it over her back, and snagged her bow. The bar on the door was heavy, but she lifted it free with her shoulder. As she did, she heard one of the thumpers fire. Yes! Blacktree men fought back!

Outside, chaos reigned.

Arrows zipped around at all angles. She could see men lying on the Flat far below. Some lay motionless. Other men writhed and screamed. Some had formed groups with shields raised to defend from above.

She saw a man on one of the defensive platforms. He clearly had just fired the thumper, which smoked from the open end. The man reached for a bow.

She looked again. The angle of the thumper told the story. That man had just fired their thumper down into their own men. He wasn't a Blacktree man. As she watched, he nocked, drew, and loosed an arrow into the group down below at the base of the steptree.

She didn't think. She didn't pause. In one smooth motion, Lidai pulled an arrow, nocked, drew, anchored, and loosed. It was a long shot. It had to be over fifty paces. The air was still and cool. The arrow flew true, disappearing into the base of the man's neck. He fell like a sack of roundnuts.

She couldn't see it in the dark, but she heard it coming. Her body moved before thought. She fell to the boardwalk, and the arrow ripped harmlessly over her, thunking into the wooden wall of her house.

Lidai blindly loosed a shaft back the way the arrow had come, then stepped quickly into the shadows next to a lattice window where light spilled out onto the balcony. As soon as she was in the dark, she moved again to the rail. She watched the trees above in the general direction of the first arrow.

Sure enough, another arrow ripped down out of the branches above to land harmlessly in the shadows next to the window where she had been only a moment before.

She saw him, straddling a branch up there. Though her eyes were still adjusting, a stray moonbeam gave her just enough light. She had already nocked and half drawn. She anchored, aimed carefully, and loosed.

The man took the arrow in his mouth. His head snapped back, then hung forward. In slow motion, his body went limp, and he slid off the branch to fall into the black below.

Lidai scanned the forest branches around the village. All she could see were dark shapes, moonbeams, and flickers from balcony torches and window lamplights. She couldn't see well enough to find targets in the shadows. Her eyes hadn't adjusted to the dark yet. Kenan always harped on her about patience. Maybe she should do as he said, just this one time.

Lidai crouched down behind a rail post, watching and waiting.

KENAN cut the rope for the last of the platform lifts connecting the house and village levels. Four more footlifts were left. He turned and hobbled to a village sentry lying on a house balcony nearby, his neck pierced by two arrows. The planks ran slick with blood, and Kenan slipped, falling on his side next to the man. The body didn't move as Kenan removed his wooden armor and harnessed it around his own torso.

He regained his feet and continued moving, crossing a rope bridge high above the Flat. An arrow ripped in and hit his spear, bisecting the spear shaft. Well, better it than him. The arrow would have hit his already wounded leg. He didn't need that. He could hear Wren in his mind and picture the wry quirk of his mouth. "One arrow per limb per night seems enough to me, Kenan."

He raked the spear shaft across the edge of the bridge planks, breaking off the arrowhead and shaft. He hardly slowed, gimping his way to the next balcony and into a dark shadow. Another arrow ripped in but missed.

Three of the remaining footlifts were just around the corner.

Below, he heard men shouting on the Flat. The thumper had killed many of the fifty men stationed there but others held their position. Blacktree men still defended their village.

Now, raiders appeared at the far end of the Flat. Two groups of eight men lined up, shields raised. The white spiders painted on the shields almost glowed in the torchlight. They left a gap between the two squads.

A man in a brass helm and a steel sword charged through the gap, riding a hissdragon. The creature stretched thirty feet long. Rows of sharp teeth glinted while arms reached forward with curved claws. The creature hissed as it sprinted directly for the Blacktree men stationed at the base of the steptree.

A second man, this one in steel armor and with a steel sword, rode a second, even larger, hissdragon through the gap. His steel helm glowed with orange light.

"He's back," Kenan whispered. He felt his knees go weak and grabbed at the balcony railing. He watched the horrific attack unfold below.

The sight of two charging hissdragons and their armored riders became simply too much for some of the remaining Blacktree men. They scattered away from their post at the base of the steptree.

Only ten men remained to take the charge. They were older, experienced men, who would not yield. They pulled back and formed a tight semicircle around the base of the steptree. Their curved line of shields bristled with sharp spears.

One squad of raiders trotted forward to follow the hissdragons across the Flat. The other group headed to a couple of platform lifts that would take them up to the village level.

What to do? Kenan pulled himself together and thought fast. Standing there gaping wouldn't save anyone. Almighty, his mother, sister, and his Anna were in danger.

The village level was lost. Kenan had no time to go down and cut platform lifts to the ground before the raiders used them. A few women still occupied the village level. Lamplight shone from a few shop windows where they worked to prepare for the returning Blacktree men. He could do nothing for them. Not yet.

But he could cut the rest of these footlifts up to the house level. The raiders would then be stuck below, and most of the women would be relatively safe, for a time at least, behind barred doors.

Not all. Three women stood on an upper balcony, visible in the lamplight shining out an open house door. All three held bows. They immediately launched a volley down at the hissdragons.

Arrows zipped back at them from other balconies or tree branches, piercing two of the women through the chest. The third stood, transfixed at the sight of her friends struggling with arrows in them. Another arrow zipped in, taking her in the head and dropping her cleanly onto the balcony. Both of the other women sagged to the boardwalk. One dragged herself back into her house, but collapsed just inside the doorway, the black arrow spreading red on her dress visible in the lamplight.

One of those lethal arrows had come from just around the corner, from the very balcony on which Kenan stood. Ignoring the pain in his leg, he raced around the corner.

Three men stood there, guarding the footlift railing posts. Two of the men had bows, one had a hammer and shield. They all turned at the sound of his bare feet slapping on the boards.

Without slowing, Kenan hurled his spear at one of the men.

107

The man with the shield calmly stepped in front of the spear, which thunked into the body of the painted white spider. The man dropped both spear and shield to raise his hammer. Meanwhile, the two men with bows turned their weapons towards Kenan, drawing arrows back.

In a split second, Kenan knew he would not survive. The man with the hammer crouched ready. The men with the bows would skewer him before he got there. He had no other choice.

Kenan didn't slow as he dove over the railing, into the black, arrows ripping by around him.

LIDAI moved about the balcony of her house on the upper level. She kept to the dark and trod lightly. She avoided looking at torches to protect her night vision. She had an arrow nocked, ready for action.

There. Across the way on another balcony, a man stood in the shadows. He had just launched an arrow. A woman out of sight shrieked in pain.

That would be the last pain he ever caused.

Lidai drew, anchored, and loosed. Her arrow flew true, striking the man in the Adam's apple. He stiffened, and his bow clattered to the boards. His body hung, suspended by the arrow pinning him to the wood wall behind him. The arrow began to bend, and his dead weight pulled him down the arrow shaft. The fletching disappeared into his neck before he collapsed onto the balcony boards.

Lidai didn't wait to admire her handiwork. As soon as she loosed, she crouched down behind the railing and rolled to the side. Another arrow ripped in from above, thunking into the boardwalk near where she'd been standing. She'd been watching, though, and she saw where it had come from. There, he crouched in the shadows of that chimney.

She didn't see the man. But she knew where he must be. She stood, drew, and loosed her arrow. Ducking back down, she watched through the gaps in the railing.

She heard nothing, but a man slid face first out of the shadows, bumping down the woven roof planks, and off the eve. No balcony waited below to catch him. He fell, and she could hear his groan as he disappeared into the dark.

Lidai waited again, impatient to target more raiders.

The noise on the Flat below caught her attention. Hissdragons! Men with white spider shields! She must get over there. Enough of this darterdragon-

and-chipmunk game. She would empty her quiver into these dragonscrape. She took off down a rope bridge at a sprint, hair and dress flying loose behind her.

CHAR clung to his hissdragon with his free hand. How his prince could ride these things with both hands free mystified him.

The time for thought passed. They were on the small shield wall of men at the base of the steptree.

Char rode his hissdragon at a glancing angle. His hissdragon reached over and snatched at a man's head with a clawed arm as it ran by, shaking the earth with its heavy, running steps. The head came away without a body. Char slashed down with his sword, cleaving away another man's spear shaft and a large part of his arm.

He circled around for another pass. His hissdragon tossed the head in its mouth and bit down. It made a crunching pop.

Prince Gharan used no such glancing tactic. The Nephilim sat his hissdragon gracefully as the animal leapt over the shield wall, using its clawed legs and arms to land on and cling to the side of the steptree. His prince leapt from the hissdragon's back and landed nimbly on the ground behind the Blacktree line.

The men all turned, but in the close quarters, shields and spears tangled with a clattering sound, like tree branches in a winter windstorm. His Prince grinned, and his eyes flashed orange. He stepped into a stance and swung his steel sword.

Limbs parted. Innards spilled. Arteries erupted in fountains of blood. His prince's eyes flashed orange with every cut and he shouted his glee.

"Four! Five! You there! Six!"

His prince's hissdragon leaned down from its perch on the side of the steptree and clamped its jaws around a man's head and shoulders. It chomped repeatedly as the man screamed before his body went limp. Blood and saliva poured out on the ground.

By the time Char got back to the steptree, no village defender lived. His prince coaxed his hissdragon down off the spiral staircase. The claws squealed as they pulled from the wood.

The White Spider squad trotting to the steptree never paused. The eight men ran right by and up the steps without a word, as planned. Other men rose on platform lifts up to the village level. Squads B and C were on their way up.

Char leapt off his hissdragon and went to one knee.

"My Prince. You fought well!" Char meant every word.

"Rise." His Prince's deep voice commanded him to obey. "Commander, please see to this operation. There is, I think, a resistance. More village men were left behind, perhaps, but I think these women will not be cowed. It is as you predicted."

"Yes, my prince. Should I leave a guard here with you?"

"No. My mount is all the guard I need. I will see you when you return to the ground, Commander. This is hard, I know, but be strong."

Char nodded and made good on the order. He turned and raced up the steptree to catch up with squad B.

KENAN fell.

One of the footlift ropes hung right where he thought it would be. In the dark, the rope seemed to fly upwards as he descended. It was within easier reach than he had planned. He almost casually reached out and grabbed it.

Dragonspit! The rope burned his hand and pulled at his earlier hand wound. His body immediately dropped and swung wildly against rope. His other hand found its grip as well. His feet wrapped around the rope. His descent slowed and soon he dropped at a controlled pace.

He saw the village boardwalk rushing up to him. He slowed more, gripping with hands and bare feet. The burning pain grew intense. He dropped the last ten feet, landing momentarily upright. He promptly collapsed as his wounded leg gave out.

An arrow thunked straight down in the boardwalk between his knees. He glared up at the balcony above even as he rolled to take cover and concealment in the darkness under an eave.

In a moment, he spotted the three footlifts at the boardwalk rail. He could cut them down here with the same effect as cutting them up on the upper level. He got to his feet, retrieved the sword he'd dropped on the descent, and hobbled over. His sword slashed as he cut one. Gears whirled nearby.

Another arrow ripped down from above. This one pierced him in the foot. Pain flared up his ankle and lower leg. An involuntary gasp escaped him. The arrow pinned his foot to the boardwalk. He felt like he'd been on the losing end of a wrestling match with a porcupine.

Yet another arrow thunked down, so close it gashed his shoulder. Even in the dark, these dragonspitting men shot well.

As quick as a darterdragon snagging a butterfly, Kenan bent, broke the arrow, pulled his foot off, and stumbled back to cover, leaving bloody footprints behind. He bled from arrow wounds to his arm, shoulder, and foot. The small sword cut on his hand had broken open and bled as well. The stitched arrow wound to his leg seemed to be holding. Barely.

Kenan needed to get some of these injuries wrapped. Whatever Alannoon had given him in that wine might still be working, because the pain hadn't overtaken him yet. But he felt lightheaded again from blood loss.

He gazed for a moment at the two remaining lift lines and thought. He had to cut them.

Before he could give it too much thought, Kenan's hands rushed into motion. He pulled off his wood armor and doubled up the breast and back plates. He put them on the top of his head and held them with one hand. Taking a deep breath to gather his courage, he moved out to the balcony rail.

He cut first footlift rope before the arrows started. Two thunked into the blackwood slats of the armor balanced on his head. He cut the last footlift just as an arrow angled in from a different direction, catching him with a glancing blow across the stomach. The arrowhead cut his stomach skin, then pierced his stomach muscle before exiting out his side.

He limped back to the building wall, dropping the wood armor along the way, and sat down on a bench there. Dragonstool. He really didn't feel good.

He couldn't stay here long. Kenan rose with difficulty, his sweat and blood-soaked cloths sticking to his skin. He retrieved the armor and limped around the dark building, putting pressure on the stomach wound. It appeared to be superficial, but it hurt and was making him feel sick. He trudged down a branch with a rail on one side, sword under his arm and dragging his armor behind him. He found a sheltered spot in the leaves.

Blacktree would have to fend for itself for a moment. He was about to pass out and would help no one if he did. At least the footlifts were cut. Well, almost all of them. There was one more, but it wasn't easy to find. He doubted the raiders would know where it was. The women were as safe from the approaching raiders as he could make them.

He pulled off his overshirt and started to cut strips of cloth.

AS Char reached the top of the steptree, an arrow ripped in from above. It struck his brass backplate a glancing blow, then nicked him along a few ribs. He moved on, pulling the arrow shaft from the fabric of his overshirt.

"Archer! To the north!" He screamed.

As he followed his men down the village boardwalk towards their designated lift points, he looked back from where the arrow came. A small, lone woman stood in the dark, another arrow already drawn. It ripped down, across the space over the Flat. One of his men saw it and reflexively pulled his shield up in cover. The arrow thunked into the wooden shield. The men ran on.

Female resistance indeed.

"Bear left. Use that building for cover," Char commanded. His men quickly complied. One man stopped and faced the female archer, shield ready. Sure enough, another arrow ripped in from the dark. The man moved and caught it on his shield. They all took cover around the building, running onwards.

They quickly came to the designated lifts. Two footlifts and a platform lift were supposed to be here. Instead, only coils of loose rope lay on the boardwalk.

Dragonspit. The women must have cut the lifts.

Well, this possibility had been anticipated. Char whistled up to the house level. In moments, several ropes dangled down.

"Climb, you dragonscrapes! Get up there and get to it." The men rushed to comply. Using their strong arms only, they climbed quickly, their bodies swaying side to side.

Char moved off to check the next lift point. Were they all cut? If so, he knew of one lift, out of the way and rarely used. He'd check that one. It went up near a rope bridge that led directly to that blond girl's house. If not, he could scale the tree in short order.

LIDAI had almost laughed as she hit the brass-helmed man in the back. He jumped like a fox stung by a bumblebee. But the shiny dragonscrape kept running. She tried another man. He raised one of those dragonspitting shields.

They had all run around a building corner. She tried one last arrow, but the man was ready for her. She hated those shields.

She would have to move and shoot from the dark.

Down below, on the Flat, the man in steel mounted his hissdragon. She eyed him. No shield, the stupid dragonstool. She watched closer. Was that orange light and glowing steam coming out of his helmet? What was *that* about?

She loosed a shaft at him. The shaft flew true but shattered on the steel plates of his armor.

She nocked another arrow, drew, and loosed fluidly. This shaft flew true as well but shattered on a plate on his shoulder. He didn't even look at her. He ignored the shafts completely as he patted the hissdragon on its neck hump.

He turned to the side, which gave her a great angle on the ear hole in his helm. That dark circle was only a couple fingers wide at a range of a hundred feet or more and at a steep vertical angle. Could she hit it?

She drew and anchored. She took a moment, sighting down the blackwood shaft, judging air currents. She'd oriented the bronze arrowhead just right. The man stopped moving for just a moment. She exhaled softly and loosed, the string flying off her fingertips almost as a surprise.

The shaft flew. She knew it would sound like a rip from his end, but from here it silently glided away.

At the last moment, he turned, looked directly at her, and casually batted the arrow aside with his gauntleted hand. Even though the hissdragon turned about, he twisted to maintain eye contact with her.

His eyes glowed orange. She could see the twin orbs of light pulsing from his helmet. What the dragonspit?

Another arrow, from somewhere on the house level, ripped by her head. It pulled at her hair and scored her at the crown of her scalp. She fell back, cursing as she went. A second arrow followed the first, ripping through the air just over her face and thunking into the house wall behind her. Dragonscrape! That was close!

Her head hurt. When she touched it, her hand came away wet. A warm line dripped down her face, around her nostril, and into her mouth. She tasted the unmistakable metallic flavor of blood.

She felt around on her scalp more. A palm-long gash had split her scalp. The arrow had cut deep enough to scrape her skull. Dragonspit! It bled everywhere! A rivulet ran into one eye, and she suddenly couldn't see out of it. She pulled a damp dishtowel from her belt and held the hateful cloth to her head. Pain throbbed to the rhythm of her beating heart.

Several men with shields and swords ran across a rope bridge, heading directly towards her. They held shields in front, white spiders showing.

Hateful men.

She ran around the building and further into the darkness, holding the top of her head. She ignored the pain as she slid into a dark shadow to wait.

Lidai saw a man approaching her hiding place. She didn't see any others, just the one man, and she didn't spend time wondering where the others had gotten off to. The white spider of his shield looked like a phantom monster floating through the dark. As he got closer, she could see him more clearly. Then his eyes turned towards her.

He took two steps towards her. She smiled and stood, bow drawn. Even with one eye, at this range she couldn't miss. She put the arrow through the man's mouth.

He fell forward, twitching.

Lidai jumped the body, moving to a new hiding place. She needed to stop the bleeding, clean her eye, and find more arrows. Then she would find a better perch to fight from.

# Chapter Eleven
## Rows of Sharp Teeth

ANNA extinguished the last lamp, plunging the bunkroom into black. She patted the back of a seven-year-old sister's head as the child clutched her leg through her dress. Anna stood steadier than she felt.

The smaller children all huddled towards the back of the room, swinging quietly in their hammocks. A few of the little ones had never awoken, still sleeping quietly in their blankets.

The women had barred the outer door in the common room. This bunkroom's door had no bar, but they did have rope. Every room had rope. Haley had just finished tying the rope to the door, pulling it tight. The rope stretched across the room to a hammock peg in a wall, holding the door firmly shut. Anna hoped it might slow the raiders.

They waited in the dark. Two of her little sisters whimpered in fear, which she understood fully. One of the sleeping children belched softly. Abidoon, thank the Almighty, slept in her mother's arms. Alannoon rocked her gently. They couldn't have the baby waking up. That'd ruin them all.

Johlick had an old bronze sword, green with weathered age. He gripped it in both hands. Where had he gotten the thing? The whites of his eyes showed in the little light coming through a small window.

Shathan stood facing the door in front of his mother. He gripped his hand knife, glanced at Anna, and frowned in resolution. Their mother pulled at her teenage son, but he pushed her away, guarding her with his lean body.

A crash sounded from the common room, metal pinging and wood breaking. Everyone in the bunkroom jumped. The raiders must have come through the lattice window and shutters.

Anna crept up to the tied door. She unbound her hand knife, pulled it free, and prepared herself.

After several painfully long minutes of boots thumping on the wood floors of the house and the occasional breaking pot, the bunkroom door was reefed open a palm width. Then it slammed back shut under the tension of the rope.

"Aah! That silting smarts," came a male voice from the other side.

"What 'appened?" Another voice asked.

"I think I ripped a mucky nail."

"'Ow'd you do that?"

"The door is tied on the other side. It won't open."

"'Ere. Let me."

The door again opened only a palm and stayed open, torchlight angling into the bunkroom. Anna readied her knife. When the arm came in, she would cut it.

A bronze sword slashed through the opening, slicing through the rope with a snap. The door swung wide. Men stood there with torches, shields, and blades. "None of that, now, lassie. Drop that knife. Come with us quietly or die standing."

Anna planned to die standing. Snarling, she raised the knife and stabbed forward.

The man deflected her knife with the flat of his sword and grabbed her throat with his free hand. She hadn't even seen him move.

Her air! It was gone! She couldn't breathe! He pushed her back against a wall. The man laughed at her, his breath foul in her face. Through spots in her vision, she could see several more men rushing into the room. Women and girls screamed. A sword flashed in torchlight. Blood sprayed and a body hit the floor. No! Johlick! Oh, Almighty, no!

Her vision narrowed and narrowed some more. Blackness. She was going to die with a laughing man squeezing her throat. She tried to stab but couldn't reach around him. She clawed blindly, but only found rough cloth and metal plates. Against her will, she started to go limp. Her knife clattered onto the floor.

Suddenly, Anna fell free. She dropped straight down, thudding forward onto her face. She coughed once, spluttered, and finally sweet air filled her lungs through a tortured throat. Her head pounded with fresh blood to her brain. She dragged in another breath. Then another.

Someone pulled a rough rope over her neck and cinched it tight from behind. Her arms were brusquely lifted behind her back, high, almost between her shoulder blades. It hurt, but her strength hadn't yet returned to fight. More rough cords were cinched around her wrists holding them together. She struggled weakly. Finally, the hands released her. As she relaxed her arms, the cinch around her neck tightened, squeezing against her neck and cutting off her blood. She started to fade out. With great effort, she lifted her hands higher against her back. The pressure on the rope around her neck eased.

Women and girls cried all around her. Haley screamed at someone but stopped with a crack of a callused palm to her face. Anna opened her eyes and could see all the women and girls being similarly bound. They choked, whimpered, and cried. One young sister appeared to be fighting her bindings and choking to death in the corner. She'd been put in a binding too short for her. None of the men moved to help her.

Something warm and wet flowed across the floor and against her cheek. Following it with her eyes, she saw the source. Shathan had been split through the collarbone to his sternum. His sightless eyes stared at her in the torchlight. He would never play a prank again.

Johlick lay on the floor, silently clutching at what was left of his arm. Where was it? She looked and found it laying off to the side. It had been sheared off just above the elbow.

Jared, with the courage of a young boy, attacked a man's leg with a wood stick. The man casually backhanded the boy, and he stumbled backwards, hit his head against a wood chest, and fell silent.

Her mother glared up at the man who rolled her over.

Anna was also roughly rolled over. A man pushed up her dress. Anna started to kick, but a rough pinch to her thigh straightened her leg involuntarily. He cinched a rope tight around her lower thighs, just above her knees. The man moved to the next girl.

Anna pushed herself up against the wall with her legs, which were free below the knees. She looked around, her tears falling from her face. Great sobs racked her chest.

"Stop that, lassie. You get too much snot in your nose, and you'll suffocate." And with that short warning, the man gagged her with a greasy cloth. He pulled a burlap sack over her head next and cinched it closed around her neck.

Anna continued to cry. All the girls did. She tried to stop, to be brave for them. But she couldn't seem to control her sobbing.

CHAR kept the operation running smoothly. Every house in the plan was

117

hit except the one beyond a rope bridge that had been cut. Three men had plunged to their deaths. On Char's orders, a secondary house had been hit instead. Women had been captured and bound. The cut lifts slowed them down at first, but his men moved quickly now. No more resistance came from any of the women. Once in the rope cinches, all fight left them. He'd seen it before.

Some of the houses on this level still had lights. No one came out. The doors had been barred. Any house not in the plan was ignored.

None burned. Char needed no diversion now. No one would come out to quell the flames. No one would pursue them. They just needed to descend and retreat to Location One. Follow the plan. They were almost done.

Some women were being lowered by rope. Many others were being lowered by the remaining footlift Char had found. Char had added to the counterweight. A man fitted each woman's foot into the stirrup. Another man stepped into the stirrup with her and held her in place against the rope. They both went down. In moments, the man came back up alone to take the next woman. It all moved quite quickly.

Most of the women cried or whimpered. Char liked the noise. It sang to him of wealth and power.

As the women were lowered, he did not count them. He would count them later, but he smiled to see so many. For now, he made sure the descent went smoothly. He scanned the village as well, looking for any more archers. And he watched the house he had forbidden to everyone. It stood dark against the trunk of a big tree. The door and window shutters were closed tight.

More women descended, by lift or by ropes tied around their ankles. Women screeched musically. One squealed loudly as the rope bit into her bare legs. She should have been gagged. But maybe they'd run out. There were a lot of new slaves.

He turned to watch. An arrow ripped through the air where his head had just been. It tinged off the side of his brass helm.

He spun and looked. There, standing in a posture of defiance not fifty feet distance, stood a woman. She had a bloody cloth tied around her head.

She drew and loosed again. Before he could act, the arrow struck him squarely in the brass breastplate. The plate dented but held. He barely noticed. He stared, jaw hanging open at the woman.

Several of his archers drew and aimed.

"Wait! Hold!" Char screamed at them.

The woman turned and ran behind a building.

"Commander?" One of his archers asked.

"Keep an eye out. If she shoots again, return arrows. Otherwise, let her go."

"Sir?" The archer asked again.

"Can you not understand me?" Char's voice was quiet. Dangerous.

"Understood sir. We're on it." The archer stepped forward, taking a knee to gain cover behind a small wooden planter sprouting green plants and red fruit.

Char gazed back at where the woman had run. He looked for a long moment, then turned back to his work.

KENAN returned to the village. He crouched in his undershirt, watching what was happening. His overshirt had been converted into many bandages. He flexed his limbs, ignoring both stiffness and throbbing pain. His body felt the pulse of adrenalin. He wasn't done.

He had his hand knife and the bronze sword. He'd re-donned the wooden armor over his undershirt. And he'd cut an arm-length blackwood stick, which he had tucked under his belt behind his back.

Women were being lowered from the house level down to the village level. From there, they struggled down the steptree. They appeared to be bound around their knees. Their hands were tied high behind their backs with a cord running up and under the dirty burlap sack covering their head. They descended bound and blind.

Others were lowered from the village level by platform lift, four or five at a time. Some of those women had blond hair sticking out below the burlap sacks. Anna! Anna was being taken! Dragonspit, no!

Nearly twenty men worked the operation. Kenan couldn't stop twenty men, wounded and on his own. He struggled to think against his hot emotions.

He remembered a hissdragon prowled the forest when he heard a man scream not too far distant, followed by a loud hiss. The scream cut off abruptly.

On the Flat below, the man in steel circled on his hissdragon. If Kenan went down there, he wouldn't survive long. The man with the crazy orange eyes or a hissdragon would get him for certain.

But he had to do something. They were taking Anna!

Kenan moved forward in the darkness. He found a man with a bow and nocked arrow standing at the balcony rail, looking out over the Flat and scanning the area from the dark. Kenan moved up behind him silently on bare feet. At the last moment, the man sensed his presence and started to spin. Too late. Kenan stepped inside the spinning bow and gutted the man with the bronze sword. The man gaped at him and a little wheeze escaped. His head tipped back, and he fell over the side of the rail, making surprisingly little noise. Kenan tried to keep the sword, but the hilt was wrenched from his hand. Kenan stepped back and faded into the night.

As Kenan circled another building, keeping to the shadows, he saw a shape move. Someone crouched down by several barrels. Kenan quietly approached, wishing he still had that sword.

"Kenan? Is that you?"

Kenan recognized the voice of the potter's apprentice, Zacharai. The boy was fourteen, but big and strong for his age.

"Zacharai? What are you doing?"

"I can fight. I have a weapon." Zacharai brandished a four-pronged bronze tool used to loosen clay from the banks of the Babelwind Brook. He also wore the older style of wood armor.

"No. Stay here. I'll come back for you."

"But Kenan, I..."

"No. It's too dangerous for you to try to make it home. They'll catch you. Stay here and don't move."

"Then how can I help?"

Kenan eyed the boy. "I don't need your help, but your family will. After. Stay here and be ready to help when I call."

"Okay, Kenan."

Kenan paused, then asked, "You got rope?"

"Yeah."

"Good. Enough to get to the ground?"

"Twice that."

"Okay. Give me half. And don't use the lifts. If you have to get away, go down to the ground and hide. If I call, come."

"Okay."

Kenan put his hand on the boy's shoulder, squeezing before he moved off.

He heard the zip of an arrow not too far away. A White Spider archer took an arrow from above, screaming in pain. Kenan thrilled that another man from Blacktree fought back. He watched as the raider struggled to move away but instead eased himself to the boardwalk. Kenan approached quietly, using his hand knife to end the man's pain before he knew Kenan was there.

Arrows zipped through the night. More White Spider archers returned arrows to the house level above.

He couldn't stop them all, but he could perhaps stop one of their leaders. Perhaps, if he could kill a leader, it would yield an opportunity.

A man in a brass helm slid down a rope from the house level down to the village level. He landed lightly on the village boardwalk, not far from Kenan. The man had a cloth wrapped around his head under the brass helmet.

Kenan slid into position, tying off the rope Zacharai had given him. He would kill this man. The White Spider deserved it and more. A cold rage seethed in him, and it became focused on this one man before him.

The rider in steel below yelled up with a deep booming voice Kenan remembered well. He heard it in his dreams. "Commander Char!"

The man with the brass helm, Commander Char, called back down. "Yes, my Prince?"

"There is a man, just there. He is wroth with you. He is planning to kill you." The man in steel pointed his sword directly at Kenan. The orange eyes pulsed with angry light. Kenan stiffened in shock. "Kill him for me, Commander, if you would."

Char spun, making eye contact with Kenan. Just one eye glared at him. The cloth covered the other eye. Char reached up and pulled the cloth down, exposing his second eye, which looked healthy enough.

Kenan stepped up, still mostly covered in darkness. He loosened his stiff and wounded limbs. He slipped the blackwood stick from behind his back, holding it hidden behind his arm. Adrenaline flowed. His body was as ready as his wounds would allow.

Char drew a sword, shining bright against torchlight. Steel! Char leapt forward and swung the broad steel sword in a wide sweep with two hands. The blow would easily cleave a man through to the heart.

Kenan stepped back, the sword tip passing a palm short of the wood armor on his chest. If the blade had only been a little longer, he might have been cut.

Char swore but recovered smoothly and stabbed with the point.

Kenan stepped and twisted to the side, then cracked Char across the helm with the blackwood stick.

Char stepped back clutching his helm in one hand, straightening it on his head. The cloth was up over one of his eyes again.

Kenan squared his shoulders to Char, staring at him, challenging him out of the dark.

Char looked back, a bright grin showing under the edge of the cloth. He looked hungry for a challenge.

Kenan stepped forward, into the torchlight. He would kill this man. And he would enjoy it.

Char stepped back, eye going wide. "You!"

"Yes, me," Kenan said. He hurled the hard, fist-sized nut hidden in his other hand at Char's leg. It cracked Char hard on the kneecap. Char jumped back with a cry of unexpected pain.

Kenan was on him like a toedragon on a chicken, the blackwood stick

121

singing in the air. Thwack, against a thigh. Thwack, on the meat of a forearm. Thwack, on the exposed inner bicep. The sword pierced outward, but Kenan parried. Thwack, to a knee. Thwack, against the bones on the back of Char's hand.

Char snatched back one hand from the hilt, then pulled his sword back with the other, attempting a slash at Kenan as he withdrew. The stick turned the blade. Thwack, against the helm again, making it ring.

Char withdrew further, retreating from stance to stance. Kenan advanced, stance to stance, staying inside Char's reach. Thwack, against the helm, again. A spray of blood arced as Kenan slashed Char's forearm with the hand knife he had drawn, reversed in his hand to hide the blade until too late.

Char fell back again, crying out in shock at his own blood. He used his sword, creating space between him and Kenan.

Kenan swatted at the sword with the blackwood stick. This time, he caught the sword's edge. The sharp steel bit into the blackwood stick. Kenan heard it split. He stepped back, out of reach.

"You?" Char said. It sounded like a question.

"We've been over this," Kenan said.

"You!" Char growled.

"Is that all you can say?" Kenan asked.

"Commander," came a call from behind Char. "Down!"

Char dropped to his stomach in an instant, never taking his eye off Kenan.

An archer stood on the boardwalk fifty feet behind Char, an arrow already ripping forward. The shaft thunked solidly into Kenan's wood breastplate.

Time to go. Kenan spun and lurched for the rail behind him.

A second arrow thunked into the wood armor on his back. He felt a jab of pain against his spine.

Kenan grabbed the rope end he had left dangling on the balcony rail and glanced at the coil left carefully on the boardwalk. He sat on the rail, arced one leg over, then another, and fell without pause into the dark. An arrow ripped by over him.

He braced for the impact as the rope played out. He knew the rope had a little spring to it, and so he... the rope ripped up and out of his hands. The shock of it tore the already injured bicep. He cried out in pain and shock.

The drop to a nearby branch didn't seem that far compared to the depth of the pit into which he had just dropped his hope. But he knew despair wouldn't help. The women were being hauled away. Anna was being hauled away! Dragonspit! He could do nothing to stop it. There were too many men. They had hissdragons and men with steel swords. He had holes and an arm that now hung useless at his side. He wanted to chase after her. He wanted to rescue her! But he could not.

He moved down the branch, tears in his eyes. He didn't see the knot of wood that caught his toe. He didn't care as he fell off the branch to the ground below.

He hit another branch with his flailing arm, spinning him as he fell. Then another, breaking his femur with an audible crack. White hot pain flared down to his toes and up his hip.

He landed in a pile of sawdust. It wasn't a big pile. Something cracked in his back on impact and his breath whooshed out of him. He didn't lose consciousness.

He wished he had as he regained his breath. A hissdragon thudded up to him, looking down where he lay. Every man, woman, and child feared death by dragon. The primal fear of being eaten alive caused nightmares for everyone. Now, he would know the reality of it.

The creature opened its mouth, displaying rows of sharp teeth. It hissed at him and lowered its nose to no more than an arm length away from Kenan's face. He could feel its hot breath on his cheek. It smelled strongly of freshly butchered meat. As understanding came, his stomached clenched.

His hand knife was there, in its sheath on his belt. He pulled it and pointed it at the hissdragon with his good arm. The blade wavered back and forth. He struggled to steady it.

A deep voice said, "Hold. Good beast. Hold."

Kenan dropped his knife. It bounced off his wood armor and into the sawdust. His arm flopped down onto his chest. His adrenaline was wearing off, and his strength ran out. He hurt everywhere.

A man dismounted from the hissdragon and strode over. He was the man in steel, eyes aglow in orange and a glowing, orange mist wafting behind his head. He took his helm off, releasing a small cloud of the orange vapors. He squatted down next to Kenan. His eyes lost their orange glow and turned an ordinary blue as he addressed Kenan.

"My name is Gharan," he said formally.

A wave of leg pain from the broken femur wracked Kenan, causing him to tremble. He struggled through it, gritting his teeth. "My name is Pissoff."

Gharan arched an eyebrow as he looked at Kenan. He absently laid a gauntleted hand on the muzzle of the hissdragon, smiling. "I like your anger. But that's not your problem, is it?"

Kenan grabbed the arrow in the front of his wood armor. It was the only position he could put the arm to ease the pain in his shoulder. "I do have a problem."

"Most men deny this. What is your problem, son?"

"There's this dragonspitter talking to me, see. And I can't seem to make him just kill me and be done."

Gharan's smile widened. "I like you, Pissoff. If half the men in my city had your spirit, we'd have already conquered the world."

"Sounds like you're a bunch of baby rabbits mewling for their mother."

Gharan's eyes actually twinkled in amusement. It didn't last. They flashed with orange, starting deep in the pupils and expanding to fill the entire orb from lid to lid. Glowing orange vapor rose from the seams in his armor and from his head and neck. Kenan stared at it.

"Your problem is pride, my boy, the arrogance of personal independence. I can work with that." And Gharan exhaled an orange vapor that settled over Kenan.

What in the deep forest was that?

The orange faded from Gharan's eyes again as he stood. He looked down at Kenan and smiled again. "Goodbye, Pissoff. Perhaps someday we'll meet again."

"Nope. I'll kill you from the dark before you know I'm there."

Gharan settled his helm on his head and remounted his hissdragon, whirling it around. He looked over his shoulder at Kenan, smiling. His eyes flashed orange once more. Orange vapor rose off him like steam. "That won't work, boy. The dark is where I thrive." He kicked the hissdragon and the animal bolted off towards the Flat.

Kenan closed his eyes, fighting to control his anger and fear. He needed a moment before he called for Zacharai.

LIDAI watched from a new perch on a house rooftop. Her scalp ached fiercely, and her head pounded. But it had stopped bleeding, thank the Almighty. It had taken her a long time to clear her eye of blood so she could see to shoot.

Raiders and Blacktree women were now all down on the Flat. The women were lined up and tied together, connected with ropes around their necks. The women waddled as they trudged off in a column, pulled by the men. At least sixty or seventy women and girls were being hauled away. It made Lidai furious. But there was nothing to do about it.

She was even a little happy. Her house had not been touched. This thought immediately made her feel guilty for being happy. Feeling guilty enraged her.

The two dragon riders circled the Flat on their hissdragons. They were too far away for a shot from her bow. The men were too small at this distance. She might hit one, but even if she did, they had armor.

Well, why not send a parting gift? She felt she should send a little message, like, "Don't come back! Understand, you dragonspitters?"

She drew her bow, judged the vertical angle, and loosed.

The arrow flew for several seconds, arcing down steeply before thumping into the meaty flank of one of the hissdragons. It screeched in pain. Served it right.

Why not another? She nocked, drew, and loosed smoothly, with no pause. Another hit, this one to the second hissdragon. The man in steel turned his head upward. The orange light in his helmet faded. The hissdragons lurched forward and ran into the night after the men and captured women.

Lidai listened as they moved off, disappearing into the dark. She could do nothing more for them. Time to go check on her mothers and sisters. People would need her help.

KENAN clung to Zacharai's shoulder. The strong boy supported nearly all of Kenan's weight.

He noted the direction the White Spiders moved. South, not east. They were headed towards the narrow end of Babelwind Brook. The entire first attack had been nothing but a diversion to draw the bulk of the village men away.

He hoped the men of Blacktree fared well but accomplished their mission quickly. They were needed back here and fast.

When they reached the Flat, village men — in whole and in part — lay all around, all soaked a grisly red. Blood had splashed over the hard-packed earth, making grim mud in the fading torchlight. Hissdragon prints intermingled with human footprints. Weapons and shields lay about. Blood congealed in little puddles.

Zacharai helped him remove the wood armor. His back stung where an arrow had broken through the blackwood slats. Several long splinters had pushed through and bloodied him.

He sat on the bottom step of the steptree. His leg throbbed in a way he feared would incapacitate him for weeks. His arm with the torn bicep hung all but useless at his side. He bled from nearly a dozen wounds. He felt lightheaded again. A giggle bubbled up.

"Kenan?"

"Yes, Zacharai?"

"What should I do?"

"Go up. Let people know they've gone and help who you can."

"What about you?"

"If my family lives, send someone for me. I'll just sit here awhile."

"Okay, Kenan. I'll be back, soon." Zacharai raced up the stairs.

Kenan leaned against the steptree. He didn't wait long before falling unconscious again.

# Chapter Twelve
# Red Waterskins

ANNA stood by the babbling brook and wanted desperately to be ugly.

She didn't know exactly where she was after marching through the night. She'd hardly been able to breathe through the greasy burlap sack over her head, much less see. The sack was so filthy it stuck to her tear-soaked cheeks.

The sack had only gotten worse. The gag in her mouth meant she had to breathe through her nose. Her pain caused her to involuntarily cry. She had no choice but to blow her nose into the sack as she struggled to walk to stay alive. The mucus made the bag stick to her chin.

She'd marched through forest duff, stubbing her toes on roots, rocks, and things that bit. She'd waded through several muddy areas and at least three streams, the largest of which had just washed her feet with its water and bruised her ankles on slippery rocks. Her legs throbbed with pain from the calves down.

She hated the binding. She would never again take the ability to stretch for granted. Her wrists were bound together high behind her back, held in place by a cord up and around her neck. If she struggled to lower her hands from between her shoulder blades, she choked. The night had been a constant battle between the pain in her shoulders and the ability to suck in her next breath.

It got worse. The women had been bound together in columns by a rope from one woman's neck to the next, and so on in a line. When one woman tripped and fell, several others were dragged down. They had all been tied to stompdragons, who pulled them along at a relentless walking pace. They didn't stop when women fell. She'd been dragged by the neck, while being kicked by the woman in front of her, for what seemed like forever before the line stopped, and they were all hauled to their feet by rough hands.

They'd been warned not to fall. Falling meant being dragged and maybe death. Every time someone fell, they were warned again. Soon, they all learned to take every step as high as their leg bindings allowed to avoid tripping. It meant throwing their feet to the side in a waddling fashion.

Finally, they'd crossed this last brook, and the march stopped. She had never felt so relieved.

The hateful burlap was finally yanked off her head and used to wipe her face clear of snot and tears. They hadn't been gentle about it. The ropes binding the women together were removed, but their own bindings at knee, wrist, and throat remained.

And it got worse, again. The women were lined up in what appeared to be a rough camp. The gray light of early morning yielded to the orange glow from a few torches still lighting the morning mist. A small dragonring protected a single tent. Other rough lean-to shelters dotted the clearing next to a wide, babbling brook. A handful of stompdragons lay on one side, noisily eating vegetation that had been cut for them. Nearby, a very large fandragon lay next to a pile of baskets, eating what looked to be the remains of one of the stompdragons. On the other side of camp, near the dragonring and the tent, two hissdragons lay on the ground, tied to a thick stake, licking small wounds. They occasionally turned to look at the people. Their eyes seemed to glare.

The women sobbed quietly. Anna wanted to scream, but had no energy left for it. She could only stand there, aching back as straight as she could make it, elbows back, chest out. She took a shallow breath. Then she took another breath. She spared a breath for a sob and to ease her burning shoulders. She straightened again, gasping for another breath.

They stood there in line for a few long moments as the rest of the women were relieved of their hoods and cleaned up. The big men with the white spiders on their shields stood all around. They looked tired as well, but not too tired to eye all of them. She didn't like their look.

One man pursed his lips at her. They all seemed to be leering at her.

They were not the worst. The worst was a man with dark brown hair, brass armor, and a cloth around part of his face. Bloodstains mottled the filthy fabric. Another bloody cloth wrapped a forearm.

Since she had the sack ripped off her head, this man had not taken his eyes off her. He looked her down. Then he looked her back up. He stared into her eyes for long moments. The rest of the men avoided him.

He never said a word, but his look made her wish she was ugly. The tiny little thought in the back of her mind said ugly was good. She'd never had the thought before. Right now, ugly would be great. She lowered her gaze.

"'Ow many?" asked a raspy voice.

"One 'undred thirteen," a man answered.

"Seriously? That's muddy good," continued the raspy voice.

"Cols," the man who watched her said, speaking for the first time. His voice was sharp and allowed no challenge. "Remove their gags. They are too far away from their village to worry about noise, now."

Cols, a man with big muscles, red paint on his arms, and scars all over, walked down the line. When the gag was pulled from her mouth, she tried to bend over and spit. The binding choked her, so she settled for hawking and spitting forward. It didn't go far. She had a hard time getting a full breath. Her throat felt raw. Her chest didn't want to stretch right. She hurt miserably.

Cols came back down the line and joined the man watching her. They both stood looking straight at her.

"She's a beauty, ain't she?" Cols asked.

Her watcher never took his eyes off her. "Yes. Stunning."

Anna looked away. She turned to look at the women to her left and right. There were a lot of them. Apparently, these animals could count. She saw women from multiple families. From her own family, she saw most of her sisters. She was the oldest and little Jaila, only seven years old, the youngest. Where were the little ones? Anna's tears started again.

Her mother stood nearby, her face proud and lips set in a thin line. Anna wished she was made of such strong stuff.

"Mother," Anna whispered, "What are..."

"Silence!" One of the guards stepped forward and backhanded her across her face. The shock of it made her lean back. Her hobbled knees wouldn't let her step. She lost her balance and fell. She couldn't catch herself and landed hard on her side, wrenching her shoulder.

She was immediately hauled to her feet by the man who could count. As he righted her, she felt his hands on her. They lingered.

"Careful with that one, Himmons. I want her to keep her teeth." It was her watcher.

"As you say, commander."

The commander didn't say anything further. His eyes stayed on her even as he continued to issue orders.

"Himmons, take your squad and cut their clothes off."

What? They were going to do what?

Haley cried anew as Himmons stepped up in front of her and cut her clothes off with a hand knife. He smiled as he did it. But his hand was sure and steady. He whistled a friendly tune, like he was shearing sheep.

All the women were now crying. Anna cried, too.

Himmons stepped up to her. The knife flashed bronze with the first rays of the sun cutting through the mist. She could feel the back of the blade against her skin. With all her will, she forced herself to remain still. Whatever was to come, being accidentally gutted was not how she wanted to go.

She had a small hope the bindings would be cut. No such luck. When he stepped away, her dress and overshift lay in rags at her feet, but her bindings remained very much intact. Her undershift remained, albeit with many nicks and slices. Thank the Almighty for small mercies.

"Water," said the commander. He said it directly to her, but several men came forward with red waterskins.

Women were watered by the men moving down the line. When the water came to her, she eagerly tipped her head back and drank what he poured from the red waterskin. He was generous, letting her gulp but not pouring so fast she spilled. It tasted metallic but she didn't care. As she needed air, he gave her the time to gasp for breath, then poured her more as she tipped her head back. She drank until she could take no more.

When all the women were watered, they stood, elbows back and chests out, shivering in the cool morning air. The undershifts were little protection against the mists. Several women wept, but most just breathed, wheezing and choking to the rhythm forced by the bindings.

The commander stepped up.

"You are now the property of the White Spiders." He looked up and down the line of exposed women and girls. "You are ours. We will bring you to Mordeen, in Midreer, where you will be sold and put to work. Your old life is over. Your new life has begun. Accept it.

"Your men are dead. Your elderly are dead. Your livestock have been taken or slaughtered. The few who remain do not know where you are. They do not know where you are going. There is no hope for you. You are now my property. Accept it. I am Commander Char Roughrock, your master."

He paused to take a drink out of a plain, brown waterskin.

"You will not speak except to answer a man. You will not speak to each other. You will not scream. If you do, no one will hear it. No one is coming for you. My men will enjoy your screams. But know that screaming may agitate one of the hissdragons. To them, screaming means food. It would not be wise to scream."

The women continued to quietly weep as the reality of the situation settled on them.

"Cols, take the smallest one. String her up."

"No!" shouted Freena down the line. "You will not touch my..." She was grabbed by the binding, choking off her words.

A young girl, smaller than Jaila, was pulled forward by her hair to an understory tree. A rope was wrapped once around the tree then tied to her binding at the nape of her neck. She was left there leaning back against the tree, wheezing for breath and staring at her mother in stark terror.

"Hareenan," said Commander Char. "If you please."

A man with a bow stepped up, drew, and loosed an arrow at the young girl. It thunked into the bark just over her head. The girl chirped a cry as the arrow parted her hair.

"Do not try to escape," Commander Char continued. "Do not try to fight us or rebel in any way. We will not bother any girl who looks to be under the age of thirteen. Yet, every time one of you attempts escape, I will personally see to her last night on this earth. Every time one of you resists, I end one of them. Do you all understand? Nod if you understand."

Anna nodded with the rest of the women. It hurt, but she saw no choice.

"Asher. Collect up the young ones. Add them to the tree."

Asher stepped into view. Anna's eyes grew wide with horror and rage. That... that... dragonscrape!

Asher grabbed a young girl in each hand and dragged them to the tree. The man was so strong it didn't matter if they fought him. Several men stepped in to help with other young girls.

"Take this one as well!" cried Freena again. "She's only thirteen! Only thirte..."

She cut off with another cry as a White Spider yanked her binding from behind.

Commander Char looked over. "Cut out her tongue. She talks too much."

"No!" Freena screamed at him. "I won't say another word, I promise! Please, no! Please!"

No, they wouldn't do that, would they?

Anna felt a little warmer, even though a cool breeze started to blow away the mist. Her cramped fingers didn't tingle any more.

Freena's tongue was cut out. Anna didn't see it from her place in line, but she heard it. Other women cried out. One vomited. How she did it with these cursed bindings, Anna didn't know.

"Now," Char called out. "Do you get the idea, chattel? Have you learned your place? You are no longer people. You are livestock. Learn your place or lose your tongue. Accept it. There is no hope for you.

"Cols! Get them all standing and ready for our prince. He's coming to inspect our new property."

Cols moved quickly down the line, pushing women into place. Some he needed to lift off the ground. Freena was stood up and warned that, "Tongue or no tongue, lovey, you'll stand or die."

Commander Char straightened. "Men! Not much longer now. Our prince is here."

A man with black hair and blue eyes, perhaps in his 200's, left the little dragonring, passed the hissdragons, and made his way over. His handsome face terrified her, but she couldn't work up enough emotion to feel her fear. The binding dug into her throat, but she seemed to be breathing easier. Her body still cried out in pain, yet it seemed distant now. She calmed.

She looked back at Commander Char. His hazel eyes met her blue, and this time she held them.

GHARAN Mordeen approached the men's camp feeling very full.

Anger still stirred in him, anger at that infuriating young woman at Blacktree and her infuriating gift with a bow. She almost ended him right there, with a single arrow from afar. If he hadn't *known* the arrow was coming in that last instant, he would be dead right now. He hadn't been so close to death in centuries.

He let his anger stir. He would return for that one.

Char had done an acceptable job with the night's work. Nearly a hundred women stood in line, with perhaps a dozen young girls tied standing against a tree. The men had been well prepared and well led.

As he approached Char, the man turned to him and took a knee.

"Rise."

"My Prince, we are ready," Char told him.

"I see. They have been watered?"

"Yes, my prince."

"Very well. How are the men?"

"Fine, my prince," Char answered. "Two have wounds and have been treated. We lost eighteen men."

"So many? To arrows?"

"Mostly, my prince. One man died of a spear or a sword. One was, well, he was gutted.

"By a knife?"

"No, my prince. By a sword. One of our own blades, it appears."

"Interesting. Do we have a traitor? Or perhaps it was done by the same man who fought you?"

"The latter, I would guess."

Gharan quirked an eyebrow at Char. "He bested you with a stick."

"Yes, my prince. I will double my form work."

Gharan nodded. Eighteen lost. Thirty-eight remained. Enough for an orderly retreat and to drive off any wildlife.

"Who was this man, Commander?"

"I don't know."

The commander was lying, but Gharan let it go. No matter. Gharan had given the village man a parting gift.

"May I inspect our goods?" The question was a formality, of course. He would do whatever he wanted. But Char was in charge. Gharan wanted him in charge. This was a difficult mission for the commander, yet he had performed quite well. There would be reward.

"Of course, my Prince. They are ready for you," Char said.

Gharan walked to the far end of the line and slowly worked his way back, eyeing each slave from head to toe in a cursory examination. One end of the line was dominated by large-shouldered women of significant height. They had well defined muscles, though a couple of the women, surely mothers, had muscles well hidden. They boasted strong, wide hips. These slaves will be bloodmothers, surely.

The middle of the line contained 133reate133s brown-haired, brown eyed slaves, clearly the dominant traits of this backwater village. They probably still wed siblings. Well, these women were mostly well proportioned. Some were mothers but many were not. Perhaps he would sell some. They would fetch a good price.

One was covered in blood from her mouth down. Even though she was too old for his taste, his gaze lingered. He liked the way the blood looked on her throat.

The other end of the line contained tall, blond, blue-eyed slaves. Blond hair was prized in Midreer. He would keep some of these. The rest would fetch a very high price. This had been a profitable trip.

Gharan stopped in front of one blond slave, older than the rest. Clearly the mother, she looked past her prime. He wondered why she'd been taken. Perhaps the blond hair attracted one of Char's men? Or did Char command it?

"What is your name," he asked her.

The woman glared at him. Glared! The females of this village were far more formidable than their males.

He stared back at her. It was time to see. It was time to ask.

"What is in her?" Gharan whispered, as if to himself. He *knew*. "Pride. Arrogance. Yes. Oh, and you have a past. You... you danced. For men. Interesting."

The slave's eyes widened in shock.

"Yes. I *know*." His deep voice purred the word. "And your spine is as stiff as a dragonpike. You've never yielded a fingerspan a single day of your life, have you? You will be an incurable problem, I'm afraid."

The older woman's shocked eyes could open no wider when his steel dagger entered her throat.

Many of the nearby slaves cried out. What a wonderful sound.

"Commander Char," he said as the woman fell over, her life blood spurting out onto the dead leaves. Unfortunately, the blood's vibrant color was lost in the gray morning light.

Char hurried over to him and stood over the slave as she gurgled her last breath. "Yes, my Prince."

"Do you see her age?"

"Yes, my prince."

"Please be sure none that old are brought back to Midreer in the future. They cause problems along the way."

"Yes, my Prince. I will see to it."

Char's heart was too soft. He *knew* it. But the commander did well, usually. He had a mind for strategy, tactics, and business. Ambition, too. Yes, plenty of ambition. Gharan liked what Char could someday become.

Gharan continued down the line and passed several true beauties. He passed them by and finished the line. These blond women would truly bring him a fortune in coin and favors.

Gharan made a mental note to have Char send scouts to villages more to the east and north of Edeer. Closer to Ulneer, there may be more caches of these beauties hidden in the smaller tree villages.

He returned to the cluster of the best slaves. One stood out from the rest. Her blond hair waved and curled at the ends. Despite the rough treatment, her beauty still shone in her blue eyes.

"What is your name," Gharan asked.

The slave wanted to defy him. He could see it in her eyes. She was much like her mother. But she was young, and her resistance had been battered this night. "Agliranna," she finally said.

"What is in her?" Gharan whispered. He *knew.* "Vanity. Yes, and pride, like your mother's. Oh, and addiction could be a real problem. A good combination."

He liked this one, very much.

"Commander Char."

"Yes, my prince." Char hovered nearby and was ready.

"This one is not for you. Or for me. This one is for my father, the Most High. She is not to be touched."

Char didn't respond. Gharan turned to look at him.

Char quickly masked his face, but not fast enough. He was outraged, covetous, and deeply disappointed.

"Did you have plans, Commander?"

"Of course not," Char lied. "Any of them will do. She should make an excellent slave for the Most High." That last was not a lie, assuming she could be cleanly broken.

Gharan turned back to his father's new slave, the blond Agliranna.

Gharan would break her. He was full and had what he needed to prepare her for her breaking. He would then mold her for her new life.

Gharan breathed on her. As he did, his eyes glowed so orange he could see them reflected in the slave's horror-struck eyes. He knew glowing orange mist wafted off his head, neck, and shoulders. He gave it no mind. He continued to breathe out on her until he was done.

He was still full, of course, but there were many slaves still to see in the line.

"She is already feeling the effects of the watering. Give her two silver-stripe seeds and see her safely to the post outside my tent. Safely, Char. Mind her by our mounts. They're in pain from the arrows."

"Yes, my prince." There was an ever-so-slight tone to Char's words. The man was careful but not careful enough.

He did obey, however, stepping up to place two small seeds in the woman's mouth. She wouldn't open for him, so he gave her a short but strong thrust punch to the stomach. Her mouth gaped open then, and he tossed the seeds to the back of her mouth. He gave her more water from the red skins.

Gharan hardly noticed his father's slave being struck. Her marks and bruises would be long healed by the time they reached his home. He had another priority right now. He moved to the young woman next to his father's new slave.

"What is your name?" He asked.

The woman didn't answer. Fear.

He reached with a finger, lifted her chin, and forced eye contact. Once established, she couldn't break it.

"Answer me," he demanded.

"Haley," she responded with a whimper.

"What is in her?" Gharan asked again. Deep fear. Envy. Jealously. He *knew*. Yes, she would do fine.

He breathed on her. Another went. His new pet stood straighter, her look settling. Good.

"Commander Char," Gharan said.

"Yes, my prince."

"This one is my choice. Have her and my father's slave brought to my tent together. If either says anything, please remove a finger from my slave's left hand. One knuckle for each word, if you please."

"Of course, my prince."

The two women shared a look. They both still feared. The water, however, was at work. They looked almost calm. Their eyelids looked a bit heavy, their eyes not quite glassy.

Gharan still felt so full. He scanned the line. There were many here. He would be mostly empty again, soon.

# Chapter Thirteen
## Under a Stalkdragon's Tail

KENAN struggled to help Wren off the shielddragon by the babbling brook, wishing for the seventy-seventh time in the last day that he would have landed on a rock instead of sawdust.

One leg still hurt from the arrow wound, even though it'd been a month since the attack on Blacktree. The broken leg healed faster than it should but still throbbed if he walked too far. His arm still hurt. His foot hurt when he stepped on it wrong. They were all just aches, really. In truth, he healed quickly.

None of it hurt like the loss of his village, of his friends, of Anna. Anna was gone. Nearly all her family was gone. Jaret had been killed when thrown by a crescentdragon. A brother had been crushed by a mawdragon. Another brother had been cut down by a sword while retreating through the forest. Many had been pierced by arrows. Jaret's house now stood empty.

The women of Kenan's family had been spared. But the men had been decimated in the attack. His switch-father had been killed by sword. An uncle and a brother were felled by arrows. A nephew still clung to life after having three arrows pulled from him. A third-uncle just never came back. No one knew where he was.

About two hundred men came back from the disaster with the mawdragon. Half of those had been wounded, some gravely. The village mourned while Kenan and Wren had spent their time under his mother's ministrations and watchful eyes.

Wren's wounds knit slower than Kenan's, who often joked he was from the strong end of the gene branch. But the thigh wound still bothered Wren. He could walk but not for long. He rode his shielddragon with the ridiculous name.

"Okay, stand still," Lidai said, holding the big creature by the nose horn. Okay belched at her. "Oh, that's gross!"

Wren smiled at her as he slid the last distance to the ground, turning it into a grimace as he thumped to the duff. He hopped on one leg, shaking the other loose after the long ride.

Kenan would have smiled at her too, had they been elsewhere.

The Babelwind Brook chattered to the side. They stood in the encampment the raiders had made.

While Kenan, Wren, and many others recuperated from the battle, some of the few remaining woodsmen had scouted out from Blacktree. They found the trail left by the White Spiders and tracked them to this encampment.

The place was set up for defense. One area had a dragonring, and the whole camp was surrounded by a low ring of fallen trees and interwoven thorn bushes. Rough lean-to shelters dotted the area, as well as piles of dragonstool from hissdragons, stompdragons, and a very large fandragon. He remembered well the fandragon.

The White Spiders had not stayed here for long. The scouts had followed the trail further south, finally losing it in the slow, deep waters of a small river flowing to the east.

Even though the trail was now cold, Kenan, Lidai, and Wren had come out to see for themselves. Kenan would not take another man's word for it. He had to see where Anna had gone.

He followed cuttings made in tree bark by the Blacktree scouts. The river flowed deep. There could have been a sizable boat. He doubted they would swim. The scouts said there had been no sign of the raiders on the south side of the river. The White Spiders must have used the river. He had no way to know for sure which way they'd gone, but he guessed east, downriver. There was nothing to the west but swamp.

Kenan and his friends were now on their way back to Blacktree. The safest place to spend the night was this cursed piece of ground next to the Babelwind Brook.

This is the place where they'd found all the cloth scattered on the ground. The women's dresses and overshifts had been cut off. Rough slashes showed the clothing had been cut right off their bodies. Anna had her dress cut off her body. Right here.

Kenan fell to his knees. Where had she gone? What had they done to her? What was he to do?

Lidai knelt beside him, taking his hand. "Hey there. We'll figure this out. We'll find them."

Wren knelt carefully to his other side. "What she said."

"Thanks. I'll be okay." Kenan wiped his eyes. "Just give me a moment, okay?"

The shielddragon thumped over, his nose down and shield crest standing vertically. He looked playful.

"Okay, stop." Wren stopped the beast with a hand gesture. "Let's give him a minute, huh? Let's get you a bath in the brook. You stink."

"He dragonspitting does!" Lidai agreed as Wren led the animal to the brook.

"Woah, little sister." Kenan sat back against a stump and held his sister's hand. "You may be the Heroine of Blacktree, but our mother will not stand for that kind of language."

She grinned defiantly. "What she doesn't know won't hurt her. Besides, she let me curse all I wanted as she sewed up my head."

"Really? She wouldn't let me curse at all as she cut open my arm to sew the thing up from the inside out. I didn't even know she could do that."

"She's full of surprises, that one." Lidai paused, then looked at Kenan. "We'll find Anna, Kenan. We'll find all of them."

"No one found anyone last time," Kenan said, voice rougher than he'd intended.

"I wasn't around last time," Lidai explained. "Wren said I'm 'tenacious.' It sounded bad when he said it, but I'm thinking I like the sound of it, now."

"He could call you a slimy dragonstool, and you'd probably like that too."

"Maybe..." she said, looking over at the brook. He could hear Wren and Okay splashing around in the water.

Kenan wanted to go after Anna. He thought about it nonstop. The river flowed to the east. He could build a rough boat tomorrow. The day after, or maybe the day after that, he could launch. Where they camped, there would be sign. He could track them through the Dragongrass plains and to wherever they were. He would find her, sneak in, and take her back. He had what he needed.

A plan formed in his mind. He would wake before the others and sneak away. He'd leave a note, so they wouldn't come after him. He had a knife and a hand-axe. He didn't need much more.

Lidai looked at him, still holding his hand. "What are you thinking?"

"Nothing."

"Dragonspit that. I know you're hatching some kind of plan."

"Nothing grand."

"Spit it out. I want to hear it."

"I... I am going after her."

"We will," she agreed.

"No. You're going back to Blacktree with Wren. I'm going after her.

Tomorrow."

"What? Are you going to swim the river? You'll get eaten by something scaly, you know."

"I can build a boat."

"Alone? I don't think so."

Kenan raised an eyebrow at her. "Because you say so?"

"No. Because we'll do it together, when the time's right."

"I'm better off on my own. I can do this. Anna needs me."

"They all need us. Kenan, we'll go back to Blacktree. We'll form a plan together. And we'll go. Together."

"I can't put you in danger."

"And I can't choose my own danger?" Her tone had a knife's edge to it. She sounded much like their mother.

"I need you and Wren to be safe. To keep Blacktree safe. If I know that, then I can do this."

She softened. "And how will you know where to go?"

"I'll track them."

"Down a river? How will you know which branch they took?"

"There can't be that many."

"Did you ever look at that map Master Medahal has in his house?"

"Of course," Kenan said. "I've sat with him while he meditates. He made me tea, and I stared at it, wondering."

"Well, I've never been invited to watch over him while he meditated or did anything else," Lidai said. "But I did go help clean his house a few times. That man has no concept of organizing his..."

"Lidai," Kenan interrupted.

"Oh, yeah. Well, I have an idea," she said.

Wren came out of the brook with Okay trailing behind. His overshirt was off, which he used to dry his hair. He'd tied his undershirt around his hips, exposing the red, puckered scars across his arm and thigh. Otherwise, he was a picture of masculine health.

Kenan turned to a staring Lidai. He reached out with a finger to her chin and shut her mouth.

"Uh, yeah." She collected herself. "What was I saying?"

"Yeah," said Wren, easing himself down next to them. "What were you saying?" Okay thumped over to a pile of stompdragon excrement and rolled in it, getting filthy again.

Lidai shook her head at the beast. "Well, I have an idea."

"Love to hear it, little sister," said Kenan.

"Well, stop interrupting me, and I'll tell you."

Kenan just shrugged at her. Wren was grinning at her. Those two were getting close. Kenan figured there was nothing to do but ignore it.

"Well, we don't know where the White Spiders came from, right? They left by the river to the south, which needs a name, by the way. I mean, how come no one named a river deep enough for a boat that's only a day away from Blacktree? I think we should name it..."

"Lidai," interrupted Kenan and Wren at the same time.

"Sorry. Anyway, that night they came from Blacktree to this place south of the village. There's nothing to the west. They didn't go south. So, they must have gone east."

"Yeah," Kenan agreed. "They went east. Everyone agrees."

"Okay, then, what if... no! Not you! Just lay there, you big monster. Well then, if they went east, they hit the Morderain River, which we all know flows in an arc to the east, then south, then back west and ends up in Midreer. The White Spiders must be from Midreer."

"We don't know that for sure," said Kenan. "They could be from the east, from Kalenteer, or even from Caineer. Really, they could also be from Ulneer to the north. The Morderain River stretches that far up."

"All true," Lidai conceded. "We don't really know. But here's the thing. I think that's all wishes and hope. We want the White Spiders to be from any of those places because we can imagine ourselves sneaking into those places to rescue our people. No one wants to do *anything* in Midreer. That's why we resist thinking they're from Midreer.

"If I were raiding," she continued, "I wouldn't mind slow going to get to my target, but I'd want a quick escape when I was done. Ulneer would be the opposite. They'd come to us down the river quickly but have a slow retreat. Kalenteer and Caineer would be slow both ways, to say nothing of crossing the Dragongrass. Midreer, on the other hand, is a run downstream on the Morderain to escape. If I were from Midreer, this is where I'd come to raid."

Wren beamed at her.

"Wren," Kenan frowned at him. "Knock that off. Almighty, that's nauseating."

"It's not," countered Lidai. "And I'm right. They're from Midreer. I'd bet my bow on it."

"Hold onto that thing," Wren said. "We'll be needing it. In the morning, let's get back to Blacktree. I want to talk to Medahal about this."

"Fine with me," Kenan said. Medahal was his Jempo mentor, and wise. The man would help them decide. "And Lidai, I think you're right, too."

She faked a look of surprise. "Well, hoist me up under a stalkdragon's tail! I'm going to go write that one down. Kenan thinks I'm right. Huh."

Kenan got to his feet, favoring the leg that hadn't fully healed yet. "Let's get a fire going for dinner. I want to turn in and get up early." He turned towards the dragonring.

Wren agreed. "We've got to go see that map."

# Chapter Fourteen
# Angles and Curves

THE three returned to Blacktree early the next afternoon, riding bareback on Okay. Kenan liked the animal well enough, but its wet skin stank. It had rained hard but was letting up. Lidai had a green-striped, wool blanket wrapped around her shoulders, but they were all soaked through. Kenan watched the activity and life of the village, knowing the inevitable end.

The guard platforms each held two men. Scouts ranged out in the forest specifically to look for enemy camps. A viewing nest, high in a central tree with a good view of the village, had been renovated and was manned all day and night to watch for an attack. Plans had been drawn to react better by cutting lifts and rope bridges as Kenan had done.

Kenan knew they'd prepared after the raid on the bathing pool. The planning hadn't worked, and they'd taken even heavier losses. Kenan knew the problem, but not the solution.

Gardens were repaired. The traders were back. The Flat buzzed with activity. People came out after the rain to get ready for tomorrow when the market would open. Older boys tossed huge, dried leaves into the barns while younger boys jumped in the leaf piles with squeals of delight. Men talked while heading back to their saw pits, and other men hauled logs with stompdragons. Half a dozen men worked to card rope, spinning it with a geared machine spun by two teen boys. Life went on.

Kenan thought they were all off task. After the passing of time, people grow lax. They forget the danger. They forget the lessons. Complacency comes with plenty of all the good things of life. The needs of spouses and children outweigh the fear of a distant unknown. The enemy watches for it.

The White Spiders would not be back soon. It had been about sixty years since the previous attack when they took 41 villagers. This time, they took 113 women and girls and killed fully half of the men. They would raid elsewhere, waiting until Blacktree grew fat again, complacent and ripe for the picking. It might take another sixty years.

Meanwhile, Anna was gone.

They stopped at Wren's shed, where Okay was left to lie in some fresh mud and chomp leaves. The three continued on foot towards the Flat.

They took a platform lift up to the village level, then walked over to a second lift to go up to the house level. Medahal's house was a couple of branches and a rope bridge over.

They knocked on the door. It wasn't locked or latched. Wren's knuckles caused the door to swing open.

"Hello?" Wren called. "Anybody here?"

No one answered, but the map hung there on the wall. Kenan slid past Wren and Lidai, into Medahal's house. They hesitated before following. Lidai hung her wet blanket on the back of a chair.

The small room consisted of both living and kitchen space. Every surface held pots, cast iron pans, scrolls, clay jars, clothes, and many other household items. Numerous cages of sticks and wicker held animals. A fat lizard the length of Kenan's forearm sat in the bottom of a cage, its reddish skin sprouting hundreds of little horns. Another cage contained several baby rabbits huddling in a corner. A larger cage made of fine wicker held a big snakeskin. A hole the size of Kenan's fist had been made in the wicker with all the little broken ends bent out. That got his attention, and he scanned the room looking for the escapee.

Wren sighed. "How does anyone live like this?"

"Kenan," said Lidai. "Shouldn't we come back when he's here?"

"He'll be okay with us here," Kenan said. "Look, here's the map."

The three gathered around the wall map. It was just as Lidai had said.

Edeer, the capital of the nation with the same name, was to their immediate north. Ulneer and the hills towered further to the north. Caineer and Kalenteer lay further to the west, on the other side of the Dragongrass. Through the Dragongrass wound the Morderain River, flowing south. Far to the south, Midreer lay against the great western ocean where the Morderain River formed its delta. Between Edeer and Midreer, the land was wild with dragons and other animals. The ocean was covered by a giant floating forest. The two nations were well divided.

"Lidai, I think you were right," said Kenan. "They must be from Midreer. It's the only thing that makes sense."

"Yeah," said Wren. "Anyone from Caineer would take the mountain passes or need to cross the Dragongrass. Kalenteer is totally out of the way. I mean, it could be them, but they'd have to go back upriver to escape as well."

Lidai sounded satisfied when she said, "You guys should have listened to me."

"You guys should have listened to me," mimicked someone behind them.

They all gasped and spun.

In a small wooden cage with the little wooden door swung open sat a colorful bird. "You guys should have listened to me," it said again.

Kenan breathed out slowly.

"Yes, you should have listened to her," said another voice behind them.

Gaping, they all spun back around. Wren lost his balance on his bad leg and fell over, shaking the whole house on its springs. A clay pot fell off a shelf and crashed to the floor. Small yellow seeds scattered in all directions.

Medahal stood by his map, looking at them. The wrinkles of age on his face added weight to his stare, but the corners of his mouth twisted up almost imperceptibly.

"Master Medahal!" Lidai cried. "You scared me! And it's a little creepy."

"Not as creepy as someone sneaking into your house uninvited," he retorted, raising his eyebrows incredibly high.

Kenan grinned at his old Jempo master. "Master Medahal, may we have a few minutes of your time?"

The old man looked at him, eyes crinkling with delight. "I haven't many minutes left, you know, boy. Why should I spend them on people who break into my home?"

Wren got to his feet, favoring his leg. "We knocked. The door was open."

"Did it have a sign? Did the sign say, 'Come in and talk to my bird?'"

Lidai laughed behind her hand.

"Not helping," Wren said to her out of the corner of his mouth. To Medahal he asked, "How did you do that?"

"Oh, I didn't do a thing. He started talking all on his own. The real trick is getting him to stop."

"Stop," said the bird.

"No, not that," Wren said. "You weren't in the room. Then you were. How'd you do that?"

Kenan was amused as Medahal answered. "Neglect. Assumption. Hastiness."

Wren looked confused.

Kenan came to his aid. "We were neglectful as we entered and did not observe. We made an assumption that he wasn't in the room. When he appeared, we hastily jumped to the wrong conclusion that he can disappear and reappear elsewhere at will."

"My boy," Medahal said, smiling up at Kenan. "You're assuming I can't."

Lidai snorted, then covered her mouth in shame.

"Oh, young woman, teleportation is a singular talent. I assure you, I don't have it. Now, sit," Medahal demanded. "Sit. All of you. You're all wet. Wren, please sit carefully. No, your leg is your problem. Just be careful not to break one of my chairs. They're not used to such a heavy load."

They all found their seats while Medahal filled a copper kettle with water from a bucket. He added some leaves from a small clay pot. Blowing on some coals in an iron brazier to get them glowing hot, he set the kettle on to heat.

"The White Spiders are from Midreer," Kenan finally said, when it became clear Medahal wasn't going to advance the conversation.

"Yes, I suspect they are. Their arrowheads are from there. And your logical deductions from my map were quite good."

Kenan admitted, "All Lidai's ideas."

Medahal turned to her. Lidai bowed her head in a convincing display of meekness. Kenan knew her better than that.

Wren, buying her subterfuge, looked at her incredulously.

Medahal pointed at her. "I take it, young woman, you are not meek? I've never seen you meek before. Quite the opposite, usually, I would say. Are you feigning meekness?"

"I... No. And yes."

"The Heroine of Blacktree, shy," Medahal tisked. "Well, real or fake, you'll need to shake it off before you reach Edeer. They'll eat a meek, young woman alive, there. Politicians, all of them."

"Edeer?" asked all three of them at the same time. Kenan continued, "Master Medahal, why would we go to Edeer?"

"Oh. Were you planning a different trip?"

"I am!" Kenan almost shouted. "I'm going to Midreer! I'm going for our families. I'm going for Anna!"

Wren and Lidai nodded their agreement.

"I see," said Medahal. "Let's assume you can build a boat. Let's assume you can float down the Morderain River and somehow survive the trip through the Dragongrass. There's spinedragons there, you know. Cranky ones. Let's say you actually reach Midreer. What will you do then?"

"I'll find... I'll look for... I'll search for our people. I will find them. I'll kill those who took them, and I'll bring Anna home!"

"I see. You and whom else?" Medahal raised an eyebrow at him.

"I'm going." Wren affirmed.

"Me too!" Lidai quickly tossed out.

"Ah, good. Three to Midreer. One is a huge blond in a land of raven-haired men. Another is a young woman, who by law will be a slave in Midreer. And a man any of the White Spiders will recognize on sight, as he who bested their captain. I'm sure you'll all do just fine."

The three sat, staring at him. Kenan didn't know what to say.

"Midreer is a large nation," Medahal continued. "Much larger than Edeer, in land and peoples. They've assimilated four city-states that I've heard, and one other I observed myself, long ago. They've founded other cities along the Morderain River as well. In which city will you look? Most cities have many thousands living there. In which part of which city?"

The group of young people grew quiet and still.

"What will you do if caught? Young woman, you are too small to be a breeder, but too pretty to be a scullery maid. A pleasure house is your likely destination. And you, boy, you're a giant of a man, but too old now to be a soldier loyal to Midreer, I would think. You're likely to be put in the fighting yards or the bowels of a ship to row the centuries away. And you, Kenan, you would be just right for the mines or the fields. But you bloodied them here at Blacktree. They saw your face. I suspect they'd string you up from their dragonwalls to die slowly, as an example to all."

Wren spoke up, "Well, none of that sounds terribly great."

Lidai elbowed him in the ribs.

Kenan said, "Master Medahal, you sound like you have a plan."

"Indeed, I do. Here, hold these cups while I pour you the tea. You'll all catch an illness from the rain." The old man took the copper kettle off the brazier and poured for each of them.

Kenan tasted his. Minty and smooth. A hint of honey, despite the fact he saw no honey go into the pot or cups.

"This is good, thank you," Lidai said.

Kenan couldn't hold himself back. "The plan?"

Medahal grinned. "You've heard it already, my boy. Go to Edeer."

"But Edeer's the wrong..."

"...the wrong direction? No, there you're wrong, my boy. The quickest path is rarely in a straight line. Angles and curves. Angles and curves," Medahal recited. Kenan knew the phrase well from Jempo training.

Medahal's arm suddenly shot into a space between two wooden boxes. He pulled out a snake, which promptly curled around his bony limb. The old man shifted his grip to hold the snake behind its head. "Wouldn't want to get bit, would I? Snake bites are no fun."

Kenan changed his angle in the conversation. "Why go to Edeer?"

Medahal smiled at him. The old man was missing several teeth. "For two reasons, my boy. First, because we sent three men there in the days following the attack. We needed King Enoch to know of our plight. He may not pay much attention to a few random raids, but an attack on one of the king's villages itself will get his attention. We lost nearly half of our population to the attack. He'll pay attention to that. Only, it's been over a month since our messengers left and they haven't returned. There's still time yet, but the elders, curse all those useless louts, are getting nervous."

"You want us to report directly to the king?" Wren sounded a little incredulous.

"Yes, that's exactly what I want, and what you want. He may be a king with a fancy title, but he's still just a man. Show him respect if you want to leave when you're done talking to him. It won't do to mock him. Yes, Lidai, I'm talking to you. The king must hear of this. You want his help. He might gather forces to move on Midreer. Would it not be better to go with an army at your back?"

"Do you think he'll really go to war with Midreer?" Kenan asked, excitement creeping into his voice.

"No, I do not. But neither will he sit still waiting for his villages to be picked off one by one. Go to him, my boy, and sway him."

Kenan felt intimidated but resolute.

Lidai spoke up. "What's the second reason?"

"You will want to see my old Jempo master. He's quite skilled and wise. It may even be possible to talk to the Grandmaster, a man of great wisdom. He may not accept you into his presence. But he might, if there is need."

"A Jempo master?" Kenan objected. "Master Medahal, Anna is out there. Right now! I need to get her before they... before..."

"Easy, Kenan. It's been a month and more, now. Whatever they planned for her, it's already done. It's already done for all of them. Midreerians are cruel and capricious, but they are not wasteful. To them, this is business. She lives. She lives and will keep living until her usefulness to them runs out, possibly centuries from now."

"I understand. But that doesn't mean I should go train in Jempo while she lives in pain."

"My boy, of course not. It means you should go gain information and allies while she lives in pain. Without information and men to go fight with you, do you think you stand a chance in Midreer? Will your death help her?"

"No." Kenan was thinking now. This hadn't gone as he'd expected. Yet hope had crept in and was growing roots. Perhaps the king would help him. Perhaps he could join an army to move on Midreer. Perhaps he could rescue Anna after all.

Medahal continued. "I will talk to the elders, curse them all. I will see you sent to the King. Then, go and find Lamech. He lives in Edeer on the east end of the fifth level. You will find him if he doesn't find you first. I will send you with a scroll to give him."

# Chapter Fifteen
## Knives in a Dress

KENAN walked along the forest road, leading their little caravan north from Blacktree. He loosely held a cord attached to his stompdragon's neck. The beast was laden with baskets, though it didn't seem to notice the weight. It twitched its head irritably at all the noise. It probably wished it were deaf and Kenan sympathized. Behind him and his stompdragon, Okay followed carrying Wren and Lidai.

"I am not," Lidai said.

"Of course, you are," Wren insisted.

"Well, what does he know? He's got to be a thousand years old."

"No one's *that* old," Wren objected. "Hey, Kenan, how old is Medahal?"

Kenan looked back. Wren rode on Okay, just in front of the hump of the dragon's back. The shielddragon was harnessed with straps and laden with baskets and gear. The beast snagged a juicy leaf and happily munched as it trod forward.

Lidai sat up behind Wren, her arms around his waist.

Kenan scowled at them. "Who?"

Wren grinned back. "Medahal. How old is he?"

"I'm not sure. Never asked." Kenan turned to continue walking, leading the stompdragon by the cord.

"Come on, Kenan," Lidai called to him. "You must have some idea."

Kenan rolled his eyes. There was no avoiding the two of them. He stepped to the side of the stompdragon. The packed dirt road here in the

forest was well defined and rutted by trader's wagons. The stompdragon
would follow it, at least for a time. He forced the stompdragon's head away
from him and down the road. The thing kept walking placidly in the
direction Kenan pointed him, stomping down on the trail with each step.
Kenan hopped up on the saddle and sat backwards, facing his friends on the
shielddragon. The stompdragon's tail swayed back and forth in his view.

"I'm not sure. It's not something you just ask someone, you know."

"I ask people that question all the time," Lidai insisted.

"Yeah, and how does that work out for you?" Wren's voice was wry.

She tried to tickle his ribs, but it apparently made his scar itch. "Ooo,
scratch right there."

Lidai grinned as she complied, leaning to the side and putting both arms
into the work.

Kenan groaned. Did he really have to watch this? "He's somewhere in
his mid-six hundreds. I think he's 645, or 650, or something like that. He's
not that old. Why?"

"He said I was pretty," Lidai said.

"Well, sis. I think he's right. You are."

"If you say so."

Wren nodded, agreeably.

Kenan fell backwards onto the neck of the stompdragon, who ignored
him and kept stomping forward. Really? Is this what he'd have to listen to all
the way to Edeer?

Wren clucked at Okay. "I thought he was older."

Lidai continued working her fingernails at the healing scar. "He looks
older."

Kenan blew air out of his mouth. "No. I think he lived hard when he was
younger."

Wren shrugged. "We all live hard."

Lidia snorted.

"What? Life is good. We live it hard."

"Is that what ages us?"

"Maybe. But not you. You'll stay pretty, always."

"You think so?"

Wren grinned. "I do."

Lidai rubbed at his scar with one hand and sat up straight, smiling and
fixing her hair.

Kenan's stomach soured at their flirting. He looked around for a sharp
stick that might fit into his ear canal. It would only hurt for a minute, right?

Lidai asked, "So, pretty or not, am I courtable?"

Wren snorted. "Of course, you are."

"Good. Know anyone interested?"

"Lian might be."

She must have jabbed him with something. He grunted and cried, "Hey! That hurt."

"Good."

"Not good. How can you court someone if you're poking at them like that? Was that your finger?"

"No. Are we courting?"

Wren said, "No," just as Kenan said, "Yes."

Kenan lifted his head and saw them both looking at him. Neither looked happy. Wonderful.

Wren blew air out his nose. "I don't know."

"You don't know much, do you?" Yet, even as she said it, her arms snaked around his middle again.

Kenan groaned. This was almost as bad as thinking about the White Spiders. He'd hunt them, find them, and deal with them one by one. He didn't need a deity. He didn't need an army. And he certainly didn't need those two lumps behind him, sitting on the shielddragon's back.

The stompdragon reached up for a flower as it walked. The motion raised Kenan up, and he faced the two of them again.

Wren nodded. "I guess we are. I just thought men decided such things."

Lidai bristled. "Men? Whatever gave you that idea?"

"Your father, for one, the Almighty keep him in peace. He told me once that he chose your mother."

"Did he? That's not how my mother described it."

"I bet."

"What's that supposed to mean?"

"It just means that women like to think they run the world, while men go out and do it."

Lidai snorted. "Right. As if you men would have an inkling of what to do without us leading you by the nose."

Wren grinned. "Hey Kenan? Have you seen my nose ring? I've left it lying about somewhere. Lidai wants it."

Lidai scowled at them both. Kenan scowled back.

Wren smiled. "You know, if we're courting, then I get to make the decisions."

"It doesn't mean that, you oaf."

"It does. And you'll have to stop calling me 'oaf'. I prefer, 'handsome,' or, 'your most incredibleness.'"

"Well, your most incredibleness, I'll let your impetuousness slide while we're courting."

"Impetuous?"

"Yes."

"Isn't that the pot calling the frying pan black? Listen, I'm not impetuous. I'm teasing."

149

"I listen. Less teasing, more complimenting."

"You listen, just like all little girls listen. When you want to."

"Oh. Really." Her hands withdrew.

Uh oh. Wren never knew when to stop. Did the man not know she had knives?

"Well," Wren stammered out a correction. "Not all women. Some women. Some men, too. It's a human thing, really."

"Uh huh."

Nice recovery, Wren. Only, she wasn't buying it. Lidai glared at the back of Wren's head. She wriggled back and slid off the shielddragon. She stomped along on the road next to the animal, all the while glaring up at Wren. The shielddragon gave her a friendly nuzzle which almost knocked her down.

Kenan hoped this would end their flirting but worried she might kill them both in their sleep.

Wren frowned down at her. He opened his mouth to speak but saw Kenan shaking his head at him.

"I do listen, you clod. And I am *not* a girl!" Lidai shot over her shoulder at Wren.

Wren didn't reply. He rode on his shielddragon, frowning in thought.

Kenan laid back on the neck of the stompdragon again, watching the trees pass above him. The view disoriented him, so he closed his eyes for a moment, his body swaying to the movement of the creature the same way he swayed to a branch under his feet.

After two wasted weeks of deliberation, the elders had sent them off with scrolls to the king, a small leather pouch of coins, and this stompdragon to help with the load. Each elder had verbal instructions for them, most of which countered the others. Kenan had already forgotten most of it.

His mother had sent him with food and lots of it. Truly, they had enough food to last them from Blacktree to Edeer and back again. She was in mourning for her husband and the sons who had died in the attack. She worked out her grief in the kitchen. The stompdragon's back paid for it now.

They'd left three days ago. Eight more to go before they reached Edeer.

Seven weeks had passed since the attack on Blacktree. Seven weeks of Anna and over a hundred village women and girls at the mercy of those animals.

The White Spiders. He saw some of their faces when he closed his eyes at night. He etched them in his mind. He made sure he would remember them. He planned to hunt them all, on his own, one at a time.

"Woah," Wren called to his shielddragon, which tossed its head up. The stompdragon stopped, too, with a little hoot.

Kenan sat up and twisted to see a man standing in the road.

"Hello," Kenan called to him.

"Hello, back," The man said with a smile as he strode a little closer. "I'm wondering if you might help me."

Wren asked him, "What can we do for you, friend?"

"Well, you can tell that little minx back there to take her hand away from that bow."

Sure enough, Lidai had her hand on her bow, which was tucked under a harness strap on the shielddragon. Kenan frowned. "And why should she do that?"

The man smiled broader as he answered, "Because if you don't, my men will riddle her with arrows."

WREN could think only of Lidai as he walked through the forest. She walked in front of him and Kenan in front of her. They were each bound at the wrists with rough-spun cords. Two armed men walked in front of Kenan and four walked behind the group.

The last man led Okay through the forest. The stompdragon had been tethered to Okay's tail. Okay didn't like it and was pulling at his lead straps. The man in back fought with him, cursed him, and struck him with his spear shaft. Wren didn't know how long Okay would stand for it. If the animal got it in his head to leave, there was little anyone could do to stop him.

The men wielded bows and arrows, clubs studded with sharp stones, and notched bronze spears. They were clearly rough men gone rogue, road robbers preying on travelers.

Wren wanted to knock them all down, snag Lidai, and run. He figured he could do it. At least, he could for a little while. His leg was healing fast, but it wasn't at full strength yet. He would falter and be caught. He would probably be skewered by one of the archers. Then what good would he be to Lidai?

The group parted the final vegetation and marched into a small encampment.

The camp contained a small dragonring, two fire pits, and several medium-sized lean-tos. A man sat near a small fire, heating something foul in a cast iron pot. Whatever it was, Wren wouldn't eat it even if he were starved, and that was saying something. A filthy woman also sat near the fire, bound to a stake in the ground.

"Wren?" The woman said his name when their eyes met.

"Miriam?" Miriam was a woman of Blacktree, relatively young at about 150 years old, and sent with the previous group to Edeer. Wren stopped cold at the exchange.

"Keep moving or die," said a rough voice behind him. Something sharp pricked his back. Oh, this man would die first.

"Run!" Miriam shouted at them. "Run now!"

The man in the camp reached across the small fire and backhanded her. "Silence, woman, or tonight will be your last. Look, we have a replacement."

Then again, maybe that man should die first.

Lidai backed into Wren's chest. He raised his bound wrists and dropped his arms protectively over her. He still wasn't sure of this match between him and Lidai. She was mighty young. Sassy, which he liked, but too often immature, which he did not.

He was fond of her, but unsure yet how far that would take them. He liked flirting with her. He thought he liked her. Really, though, it didn't matter. He would protect her all the same. He would not let these men touch her.

"Sort this lot," ordered the man they'd first met on the road. His smile was gone. "Watch the men. The smaller one's going to try something."

Wren watched as Kenan pasted on an obviously fake look of innocence. All he really accomplished was to glare harder at them all. A vein in his friend's forehead visibly throbbed as he scowled. Kenan, be careful, man.

All three were forced to sit in the dirt in a rough line with Miriam. A stout stake was driven into the ground, and cords tied from the stake to Kenan and Wren's wrists. Lidai was tied to Miriam's stake.

Okay and the stompdragon were tethered outside the dragonring. With everyone secured, the men unloaded the dragons and brought the goods into the camp.

It was quite a haul for this group. Food, water, and weapons were unloaded and laid out for all to see.

The money bag had been confiscated by the leader back on the road. Wren didn't see how they'd had a choice. Half a dozen bows had been drawn on them from just a few paces away. It had been surrender or die.

"Hey, what's this?" A man held up a scroll to the firelight.

"What's it say?" Another man inquired.

"How should I know? You know I can't read."

"You ignorant cur."

"Hey! You can't read, either."

"I bet it'll make great paper for the bushes come tomorrow morning."

"Nah, I say we just throw it in the fire." And the man made good on his words. In a flash of flame, the small scroll disappeared.

Wren watched them. Fear faded. He was getting mad. But there was little he could do. They sat on the ground, tethered to a stake and weaponless. Wren might make a move, but one man stood ready. He carefully watched all four prisoners, his bow nocked and ready to pull with a moment's notice. He looked like he knew how to use it.

Another armed man pulled a fistful of peeled nuts from a cask where they had been soaking in water for supper. He stuffed a nut in his open mouth, chewing for all to see.

Another man flexed Lidai's bow. He was too big for it, and he tossed it aside.

"Hey, here's another one." The man held up another scroll.

"Don't burn that one. Give it here. I want it," said the other man.

"Why should you have it?"

"You had one and burned it. This one's mine."

"No."

"Yes. What do you want? I can give you a knife."

"I have a knife. A nice one."

"Well, what do you want?"

"I want your arrows. You can go make more," said the man with the scroll.

"What? That's not even close to fair."

"Tell you what. You can have it if I get first go with the girl."

"Which one?"

"The new one."

"Okay. Deal."

"Yes!" cried Lidai. "Okay!"

Kenan lifted his head and shared a look with his sister. He turned back to the rogues and said, "Yes, she'll like it. Okay!"

Wren grinned, understanding dawning. "Okay!"

Okay broke his tether with what seemed no effort, turned to the camp, lowered his head with shield raised, and pushed through the dragonring. The points scored his shield, but Okay didn't seem to notice.

The guard with the bow and all the other men turned to face this new threat. An arrow flew at Okay, but it just bounced off the shield.

No one watched Wren.

He kicked at the stake, loosening it. He jumped to his feet and ripped the stake out of the ground all in one motion. He set his shoulders and pulled his fists apart as hard as he could. Or, he would have, if it had taken all his strength. It didn't. The rough cord snapped with an audible crack.

The archer turned back to Wren, but too late. Wren punched him with a hook to the head so hard the man went stiff and dropped. He never moved again.

Wren grabbed at the man's belt for a knife and tossed it behind him towards Kenan.

Without hesitation, Wren rolled to the side to avoid being trampled by Okay. The rough men were attacking Okay with spears and clubs. The animal moved about in a panic, grunting and snorting, looking for a way out. One man was trampled under the beast's stout legs.

Wren jumped the shielddragon's tail as he spun about, then rolled again to spring back to his feet right next to a man with a club embedded with sharp flint fragments. The man, who had been moving towards Okay, swung at Wren instead. Wren stepped in and caught the lower part of the haft in his open palm with a meaty thwack. The club stopped short, and the man's eyes went wide. Wren grabbed the man by the throat with his other hand and squeezed sharply. The man's wide eyes rolled into the back of his head as Wren crushed his throat to a bloody mess. Wren kept the club as the man collapsed straight down.

Another man charged Wren from behind. Spinning, Wren braced for the impact. But a knife sprouted from the man's temple, and he fell at Wren's feet.

Lidai screamed and hurled another knife at a different man. Another knife appeared in her other hand. Where had she gotten them all? And he'd let the girl ride behind him while he teased her? How had he not been stabbed?

Okay broke out of the dragonring and headed into the forest. The stompdragon hooted and followed.

The remaining four men faced Wren in the campsite. Kenan, who had finally cut himself free of his bonds, stepped up next to Wren. Kenan held the dirty stake in one hand and the raider's knife in the other.

Two of the men dropped their clubs, turned tail, and bolted into the forest. The other two failed to heed their friend's good sense and charged Wren and Kenan.

Wren swung the club downwards in a powerful blow at his attacker. His opponent was large, nearly as large as Wren. He blocked the blow with his own club, then swung from the side to crush Wren's ribs.

Wren jumped back to avoid the blow.

The man came back with a backhand attack.

Wren blocked it with his club and tried to punch the man. But this man was a fighter. He stepped back, avoiding the punch, and dragged his club along Wren's arm as he went. The sharp flints left long bloody scrapes. Wren ignored the pain and jumped back.

Kenan, having dropped his own opponent, suddenly appeared behind the man. His friend's face grimaced, and his eyes glinted with malice. Wren couldn't believe the look on Kenan's face. It was the face of death.

Wren didn't see Kenan move, but the man grunted and collapsed straight to the ground. As the man rolled back to look up at his new attacker, Kenan put the stake through the man's eye. The body quivered from muscles suddenly sent crazy signals.

"You're going to have to show me how to do that," Wren told him.

"You put the pointy end in the eye socket. Not that hard, really."

"Not that. I mean, the way you dropped him."

"You should have come to Jempo class," Kenan answered. His friend picked up a bow and a quiver of arrows.

"Where are you going?" Lidai demanded, running up to them.

"I'm going after those men."

"No! Kenan, stay with us. They're not coming back."

"Be back soon." With that, Kenan took off into the forest after the two fleeing men.

Wren moved to go with him.

"Wren, no! Don't leave us here alone!" Lidai sounded frightened, which stopped him mid-stride.

Wren turned back to her. The young woman stood with a knife in each hand. Though small, she looked anything but helpless. She looked ferocious, like a pretty badger defending her den.

Wren tore his eyes off this ferocious woman and saw Miriam. She still sat on the ground where he had first seen her. She just stared at them with big round eyes.

Wren approached her. "Miriam, it's okay. We're all okay. Let me help you." Wren untied her raw, chafed wrists carefully. The open sores were filled with sweat and dirt. "Let me help you up."

"No," Miriam said. "It's my leg. They broke it after I tried to run."

"Oh. Well, we can carry you. You can ride Okay."

"I'm not much of a rider. But okay, I'll try."

He chuckled. "Okay is my shielddragon. And yes, it'll be okay, if your leg will take it."

"It still hurts. But riding should be fine."

Wren frowned, his anger building. "We'll make it work," Wren assured her.

"What kind of name is Okay?" Miriam asked.

"A stupid kind of name," Lidai answered as she strode up, her bow in one hand and her quiver over her shoulder. She stashed a knife into a fold of her dress.

LIDAI crouched next to Miriam under a pod of yellowpetals and acacia saplings. The spot was good and so was the concealment. Lidai could see most of the way back to the encampment and had room to use her bow properly.

Kenan wasn't back yet from his chase after the last two men. What a fool her brother could be. He was likely to get clobbered. Those clubs were not for fun and games. Wren had gone to retrieve Okay and the stompdragon, and, if he could, help Kenan. The fool tower of muscle had *ordered* her to go hide and said he wouldn't go far, whatever that meant. Ordered! Worse, she'd actually done it.

She worried about Okay, though. The shielddragon had a bunch of wounds from clubs, spears, and the dragonring itself. The stakes stood stout and sharp. She wondered how far he would run before Wren caught him.

The stompdragon had importance, too. Otherwise, she would have to share Okay with both Wren *and* her brother. Right now, she didn't really want to share him with anyone.

That stompdragon needed a name. The thing tread pretty lightly for a stompdragon. Maybe something with a light touch. Sparrow? Finch? No, bird names were stupid.

What was that man up to? One minute, she thought they were making progress, then he treated her like a little girl. He let her wrap her arms around his waist. His waist! Her hands had been on his stomach! Then? Then, he insulted her. Almighty, he could infuriate her!

And she did listen. She did!

"Lidai?"

"Miriam, is there someone coming?"

"No..."

"Then, be quiet. I'm listening."

The man needed to be clear with her. He owed it to her. After all, she really liked him. No, not just liked. The man made her insides turn all upside down. She really, really liked him. No, that didn't cover it. She loved him. Really? That seemed a mighty strong word. Did she love him? Yes, she thought she did. Okay, she loved him.

Fat lot of good it did her, though.

Both of Wren's parents were gone. His father died. His mother had been taken by the White Spiders, curse every last one of the dragonspitters. Lidai spat to the side, almost hitting Miriam who looked shocked at the gob of spittle on a leaf right next to her head.

Lidai thought about saying sorry. She meant to say it. Then she thought of her father. He was dead as well. She grieved for weeks after his death. It was still hard, especially when she wanted to do something and needed permission. He wasn't there any longer. Who would she turn to for life's permissions?

Well, that's the point, wasn't it? The only one both her and Wren had left was her mother, and, as a woman, she couldn't give permission. The elders would have to give permission. And they were a bunch of do-nothing, annoying, slabdragon men. They wouldn't lift a finger if Wren didn't want the match. The situation infuriated her!

"Lidai?"

"Miriam!" Lidai almost hissed at her. "I said if you..."

"There's someone coming."

Oh. Lidai listened. Sure enough, she heard a bunch of something large coming through the forest. She recognized the low grunting.

"It's Okay."

The first they saw were tall ferns and saplings being jostled. The top of Okay's shield appeared through the vegetation. The dragon had a long red gouge from the dragonring. Kenan appeared next, towing Okay and the stompdragon by their leads out of the forest and into the encampment. They were followed by a very red and sticky Wren.

"What happened to you?" Lidai asked as she broke concealment and joined the men and dragons.

"Where's Miriam?" Wren asked.

Where's Miriam? Is that his first concern? Lidai pointed behind her with a thumb. "Wren, is any of that blood yours?"

"No," Wren said. He gave Lidai a glower before going to help Miriam. The woman moved their way, struggling to use her bad leg.

"Then where'd it all come from?" Lidai followed, pressing him.

"I don't want to talk about it."

"Did you fall in a pit of blood?"

"A what? Lidai, the forest isn't pockmarked with pits of blood. Those are spring pools."

"Well, that's what it looks like."

"No."

"Then what?"

Wren sighed, almost as if he were annoyed with her. "I... I got carried away."

"By a dragon?"

"No, not carried away. I mean, I got carried away. Like, I lost my temper with one of the men."

"Wren, what did you do? Did you slice him open and crawl inside?"

Wren gaped at her as he leaned to pick Miriam up. "That's disgusting." The woman's ribs rolled under her skin as he lifted her. He didn't look like he even noticed her weight.

Kenan approached after hobbling the dragons. "Lidai, he was just making sure the man didn't get up." He made for the gear, which was still laid out in the encampment.

In short order, Wren and Miriam had washed up and the gear was reloaded on Okay and the stompdragon that still needed a name. Miriam sat in Lidai's spot on Okay's back. Lidai should be mad, but Wren put Miriam there. Okay was his, after all. It was his right to put anyone on Okay anytime he wanted, wherever he wanted.

It didn't matter. Lidai wanted to walk. Good for digestion and all that. She looked at her brother. "Kenan, I'll lead Finch."

"What?" Kenan asked.

"Finch. I'll lead him."

"Did you name my stompdragon Finch?"

"What's wrong with Finch?"

"A finch is a bird."

"Really? I had no idea." She grinned at him.

"It's a stupid name."

"All bird names are stupid." And with that, she turned and shot a glare at Wren.

Kenan rolled his eyes. "Fine. From now on, not only will we set a watch at night, but I'll also scout ahead as we travel. This isn't happening again."

"I'm sooooo glad you're in charge," Lidai smiled sweetly at him.

Kenan exhaled at her, then trotted into the forest. He cut small limbs and green vegetation with his hand-axe as he went.

Lidai flexed her bow a bit, taking comfort from the weapon. She didn't think she was going to let it go ever again. She glanced up at Wren as he led Okay through the forest. No, she'd always keep it close. One never knew when a big man would need skewering.

THE rest of the trip to Edeer was awkward, and Lidai knew it was all Wren's fault.

Wren cared for Miriam's leg and well-being. Miriam didn't speak to Lidai and, once she'd had the pleasure of re-breaking and setting her leg, Lidai ignored Miriam. The woman clearly liked Wren.

And the stupid man fell for the woman's wiles. Didn't he know that a "Thank you so much," was really an, "I want you right now," in disguise? It seemed obvious to anyone willing to look.

The man even carried her when she went to water the bushes. Seriously! Lidai ignored Wren, too. If he wanted to occupy his time with this other woman, well, that was his business.

Kenan ignored them all.

They slept in trees at night, always with one of them awake and on guard against wild threats. Some of the dragons and all the bears could climb trees. Kenan never stayed with the other three. He always slept on a branch nearby, brooding on his own.

During the day, Kenan led the party down the road. He rarely stayed in sight. Sometimes he left short messages scratched in the dirt of the road. At least twice a day, they found a small animal hanging from a branch in the road where Kenan had left dinner for them to collect.

Whenever they needed a break, they'd find him in a branch over the road waiting for them. Drat the man. She wouldn't even know he was there until leaves rustled and he descended to the ground in front of them by one hand, dropping lightly the last five feet. How'd he even do that? Crazy woodbender.

They came upon Shallowbrook, crossing its namesake at the best ford for miles in either direction. The small village was, of course, tree bound. It only had one level with a mix of buildings. But it did have a rather nice little inn serving a wonderfully hot and spicy turtle stew. They served it out of its own shell, so large Lidai could have taken a bath in it. She enjoyed the luxuries of the inn and was able to take a real bath in a normal wood tub. She even bought a new undershift from a woman who waited tables in the common room. How they got the fabric so soft mystified her. She got the coin to pay from Kenan's money purse. He'd never notice it was gone.

At breakfast the next morning, Kenan and Wren talked right over her head about what to do with Miriam, as if she wasn't even there. Should they bring Miriam on to Edeer? The king would need to know about the rogues' attacking travelers and she was evidence. Or should they ask some people here to watch over the woman until a group passing through could bring her back to Blacktree? Well, that sounded like the best idea, and she said as much.

"Well, I don't know," countered Wren, who looked at Kenan. "Miriam said she was happy to go on to Edeer. She has family there."

Figures. They would take Miriam's opinion into account, but not Lidai's. This trip was dragonscrape.

As they were leaving, the Shallowbrook innkeeper told Kenan and Wren they'd have no problems with wildlife or rough men between here and Edeer. The King's Guard patrolled these roads. More people traveled here. "You'll be fine," the fat man said.

And true to his word, they were. When they left Shallowbrook, they traveled in the company of two other groups, both traders. The combined group numbered near fifty, with numerous stompdragons, three shielddragons, and half a dozen crescentdragons ridden by guards with dragonpikes.

They stopped sleeping in trees. Well, everyone but Kenan. Her brother was paranoid or something. And he'd taken dark and brooding to a whole new level.

One day, Lidai led Finch along by his lead. Wren walked Okay behind them. Miriam still occupied her spot behind Okay's shield, or at least she had when they'd mounted up that morning. Lidai tried not to look at her. A man on a crescentdragon overtook them. He said good morning to Wren and that woman, asking how they'd slept. The man clearly thought them husband and wife. Wren had laughed and quipped, "No, we're not married, though I would have been honored."

When the dragon rider smiled down at Lidai, he recoiled as if someone had just flung dung in his eyes. What was his problem? Men.

They knew they were approaching Edeer as they started passing solitary homes in trees. They hadn't seen or heard any dangers in the forest for days, and here people lived by themselves outside any kind of dragonring. They even passed one small home of stone and logs built on the ground. A home built on the ground!

Gardens were scattered through the forest with people tending them. They grew their gardens bigger here than in Blacktree. Lidai heard there were a lot of people in Edeer. Foraging would be problematic.

Finally, they crested a hill. A field of low-bush berries had been planted along the hillside where several great trees had fallen years ago. The terrain afforded a beautiful view of the city. The trees of Edeer dominated a wide valley. In those trees, hundreds, no, thousands of buildings were perched at many levels, buzzing with the activity of people and livestock. Smoke curled up from so many chimneys that a huge, wispy cloud of blue swirled away through the trees as far as she could see.

Lidai jerked Finch's lead. It was time to dump this woman at her relative's place and be done.

"Easy, girl." Wren stepped up and put a massive hand on her shoulder. "Just take in the sight."

Girl. Right. Lidai saw it all through a haze of red.

# Chapter Sixteen
# Finding a Nobody

"NOW that's a dragonring."

Kenan heard Wren, but it didn't really register. They all gaped up at the massive wall around the great trees of Edeer.

The ground sloped upwards at a sharp angle, covered in low yellowberry vines. Fifty feet up, a tall stone wall stood just as high again to bar the way. The top of the wall sprouted sharpened blackwood stakes of many sizes and at many angles, some tipped with bronze. The tallest of stalkdragons couldn't have peered over the top. Big thumpers, most made of wood, but some a shiny new bronze, sat on top of the wall and on defensive platforms built on branches over the wall. Men holding crossbows watched from above.

Kenan nodded to Wren. "Seriously. Why even bother building in trees?"

A whip cracked over their heads. Kenan spun, dropping into a Jempo stance. Okay snorted. Lidai and Miriam gasped at the same moment.

A fat man on a massive shielddragon on the road behind and glared down on them. He held a whip. "Get you gone, or I'll get you going."

"Snap that thing again..." Wren began.

Kenan stood, adjusting to a relaxed posture. "We're on our way, good man. Just a moment."

Wren gave the fat man one last look. Lidai had an arrow nocked.

"Put that thing away, girl," Wren told her. "We're not here to start a fight."

Kenan agreed. "Yeah. Let's go."

His sister stomped her heel before putting the arrow back in her quiver. The group got the dragons moving again.

The road, now wide and hard packed, turned and directly approached an opening in the dragonwall. The gates hung huge, covered in green bronze, and open for the day. Streams of people entered Edeer in the morning sun.

The guards at the gate wore bronze mail and carried blackwood shields with green trees painted on them. They leaned on their spears and generally looked bored. They didn't stop anyone.

The group moved through the gate, which looked more like a stone tunnel on the inside.

Once through, they would have stopped in wonder if the fat man on the huge shielddragon hadn't been right behind them.

The giant trees of Edeer towered over the entire city. Above, defensive platforms ringed the city inside the dragonwall. Inside and above them, massive buildings were built on every available branch and against every stretch of tree trunk. Lifts of all sizes reached the levels above. Some lifts were so large they were lifted by bronze chains. Wooden stairways, ramps, and spirals stretched up to buildings everywhere.

The city spilled down onto the ground. Elegant wooden buildings of Woven planks lined streets of river stone and roots. Signs hanging above doors declared inns, taverns, and shops. A massive stone ziggurat loomed near the center of the city.

The city Flat, just inside the gates, bristled with tall tents, market stalls, and stacks of goods. In the center, a large round pool splashed with fat drops of water dropping from somewhere far above. Dragons stood drinking around the edge.

People, animals, and dragons moved everywhere. The noise almost caused Kenan to cringe.

"You there! Where's your tags?"

Kenan turned. A thin man in a black overshirt looked at him. He stood next to a tall man with a neatly trimmed beard who eyed them all. A squad of Edeerian soldiers stood nearby.

"What?" Kenan asked.

The man with the black overshirt asked, "Where's your tags? Are you from Edeer?"

"The nation, yes. The city, no." Kenan didn't like the way this man looked down at him.

"Come with me." The man turned to go.

"I don't think..."

Half a dozen guards were standing nearby, now watching Kenan and his group. One thumped his spear on the ground and pointed towards the back of the tall man. The man with the trimmed beard continued to eye them. He looked dangerous.

"I think we should go with him," Wren said.

"Yeah," Kenan muttered. They followed.

The man led them to a building with a sign above the door. It read, "Clerk of Southbreach."

"I thought they called this city Edeer," Kenan said.

As Wren helped her climb down off Okay, Miriam said, "Southbreach is the name of the gate and the Flat."

"Why does the Flat need a name?"

"Because there are five," Miriam answered.

"Five?" Kenan could hardly fathom a place large enough to need five Flats. Yet, here it was, towering over him.

They tethered the dragons outside before the four of them went into the building, Wren helping Miriam limp along in her splint.

Inside, a long, whitewood counter split a room lined with tables covered in scrolls. The trees from the guard's shields were also painted in here on the walls. The tall thin man waited on the other side of the counter.

"Name?" he asked.

"Kenan Blacktree. Yours?"

"I am Golgatta Southbreach, minister of the green gates of Southbreach, warden of the showering pool, cleric of the turning root, filer of..."

"Got it." Kenan didn't have all day. "This is Wren Blacktree, my sister Lidai Blacktree, and Miriam Blacktree. Want to guess where we're from?"

Golgatta made a small note in an open scroll on the counter. "I see they still grow them impertinent in your little... village."

"Im-pert-a-nent," Lidai said, picking her nose. "Me no speak big words so good. What means impertinent?"

"Lidai," Kenan said in a warning tone. She flicked her finger at Golgatta and clamped her lips shut on a smile.

Golgatta cleared his throat. "Ahem. What is your business in Edeer?"

Kenan responded, "We're here to bring Miriam to relatives and to see the king."

Golgatta just looked at him.

Kenan shrugged. "Is there a problem?"

"You're here to see the king, you say." The man smirked at them.

"Yes. What of it?"

"Oh no, good man. Not a problem at all." He still smirked at them. "The king receives visitors the day after restday. Unfortunately, you'll have a few days to wait."

"I see," Kenan said. "We'll find an inn."

"Do you have any goods?" Golgatta asked.

"Just traveling supplies."

"Weapons?" Golgatta was reading from a list and making notes on the scroll.

"Just what we need for ourselves."

"Skills?"

"I'm sorry?"

"Skills. What do you do for a living?" Golgatta clarified.

"Well, I'm a woodbender. Wren does lumber," Kenan answered.

"And the woman?" Golgatta pressed.

"I tend house..." Miriam answered.

Golgatta talked over her. "And the girl? Does she have a skill?"

"I disembowel clerks," Lidai answered with a sweet smile.

"Ahem. I see." Golgatta didn't look at her.

Kenan was done with the clerk. "Is there anything else?"

"Yes. Several." Golgatta read from the scroll. "First, you may keep your weapons. It is, however, illegal to draw them inside Edeer except for self-defense, as adjudicated by a captain of the King's Guard, at a minimum."

"Second, keep the peace. Disruptions are illegal.

"Third, vagrancy is illegal. I have assigned you to go to The Goosedown Filler. You'll find it right over there." Golgatta pointed across the Southbreach Flat. "Be there tonight, or the guards will be told."

Wren smiled. "Strange. I thought we'd be tolled."

"Ahem. They you, yes. Lastly, you must have your tags with you at all times. I will get them for you."

Golgatta brought out a small box overflowing with braided cord loops. He reached in and brought out four yellowwood tags, each about palm sized. Golgatta wrote on each with his quill pen.

"If a guard asks, you must show your tags. Each comes with a toll of a silver Edeerian crest." The group looked at each other. Golgatta watched them. "You can pay the tag fee, can you not?"

"Yes," Kenan mumbled as he pulled out his small coin pouch. This would cost nearly half of their money.

"Very good. I'm writing your inn on your tag. That is where you're expected to be. No people are allowed outside after dark on the ground level. Failure to abide by the curfew is..."

"...illegal?" Lidai finished for him.

"I'm afraid so," Golgatta confirmed.

"Got any more laws?" Kenan asked. He couldn't help but let a little growl out with it.

"Many. Do you wish to read the legal scrolls? I can provide you access to our scroll room, or you can purchase copies with a seven-day notice."

Kenan shook his head. The group filed back out the door, hanging tags around their necks. After collecting up Okay and Finch, they crossed the Southbreach Flat, making their way around the pool and drinking dragons.

They crossed the Flat to The Goosedown Filler.

THE Goosedown Filler was a huge structure of painfully straight planks, each painted a different bright color. Kenan thought it was perhaps the ugliest building he'd ever seen. Many windows dotted the straight walls. Even more stone chimneys stuck up through the plank roof.

The stable for the inn was squat, long, and twice the size of the inn itself. Boys raced out to take Okay and Finch away. The stablemaster, a man of height and immense girth, strode up to the group.

"Good morning to you, good men. Are you staying in our inn?"

"Yes, if we can," Kenan said. "Can you stable our dragons?"

"Oh yes. Pitch! Grand! Take those two into the empty stalls down on the left. See the dunnage taken to the rooms of..."

"Kenan Blacktree."

"Yes, just right! Master Kenan. I suspect that'll be the green-yellow room."

"Thank you..."

"Gruntle," answered Gruntle.

"Master Gruntle?" asked Lidai.

"No, just Gruntle, young woman. Is there a problem with my name?" His words challenged, but the man's eyes sparkled in amusement.

"No, no," Lidai said. "I actually quite like it."

The stablemaster grinned broadly at her. "Well, you good folks have picked the right inn! We're reasonably priced and convenient to the Flat and the breachgate. I'll tell you what, I'll see you get lamb tonight, fresh off the spit and on the house. How does that sound?"

They were agreeable and the group moved inside.

It turned out Gruntle was more than just the stablemaster. He apparently owned the inn. As they entered the large, cheery common room, the maids jumped quicker, the man behind the bar nodded to him while filling a horn from a barrel tap, and a young boy scampering past with an armload of firewood stopped and bowed.

"Off with you, Seth. That goes to the green-yellow room." The boy sped off.

There were no other patrons in the common room.

"Breakfast is all done, of course. Getting here mid-morning presents some challenges, wouldn't you say? But I'll get you some birchbeer. Take a seat and I'll see it done." Gruntle moved to issue orders to the barman and maids.

"Is this place for real?" Lidai asked.

This inn was far larger than any building they had in Blacktree, even the meeting house. The wood glowed from polish. The firelight in the giant stone fireplace warred with the light streaking through the latticework

165

windows.

Gruntle himself delivered four horn mugs of a fragrant liquid. They all took a sip. Kenan immediately liked it. Smooth and a little sharp, not too sweet, and with a tang of alcohol.

"How long will you be here?" Gruntle asked, getting down to business.

"Four nights, probably. We'll need room and board for us and stabling for our dragons," Kenan answered.

"Very good, Master Kenan." Gruntle told Kenan how much it would cost. Wonderful. They'd been in Edeer less than an hour, and the mawdragon share of their money was gone. Lidai, for some reason, looked guilty. The girl was always up to something.

A pretty maid showed them upstairs to their rooms. The doors were slashed with differentiating colors, each door with a base color covered with a stripe. When they reached a door with a green stripe over yellow, she opened it and stood back to let them in.

The small room had one window, a small cast iron stove, and one bed.

"Uh..." said Lidai.

"I think..." said Kenan.

Wren stared at the bed and spluttered.

"Dinner's at sunset. Food's included, but drink and tips are extra," said the maid, playing with her hair. "I'll be there tonight. Don't forget." She smiled up at Wren. He smiled back. Lidai glared at everyone.

"Well, we'll make the best of it." Kenan tried to make it sound brighter than he felt.

They collected Miriam in the common room, then headed out to find her relatives.

LIDAI stood quietly on the balcony, wondering if a fall from this height would kill a person.

They were outside Miriam's relative's house, which hung from a branch high up. Fifth level? Maybe sixth. Lidai had lost track.

From The Goosedown Filler, they'd made for a lift. But, to their surprise, the lifts were not free. Wren argued with the man running the lift for a while. The rain powering the lifts was free, so why was the lift not free? The man just shrugged and said, "Nothing's free. No such thing as free."

Lidai supposed that was true, though Wren didn't seem to like it.

So, they had moved to one of the ramps. The ramps were free for cargo haulers, but people on foot had to pay. A ramp that cost money to walk. What kind of foolishness possessed these people?

Finally, they'd figured out the stairs were free. They'd taken a spiral staircase up. It wasn't carved like the steptree, but it worked the same way. With her bad leg, Miriam couldn't climb on her own, so Wren picked her up and set her on his shoulders. She was still underweight and perched up there like a child, smiling at everyone. Her dress had hiked up onto her thighs like a child, too. Only, those were not a child's legs, skinny or no.

Lidai had not been impressed.

After many steps, solid timber bridges, a couple rope bridges, and what seemed like miles of balcony boardwalk, they'd finally made it to Miriam's destination. Her sister seemed exceedingly happy to see her. Lidai was exceedingly happy to see her go.

How long would the woman scream before hitting the ground? Lidai peeked over the railing. Almighty, she wouldn't even reach the ground. But she wouldn't survive the fall to the boardwalk two levels down, either. It would be glorious.

She wouldn't really do it, of course. But she could dream. Not really. Well, probably.

"Thank you all, so much!" Miriam said to the three of them. "I owe you my life! I thought I was dead, but now I live! My sister will send a message to my husband. He'll join me here. I can't wait!"

Husband? Huh. Bet she wouldn't tell him about Wren.

"You are most welcome," Kenan smiled at her.

"We're just really happy to have helped," Wren added.

Lidai kept glowering.

Miriam smiled up at him. "Wren, you were so helpful." Turning to her sister, she said, "He carried me for miles. He helped me when I couldn't stand."

Miriam and her sister beamed at Wren. If Lidai hurled both women over the rail, she wondered which one would impact first. Lidai frowned at herself. That was dark. But still, would it be the heavier woman? Or the one with the biggest dress? She didn't know but enjoyed thinking about it.

They were all invited in. Kenan declined. They must get to the palace to see the king. "But thank you for the kind offer," he finished. "We'll stop by to say goodbye before we leave."

Miriam thanked them all again, hugging first an awkward Kenan then a smiling Wren, who fully engulfed her thin body.

Then the woman turned to Lidai.

Lidai stiffened. The woman approached Lidai, arms out and hands open. Lidai thought about running away, or stabbing her, or really throwing the woman over the rail. She didn't do any of those things, of course. Kenan wouldn't let her. Before she could think of anything else to do, the woman wrapped her thin arms around Lidai.

Miriam whispered in Lidai's ear. "I'm no threat, Lidai. You're young, but not too young. Trust, persistence, and patience. Be yourself. He will love you in time if he doesn't already. He talks about you. I've seen him watching you."

Lidai felt her body ease.

Miriam released her, smiled, and limped for the house and her waiting family.

As they walked down the boardwalk and out of sight of the house, Wren asked her, "What did she say to you?"

"She said you have bony shoulders and a thick neck," Lidai said, but she smiled quietly to herself.

MAYBE they should have brought Okay with them to the palace.

The king's palace was located far up the largest tree in the center of the city. A sign said they were on the tenth level. Tenth! Kenan could hardly believe the scope of this place. Blacktree only had two levels and Shallowbrook just one. This place had a dozen levels or more, stretching through many enormous trees for a mile at least.

Huge bronze chains suspended a wide timber balcony in front of the palace. The gates of the palace were plated in aged, green bronze. The palace itself had been built around the narrowing trunk of a great white tree. The walls were stained timber and the roof plated with lead sheeting with bronze trim. The planks of the structure glowed in the early afternoon sun, bright this far up in the tree.

People mobbed the balcony. Most were shouting towards the palace, demanding to be seen by the king. Other people apparently protested a tax, and yet another group chanted about how a god would rain fire down on them all. Fools. The crowd noise drowned out all else.

Kenan couldn't imagine getting any closer. He'd need a shielddragon to push through.

"This is foot tiles!" Wren shouted in Kenan's ear.

"What?" Kenan shouted back.

"Food aisles! It's food aisles!"

Kenan just looked at him.

"He said," Lidai shouted into his other ear. "It's two piles!"

Kenan shook his head at them. "This is futile! Let's go back!"

"What bat?" Wren shouted, looking around.

"I didn't mean any flack!" Lidai countered, looking stubborn.

This was ridiculous. Kenan shook his head again and walked away. They followed.

"What should we do now?" Wren asked when they were far enough away from the crowd to hear each other.

"I'm thinking we go find Golgatta," said Kenan. "He said it was days until the king heard petitioners. But here they are."

Wren added, "I saw the man-door on the gate open and accept a couple people. Why would they do that if he wasn't taking petitioners?"

Golgatta, it turns out, was not there when they reached the Southbreach clerk's office. The young clerk on duty told them the king takes petitioners when the king wants to take petitioners.

Great. Just great.

They went back to The Goosedown Filler. After searching around, they found Gruntle in the stables.

"Gruntle," Kenan said. "We have a question for you, if you don't mind."

"Ah! My Blacktree friends! Loose the goose feather shafts!" Gruntle smiled broad for them as he watched Pitch and Grand maneuver a table-sized leaf into a stall for an excited Finch. The dragon snapped its beak-like jaws, trying to get to the food.

"Right. We were wondering about the king," Kenan said.

"Really? That's pretty high up for you three," Gruntle observed. "Meaning no offense, Master Kenan, Master Wren. The king is a mighty important man."

"Yes. But we need to see him."

"Uh huh. What about?"

"Blacktree was attacked. We need the king's help."

"Attacked?" Gruntle seemed concerned. "What kind of attack?"

Wren spoke. "Raiders from Midreer. They took over a hundred of our women and killed twice as many men."

"So many?" Gruntle looked deeply concerned. "Come, let's go sit."

Gruntle led them out of the stable and to a stompdragon cart. He eased himself down on it, facing the three youths. There was no place for them to sit, so they stood.

Gruntle's brows lowered, uncharacteristically serious. "Tell me what happened."

The three of them told Gruntle everything, from the raid over sixty years ago to the larger attack on Blacktree only a couple months ago. He listened intently, asking clarifying questions, and sympathized at all the right parts.

"So," Kenan finished. "We're going to go find them and kill as many of those dragonsphincters as we can."

Gruntle nodded. "Don't blame you, Master Kenan. Don't blame you a bit. Before I help you, I do have some more questions."

"Go ahead," Kenan said. "Or, uh, loose the goose feather shafts."

"Just right!" Gruntle laughed. "First, girl, can you really hit a partridge on the wing?"

Lidai smiled at him. "Usually."

"Hmmmm," Gruntle said. "And you, Master Wren. Did you really kill a man with a single blow of your fist and crush a brigand's throat with one hand?"

Wren looked mortified. "That sounds horrible, the way you..."

"And you, Master Kenan." Gruntle raised an eyebrow. "Three armed raiders with one bucket?"

"Don't ask him about that," Lidai pleaded. "He's already got a big enough head over it."

Gruntle laughed. "Okay!" He boomed, and the shielddragon poked his head out of his stall to grunt at them. "You three need to talk to someone, for sure. But not the king."

"But we were told..." Kenan began.

"All the outlying villages think the king's the man in charge. They see his tree sigil on the soldier's shields, after all." Gruntle lowered his voice. "But he won't help. First, it'll take you a month before you get to see the king. Assuming you got a number today?"

"Uh, a number?"

"Just right. Second, the king can't do a thing about it."

"But," Lidai said, "he's the king!"

"Yes," Gruntle confirmed. "Do you know what that means here?"

"Well," Lidai stammered. "It means he, you know, reigns. That's what a king does. Uh, right?"

"No. Not in Edeer. The king has a palace and leads the military. Just right. He also chairs the High Council. But Edeer cannot act without the support of the Council. They rule Edeer in practice. You need to see a high councilor."

Wren inquired, "Is that like an elder?"

Gruntle smiled at them all. "Just right, like an elder. Only a lot more powerful."

"So," Kenan asked. "How do we see a high councilor?"

"You don't. You see a high councilor's secretary's assistant. If the assistant thinks you need to be heard, you see the secretary. The secretary will decide if the councilor needs to hear about you. Then maybe - maybe, mind you - the high councilor will see you. But only if he decides it's worth his time."

"Dragonscrape," Lidai spat.

"That's ridiculous," Wren said. "He's not hidden away in some room, is he? He does come outside from time to time, right? Why can't we just go see the councilor directly?"

"No, Master Wren. That's ridiculous. You'd be chased off by his bodyguards before you reached a stalkdragon length. Then you'd be picked up by the city guard and tossed into a cell. You'll lose a decade in there, my boy."

"So," mused Wren, "they don't really care."

"No, that's not it," Gruntle refuted. "They care. Probably. Well, maybe. It's just that they're busy. And important, like. Not like you or me. Everyone wants to talk to them."

Kenan thought about the crowd at the palace today. "So, do you know one of these secretary's assistants?"

"No, not me. I'm nobody. But I know someone who knows one. I'll send word tonight and see what I can set up."

"When do you think we'd get to talk to them?" Kenan asked.

"The assistant? Oh, it'll be a day or two, for sure. Maybe more. I'll tell them the matter is important. Look, our country lost half of one of their villages. That's not a small thing. I think you'll get a reaction of some kind."

A reaction. Well, that's not nearly enough, Kenan thought, but better than nothing.

THE common room of The Goosedown Filler bustled with activity. Barmaids hustled around the room, taking orders, bringing food and drink, and dodging some of the more handsy patrons. The women didn't seem offended. They seemed to play it as a sport.

Maids refilled lamps, put wood on the fire, and wiped down tables. The barman filled horns with birch beer, wine from barrels, and stouter liquids from smaller casks and bottles. The air hung heavy with smoke from people smoking pipes stuffed with half a dozen different tobaccos and other herbs. The smoke didn't seem to bother a tall, redheaded boy playing a flute while a sallow young man juggled many balls of different colors.

Kenan's head was a little light from it all. He'd had two birch beers and knew he'd reached his limit, despite a full belly of the best lamb he'd ever tasted. He didn't know all the smokes and suspected one or two of them weren't helping him think.

Wren took it all in with a goofy grin plastered on his face. He'd had four of the drinks and raised a hand for another.

Lidai had fallen over onto Wren's shoulder. He put an arm around her, keeping her upright. She snored into his collarbone.

"What are you doing?" Kenan asked him.

"What do you mean? I'm having an after-dinner drink."

"No. I mean, what are you doing with my sister?"

"I'm propping her up."

Kenan gave him a flat look.

"Well, if I didn't, she'd likely fall on the floor and break her pretty little nose."

Kenan maintained his flat look.

"In truth, Kenan, I don't know. She's too young for me."

"No kidding."

"She doesn't think so. Technically, she's not."

"She's my sister, Wren."

"Every woman is someone's sister. I like her."

"Do you love her?"

"Woah, there, Kenan. You're out of line."

"I am not. I'm her brother."

"So?"

"So, she has no father now. I'm the oldest man in her close-family." Nehamane would have been, if he hadn't been taken by the White Spiders. Of course, Nehamane would have botched it.

"Oh." Wren looked at Kenan. He could see him working it out through the smoke and drink. "Well, I'm pretty sure she has no idea what she's doing or what she wants. She's only thirty-four."

"And you're thirty-four as well?" Kenan asked.

"You well know I'm eighty-four."

"Right," Kenan said. "Old enough to know how to treat a girl honorably."

"She's not a girl. She says so."

"So, since she's a woman, you can take advantage of her?"

"What? Kenan, I would never!"

"I know, I know," Kenan placated, hands out. "But you might hurt her. Break her heart. You know, girl stuff."

"It's not girl stuff. But yes, I'm aware."

"So, be careful."

"What do you think I've been doing?"

"I have no idea what you've been doing."

"Well, that makes two of us." Wren grinned wryly at Kenan.

"Three," Kenan corrected, smiling fondly at his sister as she snorted in her sleep. How many of those drinks had the girl drained?

Wren waved his empty horn in the air. A passing serving woman snatched it out of his hand. "I'll be careful. I'm working on it, you know, figuring things out. I don't want to rush anything."

"That's the smartest thing I've heard you say all day."

"Well, the night is young!" Wren grinned and took the drink offered by a pretty barmaid who appeared next to him.

Kenan shook his head. "It's not that young. I'm almost ready for my hammock."

"You don't have a hammock in our room."

Kenan frowned. "No. Neither do you. We've got that soft, ugly contraption sitting on the floor. Who sleeps on the floor?"

"How, exactly, are we all going to fit in that thing, anyway?"

Kenan shrugged, then said, "Well, I know one thing for sure."

"What's that?"

"I'm sleeping in the middle."

"Ha!" Wren slapped the table hard enough to make Lidai snort again.

Kenan finished his drink with a long pull.

"Hey, Kenan," Wren said quietly. "There's a man over by the door. He's watching us."

"Where?"

Wren kicked him under the table. "Don't look, you drunken patedragon! Casual like."

That made sense. Kenan stretched and caught a glance.

The man was older. He had thinning gray hair and looked to be north of 700. But he still carried a powerful build. His face boasted several scars, and his forearms were covered with them as well. He hid one of his eye sockets with a yellowwood eye patch painted a garish red.

"Who do you think he is?" Kenan asked Wren.

Wren scoffed at him. "What, do I have a city census tucked in my belt?"

"Okay. Just keep an eye on him."

"No need," Wren said.

"Why not?"

"Because he must have seen you look. He just left."

Kenan turned and saw the man had, in fact, disappeared.

"Good news, my young Masters!" Gruntle boomed as he thumped over. Lidai groaned, covered her ear with one hand, and tried to hide in Wren's armpit. Disgusting.

Before they could ask him, Gruntle continued. "I talked to my friend. He's going to talk to the secretary's assistant first thing in the morning. Apparently, you're not the first here with the news of Blacktree. They know your village got hit and someone will want to talk to you."

"Excellent! Thank you!" Kenan said. Now maybe he'd get to go to Midreer, kill Char and Gharan, and rescue Anna.

"Hey, Gruntle," Wren said. "Do you know who that older guy was over by the door?"

"What guy?" Gruntle turned his girth to look around the room. The tall, redheaded boy bowed as he finished one song, then launched into another, his fingers flying over his flute. The silver instrument looked too expensive for one as young as he.

Wren said, "He was sitting over there."

"How old?"

"Not ancient, but like 700 or more. He had a red patch over one eye."

173

"That isn't young, boy. Even for me, and I'll be 487 next month. I didn't see anyone like that tonight. The patch, though," Gruntle rubbed his chin. "That'll narrow it down. I know several who've lost an eye."

"Okay. If you find out who he is, can you let me know?"

"Of course, my boy. Just right. Now, enjoy the evening, though somebody had better get this lass up to bed before it gets too late. Here." He reached to another table and snagged a big wooden bowl. Wiping the bowl out with his apron, he handed it to Wren. "She'll need that come morning. Bring it up with you, but make sure she washes it when she's done. Mind me. I can't stand the smell of sick up."

This seemed incongruous to Kenan. "But Gruntle, you run an inn and barroom."

"Indeed, I do. But a father can sire a son without changing nappies, can't he?"

Wren scooped up Lidai in his big arms. Kenan took the bowl and followed him upstairs. As he climbed, his mind remained focused on the old man by the door.

# Chapter Seventeen
# Dragongrass

ANNA stood on the tower at the rear of the large boat floating down the Morderain River and wondered if she could swim to shore, towing her sister Atarra, before getting caught. And, she wondered, what would catch her first?

The White Spiders hadn't stayed by the Babelwind Brook long after that first dreadful day, when the unspeakable happened. It had been a long day for most of the women. When a man finally fell asleep, the woman had been hauled away and given a simple chore to occupy her hands. None were allowed to sleep until late in the evening. Even then, huddled together for body heat early in the dark of pre-dawn, they had been unkindly roused by booted feet.

Only the young girls and Anna had escaped their attention. She was apparently being saved for the Most High, whoever he was.

The White Spiders had tied them again, each woman's wrist tied to the wrist of another, forming lines. At least the binding cords to their throats had been stowed away, and she felt ashamed to be relieved. Stompdragons pulled them south through the forest at a fast walk, making any attempt to work at the knots at their wrists futile, not that anyone had energy for an escape attempt.

Talking had been forbidden. No one dared try, not with Freena to remind them.

The huge fandragon had been laden with large baskets. The young girls were hogtied and unceremoniously dumped into the baskets, two or three girls to each container. If they struggled or cried, the men beat the baskets with sticks.

The hissdragons had brought up the rear. No one wanted to dawdle. They looked hungry and eyed the women constantly.

In half a day's walk, they'd come upon a small river with two large boats about fifty or so feet long. The boats each had a narrow main deck just over the keel and exposed ribs over a layered plank hull. Each boat had a fore deck set only hip high over the main deck, and a rear deck set only a little taller, though it boasted an enclosing wall and a small door. Above the rear deck stood an open tower, each with a mid-level platform and a top platform. Notches pocketed the wales along the edge of the boat for long oars.

The boats held a stockpile of simple, short smocks of rough wool. They were distributed among the women but fell short of the number needed. The larger women were left without. The young girls were given wool blankets, which stank of body odor and urine, but they looked warm.

Everyone and everything had been loaded onto the boats along wide, timber gangways. The two hissdragons were loaded into one boat. Men butchered the stompdragons for meat, which was loaded last and thrown in a bloody pile in the other boat.

Then off they went, downstream to the east. The fandragon slid into the water and followed the boats under its own power. In the shadows of the trees overhead, only its fan marked its presence.

By noon, a tributary joined the river. Then another. By evening, the width of the river offered protection from anything on shore.

The lead boat had been rowed by soldiers at first, but soon the larger Blacktree women replaced them. It contained most of the raiders and women. The first boat towed the second with a thick rope.

Anna, Haley, and Atarra had been kept in the rear boat with the younger girls, the hissdragons, Char, and Gharan. Half a dozen men were rotated on and off this boat to steer, perform various manual labors, and guard the young girls. Keeping the girls separate from the Blacktree women kept everyone in line.

So did the red waterskins. The women had been generally fed and watered quite well. But they only drank water from red waterskins. Anna had seen officers putting powder in the empty skins before refilling them, so she knew it wasn't just water. There was nothing she could do about it.

She had been forced to take two silverstripe seeds each morning and evening. At first, she fought it. Within a few days, she willingly opened her mouth for the seeds. They dulled the emotions of what was happening. Plus, Gharan gave her more pain if she fought. She no longer resisted the seeds. Haley and Atarra hadn't been fed the seeds. Those were for Anna alone. She didn't understand why and was beginning to no longer care.

The treatment of the women had not improved. Nights were long for them.

In the mornings, Haley would emerge from under the rear deck and stare out at the passing riverbank. She wouldn't make eye contact with anyone.

Atarra, only nineteen years old, didn't watch the riverbank. She slept most of the day under the fore deck. If she was awake, she cried. Char didn't seem to mind either the sleeping or the weeping.

As the days passed, larger tributaries joined the river. Soon, their river joined an even larger river. And then, to her shock, the trees ended.

Anna had always thought the world must be covered with trees. But it was not. Vast rolling hills of huge grass covered the land here. It grew right up to the riverbank. The blades stood taller than a man, broad, and sharp edged. White blossoms grew at the tops of narrow stalks. She inhaled to see if she could smell the blossoms from the boat, but she couldn't smell anything. Her sense of smell had faded soon after she'd started taking the silverstripe seeds. She had no idea if it would ever come back.

In the Dragongrass, dragons dominated everything. Swampdragons lay in the water and on the black dirt riverbanks. Small herds of stalkdragons towered over the plains and swamps. Fandragons loitered on muddy flats, rasping out warning grunts to the larger fandragon tagging along with the boats. A large herd of grinderdragons ate bright green shoots in the water, their duck-billed mouth-plates grinding the vegetation to juicy green pulp. Darterdragons hunted crustaceans on the water's edge. One day, she saw a massive mawdragon moving on the sand along the edge of the grass. Just beyond the wall of vegetation, the dragongrass rustled. The big mawdragon pounced and something screamed. Blood fountained into the air, staining the sandy shore.

As they entered the Dragongrass, the reason for the boat towers became evident. From the boat, all Anna could see was water, mud and sand, and the tall grass. But from the tower, she could see over the grass. If anything large approached, the men called warning. Spinedragons worried them in particular.

The women and girls were occasionally allowed up onto the platform to see. It hadn't occurred to her why they would be treated to this kindness until she climbed the ladder and saw for herself.

The land lay feral. The Dragongrass undulated like a green ocean dotted with white flowers. Birds flocked. Insects swarmed. Fish schooled. From the elevated tower, she could see it all. A family of otters frolicked in the water, lazily toying with an irritated swampdragon, which had legs longer than any she had seen to the west of Blacktree.

In the distance, the green grass broke around a lumpy gray outcrop of rock. Then a dark gray log lifted up, all by itself. She strained her eyes and saw the shorter neck of a stemdragon, cousins to stalkdragons, chewing something. But, if that wasn't a rock outcrop, it must be a massive herd. Indeed, the stemdragon lowed a mournful call to her and thousands of stemdragon heads and necks stuck up out of the herd, all chewing the roots and duff of the Dragongrass.

Four large hissdragons stood out of the grass, not far from the herd. The stemdragon heads all swiveled on their necks to regard these unwelcome visitors. Stemdragons near the predators lowed urgently and moved away, but the massive herd didn't react. The hissdragons dipped back down below the grass, leaving a wake as they approached to single out their next meal.

Something caught Anna's eye near the bank. There, ten or more of the largest toedragons she'd ever seen watched the boats from concealment, only their snouts and eyes visible. She shuddered at the sight.

A massive turtle floated with the current nearby, a large dragonfly resting on its back. The turtle poked a head larger than a dinner tray up out of the water where it regarded the toedragons. The toedragons regarded it back. The turtle extended its legs into the mud and stopped there in front of the pack of predators. They were still challenging each other as the boats left them behind and out of sight.

A small herd of wild shielddragons wallowed in a muddy flat. One grunted at her. She watched it, thinking of her brother.

A hummingbird, iridescent green with a bright red throat, landed on the tower rail. She studied it for a moment as it worked its throat and twisted its head about to watch her in return.

It should have all been beautiful, but Anna did not find beauty in any of it. The environment looked to her like the thick stone wall around the pen of her brother's shielddragon. It walled her in. There was no escape. She could judge the distance to the bank, the distance to the fandragon, and from the tower she could see where the swampdragons were. She might make it to shore. She might make it with Atarra. But even if she could make it, there was nowhere to go. They would not survive. There was no escape.

The hummingbird zipped away with no warning. It took hope with it.

Atarra, standing next to her on the tower, whispered, "There's no escape, is there." They were her first words since their capture.

It didn't sound like a question. "We'll work something out. Be brave, Atarra. We'll make it back."

She looked down at Gharan and Char, both standing on the fore deck. Gharan saw her and smiled, nodding as if to confirm Atarra's words. There was no escape here. Here, there were dragons, enough to ensure a messy death.

The larger women's backs flexed as they worked the front boat's oars in the water, pulling them all farther away from home.

# Chapter Eighteen
# All Sorts of Mischief

IN their room at The Goosedown Filler, Kenan lay sweating between his friend and his sister. He wondered if it was safe to gag Wren with a dirty sock.

The bed sagged in the middle and was far too soft. Lidai, it turned out, kicked in her sleep. Kenan felt a little pity for her future husband, until he looked at Wren with his gaping mouth right next to Kenan's face. The sounds emanating from the man shook the dust off the headboard. Kenan thought perhaps there might be a little justice in the world.

The iron woodstove had gone out, to his relief. The window stood open, the glass and lattice creaking in a light breeze outside. Still, the room sweltered. Kenan suspected the common room fireplace was right below this room, give or take. Or maybe it was his companions pushing at him on both sides.

Wren drooped a leg over Kenan's thigh. That did it.

With not a little effort, Kenan pushed the offending appendage off and quietly extracted himself from the bed. Wren and Lidai groaned in their sleep, then rolled towards each other into the sagging middle. Their arms and legs entangled.

Well, that was just great. Kenan rolled his eyes while he donned his overshirt. The heat, it turned out, was from the two in the bed. The room felt a little chilly, though the boards under his feet were warm. He could probably sleep more comfortably on the floor.

He heard something outside. Was that the scuff of a boot on stone?

Kenan sat slowly onto the edge of the bed and worked on his boots. He tucked his hand knife into a boot top.

What was he to do about these two? Wren had an arm draped across and around Lidai's hip. Not good. What would their mother say? Was this Kenan's problem? Sure, he was her oldest male relative. He was also, technically, not a son of her father. Kenan's father had left when he was a babe. What authority did he have over the girl?

A slight scrape of something on wood sounded from outside followed by a faint grunt. Kenan retrieved his short staff from where he'd left it between the mattress and the headboard. While he was there, he flipped Wren's arm off Lidai's hip.

Lidai looked so very young as she slept. She snored softly. Kenan judged her quite lovely, as far as sisters go. He could almost imagine her quiet and demure. Almost. The girl would eventually wake up, shattering the peaceful illusion.

Another scuff drifted up from outside. Someone was climbing the wall outside, under their window.

Kenan walked lightly over to their gear piled in the corner of the room. He stepped carefully, not knowing which boards might creak. He fetched another knife, tucking it behind his belt, and grabbed a coil of rope off the side of a saddlebag. He silently moved back over to the bed to await the unwelcome visitor.

Wren's big hand comfortably cupped Lidai's hip again.

Kenan sighed. He thought about correcting it once more, or maybe even waking the man up. Unpleasantly. Well, he'd be awake soon enough.

A hand appeared on the windowsill.

Kenan quietly tied the rope off on the bed post.

After a few grunts from outside, a man's head appeared, peering through the opening. It must be darker in the room than Kenan thought. Even though there were only a few feet between them, the man's eyes held no alarm. Kenan just watched.

The man lifted himself up with some effort, grunting softly from the exertion. Lidai and Wren snored on. Finally, the man squatted in the window opening, again staring and watching. He didn't move for some time.

Kenan got bored. "Hey there. Would you like to come in?"

The man's eyes went wide, his fingers slipped, and he dropped away in an instant.

Kenan threw the rope out the window and followed headfirst.

The man thumped off a stack of barrels and onto the ground. It wasn't an easy landing. But the man scrambled back up and took off running across the dark Southbreach Flat. A sword flapped near the back of his belt.

Kenan cinched his hand on the rope. The rope went taut, and he heard the bed scrape across the floor above. As his body swung, he let go and landed lightly on the packed earth near the stables. He was already running after the man.

He gave chase across the Flat, jumping several dragon tails and dodging around closed market stalls. The chase continued down a street, through an alley, and down another street.

At one corner stood a pair of city guards under a torch post. The intruder ran past so fast a guard only had time to raise a hand after him. Kenan rolled under a guard's attempted grab. The guards gave chase as well, but quickly fell behind.

Kenan gained on the intruder. The man puffed as he ran, beginning to slow. They both turned into an alley. Another few steps and Kenan would have him.

Something snagged Kenan's leg.

At full speed, Kenan lost all control. He landed on his chest, head turned to the side, and skidded on the packed earth.

Three men jumped on his back while three others watched.

WREN'S eyes snapped open as the bed was jerked across the floor. He disentangled himself from Lidai and sat up, trying to orient himself. Where was he? What was happening? Something had yanked him from a most pleasant dream.

Lidai sat up next to him, rubbing sleep out of her eyes. She mumbled, "What's going on?"

Wren heard the thump of boots on the ground and men running away from the inn. Kenan was nowhere to be seen, but a rope led from the bedpost through the open window. What had that crazy woodbender gotten himself into this time?

Wren hopped out of bed, reaching for his boots. "I don't know, but Kenan just left via the window."

"What?"

"Kenan jumped out the window."

"Is that all?" But she rolled out of the bed and over to the pile of gear. She bent half over the pile in her undershift, pawing around for something. If he knew her, she probably wanted her bow.

Wait. Lidai was in her shift, right in front of him. He felt his face flush, but he couldn't look away.

She turned to look at him over her shoulder. She smiled wickedly and put her hand on her hip.

Wren sat with his mouth hanging open. He couldn't think or say anything.

"We don't have time for you to do a painting. As if you could paint, you big lout."

Wren shut his mouth and rushed back to lace his boots. He kept his eyes on what he was doing. After his boots, he stood, threw on his overshirt, and cinched it with a belt.

"Are you decent?" Wren asked.

"Always."

"Right." He turned to see a fully dressed Lidai throw her quiver over her shoulder.

"Lidai, you can't go out like that."

"What's wrong with it?" She pawed at her dress, exposing a knife sheath.

"Nothing. You look... well, never you mind. But leave your bow and arrows here. We can't afford to get you out of a cell if you're seen."

Lidai huffed but tossed bow and quiver on the bed. "Let's go. We're wasting time."

Wren followed her down the stairs in the dark and into the common room. Coals from the fireplace gave off a faint glow.

"Hurry, Wren! We'll have no idea which way they went!"

"I think we'll figure it out." Wren stopped at the door and snagged a walking stick someone had left. It looked stout enough to knock the sense out of a man.

Lidai had the door unbolted and was already through.

Wren caught up in the dooryard. "Slow down, Lidai! We can't be caught running around the city at night! Remember the curfew!"

"Oh, that's dragonscrape," she spat, but slowed to let Wren catch up. "How are we going to find him?"

"That way," he pointed across the Flat.

"How do you know?"

"Men know things."

"I hadn't noticed. Must be your age."

"Hey now. Not nice. See those two stompdragons over there? Why are they awake? And which way are they both looking?"

Lidai nodded. "That's almost smart."

"Almost," Wren agreed with a smile for her.

They moved off down the street. They heard a man shout a word and moved that way, careful to stay in the shadows. They saw a lit torch post with one guard. As they watched, a second guard came into the light, stopped, and bent at the waist, breathing hard. Wren led Lidai down an alley and around the guards.

Just when Wren wondered if they'd have to get help, he heard a groan in an alley up ahead, followed by a thump and another groan. Someone was taking a drubbing.

"Go quiet," he whispered to Lidai. "We need to know what's going on before we interfere." She nodded to him. He noticed she had a sling in one hand, using the other hand to hold a stone in the sling pouch. He smiled at her in the dark.

"I can tell you're smiling."

Wren didn't respond and kept to shadows. He approached the entrance to the alley.

In the dark, he almost missed the young man squatted down next to a barrel. He looked to be on watch, but he kept looking down the alleyway, clearly wanting to be in on the action. Every time he looked into the alley, Wren crept closer, pausing whenever the young man turned back.

Wren got very close. The young man had his back turned but was peering around now with wide eyes. Something had alerted him to danger close.

Wren took two big steps and struck him in the temple with the walking stick. The lad's eyes rolled up into his head, and he dropped. Wren caught him and eased him down, silently.

"Remind me to never turn my back on you," Lidai whispered to him. How had she gotten so close? Had she been right behind him the whole time?

Another thump came from the alleyway, followed by another groan. A man was asking questions in a muted voice.

Time to see if they'd found Kenan. Wren and Lidai slipped into the alley, saw a group of men, and quickly ducked down behind a crate.

Six men stood in the alley. One man crouched down next to a prone man whose hands were tied behind his back. Another sentry probably stood guard further down the alley.

Wren peeked back up over the crate. The narrow alley contained a few barrels and crates but was otherwise empty. A couple of clotheslines stretched above with bedsheets rustling in the light breeze. Some yard tools hung from pegs on one of the walls. The crouching man punched the tied man in the jaw again, and he groaned. It was Kenan.

Lidai put a hand on his shoulder and whispered to him, "There's too many."

Wren grinned and shook his head. "There's not enough." He stood up and charged. On the way by the tools, he dropped the stick and snatched a bronze sledgehammer. The big tool felt good in his hands.

A stone whistled past him, and a man fell to the dirt clutching his throat.

Wren reached the first man and swung the sledgehammer at his head. What remained of the man's body fell over backwards. A second man brought up a short staff. The sledgehammer shoved it out of the way, the heavy, bronze head crushing the man's shoulder. Wren reversed the swing, catching the man in the armpit on the upswing. The arm came away with a ripping sound, and the man fell with a short scream. Wren needed to finish this fast before the guards came.

Another man brought up a studded cudgel. But a stone whistled in from the dark and hit the man in the temple. He fell with a little whimper.

The man who had been crouching grabbed the sledgehammer handle with both hands. The man was big, but so was Wren. The two muscled the handle back and forth, up and down.

A stone struck the man behind the ear. He fell straight back, and Wren swung the hammer as if he was driving in a stake. The man's chest crushed under the blow. He did it again. Then, because he couldn't help himself, once more.

Wren hefted the hammer. Blood ran down the haft and over his fingers. The remaining men turned and ran away towards the far end of the alley. It was a dead end. Wren wasn't sure where they were going. One fell to a stone in the back of his leg but lurched back to his feet, limping away. Another stone followed, but Wren heard it thwack off the wood siding of the wall at the end of the alley. The men crawled up over the wall and disappeared.

Wren bent down. Kenan groaned into the filthy ground of the alley. Wren cut the cords binding his wrists and helped his friend up. Lidai trotted up to them.

"I'm going to start charging you," Lidai said to Kenan.

"Foh wat?" Kenan asked through gritted teeth. He'd been struck in the mouth and his lips and jaw swelled.

"For rescuing you. I'm pretty sure that's above and beyond for a little sister."

The man without an arm sighed and stopped breathing. His eyes stared up at the night sky. Wren dropped the hammer onto a barrel and left it there.

The other men lay unconscious or dead in the dirt. Wren pawed over the big man and found a knife, coin bag, and a small scroll case tucked behind his belt. He also took the man's tag from around his neck. He noticed the man had a tattoo on his arm in the shape of a toedragon claw.

"Wat'd oo find?" Kenan tried to ask him.

"I'm not sure. What do you make of that?" Wren pointed to the tattoo.

"Noh soor."

"Guys, people are coming," Lidai said to them. Sure enough, Wren could hear boots thumping down the street. Torchlight reflected off the woven plank walls. In the direction the men had run, a light came on in a window. Nearby, a door opened and a portly man with a lamp stepped out.

"It's time to go," Wren said. He'd have to talk his way past the oncoming guards or thump them senseless.

"No, noh tha' way. Thes way. And cahful," warned Kenan. "Tha's a twip line."

Wren and Lidai followed Kenan out, stepping carefully over the thin cord stretched across the alley. They ran past the man with the lamp, startling him. He stepped back inside, slamming his door shut.

The end of the alley looked like a dead end, but a small opening to one side meant they didn't have to scale the wall. They fled down a dark passage, out onto another street, and away.

They got lost twice before finally making their way back to The Goosedown Filler.

THE rope still hung from the dark window of the inn, which was a good thing since the inn door had locked itself when they left. In no time, they were all up and back into their room.

Kenan pulled the rope in and coiled it back up. Lidai shut the window.

With that done, Lidai approached Kenan. "Got any holes that don't belong?"

Kenan gave her a look, then shook his head.

"Good. Sit down. Let me see." Kenan sat on the bed, and she took his head in her hands. She probed around his eye sockets, his jaw, and pushed on his nose.

"Ow."

"Don't be a baby. Doesn't even look like you broke anything."

"I haf a few teef that feel woose."

"I bet. Your lip is as big as a patedragon tail. You'll look like you took a beating for a week, but you'll be just fine."

"Tanks."

Wren sat on the iron woodstove. "Wow, that lip is something else. You look like a moose. So, what happened? Why'd you run off?"

"Welp, one of them twied to get in our woom. Climbed the wall."

"Why?"

"I dunno. He didn't schtick awound to chat about it."

Wren shook his head. "And you thought it a good idea to go after him alone?"

"Welp, he moofed pwetty fast. I had to know whaya he was going."

"Next time, let him in. We'll handle it together."

"Agweed."

Lidai chimed in, "And maybe you ought not charge off alone. You're going to get yourself killed."

"Sowwy. I just, welp, I just was itching foh a fight."

"Me too. But we're in this together. We go where you go. You're not just going to get yourself killed, you're going to get us all killed and condemn Anna to a life of slavery. So, just stop it."

Kenan felt some guilt. His little sister had a point. There was no sarcasm in her voice, just concern. Kenan nodded to her. Then, just in case she thought she had the upper hand, he winked at her. It hurt but was worth it.

Wren pulled out the little wooden scroll case. Both Kenan and Lidai caught the action and watched with interest. He popped off the end, and a small scroll slid out into his palm.

Lidai pulled her tinderbox out of the gear pile, struck a spark, and quickly had a small stick burning for light. Wren opened the scroll to read it.

Lidai asked, "Well, what's it say?"

"Nothing."

"Nothing?"

"On account of it not having a mouth."

Kenan tried to snort but ended up choking.

Grinning, Wren said, "It's not writing. It's a sketch."

"Of what?" Lidai asked.

"Of the inn." Wren held the scroll up to them. Lidai adjusted the light. The scroll showed a rudimentary drawing of the front of the Goosedown Filler. Their window had been circled.

"Think it could be a mistake?" Lidai offered.

"Maybe," said Wren. "But that seems mighty coincidental." Kenan nodded at his friend.

Someone pounded on the other side of the wall. They heard a muffled, "Shut up!"

Lidai's little stick burned to her fingertips, and she shook it out. She whispered, "Do you think they're coming back?"

Kenan, his night vision now ruined, whispered back, "No. Noh tonaght."

Wren rumbled, "It's still early." He yawned. "They could."

It made Kenan want to yawn. He tried to stifle it, failed, and groaned in pain as his jaw flexed.

"You two go to bed," Lidai whispered. "I'll take first watch."

Wren didn't even hesitate. He ripped off his belt, overshirt, and boots, flopping into bed before Kenan could unbuckle his belt.

Lidai helped Kenan out of his overshirt. He'd stiffened more than anticipated. "Lay back, Kenan. You need the rest. We have a big day tomorrow."

Wren mumbled, "Lidai, wake me for second watch." He was snoring in seconds.

Lidai smiled at Wren as Kenan laid back on his side of the bed. The sag in the middle wasn't too bad if he stayed near the edge.

"Kenan, I think I like that man."

Kenan thought it an epic understatement. He drifted off wondering if he should ask to be woken when the two traded watch. Alone, the two could get up to all sorts of mischief.

# Chapter Nineteen
# Words from Nowhere

Kenan winced at the innkeep's look.

"Almighty! What happened to you?" Gruntle stood at the group's table in the common room the next morning.

"I had a little scuffle," Kenan replied. Gruntle dashed his hope the bruises wouldn't be too noticeable.

"Was it with a mawdragon? Did a mawdragon get into your room last night?"

Lidai giggled. Gruntle winked at her. Kenan took another spoonful of nutmash. He'd asked for it with a lot of cream. He could suck the delicious slurry down without hardly chewing.

Wren, using the story they'd agreed on before coming downstairs, cracked his knuckles. "We ran into... a little disagreement last night."

"Oh, just right. Master Kenan, I urge you to avoid fisticuffs with a man so muscled as our Master Wren."

"I'll keep that in mind, Good Master Gruntle."

"Ho now! 'Good Master?' Clearly you want something!" Gruntle smiled broadly and tucked his thumbs behind his apron string.

"Not much. Will the secretary's assistant come this morning? Or are we going there, wherever there is?"

"No, no. He's coming here. He should be here any moment. Eat up, while you can. If he takes you into the ziggurat, you'll be there awhile. Here, I'll have a lunch made up for you, on the house."

Wren answered, "Oh, no. We can pay."

"I won't say no!" Gruntle said with a laugh.

Lidai asked, "We're going to the ziggurat?"

"Well, I can't say for sure," Gruntle said. "But if you end up talking to the secretary, I suspect that'll be at the ziggurat. It's where the High Council and all their support staff do their work."

"I've never been in a ziggurat before." Lidai sounded excited.

"Well, it's a building like any other. Bigger. Stone. But it keeps the rain off their heads. I... wait, Seth! No, boy, not there. Excuse me, please, young Masters. Mistress Lidai. Seth, take that over..."

As Gruntle moved away, Kenan smiled, which brought a wince of pain. He took another slurp of nutmash slurry. He sighed at the flavor of cream and honey.

Wren scraped the bottom of his bowl and began eyeing Lidai's half-eaten, whitewood plate of fried sausage and eggs.

"Oh, go ahead. Listening to Kenan slurp has killed my appetite."

Kenan looked directly into her eyes as he slurped another spoonful as noisily as he could. Lidai returned his look. She was getting better at those. But not good enough. He smiled at her as he swallowed hard to exaggerate the noise.

It wasn't long before two men in colorful robes and gold jewelry entered the common room. One was young, clean shaven and narrow-chinned. The other looked older, graying at the temple and beard. Two armed guards followed them in and took posts at the door. Conversation in the room quickly faded as the men scanned the room.

"This must be them," Wren said, as he licked his fingertips clean.

Every soul in the common room stood and nodded respectfully to the two men. Those wearing hats doffed them. Kenan was caught off guard at the show of respect. The three from Blacktree were the last to their feet.

Gruntle hurried over. "Ah! Secretary Abram! Ah, Master Secretary, uh, Master Abram. Secretary. Thank you for gracing my modest inn! I am the innkeep, please call me..."

"Master Gruntle," Secretary Abram answered. "Indeed, I know of this inn. You have the best lamb in the city."

"Oh, Master Secretary, that's mighty fine of you to say. I only wish it were true."

"Your modesty befits you, master innkeep, but I know it to be true. My assistant Eleenan here has his friend get me an order every few weeks."

"Your Eminence! If I had known those orders were for you..."

"None of that. Abram will do fine in your own common room."

"Yes, as you say, Master Abram. I didn't expect you to come yourself!"

"When I got word you had guests from Blacktree, I would allow no delay. I must speak with them at once."

"As you say, Master Secretary. Please, this way." Gruntle started to show them towards Kenan's table.

"No need, good master innkeep. I see them."

The two finely dressed men approached Kenan's table with Gruntle following, washing his clean hands in his apron.

Kenan didn't know what to do. Should he take a knee? Shake his hand? Salute with his fist as he'd seen soldiers do? He settled for a Jempo bow, left fist in right hand in front of his chest, bowing from the waist and maintaining eye contact.

Master Secretary Abram smiled at him. To Kenan's surprise, both men returned the bow in perfect form. "My friends from Blacktree, I presume?"

"Yes," Kenan answered. "I am Kenan..."

"And you are Wren, and this is the lovely Lidai," He answered.

The three glanced at each other.

"My master is most well informed," said Eleenan. "Please, may we join you at breakfast? We have not yet eaten."

They all sat down. The entire common room followed suit and immediately broke out into a loud buzz of conversation. Many eyes strayed to the Blacktree people.

Gruntle stepped forward and asked the secretary's preference. Eleenan's order was taken as well, then Gruntle was off to the kitchen. The big innkeep moved with a surprising burst of speed.

"So," Secretary Abram started. "Should we begin with what happened to you?"

Kenan touched his face. "Oh, this. It's nothing. A squabble, nothing more."

"I see. So, where should we begin?"

"We begin with Anna," Kenan said.

"Who is?"

"My betrothed."

Wren leaned forward. "And my sister."

"Does this story begin with your Anna?" Abram inquired, looking back and forth between the two men.

"Not really," Kenan and Wren said at the same time.

"And you, Lovely Lidai, where do you think this story begins?"

"Me?" Lidai looked shocked to be addressed by a man of authority.

"This story begins with you?" Abram asked, amused.

"No, sorry. The story begins nearly sixty years ago, before I was born."

"So long ago? Nearly sixty years ago, in Blacktree..." Abram touched his beard in thought. "That would be the raid on your bathing pool, and a skirmish at Babelwind Brook, would it not?"

"Good memory," Wren said.

"Indeed," Abram agreed. "I know this story. A raid by slavers took a number of women. They escaped down a river, is this right?"

"Yes," said Kenan. "Several men were taken as well, including my brother Nehamane. Men were killed in the raid."

"I'm sorry for your losses. But that was some time ago. What does that have to do with your visit here?"

"The men who attacked us then had a sigil on their shields and armor."

"Perchance was it a white spider?"

Kenan's blood ran cold. "You know of them?"

"Indeed. Continue, please."

"We were attacked again, about two months ago now."

Secretary Abram's mouth tightened in a thin line. "I've heard but don't know the details. How bad?"

"Bad. They attacked the village itself, in force. We lost half of our men in the attack, as well as women and children. Over one hundred women and girls were stolen from their homes."

"Including your Anna." Abram wasn't asking a question.

Kenan answered anyway. "Yes."

"Two months is a long time to wait to send for help. Blacktree is hardly more than a week or two away."

"Another group was sent, but they were attacked on the road. We didn't know they hadn't made it through."

"The White Spiders?"

"No, I don't think so," Kenan answered. "They used shields and weapons with various markings, none with the white spider, and most of it old and not well maintained."

"Brigands. Unfortunate that they still ply the roads far from Edeer."

"Unfortunate," Wren growled, "is not the word for it."

"Yes. My apologies. How do you know it was brigands? Did you see them?"

"We were captured by them."

"The Almighty himself must have been with you for you to have escaped with your lives."

Kenan quirked an eyebrow. "It wasn't the Almighty. It was Okay."

"Okay indeed. It gladdens me that you're here, safe."

At Abram's pause, Kenan noticed the common room had gone quiet. Every ear was turned to their table.

"Well," said Abram. "Eleenan, we must return to my office. Please have the good master innkeep have his meals boxed for us. Kenan, Wren, and Lovely Lidai, would you please join me? I would hear more."

They rose and left the common room, the two guards trailing. Outside, another six guards stood sentry in full bronze armor, swords, spears, and tree-painted shields.

As the secretary moved off across the Flat, the soldiers formed a perimeter around them. Kenan felt rather intimidated by the show of force.

Many eyes from the Flat followed the group.

Seeing their looks, Abram explained. "I'm afraid I lost my freedom to travel about alone many decades ago. Now, tell me. Please, tell me everything as we walk."

The three described the attack on Blacktree in detail as the party made their way through the city. Abram made no notice of Eleenan as he caught up carrying a towering stack of wooden boxes smelling of bacon. The thin man had to lean to see around the boxes.

Kenan gave Lidai most of the credit for harrying the attack. Lidai told the secretary about Kenan's efforts to slow the attacker's advance. Kenan blushed when she described the bucket.

Wren described the ambush of the counterattack. "Mostly, I was almost eaten by a mawdragon."

"How did they get a mawdragon, anyway?" Lidai asked.

"Oh, it's really not that hard," said the assistant Eleenan from behind the boxes. "Find one, and let's face it, they're not hard to find if there's one around. Lure it with meat into a cage. As long as you feed it enough, they'll stay without much hassle."

The three turned to the younger man.

"I've not done it, mind you. I, well..."

"He's read about it," Abram supplied. "Our Eleenan likes his scrolls."

When they were done with their story, Abram said, "Young woman, do you have an interest in our archer corps?"

"Uh...but I'm a girl."

"Some women serve. There's a whole company of them up near the village of Brookstone. I'm quite serious. They train for many years to attain your skill. You obviously have a gift."

"Thank you. Maybe. Someday."

Wren grinned at her look of surprise. In return, she poked him in the short ribs.

"Master Secretary," said Kenan. "We're here to ask for help from the king and council. We need..."

"Yes, I know what you need," the Secretary said. "We will discuss it further once in my office. Eleenan, not the main door. Let's go through the officer's door, if you please."

Eleenan, with his boxes of food, trotted to the front of the procession and led the group around a corner. The ziggurat loomed ahead.

The structure dwarfed the buildings on the ground and reached up into the branches of the surrounding great trees. Made of worked stone, it angled up on four sides. A square, stone structure stood at the top, reached by a long flight of stone stairs. The edifice stood alone. No bridges or balconies connected to it.

A stone wall with low towers surrounded the ziggurat. The wall bristled with bronze thumpers and archers. Men kept watch from the towers.

The group angled to a side of the ziggurat, skirting the wall. They came to a narrow gate, and the guards let the group through without challenge. Eleenan led the way.

"Who built this thing?" Lidai asked, her eyes wide in wonder.

Abram smiled at her. "Our forefathers, as an edifice to the Almighty."

Kenan looked away and breathed out his nose.

"It must have taken decades!" Lidai said.

"Centuries," Abram corrected.

Up high, on the top of the ziggurat, a fire burned.

Kenan pointed. "What's the fire for?"

Abram sighed. "There aren't many priests left. But a few remain to offer burnt sacrifices to the Almighty."

Lidai asked, "What are they burning?"

"Animals."

She grimaced. "Not alive, I hope."

"Oh no. The animals are humanely dispatched and then burned on an altar."

Wren asked, "Why?"

"As a blood offering. It has to do with Adam's original sin. Only blood will suffice for the Almighty."

Lidai grimaced. "Sounds barbaric."

"Turning away from the Almighty is barbaric. What we do to each other and ourselves is barbaric. There is a price for everything we do. Nothing is free. This is His price."

Kenan rolled his eyes. "If you believe the priests."

Abram nodded.

They crossed the small space between the wall and the ziggurat before entering through a small doorway in the stone. Two guards in brass armor stood watch. They stiffened to attention at the sight of the group.

Most of the secretary's guards stopped at the doorway. One followed Eleenan in. Another followed at the rear.

Kenan didn't like this. The stones above loomed over him, cutting off the trees, the breeze, and the sun. He wondered if he'd ever see daylight again.

The darkness inside yielded to lamplight. The guards each took one of the wall sconces for additional lighting. The narrow passageway opened to wider hallways inside, well-lit and hazy from lamp smoke. Men in robes and guards in armor moved about.

As they approached a set of steps leading up into the ziggurat, Kenan saw a man he recognized pass by. The man stood tall and lithe, with a neatly trimmed red beard. He looked like his switchfather's garden scarecrow. The man gave a sour look to Eleenan but otherwise ignored the group. Kenan almost stumbled when he noticed the man's tattoo of a toedragon claw on his wrist. Kenan stared at it. When he looked back up at the man's face, they locked eyes. The man stared at Kenan, amused. Then he was past the group. Kenan turned and the two looked at each other for a moment longer before the man turned back and walked away with a long stride and a little jaunt.

"Who was that?" Kenan asked.

"Who was who?" Abram asked back.

"That man with the neat red beard."

"The one who doesn't like Eleenan?"

"Yeah. I saw him on the Southbreach Flat."

"He doesn't much care about Eleenan. It's me he doesn't like, and he knows better than to give me that look here."

"Why?"

"His master doesn't like me, I'm afraid. Or, more appropriately, his master doesn't like mine."

Kenan frowned.

"It's politics. Patience, Kenan. We're almost there."

They reached a large room, decorated with tapestries hanging on the walls and fine furniture covered in leather, brass, and cushions. Braziers smoldered in the corners and lampstands bathed the room in a warm glow. The ceiling of massive stones hung high over the floor, threatening them all through the swirling smoke.

"Please, my friends, wait here. Drink will be brought for you." Abram straightened into a more formal pose and cleared his throat. "I adjudge this matter worthy of my master's attention, High Councilor Enosh, of the Seven, Guardian of the Sea Branch, may he live for a thousand years." And with that, he turned and left, the door closing them in.

"HOW much longer will we have to wait?" Lidai asked.

Kenan had answered the first time. He rolled his eyes each time after. Now, he just paced the room and ignored her. She sat on a leather chair, legs tucked under her and her chin on one palm, propped up on the plush arms of the chair.

Wren stood by the brazier warming his hands. He smiled at her, the besotted fool.

Drinks had been delivered, as promised. The wine was really quite good. They were given glasses - real glass – to drink from. Kenan rubbed his thumb across the smooth spirals of the glass. He'd only ever seen glass windows. He didn't know glass could be used for other objects, and in such colors. What else could be made from glass? Broken glass could cut with deadly ease. Could glass be used for spearheads? Swords?

Kenan would think on anything but the ceiling. If he spent too much thought on where they were standing—for far too long—he feared he would embarrass himself and run screaming from the room.

Wren reached down and picked up the brazier by its stem. The thing had no feet. Below the metal bowl of coals, an iron pole had been set in a hole in the floor. He held it down low, inspecting the stem and how it fit in the hole. It wobbled precariously, and he almost toppled the whole thing onto the floor.

"Careful there. Wouldn't do to burn the room down with us inside," Kenan said.

Wren grinned at him and set it back in its hole. "No, I suppose it wouldn't."

Kenan resumed his pacing, looking down, left and right. Never up.

The man with the tattoo had a master who didn't like Abram's master, this Councilor Enosh. The toeclawed man's master, whoever that was, must not want Blacktree's story told. That must be why they were attacked last night. But why? It didn't make sense.

Lidai took a great breath and exhaled an exaggerated sigh. "It's been hours. Days, probably. You think they'll let us use the privy soon?"

Kenan stopped to observe one of the tapestries again. It showed Enoch being taken up to heaven by the Almighty. Another showed Adam and his wife in the garden, looking at a tree laden with ripe fruit. A large lizard-looking creature had been cleverly woven into the branches. Another showed the pair dressed in hides, walking sadly away from the garden which was guarded by an angel and a flaming sword. Other men were depicted on tapestries doing great deeds of battle. One wrestled a hissdragon with his bare hands, which seemed entirely unlikely. Was that supposed to be Seth?

This councilor Enosh clearly identified himself with the line of patriarchs. He was even named after one of them.

Well, come to that, so was Kenan.

"Hey, Kenan," Wren said. "How do you suppose they set those ceiling stones? And how is the smoke getting out?"

Kenan stopped and stared at the floor.

Lidai said, "Wren, I don't think he likes the ceiling."

"Oh. Sorry."

Kenan paced some more, eyes on the floor.

Lidai sighed for the seventy-seventh time. "How much long..."

The door opened. Eleenan strode in, hands in sleeves and back straight. Two guards followed him in, taking station next to the door. "Prepare yourselves for an audience with the High Councilor Enosh, of the Seven, Guardian of the Sea Branch, may he live for a thousand years."

Kenan wasn't sure what exactly he needed to do to prepare.

A tall, thin man over 500 years old strode confidently into the room, dressed in layers of multi-colored robes and an air of dignity. Gold hung about his neck and down his chest. His fingers sparkled with jewels. His gray hair was neatly brushed back off his forehead.

Secretary Abram followed with another two guards.

Kenan again wasn't sure what to do, so he gave Councilor Enosh a Jempo bow. Abram smiled, hid it with a finger, and shook his head slightly.

Enosh spoke with a reedy voice. "Kenan Blacktree, is it? We don't bow to each other in the ziggurat. Here, we are all free men."

Kenan straightened. His face felt warm.

"And this is the mighty Wren Blacktree. And you are, of course, Lidai Blacktree. Word of your beauty has reached my ears, my lady."

Lidai, standing by her chair, blushed crimson and toyed with a lock of her rich hair. High Councilor Enosh took her hand, kissing her knuckles. Her blush deepened. If she kept blushing, she might burst into flames.

Enosh continued, "My apologies, friends, for keeping you waiting. The business of the city demands my time. Please sit, all of you."

Enosh sat in a chair, sinking into the cushions. Lidai sat back in her chair, and Kenan and Wren followed suit. Eleenan, Abram, and the guards remained standing. Two of the guards moved to either side of Enosh's chair. They just stood there, but Kenan got the impression they were ready to strike if he so much as twitched.

"Kenan Blacktree. Have you run into trouble in my city?"

"Um, no. Oh, my face. Yes, but it was just a misunderstanding, I'm sure. You should see the other man."

"I see. I can put in a word with the King's Guard..."

"No, but thank you. I've had worse falling out of a tree."

"That's the truth," Lidai confirmed with a grin. "He's a woodbender."

Enosh smiled at them. "I see. Well. I have heard of the attack on Blacktree. Word reached me some time ago. We sent an envoy but have not heard back. You are the first from the village itself to present themselves. You have my sympathies and apologies for our failure to protect you and your village."

"Uh, thank you, High Councilor," Kenan said.

"Feel free to call me Councilor, if it pleases you. Enosh will work, as well."

"Thank you, Councilor. This is, of course, why we have come. We must go to Midreer to rescue our people."

Councilor Enosh went still for a moment. Abram approached and whispered in his ear.

Kenan didn't wait for them to finish. "We'll need your help, Councilor. We're ready to leave as soon as you say the word. When can we go get them?"

"Get them?" Enosh seemed quizzical and glanced briefly up at Abram before looking back at Kenan. "Oh, I am terribly sorry, young Kenan.

There is no going to get them. If, indeed, they were taken to Midreer, they are lost to you for all time. You must know they will by now have been sold and scattered, if they even survived the attack and journey."

Kenan felt his stomach sink. "That can't be."

"Has no one told you? I fear I have been too blunt again. Abram, tell them. Express my compassion."

Abram took over. "Kenan. Wren. You must understand. It's been two months. Even if you could mount a rescue attempt, it will be another month, or more likely two, before you get there. In four months or more, they will be gone. They will have new names, new owners, new cities. Even if you could find one or two of your women, a rescue from Midreer is impossible. They are a violent people, bred to war. Without knowing exactly where they are, the task is, I'm afraid, completely impossible. There is nothing for you to do. I'm terribly sorry, lad."

Kenan had a lump in his chest somewhere under his collar bones. Wren stared at the floor.

"What, that's it?" Lidai shattered the silence. "Oh, I'm terribly sorry but just forget them all? Is that what you offer a grieving village attacked by foreigners inside your own nation's borders?"

Every man in the room stared at her. One of the guards let his mouth drop open.

Abram warned, "Lidai, be carefu..."

"No, I will not. This happened before. It will happen again. When was the last king's patrol we saw through Blacktree? Three years ago? Four? You could have prevented this!"

"Are you finished, girl?" The reedy words from Enosh held the glint of a sharp knife, but it was not enough. Lidai opened her mouth again.

"Yes. She is," Kenan interjected, looking at her fiercely. Wren reached over and put a hand on her shoulder. Lidai shut her mouth with a glare for everyone.

Abram said, "High Councilor Enosh is offering his precious time and assistance. Kenan, please do not abuse his generosity."

"My apologies," Kenan offered. "High Councilor Enosh, Secretary Abram. In Blacktree, we are free to speak our minds. Even our women talk when they ought not."

"So, I see," Enosh said. "Be that as it may, the girl is correct. This could have been prevented."

Abram bent to whisper to Enosh again, but the councilor held up his hand.

"No, they should know," Enosh said. "They are not from our city and, unless I miss my guess, have never strayed far from their village. Kenan. Wren. The White Spiders are indeed, we believe, from Midreer. Further, they have struck other villages, not just Blacktree. They disappear for months or years, then strike again, taking mostly women and girls."

"You knew?" Kenan asked incredulously. "You've known this whole time?"

"Yes. They have been raiding for over a hundred years. They strike to our south and east. There are dozens of our villages spread out over a large area. We knew they would strike again, but simply did not know when or where."

The three looked at each other. Kenan was confused. "And you did what? Nothing?"

"We did something. Many times," Enosh stated simply. "We chased. We laid in wait. We got into a few skirmishes with them. But we have been unable to stop them as of yet."

"We had no warning," Wren said.

"Such is the nature of slaver raids. They scout, searching for weak spots. They strike where we are not. We could have prevented this by posting a garrison in your village. Unfortunately, the king cannot afford a garrison in every little village and hamlet. It's not practical."

"Practical?" Wren said, his voice holding an edge.

"What he means to say, I'm sure," Abram supplied, "is that the king does not have the resources to keep every village and every citizen safe at all times. Safety is not a guaranteed part of life, as you learned on the edge of a Midreerian sword, young Wren."

Wren frowned but reluctantly nodded.

Councilor Enosh continued, looking at Kenan, "I cannot bring your women back. I cannot go and find your betrothed. I cannot go and find your brother, missing these many years. What I can do is maneuver the High Council to petition the king."

"What would you petition?" Kenan asked.

"Ah. Now that, young man, is exactly the right question," Enosh said.

Abram turned the question back on Kenan. "What would you have the king do?"

Kenan had a ready answer. "Send an army south. I would join them."

Enosh watched Kenan while Abram responded. "An army? I wish it were so, Kenan. I really do. But you don't understand the larger situation."

"What larger situation?" Wren asked.

"Ulneerian diplomats have been making great demands on us from the north. They demand greater tributes, larger wagons, and more ships. Trade with them is better than ever before, trade we desperately need to survive. They demand better trading terms, and we give them. Why? They have a larger force made up of larger warriors with better weaponry. An army of all of our fighting corps could not hold them back for long, and I speak generously of our military. They're good but outmatched. Ulneer has not attacked because they like our trading terms, and we have a strong position here in the city. You would have us drain our city and our nation of our military to travel south and leave all other Edeerian women defenseless?

"Further, if we went south, and if we armed every man, woman, and child old enough to throw a stone, we would be outnumbered by the standing Midreerian army twelve to one. They are bred for war, literally born into it and raised to fight. They could meet us with a tenth, nay, less and wipe our entire nation off the earth. We would already be conquered if we were easier to reach. The Dragongrass protects us to the west and deep wild lands to the south. The floating forest protects us to sea."

Kenan and Wren stared. The sheer scope of it boggled Kenan's mind.

"That, lads, is the bigger picture, without even mentioning the recent rumors from Caineer or losses to privateers at sea. No, I'm sorry Kenan. An army is not an option."

Kenan looked at his feet. "I understand. I didn't know."

"Now you do," Abram said, soothing with his tone. "So, lacking that, what would you have us do? Kenan, think, and be specific."

Enosh eyed them all quietly.

Kenan thought for a long moment before sharing an idea. "Routine patrols are not enough. The White Spiders will see them coming. What if we opened up a village? What if we made it somehow ripe for them? Then we could lie in wait and catch them in the act. If we bloody their nose, make them second guess their scouts, they'll think twice about returning.

"When they retreat, a small group can follow them back. We'd know where they're based, and where we can start looking for our families."

Enosh replied, "That, young man, is a very good idea."

"Are you certain?" asked a thin voice at the door.

The guards jumped along with everyone else but did nothing as an old man who must be well over 800 years old pushed his way into the room. His cane clicked on the floor. He was dressed as Enosh, with as much gold and gems.

"Councilor Tardain. A pleasure, to be sure," Enosh's voice held no warmth.

A man back in the doorway announced, "High Councilor Tardain, of the Seven, Great Defender of the..."

"That'll do!" Tardain said in a high voice that echoed off the wretched ceiling. "Everyone knows who I am." The old man tottered on his cane over to the group. Other men and guards rushed into the room behind him. One pulled over a chair for the old man.

"A footstool as well, boy." He leaned over to Lidai. "It's my knee. Hasn't been the same since the battle of 1207!"

"This was a private meeting," said Councilor Enosh.

"Was it? Well, what were you talking about? And won't you introduce me to our delegates from Blacktree?"

"Tardain, you must know..."

"If I knew, I wouldn't be here. Now, what's all this business in that little hamlet to the south?" He directed the demand at Kenan. "And Almighty, boy, what happened to your face?"

"Is it that bad?"

"You look like you got into a fist fight with a mawdragon. They've got tiny little arms, but they're pretty big up close, you know."

Wren smiled.

"No, High Councilor. Nothing so dramatic, I'm afraid. Just a disagreement amongst friends."

"Friends, eh? Don't I know it. Now, what happened in Blacktree?"

"Well, High Councilor, we were attacked by Midreerian raiders and..."

Enosh interrupted. "I suggest we pick this up later at a more..."

"No time like the present!" Tardain screeched with a toothless smile. "That's what my aged mother still likes to tell me, the old crone." Tardain winked at Wren. "My, you're a big one. Got Ulneerian blood in you, do you? It's that shade of blond hair that gives it away, you know."

Wren said, "Uh, Ulneerian?"

Tardain turned his watery, dark eyes to Enosh. "Well, High Councilor?" The title dripped with false honor. "Bring us into the fold, as they say."

"Tardain, now is no time to..."

"To do what?" another voice asked from the door. The voice boomed from a man in his prime. A round man, no more than 300, came through trailing a long robe and his own retinue. By his gold and jewels, he could only be another high councilor.

Enosh put his head in his hands.

Kenan's mind spun. Three high councilors? No, another came through the door, with another announcement and his retinue. Then another. And another.

"You called the entire council," Enosh accused Tardain. The old man just smiled at him. The look in his eyes told Kenan the old man had lost nothing above his skinny, wrinkled neck.

"What are we called for, exactly? What's going on?" The last councilor through the door asked.

"Always the last to know, eh, Gretheenan?" Tardain smiled happily at everyone. A smattering of laughter made Gretheenan frown.

Conversations in the now crowded room sprang up in every corner.

Kenan had never felt more ill at ease in his life. Wren rose and backed away to stand against the wall next to a guard, who eyed him sideways.

Lidai shrank into her chair.

Enosh stood. "Councilors!" he boomed. "High Councilors! There has been an error, I'm afraid. We are set to meet next week at the usual..."

"Error, indeed, Enosh!" Tardain cackled. "We should all have been called to meet our good delegates from Blacktree!"

"Blacktree?" asked another councilor. "That backwater hamlet down in the lowlands?"

"Don't they just breed sheep down there?" Someone else inquired. "How much trouble could they get into?"

"Breed *with* sheep, you mean," another man laughed.

"Councilors, please, order!" Enosh yelled.

"I'm eldest!" Tardain shouted. "I call order!"

"Not unless the king is absent," a man quietly said from the door.

Everyone stood and faced the door except Kenan and Lidai. This was all moving too fast.

"His Highness," came a shout from behind the king. "Guardian of the towering trees, Defender of the dragonwall, Savior of the red snows, Slayer of the great behemoth, I give you King Enoch of Edeer! May he live a thousand years!"

"It's a bit much, don't you think?" Tardain whispered to Kenan and Lidai, who had finally found their feet. As everyone watched the king come into the room, Tardain slipped Kenan a small scroll. Kenan stared at it for a moment before tucking it away.

The king was much younger than most of the high councilors. He looked no more than 250 years old. His dark brown hair showed under a thin band of gold. He wore no robe but rather steel armor over a rich fur tunic and a steel sword at his hip.

His retinue filled the rest of the room behind him. As the king walked, people bowed to him. Kenan followed everyone's lead.

The king turned to Enosh. "High Councilor Enosh, what is the meaning of this meeting? Why was the High Council called on such short notice? I presume you have an emergency to present to us?"

"My King, there has been an attack on one of our villages. Many were killed or taken."

"I see." The king frowned, glancing at Tardain, then looking back to Enosh. "And which village was this?"

"Blacktree, your Grace, in the southern reaches."

"Yes, I do know the villages, thank you, High Councilor. When was this attack?"

"Your Grace, approximately three months ago."

"And the emergency now?"

"Your Grace, there is no emergency now, only plans to be made to deal with the growing threat from these raiders."

"And you saw fit to call us all here?"

"Your grace, I did not..."

"No, your Grace," Tardain interrupted. "I thought it best if we all heard of this threat, and the harm done our good people in the important village of Blacktree. I thought it wise to hear directly from those who suffered through the incident."

"You did. Well, this seems out of order. But since we're all here, we might as well hear about it. Will it take much time?"

"No, your Grace," said Tardain. "We have delegates from Blacktree here with us right now."

The king looked around the crowded room. "Do we? Where are they?"

It took some shuffling to find Kenan ensconced behind a group of taller men and Wren pretending to be a guard. Abram escorted both to stand before the king.

"These are the Blacktree delegates?" the king asked. "Not elders, then. You are young for such an honor."

Enosh said, "Your Grace, they were active participants in the defense of the village, heroes of the engagement."

"Indeed?"

"Your Grace," Kenan choked, cleared his throat, and tried again, "Your Grace, please forgive me. I do not know how to honor you. We are simple people."

"Simple people are blessed by the Almighty. Please, your presence here is honor enough. What is your name? And are you well? You've been in a fight it seems."

"I am Kenan. This is Wren, both of Blacktree. And I have brought my sister to your city as well. I am fine, your Grace. Thank you for asking."

"Very well. Is your sister here, among the crowd? I will hear your story. I hope it is brief. But first, let us get more comfortable."

With much commotion, guards rearranged seating under direction of secretaries to make the room into an impromptu council chamber. The king sat in a chair at the front with the high council arranged to either side. Everyone else stood facing the council and the king. Kenan and Wren were placed in front of the arrangement. Lidai was whisked to the back of the room by Abram.

Kenan started with an apology. "We had a scroll from the elders of Blacktree for you, my grace. Unfortunately, it was lost on the road."

"We don't need a scroll," King Enoch said, waving it off. "We have you. You are first-hand witnesses to the event, are you not?"

"Yes, your grace. We both are."

"Then tell it. The highlights, if you will. The details can be relayed later."

So, Kenan told the king and council an abbreviated version of the events at Blacktree. Wren nodded here and there, adding to the story when they reached the part about the mawdragon ambush on the village response force.

When Kenan reached the numbers lost to the raid, Enosh asked, "And how many people did your village hold before the attack?" Kenan told them.

"What?" A councilor gasped. "Why, that's half the village!"

"Oh, the brazen creatures!" said another.

"They've gone too far!"

"Really, Joseph, when was it not far enough?"

"We must do something!"

"We must not! We cannot leave Edeer exposed. Not now!"

"Order!" shouted the king. He didn't look angry. He looked like he used the word routinely. They all quieted.

"Your grace," said Tardain. "Should we not put our generals to this issue and let them recommend a plan?"

"It's been over two months!" exclaimed another councilor. "We must do something."

"It's been too long. What can we possibly do?"

"We should take decisive action!"

"Decisive action must be taken," agreed Enosh. "But we have a plan to..."

"A plan from a young woodbender?" Tardain scoffed. "Young man, I mean no disrespect. But we need a plan from experienced men in the art of war. For make no mistake, Edeerians. This is war!"

"It is not war," countered another councilor. "These are raiders. We need to show them a heavy hand, not mobilize our army."

Kenan stood quietly next to Wren. He watched the king, knowing the king controlled the course of this meeting.

The king noticed. "Kenan Blacktree. You have a thought. What do you say?"

"Your grace, I am just a villager, a woodbender as High Councilor Tardain says. But I am a villager who has seen the raiders. I fought against them. I killed some of them. I have pressed against the white spider on their shields. My blood is on their swords."

The high council watched him with interest. The king nodded for him to proceed.

Kenan thought for a moment. How could he explain this to them? Words came to him from nowhere. "We take the nuts and animals from the forest, as is our right. We process them and consume them. We store them in our granaries. We sell them to traders to support our village. At auction, we sell the dragons from our forests, the wool from our sheep, the pigs from our pens. We take, we are sustained, and we grow.

"This is how these raiders see us. They come to our forests. They seek out the best they can find, and they take. Not our food. Not our animals. They take us. People. They take the women of our villages, women in their prime and girls yet to lower the hems of their dresses. They come and they take us like animals from the forest!

"My betrothed, my Anna, was taken. She has surely been beaten into submission, violated in unspeakable ways, and then stood at auction to be sold like a common ewe! Over a hundred of our women and girls have suffered this fate from this attack alone! They were nothing to them but animals, animals to be sold for profit. In the end, our women were nothing more than these." Kenan scattered a small handful of his last coins on the floor. The clatter bounced off the oppressive ceiling and echoed throughout the chamber.

"We do not know and would not presume to advise any of you of what should be done. I only implore you, do *something*. Let no more wives be taken from our great nation. Let no more young girls be tied up and slung over evil men's shoulders to be carried into the night. We are bleeding the women of our nation. Please, no more!"

"Hear, hear! Well said, lad!" exclaimed a councilor.

"I agree! He's right!"

"Hear, hear!"

"Well spoken, lad. I am moved," Tardain said to him. He turned to the king. "Something must be done, Your Grace. None here think differently. But it must be done right. Our generals should advise us. They will know the way." Several councilors voiced agreement.

"This is an issue for the king's guard. They know the region," Enosh countered. "We have the men to deal with this, with speed and adaptability."

"Very well," said the King. "A vote, then. To the generals?"

Five hands were raised.

"To the king's guard?"

Two hands were raised.

"My vote is moot. Our army's generals will convene to discuss this. When is their next meeting, Tardain?"

"Your grace, we just missed it this month, I'm afraid. Next month they are meeting with our navy captains at Archmouth. The following month there is no meeting. So, three months, your grace, give or take a week or so."

Kenan couldn't believe it. Three more months, just to start talking about maybe making a plan? He opened his mouth to object, but the king spoke first.

"Kenan Blacktree. The council has ruled. It is done. Meanwhile, I have a task for you. One of my scribes will meet with you to record the details. Please think on this grievous attack on our nation and your village. Any detail, no matter how small, can be used against these raiders. Do not leave the city and receive my scribe when he comes. Do you understand?"

"Yes, Your Grace," Kenan choked out.

The king nodded to him before turning to a man in his retinue who scurried over. The king whispered to the man for a moment. Finally, the king rose and left. This was apparently a dismissal, for the high councilors stood after, and, one by one, they and their retinues left the room, talking amongst themselves.

Kenan turned to Wren. The big man looked about to follow the leaders of Edeer out of the room, and he didn't look like he had nice things to say to them. Kenan forestalled him with a hand to his big chest.

"Easy, Wren. We need those fools on our side."

"Fools is right," Lidai said, approaching with Secretary Abram from behind. "Those idiots wouldn't know their elbows from their..."

"Have a care, Lidai," Abram said. His face held warning, but his tone sounded friendly. "Perhaps you should make your language as lovely as your face, don't you think?"

"Secretary Abram," Kenan said. "It doesn't seem like we've made any progress at all! Three more months? We don't have that much time."

"Are you certain? Young Kenan, you have nothing but time. The White Spiders will attack again, but not so soon, I suspect. Some attacks came within months, but most came after a year or more. I must study the history of their attacks further."

"Study?"

"Yes, study. Much can be learned. How large is their force, and has it varied? If so, when? Where do they attack, and during what season? Is there a pattern? The Nephilim, is he always part of the attack? If not, when does he appear? Can we find a pattern to correctly decide where to provide them with your ripe target?"

"Is that what we're going to do?" Wren asked. "Kenan's plan? They just said the generals will..."

"There's what the politicians say must be done, and there is what gets done while they talk about it." Abram's eyes sparkled. "We will gain the generals approval and prepare until then. Now, take this." He handed Wren a small scroll. "This is a note for our good innkeep at The Goosedown Filler. Gruntle will hold your dragons in his stable until you need them again. No objection. I have seen payment made."

"Uh, thank you," Wren said.

"You are most welcome. And I suspect, you will make it up to me while this issue is settled."

Kenan raised an eyebrow at the man but said nothing.

A scribe stopped at the group long enough to give Abram a small item.

"Lastly, my friends from Blacktree, you did well today. But I have one more thing for you before sending you to your dinners."

"Dinner?" asked Wren, eyes brightening.

"And what are we to do?" Kenan asked.

"Take this scroll. It is from the king's own secretary."

"What's it say?" asked Lidai.

"How am I to know, Lovely Lidai? I wouldn't dare break the royal seal. It is yours. Break it and tell me."

"We will," Kenan said. "But later." He had a sudden urgent desire to see the sky again. This stone over his head had him crawling out of his own skin.

"Fair enough. Farewell, my friends. I will stop by the inn come morning to talk further. I never did get good Master Gruntle's breakfast."

# Chapter Twenty
# Trussed Up Like a Piglet

OUTSIDE the ziggurat walls, Kenan stopped, stared up into the branches of the great trees of Edeer, and breathed a huge sigh of relief. Nothing was above him but the city of Edeer and trees, the way it was meant to be. The sun slanted in from a sharp angle. More time had passed than Kenan had thought.

"Almighty!" Wren exclaimed as he stretched. "That place is oppressive."

"The people or the stone?" Lidai asked.

"Yes," Wren smiled down at her. "Yes, to both."

"Agreed," Kenan said.

"Kenan," Wren said. "I had no idea you could be so eloquent! Your blood is on their swords? I can't believe you had it in you."

"Me neither," agreed Lidai. "How'd you do it?"

"I really don't know. The words just came to me."

"You've never spoken like that before," Wren said. "Friend, it's usually hard to get you to say more than a handful of words in a row."

"You should hear him around Anna," Lidai countered with a twinkle in her eye.

Which, of course, darkened Kenan's mood. "I could use a drink with Gruntle."

"Me, too."

"Me, three," Lidai said quietly. "I'm sorry, Kenan. Can we go?"

The three made their way through the city. The area near the ziggurat contained beautiful buildings of woven plank, stone, and huge glass windows. As they neared Southbreach, they passed through a district of shabbier buildings, with taverns, seer shops, and shrines. It seemed the Almighty, if he existed, wasn't the only god of Edeer.

Kenan stopped to look at one of the statues. A small fountain gurgled under a bull made of brass. The fountain pool below glittered full of small coins.

"Who would just leave coin here?" Lidai asked.

"And why?" Wren agreed.

"Because the great God Beellal provides to all who worship him," said the little man who sat on a stool next to the shrine. Kenan had thought him a beggar.

"Provides? What does he provide?" Wren asked the man.

"Wealth. Success in your endeavors. Blessings be to all men who drop a coin to the Great Beellal."

"Uh huh." Kenan turned away.

"There's a god for making money?" Lidai asked herself.

Wren frowned. "Most common god of all, seems to me."

"There's a god for everything," Kenan muttered. "None of it's real." But he thought of Gharan's glowing eyes.

As they walked down the street, hawkers cried their wares and men sat on barrels drinking from wood cups. Noxious smoke hung in the air. A brief scuffle broke out, and a man was cut. All involved rushed away into alleys.

A woman in her overshift grabbed Wren's arm. She cooed to him, "A copper coin, my big man, to lose your mind for a moment."

"Uh, what?" Wren looked confused.

"I don't think so," Lidai said. She produced a knife and twirled it between her fingers.

The woman eyed her for a moment, shrugged, and moved on to the next man.

"Was she just..."

"Yes. Ignore her," Lidai said, pulling his arm onward. "I don't like this part of the city. Let's move on."

"You're about to like it less," Kenan said.

Lidai's frown deepened. "What do you mean?"

"We're being followed."

"We're being..."

Wren grabbed her shoulder. "Don't look back, Lidai! Dragonscrape, it must run in the family."

Kenan walked on. "It's the old man from the common room. The one with the red eye patch."

"You saw him?" Wren asked.

"Yep. And he's watching us."

"Can't be a coincidence."

"Nope."

Lidai asked, "What're we going to do about him?"

"Let him follow," Kenan answered. "And be ready."

Kenan led them further down the street and ducked into an alley. The group maneuvered around a pile of garbage, then between stacks of barrels. He found a gap in the stacks.

"This will do," he said.

"Good ambush spot," Wren agreed.

"Where am I going to go?" Lidai asked.

"In there," said Wren. She squeaked as he quickly pushed her into the gap between barrels, turned around, and crammed in backwards after her.

"I can't see anything back here!" she hissed, pushing on Wren's back.

"Can't do anything back there, either. Stay put. And stop poking me. If you stick me with another knife, I'll gag you."

A growl drifted from behind Wren, but the scuffling stopped. Kenan shook his head but appreciated Lidai being out of the way for this.

They waited.

They waited some more. Kenan began to wonder if the old man had seen them turn into the alley.

Finally, Lidai's muffled voice said, "I don't think he's coming."

Kenan agreed. They stepped out of their hiding place. And the man with the red eye patch stood right there next to them, scowling at them all.

Kenan reacted first. His hand flew out to strike the man's temple. But the older man stepped under it and struck Kenan's hip with a stout finger. Kenan lurched off balance and somehow fell to the filthy alley floor.

Wren grunted and moved to attack with balled fists. In a moment, he landed next to Kenan, eyes closed and unconscious.

Kenan rolled, extended a leg, and came up in a crouch. The old man caught a knife Lidai hurled at him and returned it to her as fast as a striking viper. Kenan heard Lidai squeak again.

Kenan lurched forward with a feint ridgehand to the man's neck followed by a real spearhand to the groin. The man subtly twisted, and Kenan missed.

A finger poked Kenan hard in the throat just above the collarbones, stopping him short. The man instantly dropped out of sight. Kenan felt a push just above his knee, and he was falling backwards, out of control. His head thudded off something hard, and the alley went black.

Sometime later, Kenan opened his eyes to find Wren looking down at him, shaking his shoulders.

"I'm awake. I'm awake."

"So am I!" Lidai cried. "I have been the whole time. Kenan's fine! Now, come untie me!" Lidai lay on her stomach, her hands and feet tied behind her back as neat as a piglet being taken for slaughter.

"You okay?" Wren asked him.

"I'm okay. Just took a thump on the head when I fell."

"Me too. I think. I'm not sure."

"You'd better go untie her. She'll stab you if you don't hurry up."

"Suspect you're right." Wren went to Lidai, who stopped squirming long enough for Wren to cut her binding cords. She got to her feet and brushed off her dress.

"Eeeeew! What's that?" She produced a knife and poked at something dark and slimy stuck to her bodice.

"What happened?" Wren asked Kenan. "You went down so fast I didn't even see what he did to you. I tried to hit him and, well, I don't know. I just fell. Something hit me in the temple and that was it."

"I don't know. I haven't been schooled like that since the last time I sparred Medahal." Kenan rubbed the ache at the back of his head.

"He caught my knife and threw it back at me," Lidai said in wonder. "See?" She pointed at a knife stuck in a barrel next to her. "I didn't know a man could do that."

"Yeah," Wren said. "Let's steer clear of that crusty old patedragon. If we see him again, I'm headed the other way."

"I don't think that's going to work," Lidai countered.

"Why?"

"Because of that." Lidai pointed at a scroll case lying in the alley. "He caught me, quick as you please, folded me up I don't know how, and tied me up. He put that thing in my mouth like I was some darterdragon with a bone."

Kenan asked, "Did he say anything to you?"

"Yeah. He said, 'It wasn't supposed to go this way. See you tomorrow, child.' He had a gnarly old-man voice and his breath smelled like mint. That's just not right."

"Seriously?" Wren said.

"Serious as a mawdragon with a toothache."

Kenan picked up the wood case. "Well, that makes four."

"Four what?" Lidai asked.

"Four scrolls. This one, the king's, Abram's scroll to Gruntle, and the scroll from Tardain."

"What scroll from Tardain?"

"The one he handed me when the king came in. I don't want to read them here. Let's get back to the inn."

WHEN they entered The Goosedown Filler, the linen maid flirted with Wren again, earning a scowl from Lidai. But soon, drinks were poured, and a meal of deer meat stew was ordered from the kitchen.

"This one's from Abram." Kenan read it. "Yeah, it says what he said it would." Kenan rolled it back up and gave it to a passing barmaid, asking her to deliver it to Gruntle.

She smiled at him with one hand on a pleasant hip. "He's in the kitchen. Stews almost ready, and he don't trust nobody to finish it." She touched Kenan's shoulder as she smiled at him. "I'm Denah. I'll see it done."

"Thank you, Denah," Kenan said, giving her a smile. He didn't watch Denah go, though he saw Wren did.

Lidai saw it too and kicked the big man under the table.

"Ow! What was that for?"

"You know."

Kenan ignored them both and opened the next scroll. "This one's from Tardain."

They all gathered around to read it in the lamplight.

> Delegates from Blacktree. We must talk. Please meet me at The Bark's Bite, an inn on the third level, to the east. Leave word with the barman. I won't be far away. -High Councilor Tardain.

"Well, that's not ominous or anything," Lidai said. Wren quirked a grin at her.

Kenan nodded agreement. "He sounded like a crazy old fool, but I think he got his way today, and I think he made it happen. I don't trust him as far as I can toss him."

Kenan removed the king's scroll from its case. Kenan broke the green wax seal and read.

> Brave men of Blacktree. While I must wait until the generals discuss this unfortunate situation, you are under no such restraint. I implore you to go to the Old Pine Tree school on the fifth level. Seek out my old friend and mentor. Lamech will help you. -Enoch, King of Edeer.

"Who the dragonspit is this Lamech?" Lidai asked.

Wren frowned at her. "I was only half-done reading that. And you're prettier when you're not swearing."

She frowned at him, then smiled, then frowned again. It gave the men a chance to finish reading.

"Well, both Master Medahal and the king himself says we should go see this Lamech," Kenan said, looking at both of them. "What do you think?"

"I think you should open that last scroll," Wren said. "I want to know what Old Patch Face had to say." He shuddered.

Lidai asked, "What's wrong?"

Wren shuddered again. "The idea of losing an eye. There's something about the eyes. Gross."

The writing on this scroll jerked and bled in blotches. The paper was scratched and torn from the nib. It looked as if written by a child.

*Young ones from Blacktree. Come to see my master here*
*at the Old Pine Tree school. Ask for Lamech.*

Wren chuckled. "Think someone's trying to tell us something?"

"Who?" Kenan frowned at him. "Do you think Old Patch Face is part of this school? I don't think we should just run to them without digging for some more information."

"What kind of information?" asked Denah as she brought them three bowls of steaming stew. Her curly black hair bounced as she walked, but Kenan ignored it. He liked blond hair. Anna's hair.

"Information about the school up on the fifth level," Wren said, smiling up at her. The woman ignored Wren and looked back at Kenan. Lidai smiled at her as well and not in a friendly way.

"Which one?" Dinah asked. "There's, oh, three? Maybe four."

"The Old Pine Tree school."

"Oh, the fighting school. Yes, it's Master Lamech's."

"Who's Lamech?" Kenan asked her.

"He's a bit of a patriarch. Lamech, son of somebody or other. He has a direct line back to Adam."

Lidai snorted. "We all have a direct line back to Adam."

Denah smiled prettily at Lidai, but there was no warmth in her dark eyes. "As you say, miss," she said and bobbed the briefest of curtseys. She turned back to Kenan and the warmth returned. Kenan noticed and smiled back. "Lamech is an old general here. War hero and stuff. I don't know him, mind. Wouldn't know him from Adam. But I did see him once, from far off. He doesn't come out of his school much, so I hear."

"Is he, well, is he a good man?"

"For that, I wouldn't know. I've heard the army consults with him. He meets with the generals now and again. I hear they ask him all sorts of questions about what they should do."

"Where did you hear that?" Lidai asked.

"I hear things. A girl has friends. Well, most of us." She smirked at Lidai, and with one last smile for Kenan, the pretty, plump brunette sauntered away.

"If I were you," said Wren to Lidai, "I wouldn't eat another thing that woman brings you."

Kenan nodded agreement.

Wren looked at Kenan. "You, you're safe to eat whatever she gives you."

Kenan made a face. "I just want her to like us so she'll spill more gossip. Seems to me, barmaids know more than anyone else in this city."

"Agreed. Except maybe an innkeep." Gruntle bustled over, thumbs tucked into his apron. "Master Kenan, Master Wren. And pretty young Lidai. How is the stew?"

"Mmmm," Wren hummed around a mouthful.

"You're going to burn your tongue again," Lidai said.

"Just right!" Gruntle beamed at his guests.

"Master Gruntle, can we ask your advice?" Kenan asked.

"But of course, Master Kenan. What can I help you with?" The man leaned over and put his elbows on their table. He looked like a happy conspirator.

"It's been recommended we visit a Master Lamech at the Old Pine Tree School. We were wondering what you know of the man."

"Oh! Master Lamech is well known in Edeer, young Blacktreerians. Blacktreers? I'm not quite sure how to say that. Anyway, he's a war general from many years ago. Fought in the Red Snow. Battle hero and all that. He campaigned against Midreer, Ulneer, and just about everyone else."

"Is he trustworthy?"

"I couldn't say. I don't know the man. I haven't seen him for, well, a hundred years or more, now. Bearish man. Big in the chest, you know, like Master Wren here, only not so tall. Pardon me, Master Wren, if that's offensive."

Wren waved him off through mouthfuls of stew. He was already near the bottom of the wooden bowl.

"Should we go see him?" Kenan asked as he mashed the tender vegetables in the stew. There was no way he could chew the meat with his sore teeth.

"Well, who recommended him?"

"Uh, well, the king did."

"What? You saw the king?" Gruntle all but shouted. Heads turned their way.

"Quietly, Master Gruntle. We saw him and talked to him, yes. He said we should go see this Lamech." Kenan showed him the scroll.

Gruntle read it quickly. "You have no choice. The king said you should go. Go."

"I'm not sure we can trust the king," Kenan whispered, careful of the people at the other tables.

Gruntle stood straight and looked down at them. He waved pretty Denah towards a table across the room.

"Master Kenan. I don't know Lamech, at all, really. But I think you can trust him not to thump you over the head and dump you in some alley. As for the king, I trust him. He's a better man than people say. I've kept watch." Gruntle tapped the side of his nose.

"Sounds like we should go," Wren said, as he scraped the bowl clean.

Gruntle smiled. "Just right."

Kenan was wrong about the deer meat. It was tender and delicious.

# Chapter Twenty-One
# Trials of Acceptance

THEY waited in the common room for Abram until mid-morning. He didn't come. So, the group spent the rest of the morning gathering their gear and vacating their room. Wren carried a large share, but he didn't mind. He wanted the exercise.

They had no idea where they were spending the next night. Gruntle might let them stay an extra day, but they had agreed not to ask it of the amiable innkeep. They left the inn laden with their belongings and headed up to the fifth level.

Wren looked over the railing. His head spun for a moment. "Phew! We're up high!"

Lidai stopped for a break at a landing. She looked up in wonder at the city arrayed around them. "And there's so much more still higher."

Kenan grinned at them. "You guys should try harvesting gopherwood nuts."

Wren scowled at him. "No, thanks."

They continued up the stairs, reached the fifth level, and walked across the boardwalks of balconies and timber bridges. Some of the branches hung so wide that people strolled along side by side on the bark.

The city buzzed with activity. Dragons moved down below. Someone had domesticated a stalkdragon. The beast pulled at a laden sledge and blinked up at them. People walked and talked in all directions. Some carried heavy loads. Others carried baskets and sacks. Some sat and worked at tables in the pleasant sunshine streaking between the great leaves above.

They had to inquire for directions a couple times, but they finally stood in front of a large structure with many protruding rooms and out-buildings.

The large, redwood door held a simple sign in black lettering, which said, "The Old Pine Tree School."

A boy sat on a crate next to the door. His face was clean, but his legs and bare feet were smudged with layers of dirt.

"Hello," Wren said with a smile. "We're here to see Lamech."

"I know." The boy didn't move. His solemn look was a little creepy. Wren tried again.

"Can we go in and see him? Or do we knock?"

"I'm to take you in."

"Oh. Well, thank you. That's mighty nice of you, son."

"Do you have a son?"

"Well, no. Not married. Not yet." Wren avoided a glance at Lidai.

"Oh. But lots of people have kids and ain't married." The boy still didn't move.

"You're right, of course. Um, could you take us in, then?"

"I could."

"I see." Wren scrummaged in his belt pouch and came out with his last copper coin. He flicked it to the boy, who snatched it out of the air and made it disappear. It happened so fast Wren didn't see where the coin went. "Cool."

"Yeah, thanks." The boy got up and pushed open the heavy door, grunting a little with the effort. The door hadn't been locked. A small chime sounded faintly inside.

They entered a small room with benches. Cloaks hung on pegs on every wall. When they all were inside, they had little space to move.

The boy stood in the entrance to a hallway leading further into the building. "What you got there?"

"Oh, this is our stuff," Lidai said.

"What stuff?"

"Our gear. You know, clothes, food, rope. Stuff."

The boy smiled shyly at her. It was the first real expression Wren saw on him. "Could I have some?"

Lidai quirked a pretty eyebrow. "Our stuff?"

"Yeah. Food. What you got?"

Lidai dropped a bag from her shoulder. "Oh. Sure, of course. I have a palm of bread heel somewhere in here."

"Got any butter for it?"

Wren chuckled at the boy. Kenan was studying the view down the hall.

Lidai looked at the boy. "Um, no. But you can have the heel if you want it."

"Nah. Just had breakfast."

"Okay..."

The boy pointed to the floor. "Drop your stuff here."

Kenan eyed the boy. "Will it be here when we get back?"

"Kenan!" Lidai scowled.

"Most of it," the boy told them.

Wren shrugged, then dumped his gear to the floor. The others followed suit.

"Got any knives?" The boy asked.

Wren glanced at Lidai. "Some."

The answer seemed to satisfy the boy. He turned and walked down the hall. Wren shrugged at his friends. Kenan followed the boy down the hall and Wren followed after Lidai.

The hallway was flanked with doors, which were ignored by the boy. In short order, the hallway emptied into a large, circular room. The floor was yellowwood, polished to a gleam, and fifty feet across. The circular walls held lattice openings without glass. Light spilled across the room and a breeze wisped lightly throughout. Blackwood beams in intricate trusses supported a woven whitewood ceiling. Around the edge, a double tier of raised benches circled the floor. Gaps in the benches gave access to weapon racks and doorways to other parts of the building.

Three people stood in the middle of the room. A thin, wiry man in a simple green overshirt and brown belt stood to the left. A barrel of a man with a keg of a belly stood on the right wearing only a kilt. In the middle stood a thin woman well into her twilight years. She wore a simple gray dress belted with a thin cord.

A half dozen older men and women sat over to one side, quietly watching.

The boy turned back to Wren and his friends. "Take your shoes off."

A round man with a wreath of white hair under a bald pate growled from the group of onlookers. "Please, Tadd."

Tadd scowled, then turned to the three. "Take your shoes off. Please."

They all stooped and removed their boots, placing them against the wall.

"Need those knives, now. Uh, please."

Wren didn't much care. He relinquished his hand knife. Kenan hesitated but muttered something and gave Tadd his hand knife.

"The one in your boot, too. Please."

Kenan looked at the boy, who stared back unblinking. Then he stooped and removed the long knife hidden in one of his boots against the wall. He handed it over. "Careful, boy. It's sharp."

Tadd tucked the bare blade behind his belt without much care at all. He turned to Lidai and waited.

"What?"

"Um, please?"

She stared at Tadd a long moment. She glanced up at the people in the room, then back at the boy. She turned, showing them her empty belt. Tadd

216

stared with too-big eyes. Finally, she parted a fold in her dress and pulled a hand knife from a sheath. "Here you go."

Tadd took it and waited, looking at her.

"Really?"

"Yes, please."

She parted another fold and gave him a small throwing knife.

The boy took it and waited.

Wren grinned at her. What was she waiting for? Clearly, they were on to her.

Finally, she parted another fold to the side and gave him a narrow dirk. Wren was pretty sure it's the one she pricked him with while on the back of Okay.

Tadd took it and waited.

"That's it. That's all I have."

"Boy," came the growl from the big man in the stands. "Search her. If she resists, she leaves."

Tadd shrugged and stepped forward.

"Oh, I don't think so..."

The boy's hands darted to the dress, came away with another knife. He made it disappear behind his back. She looked ready to drub the urchin.

Wren knew this look well. "Lidai, we need to do this. Unless you want to go meet with the creepy old Councilor?"

Lidai folded her arms and suffered the indignity of the search. "Careful, Tadd. If those hands stray..."

Tadd ignored her and set to work. He tucked several more throwing knives from the folds of her dress into his belt. He found a knife strapped to her ankle. He found one behind her belt in the small of her back. Wren's grin turned into full blown amusement as she eyed the boy sideways.

Tadd looked up at her with owl-like eyes. "Lower your arms, please."

Lidai complied with a huff. Wren hid a grin.

Tadd found a thin blade up the left sleeve of her arm.

Lidai glowered at him. "You're not getting that bread."

He found one more through a hidden slit on her upper right arm. Finally, the boy walked away sprouting knife hilts.

Kenan looked a little surprised. "Seriously, Lidai. Did you rob the entire kitchen when we left?"

Wren barked out a short laugh. Lidai scowled at him as she re-crossed her arms. Almighty, she was adorable when she did that.

Tadd approached the older people on the benches, bowed, and laid the knives out on a bench seat, carefully arranging them by size and shape. The audience silently stared while Wren awkwardly waited. Finally, Tadd left with a little skip in his step.

Silence hung in the room as the audience watched the three from

Blacktree.

Wren studied the group of older people. He looked for an eyepatch or a missing eye. But each had two good eyes. So, where did Old Patch Face go? Was he even here?

Finally, the old woman of the three in the middle stepped forward. "Welcome to the Old Pine Tree School. Welcome to your first trial."

Wren frowned. Trial? Well, that seemed ominous.

"I am Maryleen Archmouth. I manage this school. This large man next to me is Belroon Chimney. This other man is Trime Brookstone."

Wren caught movement and watched as Kenan performed his Jempo bow, holding it. He wasn't sure he could mimic it well, but he tried. Lidai did the same.

All three of the people in the circle formed the exact same pose and straightened. When Kenan finally straightened, Wren and Lidai did too.

Maryleen smiled at them. "I see my old friend Medahal Blacktree is still teaching."

Kenan replied. "Yes, Maryleen Archmouth. He is my treasured mentor."

Well, that seemed pretty formal. Should he bow again? No, Kenan didn't. Enough of all this formal bowing. Wren decided to be himself. He tucked his thumbs behind his belt and stood with feet at shoulder width. He smiled at them all. A good smile smooths over many concerns.

He smiled over at Lidai. She stood with her weight on one leg, hip out, and arms crossed. If her eyes could strike fire, she'd put the flint miners out of business.

Maryleen stepped back. Trime stepped forward.

Hair black and eyes nearly as dark, Trime moved with lithe grace. His trimmed black beard sparkled with a few flecks of gray.

"The trial you face is the Trial of Acceptance. Fail this trial and you will be ejected from the school. Succeed and we will provide."

Wren nodded. Simple enough.

The big man on the right stepped forward. Belroon's brown hair and beard stuck out in every direction. His chest hair was matted from a recent workout, or maybe it was always like that. His arms, calves, and shoulders bulged with muscle and bristled with hair. He crossed his arms over his round gut, and his forearm muscles rippled as he drummed his fingers on one bicep.

"Each one of you will face one of us. We will spar unarmed as well as armed with blunted weapons. We are looking for courage, so do not shrink back. We are looking for what skills we've heard you already possess and to gauge those skills. We are looking, in short, to see if you're worthy of our time, yah?"

Wren nodded. Got it. Give a drubbing, take a drubbing, and maybe learn some stuff. Let's get this thing going.

Belroon cracked his knuckles. "Now, which one of you sorry children is first?"

Wren stepped forward without hesitation. "That'd be me, round man."

"Yah! Boy, I'd hoped you'd say so." Maryleen and Trime walked calmly to the side, pulled large hammers off the wall, and returned to give one to each of the men. They took a seat on the benches near Lidai's knives.

Wren cracked his own knuckles and smiled at the large man. He was much shorter than Wren but might outweigh him.

Wren swung the hammer. It felt light in his hands. It had a long handle and bronze head, but much smaller than the hammer from the other night. This wasn't a tool. It was a weapon. Wren spun it around a few times in his hand. It felt light enough to use one handed and should be quick with two.

"Well, boy?" Belroon picked his teeth with a dirty nail. His hammer hung down at this side. "What're you waiting for, yah?"

Wren wasn't going to hold back. If these people wanted to see what he had, he was going to show them. He charged in, hammer twirling in one hand.

Wren struck from above, aiming to bury the head in the man's shoulder. Belroon's hammer still hung at his side. As the blow came down, the man stepped to the side with an expression of amusement on his broad features.

The hammer thudded against the yellowwood and left a dent in the soft material.

Belroon retreated a couple of steps. "Oh, now. I suspect you'll regret that, boy."

Wren swung the hammer around, took a big step, and attacked from the side. Belroon stepped back again, and the hammer missed.

"Is that the best you've got, boy?"

Wren saw red. This man was going to pay.

He swung wildly, left, right, up, down. He swung diagonally. Each blow could kill a man if he connected. Wren didn't care. And it didn't matter. He couldn't seem to touch the round man.

Belroon swiveled and stepped. He bent back and pivoted. He ducked under blows faster than a man his size should be able to. All the while, he laughed.

"I could have dropped you like a stone at any point, boy! When are you going to impress me, yah?"

Wren attacked with one arm then punched with the other. The blow nearly caught Belroon on the chin, but the man spun away at the last moment.

Belroon stepped back. Wren didn't follow. He put his hands on his knees and gasped for air. He didn't want to stop, but he had no choice. He had to find his air again.

"Well, boy. You've got some promise after all. But you need some conditioning, yah. The tired man dies first, you know, boy."

"Well," gasp for breath, "I'm not," gasp for breath, "done yet," gasp for breath, "fatty."

Belroon frowned. He moved in, raising his hammer for the first time. Wren swung, but to block the blow first. Belroon's hammer deflected wide. Wren used this movement to punch for his face.

Only Belroon wasn't there anymore. The stout man ducked under the blow and out of sight.

Wren felt a painful punch to the meat of his inner thigh, which dropped him to a knee. Another punch to his cheek dumped him over. His head rang, and his leg spasmed in pain.

Belroon looked down on him, mirth on his face. His whole body bounced as he chuckled. "That's not half bad, boy. There's hope yet. Want to learn, yah?"

Wren struggled to comprehend. What in Almighty's creation had just happened? But he understood the question. He wheezed, "Yes, please." He gave Belroon a weak smile, the best he could manage given his reeling head.

"Hah! Yes. Control, boy. You must learn when to start and when to stop. I will teach you, yah." He turned back to the bystanders. "I'll take him!"

With that, he dropped his hammer by Wren's head and stomped over to sit beside Trime. "When's lunch?"

LIDAI watched as Wren rose on unsteady feet. Thank the Almighty he wasn't hurt. Those hammers looked dangerous. He limped over to a bench and started rubbing his thigh. Well, not hurt bad, anyway. The blow had landed opposite the scar from Cols' blade.

She looked at Kenan, who looked back at her and nodded. Right. She was next.

Lidai stepped forward, and Maryleen rose. Her arms hung loosely at her sides. She held her posture straight for a woman of her advanced age. She was, well, willowy.

"Child, go pull that target away from the wall." Maryleen pointed at a square target made of pressed reeds. A red circle a palm across marked the center.

Lidai went to it. The target hung on a wood rail frame on hide-wrapped skids. With some effort, Lidai dragged it out from the wall. Child, was she? Well, her anger fueled the exercise. She had to put her whole weight into it to get it to move.

"That's far enough, child. Now, come here."

Lidai stalked to the old woman, stomping on the floor harder than strictly necessary.

"Take these." Maryleen handed her three throwing knives. The edges had been blunted but the tips were sharp. "See what you can do."

Lidai spun. With three quick flicks, all three knives sprouted from the center of the target. Bronze clicked against bronze as they struck so close they touched.

"Ah. The girl has done this before." Maryleen walked slowly to the target, pulled the three knives, and adjusted the back of the target. It slid to the side, exposing a counterweight on the other side. She gave a downward pull on the target, using all her frail weight. The target spun in smooth circles around a center axle.

Maryleen returned to Lidai. Lidai eyed her. This old crone was in for a surprise.

Maryleen handed her the blades. "Again."

Lidai turned and eyed the target, gauging its rotation.

"Don't dally, girl."

Lidai hurled the first knife. It struck inside the red spot. She aimed again and hurled. The third knife came quicker. All three stuck in the red circle.

"I see. This girl likes her blades. I pity her future husband, the poor fool."

Lidai stomped her foot. She just couldn't help herself. This old bat thought she could rile her up? Well, it was working and Lidai let her anger boil.

"Well, girl? Go and get them."

Lidai stomped over and retrieved the blades.

"Stay there, girl. Hit me." Maryleen held her spindly fingers up to form a circle around her gray eyes. "Right here."

Lidai hesitated. Really? Throw a knife at her?

"I mean it. Do your best, child."

"I. Am. Not. A. Child!"

With the last word, she threw the knife. The old woman didn't have long to live anyway.

Maryleen casually stepped to one side. The blade traveled the room and clattered against some swords in a rack.

"Just one, child?"

Lidai huffed and threw two more.

Maryleen stepped back to the side. She stepped like she stepped walking across the room, upright and carefully. The second knife flew by. The third knife she snatched out of the air and returned to Lidai.

Lidai saw it coming. Old Patch Face had taught her this lesson. But the blade came too fast. She fell backwards, the blade whistling through the air over her shoulder.

When Lidai sat up, Maryleen stood over her. "You are a child to my eyes. Now, go get that bow and quiver, over there." This time she used a bony, pinky finger to point. She clasped her hands in front of her, patiently waiting.

Lidai climbed to her feet and brushed off her dress, though there was no dirt or dust on the floor. She stamped her foot, glaring at the old woman, but turned and huffed over to the wall. The bow looked just like hers. She pulled it off the wall and tested its draw. It had the same strength as hers. How did they...

"Don't forget the arrows, child. You'll need those."

Lidai shot the old woman a look. She drew an arrow, testing its length and weight. They felt just like hers.

"The whole quiver. Mind me, child. I haven't got all day."

Lidai shouldered the quiver hard enough the arrows rattled. She thumped back over to Maryleen.

"The target."

Lidai turned. The target still spun on its axis. She nocked, drew, and released smoothly. An arrow pierced dead center on the red circle.

"Again."

"I'll damage the arrows," Lidai replied. She let smugness ooze out, but not too much. She'd save that for the trickier shots sure to come.

"As you wish. Trime, your assistance, if you would?"

Trime rose and brought a basket of green apples.

Maryleen turned back to Lidai. "Are you ready, child?"

"What do you think?"

Maryleen frowned at her, raising an eyebrow. She turned to Trime and nodded. He tossed a big green apple up into the air.

Lidai was already nocked. She drew, sighted down the shaft, and burst the apple into pieces. The arrow thunked into the ceiling and quivered there.

"Again. Faster, if you wouldn't mind, Trime."

An apple sped into the air. The result was the same.

"Good, child. Trime, two, if you wouldn't mind."

"Two?" Lidai gasped.

Trime used one hand to toss two apples into the air at once. The first burst almost after it left Trime's hand. The arrow thunked into the wall just above the hall doorway. Kenan ducked, shooting her a wide-eyed stare.

She drew another arrow out of her quiver, nocked it smoothly, and drew. Where was the dragonspitting thing?

The apple thudded to the floor.

"I see," Maryleen tsked.

"Wait," Lidai said. Her anger was losing its battle to the challenge. This was fun. "Again."

"As you wish it."

Two more apples flew into the air.

Lidai drew and sighted down her shaft. She judged their path, took two steps to the left, and loosed.

The arrow burst one apple and scored the second.

Wren clapped for her. She smiled at him and loved him for it.

"Interesting. We're not done yet, child. Come with me."

Maryleen led her to a window. They looked through the lattice. "Do you see the green apple. There, on the barrel."

Lidai looked around on the balcony outside, then further to the next structure over.

Maryleen put her hand on Lidai's back.

Lidai shrugged her off. "Where? I don't see it."

"Look further."

People walked to and from on balconies and bridges, going about their daily business. Finally, she saw it, two balconies beyond where she had been looking. It must be over 400 feet away!

"Have you lost your mind? No one can make that shot."

"So certain, child?"

"I'm certain this bow won't reach that far, let alone hit anything."

"Give me the bow and one arrow."

"What?"

"Do not ask me to repeat myself, child."

Lidai thrust the bow into her hands. She drew an arrow, thought about stabbing the willowy old crone with it, but instead handed it over, nock first.

Maryleen calmly nocked the arrow and drew the bow. She drew it back a long way, behind her head. The bow limbs creaked. How strong was this old woman? She calmly sighted down the shaft, which she aimed up at a steep angle. The bow released, and the arrow flew.

Lidai watched it go. As it got closer to the target, she could see it would be close. People walked by the barrel. Finally, though she could hear nothing of the impact, she watched the apple burst.

A man nearby jumped, turned, and raised a fist towards the school.

Lidai looked back at Maryleen. "I... I never... I didn't..."

"That's quite all right, child. Come, there is one more trial for you." She walked to the center of the yellowwood floor and Lidai walked silently behind her. She'd been wrong. This woman had something to teach her.

"Belroon, would you please assist."

"With this little sprite? Yah. Gladly, my Lady." The big man came over.

"Thank you, my friend. Now, this girl has another knife tucked between her shoulders, hidden under her hair. A small one, I think. I want you to take it from her and shear her like one of the sheep from her little village."

Lidai stepped back. "Oh, I don't think so."

Wren stood.

"Boy," Maryleen stopped him with a bony finger. With a flick of her wrist, she produced a knife and pointed it at him. "Move from that spot, and I'll skewer you where you stand."

"Wren!" Lidai yelled, never taking her eyes off this beast of a man. "Stay there! I can handle this slabdragon!" She tossed her head to clear her dark hair and deftly retrieved the knife. It was small, but enough to gut Belroon if she cut him low enough.

The man thumped his way toward her. She backed away, knife raised. Belroon's round gut, she saw, was crisscrossed with scars. Great. He clearly didn't fear her little blade. Suddenly, she felt small. Hope fled.

When he got close enough, she desperately slashed.

His massive arms moved faster than she could believe, blocking her painfully with his forearm and redirecting her down. Her knife slid past him lower than she'd intended, and he stepped to avoid the edge. He caught the meat of her thumb in his fingers, pulled her arm close, and twisted. The blade pointed back at her. He gave it a little shove, so the tip came close to her eye.

"You're dead."

He rotated her arm around. She tried to strike him, but the way he held her hand, she couldn't reach him.

The blade was again pointed at her from underneath. He tapped the butt of the hilt with a meaty palm. "Dead again."

He twisted her wrist, forcing her arm to roll around. It hurt at wrist, elbow, and shoulder. She cried out. He easily pulled the knife from her fingers. She was twisted about, and her feet left the floor. She saw floor, ceiling, and floor again before thudding to the yellowwood on her stomach.

The man knelt on her back, pinning her hand there.

"No!" she heard Wren yell.

He couldn't interfere. "Wren! No! Stay there!"

She felt a tugging at her scalp. She stiffened her neck so as not to be slashed as her thick brown hair was cut. It fell in piles around her head. Tears leaked from her eyes and ran down her cheeks. Anger yielded to humiliation.

Maryleen bent over her, making eye contact. "Child, you think this cruel. But in time, you will understand. Now, do you ever want to be so helpless again? Do you want to learn to pierce a man's heart at such range?"

Lidai wanted to shout no with all her heart, just to throw this back in the old woman's face. But her mind considered this trial. Could she do things Maryleen had done? Could she do them better? And how would she ever stop a man like Belroon? Would these skills one day save Wren's life? For

Wren, then. She swallowed her pride and her tears.

"Yes."

Maryleen straightened. "Maturity, child, and vision for what can be." She turned to the onlookers. "She is acceptable. I will teach her."

Belroon was done with her before the old woman reached her bench. The air was cold on her scalp.

KENAN stood rooted to the floor as his sister struggled to regain her feet. She stumbled on the hem of her dress as she stooped to collect those beautiful dark brown strands. She held them in a fist as she walked slowly, head bent, to Wren. His big friend engulfed her in a hug, holding her shorn head in one big hand.

Wren, with tears in his eyes, stared at Kenan.

Right. If they wanted to see him perform, they would see the real him. They would pay for humiliating his sister.

Trime strolled casually out to the middle of the yellowwood floor. He clasped his hands behind his back. He wasn't a big man, slightly shorter than Kenan. A shock of black hair fell across one eye, the other darkly shining at Kenan.

Kenan walked forward, stopping just out of reach. Kenan placed his left fist in his right hand against his chest and bowed. He held the bow as he watched Trime.

Trime repeated the bow, holding it for a moment. The two stared at each other. Trime straightened first. Only then did Kenan do the same. The deference of initiating and ending the bow was the only honor this man would get from him.

"Woodbender, would you prefer unarmed or armed?"

"Oh, armed, please."

"Please go get any two weapons you prefer."

Kenan walked to the wall. He spied the short staves. He bowed to them before taking two off the rack. He returned, placed one on the floor out of reach of Trime, and backed off.

Trime strode forward, stooped, and collected the staff. "As you wish."

Kenan twirled the staff. The heft and length were similar to his. Trime stood idly, staff in one hand pointed at the floor. Well, he knew how to hold the thing at ready.

Kenan stepped forward. Trime did not move.

Kenan stepped forward again, feinted to the left, to the right, and cut downward at Trime's head.

The man stepped to the side and slapped Kenan with an open palm. Kenan staggered back. Trime's staff remained in one hand, pointed at the ground.

Oh, this was on.

Kenan leaped forward, the staff in two hands, striking and defending in quick succession. Trime put his staff into action, parrying, feinting, and striking. The two staves clacked out a beat. No other noise could be heard in the room for long moments.

That is until Kenan cried out from a strike to the ribs, quickly followed by another strike to the shin and another to the upper arm. Trime's staff slid in under Kenan's arm, putting his shoulder in a lock. Kenan knew what came next. He had no wish to have his shoulder dislocated so he dove and rolled out of the lock. His staff clattered across the floor.

Trime looked at him, staff back at ready position. "Good, but you came on too fast."

"Then you'll like what comes next."

Kenan dove for Trime's knees, sliding in under Trime's staff attack. He wrapped a forearm around a calf, intending to take him down. Trime gracefully stepped out of the maneuver. The leg was suddenly gone.

"Far too hasty. Strange, for a woodbender. I'd thought you'd be more patient."

Kenan rolled backwards, slid a leg back and rose to his feet, ready in case Trime pressed the attack. Instead, the man stepped back, carefully laid his staff on the floor, and kicked it away with a bare foot.

Kenan watched him warily as he circled the man. Trime turned with him but let Kenan spiral into unarmed combat range.

Kenan snapped a kick at Trime's thigh. The man stepped back. Kenan snapped a roundhouse kick at Trime's head, then reversed it into a hook kick.

Trime ducked under it so easily Kenan backed off a step in surprise.

Okay, time to get in close. Kenan snarled at him, advancing first with a simple shovel kick, followed by a series of jabs, hooks, ridgehands, and thrust punches.

Trime parried and struck back, forcing Kenan to dance. And dance they did, back, to the side, and around. Each blow, each block turned the men. Never in a straight line, they moved at angles and curves.

Kenan landed a blow on Trime's shoulder. It was meant for his throat, but the slippery fish twisted on the balls of his feet.

When Kenan pulled back, faster than he had struck, Trime's hand clung lightly to his wrist.

So, this was how he wanted to play it. Well, Jempo had many forms.

Kenan felt his arm being subtly redirected as he withdrew it. It happened in the blink of an eye, but he could tell. He knew what to look for.

Trime's other hand came in, quick and loose. Not a strike.

Kenan's other hand parried the grab, then he laid it softly on the man's elbow.

The bending began.

Kenan was the first to put a lock on Trime's arm, folding him at the elbow. But Trime countered the lock and put Kenan in a side wrist lock. Kenan knew the counter, twisted out, and put Trime in a pointer wrist lock. Trime countered that by rolling his whole body in a circle and put Kenan in an underhand lock.

Back and forth, they locked, countered, and locked again. Kenan knew, from a bystander's point of view, it looked like a child's game of palm-pat-make-the-cake.

This was no game. Whoever lost could suffer a dislocated joint or broken bone. It looked graceful, but bending was vicious.

Finally, Kenan felt the man's foot on his toes. He lost focus for a moment, trying to adjust against a foot trick. That was all Trime needed.

Trime spun Kenan's arm around in a painful lock, stepped forward, and grasped the tip of Kenan's thumb in the crook of a finger.

It looked childish. Yet, Kenan felt intense pain in his thumb, hand, wrist, elbow, and shoulder all at once. What was this?

"Maybe you should take a knee, Woodbender."

Kenan was forced to a knee.

"Perhaps you should turn to the left."

The pressure and pain forced Kenan to spin left on his knee. He groaned through the pain.

"Not that way? Okay, right."

Kenan found himself painfully spinning to the right.

Trime just stood there, holding the tip of Kenan's thumb, applying rotational pressure. His other hand he held loosely behind his back.

"To the floor then."

Kenan fell hard to the floor on his side. Before he could move, Trime squatted down, one knee on Kenan's ribs, the other on his head, with his arm in a lock somewhere over his body. He realized this show was over.

Trime spoke softly and casually in Kenan's ear. "Far too hasty, Woodbender. You let the emotions of your environment dictate your tactics. Never a good idea."

Kenan tried to look up, but the knee forced his head back to the floor. His neck strained from the pressure. Kenan gritted his teeth.

Trime spoke softly to him. "The Almighty shines on you today."

"I seriously doubt that," Kenan rasped, trying to keep the pain from taking over.

"Oh, a skeptic? We will see."

Kenan groaned. The pressure intensified. "Nice thumb trick."

"Yes, it is. Would you like to learn it?"

"Very much."

"Well, then. You must learn patience. You must learn the truth of the world. These are things I can help you with. Agreed?"

"Yes."

The pressure was suddenly gone, and with it, the pain. Kenan rolled away and leapt to his feet. Trime stood erect, hands behind his back.

Kenan bowed, and Trime returned it.

"I will accept this man. He has already come far. He has further to go." Trime turned and walked to his bench.

Kenan shook out his arm. He collected up the staves and returned them to the rack. He bowed to the weapons before carefully placing them back where they belonged.

The three companions were brought to the center of the room to stand before Maryleen and an older man, the one who'd spoken to the boy earlier. He had gray hair and eyes. Though older, he carried a barrel chest and rounded shoulders. His face, crossed with scars and mottled from centuries under a helm, scowled at them all.

"I am Lamech, secondson to Enoch, who was taken by God. I founded this school and have trained warriors here for longer than you've been alive. I trained everyone in this room, save you three. I trained Medahal, whom you know. I trained legions of soldiers. And I am still learning. If you stay, you must learn as well, at great cost in sweat and blood.

"Do you accept entrance here? I guarantee nothing but what the Almighty wishes."

"Yes."

"Absolutely."

"Yes, please."

Lamech stepped forward and hung a red tag around Lidai's neck. It hung loose over the yellow city tag. "Your hair will grow with your mind and heart, little one." Kenan's sister beamed up at him. Beamed!

Lamech stepped to Wren and hung a red tag around his neck. "You will become a great warrior, boy. But your heart will carry a heavy burden. You can bear it, I think, but not alone."

Lamech stepped over to Kenan and hung a red tag over his head. "You have learned much, but you also lack much. Your skills we can increase. What is broken here," he poked Kenan in the sternum with a strong finger, "we cannot mend. You may find a way, boy."

Kenan hesitated, then nodded even as he noted the man's breath smelled of mint.

"Now," Lamech said, "we will find you a room, feed you, and tuck you children into bed. Tomorrow, you fix my battle hall. Then, you train."

# Chapter Twenty-Two
## Knowing What Will Happen

ANNA glanced over the wale of the boat tied to the end of a spindly dock. She eyed the silty water, swirling in patterns like pouring cream into hot tea. What hid in the opaque depths? Did it have teeth? Did it kill with venom? Or would something wrap her up and pull her under, holding her there until she inhaled the dark, milky water into her lungs? She'd seen all that and more on her journey south along the Morderain River.

They'd moved swiftly down the river in the two longboats, one towing the other. The larger women got used to rowing. The heavier set women became leaner, and their backs now bulged with tan muscle.

One night, while anchored in the middle of the river, a woman had jumped overboard at night and tried for shore. She dove and swam, making the shoreline quickly. Right after she disappeared into the blades of dragongrass, a big swampdragon lurched up out of the water and followed her. As they all listened, she heard the screaming of the woman as she was dragged back into the water. She went under with a splash and was heard no more.

Another night, one other young woman made the attempt. That night, a bright moon told the story. She'd tried to swim fast but mostly just splashed around. Two swampdragons, the White Spider's fandragon, and a very large snake made for her. The snake got there first, coiled around her, and dragged her under. The two swampdragons veered off, but the fandragon came in to fight for the prize. Pieces of the woman and her smock floated down the river as the animals wrestled over the meat. Eventually, the fandragon won, downing what was left of the woman followed by part of the snake, headfirst.

The fandragon crawled up on a mudflat and lay there, half the snake swallowed, the other half hanging out of its mouth, coiling and uncoiling in death throes. Dawn nearly came before the snake's tail stopped moving. Only then did the fandragon swallow it fully.

No one tried to swim away after that.

One day they had rounded a corner to see a point in the river covered with fandragons. The White Spider's big fandragon left the boats and crawled up to challenge one of the wild males. Even though the domesticated fandragon was much larger, they were still groaning at each other when the boat left the point of land behind. Anna didn't see the fandragon again.

After many more days of travel down the river, they'd come to a large lake. The river outlet, she overheard, emptied into the lake directly opposite from the inlet. But the boats veered off to the right and followed the shoreline around the lake.

The shore here was not solid land but rather swamp and floating vegetative mats as far as she could see. They'd seen life everywhere, including many dragons. Stalkdragons wallowed in the shallow water with one or two always standing tall, watching for danger. Swampdragons lay under the floating plant life, watching them pass. Sturgeon, some not much shorter than the boats, swam alongside. Turtles sunned themselves, insects flew everywhere, and fish schooled. Once, several fish had jumped right into the boat. Men clubbed them to death and set about filleting the meat.

Anna had watched as a massive dragon, something like a mawdragon but with a longer snout and a big fan on its back, swam towards a pod of stalkdragons. One of the soldiers on the tower yelled, "Spinedragon!"

The stalkdragons saw it coming. These were especially large stalkdragons and didn't shy away from the big carnivore. The three largest moved to intercept, turning their backs to the spinedragon, which angled for a better approach. The stalkdragon tails stretched to an amazing length, ending in a long, thin taper. As the spinedragon got closer, the three whipped their tails, creating a deafening crack of sound. Many of the women on the boats covered their ears.

The spinedragon was large, but the stalkdragons dwarfed it. It circled a few times, glaring at the stalkdragons. Then it noticed the boats.

A soldier on the front tower had yelled, "It's coming this way!"

Another had screamed at the women, "Faster, you silty mud floppers! Do you want to get eaten? Faster!"

The water, she'd seen, was only five or six feet deep here. The spinedragon could swim so fast! It left a wake in the water as it dipped its long head below the surface, pushing with its tail. Water rolled up over its big body, parting on the tall fan with twin splashing waves.

Fortunately, the boats had had enough lead on the spinedragon and passed it by. It stopped near the edge of the muddy shelf under the water and stood up, lifting itself out of the water to stand on its hind legs. The animal was as big as a mawdragon, maybe bigger. It watched the boats leaving and many of the women and soldiers sighed in relief. Cracking open a massive maw, it roared defiance.

Suddenly, the water next to it had heaved upwards. With a great splash, the spinedragon was pulled off its feet and dragged into deeper water by something dark and gargantuan. It was gone in an instant, leaving nothing but a big, circular wake.

No one on the boats had said anything for some time. But neither did anyone say anything as the ruddermen steered the boats a little closer to shore.

After a few days on the lake, they had come to the river outlet. The boats were anchored, untethered, and soldiers redistributed so both boats could row. They raced down some minor rapids, across a deadwater area, and down another set of rapids. No one stayed dry, but they otherwise made it with many cheers. To Anna's shock, even some of the women cheered. It didn't last.

The boats had been beached at a campsite protected by a dragonring. The women were put to work. Anna spent the time lashed to a tree, trying not to listen. She was fed and watered, but never cut down until they were about to leave. She had but a moment to clean up in the river before they tossed her in the rear boat by her hair. Her rough-spun smock tore open from ribs to thigh, nearly becoming useless. She held it closed as much as possible.

The campsite brought the return of the great trees. Not as tall as the black trees, these trees were wider at the trunk and spread further out. Some had branches and leaves drooping nearly to the ground.

A few days later, they had come upon a small village perched on a single branch of one of the great trees. A group of people with red skin tone and onyx hair stood on an offshoot branch and watched the boats pass. Despite the chilly morning air, the people wore nothing but loincloths. Three leaned on spears tipped with stone heads.

Char had stood next to her on the boat watching the village. Though she hadn't asked, he said, "No one knows how they survive out here by themselves. Men say they use magic. Others say they're more dangerous than a mawdragon and more cunning than a toedragon. Some say they turn into bears at night. I don't know, but I suspect they're just excellent in their environment."

Anna hadn't responded, but she gave a little wave to a group of children staring at them solemnly. One little girl cracked a smile at her and waved back. On a whim, Anna pointed to her own chest and loudly said, "I'm Anna!"

The little girl had smiled wider, pointed at her chest, and said, "I'm Attitasha."

Anna hadn't smiled in weeks. It felt good, until Char kicked a knee out from under her. She fell to the deck with a thump to her head, groaning.

Char had looked down at her and demanded, "Do you think you're smart, slave? No one will follow you this far. No one ever has. Accept your fate if you want to find happiness ever again. Your future belongs to the Most High. Find happiness in his children. It's all that's left to you."

Nearly a week after that, they had come to another village, this one with a full dragonring of a short stone wall, a moat, and three layers of varied stakes. They needed the protection because the buildings were on the ground. Built of stone, they looked like they could keep out any creature or man.

Gharan and Char left the boat, which was enough to jar Anna back to the present moment. People with mostly black hair and tan skin moved about the village, using stompdragons and slabdragons for labor. A man ran down the lone spindly dock to meet the boats. He helped them tie up, one to each side of the dock. Gharan and Char followed the man to the village, the White Spiders all watching them go. Everyone wanted off the boats.

Anna eyed the water. Cloudy water or no, hungry animals or no, this was her chance. She slipped over the side of the boat and gently eased herself into the water.

The current seemed slow but strong. It immediately grabbed her and pushed her against the boat hull. She dunked under the water and felt her way under the boat, through the dock supports, and under the next boat before popping up for a breath. No one raised an alarm.

She breathed in and out several times deeply, then dunked again and let the current pull her downstream. She found a rock and held it to keep her under. Anna held her breath for as long as she could. When her lungs burned and her eyes bulged, she dropped the rock and kicked, breaking the water surface. She gasped for breath and wiped the water from her eyes. No one was in sight.

Yes! She'd done it!

Did she dare to swim across the river? The far bank would mean less people to search for her. The near bank was closer to the village, which meant fewer dangerous predators, at least for a while.

She feared the men more. She made for the far bank, all the while the current pulled her downstream. She swam carefully with slow, gentle movements to eliminate splashing.

When she pulled herself up on the opposite shore, which was covered in tree roots and rocks, she heard the first shouting from the village. It was distant now, a mile or more upstream. Anna quickly moved into the forest.

She found some vines, which she pulled down and used to bind her smock closed. She was *not* going to escape with her woman parts showing. She pulled down a couple more vines and continued deeper into the forest.

Soon, she came upon a short rock face, a generally rare feature south of Ulneer. Some of the stone had jagged edges. She found a loose stone and pulled it free. Breaking it, she had a rough stone about two palms long with a somewhat sharp edge. She missed her hand knife, but this would do for now.

Where was she going? Deeper into the forest was not a plan. Deeper meant eventual violent death by something hungry. She could go further south and hope to reach another village and perhaps convince them to send her back north. No, that didn't seem likely.

She had to have faith in her father and in Kenan. Someone would come for her. She just needed to find a safe place where she could wait until they came.

Anna made a decision. She turned north and kept the river to her left, just out of sight. The White Spiders would come after her. She didn't want to be spotted from one of the boat towers or from the village she would pass. She found some flowers she knew were edible and would give her strength. She cut through the fibrous stalk with her rock to harvest them. She ate one and carried the other two tucked behind a vine belt.

She also found a cluster of nuts. She climbed the tree and discovered only a couple of the nuts were ripe for picking. She took the ripest and left the rest. She carried it in her free hand for a later meal.

She walked on for a short time when something moved in the underbrush ahead of her. She couldn't see the body, but a long dragon tail flicked up into the air above some ferns. It screeched. She knew that noise. She dreaded that noise. Toedragons.

She desperately wanted to run, even though she knew to run was to invite chase. She had the scar on her back to remember the lesson. She slowly backed away, holding her piece of rock out in front of her, the nut clutched in her other hand.

The toedragon stepped from the underbrush, head low and arms outstretched. The tail stood vertically and waved back and forth. This toedragon seemed average in size. She might be able to fight it off.

She heard something move behind her. There were more. The first toedragon was herding her into the pack.

Anna might fight off one or two average toedragons, but she couldn't stand against a dozen of them. She turned, hurled the nut at the toedragon in front of her, and bolted into the underbrush.

The pack gave immediate chase, gaining quickly.

Ahead, she saw the river. Though the river ran wide here, the massive tree branches still spanned the entire distance. Gaps in the coverage allowed sunlight to highlight areas in the middle of the river. One of the White Spider's boats floated through a spot of sunshine.

She'd been wrong. She didn't fear men more than dragons. It's better to be this Most High's concubine later than in a toedragon's belly now. She didn't want to die. She wanted to live! She'd never wanted a thing more than to be in that boat!

Something hit her from behind and drove her into the ground. She slid along the forest duff, stuffing her mouth and smock with dead leaves and bugs. Pain flared as claws dug into her flesh through the smock on her back.

Anna thrashed. She wasn't going to be sliced open again. She fought the weight on her back and finally rolled. She brought the sharp stone around and drove it against the toedragon's side, pulling it along its ribs and getting blood. It screeched in pain and kicked her away, its long claw catching her upper arm.

She heard the rest of the pack. They were almost on her!

Anna scrambled to her feet and dashed away just as the pack broke through the underbrush behind her. She hurled the stone behind her at the lead toedragon, which took the missile in its open mouth. Several teeth broke off, and the creature screeched in pain. Other toedragons stopped to regard the leader, now spitting blood onto the duff. It slowed the pack enough for Anna to gain some ground.

In moments she neared the water. Unfortunately, the toedragon pack had caught up and were nearly on her again.

She reached the riverbank and, without pausing to gauge the water, she dove in headfirst. Underwater, she kicked and pulled, attempting to get as far from shore as possible. When she could go no further, she broke the surface, shook her head, and wiped her eyes. Her back burned where claws had punctured. Her arm had a deep scratch from the kick.

The pack stood on the riverbank screeching at her. They seemed reluctant to get into the water. They each turned in unison to look downstream. There, Anna watched as half a dozen swampdragons slid from the riverbank into the water. They turned and started swimming directly for her.

Anna felt her stomach lurch. Instinctively, she swam hard for the boat. It had turned and was rowing towards her.

A glance behind showed the swampdragons gaining on her quickly. Her smock slowed her down, but she didn't stop to remove it. She swam for her life.

The boat was still too far away when something cold and hard clamped down on her foot and pulled. Anna kicked out with her other foot and connected with a rough swampdragon snout. It didn't let go.

Anna was pulled under the water. She'd had no time to draw breath.

Her leg was twisted around by the swampdragon, and she rolled around and around in the water, helpless against its brute strength.

Another swampdragon bumped into her from behind. She tried to hold it at arm's length, pushing against its bulk. Strong jaws clamped down on her arm around her right bicep. With horror, she realized the rest of her arm was in its mouth.

This was it. Her arm would be ripped off, followed by her leg. She'd pass out from blood loss in moments, or she'd inhale muddy water. Either way, she would never see Blacktree or Kenan again.

The swampdragon on her arm suddenly opened wide and released her. She was turned about a few more times, then her ankle was also released. She stopped spinning and just lay in the water, weightless, utterly exhausted.

Her lungs burned. She needed air. Which way was up? She tried to blow some air out to follow the bubbles. She had no air. Frantically, she twisted about. She could see no more than a few feet in any direction. One direction seemed brighter, so she began to pull that way.

Something hit her on the head. She brushed the swampdragon away, only to find it was hard and flat. An oar! Anna clutched at it and was pulled quickly to the surface. She gasped for breath and held to the oar.

She heard rough voices, male and female. "There she is!"

"The concubine! Pull her in! Quickly!"

"Don't let it get 'er again!"

"There! Another swampdragon. Shoot it, now!"

"Spears ready! One might try to board!"

"That one there is a big one! Never seen one so big."

Finally, the men pulled her from the water and into the boat. All she could do was breathe. Her back and arm burned. Her shoulder throbbed from being wrenched. Her ankle and knee screamed in pain. But she could breathe. She could draw breath for another day. For that, she would thank the Almighty.

The hissdragons in the boat hissed at her, loud in her ear. She looked for them and edged away.

"Almighty," said a woman. Bethany, she thought it might be. "I thought you were dead for sure."

Anna squinted up at her. "Not helpful."

"Sorry," Bethany said. "Here, you're bleeding. Maybe I can get these bound before we get back to the village."

Cols stood in the middle of the boat, scarred arms crossed and face set in a scowl. Anna avoided his eyes. They were beady and wild. She didn't know what he would do. Would she be made an example against escape?

The boat rowed back to the village. Anna was bound around the neck and with wrists high between her shoulder blades while Bethany put salve on her wounds and bandaged them, careful to cover her with rags. Anna's smock was gone, lost to the river. The bandages weren't a dress, but at least she wasn't completely naked. Her back, she was told, was not bad, though it burned as if poked by hot coals. Her arm was marked with punctures and would bruise deeply, but it hardly hurt. Her ankle was the worst. The swampdragon had rolled her entire body by the ankle. Not only was the skin there torn all the way around and off in places, but the joint itself seemed torn and swollen. She could put no weight on it.

While Bethany worked, Anna whispered, "Thank you."

"Shh. Cols is too close. He'll hear you."

Anna checked. Cols didn't seem to notice. "He's fine. You're very kind. Please, accept my thanks."

"I was ordered to help you."

"Well, thank you all the same. I see the kindness in your work."

"Heh. It's not exactly what I've been known for."

Anna smiled at her. "That was a different life."

Bethany gave her a look and nodded.

Anna changed the subject. "How are you holding up?"

"I was no virgin, and I got an officer. This is hard, but I'll survive."

"You're strong."

"Maybe. Himmons may keep me. If I please him, he may marry me."

Cols barked, "No talking!" He smacked Bethany on her rear end hard enough to make her eyes bulge. She swallowed back a cry. She looked to Himmons, but he said nothing.

Anna tried to apologize to Bethany with her eyes, but the young woman wouldn't look at her.

The boat tied up at the spindly dock again and, soon after that, the other boat reappeared from upstream and tied up as well.

Anna was transferred to her boat. Gharan waited for her. He didn't look pleased. He reached behind her, seizing her by the binding and cutting off her breath. He marched her back to the rear deck, to the door to the small room below. Anna hopped and struggled to keep her weight off her ankle.

He said into her ear, "Where did you think you'd go, concubine slave? How would you possibly survive traveling back through the Dragongrass?"

Anna answered. If he asked a question, she must answer. She rasped through her binding, "I planned to steal a boat from the village after you left, then make my way back."

Gharan smiled at her. "Lie."

Anna winced. "I planned to stay with the red people. When my betrothed came for me down the river, he would find me there."

Gharan looked thoughtful. "Char, what do you think?"

Char stood nearby, a hand on his sword. "I think, my Prince, she is telling the truth. And it's a plan that might have worked."

"Yes. Disturbing. I thought we were past that possibility."

"Yes, my Prince."

"Very well. On your next trip north, kill them all."

"As you say, my Prince. It shall be done."

"But not that little girl who spoke to this concubine slave. Bring her to me. Oh, and this evening, up this one's dose to three seeds. And see its wounds cleaned daily. This will delay its delivery to my father. He will tolerate a scar to its leg, but not an unhealed wound."

Char nodded.

Anna's binding was removed, but she was lashed to the barrels on the rear deck. Char eyed her, a little quirk to his mouth. He resembled Kenan a little, and it bothered her.

IN a few hours, they left the village behind. One of the older women had been traded for supplies and a stompdragon, which was promptly slaughtered to replenish the feed for the hissdragons.

Anna stayed lashed to the barrels on the rear deck. Otherwise, she was well tended with water, food, and medical care. Her arm felt better first, and her back next. Her ankle throbbed for many days, especially if she tried to flex it.

She watched this southern forest glide by her. The leaves on the giant gray trees hung heavier than they did in the north. The branches were stouter and the whole effect wider. The flowers here seemed brighter. The temperatures warmed, even though the year was getting late.

The river joined another large tributary. One of the soldiers called it out loudly, although everyone could see it. "We've reached the Kalezane River, my Prince!"

Anna didn't care what it was called. She only cared about the boat she saw being oared up the Kalezane branch. If a boat was going that way, there were probably people that way. She remembered an old map on Medahal's wall. Kalenteer was up there, she thought, a nation separate from Midreer. If she could get a boat, she would go there and wait. Kenan wouldn't find her there, but it might be a safe place to go to ground. In time, she could earn passage or steal a boat to travel back to Edeer, to Blacktree, to home.

The river turned westerly. In a few days, they passed another village. This one boasted a large stone dock with a fortification at the end. Again, the buildings were stone and built on the ground. Why would they build on the ground when the trees were right there? It looked strange to her eyes.

More boats passed them going upstream. Others moved downstream, towards Mordeen.

A few days later, they approached a city. Several large stone piers extended into the wide river. Boats were tied alongside with cargo of crates, barrels, and baskets of goods being transferred to and from the docks and boats. A tall wall, at least three times as tall as a man, protected the city from all sides. A low wall protected it from the water. There must be a thousand people there, no, more, all bustling in the busyness of life.

Anna mumbled, "I never thought I'd see a real city."

Cols was just climbing down from the tower. "What was that, Princess?"

Anna just looked at him.

"A city, did you say? That ain't no city, Princess. That's Mallain. Just a muddy village. We're stopping there for a bit of trading. Might find something I want there..." Cols trailed off in thought.

She got mad at him but didn't know why. "Why are you even on this boat?"

"'Ad to talk to the Commander. But why am I explaining this to you, Princess?"

"I don't know."

"Neither do I. But I need a new girl, so this is as good a place as any to change 'er out."

Anna's jaw dropped open. "Change her out?"

"Yeah. Mine stopped being fun. This place ain't big enough to 'ave a proper women's auction, say nothing about a girl's auction, but I know a man 'oo can get me what I want. I've 'ad my eye on one for a couple years now. She's got red 'air."

Anna could only stare as Cols walked by the young Blacktree girls, still sitting in a group under guard. The men were getting ready to tie up against another boat.

Char and Cols left the boat, crossed the intervening boat, and talked to a man on the dock. Soon, goods were being unloaded and loaded. Several women were led away and down the dock, disappearing into Mallain. One of them was Bethany, face streaked with tears and hands bound behind her back. Five new women and a young teen girl, all with tan skin, black hair, and wearing simple smocks, climbed into the boat. The women chatted back and forth amiably. They didn't seem worried about being traded and loaded onto a boat bound for the Almighty only knows where.

Cols came back with a young girl, perhaps no more than twelve years old. He held her by the red hair on the back of her head. She looked resigned, but her face held a trace of fear. She looked like she had an idea of what lay in store for her.

What kind of life did this girl have that she knew what was going to happen? This saddened Anna in a way that none of her experiences so far had.

They left and continued downriver. The next day, they passed a larger village, twice the size of Mallain with at least four times the population. The walls stood twice as tall. Towers protected the waterfront. Bronze thumpers pointed out over the water. She didn't know they could be made from bronze.

Further down river, they passed two boats locked in mortal combat. Grapples pulled and bound the boats together. Men fought with axe, sword, and crossbow. One man pointed a small thumper at another and fired the weapon. It cracked in a way she'd never heard, making her flinch in terror. Flame shot out the end of the weapon. The victim's shield showed a dark hole. The man's head fell forward, and he slumped over the wale and into the water. The thumper, no, *firepole* she'd heard it called, shattered its barrel. The owner of the weapon tossed it to the bottom of his boat and drew a sword.

Their boats didn't slow. The pulling boat rowed harder, and Char readied a crossbow. No one bothered them as they pulled down river, leaving the others behind to their fight.

The river ran a mile wide after the Kalezane joined the Morderain. Boats moved to and from in all directions. Hundreds of fishermen in small boats hauled nets full of fish. Big war vessels with layers of oars moved about, sometimes firing a bronze firepole at a floating log in practice. Vessels with sails soon dotted the river. Anna had never seen a boat with a sail before. Some moved downwind, and she could see how it worked. Others angled upwind, which made no sense at all.

Days and villages passed by. The forest thinned and eventually stopped. Worked fields stretched up both slopes of the valley. The scope of the fields addled her mind. As far as she could see left or right, fields full of crops were worked by people and dragons. They plowed and harrowed, hauled manure, and harvested crops. Most wagons, carts, and sledges were pulled by dragon, but a few were pulled by oxen.

She gaped at a man riding what could only be a horse along a road near the shore. She'd heard of horses but had never seen one. She'd pictured it like a furry stompdragon, but that wasn't it at all. This animal's body was long and sleek. Beautiful brown hair streamed behind it as it galloped along the road. The man sat in a saddle of sorts and had no trouble staying on the animal's back. The speed of the horse made her wonder. With a horse, she could outrun aggressive dragons and be back in Blacktree in no time.

The horse whinnied as it raced past several warriors riding on hissdragons. One warrior raised a fist and shouted something, but the horse rider made off as if he didn't notice them at all. The horse soon disappeared out of sight ahead of them.

They finally passed a real city. The shoreline wall stood at least a hundred feet tall and was supported by even taller towers. The wall stretched for at least five miles along the river. Open gates led into an enclosed harbor where she saw more boats and men rolling barrels on floating docks. A second harbor sat low, unwalled, and overrun with boats of all sizes and men moving cargo. One man, impossibly big, carried a barrel on each shoulder down the dock. He stood twice as tall as the other men. Anna gaped as he rounded the corner and vanished behind a tall, two-masted cargo ship. His head and arms reappeared behind the main deck as he walked. He must be twelve feet tall, at least! Did people here grow so tall? Or were the silver-stripe seeds affecting her mind?

The city spread out over a low hill rising behind the walls. Another wall inside the city ringed a smaller, inner city, and an inner wall ringed a large stone structure dominating the top of the hill. Tall towers looked out over the entire city.

"What is that?" Anna asked no one in particular.

A soldier watched her. Many of them did. They seemed enamored with her for some reason. "That's Achetai, city of the Nephilim 'aran Lamar."

"Nephilim Haran Lamar?"

"Yes. Like our prince."

"Gharan?"

"Yes. Prince Gharan is also a Nephilim of the Most High. 'Aran Lamar founded Achetai and defeated Kaitong's armies. 'E rules all south of the river now, though 'e almost lost the city long ago. Our Prince Gharan saved it. Tensions ain't been great since."

"Oh. But what's that?" Anna pointed at the tall stone building on top of the hill."

"That's Lodestone Castle, 'ome of 'aran Lamar."

"Castle? I've never heard of a castle."

"Castle," the soldier explained. "Keep. It's a city's last line of defense and center of power. Castle."

"Oh. It's... foreboding."

"Foreboding?" The man asked.

Anna shuddered. "Yes. I don't think I ever want to go there."

"That's good. Because I doubt you will. You're going to Mordeen with us."

"What's Mordeen?"

"'Ome, lovey. Mordeen is 'ome."

They left Achetai behind and passed an unending array of crop fields and many other villages. This nation was *huge*. How would anyone find her here?

Though they'd anchored in the river upstream, now they floated on through the night. They passed other villages. She could see the lamplight from the windows. Torches lit docks as men bought and sold at all times of the day and night.

Eventually, the boats made for the docks of a smaller city on the north side of the river. Gharan pulled Haley out from below the rear deck and stood her to face the city.

"That, concubine, is your new home. Mordeen. I founded this city in my father's name over six hundred years ago. It grows faster than any other in

Midreer, perhaps in the world."

Anna frowned and squinted at Gharan. He didn't look that old.

Haley smiled vacantly at the long lines of docks reaching out into the water. They were wide and stone, but unwalled. Each dock held numerous ships and boats, and everything seemed covered in cargo and men. Each dock led to its own gate through a short, stone, shore wall and into the city. Towers dotted the walls, much like Achetai, only not so tall. Bronze firepoles poked out over the edges on top of each tower, their dark muzzles threatening to destroy any ship that didn't belong.

The city rose on a hill behind the wall and curled up and to the east where a tall bluff stood over the river. A dark castle with two tall towers sat on top of the bluff, with more firepoles pointing out over the waters.

A small town had formed east of the main city with their own docks reaching into the river. A beaten road connected Mordeen with this outlying village.

Gharan continued talking to Haley, pointing up at the castle. "That is Blackstone Castle. My castle. You will live there and serve me." Haley didn't react.

Anna watched the castle as they approached. The stone was indeed black. The castle loomed over them. She'd thought Lodestone was a foreboding castle. Blackstone was smaller but far more disturbing.

And she was going there.

# Chapter Twenty-Three
## To Pick a Nose

KENAN danced with Trime on the polished yellowwood floor in the Old Pine Tree School. And he hated his boots.

He wore heavy bronze armor, something his body wasn't used to yet. There was a trick to moving, to speeding up your movements and slowing them down a little more gradually. Momentum, he learned, affected his movements and his joints in unexpected ways.

A heavy breastplate protected front and back. Shoulder plates curved down, making overhand movements awkward. Narrow, bronze splints hung down from a wide belt, covering him with a skirt of metal around his hips to mid-thigh. His overshirt stuck out underneath. A helm sat uncomfortably on his head. Both forearms were wrapped in bronze bracers.

He didn't mind any of the armor. He didn't tire from it as easily as those first days. His strength grew fast now, faster than he thought possible.

The boots. The boots were the problem.

He wore simple leather boots. A hide had been wrapped skin side out around the soles and greased with fat. They slid on the polished floor, constantly challenging his footing and balance.

To be fair, Trime wore identical boots and armor, though he didn't seem to be having much of a problem.

Kenan hitched his left arm to adjust the small, wood shield on his bracer. A strap didn't feel tight enough.

Trime, curse the man, saw the motion and slashed at the shield with his bronze sword. It worked. Kenan's feet slipped, and he thumped to the floor, remembering at the last moment to keep his grip on his own sword hilt.

Trime tsked. "If your shield straps don't feel too tight, they're not tight enough."

"Yeah. Got that."

Kenan struggled to regain his feet on the slippery floor. A sheen of fat gleamed on the polished wood, his sword, and his armor. He had the stuff all over him.

"What kind of fat did you say this was?"

Trime smiled. "I didn't."

"Right." Kenan lunged forward with sword tip whistling, balancing on the slick footing. Trime turned the blade away on his shield and slashed down. Kenan lurched to the side, holding his shield up. His foot shot out, and Kenan landed on the floor again.

Trime stood straight and smiled down on him, shield and sword behind his back. Other than his boots, he had absolutely no fat on him.

Kenan jerked his body in frustration.

"Am I making you mad, Woodbender?"

Kenan breathed in through his nose and out through his mouth. "No."

"I see." Trime's smile never left his face.

Kenan struggled back to his feet. "What's the point of this, this, slickness?"

"Can you not see it?"

"No."

"Ah. Well, perhaps you will tomorrow."

"No, I want to know now."

"Woodbender, how long does it take someone to bend window lattice?"

Kenan breathed in, slowing himself down. Trime was prone to these changes in conversation. "Many years."

"So, I hear. Come, see."

Kenan struggled to move across the smooth wood. Trime had no trouble at all. Kenan stamped down his impatience and watched him. Ah, step heel to toe. Kenan tried it and quickly joined him at the window.

Trime laid a hand on the lattice. "Beautiful, is it not?"

"Yes. I've made many."

"You made this one."

"What?" His work wasn't fine enough to be used here in Edeer.

"Yes, Woodbender. See here? Your mark, I believe?"

Yes. There it was. His mark stood out against the white of the wood, a tree branch bent in spiral.

"Well, this one is especially beautiful, then." Kenan smiled wryly at his teacher. He was getting his teacher's point.

"Years, you say, to make such beautifully intricate work. Can you describe it to me?"

"Certainly. First, I must find the right grouping of branches in the right type of tree. This one is from a blacktree, which has white wood, as you can see. For a lattice so large, I would need to graft other branches in. As they grow, I twist and bind them, each in its place. The branches grow together, see, here at the crosses. Some branches grow too large, so I restrict their girth with cord. After many years of routine adjustments, I can harvest the lattice. This one probably took ten years. It's how I made a living."

"I see. What if you tried to grow a lattice from both directions?"

"I don't think that would work. The piece would be weak here, in the middle."

"I see. So, patience, with many steps in the right order, yields great reward?"

"Well, yes, and I see your point."

"Yes, Woodbender. I cannot teach you one thing until you've mastered the first. Each in its order, one day at a time."

"Fine. I'll wait."

"Good. Yet, I will give you a clue about your footwear."

"Okay."

"You have been in a battle. What happens?"

Kenan paused in thought, analyzing the bad memories. "Movement. Lots of it. Pain. Sweat and blood. Desperation."

"You see?"

Kenan imagined the blood on the boardwalks, his feet sweating from exertion. He remembered slipping and falling. "Yes, I see. Footing is not guaranteed."

"Very good. And, once you master this, regular footing seems easy. Remember, all your strength comes from the ground. Should we try once more? I do believe you have time before you must clean up this mess and get to archery practice."

"Yes. One more time. Thank you, Master Trime."

"You learn, Woodbender. Never stop. Learning is a wonderful spice of life."

WREN smiled as he ran. He ran along a boardwalk, then ran up a stairway to the next level. He ran along another boardwalk. His red tag bounced on his chest, and people hurried to step out of his way.

He ran over a bridge. He ran down another balcony, jumped the rail, and landed on a broad branch. He ran down it, the bark providing traction for his leather boots.

He breathed easy after two months of running. He hardly sweated, and what sweat he produced evaporated into the cool winter morning.

Lidai ran next to him. He didn't mind running if he did it with her.

"I hate this." Her hair had grown back in. Well, a little. She looked cute with short hair. Long hair was better, but still. It stuck out around her ears. Those were nice ears, too.

"I know you do," Wren said through his smile.

They ran down the branch and across a plank to another balcony. They reached a lift rope, stretching from above down to lower levels below. The lift loop was not in sight, but they didn't need it. "After you, cute one."

Lidai frowned at him. Even that he found absolutely adorable. She wrapped her boots around the rope, grabbed with her hands and descended. She gripped it differently than he. She used her fingertips. He knew she had calluses there from countless hours of archery.

He would have liked to go first, but she was wearing her new dress. If she caught him taking a peek up, he'd never hear the end of it. He wrapped his boots and callused hands around the rope and followed her down.

Someone below engaged the lift. The rope suddenly moved, dropping with him faster than it should have due to the added weight. Shouts sounded from below. Oops.

"There! Jump there!" They leapt off the lift line, rolled on a boardwalk, and continued to run. The motion was smooth and athletic. Wren took a quick glance below to verify everyone was okay. They ran on, quickly leaving the shouting behind.

Lidai asked, "Do you think the running will ever end?" Her red tag bounced on her chest.

"Did those buckets end?"

That first few weeks, Lidai had been forced to lug large buckets of water around the school. She mopped floors, scrubbed pots and pans, and washed tables. Whenever the buckets were less than three-quarters full, she lugged them to the cistern and filled them again. She went everywhere with the buckets. They sat under her hammock as she slept. The three shared a small room, so he knew.

Her shoulders rounded during that time. After she was relieved of the buckets, she got a new bow with a stronger draw.

He liked her shoulders. The muscle wasn't masculine. Her shoulders rounded in gentle curves. They looked great on her.

"Buckets are Kenan's thing," she said.

"Yeah. That's never getting old."

She chuckled as she ran by his side. Her dress wasn't full of folds, like she'd always worn. This dress hung light and fit her curves. He liked her new dress very much.

"Stop looking at me. You're going to fall over a railing. Let's go right."

They turned right and ran across a timber bridge. Neither lost their wind on the run, which finally ended back at the school. They ran in and straight to the conditioning room.

Wren dropped forward and did push-ups. Lidai did so as well, though not as fast as he did. His hands came off the floor between each push.

They moved to a rack of iron weights. He grabbed two. Both together probably weighed more than she did. She grabbed smaller weights, and they grunted with the effort of exercise. They shifted from exercise to exercise, never pausing for a moment.

Kenan ran in. He leapt for the pull-up bar, grabbing it with both hands. He did a few pull-ups that lifted his upper body above the bar before switching to one-armed pull-ups. Wren could do it, but Kenan made it look easy.

Kenan caught him looking. He smiled as he switched hands.

Wren rolled his eyes. "I can do that, too, you know."

"Sure, you can. But how about this?" Kenan grabbed the bar with both hands, swung about, and landed with his feet on the high, wood bar. He stood tall to the ceiling, arms over his head, and didn't even wobble.

It was Lidai's turn to roll her eyes. "Show off."

Wren smiled at the siblings. He loved them both. In different ways, of course, but he loved them.

Lidai waved as she ran from the room. "I'm off to morning archery. See you boys at breakfast."

After she left, Kenan looked at him. "Going to pop the question soon?"

Wren frowned as he lifted a bag of sand up over his head with one arm, then the other. "How can I? I should really talk to her mother first."

"Or you could just ask me."

"May I?"

"What? This is how you ask? While lifting weights? With two words?"

"Well, what did that old fart say? 'No time like the present?'"

"Yeah, well, there's the matter of bride price. What you got to give me?"

"You slabdragon! You know what I have: a house and a shielddragon. I don't have anything else."

"Yea, me neither. That's why I need the bride price. You know, to live life large." Kenan stood on his hands, pinching his overshirt between his thighs. He lifted one arm to stand on one hand. Then he lowered and raised himself by one arm.

Wren looked at him, disgusted. "Well, you'd better keep waiting."

"Ha! Well, patience is a virtue, and all that. Tell you what. I'll cut you a deal. She can't be worth too much. She stabs people, after all. That'll be you, some day. Mark my words."

Wren grinned as he picked up a large stone, rolled it up to his shoulder, and set it back down.

Kenan gracefully flipped back to his feet and strode over to him. His friend looked serious. Wren did a few more pulls on the stone before he stood to talk for a moment. He hoped they didn't get caught just standing here.

Wren wondered what Kenan was about. "It'd better be a good deal."

Kenan smiled. "Oh, it is. Trust me. Here's what you do. You go pick Lamech's nose. I need to see it, now. Pick his nose, and I'll give you her hand."

Wren reached for him. "You dragonscrape!"

Kenan ducked the grab and danced out of range, smiling ear to ear. "You can do it. I know you can." With that, he raced from the room. Wren knew he had knife practice.

Wren lifted the stone again. A teenage boy entered the room, took one look at Wren, and ran back out. He wasn't sure why they were so intimidated by him.

He had gotten to know many of the other students. Hundreds trained in the Old Pine Tree School. Almost all of them only trained for an hour or two a day in rotating shifts. Some trained all day. Other than Wren, Lidai, and Kenan, only Tadd lived at the school. Lamech hadn't adopted the boy, but they acted the parts often enough.

He lifted the stone one more time. He wanted to be sweaty for what came next. He pulled off his boots and shirts, replaced them with a kilt, and ran from the room. He had rolling practice.

Wren found Master Belroon in the rolling room. Clean reeds covered the floor in a soft mat. Both men wore only kilts.

"You're late, boy. Let's get to this. First, take-downs. You remember what I taught you yesterday, yah?"

"Of course, fat man. Give it a go, if you've got the stones."

"Yah! I'll show you stones..." Master Belroon crouched low, feinting first left, then right. They circled each other on the reeds. The older man darted in to snag a calf. Wren lifted his foot out of the way and smiled. Belroon punched him in the nose.

Wren jumped back. He felt at his face. His nose wasn't broken, but his hands came away with blood. "I remembered the lesson! What was that for?"

"That's for getting cocky, yah. And to remind you, boy, there is no such thing as a fair fight. You ready to roll?"

"I was born ready."

"Yah? Well, take me down, if you can."

Wren finally succeeded in taking the man down to the reeds. Before he could celebrate his success, the round man twisted, pushed his knee, then rolled. Wren was in triangle choke before he could figure out what had happened. He tapped Belroon's leg, and the man let him go.

"Good take-down, boy. You've got archery, unless I miss my guess, yah? After lunch, come to the fight room. Come in full plate. The heavy stuff, yah? And the bronze shield, the big one."

"What are we going to do?"

"Ha! Like I'd tell you now. Get going, yah? She'll skewer you if you're late."

Wren took off running.

Mistress Maryleen skewered him with a look as he arrived, only panting slightly. Those light blue eyes were somehow sharper than a steel sword.

Wren was passable with a bow. He would never match Kenan. And Lidai made them both look like children with the weapon. But he practiced. He knew he needed a full harness of tools.

LIDAI watched Wren, who worked his big bow in only a kilt. She watched him, shirtless, and couldn't help but admire him. The bow looked like a dragonring stake, it was so large. He drew it with no apparent effort. He loosed, and an arrow the size of a small spear thudded into a target. Off-center, but still a deadly strike.

He caught her looking and winked.

Mistress Maryleen caught him winking, too, and scowled. He blushed and nocked another arrow.

"What you see in that lout is beyond me, child."

Lidai smiled at him as he drew and loosed again. She liked the way his back bunched with muscle. "Well, if I am just a child, Mistress, I can't be expected to have sound judgment."

Maryleen looked down and turned her scowl on Lidai. Lidai didn't look up. Those frowns didn't bother her anymore.

"Indeed. Listen, girl. You share a room with that boy in a man's body. Perhaps it's time you got your own room. No. It's past time. How you're not already with child is beyond me."

This got Lidai's attention. "Mistress Maryleen. My brother also shares the room. Wren and I spent time on the road and two months in that room. He hasn't touched me. He's an honorable man."

Maryleen sniffed. "Perhaps. Still, you've grown close to him, girl. Very close. I may be old, but I'm not dead. Not yet. No woman fights while carrying. Not in Edeer. Not while I'm here."

Lidai frowned.

Maryleen caught it. "You still want to fight, do you not?"

"Yes, Mistress. This isn't over. When the White Spiders return, it'll be through a hail of arrows in the night."

"Indeed. Child, you have a poetic streak. I think you'll benefit from a few lessons from a scribe I know."

"As you wish, Mistress."

Several of the men started pushing each other, trying to distract their friends from their shots. Missing a target meant push-ups. Laughter broke out on the far end of the line.

"Look at this lot. Think you can show these miserable boys how archery is done?"

"Yes, Mistress. I certainly can."

"Boys! At rest." The dozen men pulled their bows back to their sides, tips on their boot. Or in Wren's case, his bare foot. He'd forgotten to put his boots back on, again. The men all stared ahead at their target, as they were trained. Never take your eyes off the target.

Maryleen walked behind the line of men. "Look at your bows. They're bigger than what I would choose. I can't even draw some of them. Your arrows are heavy and can pierce armor. Dangerous tools. You've improved but have a long way to go." She stopped and stepped in front of Wren. She studied him from his bloodied nose down to his bare feet. "A long way, indeed."

She continued her walk, hands clasped behind her back. "Your bows are powerful because they must be. Arrows must penetrate where they can. Yet, look. Look at your targets." Not a single arrow landed in the palm-sized bullseyes.

Maryleen stood and contemplated the men. "How big, do you think, is the face opening on a standard bronze helmet. You. Wren is your name? Miserable name. How big?"

"About a palm, Mistress Maryleen."

"Indeed. Imagine those targets are charging soldiers. Twelve of them. Use your brains, if you have any, and picture it. Need I point out the bullseye is the open face of a helmet? Now, watch, you miserable lot. Watch how you would fare against a single trained archer." She nodded to Lidai.

Lidai had her new bow in hand and a full quiver on her back, as she did during every moment on the archery range. She deftly grabbed four arrows. Three she held by the nocks between the fingers of her right hand. The fourth she nocked as she sprinted down the line. She drew with her right and loosed. She nocked her next arrow as she drew and loosed again. Drew and loosed again. Drew and loosed again, all while sprinting between the men and the balcony rail. Four arrows thudded into the bullseyes of four targets. They were dead center.

The targets seemed close to her, and huge. She could do this with targets the size of a walnut at twice the range. She stopped at the far end, spinning back in a crouch on her heel. As she did, she drew four more arrows. She hit four more bullseyes as she sprinted back down the line.

A man tried to trip her. She kicked him high on the inner thigh as she leapt over his foot.

By the time she reached her starting point, four more arrows were once more in her hand. She stood as tall as her frame allowed and, in less than two heartbeats, she had four more bullseyes. Every target was stuck with an arrow in the middle.

Maryleen stepped forward. "A girl with a bow just killed all twelve of you before you could get to her. What do you think now, boys? Do you think you should take your practice more serious?"

The men stared at their targets, but Lidai could see they were struggling with this lesson. One man kneeled, rubbing his leg. The biggest man just stood there, tall and smiling. Though he looked at his target, she knew he smiled for her.

He flexed his calf. Dragonspit the man. He knew she liked his calves. Something pleasant and increasingly familiar twirled low in her belly.

Perhaps Mistress Maryleen was right. He was going to be a problem. There was wisdom in the old woman. Lidai was just starting to see it.

The men were dismissed to midday meal. Lidai joined her Mistress.

"What is on your mind, girl?"

"I think... I think I will take you up on your offer, Mistress. Wren would never touch me before marriage. He loves me and he treasures our future more than our present. I am not so sure I have such... restraint."

"Ah. Good. We will move your things during evening meal. Take something to eat for later. Now, go get your midday meal, before that gaggle of young peacocks eat all of it."

Lidai turned to go.

"Oh, and young woman?"

She trotted three more steps before she realized that was her.

"Yes, Mistress?"

"Meet me in the Battle Hall after midday meal. I want you to see something."

After lunch, Lidai sat on a bench in the Battle Hall, idly twirling her knife. She wasn't supposed to have her own fighting knife yet, but no one had checked her upper thigh that day at the acceptance trials. She still had it and had taken to carrying it again.

She liked it here at the school. The work was hard. She always sported bruises and nicks on her hands from the knife play. She went to her hammock tired every night. But she was preparing for something, something important. She gave the training her all.

She heard the telltale swish of Mistress Maryleen's dress as she walked slowly towards the Battle Hall. Lidai stashed her blade in her thigh sheath and straightened her dress just as the old woman entered the room.

"Ah, early again. Good." Maryleen shuffled across the floor.

Lidai knew the shuffle was real. The woman's hips bothered her. Yet, Lidai had been dumped during training on her backside by her Mistress more times than she could remember.

Maryleen sat next to her. "You almost connected with me at sparring practice yesterday. Your little fists come in a flurry."

"I remember ending up on the ground, locked out at the wrist, Mistress."

"Well, yes. Still, you're getting better, and with blade and bow as well. I must admit, you have a gift with that bow. You almost remind me of myself, many centuries ago."

Lidai stared.

"Yes, I said it. You won't hear it again soon, young woman."

Lidai nodded and smiled.

"How well do you think your strikes would fare against the likes of Wren? No, not him. Belroon? Trime? Any of these blockheaded men?"

"If I caught them unawares..."

"If you catch them unawares, gut them like a fish. No, I mean in a battle. They can outrun you. They can overpower you. Your blade means nothing to heavy armor. Your strikes will seem as a child's. Do you wish to be a child, again?"

"No, Mistress."

"Indeed. Ah, here comes Belroon now. No, you are not to spar with the man today. You are to observe and learn."

The big man stalked into the room. Wren towered behind him. Both men wore full armor head to ankle in heavy bronze and carried massive shields the size of a small dinner table. The metal suits made them look even larger than they were. These were huge men in heavy plate. The sight intimidated her, even though she knew Wren would never hurt her.

She thought that much armor would, well, clank more than it did. It should scrape or clang or something. Their heavy boots made more noise. At least Wren had found his. He'd left them in the conditioning room again.

Master Belroon crossed the yellowwood floor to a rack of great axes. The edges were blunted, but Lidai knew they were still deadly. He grabbed two without ceremony and thumped back to the center. He tossed his student one of the weapons. Wren caught and twirled it in one smooth motion. The man grinned at her through his helmet guard, then almost dropped the thing. Lidai laughed.

"Yah, you like that axe, boy?"

"I've been waiting to heft one. We've always practiced with hammers."

"Yah. Well, today, you don't get to use it. Just hold her, like she is that little girl over there."

"What?"

"You heard me, boy. Just hold her. If you swing her at me, even once, I'll have you scrubbing pans with the new accepted. For a month."

Wren grunted.

Lidai settled in to watch. This was turning out to be more interesting than she'd thought.

Wren tilted his helmed head. "But what am I to do if..."

Belroon lurched forward, swinging his axe at Wren at full strength.

Wren crouched and braced himself on his shield. The blow tottered him a bit, but he held.

"Good. Here I come again, boy. Be ready, yah?"

Belroon attacked again, this time with multiple swings of the heavy, bronze axe. Wren caught them all on his shield, twisting one way then the other. He gave ground under the onslaught.

"Is this all I've taught you, boy? Why do you not move? Drop that slab of wood. You will no longer have it. Someone took it from you, yah?"

Wren casually flipped his axe up, so it hung on his shoulder, then pulled at a strap or two on his shield arm. The heavy bronze and wood shield slammed to the floor.

"You will replace those floorboards tonight, yah? No sleep until it looks new. Lamech will have your hide. Now, do not get hit, or you will be months recovering."

Belroon stepped forward again, swinging his axe wildly over his head.

Lidai covered her mouth with her hands. Almighty, was she watching Wren's last day?

The axe came across at the neck. Wren dipped under it. The axe swung around, moving quickly with Belroon's strength. Wren stepped back to avoid the blow, then back in to keep his ground. The axe whirred low to crush Wren's knee. Wren simply lifted his foot high off the ground as the axe passed under.

Belroon growled and came at him with an overhand strike. Wren stepped to the side. The axe arced down and thudded into the floor, breaking a board.

"So, who's going to fix that one?" She could hear the smile in Wren's voice.

Belroon growled again, tearing the axe free, spinning, and swinging a backhand blow to Wren's ribs.

Wren dropped to the floor, his face at Belroon's feet. He instantly pushed himself back up as the axe whistled harmlessly overhead. The man rose vertical again mostly by the strength of his arms alone.

The return swing was aimed at the arm holding his axe. Wren pivoted and the axe missed again.

Finally, Belroon came at him overhead again. Wren lifted his own axe and batted the blade to the side.

"That was not a swing at you, Master."

"Getting cocky, again, yah, boy?"

Belroon swung again at Wren's head. Wren ducked as before, but this time he was struck across the helm by the edge of Belroon's shield. Wren dropped to the floor with a clatter of armor plates.

"Good, boy. You need more practice. For the next week, you are not allowed to strike me. Only defend."

"But how will I learn to get through your defenses if I can't attack?"

"You don't hear me, boy. By learning to defend, yah? Offense is much stronger when combined with defense. You must learn this. It is time. Now, again."

Maryleen touched Lidai on the arm. She jumped. She'd been caught up in the odd dance between the two fighters and had forgotten the old woman was there.

"Let us go. Have you learned the lesson?"

"Yes, Mistress. I am no match for a big, armored man. I must dodge away and look for opportunity."

"Good. We will practice, but not with these elephants tromping everywhere. We will go to the sparring room. Come. I have brought a big man for you to practice with."

What the dragonspit was an elephant? Lidai followed Maryleen from the room, leaving behind the sound of shouts, grunts, and a massive whistling axe.

Practice that afternoon interested her. She learned to parry, duck, and dodge out of a large man's grasp. She thought it would come in handy, in battle and, perhaps one day, in a home. The thought earned her a painful strike to the stomach, so she put her mind to the training.

DURING the evening meal, Lidai moved her gear out of the room she'd shared with Kenan and Wren. It looked bigger without her hammock or the changing screen. She shared her new room with Tadd. The boy had no interest in her, but she still took the changing screen.

She stood in the middle of Wren's room and looked at his hammock. His boots lay underneath. He'd forgotten them yet again. She heard footsteps coming. She steeled herself.

Wren and Kenan came through the door. She smiled at them, then couldn't hold it.

"Hey Lidai! Why weren't you at..." Wren trailed off as he saw her missing hammock.

The look on his face broke her heart. "Kenan, would you give us a minute?" Her brother nodded, patted Wren on the shoulder, and left. He closed the wood door behind him.

"What's going on, Lidai? You're not going somewhere, are you?"

"No. I'm not. Not from the school. But I can't stay in this room any longer."

"Why not? I haven't pressed you, have I? You know I would never..."

"It's not you."

"You had better not say, 'it's me.' Those are never good words, Lidai."

"Well, it is me. But not like that."

"Well, what is it like?"

"I'm not a child any longer."

"We've been over this. I noticed, remember?"

"Yes. Well, I finally noticed, too."

He took a step closer. "What does that mean? I don't understand."

"Women can't fight while carrying."

"Carrying what?"

"Carrying a child, you lunk. Pregnant women cannot fight. The life of the child would be at risk."

"You're not... not with..."

She punched him in the arm. "No! Of course not!"

"Well, I didn't think you would be. I mean, we've never..."

"No, we haven't."

He reached out to her. She stepped back.

"Lidai, I would never ask you to do anything like that. I want to marry you, in the proper way before the Almighty."

"And I you. Someday. Soon, I hope. I know you would not pressure me. You're not the problem."

"Then what is the problem?"

"I am. I want to curl up with you like we did that night in the inn. Remember? I want to hold you, always. I want, well, other things, too."

"Yes, me too. But I won't let it happen."

"And if you woke with me in your hammock in nothing but my skin, what do you think would happen?"

Wren just looked at her.

She breathed out her nose. "I thought so. I can see it in your eyes at this very moment."

"Lidai, I'm sorry I tease you."

"I love it. Don't stop. But if I don't sleep in my own hammock in my own room, I'll end up in yours."

Wren smiled at her. "Of course, you would. Just look at me! I'm irresistible!"

Lidai laughed through watery eyes. "You are, you oaf. Now, let's bring Kenan back in so I can hug you."

The door opened immediately, and Kenan stuck his head in, grinning. "You know, I can fix this. Just say the word and show me a big sack of coin or one particular booger."

Lidai smiled at him through her tears. "Shut up, you dragonscrape." Then she stepped up on the tops of her man's bare feet and took him in her arms. Wren enveloped her and she leaned into his muscled chest. It smelled like sweat and dinner, but she didn't mind at all.

# Chapter Twenty-Four
# A Scribe's Work

KENAN finished his morning exercises, then dunked his head in a barrel of rainwater. He shook his head, droplets spraying everywhere.

"Hey, careful there!" A female student brushed her sleeve where some stray water droplets landed. She smiled at him and winked with a bright blue eye. Though senior in rank, she was at least twenty years younger.

"Sorry, Jenn. It's a new year, and it's going to be a good day."

She smiled at him even broader. Her teeth dazzled him in the morning light. "1603. It goes by fast. Why's it a good day?"

"Well, tonight I'm going to give Wren permission."

"Really? That's wonderful! I don't remember a betrothed couple in the school ever before."

"Never too late for a first."

"Oh, I agree." She stepped forward, brushing a long lock of light brown hair over her ear.

Kenan frowned at her, and she stopped short. "Oh, sorry," he said. "I was just wondering. Do you think I should ask Lamech first? I didn't think about it from the school's position."

She looked thoughtful, then nodded. "Not a bad idea. He'd probably appreciate it."

She took one last step, too close. "Oh, and I heard him tell a girl to go find you. He wants to see you before breakfast."

"Really? About what?"

She laid a hand on his arm, squeezing his forearm muscles. "Kenan, if you want me tell you everything, you'll need to bring me a bottle of wine."

Right. This was getting out of hand. The woman radiated beauty and interest. He knew this sort of thing happened here between students. Often, so he'd heard. Small practice rooms were hidden away all over the sprawling structure. But he wasn't getting caught up in it. He had interest, but he wasn't ready yet. Her blue eyes looked very much like Anna's.

"Jenn, I..."

"Yes?"

"You're gorgeous. But I'm not ready."

"Oh." She looked disappointed and a little quizzical.

"It's nothing to do with you. You know I lost someone."

"Yes. I know. Too soon?"

"Maybe. You remind me of her. Besides," Kenan grinned wryly. "I can't see you that way after you've dumped me to the floor half a thousand times and given me bruises on top of bruises."

"Bruises on top of bruises? That'd be cruel. You know I'm always careful to give you new bruises." Her eyes sparkled with mischief.

"So kind," He laughed. "Sorry, but you'll have to find someone else to torture with those blue eyes."

She smiled at him. "I accept the challenge. Who do you think I should pick?"

"Lamech," He grinned.

"Lamech?" Her lip curled. "Uh, I don't think so."

"What? Don't like them big?"

"Oh, I like them big, the bigger the better. I don't like them... well, in charge."

"Not into authority figures, huh?"

She shook her head. "I like them big, stubborn, and a little malleable. And a challenge, if possible."

He laughed. "I'm not big and, trust me, I'm not malleable."

She laughed. "No, I suppose not. I'm drawn to the challenge."

"Well, challenge someone else, if you don't mind."

She cocked a well-formed hip and put her hand on it. "In exchange for what?"

Kenan regarded her more serious now. "Why does there have to be an exchange?"

"I'm a merchant's daughter. Life is exchange. Now, I'll leave you alone in exchange for what?"

He looked at this beautiful woman. She could get almost anything she wanted from any man in the city. What could he give her? "How about this. If you ever need someone to back off, I'll see it done."

Her eyes flashed and she touched the green tag hanging from her neck. "You think I can't fight my own battles, Red-tag?"

Good point. "Sorry. Right." He grinned. "How about a stompdragon with a goofy name?"

She glowered at him.

He laughed. "No stompdragon. Okay. Then I have one other thing."

"Yes?"

"I'll be your friend for life. You need help and I'll be there. I need help and you'll be there. I have no siblings my own age. I'm offering myself as your brother."

She eyed him. "That was... unexpected."

"In a good way. Right?"

She stuck out her hand, and he shook it. She said, "Done. Now, about Wren and that archer, are you going to ask Lamech?"

"Yes. When I report to him, which," he checked the sun, "I had better go do." He turned to leave, but said, "Jenn, are we good?"

"Yeah. I just don't like to lose."

"You didn't lose. You won. We both did."

She smiled. "The best kind of exchange."

She was one of the most beautiful women he had ever seen. One day she would make a man very happy or truly miserable. Probably both. He pitied whomever it would be.

It didn't take long to find Lamech in his private office, eating his breakfast at his desk.

"Master Lamech. You wished to see me?"

Lamech never looked up. "Yes, boy. Go to my private dining room. You have a visitor."

"A visitor?"

"Did you not hear me?"

"Thank you, Master." Kenan bolted away before he got the glare. He'd ask about Wren's permission later.

In the private dining room, he found Wren and Lidai talking to a man he hadn't seen in two months, despite the many messages he'd sent. "Secretary Abram!"

"Ah, young Kenan. Please, won't you join us? I brought breakfast from the good master Gruntle. He sends his kind regards. It's still hot and quite good."

Kenan sat. "Thank you! You didn't need to carry it all the way up here."

"Oh, I didn't. Eleenan did. But I sent the lad back. There's so much for him to do."

"Master Abram, where have you been? I've sent word many times."

"Yes, dear boy. I got them all when I returned."

"Returned from where?"

"Ulneer. The trade dispute rages on. Those people have ambition as large as they are." He eyed Wren. "You know, Wren, you look Ulneerian."

Wren mumbled around a mouthful of food. "So I've been told."

"Your words, full of breakfast or not, are still of Blacktree, lad. No accusations from me."

Lidai smiled at them both.

Kenan wanted to know more. "When did you get back?"

"Oh, a week or so ago. Nothing but fires to put out since, I'm afraid. But I came as soon as I could get away."

"Do you have news?"

"Indeed, I do, young Kenan. Yes. I have information, and much of it."

Lidai pointed her eating sticks. "Did you learn it in Ulneer?"

"No, my Lovely Lidai. I did not. By the way, your hair is quite fetching so short."

Wren nodded. "Like it long, too."

Lidai beamed again. "It's growing."

"And so are you," said Abram. "All of you. I had a talk with Master Lamech."

Lidai's eyes bulged. "Really? About us? What'd he say?"

"You know I won't tell you, young one. But it wasn't bad. Well, not all of it. And that's high praise from my old Master."

Wren swallowed his food. "You trained here?"

"Yes, I did. Oh, many, many years ago. Still, I remember a few things I can't do any longer." The older man smiled at them.

Kenan took his bowl of food and pulled off the wooden cover. Fried eggs over nutmash, with bacon laid on top. Steam from the food hit his nose. He missed Gruntle, and his kitchen. "Master Abram, what's your news?"

"Oh, yes. We can eat and talk. I'm sure you'll need to get to classes soon."

Wren nodded as he spooned buttered nutmash into his maw. The school only served unbuttered, so this was a treat.

"Well, where do I begin? Yes, with Blacktree, of course. The first envoy never made it to Blacktree. No one knows what happened to them. The king sent another envoy and an entire platoon of his guard to your home. I understand they're to stay and patrol until called back. Your village is as safe as we can make it."

The three nodded over their food. Kenan was thankful for this news.

"High Councilor Tardain sulked for a week after you stood him up. His Toeclaws cannot reach you here, so do not concern yourself over the likes of him. His gout has flared up again, so he's more irascible than ever."

The secretary's words brought Kenan's head up from his bowl. "What did you say?"

"I said, young Kenan, that the man is in pain and shouting at nearly everyone."

"No. Not that. The Toeclaws?"

259

"Oh, yes. I've discovered he has some influence over a gang on the ground level. They call themselves the Toeclaws."

Kenan stared. "Do they tattoo a toedragon claw on their wrist?"

"Why, yes. How do you know that?"

"Master Abram, these Toeclaws attacked us on our first night in Edeer. They tried to break into our room. Remember my face? It was them."

"Really? Interesting..." The man trailed off in thought.

Lidai deftly used her eating sticks to pluck a bacon slice from her bowl, which she used to gesture. "Why is that interesting?"

"Because, dear girl, there's only one reason I can think they would want you out of the picture at that time. Yes, very interesting. I think I may have cracked open something big."

"What is it?" All three asked at once.

Abram looked at them all. "Well, if the Toeclaws tried to silence you when you arrived, it must be because of what you knew. You clearly had nothing else they'd want. And the only news you brought worth mentioning was the attack on Blacktree. They wanted to delay that news from reaching the Council as long as they could."

Kenan asked the obvious. "But why?"

Abram said, "Could it be to give your raiders more time to operate?"

Kenan pondered this for a moment. "A city gang would have no reason to aid a foreign raiding force. Unless they were paid, or... or ordered."

"Quite right. And who said simple villagers were dull witted? You're right, of course, young Kenan. If Tardain ordered the attack on you, he did it to aid the foreign raiders."

Wren asked, "This could get him in trouble, right?"

"This could get the man hanged."

They all sat looking at each other for a long moment.

Abram cleared his throat. "Enough of this talk. Leave this to me. This is not why I came."

Wren swallowed more of his breakfast. "Why did you come?"

"Well, to see this lovely young woman, for one. But also, to tell you of the generals."

Kenan straightened. "They've met?"

"Yes, though they've not discussed your situation. However, I have, with several of them as we traveled to Ulneer. I happen to be friendly with some of them. We go back quite some ways."

"What did they say?"

"They like your plan. They did point out it's been tried in the past. But not the way you've suggested. They want to talk to you."

"Me?"

"Yes, Kenan. You. All of you. They will meet in a month or two to discuss it themselves. But I think this will work."

"Finally!"

"Quite. But this is not all. I have not been idle despite my absence. Or, should I say, Eleenan has not."

"What did the scribe do?" Wren asked.

"Oh, don't let his scrollish ways and thin frame fool you, young Wren. At my insistence, young Eleenan spent ten years at this very school. He has the black stripe."

"Really?"

"Yes. While I was gone to Ulneer, he accomplished much. First, he studied the history of the White Spiders for many weeks and from many sources. He put together a map, dated and cataloged. This may seem like idle scribe work, but it is not, I assure you. With this information, he determined many likelihoods. The Nephilim does not join on every raid. He attends every third, sometimes fourth attack, though he's not consistent about it. This means he will likely not be on this next raid unless they raid elsewhere for a while.

"Next, he determined the next town to be attacked. Fallingwater, about two weeks to the west. I agree it to be the most likely location for the next raid, based on the pattern Eleenan discovered.

"He was able to approximate the timing of the raid. The town will be attacked in about four months, we think. They'll wait until after the spring rains. Apparently, there is a lake full of spinedragons blocking the way upriver. He thinks they'll wait until the water level drops and the monsters return to the swamps. His deductions seem sound."

Kenan was amazed and said so.

Abram smiled. "Yes, but he wasn't done. The lad took it upon himself to go to High Councilor Enosh, who approved preparations for your plan."

"He did?"

"Yes. Then, Eleenan traveled to Fallingwater with a king's patrol. He talked to the elders there. The town is quietly preparing. He convinced them to move their women out, as many as would go. Some are, well, somewhat stubborn. No offense meant, young Lidai. He left the king's patrol there. Do you know who he chose for this patrol?"

Kenan bounced in his seat. "Well, no. Please tell."

"He chose the Brookstone Brigade, as they call themselves. They're not really a brigade, mind. They're really just a company. But they all have something in common. Each soldier is a blond woman in her prime. He stacked the village with blond woman who can defend themselves. Clever lad! They're all now playing the part of contrite housewives. I'm sure they're driving the men of Fallingwater mad."

The three friends from Blacktree grinned at him.

Abram grinned back. "The boy wasn't done. He also brought the three best scouts he could pick from the king's guard. He chose woodbenders, each of them. He sent them to watch the approach river. Fallingwater is as far upstream as a large boat can go."

Kenan stared at Abram. "We'll see them coming."

"Quite! But there's one more thing. For this, I'm going to have to increase his pay. The lad's sharp. He wondered how they could attack your village with such precision. The raiders knew just which houses to hit. They knew exactly how your men would react. There's only one way to accomplish this, he reasoned. They must have had an inside man."

Lidai gasped. "Asher!"

Wren smacked a fist into his hand.

Abram asked, "What's an Asher?"

Kenan explained. "Asher is not a what. Asher is a man. He came to our village a few years back, in need of help. We took him in and he stayed. He was a bit unpleasant."

Lidai grinned wickedly. "He's not around anymore. He fled just before the raid when we had a... disagreement."

"The logic is sound, and now we have evidence. Multiple evidence, actually. Yes, not only did Eleenan suspect there was such a person, but he also looked for him. It didn't take him long. The Brigade trussed the fool up and lit a fire under him. Literally. It didn't take long to break him. He now works for me."

"You've met him?"

"No, he still resides in Fallingwater. But we've made sure he has turned. A threat and an offer will turn many minds. Midreerians are quite greedy, in general. Slavers are greedy like no others. I promised him things he couldn't turn down."

"Please let me make sure I understand," Kenan said. "We've made the town ripe for a raid, we'll know they're coming, and their inside man will lead them to slaughter."

"It appears so, yes. This is the plan. Your plan, Kenan, with a little help from Eleenan."

"I owe him."

"Quite. You can return the favor later. For now, sit tight here. Master Lamech is helping me build an ambush force. We'll catch the raiders before they hit the village."

"Master Abram, thank you. But if you don't mind, I have a favor to ask of you."

"Ask it."

"Could you talk to Master Lamech? We must be part of that team."

Lidai and Wren nodded enthusiastically.

"Well, young people, I have bad news. Lamech will not allow it, I'm sure, unless his rules have changed. His students are not allowed to serve in combat until they've attained the black stripe."

Lidai almost leapt from her chair. "What! That could take years!"

"It usually does take years, young Lidai. Usually. But I know you're training long hours. And I've heard things. Stay here. Study. Learn. Practice with your every waking hour. You may yet go.

"Now, breakfast is over. Unless my memory deceives me, that chime means you are now late for your first class of the day."

"Thank you, Master Abram. Thank you so much for seeing us."

"Oh, young Kenan, your exuberance is all the thanks I need. Now, off with you. The chime has ended. You're late."

Wren leapt to his feet and bolted from the room without another word. Lidai followed hot on his heels. Abram chuckled.

Kenan remained in his chair. "Master Abram. One more word, if I may?"

"Of course. What is it?"

"Tardain is not as stupid as he appears. He will not go down without a fight. If you challenge him..."

Abram chuckled again. "Thank you for your concern, young Kenan. I have observed High Councilor Tardain for many years. I know how to maneuver around him."

Kenan nodded, rose, and bolted from the room. Master Trime would not be pleased if he kept him waiting.

# Chapter Twenty-Five
# Praying to Nothing

KENAN looked down at the teenage boy on the floor of the small practice room and wondered if he had ever been so headstrong and foolish.

Releasing the boy's wrist, Kenan stepped back. The boy rolled away and hopped back to his feet, his red tag flopping around on his chest.

"Meshek, what did you do wrong?"

"Nothing, Kenan. You're just too quick."

"Am I? Go again."

The boy sighed and rose, shaking his arms loose. Making eye contact, he crouched, resolute. His body swayed back and forth like a darterdragon, probing for a chance to grab. Kenan gave him an opening, and the boy saw it. He could see the openings easily, and he was plenty quick enough. These weren't the boy's problems.

Meshek feinted before darting in, clutching Kenan by the wrist. Then, without hesitation, the boy's other hand balled in a fist and arced in to strike Kenan in the head. Meshek moved incredibly fast. His body twisted with the strike, putting weight behind the punch.

Kenan rotated his body with exaggerated slowness inside the hook punch. Meshek's blow would no longer have force. Kenan dipped again with exaggerated slowness. The hook passed just over his head, and he touched Meshek's forearm. The boy felt it, but it was too late. Kenan locked Meshek's wrist on his shoulder, dipped further under his arm, bent his elbow, and locked his wrist underhand. He did it all slowly. The boy stood on tiptoes and yelled in pain. Kenan stood casually upright. The boy didn't notice Kenan had the edge of his foot in the bend of the boy's knee. A slight twitch with his leg caused Meshek to pile onto the floor.

Kenan still had his wrist. He turned and sat on Meshek's ribcage and locked the boy's elbow in an arm bar.

"Hey, get off!"

"And why should I do that?"

Meshek struggled, but between the lock and Kenan's weight, there was little he could do. Finally, he tapped out.

Kenan released him, rose, and stepped away. Meshek got to his feet again. His face flushed in embarrassment.

"Did I move too quickly this time?"

Meshek scowled at him. "No."

"No. But I still avoided your attack and locked you out. How?"

"You're a sneaky cuss."

"I am. But that's not how."

"Because you know more than I do."

"True. I do. I have more training and more experience." Kenan tapped the green tag hanging on his chest. He'd learned this lesson first from Trime, and again from Lamech during the Trial of Teaching, weeks ago now. And he'd thought the Trial of Acceptance had been hard. "But that's not how I did it, either."

"Then how?"

"How do you think?"

"How am I supposed to know?"

"Young Meshek, you're supposed to figure it out."

"Oh. Why?" The boy paced the room. His agitation dwindled, and his breathing slowed as he thought.

"You can guess why."

"So I'll learn it better."

"Yes." Kenan had been in this same place only months ago. He remembered it with chagrin. Kenan thought fondly of his Masters, grateful they'd put up with him.

Meshek shook his head and looked at Kenan. "I really don't know how. It's like you knew what I was going to do before I did it."

"Ah. Interesting."

"Did you? Did you know before?"

"I did."

"How?"

"How does a human body move, Meshek?"

"Because I will it to."

"Yes. But more physically. This is not a trick question. How does a body move?"

"With muscle."

"And?"

"And skeleton, ligaments, all that stuff."

Kenan nodded. "Right. And a body only moves so many ways."

"Master Trime says that when we're bending."

"True, he does. It's what makes bending work. It makes other things work, as well."

"When I strike, there are only so many ways I can punch you?"

"Correct."

"What, do you just pick one and hope you're right?"

"No. I watch you, your hips, your feet, the way you pull back with your arm. I can see it in your back foot's big toe. I know which strike you'll throw."

"That's not fair."

"Who told you fighting is fair?"

Meshek opened his mouth, then shut it and looked at the floor. Finally, he looked back at Kenan. "Can you mask it? Trick someone into thinking you're throwing one strike when you really throw another?"

"Yes. But not when you're angry. Not when you're rushed or distracted."

"Oh."

"You see?"

"Yes. I come in too hard, too fast."

"Yes! You think you're going to knock my head off, but really you're just making it easy for me."

"So, I should hold back?"

"Not always, no. But you should probe and watch for safe openings."

"Which ones are safe?"

"For now, they all are. In time, you will be taught to look for baiting."

Kenan continued to work with Meshek. He noticed Trime quietly watching from the doorway. The man quirked a grin at him.

Lidai stood on the archery balcony behind three teenage girls and watched them struggle to find their anchors.

One of the girls scratched at her shorn scalp. Lidai smiled at the back of her head.

"I don't understand why he had to cut my hair," the girl whined. "I could have put it up."

"Yes."

"You agree, Teacher Lidai? It's cruel and unnecessary."

"Yes and no."

The girl looked at her, the frown turning into a scowl. "Why did he shear me? Why were we all debased by that, that, animal!"

"Animal, is he?" Wren had done the shearing. It turned out Masters usually only observe Trials of Acceptance, not participate in them. Green cards or black stripes usually do the testing for initiates. The three from Blacktree had been a special case.

"Yes. He's a brute of a man."

Lidai smiled to herself. "Yes. Yes, he is."

The girl saw her look and misinterpreted it. "Do you think this is funny? Why'd he do it? Why did that, that ox cut my hair?"

"Because with a proper anchor point the string will pull loose hair. You'd be bald on the sides of your head within a week." And other reasons, Lidai knew, but she also knew these girls weren't ready to hear it.

Another girl added, "On one side of our head, you mean."

Lidai's dark brown tail swung back and forth on the back of her head where she had it properly bound with a red cord. "No. On both sides. You will learn to loose arrows both right- and left-handed, starting this afternoon."

"Really? Why?"

"Because one day in the future, a true brute of a man may come for you. He won't want your hair, girls. You must be ready, regardless of which direction he attacks."

"Oh."

The first girl scowled. "I could have put it up, like yours is now, in a tail or bun or something."

"Yes."

"He could have just asked."

"Yes."

"But instead, he sat on my back and sheared me like some farm animal!"

"Yes, he did."

"One day I'll stick him with an arrow when he's not looking."

"Not if you can't find your anchor for this range. Trust me on this, you won't want him closer."

"I can handle that man."

"No. You cannot. Not yet and probably not ever. There are only three ways for a girl to drop a big man and none of them are safe."

The girl scratched again at her scalp. "What ways are those?"

Lidai smiled at her. "You can stab him in the back, you can pierce him with an arrow, or you can trip him into your hammock. Here's a hint, girls. Only two of those should be done up close."

The girls all giggled. When the laughter subsided, they grew serious and turned to regard their targets once more.

"It's too far."

"No, it's not."

"It must be 150 feet."

"Well said. That's exactly what it is."

The girl tapped her foot and tried to toss her hair, which looked funny with only stubble. Lidai smiled broader.

The girl spun back to her target with a huff. "Fine." She nocked and drew again, trying to find an anchor behind her neck. It was, after all, a very long poke for her. She placed a thumb on her hairline and sighted down the arrow before loosing.

The arrow fell short, skipping off the boardwalk under the targets.

The girl spun around with defiant victory in her eyes. "I told you. This bow won't reach."

Lidai held out her hand. The girl paused, suddenly uncertain. With a scowl, she handed it over. Lidai drew an arrow from her quiver, nocking and drawing in one smooth motion. At this range, she could bullseye the target without an anchor, but she wanted the girl to see. She drew back into her fourth anchor, thumb forward and tickling the back of her ear. She looked to make sure the girl saw. Then, without taking her eyes off the girl, she loosed. The girl didn't look away either, and the two held eye contact as the arrow flew downrange. The girl flinched at the distant thud of the arrow into the target.

Finally, the girl looked at the target. Lidai knew the arrow had hit dead center.

When the girl looked back, Lidai said, "You must look beyond what you can see, beyond what you know. Do you understand?"

"I'm not sure."

Lidai nodded. "Unsure is fine. At your level, sure is not. Tell me, which was your problem? The long range or what was or was not in your head?"

The girl looked at her feet and bobbed a curtsy. "I apologize for my shortcomings, Teacher. I am my problem."

"Everyone has shortcomings. Wise is the woman who knows she is her own problem. Very wise is the woman who knows her own problems and deals with them."

The girl bobbed another curtsy and took her bow back. The other two watched the exchange closely.

Lidai smiled at them all. "Did you see my anchor? Yes? Good. Now, find your own. Every skilled archer has their own anchor points, each prepared for different situations and ranges. I cannot find yours for you. You are each taller than me with broader shoulders. You must find your own. Continue."

The girls all drew their bows and fumbled to touch one part or another on their head or neck. Arrows flew downrange. Some even hit the targets. Lidai moved from girl to girl, watching and offering suggestions as they practiced.

Maryleen sat on a chair two balconies away, watching. She smiled. Almost.

Lidai saw but didn't let on that she knew her Mistress watched. Maryleen was using the sitting pillow Lidai had made for her chair. Lidai smiled instead at her students and corrected a girl's stance by tapping her knee with the business end of an arrow.

WREN stood in the practice room, stamping his feet into his boots. His arms were dotted with small round bruises, but he was ready for another lesson with sticks.

He had mastered the hammer. The axe came to him so naturally he was besting Master Belroon now. Well, sometimes. He liked the sword, though Master Trime shook his head in disdain. "You use it like an axe. You must cut. Slide. Slice like you're removing violetfruit off the vine." Wren hadn't gotten the knack of it, so he'd been sent to learn stick work from Jenn.

Back in Blacktree, Wren had seen Kenan use sticks with Master Medahal. It'd looked simple then. After three lessons a day for two weeks, he knew now there was so much more to it.

Jenn came into the practice room, her light dress swishing at the jaunt in her step. The pretty woman dazzled Wren with a smile. Wren returned it. She'd had an embarrassing misunderstanding followed by a quiet word with Lidai that left the two acting like darterdragons staring each other down over a dead chipmunk. He didn't like being the chipmunk, dead or not.

Despite that, Jenn and Wren had become friends, of a sort. He was aware of her beauty but thought of her more as a little sister. She reminded him of Haley. For her part, he didn't think she returned the familial feelings. Jenn had some kind of hunger and was far too competitive.

Jenn bowed to the stick rack, took two arm-length sticks, and tossed one to Wren. He caught it, bowed in respect, and twirled the simple length of wood to adjust his hand position.

She raised an eyebrow at him. "Are you ready with that stick, meathead?"

"Yes. Bring it on, woman."

"I'll make you beg for it."

"I doubt that."

"We'll see." And with that she launched into a series of strikes.

Wren parried with his stick. They clacked a beat in the room for what seemed a long time. Then he stepped in, caught her wrist, rolled the stick over, and disarmed her. He stepped back with both sticks.

"Good. You're getting better. Now, can you do it distracted?"

"Distracted, how?"

"Let's strip to the undershift."

Wren stiffened. "Jenn! I don't think so."

"Down to the skin?"

"No! We've been over this. Be serious."

She smiled at him. "A girl can hope. Fine. I'll improvise. Let's go."

Wren went on the attack, though they were soon dancing in offense and defense with sticks clacking. She grabbed his stick viper quick and twisted it around to the side. He knew that meant a disarm. He countered and she changed to a different disarm. He countered again, punching for her head. She ducked under it, stepping inside his reach. He tried to step back, but she had his foot hooked in hers. She stood on tiptoe, craned her neck, and kissed him on the tip of his chin.

His back stiffened, and he fell over backwards. She sat down on his hips, holding both sticks and looking down on him. Her long ponytail swayed as she shook her head. "I've got you."

"Ha! So, you do!" Wren grinned, grabbed her by one upper arm, and easily tossed her across the room. By the time she got to her feet, he was standing and had another stick off the rack.

Jenn's blue eyes shot daggers at him. "This isn't wrestling class where you toss people about. We're not rolling. This is stick class."

"Really? Seemed like kissing class."

Jenn gripped both sticks tightly. "I was just being playful."

"I noticed."

"Okay, then. Let's play." Jenn held up both sticks and circled him. Her eyes were no longer playful. She didn't like being man-handled.

Wren had enough. This girl was his friend. Friends don't kiss. Time to set things straight.

"What's wrong, big man? Lidai got your spine in her hammock? Does she keep it there for safe keeping?"

Wren grinned at her. "Not nice."

Jenn cooed back at him. "Does she let you take it out once in a while? Maybe when she thinks you have need of it?"

Wren stepped forward and swung his stick at her head with the full weight of his arm behind it.

Jenn stepped and dipped under it. Before he could blink, he felt meaty thwacks in turn on his bicep, stomach, and thigh. He danced back but she advanced. Thwack on his forearm. Thwack on his wrist. That one hurt bad. Crack over the top of his head.

Wren fell and rolled away to make distance.

Jenn stood, hands on hips, sticks out to the sides.

Wren growled. "That was low."

"So it was, meathead. What did you learn?"

"Two things. First, I relearned to protect myself from attack, even an attack from those much smaller than me."

She crossed her arms. "And?"

"Never trust a beautiful woman."

Jenn smiled. "Both are true. But you'll pay for that."

The dance began again. Wren defended and attacked. He took several blows. But so did Jenn. She got angry at the hits. She brought her second stick to bear, and Wren was attacked from both sides. He twisted and turned, blocking every strike with his own stick. He gave ground, turning as he did so in the small room.

He watched as frustration built on Jenn's pretty face. Finally, she screamed and struck hard at his knee. Instead of blocking, he stepped over the stick and struck with his. She blocked but didn't notice his foot. When she struck again, he blocked and pulled her heel with his big toe. She fell to the side. He disarmed her of one stick as she went down.

Jenn breathed hard lying on the floor and glared up at Wren through a lock of hair that had escaped its binding ribbon. He stood calmly with one stick held only a palm from her temple.

He smiled down at her. "A strong offense uses initiative, and strong defense brings opportunity."

She blew her hair out of her face and grinned. "That's Master Belroon."

"Yes. Never kiss me again. I don't see you that way."

"I know."

"I don't think you do. My spine is mine. It's my heart I've given to Lidai. Next time, I'll tell her what you did."

Jenn climbed to her feet and challenged him. "I don't fear the girl."

"Then you're not as smart as I thought."

Jenn huffed a little before smiling. "Fine, meathead. No more distractions. Well, not that kind. Be wary, though. I'm sneaky."

"I know."

"Good. Come with me."

Wren followed Jenn to another practice room. This room's weapon rack held blunted bronze swords and a variety of wooden shields.

She bowed to the rack and picked two bronze shortswords off the wall. They both curved with half-leaf blades, sharp on only one side. One was heavier than the other. "Ready?"

"No shields?"

She grinned wickedly. "Do you think Lidai will let you have one?"

Wren gave her a wicked grin in return and took the sword Jenn offered him. He stepped safely back out of reach. The sword reached about as long as his arm.

"Okay," Jenn began. "They're heavier than the sticks. I need to move differently to accommodate them. You may not with your sword but test it. I can get you a heavier blade."

Wren swung the blade around. He could twirl it almost as fast as the sticks.

Jenn walked to the rack and selected a heavier blade. "Try this."

Wren felt the weight and grunted as he swung the blade back and forth. "Wouldn't I be quicker with the lighter one?"

"Yes. But heavier blades take abuse better and penetrate armor. Plus, in combat you'll need to accommodate a heavier weapon than a stick."

He gave her a wry smile. "Really? Never worked with heavy weapons before."

"Shut up."

"How is stick work like sword work?"

"They're the same, meathead. See?" And she attacked him.

Wren twisted and parried. He attacked back and she did the same. Back and forth they went, twisting around each other, striking low and high. Finally, Wren's sword was rolled out and Jenn suddenly had them both. The moves were the same as stick work.

Jenn smiled. "You see?"

"Yes, Teacher. Thank you."

"Oh, knock that off. You teach classes, too."

Wren grinned at her.

"Oh, is that how it is? Feigned respect?"

Wren nodded. "For now. Be wary. I'm sneaky."

Jenn shook her head at him, though she smiled. She tossed him back the sword and moved in for more sword practice. She cut up, down, and diagonally. Wren parried or blocked each one. He found openings, and she danced back. Later, he almost disarmed her of her sword. She taught him how to avoid the edges when disarming.

Swords and sticks weren't *exactly* the same.

BELROON listened from the next room. The boy had learned much, but not how to talk quietly. Still, he had control and skill.

Belroon didn't often teach those so old as Wren. Most of his students were children or teens. A few were young adults. Rarely were they older than sixty. Wren had surprised him with his ability to learn. Belroon thought the man would be difficult to teach. Instead, he'd been a delight.

It wouldn't be long, now, if for no other reason than the boy was wearing him out.

KENAN sat with Wren and Lidai eating their evening meal. He wished he wasn't so picky about his food.

Wren wasn't picky. Wren gulped down whatever was put in front of him. He inhaled the stew like Finch when he found a flower. Finch never cared what color the flower was, only that it would fit in his mouth.

This stew had the color and texture of something that came out Finch's back end. Lidai ate half of it, but now poked at her bowl with her spoon. She looked up at Kenan. "Hey, have you heard back from Secretary Abram? How long has it been?"

"No," Kenan responded. "Not since that last scroll when he told us about the generals. That was, what, month ago? More." The generals had finally met about the White Spiders. The three had been called to the meeting but failed to get the invitation scroll. The messenger had simply disappeared. Lost messengers weren't unheard of in the forests, but not in the city of Edeer. Abram had been in a fit about it. Still, the generals approved the plan, and all was a go. The three of them were to stay at the school and learn.

Lidai rolled her eyes while Wren tipped his bowl to drain the dregs into his mouth. "Stay and learn," she said. "Well, we've stayed, and we've learned. I'm ready for the Spiders. I want to be there when they come."

Wren swallowed the last of his stew. "Me too. I have a score to settle."

Lidai pushed the rest of her bowl over to him. "Exactly."

Kenan swallowed another bite of something that didn't feel right in his mouth. "We need to stay focused on the black stripe if we want to be allowed to go." He shook his head as he said it. They'd had this conversation so many times he could predict what someone would say next.

But Lidai surprised him. "Have you noticed how fast we learn, lately?"

Kenan quirked an eyebrow at her. "How so?"

Lidai pointed with her spoon. "When we teach. I've learned more teaching some of the time than I did when I was a student all of the time."

"Yeah. I noticed that." Kenan fingered his green tag. "I think it's part of the process."

"Yeah. But it's happening fast. Mistress Maryleen found me a new sparring partner because I almost took her to the floor last week. I could have done it. We've only been here eight months. Most of the other students have been here years. And the teachers many years."

"Pushing nine months, now." Kenan waved his spoon back at her. "We train longer than anyone else in this place. We train, what, sixteen hours a day? Every day but rest day. Most of the other students only train a couple hours a day, if that."

Wren waved his spoon, too. It dripped a brown gob of something onto the tabletop. "Some train more."

Lidai turned to him. "Yes, but only for six hours a day, give or take. That's a lot, but we double them and more. We train six days a week."

Kenan eyed the glob on the table. Was it still moving? "I heard Master Belroon talking the other day. I don't think they've ever pushed anyone as hard as they are us."

Lidai's eyes brightened. "Do you think we'll be called soon to the final trials?"

"Maybe," Kenan said. "I hope so. Here, Wren, you want the rest of my... whatever this is?"

Wren didn't even pause as he finished Lidai's bowl. He dragged over Kenan's, then frowned at him. "There's not much left."

"There's enough. Polish it off for me."

"I like the jiggly bits."

Lidai's eyes bulged, and she covered her mouth. To hold back a laugh or her gorge, he wasn't sure.

"What are those?" Kenan asked, poking at the glob on the table.

"I think it's dragon fat," Wren said.

"Who would eat dragon?"

"Meat's meat. I'd eat one. I think we've all eaten one."

Lidai shook her head. "I'd have to be really hungry." Hearing bare feet padding on the wood floor, she and Kenan turned and looked behind Wren.

Tadd ran up to the table. "Master Lamech wants to see you, all of you. He's in the temple."

All three stood and left with the boy. Kenan felt something foreboding come over him. He knew Master Lamech prayed three times a day in the small, school temple. Kenan didn't like it in there. This was a weakness of his master's, and he didn't like seeing it. Besides, what good could come of a meeting in the temple?

Tadd paused at the open temple door. Kenan saw Lidai hand the boy a heel of buttered bread and tussle his hair. The two had become close. Tadd took the tussle like a champion and stuffed the bread into his mouth before sprinting away.

The temple was small. It could stand perhaps two dozen people, though Kenan knew they all knelt during one of their services, or whatever went on in there. Sounded a lot like storytelling.

Two men knelt there now, hands out and palms up. Lamech was one, and he prayed aloud in his gravelly voice to nothing Kenan could see.

"...and Almighty, we give you thanks for all your many blessings, including the three young people you've brought to us. We thank you for their growth and for their service here at this school. We thank you for all this as the father of Enoch, Adam, and us all. We wait for you. Amen."

Kenan looked at his feet. He felt grateful his master thought highly of them. He felt a little disdain at the direction it was pointed. It's a dragon eyeing a leaf in the wrong tree.

Both men stood and turned to the three. The other man with Lamech was High Councilor Enosh.

"High Councilor!" They all clapped fist into palm and dropped into a Jempo bow.

"No need for that, my friends. I count Lamech a good friend, but I was never a student here."

"Bow again, anyway," Lamech barked.

They all complied without hesitation.

Enosh objected as they bowed. "Oh, thank you. But truly, there is no need."

Lamech said, "High Councilor Enosh has news."

Kenan stepped forward. "The White Spiders?"

Enosh's lips pressed into an unreadable line. "Yes. A small party of them rowed up the Fallingwater River a month ago. But then they turned and rowed back down. We don't know why."

"So, they could strike anywhere, at any time?"

"Of course, young Kenan. That has always been true. Young Eleenan, however, believes they were scouting out the best place for a remote staging base. They were spotted rather close to Fallingwater Village. Our scouts remain vigilant and are searching. They may have left for a different village. We'll know more soon, I'm sure. We're sending messengers to other nearby villages and hamlets."

"But that's not why you came. What's going on?" Wren asked. "It's not good, is it?"

"Actually, Wren, that is why I came to see Master Lamech. However, I have more news for you. I'm afraid you're quite right. It's not good. Secretary Abram is missing."

Lidai covered her lower face with her hands, eyes wide.

Kenan hung his head. "I feared this."

"Yes. Young Kenan, he told me of your warning. Abram was, if nothing else, a man of details. Tardain has been throwing spears at every turn and laying traps at every crossroads. I fear Abram was caught in one."

Lidai stepped closer. "What are you going to do?"

Lamech growled. "That is not for you to know, girl."

"Lamech, please. Would you allow me a little leeway, old friend?"

Lamech nodded and glared a warning for his students.

Enosh continued. "I don't think Secretary Abram has been killed, though he may not be comfortable. He is rather valuable to me, you see, and knows much. Even if Tardain can get anything out of the man – which I very much doubt – he's valuable for ransom. Tardain loves nothing more than coin and he knows I will spend a large sum to get Abram back. We will see my secretary again. Rest assured, I will find him."

The three nodded to him respectfully.

Lamech turned to them. "You've heard from the High Councilor. Pray for your friend Abram and heed his advice."

Enosh nodded, his reedy voice humming agreement. "Yes, my young friends. Heed him. Stay and learn. I hear your studies go well."

Lamech grumbled. Kenan knew Lamech didn't like to discuss student progress openly.

Kenan nodded and smiled. "Thank you, High Councilor. We are striving for the black stripe so we can join the team against the raiders."

"You'll have the stripe soon, no doubt. Easy, Master Lamech. I hold no sway over your school. Only, I have faith in these young people from our little village to the south."

Lamech glared at all three of them. "We'll teach them a little more. Probably. If they're not late to their next class."

The chimes sounded distantly.

The three bowed to Lamech and Enosh. Lamech dismissed them and they ran. All three were teaching tonight.

# Chapter Twenty-Six
# Never Alone

FOUR days later, Kenan walked the school's rooms and corridors alone on rest day, completely restless. Wren and Lidai had gone to see Okay and Finch. He should have gone, but they clearly wanted some time to themselves. He understood. He'd give an arm to spend time with Anna.

Better to not think about Anna.

He thought about Abram instead. If the man was a prisoner of high value, would he be locked up? Tortured? Or would he be living comfortably and tempted to betray Enosh? Who had him? High Councilor Tardain, personally? No, he wouldn't be close to it. He'd stay removed and let others make the mess.

He paced up and down the same corridor twice. He walked through the empty Battle Hall, out the main entrance, and around the complex three times.

No, Tardain wouldn't be holding him directly. He'd use the Toeclaws. Kenan didn't know where to find them, but he would. He had to start somewhere. He remembered the tall man he saw in the bowels of the ziggurat, the man with the red beard. If he could find him, then he would find the Toeclaws and maybe Abram.

Was Abram in the city? How hard would it be to smuggle a prisoner out one of the dragonring breaches? Not very hard, Kenan feared.

He cut back through the kitchens, quiet at mid-morning, and found Tadd.

"Hey, Kenan!"

"Hey there, Tadd."

The boy acted eerily solemn around a group of people but get him one on one and there was no shutting him up. "What're you doing?"

Kenan looked at him. Here we go. "Walking."

"Where're you going?"

"Through the kitchens."

"Can I come?"

The sole cook in the kitchen chopped nuts at a bench. He looked at Kenan, pleading with his eyes.

Kenan sighed. "I suppose."

Tadd fell in beside Kenan, looking up at him as they left the warm room. "Where did Wren go?"

"With Lidai, to go see our dragons."

"Okay?"

"Yes, and Finch."

"They're good dragons."

"Mostly."

"They eat a lot." The boy said it like no one could possibly know dragons eat a lot.

"Yes, they do."

"What're you doing today?"

"Walking."

Tadd snorted. "You said that, but I thought you were just talking down at me. Just walking? That sounds boring."

"It helps me think."

"What're you thinking about?"

"Stuff."

"What kind of stuff, Kenan?"

"Adult stuff."

"It's not about some girl, is it?" The boy frowned at him and looked a little disgusted.

"Not this time, Tadd."

"Good. Lidai is okay, mostly, but the rest are gross."

"They're not gross, Tadd. They're just different from boys."

"I guess," Tadd said, though he didn't sound convinced.

They passed through the main dining hall and across the archery balcony. Tadd jumped up on the rail, spread his arms to his sides, walking along it. The drop would kill him if he fell the wrong way, but he never did.

"Tadd, one of these days you'll fall. Then what?"

"I don't know. I'll catch myself. Or see heaven, I guess."

"Do you think there's really a heaven?"

"Yeah. Lamech says so. He's never wrong."

"I suppose you could be right." Kenan scratched at his short beard.

"Of course, I'm right. Lamech says I'll grow up to be a great warrior."

"Probably."

"But I have to grow taller first. How tall do you think I'll get? As tall as Wren?"

"Could be. How tall were your parents?"

Tadd hopped off the balcony rail and eyed a basket of apples left from yesterday's archery practice. "I don't know. I don't remember them at all."

"I'm sorry, Tadd."

Tadd trotted over to the basket and helped himself to a couple. They were old and more than a little wizened, but he didn't seem to mind. "It's okay. I remember my switch-parents, but they died in a fire."

"I didn't know that. Tadd, that's awful."

The boy shrugged his shoulders. "It happens. But then Lamech took me in. I've been here most all of my life."

Kenan realized the boy was talking about four or five years at the school, at most. He smiled at his perspective but felt sad. He didn't remember his own father, who'd died long ago.

Tadd interrupted his thoughts. "Where are we going?"

Kenan looked around. They'd left the school balcony and walked across a timber bridge towards the city center. "I don't know. Just for a walk through the city. That sound okay?"

Tadd rubbed his chin as if to consider whether it was acceptable. "I guess. Can we go down levels? I'm not allowed to the ground level without an adult. Can we go there?"

"Sure. Maybe we'll go visit Okay."

"That'd be great! Wren is training him to be a battle dragon, did you know? Okay will be a great battle dragon. I bet he'll charge enemy shield lines and trample swordsmen as if they were darterdragons."

"I think you're right."

"Someday, I'll have a dragon. Not a shielddragon. Or some stupid stompdragon. Oh, sorry Kenan. Finch is great and all. But I'll have something big, with teeth. Big teeth. Do you think I could have a mawdragon? Do people ride mawdragons?"

"I don't know, Tadd. I think they're too bad tempered. But then again, people ride hissdragons."

"Nah. No one could ride a hissdragon."

"Have you ever seen a hissdragon?"

Tadd nodded, eyes brightening. "Yes, once. A trader brought one into the city in a big cage. I remember Lamech being very upset that the breach guards had let it through."

"I imagine. What'd it look like?"

Tadd smiled at the memory. "Huge. It had tons of teeth. I mean, great big teeth! Not as big as a mawdragon. Wren says mawdragons have massive teeth."

"He would know. Did you hear the hissdragon hiss?"

"Not at first. At first, it just laid there. I think maybe it was sleeping. But its eyes were open. Creepy. A crowd gathered around, and so the merchant poked it with a dragonpike. That woke it up. He poked it a bunch of times, and it got all angry-like. It hissed and screeched at everyone. It grabbed the dragonpike and broke the end right off. The man got all scared. I don't think he was very smart."

"I bet."

"Yeah. It twisted and turned all about in the cage, thrashing the wood bars. One of the bars broke and everyone got scared and ran away."

"Did you run away."

"No."

"Really?"

"Well, yes. At first. But I hid behind a cart and watched."

"What happened?"

Tadd turned sour. "Nothing. Lamech came back with a bunch of guards. They shouted at the trader, and he took it back out through the breachgate. I guess there's a rule or something. I never saw it again."

"Yeah, there's lots of rules here. Well, rest assured, people do in fact ride hissdragons."

Tadd brightened. "How do you know?"

"I've seen it. Twice."

"Woah, really?"

"Yep."

"That's awesome. Tell me all about it!"

So, Kenan told the boy an abbreviated and much-edited story about what happened on the Flat in Blacktree. As he talked, they descended steps and ramps, finally coming to the ground level.

They were near the Trenchbreach Gate on the east side of the city and had a couple miles to walk to get to The Goosedown Filler. He looked forward to seeing Gruntle. They moved off, winding their way through the busy streets.

Tadd almost vibrated with excitement at the concept of riding a hissdragon. "How come they don't just turn and bite the rider?"

"I don't know. Maybe they'd already been fed?"

"They stand so tall. How does a rider mount?"

"The hissdragon squats down. There are stirrups hanging from the saddle, just like a shielddragon or any other mount, really. The rider steps on the hissdragon knee and can reach the stirrup."

"Oh. That makes sense. Do they have reins?"

"Yes. But instead of a bit, like an ox, they were looped around the back-most teeth of the lower jaw."

"Really? How come the teeth don't cut the leather?"

"I'm not sure. Maybe the teeth aren't as sharp back there? I saw one up close, but I wasn't checking for chafing of the reins."

Tadd laughed. "You're funny, Kenan."

"Most people don't think so."

"Well, I do. And my opinion is the only one that counts."

Bemused, Kenan had to ask, "Why's that?"

"Because it's mine." And Tadd nodded as if that was that.

Kenan smiled at the boy, then looked ahead as they walked. For a rest day, the streets bustled with people. Most of the city didn't observe the rest day like Lamech and the school did, but often there were fewer vendors about.

Today, however, vendors hawked their wares, women led processions of children all holding hands, and men pushed barrows and rolled barrels. Stompdragons, shielddragons, and more pulled carts, wagons, and sledges in every direction. Dark clouds loomed in the west. Rain was coming and the people of Edeer bustled to get their chores done in the dry.

A small man in a green overshirt walked across the street ahead. He carried a horn cup of something liquid and a sword hung at his belt. Something about the way the sword hung on his hip caught Kenan's attention. It was farther back than most wore it. He watched the man as he crossed the street and entered a side street. Just before he entered the narrower street, his face turned enough for Kenan to see it. Kenan recognized the man. It'd been dark, and he could be mistaken. But it might be him.

What to do? Should he follow? No, he had Tadd with him. But what if the man led him to something important? This was his opportunity. He could wander the city for days without luck, and here this man walks past him on his first trip to the ground level in weeks.

Kenan made a decision. "Tadd, what would you do if you had to follow someone?"

"What do you mean?"

"What would you do if you saw someone, and it was important to follow them unseen."

"Oh, easy. Mark his appearance from behind. Blend in. Follow at a distance."

Kenan looked down at him. "You've done this before."

"Sure." The boy nodded sagely. "Girls are always up to something. It pays to know."

"You follow girls?"

"Of course. A man has to know what his enemies are up to."

Kenan smiled at him. "Okay. There's a man I want to follow."

"The one you were just watching. The skinny guy."

Observant boy. "Yes. Him."

Tadd's face lit up. "Yes! Let's do it."

"I thought you'd say that. It might not be safe."

"Is anything really safe?"

"Good point. You're smart for your age."

"I know."

"Not too modest, though."

Tadd nodded, as if considering Kenan's words. "I'll work on that."

"Good. But not now. Let's follow him. At the first sign of trouble, you bolt. You hear me? I can take care of myself, but you need to get taller first."

"You sound like Lamech."

"Well, Lamech's always right."

Tadd frowned at him but couldn't argue against his own words. "Okay."

"Promise?"

The boy made his customary solemn face. "I promise."

"Good. Let's go."

They turned into the side street. People moved in and out of shops lining the street, which were mostly cloth traders. Kenan and Tadd jogged, weaving through the crowd to make up lost ground. At the next intersection, they stopped and looked around. Kenan caught sight of the man's head as he turned onto another street up ahead. They jogged again, then approached the next corner carefully.

This narrower street had far fewer people. The man was ahead, walking with a purpose. His sword scabbard bounced against the back of his thigh. Yes, it was definitely him. Kenan and Tadd slowly followed.

Kenan reached down for Tadd. "Take my hand."

"What? No, that's for girls. Why?"

"Because if he looks back, he'll see a father and son, not two people following him."

"Oh. Okay."

The boy's hand felt warm, almost hot, in his palm. Tadd started to skip.

Kenan nodded. "Good idea."

Tadd started to whistle to himself. He was out of tune.

Kenan shook his head. "Too much."

The man stopped, looked in all directions, including right at them. But he didn't seem concerned as he turned down an alley. Kenan marked the spot as they approached, then walked by the alley mouth without looking.

Tadd looked. After they passed, Kenan asked him, "What'd you see?"

"It's a narrow alley. Lots of crates and stuff. The man was just standing there, cleaning his nails with a hand knife. He looked at you but went back to his nails."

"He was checking his tail."

"What's that mean?"

"He's going somewhere secret. He wanted to be sure no one was following him."

"Oh. Smart."

"Yes."

Tadd shook his hand free. "What're we going to do?"

"Wait."

"Boring. But okay."

They took seats on the steps of a shabby-looking inn. Tadd took out his hand knife and started to clean his own nails. Kenan had never seen him clean his nails, which were perpetually filthy. For that matter, he'd never seen him clean anything. "What're you doing?"

"I'm waiting. I'm being inconstituous."

"Inconspicuous."

"Yeah, that."

Kenan grinned. A rain barrel sat next to the steps with a wooden dipper floating on the surface of the water. He borrowed it and took a drink. He offered some to Tadd.

"No, thanks." Tadd flinched. "Ow."

"Did you cut yourself."

"No."

"Uh huh."

Tadd huffed and wiped his finger on his shirt, leaving a thin blood stain. It blended in with all the other stains. "Do you think we've been here long enough?"

"We just got here."

"I'm bored."

"I can tell. Eat an apple."

Tadd took one out of a little belt pouch but didn't eat it. "So, what're we going to do."

"In a minute, we'll walk back by the mouth of that alley. I won't look, but you will. You'll tell me what you see."

Tadd took a juicy bite of the little apple. It sounded half rotted. Kenan asked, "Is that any good?"

"Yeah." Tadd took another bite.

"It sounds gross."

Juice rolled down over Tadd's chin, leaving a clean streak. "It isn't. I like them like this."

Kenan drank some more water while Tadd finished the little apple and tossed the core into the street. The boy wiped his hands on his overshirt, put his hands on his bony knees, and sighed contentedly, finally falling still.

Kenan counted five heartbeats before Tadd started fidgeting. Kenan looked at him. "Got ants in your undershirt?"

"Kenan. No. I'm not wearing an undershirt. Let's go."

"In a minute."

"Why?"

"We need to give him time to decide no one is following him."

"Oh."

They waited on the step. Tadd fidgeted.

Finally, Tadd asked, "But how does he know how long to wait?"

"I don't know."

"How long will he stay?"

"I don't know."

"So, he could be gone already."

"I suppose."

"So, let's go now."

"Tadd, give it a moment more."

Tadd sighed, took two more breaths, and said, "Now?"

Kenan got up. "Fine."

Kenan took his sticky hand again, and they walked back by the mouth of the alley. Kenan looked the wrong way, but Tadd took a quick glance.

After ten paces, Kenan asked, "Well?"

"He's not there."

"Okay. Now, we need to be quiet."

"I can be quiet."

"Yeah, when your mouth is closed."

Tadd shot him a glare, and Kenan smiled at him to take out the sting. They both slowly entered the alley.

Crates, barrels, and debris lined both sides of the narrow passage. A single path littered with trash wound through it all. They saw no one as they crept down the path, Kenan in the lead.

Kenan saw a barrel stave and stooped to pick it up. It felt solid, wider in the middle, and about the length of his arm. He used it to flick debris out of his way, checking for traps and anything stinky.

A mischief of rats chased a darterdragon, this one smaller than a chicken, out from under a stack of empty crates. It chirped as it ran, clearly afraid of the rats pursuing it.

Tadd whispered, "I didn't know there were any..."

Kenan shushed him, and Tadd fell silent.

They neared the end of the alley where the way was blocked by a solid stone wall behind another stack of empty crates. From behind a pile of barrels, a large man stepped into the path. His eyes were small and set close together in a square face framed by a square beard. He wore a dirty brown overshirt, leather vest, and held a stout hammer in his hands. His arm muscles bulged as he thumped the hammerhead into his open palm.

"Who are you?" The man demanded.

"I'm Kenan Blacktree. Who are you?"

"I'm here to tell you to leave."

"Where's the small man in green?"

"Who?"

"He came this way."

"You're mistaken. No one came this way. I can't help you."

Kenan grinned at the man. "Oh. Terribly sorry. But you promised."

The man looked confused. "What did I promise?"

"Not you. The boy. He promised."

Tadd began, "But, Kena..."

"You promised." Kenan kept his eyes on the man with the hammer.

"If I have to."

"Now. Go."

Tadd turned and sprinted back down the alley. The man's confusion deepened.

Kenan explained. "I had to get the boy to leave so he wouldn't see what comes next."

Decision replaced confusion in the man's dark little eyes. "Too bad. He'll never know what happened to his father."

"I'm not his father, though I'd be honored."

"Whatever. You didn't leave on your own. Now you'll die."

"Everyone does, sooner or later."

"Sooner for you." With that, the big man lifted the hammer over his shoulder to strike.

The motion seemed ridiculously slow to Kenan. He brought the stave up and poked the end into the man's throat just below his Adam's apple.

The man's eyes bulged in shock. The hammer never came forward. He dropped it to put both hands to his throat as he tried to draw breath. The hammer fell with a thud.

Kenan whipped the barrel stave up, around, and into the man's groin. The man's knees buckled, and he dropped to his knees on the filthy alley floor.

Kenan whipped the stave around again to hit the man on the temple. The man's eyes rolled into the back of his head, and he fell forward. Kenan caught him and eased him down. The man still breathed, but Kenan judged he'd be unconscious for a while. A strike like that to the temple was no small thing.

Kenan took the man's belt pouch. When someone found the man, they might assume Kenan was a thief and nothing more. Kenan checked his wrist. Sure enough, it had the Toeclaw tattoo.

Kenan looked around. He saw no door, but did see crates, barrels, debris, and a pile of straight boards. There must be a door somewhere. Where did the path go? Besides, no one sets a guard without something to protect.

Kenan eyed the boards again. They were straight, knot free, and ugly to him. Who used a straight board? But the way the pile lay kept his attention. It wasn't quite right, and the path led to it. He looked the pile over. Reaching out, he grabbed the edge and lifted. The entire arrangement rose smoothly on leather hinges. It wasn't a pile of boards but rather a hidden door. He listened but heard nothing. Carefully, he lifted it all the way up and past the balance point. It stayed open.

A set of stone steps led down to a room below ground. He'd had no idea people would build a room under the ground floor. Yellow lamplight flickered somewhere inside, and he heard male voices talking quietly.

Raindrops began pattering on the roofs above. A fat drop landed in the part of his hair. The first drop of a storm *always* seemed to find the part in his hair.

He knew he should get help. He knew it wasn't smart to go in alone. But he wanted information, and he didn't care who stood in his way. He could do this. He knew how. And he wanted to. Besides, why get wet?

With a grim smile, Kenan slowly and quietly made his way down the uneven stone steps.

The stone wall of the building foundation stretched ahead on one side and a wood partition wall ran on the other, making a short hallway. Ahead, he could see a low wood wall with a couple of arrow slits in it. A crossbow stood against the far wall, glowing in the lamplight from a room to the side. He eased his way forward.

One of the male voices said in a raspy voice, "'Ow much longer do we 'ave to wait?" The Midreerian accent made Kenan's adrenalin flow.

Another answered. "Not much longer, I'm sure. He'll be here."

"'E better be, Rillain. We need to be out of this cursed place and through the Eastbreach in time to reach camp before dark."

Rillain said, "It's not so bad here. Have some more wine."

A third man with a Midreerian accent said, "It's not bad wine."

The raspy voice said, "True. Better than we brought with us, but not as good as Mordeerian ale. That stuff will curl your chest hair."

Rillain asked, "Really?"

"Oh, yeah." The man's raspy voice drew out the word. "We 'ave some right good ale with us back at camp. But the Commander won't let us 'ave much. Say, can we take some of this wine back with us?"

"Of course, Cols," Rillain answered. "There's room for a barrel on the wagon."

Kenan remembered Cols.

Cols rasped, "There's room for two."

"Well, you'll need room for our gift."

"What gift?"

Kenan could hear the smile in Rillain's response. "We have a gift for you to take back to camp. The prisoner alone will be no fun for you on your journey back. But we've brought you someone much more to your liking, I think. Harrel, go fetch her."

Kenan heard footsteps go up a wood staircase.

Cols said, "'Er? You 'ave a girl for us?"

"A token of appreciation," Rillain said. "Your last score was worth quite a bit, and our patron's share was more than expected. He wants to show Gharan how much we appreciate this arrangement."

Footsteps came back down the wooden staircase. A female voice whimpered behind a gag.

Cols seemed pleased. "Ooo, a blond. Most generous of you lads."

"Yes," Rillain said. "Old enough for good wholesome fun, but young enough to fit into a barrel."

"And if she cries out at the breachgate?" Cols asked.

"She won't. I have some seeds for her. Enough for both of them. They'll be too stupefied to say anything for many hours."

"'Ours?" Cols asked. "'Ow many 'ours?"

Rillain answered, "Oh, probably all day."

Cols said, "Cut 'er dosage. Give 'er enough to get through the breachgate but not enough for the day. We'll 'ave first go with 'er before we reach camp."

"Good idea," said the other Midreerian. "I'll go first."

Cols said, "No, you won't. I'm lead. I go first."

"Okay. I'll go second."

"Of course you will, you stupid lump. There's only the two of us."

"Easy, my friends," Rillain placated. "I'm sure you'll both have a good time. As you say, Cols, you're lead. I'll leave it to you."

Kenan remembered Cols from long ago, next to the women's bathing pool. They weren't just Midreerians, but White Spiders. His anticipation grew.

Rillain sounded local. Kenan didn't hear any other voices.

Three men. No, four. Someone brought the girl down and didn't go back up. He could take four men, alone. Probably. Kenan made his decision and stepped around the corner into the lamplight, leaning on his barrel stave. "Hey there."

The men started where they sat in simple, wooden chairs. The three men sat around a small table covered in lamps, candles, bottles, and cups. Two more men sat in chairs on the far wall, and between them sat Abram, stripped to the undershirt, bound, gagged, and head lolling. A thin, yellow-haired girl, perhaps just under twenty years old, stood in her undershift in the middle of the room, gagged and hands bound in front of her. She looked terrified. A sixth man, Harrel from the window at The Goosedown

Filler, stood in his green overshirt beside the girl with his sword sheathed far back on his belt. He held her in place with one hand clamped around her upper arm.

Not four to one. Six to one. Kenan hesitated but didn't shy back.

The men at the table jumped to their feet. Rillain, tall, lithe, and with a neatly trimmed, red beard cut to a point, stared at Kenan and said, "You."

"I get that a lot." Kenan recognized Rillain.

"I remember you," said Rillain. "You were in the ziggurat, with him." He hooked a thumb towards Abram.

"Yes. I'm Kenan Blacktree. He's why I'm here." Kenan pointed at Abram as well, who now lifted his head and looked at Kenan with bleary eyes. The secretary's cheek had been slashed, and his beard crusted with old blood. He cracked a weary smile.

"That so?" asked Rillain. "Where's Heen?"

"Heen the Hammer?"

"Yes. Wait. How did you know we call him that?" Rillain's smooth voice sounded refined.

Kenan grinned. "Just a guess."

The men guarding Abram stood, hands on sword hilts. The two Midreerians also grasped sword hilts. No one wore armor, but they all carried swords.

Kenan smiled at them all. "You left your crossbow by the door."

Cols snarled, "We don't use crossbows, tree rat. Besides, we won't need one." The man stood shorter than he remembered, but the scars all over his face and arms were distinctive.

"We'll see about that." Kenan stepped forward, twirling the barrel stave in one hand.

The girl broke free from Harrel and ran for a corner, unknowingly providing a useful distraction and delaying the other men. Harrel grabbed for her but missed. He stopped and turned back to Kenan. He stood closest so he reached back and drew his sword. He met Kenan with a diagonal overhand slash. Kenan, however, was ready.

The combat once more seemed painfully slow. Kenan angled out of the way of the blade and thumped the man's lead kneecap with the stave at the same time. Harrel grunted and fell, sword clattering across the stones of the floor. Kenan struck him in the head with the end of the stave. Harrel went quiet.

Kenan stepped out of reach just in case Harrel's head was harder than it looked. He pointed at the girl cowering in the corner. "You can't keep the girl, either. I'm taking both."

The Midreerians hesitated. They knew danger when they saw it. The two men guarding Abram weren't as experienced. They both charged Kenan, polished bronze blades shining dully in the lamplight.

Kenan stepped to the side to put his back towards a wall and, at the same time, parried a sword thrust from the first man. A slashing blade from the second man came next, which he ducked under. He delivered him an uppercut with the stave to the inside of a thigh, then a reverse strike to the man's head. The stave whooshed through the air as it spun. The man went down with a groan.

The first man recovered from his lunge and swung from the side. Kenan spun into a back stance and blocked the blade with the thick part of the stave, which was cut nearly in two. Kenan kicked the man just below the knee and released the stave. In a blink, he snatched up the man's sword hand. A quick turn, and the man's wrist dislocated, leaving Kenan with the sword. He slashed the man across the eyes. He fell back with a spray of blood and a whimper.

It took less than ten heartbeats. Three men writhed and groaned on the floor. Now it was three to one. Kenan knocked the stave from the sword edge where it clung. The wood clattered to the floor.

Rillain stepped forward. In one hand he held a long, thin sword made of steel. Brass and steel formed a protective basket around his sword hand. "Enough!"

Kenan nodded. "I agree."

"You do?"

"Yes. Give me the man and the girl, and I'll leave without harming anyone else."

"No. You misunderstand."

Kenan grinned at him. This was fun. "Enlighten me."

"You've taken down enough of our men. I'll do this myself, in the name of my father." As he said the last sentence, Rillain's eyes flashed orange and red.

Kenan nodded. "Oh. You're one of those."

"Fought a Nephilim before, have you? Rare, to have survived the encounter. Or did he breathe into you?" Rillain sidled closer, sword extended. "He did, didn't he?"

"Not sure, but I know you all have a problem with personal space." Kenan stepped back. His bronze sword was wide, short, and heavy compared to Rillain's elegant blade.

Rillain nodded. "He must have. But it matters little. I can't let you leave this place. Time to die." Rillain lunged.

Kenan was ready. He dodged to the side and swiped down near the base of Rillain's sword in an attempt to disarm him. Rillain's blade swept down from the blow, but he didn't lose his grip. Instead, the blade twirled around, whistling, and flicked in again.

Kenan parried it and lunged. Rillain stepped to the side and slashed. Kenan rolled to the side, away from the blade, and came back to his feet with sword ready.

The man slashed across the eyes still cried out where he lay. Boots tramped on the floor above.

Rillain allowed him no rest. He came in, blade flicking left, then right. Kenan parried, dodged, and blocked. He used the motion to hide his free hand drawing his hand knife from his belt. He held it reversed in his palm.

Kenan's patience paid off. Rillain left an opening. Kenan took it, slashing in with his sword. The opening was a trap, of course. When Rillain blocked and countered to close the trap, Kenan was ready and dodged under and in close, as he'd planned. He slashed with this hidden hand knife, attempting to cut Rillain across the thigh above the knee. It should have been a crippling cut, but Rillain somehow saw it coming and adjusted his stance. The knife scored a shallow slash in the thigh muscle.

Rillain danced back, eyes flashing deep red now. "Oh. You are quite good! I recognize the style. You're a student of Lamech."

Kenan shook his head. "Who? I don't know this Lamech. Is he ugly?"

Rillain smiled. "You fight like him. His speech is all over your tongue, boy. Now, let's finish this." Rillain moved in.

Kenan had never dropped his sword point. He used it to deflect the steel blade. Rillain came in fast, his eyes flashing orange and red. The steel blade flicked with incredible speed. Kenan parried and gave ground. The blade came closer. He parried again and again. The Nephilim was too fast. Kenan gave more ground and took a shallow gash on his shoulder. The blade flicked in again, then again. Kenan parried and dodged until his back foot hit a wall.

Rillain's eyes flashed. "I have you."

"Not yet, you don't." Kenan threw his hand knife underhand.

Rillain caught the knife by the handle. His sword never wavered.

Kenan thought he might have gotten himself in trouble this time.

Kenan heard a twang and felt a sharp pain in his chest. He looked down to see a small bolt sticking out of his left chest muscle. The fletching had been dyed red. It should have hurt more than it did, but the pain left almost immediately.

"Hey," Kenan said to Cols. "You lied."

Cols held a miniature crossbow in one hand. The device still pointed at Kenan. "Yeah. I do that. So, 'ow does that feel, tree rat?"

"It doesn't hurt at all."

The Midreerian nodded. "It shouldn't."

Kenan felt a numbness spreading across his chest and down one arm. Uh oh.

Rillain objected. "I wasn't done with him."

Cols rasped a short laugh. "You are now. No time to finish your fancy duel, and your light show don't impress me none."

To Kenan, Cols said. "We coat these with the venom from a spider we find in the southern reaches. They're big and white. Nasty things. A bite will drop a man in moments. Kill 'im in less than an 'our."

Kenan's face felt hot. "I don't much like spiders."

Cols chuckled. "Don't worry. There's not much venom on that little bolt. It ain't going to kill you."

Blood pounded in Kenan's ears. His sword slipped from numb fingers. It clanged onto the floor, the sound louder than it should have been. He stumbled towards the exit, but the other Midreerian moved to block him, bronze sword out and ready. The man sneered, reminding Kenan of his brother, Nehamane.

Men pounded down the wood stairs from above. Reinforcements. Kenan looked around, the room lurching a little in his wavering vision. Abram had fallen to the floor. The girl crouched in the corner with a stool in her hands held over her shoulder to strike at anyone who came near.

Cols dropped the small crossbow on the table and hooked his thumbs behind his belt. "You can fight, I grant you that, tree rat. But we're taking our prisoner and our gift back with us."

The other Midreerian objected. "We should take him, too, Cols. I recognize 'im. 'Ee's the one 'oo gave Commander Char a 'ard time in that village last year. What was it called?"

Cols looked Kenan in the eyes and rasped, "Blacktree. Yeah. I remember you from long ago." He winked a beady eye.

The other man said, "Yeah, that's it. Good 'aul from that place. Lots of blonds."

Kenan felt nauseous, and his knees were getting weak. There were no windows, no other doors. There was no help. This was the end. Kenan had to know. "Where's Anna?"

Cols frowned at him. "'Oo?"

"Anna. Tall. Blond, wavy hair. Really pretty."

"Oh, yeah. I know the one. 'Ard to miss 'er."

"Where is she?"

"Oh, she's dead."

Kenan gulped, tasting bile. "What?"

"Dead. She fought back, and we 'ad to end 'er, though not before a good time was 'ad by all. And I mean all of us."

Kenan stared. "No."

"Yes. She stopped screaming, after a while."

The room spun around Kenan. Men groaned on the floor. Harrel awoke and cursed, one hand going to his head, the other to his knee. The reinforcements stood ready with swords out. Too many.

Cols clucked out of the corner of his mouth. "I can see how you bested Char. I thought 'e was going soft on you people, but now I see it was you.

Well, you've got silty skill, tree rat."

Kenan looked at him. The edges of his vision grew hazy. Something hit him in the back of his knee, and he fell to the floor.

"Don't you worry, tree rat. We won't be killing you just yet. 'Ey, Rillain, we'll take 'im, too. Got room for one more barrel?"

Rillain stopped glowing. He grunted, cut Kenan shallowly down the sternum with the tip of his sword, and sheathed it. "We'll make room for him. Just promise me he'll suffer."

The room faded to gray. He felt Rillain kneel beside him and use his finger to open the wound on his sternum, rubbing his finger on the bone. It should have hurt, but he didn't feel a thing. Rillain lifted his bloody finger and drew it across Kenan's forehead. "Enjoy Midreer, boy. You'll wish I killed you here and now, before they're done."

As Kenan lost consciousness, his last thought was to wonder why he ever thought he could do this alone.

In the black, he heard a small, still voice whisper. "You're never really alone."

# Chapter Twenty-Seven
# The Cost of Independence

TADD bolted down a busy ground-level street through the rain. People hurried to finish their tasks before everything got completely wet and covered in mud. Dragons hooted and roared as their drivers slapped them with reeds. Carts bounced over uneven paving stone and through puddles. Everyone rushed to get into a building or to a dry zone.

Under the great trees of the city, rain didn't fall evenly or in sheets. Enormous leaves above directed water into concentrations of fat drops and rivulets called dowsings. Suspended canvas tarps caught many dowsings to direct them into cisterns for use by people, privies, and lifts. Others splashed against rooftops and balconies above, only to be formed into dowsings again as the water fell through the trees.

The water that eventually reached the ground soaked some areas while others were left dry for a time.

So it was that Tadd jumped a puddle to land on dry stone and left watery footprints as he ran into a dry area. The dry zones contained many more people now. Some milled about, looking for a way to proceed around the dowsings. Others stopped and set up canvas tarps right in the middle of the street. The area wouldn't stay dry. As the rain intensity and wind changed, so did the dowsings. In the end, everything without a roof would be wet.

Tadd was already wet. He bolted through a small square surrounded by taverns and past an idol to some god or another. He ran directly through another dowsing and out the other side, ducking under a man holding hands with two wives. He bolted in a shop door, past a display of fragrant round pastries, and rolled under the fat baker's reaching hand. The man moved far too slow. Tadd was through a door, through the kitchen, and out the rear before the baker finished yelling at him. He left behind a trail of water through the shop.

He sprinted down an alley. The round pastry he found in his hand looked good. Should he save it for later? No, he'd eat it now. If he was caught with it, he might get in trouble.

He knew another shortcut and took it, stuffing the last of the pastry in his mouth. It'd been filled with mincemeat. Delicious.

He wasn't supposed to be on the ground level without an adult, but he often found himself down here anyway, usually by accident. He knew the way. He ran down the alley, out onto a street for twenty paces, then down another alley. He ran towards several boys who looked like they were up to something bad. They lined up to bar his path.

Tadd never slowed as he threw one of his knives at the biggest one. The boy saw it coming and yelled, "Oy!" The big boy tried to fall back but wasn't quick enough. The butt of the knife handle hit him between the eyes and bounced back. Tadd deftly caught it out of the air, ran up the chest of the falling boy, leapt, and was past them all without so much as a giggle. His face was solemn as he ran, though he didn't realize it. He had a mission and meant to complete it.

He sheathed his knife and pocketed the iron ring he'd found on the falling boy's finger. It probably wasn't worth much. But maybe he could sell it to pay for the pastry? He should do that. Yes, he would. Later. Someday.

He ran down another street and broke out into the Southbreach Flat. A huge dowsing showered down through the air to fill the large pool in the middle of the Flat. He turned without slowing towards The Goosedown Filler.

WREN stooped in the stables of the inn and picked up the last leaf of the stack. The fresh leaves, each the size of a tabletop and nearly a palm thick, weighed more than Lidai. He didn't have any trouble picking them up, but he was glad the chore was done. He slid the last leaf over the door to Okay's stall. The shielddragon, nearly fully grown, munched on the pile of greenery.

Finch ate far less than Okay these days. He only needed one of the leaves. Okay ate a dozen a day.

Lidai sat up on the half-door of Finch's stall, scratching the dragon between the shoulders with the end of her bow. She looked beautiful at all times, but the pretty orange flower in her hair brought out the color of her hazel eyes. The way she cocked her head at the stompdragon took his breath away as he approached.

Finch looked up at her while he happily chewed the juicy vegetation. Green drool glopped to the floor and Lidai recoiled. "That's disgusting."

Wren stood leaning on the door next to Lidai, looking down on Finch. "It sure is."

"I don't know what Kenan sees in this thing."

"I'm not sure he sees anything in him. He doesn't seem affectionate towards him."

"So, why doesn't he sell him or something?"

Wren shook his head. "I think he's keeping him in case he needs him."

"Oh." Lidai looked thoughtful. Did she know her nose crinkled a little when she did that? Absolutely adorable. She adjusted the flower in her hair, and Finch hooted. She smiled at the dragon and plucked it out. The dragon accepted it eagerly.

The rain pounded down outside the rear of the stable in a dowsing. It slowly moved off towards the dragonring.

Wren watched it go, then took her hand in his. Her fingers looked small in his calloused hand. He said, "I think he's right."

"About needing Finch? Why?"

"Something is coming. The White Spiders will return. We'll have to go meet them."

"I agree," she said. "Something is coming. Or, apparently, someone."

Tadd dashed into the front of the stables and ran towards them. His dripping overshirt clung to him.

Lidai hopped down off Finch's half-door. Okay stuck his beaked snout out over his own half-door and grunted at everyone.

"Tadd," Lidai said. "What's going on?"

Tadd breathed hard and had clearly been running for some time. The boy's round eyes looked at the two adults and Okay. Were those crumbs pasted to the skin around his mouth? Tadd gasped out between breaths, "It's Kenan."

The tone and the words straightened Wren to full height. "What about him?"

"He's in trouble. He saw a man he wanted to follow. So, we followed him to an alley. Only, there was another man there. Kenan told me to bolt, so of course, I did what he said."

Lidai nodded to the boy. "Uh huh. How long did you stay?"

"Well, long enough to hear him get in trouble with a bunch of men. But then a wagon came, and I had to leave."

Wren's brow wrinkled in concern. He gave Lidai a look before asking Tadd, "Can you take us to him?"

Tadd frowned at him. "The question is, can you keep up?" And the boy turned and darted back out into the drizzle at the front of the stable.

Wren looked at Lidai. He saw the agreement in her eyes. They both sprinted after Tadd.

They passed the dowsing showering into the pool on the Flat. The noise drowned out their footsteps. Various dragons in harnesses and saddles swarmed the pool to drink the fresh water. A huge stalkdragon lay full length in the wide pool. Wren reminded himself to never drink from that pool again.

Tadd waited for them at the edge of the Flat. When he saw them coming, he turned and ran off. They followed as quickly as they could.

Tadd waited for them several more times as they made their way across a quarter of Edeer. Wren was glad he'd been working on his stamina. He needed it to follow this little dragonscrape of a boy.

On one street, a small flock of goats got in their way. There was no sign of Tadd. Lidai used her bow to swat a path clear. "Why didn't you bring some kind of weapon?"

Wren shrugged as he pushed through the herd. One tried to head-butt him on the thigh. He snatched it up under an arm. "Didn't think I'd need one."

"No one ever thinks that."

"Sure, they do. Before a battle, they do."

She cleared the goats and turned to him with arms folded across her chest. "Put that thing down."

Oh, she was feeling a little imperious, was she? He didn't like to fight with her. He knew just what to do. As he reached her, he scooped her up in his free arm and kissed her full on the lips.

She and the goat both struggled and squirmed. "You oaf, put me down this moment!"

Wren dropped the goat, who bleated and ran for the rest of the herd. Lidai he kept in his arm.

"I said, put me down!"

"Well, I put down one cranky goat."

She stiffened in his arms. "Did you just call me a goat?"

He smiled down at her until something sharp pricked him in his bottom. "Ow! Did you just stab me again?"

Lidai landed on the wet paving stones with lithe grace. He caught a flash of her ankles as her dress hem flared.

She glowered up at him through wet locks plastered to her face. She tucked away a blade into her sleeve. "You know better than to man handle me. I am not a goat!"

Wren rubbed the spot on his bottom. "I noticed."

A young voice said, "You two have the strangest flirting."

Lidai turned to Tadd. "And exactly how, young man, do you know what flirting is?"

"A girl told me that's what it is. I'm pretty sure that's all girls know how to do."

Wren grinned. "I think you're right, Tadd."

Lidai moved for her young roommate, but the boy danced out of reach, turned, and sped away. Wren grinned at her. She glowered back and raced off after Tadd. Wren followed. The little stab wound didn't slow him down. She'd barely broken the skin.

People were still on the streets, mostly between dowsings. Dragons pulled carts, and men worked barrows. Few women were about, but men moved in every direction. An old shielddragon with bunted horns pulled a big, four-wheeled wagon full of barrels, and a slabdragon pulled a two-wheeled wain stacked high with big green leaves. Tadd's slight form wove between them. Lidai and Wren were forced to go around.

Tadd finally turned into a narrower street, looking back to make sure they saw. Wren pointed, "There!"

Lidai said, "I see him." They sprinted to follow.

They passed a bunch of cloth shops before turning down an abandoned street, empty of people who were avoiding the dowsings. Water fell from roofs above, pounding down on them. They tried to avoid the worst of it, but it was no use. They were thoroughly soaked.

Wren appreciated the sight of Lidai running in front of him in her very wet and clingy dress.

She didn't even look over her shoulder as she called back, "Stop looking at me."

"How do you always know?"

"I have a special power. Now, where did that little scoundrel go?"

"I'm right here," Tadd said. Indeed, the boy stood next to an empty crate at the mouth of an alley, looking at them solemnly. The alley looked just like all the other alleys they passed.

Wren asked, "Did Kenan go down there?"

Tadd nodded.

"How do you know it's the right one?"

Tadd said, "Because of the core."

"What? What core?"

"The apple core."

Sure enough, a small apple core sat in a shallow puddle near the entrance to a nasty looking tavern. Wren shook his head. "Sometimes, boy, I'm not sure about you."

Lidai poked him in the stomach. "Leave him alone. He did great." She reached for her quiver and pointed with several arrows now in her hand down the dark alley. Rain dripped off the eves, but the worst of the dowsing seemed to have moved on. "Now, Tadd, have you been down there?"

"Yes. Kenan and I went down. But then he sent me to find you."

"What's down there?"

"Rats." Tadd shuddered a little. "And a darterdragon. I didn't know there were uncaged darterdragons in the city."

Wren nodded. "Nothing keeps them out."

Lidai stomped her foot, impatient with them. "What else did you see?"

"Just crates, barrels, and a man with a hammer."

Wren nodded. "Right. We get the picture. Let's go."

Tadd stepped toward them. "Can I come?"

Wren shook his head, but Lidai said, "Yes. Watch behind us."

Tadd nodded with his serious expression and followed them. Wren took lead, seeing many footsteps in the mud of the alley.

From behind, Lidai said, "Wish you had a weapon now?"

Wren scooped up a crate to use as a shield. "Maybe."

"Can't say I'm right?"

He chuckled. "You're right."

"Thank you."

"I just don't want you to stab me again."

Lidai laughed softly. It sounded like beautiful music to him.

It didn't take long before they reached the end of the alley. In the gloom of the storm, they saw stone walls, stacks of empty crates, and a pile of boards. The many boot prints went right up to the pile of boards. Wren immediately noticed how it was all one piece.

He said, "Here." He avoided a trap at the natural pull point and pulled instead on the true handle.

Lidai jumped back as he lifted the door to the side. She had an arrow nocked and pointed it down into the basement. "How'd you know that was a door?"

Wren shrugged. "Seemed obvious."

She scowled at him again, but he ignored it. A light flickered down below.

The door stayed open. Wren led the way down with his crate held in one hand before him. Lidai followed, ready to loose. Tadd followed, watching behind.

They soon saw the little wall with the arrow slits. Wren could see how it could be used to loose arrows at anyone trying to get into the basement. Thankfully, no one was there.

They eased up to a corner in the wood partition wall. Wren peeked around. A single candle burned on a table. Half a dozen chairs stood haphazardly on the floor and against the walls. Stacks of crates sat under a set of stairs going up to the main floor. Blood had been spattered and pooled in places on the floor. A lone man lay dead in a corner. He had a cut across both eyes, and a stab wound puckered his neck. Blood pooled around him.

Lidai whispered, "What happened here?"

Wren whispered back, "I don't know." Someone walked across the floor above them. "We're not alone in this building."

Lidai kept her bow pointed at the stairs, but no one appeared. Wren saw Tadd had a knife in his hand, reversed with the blade hidden up a sleeve. His wide eyes were glued on the corridor leading back to the hidden door. Good lad.

Wren studied the blood markings. Over there was where the dead man was slashed across the eyes. That spray of red was the slash. That smear through the blood was him getting dragged over to the wall before someone ended his life. A mercy, perhaps. Wren looked around some more. Someone had been cut here. And there. And someone lay here in a small puddle of blood. He could see where they had been rolled over.

"Wren," Lidai hissed quietly. "What are you doing?"

"Shush. Give me a moment."

Lidai's eyes opened wide. "Did you just shush me?"

Wren shook his head. "No. Now, shush."

Tadd shook his head but kept watch.

What was that line of blood? It didn't look like a dribble from a wound. The line was really a series of arcs made by something. What would make that mark? Something with an edge. Something round, rolling, with an edge...

"Tadd."

The boy turned to him. Wren noticed, for perhaps the first time, the intelligence there in the boys eyes. "Didn't you say there were barrels in the alley?"

Tadd shrugged. "There were."

"But there's not now."

"Nope."

"And a wagon came."

"Yes."

Lidai eased the tension on her bow. "Didn't we see a wagon of barrels not far from here?"

The three all looked at each other. Moving quickly from the room, they bolted back down the corridor and up through the hidden door. Outside, Wren eased the pile of boards back in place. Tadd and Lidai had already run down the alley. He tossed the crate into the mess and caught up to them on the street.

Tadd pointed. "This way is faster." He turned down a narrower street. Lidai followed, so Wren did as well.

They emerged on a main street through the city that angled in towards the Trenchbreach Flat. As the storm let up, people emerged from their homes and shops. The street wasn't choked with people, but it would be soon. They ran across the stone pavers as fast as they could in the gray, post-storm gloom.

When they reached the Trenchbreach Flat, they skidded to a stop on their heels.

Lidai softly gasped. "Oh no."

The Flat was completely clogged with people, dragons, market stalls, and vendors. Even at his height, Wren couldn't see past the first slabdragon pulling a sledge of what could only be dragonstool.

Tadd said, "Dragonstool."

Lidai looked down at the boy with a shake of her head, but Wren only nodded. How would they find them in this crowd?

He saw a rain barrel. It had a top with a small clay pipe leading down into it through a hole. Above that, a second-floor balcony hung out over the Flat. People streamed down the street behind them, pushing them into the Flat.

"Lidai, we're going to get pulled into the Flat with the people. We need to move. Go over there to the side. I have an idea." Wren didn't wait for her to do as he said. Honestly, he didn't think she would. She rarely did.

He hopped up onto the barrel, then leapt upward. He caught a balcony support in one hand. In moments, he pulled himself up and stood on the balcony.

Even at this height, parts of the Flat were still not visible. The tops of the plates along the backs of slabdragons obscured some areas. Still, he spotted four shielddragons pulling wagons. None of those wagons contained barrels. He crawled over the railing, maneuvered to hang from the edge of the balcony, and dropped the rest of the way to the ground.

To his surprise, Lidai and Tadd stood where he'd told them. He fought the crowd and reached them. "They're not here."

Lidai asked, "Do you think they made it out already?"

"Doubt it. The Trenchbreach gate floods during a rain like this. They need a drainage pipe. Anyway, maybe, if they got there before it filled. But I doubt it."

Lidai thought, which crinkled her adorable nose. "They're either out, on a side street, or still back on the street where we passed them. In the rain, maybe they got stopped. Let's go back along that street, whatever it's called."

Tadd said, "Mahalalel."

Wren looked at him. "What?"

Tadd shrugged. "Mahalalel Street."

Lidai looked at the boy. "You've been down here alone, haven't you? We'll talk about it later. Let's go." She made good on her words and ran off. Wren smiled as he followed her.

They cut through a side street and hit the original street, apparently called Mahalalel Street. He looked back towards the Trenchbreach Flat but saw no wagon of barrels. "They're still ahead."

Lidai nodded and moved onwards.

No street of Edeer ran straight. They wound around enormous trunks and roots. As they ran along a curve, they entered another dowsing. Lidai scowled up at it, getting water in her eyes. "I thought the storm was passing." She tested her bowstring.

Wren kept moving, passing under an enormous root that arced up and back down into the ground. "Its last gasp, I'd guess."

Ahead, a small crowd stood under eves and balconies watching a man covered in a hooded cloak struggle to put a new wheel on a cart full of firewood. Another two men worked to help him. A fourth man, the owner of the cart by his frayed, straw hat and shabby clothes, stood by and offered suggestions through a wide smile. A stompdragon hitched to the cart licked water off the paving stones.

Behind them, the old shielddragon with bunted horns stood placidly. A man standing on the front of the wagon yelled at the beast and whipped at it with a long reed. The dragon stood still and took little notice.

Neither did Wren. For standing on the wagon next to the screaming driver was Cols. He wore a cloak with the hood up. His scarred arms crossed on his broad chest, though they weren't red now. He frowned down at the man with the cart. Then he looked up and made eye contact with Wren.

Recognition passed between them. Cols smiled.

Wren said to Lidai, "Kenan's in big trouble."

"How do you know?"

"Because that man," he said, pointing, "is a White Spider."

The woman never even paused. Almighty, she was so quick. In a split second, she drew an arrow and launched it at the man. It ripped through the dowsing, tracing a line in the falling water.

It should have struck Cols in the throat, but he dodged to the side. The arrow took him in a shoulder and went clean through.

A woman screamed. Several more followed suit. Chaos erupted on the street as people scattered in all directions.

The rain slowed and stopped.

Wren dashed forward towards the stompdragon. The owner of the cart ran out of the way and into an alley, turning back to look one last time with a smile on his face. The three men working on the cart threw back their cloaks and drew bronze swords. The Toeclaw tattoo stood out against the pale, damp skin of their sword hands.

The stompdragon never stopped licking the wet stones. Wren jumped, running up the neck of the stompdragon and along its back. He saw a single arrow rip in and through the necks of two of the men. Both fell bonelessly to the ground. The third man charged Lidai. Good luck to the fellow.

Wren jumped to the cart and snatched the woodman's axe he'd seen on the wet firewood. He leapt for the shielddragon's face. The animal was old but not dead. Its eyes widened at the sight of a man flying through the air at it, and it lowered its chin in a protective posture. Perfect.

Wren landed between the big, brow horn bases. The tips had been cut off years ago. He scrambled up the shield, hidden from the people on the wagon. He crested the shield, set a foot, and jumped for the animal's back. It shifted, but he adjusted. He'd spent his entire life living in trees, and he knew how a shielddragon moved.

The wagon driver held leather reins, but he dropped them and reached for something at his hip.

Wren sprinted down the tail slope of the beast and jumped for the wagon. The axe in his hand was ready for attack or defense.

He didn't see Cols. The wagon driver fumbled with his wet cloak. Behind him, two men with crossbows crouched on the barrels. One man loaded his crossbow while the other lifted his to point directly at Wren. Wren held the head of the axe across his chest and hoped the Almighty might spare him.

An arrow ripped in from an angle and took the crossbowman in an eye. His head snapped back, and his body followed. He triggered the crossbow and with a thump, the bolt shot straight up into the air.

The other crossbowman looked up in time to catch Wren's axe across his neck. The head fell down between the barrels loaded into the wagon. Hot blood fountained briefly.

Wren twisted from his crouch on the barrels, sweeping the axe around. The driver wrenched his sword free just as the axe sheared through his leg below the knee. The sword dropped from his spasming and falling body. As the man hit the barrels on his back, Wren buried the axe in his chest.

Two men sprinted away back down the street. Wren pointed and screamed, "Lidai! There!"

Another arrow ripped past his head and took one of the men in the back. He staggered but both men ran on and into an alley.

Wren twisted about, scanning. He was the only person alive on the wagon. Two men lay next to the cart. Another lay in the street with a knife handle sprouting from his open mouth.

Lidai stood on a second-floor balcony. How'd she get up there? She scanned the area looking for targets. The only other person in the street was Tadd, who approached the man with the knife in his mouth. The boy squatted down and pulled the knife out. He went to wipe it on his own shirt.

"No, Tadd. Use his shirt."

Tadd nodded at him and did as instructed.

Wren retrieved his axe from the driver's chest. The man groaned. Apparently, he wasn't dead yet. He would be, soon. Blood pulsed out of him. Wren wiped the axe on the crossbowman with the arrow in his eye. Wren shuddered. Something about eye wounds made his stomach clench.

Wren hopped down off the wagon and went to the shielddragon. He took him by the nose horn and made soothing noises. It looked a little agitated. Old or no, a stampeding shielddragon wouldn't help anyone.

Lidai called to him. "Did you see where he went?"

Wren looked up at her. The breaking storm allowed a single ray of sunshine to land on her. Almighty, she was radiant.

"Stop that, oaf. I said, did you see where he went?"

"Who?"

"The White Spider."

"Oh, he went back down the street. He was the shorter one."

"Dragonspit. I hit the taller one."

"That's okay. They both have arrow holes. They won't get far. Look. Here comes the city guards."

A troop of a dozen city guards ran up in formation. The sergeant, a tall man with a scar across his face, issued a command and they all formed up and drew their swords to face Wren, Lidai, and Tadd.

The sergeant pointed at them. "Drop those weapons!"

Lidai put away her arrow and leaned on her bow. Tadd dashed to the side and disappeared behind a vendor stall full of green ribbons and decorative cords. The guards looked grim at the sight of all the bodies. Blood ran down the street and into gutters.

Wren nodded and dropped the axe into the cart of firewood. "We're students of Lamech. We just stopped a kidnapping."

The sergeant looked at him. "Uh huh." He looked up at Lidai. "You, there. Girl. Drop the bow."

Wren flinched. Lidai scowled down at the guards but laid the bow carefully on the balcony floor.

"Listen, friend. I can show you we're truthful. We stopped a kidnapping of one of our friends."

The sergeant looked around and made a decision. He turned to his men. "You three, go get that girl. If she gives you any trouble, bind her. Otherwise, treat her like your little sister. Rear rank, form a perimeter. No one comes in or out. If this man tries to leave without me, cut him down. You three, with me."

"I'm Wren Blacktree."

The officer frowned at him. "I'm serious."

"Uh huh."

"Listen, boy. I don't care how big you are, we'll cut you down if you so much as twitch. Understand?"

"Got it. Here, take my hand knife. It's the only blade I have. Please, follow me." Wren handed him the knife and led them to the rear of the wagon. A dozen barrels were bound on the wagon's flat bed. Wren pulled a line to release the binding and took down a barrel. It bumped off the ground. Something sloshed inside.

The sergeant waved his sword a little. "That doesn't sound like a person."

"Easy, sergeant. No, it doesn't." Wren pulled the bung and wine poured out.

As one of the guardsmen righted the barrel to keep the wine from draining, Wren pulled down another barrel. He knew immediately it was empty.

Wren smiled at the guards. "Why one barrel of wine but the other empty?"

The sergeant nodded to one of his men. "Get up there and check them all." The man sheathed his sword and climbed up on the wagon.

He tossed down two more empty barrels. Then he said, "Ug."

"What is it?" asked the sergeant.

"A head."

"What kind of head?"

"A man's head."

The sergeant looked at Wren and kept his sword ready. Wren shrugged.

The man above said, "This one has something solid in it."

The sergeant ordered, "Open it. Carefully."

The guard removed the top of the barrel. "Cabbages."

The officer frowned. "Cabbages?" Cabbages were transported in crates. No one would waste a good barrel on cabbages.

Wren looked blandly at the sergeant. "Might I suggest the barrels in the middle?"

The sergeant nodded and the guard in the wagon tested their weight. "This one has something solid as well. Heavier than cabbages. There are some holes drilled in the side."

"Let's see it, son."

The guard opened the barrel, stiffened in surprise, then eased the barrel over on its side. A young girl lay curled in the bottom, snoring softly.

The sergeant leapt into action, Wren all but forgotten. The other guards soon found Kenan and Secretary Abram in their own barrels.

Lidai walked around the barrels and bodies lying in the street and stood next to Wren. Someone had draped a cloak around her shoulders. She nodded back at the axe on the cart. "You found a weapon, I see."

"Yeah. They seem to be lying about."

A guardsman pulled Kenan out of a barrel and laid him on his back on the wagon bed. "He's okay. They're all okay. Looks like maybe they were drugged."

Wren nodded. That made sense.

But Lidai rolled her eyes. "Of course, they were drugged. It's the only way to get them out of the city without them making lots of noise."

Wren smiled down at her. "Easy, pretty flower. They're just doing their jobs."

"No, that won't work. You're not going to call me 'pretty flower.' Find something else." But she looped her wet arm through his and leaned into him.

KENAN lay on the hard wood of the wagon bed. He couldn't move a muscle and he felt like he should be sleeping. He had been sleeping, but now he was awake, struggling to regain his mind. His head felt so fuzzy. He wanted to go back to sleep.

He tried to lift his head. It didn't respond. He tried a hand. Nothing. So, he relaxed and concentrated on breathing deeply, which usually helped him fall asleep. Sleep would be good.

He heard his sister. "At least he'll be alright."

Wren spoke next. "He'll probably have a wonderful headache when he comes to."

"Serves him right."

"Lidai! You can't mean that."

"I do. He's always going off on his own. He gets into trouble. Then he gets us into trouble."

"Well, that's his way. He does things alone."

"His stupid way is stupid pride. It endangers you. And me. For Almighty's sake, he took a boy down that alley! They could have both been killed."

"You're right, of course. But still, don't be too hard on him when he wakes up. He's had a rough day."

"He brought that on himself. It was stupid to take them on alone."

"I agree. He was stupid. You're right."

"Say that again."

"He was stupid."

"No, the other thing."

"You're right, honeyface."

"Not on your life, big man. Honeyface? I won't let that one stick."

Wren chuckled, but Kenan felt his heart fall down to his spine. Stupid. Yes, he was stupid. Prideful. Arrogant.

Something inside pulled him down. He deserved his barrel and a future of pain. He deserved a life without Anna, his dead love. She would never smile again. He had earned it all with his foolish independence.

God Almighty hated him for sure.

THE smiling cart owner sauntered down the soggy alley. He whistled for a minute, then stopped as he turned down an even danker alley. Very little light reached the alley floor here. The air hung thick with the smell of rodents and nightsoil flung down from windows above. A shadow stained a stone wall just right. He slid into the shadow, but he couldn't stop smiling. He looked forward to this.

Two men struggled by the mouth of the alley. They looked injured.

The taller man stopped. "This way," he breathed, and leaned against the stone corner to steady himself.

The other man held a shoulder. Blood seeped down his overshirt. "No. I'm 'eaded that way," he rasped. "I 'ave my own way out."

The man named Harrel nodded, limping into the alley alone. He staggered and fell against the wall but pushed himself up again.

With effort, the cart owner pushed his lips down to hide his white teeth. He needed Harrel to come close. He could be invisible when he wanted to.

Harrel worked his way down the alley. He limped for some reason. Was that an arrow sticking through him? Yes, the man had been pierced. A sharp arrowhead protruded from below his breastbone, just off center. That girl knew how to use a bow. He wondered how far the shot had been.

Harrel was in pain, but that's not why the cart owner had been asked to come here. Why was not something he wondered about much. He trusted. He always had.

This wasn't his usual role. But he would play any role or do any task asked of him. Being part of the plan made him smile.

"Who's there?" Harrel gasped. He was close and must have seen white teeth.

"Just me." The cart owner stepped forward.

"Who are you?" Harrel breathed. His eyes held suspicion, but his body slumped. He leaned against the wall and pressed his face against the stone.

The cart owner's smile widened as he said, "Harrel, how do you feel?"

Harrel leaned against the wall, clutching his knee. "Cold. Tired." Harrel's voice was weak. "Ain't you the guy with the firewood?"

The cart owner nodded. "I'm sorry for you, Harrel, but you're near your end."

Harrel closed his eyes and shuddered, falling to one knee. "I don't want to die."

The cart owner squatted down with him. "I know. But I have good news. You only need to do it once."

Harrel just looked at him. Well, it did seem like small consolation.

The cart owner asked, "What do you think comes after, Harrel?"

"How do you know my name?"

"God Almighty knows everything."

"Are you him? God?"

"No. But He sent me here to help you."

"Help me with what?" Harrel coughed blood onto his lower lip and chin.

"Help you understand something."

"What," Harrel coughed again. "What do I need to know?"

"You need to know God is real."

"God Almighty?"

"Yes." The cart owner smiled broadly. "And He cares about you, deeper than you could possibly know."

"I..." Harrel sat down, leaning heavily on the wall now.

"Yes?" asked the cart owner.

"I don't believe you. God doesn't care."

The cart owner's smile fell. "I'm so sorry, Harrel."

Harrel glared at him and coughed weakly. "Will I be judged? I heard I'll be judged."

"You will. Everyone will."

"Will God accept me?"

"That is not my place. I don't know. But He's a perfect judge."

Harrel shuddered again.

"A time will come, Harrel, when men will know their place with God. God himself will come to them. God himself will live in them. Until then, we can live righteously, have faith, and love God."

"I, I don't know," Harrel wheezed. "I don't know if God will love me. I've been bad."

"You have little time left, Harrel. But you can always start, right now. Love, have faith, and do what is right. Do it for God."

Harrel reached out and the cart owner took his hand. Harrel nodded slowly, then breathed out, "There's something."

"What?"

"Something I must tell you."

"Say it, Harrel, if you must. But relax as much as you can."

"Okay." Harrel slumped further and breathed a few times, his chest barely moving. "Fallingwater."

"Yes. It's been raining."

"No. The town. Fallingwater."

"I've heard of it. What about it?"

"They're coming."

"Ah. The White Spiders. Why did you tell me?"

"It's..." Harrel's eyes lost their focus. "It's the right thing to do." Harrel rattled out one more breath and died.

The cart owner released Harrel's hand, stood, and smiled down at Harrel's corpse. "Only our Father can know, but perhaps we will talk again one day. I hope so, Harrel. I hope so."

The cart owner smiled upward and spoke to God for a moment. He walked back down the alleyway. When he got to the street, he turned and walked towards the Trenchbreach Flat. He must go to Fallingwater.

The streets grew busy again. A woman passed him, returning his smile briefly. She towed a young child by the hand. The boy broke free and approached the cart owner, smiling up at him.

He stopped and smiled down at the boy before squatting down to see him eye to eye. The mother put her hand on the child's shoulder protectively.

"Ah, young man. How are you this fine day?"

The boy-child squinted up at the dripping leaves above them. "It's raining."

"Oh, I know. But that's also good. Hey, what have you got in your hand, there?"

"I've got a bug."

"What kind of bug?"

"A beetle. A yellow one."

"Oh, can I see?"

"It'll get away."

"No, I promise it won't."

The boy-child opened his chubby fist, and a little yellow beetle extended its legs to walk around on his palm.

The boy smiled up at the cart owner. "I like bugs. Do you like bugs?"

"I do. Are beetles your favorite?"

"Yep. What's yours?"

"Oh. I love dragonflies. Have you seen any?"

"Not today."

"Well," the cart owner said, standing. "I'm going to go find some. Love the Almighty and love your mother."

The mother gave him a quizzical look before turning the boy away. They moved off, the boy looking over his shoulder at the cart owner, his hand clutching the beetle. The cart owner waved as he moved towards the Trenchbreach gate, a smile on his face. He knew he must go to Fallingwater. He had another part to play in the great plan.

# Chapter Twenty-Eight
# A Wheel of Cheese

ANNA stood on the roof of her castle prison and planned how to get into the room below the ground. They called it a vasement. She might have wondered why they needed a room below the ground, but she didn't care. She just needed to get down there, to the vasement.

Standing on the rooftop between two lofty towers afforded her a panoramic view of Mordeen and the Morderain river valley. The small city stretched a mile to the west and curled down to the Morderain River. Even after a month, the place seemed strange to her eyes. Every building was made of stone or mud with clay tile roofs. Every building was on the ground. The ground!

The great city held many thousands of people. A tall dragonwall surrounded Mordeen, not that it needed it. Any wild dragon coming within sight of Mordeen would either be flying or would be chased down and captured for human use or killed for sport.

Vast fields of cropland or dragongrass extended out onto the fertile river plains and up into the low hills on both sides. Far to the north, the tops of giant trees showed gray in the distance. Sometimes she came up here just to stare at them.

On the southwest corner of the city, the giant stone wall extended a short distance into the Morderain River. Protected by a shorter wall, the waterfront extended in stone docks out over the waters of the wide river. Ships and riverboats tied at the docks bustled with activity. The men looked like ants from this distance, carrying crumbs into their tunnels.

Anna watched all this and traced her planned route out. She would avoid the docks. She would get what she needed from the vasement, gather up her rope and the food she'd stashed in her room, cross the castle courtyard in the dark, and go over the wall to the east. There, fields grew crops right up to the shallow wall moat, and a road led down through the fields to the little outlier village called Mud Hole.

But she wasn't going to Mud Hole. Once over the wall, she'd leave tracks towards the little village, before escaping northwest, through the fields and hills. She'd heard bladegrass grew for miles to the north, but eventually the land sloped down and the great floating forest began. If she could make it to the trees, she could survive. She knew how to gather food in the forest. Kenan could walk the trees. She would learn. She would carefully navigate them northward. It would be a long journey, but if she kept heading north, she would eventually find Edeer and home.

Standing on the roof, she thought about where Gharan kept what she needed to escape. They were in a small brown sack, or maybe a jar. She had searched the castle at night not long after she got to Mordeen, Gharan's own city. She hadn't found them. They must be in the vasement.

She had a plan. She knew how to get out of the castle. She knew how to get out of Mordeen. She knew where she would make them think she'd gone, and she knew where she would actually go. The voyage back to Blacktree would be arduous, she knew, and dangerous. But if any woman could make the trek home alone, it would be her. She would tell Kenan where her sisters were, and they'd return to rescue them.

But first, the vasement. She had to get what she needed from the vasement.

Anna left the roof. A stairwell lined with bows and quivers of arrows led her down multiple floors. Her guard was there.

"Hello, Yarro. Still don't like heights?"

Yarro just looked at her, which was disconcerting enough. He must be the ugliest man she'd ever seen. His skin shone dark with old oil and his naturally dark complexion. His black hair was matted to his head, curling and greasy. He didn't like her or his task to guard her. He definitely didn't like that he couldn't have her. She saw it all in his sharp, dark eyes.

Anna swayed down the hall. She felt Yarro's eyes on her and was amused. It was the only way she had to hurt him back.

She descended another stairway to the main floor. As she strolled through the main dining hall, she saw Haley. Her sister sat quietly near the fireplace with two other women who'd been here when she'd arrived. None spoke. They sat quietly, expressionless, staring at the fire.

Anna hadn't spoken to Haley in a week. Her sister wouldn't respond. There was nothing for her to do. They all greedily drank the water in the red skins. Nothing else mattered to them, anymore.

Not to Anna. It was true, she loved the water. But she had something else, something better.

As she walked the hall, she glanced over her shoulder. Yarro still watched her. The man wore a rough overshirt, over which he wore a bronze breastplate. Heavy leather guards wrapped his forearms and a thick flap of hide hung down over the backs of his hands. His belt held a bamboo stick. She eyed the stick.

"Yarro, have you seen Char lately? Haven't seen him for a month or more."

Yarro said nothing.

"Is he on a special mission? I heard he went north."

Yarro scowled at her more. She knew he wouldn't answer the question, but she could prod him.

"I bet Atarra misses him."

Yarro grunted and followed her. He could talk, and often wasn't nice about it. But he was usually quiet when in the castle.

Anna strolled up to the privy door. Yarro stepped up right behind her.

Anna looked over her shoulder at the ugly man. "You coming in with me, Yarro?"

Yarro just looked at her.

"No?"

The man stepped back.

"As you wish." Anna stepped into the privy and closed the door.

She lifted her dress and undershifts, then sat, listening for Yarro. Sure enough, he moved down the hall. The man didn't like to hear a woman in the privy. How strange for a breeding master.

As soon as he was out of earshot, she stood and looked down into the privy hole. It was narrow but opened into a much larger box below. The pit drained by a small hole in one corner. There was space down there for several people to stand shoulder to shoulder. Why they'd be down there in the night soil and fluff-leaves used for wiping was not a concept she dwelt on for long. She had other priorities.

Anna bent down further, putting her head through the hole. Yes, right there. She could see the small door with the little wooden latch down near the bottom. Anna pulled her dress up over her head and hung it on a peg. Her overshift and undershift followed.

Bare, she sat on the privy with both feet dangling in the hole.

She wiggled her hips to get through the opening. Her chest and shoulders provided a greater challenge, but she wriggled until she made it through. She hung inside the privy vault, hanging on only by her hands on the privy seat. Her feet kicked in the air a couple of feet over the soiled floor.

She let go and dropped with a little splash. Her feet slid and she sat down hard in the slime, mud, and crumpled fluff-leaves on the privy floor.

There was a time this would have nauseated her. But she had her mind only on what was in the vasement. It had to be there.

Standing, she saw the little door right in front of her, down low. The latch twisted easily, and the door swung outward, into the vasement. Anna crawled through without difficulty.

The hall beyond had almost no light. Anna felt around, eyes wide to take in what faint light shone from between the floorboards above. She saw the shadow of Yarro pacing. To the right, a square of light outlined a small door where they dumped the privy soil. To the left, she saw a door for humans. She moved down the hall, through the door, and entered a storage room. She found a rack of candles hanging from their wicks. She grabbed a pair. But she had no way to light them.

She fumbled around. She bumped into barrels, stacks of crates, and bins. She finally found a lamp on a shelf, so she dropped the candles. Yes! The lamp had its own striker. She worked the little rod of metal against the stone, watching sparks fly. Finally, the wick caught. Light!

The vasement room had no windows. She saw rough steps leading up to the main floor. A heavy door nearby led to the kitchens, situated outside the castle. Most of the vasement was filled with food: great barrels, little casks, stacks of cheese, crates, bins, and hanging nets full of onions, garlic, and other root vegetables.

She wished she could smell it all.

In the back corner of the room and inside a chest, Anna found some jars. Many of them were crowned with a thin layer of dust. Others were not. They must be in one of these.

She opened the first. Little dried white mushrooms fell out. She had no idea what they were and didn't care. She opened the second. It contained some kind of spice, but it was hard to tell what it was. She opened the third. It was filled to the brim with silverstripe seeds. Yes, finally!

Anna capped the jar and made for the privy box. She had to get back. Yarro would wonder what was happening.

She darted down the hall and climbed back into the privy through the little hatch door. Standing to her full height, she looked up at the hole in the seat, above. She reached. Not even close. She jumped and stretched. There was no way.

She was so stupid! Why hadn't she brought a rope? A cord? Anything?

Wait. What she needed was a stool. A small stool with three legs, like the one Kenan's mother used to reach the upper shelves of her kitchen would work. Yes! She just needed to find a stool.

She climbed back through the little door and retraced her steps to the vasement. The wick on the lamp burned low, too low. She realized the lamp had no oil. It just burned the residual oil in the wick.

She quickly searched the vasement storage room. There was no stool.

Well, maybe she didn't need a stool. Wouldn't a wheel of cheese work just as well? It would fit through the little door hatch, too.

She set the lamp down on a crate and ran back to the privy. She carefully set the jar in the muck on the floor. She needed to be careful.

She went and pulled at a wheel of cheese. It was big, at least a foot and a couple palms in diameter and several palms thick. She couldn't lift it, but she could roll it. Grunting with the effort and slipping from the filth on her feet, she rolled the wheel. As she left the storage room, the lamp went out. She hardly noticed.

The little door was located near the floor. She rolled the cheese over the lip and into the privy vault. Once inside, she flopped it over onto its side. Light shined down through the privy hole.

Anna scooped up the little jar and stretched for the privy hole, going up on the tips of her toes.

She still couldn't reach!

Yarro knocked on the door above. "Everything alright in there?"

Anna stretched again. She tried to jump for it, but still couldn't reach the hole.

She looked down, past her legs streaked with filth, to the wheel of cheese. The wheel had been cast significantly wider than it was thick.

Anna stepped off the wheel, carefully setting the jar to the side, and with effort, flipped the wheel up on its edge.

She had hair in her mouth. She brushed it away. Some stuck in her mouth, and she reached in with filthy fingers to pull it out. She spit into the corner. She didn't think about the taste of the filth or what it was. She only thought about getting up through hole with her prize before Yarro found out what she was doing.

She eyed the hole above. She scooped the jar back up and put one foot on the top of the wheel. It wobbled.

Yarro knocked harder.

"Well," she mumbled, "here I go."

She jumped up with her other foot, balancing on the wheel. One hand grabbed for the seat. Her fingers curled and caught the edge. She got it!

The wheel of cheese fell over with a splash. Anna dangled by one hand from the lip of the privy seat hole above her. She grunted loudly with the effort of holding on tight and the stress on her arm.

The knocking stopped abruptly. Anna almost giggled to herself. Almost.

With great effort, she pulled herself up enough to lift the jar up through the hole and place it carefully onto the seat. As soon as it was safely stowed, she grabbed the edge with her free hand.

The effort to pull herself up and wriggle through the hole took everything she had. By the time she sat on top of the seat, she was exhausted and breathing hard. Filth streaked her most of her body. She was sweating and shivering from exertion.

She had the jar of silverstripe seeds. Anna felt elated! Now, finally, she could leave. Anna wiped her body down with her undershift before dropping it down the hole.

Yarro knocked hard on the door.

"Just a minute," Anna called through the door. "I had a rough moment. Must have been the fish. I'm almost done."

She donned her overshift and then her dress.

Did she stink? She must. She couldn't tell, but she didn't care. She had the seeds!

She lashed the jar high up on the back of her thigh with a strip of cloth from her overshift. It didn't seem secure enough, so she ripped another strip off and lashed it again. There. That would have to do.

The knock came again through the thin, wood door.

"Yarro, give a woman a moment!" She called through the door. "I'm almost done!"

She straightened her dress and felt for the jar. She didn't think it would be noticeable under her dress.

Finally, she turned the latch and pulled the door open.

Gharan stood on the other side, staring at her with his crazy blue eyes. His white clothes positively glowed in the beam of light angling down through the privy window.

He held a hand up to his nose and closed his eyes in disgust.

"Gharan! How very nice to see you. You look... glowy. Not that glowy, but white glowy."

He just looked at her.

"Um, what happened to Yarro?"

"He is in the basement, cleaning up your mess."

Oh. Not a vasement. Basement. Right.

Wait. Her mess? No. Oh no!

Gharan made no move toward her. But she could not leave the small privy room. He barred her way.

Yarro arrived. "She 'as them. Plus, we're down a wheel of cheese."

"No, we are not." Gharan said, looking at her. "She eats only that cheese, until it's gone."

"As you wish, my Prince."

Gharan held out a hand to her. "Agliranna Blacktree, give them to me."

"No!" Anna screamed. "They're mine!" And with that, she made for the privy hole.

Yarro grabbed her from behind and pulled her into the hallway. Anna kicked, screamed, and clawed. The man didn't seem to care. He found the jar, deftly reached up her dress, and pulled it out with a rattle.

"Apologies, my prince. May I suggest a cell in the breedery for now? We will make it comfortable for 'er."

"Yes," Gharan replied, holding his nose. "Good idea, Yarro. Be sure to make it very comfortable. The Most High will be here in another moon or two, maybe three. She must be presentable. And let's drop the dose to two seeds, if you please. She's barely lucid. She must understand."

Anna asked, "Understand what?"

Gharan smiled at her. "You must understand there is no escape. You must accept your fate. You are the Most High's concubine. You are his."

Anna lost her breath and her fight. Yarro slung her over one round shoulder. As she was carried out, she saw Gharan pull a cloth to hold to his nose. By his eyes, she could tell he was smiling. His eyes flashed orange once, then returned to blue.

Yarro carried her out through the castle barbican, through the castle courtyard, and into a tall, square building.

"You know," Anna said into his back. "It's called a basement."

Yarro grunted.

"I had no idea," Anna said. She could hear the smile in her voice. She just couldn't help it. Blood had rushed to her head, and she felt high again.

"Dragonscrape, you stink bad," Yarro muttered.

"I wouldn't know," Anna mumbled, then giggled.

"No. It's the mucky seeds. They take away your silty sense of smell."

"I knew that," she laughed.

They passed a line of cells. Thick wooden bars and plank doors barricaded prisoners into small stone rooms. Some of the rooms were so small the prisoner could only stand. Others were more spacious.

Most of the cells held pretty blond women. Her sisters' hair hung scraggly and their faces dirty, but they all appeared well fed. One gripped a red waterskin in a clenched fist.

Atarra pressed her face between the wood bars. Her eyes followed Anna as she was carried past. Anna wanted to say something to her, but she didn't know what. So, she just smiled.

Atarra smiled back at her. It wasn't friendly. Or sane.

# Chapter Twenty-Nine
# Friend

KENAN trudged along the road outside the Southbreach gate. The dragonwall stood high to his left and cultivated berry bushes lined the road to his right. The limbs of the plants hung heavy with green berries growing in the bright sun. He passed several people thinning the berries and collecting the hard, green fruit into baskets. He wondered what they would do with them.

"Tadd, what do they do with the green berries?"

Tadd, walking beside him, shrugged. "I don't know. They're green. What good are they?"

"I don't know."

Tadd screwed up his face in thought. "Could probably shoot them out of a thumper."

"Probably." Kenan grinned at the youth. But as Tadd chatted on about thumpers and damage from different types of projectiles, Kenan thought about Wren.

They weren't getting along well anymore. Kenan felt awkward around both Wren and Lidai. His rescue on Mahalalel Street had changed their relationship. He didn't know what to do about it, so he kept his head down and trained harder. Wren tried to start conversations, but Kenan avoided him as much as possible. He hadn't talked to Lidai once in the weeks following the event.

He'd been stupid. Dangerously stupid. He'd endangered them all.

And Anna. Sweet Anna. She was gone.

Wren had asked him to come see him today at the dragon training grounds. His friend tried to reengage Kenan constantly, which annoyed them both. Kenan had declined again, yet here he was.

Dust rose ahead, and he could hear dragons grunting and men shouting. A crescentdragon trumpeted and several others returned the call. The berry pickers didn't look up from their work. Tadd skipped ahead, excited to see the dragons practice at battle.

Lamech had ordered him to come here today. He grumbled something about understanding battle resources. It made sense. Kenan would pay attention, but he didn't have to like it.

He just wanted to train. He needed to be better. He needed to increase his skill and speed. He needed to work on his awareness. He must become a true warrior. With enough training and strength, he could have defeated those men.

Couldn't he?

"Hey, Kenan! Come on! We're almost there!"

"I'm coming." Kenan picked up his pace.

The dragon training yard came into view. The large, open area had been beaten raw and flat by decades of big dragons stomping around. The dry dirt puffed as it was kicked and trampled by the animals.

Most of them were crescentdragons, saddled, harnessed, and protected with bronze plate shaped to fit them. Men rode them in formation, carrying shields and dragonpikes. They ran in long lines, curving one way or the other. A man shouted and the line changed into a wedge, then a zig-zag pattern. Another shout came and they all turned as one, wheeling around in a circle. They looked like a flock of birds, moving in unison. He could see the use in battle.

To the side, dummies made of old clothes stuffed with reeds stood staked in a line. The dummies carried shields and supported wood swords and blunted spears which bristled towards a staging area. There, several shielddragons stood facing them, snorting in aggression. Men rode their backs, carrying their own shields and spears.

One of the men saw Kenan and Tadd approach and waved. Wren's grin shone through his bronze helm. Tadd waved back, putting his whole body into it. Kenan just nodded once in acknowledgment. This was business, not a social call. If he had to be here, he would learn what he was sent to learn and be done with it.

An order from a group of men standing to the side reached Kenan's ears. The riders kicked their shielddragons, who charged towards the dummies. Kenan watched as Wren set himself. The shielddragons lowered their noses and raised their frills. The dummy line was trampled, fake weapons and reeds flying in the air with ribbons of torn clothing. Wren skewered one of the dummies with his spear as they passed. Okay snorted and grunted, looking like he was having a great time.

A shout came from the group watching. The riders wheeled the shielddragons around in unison and charged again. Kenan could see it from the dummy's perspective now. The beasts ran shoulder to shoulder. All he could see was horns, bony frills, and the men's helms and spears as they attacked. The rest of the dummies were destroyed in a shower of reeds.

The man in charge, an older man who leaned on a stout blackwood staff with the onlookers, shouted, "Halt! Circle formation!"

The shielddragons skidded to a halt and formed a protective circle, horns facing out.

"Face south! Wedge!"

The riders turned their mounts to the south, Wren now in the center. He stepped Okay forward one step, forming the wedge commanded.

"Men, dismount! Scatter fifty paces!"

The men all leapt from their dragons and ran away from each other, then stopped. The shielddragons never moved.

"Call and mount!"

The men all yelled a name, Wren calling, "Okay, here!"

The shielddragons all trotted to their riders and took a knee for mounting. Using the dragon knee as a step, the men vaulted up onto their backs and into saddles.

Kenan leaned his shoulder on a post and watched. Tadd bounced on the balls of his feet, cheering for Okay.

Beyond, on the other end of the dragon ground, the crescentdragons wheeled, churning up a great cloud of dust. They charged a line of orange gourds on the ground, and the men on their backs pierced some of them with their dragonpikes as they passed.

Wren and the other shielddragon riders reformed a line and charged in a different direction towards a cloth covered framework somewhat resembling a hissdragon. The animals thundered as they charged past, shaking the ground. Kenan could feel the vibrations through his feet.

Despite himself, the sight impressed Kenan. To fight a man was one thing. But to stand against a charging line of shielddragons?

The line collided with the fake hissdragon. The shielddragons hit horns first, splintering the contraption to pieces.

Tadd turned to him. "Pretty good, huh?"

"Yes. I'm impressed." Who could stand against that?

"Glad I'm not a White Spider."

"Me too, Tadd."

A break was called. Wren rode Okay over to them. "Hey Tadd! Want a ride?"

The boy moved so fast Kenan didn't really see how he got up Okay's side and into the saddle. Wren, still in his saddle, laughed in amusement.

Kenan smiled a little. The boy's enthusiasm couldn't be contained. It spilled out to those around him.

Wren showed him how to push on the short horns around the shielddragon's frill to get it to move in different ways. After a few loops around the shielddragon training area, Wren slid off Okay's back and let Tadd ride him alone. Okay watched Wren walk away and grunted after him.

Kenan shook his head. "You let him do that by himself?"

"Yeah. When Lidai isn't here."

Tadd pulled at Okay's frill spikes near the sides and the animal turned in circles. "No, Okay! Go forward!"

Wren smiled and called, "The top spikes, Tadd. Remember? Push the top spikes together." Soon, Tadd had Okay walking around in lazy circles. The boy's face split in a giant smile.

Wren stood by Kenan, looking more serious. "Couldn't get out of it, huh?"

"Out of what?"

"Coming here."

Kenan shrugged. "Lamech said I needed to see."

"What do you think?"

"Impressive. I have no idea what I'd do if charged by a line like that."

"Die, most likely. Still, there is a way."

"What's that?"

"Dive low between them, if you can. They're unlikely to step on you. Shielddragons don't like stepping on things that pop open."

Kenan grimaced. "That's... disturbing."

"Well, you asked."

Kenan grunted at him.

Wren looked at him. "We need to talk."

"Wren, no. I don't..."

"Then you need to go talk to your sister."

"She's my switch-sister."

"Right. You two don't talk much since that day with the barrels."

Kenan avoided Wren's eyes. "No, we don't."

"That's just stubbornness. And foolish. Go talk to her."

"Perhaps."

Wren folded his arms. "No perhaps about it."

"Look, you two may be a thing, but that gives you no right to..."

Wren squared himself to Kenan. "I'm your friend. I have every right."

Kenan looked up at him, then down at his feet. Wren continued. "Do you know what your problem is, Kenan?"

Kenan frowned as he looked back at him. "I'm sure you'll tell me."

"I will. Your problem is you think you don't need anyone."

Kenan shrugged. He wasn't going to take this much longer.

Wren pointed at him. "I'm going to do something about the White Spiders. But I'm not going to do it alone. Grow up, Kenan. No man can take on the whole world."

Kenan turned and walked away.

Wren followed him and pulled at his shoulder "Kenan! I'm talking at you!"

Kenan spun, brushing Wren's hand off, and growled, "And if it was Lidai? Helpless and a slave? Would you take on the whole world then to get to her? What if they were torturing her? Abusing her? What if, when they bore of her, they just slit her throat?"

Wren's brows lowered and he growled back, "You leave Lidai out of this."

Kenan sneered. He didn't understand his own feelings, but this felt good. "Oh. Did I strike a nerve?"

Wren pushed Kenan with a big hand, forcing him to stumble back. Pointing a finger, Wren advanced. "We're doing something here, Kenan. And you're not being a part of it. Don't shut us out."

Kenan grew cold. His entire demeanor shifted to something else. "Don't touch me again."

"What's wrong with you?"

"Me? What's wrong with you? I did what I had to do in that alley. If you had a chance to help someone you loved, you'd do it, too. Don't deny it."

"Of course, I would. But I wouldn't walk into the bear's den alone if I didn't have to. Think, man! You could have watched and sent Tadd back for us. But no. You think you don't need anyone. You'll only succeed once you figure out it's really the opposite. You need to learn to trust. You think you're so good no one can stop you."

Kenan narrowed his eyes. His feelings clarified, pushed by something to the forefront of his mind. "No one can."

"That's stupid. You're full of yourself, full of pride at what you think you know."

"I know a lot. I'll kill them all."

"No one can. I can't. You can't."

Kenan grated, "You're wrong."

"You couldn't even handle a few thugs. You can't handle the White Spiders. And you can't handle me."

A part of him knew this was wrong. But a big part of him latched onto his confidence and strength. "Try me."

Wren moved to shove him again. Kenan stepped inside and punched Wren just below the bronze breastplate. Wren grunted. On a smaller man, it would have knocked the breath out of him. But Wren was not small, and he knew how to breathe to counter the strike.

Wren kicked out with a foot towards Kenan's shin. Kenan changed his stance, causing the kick to miss. He shuffle-stepped forward and punched upwards, hitting Wren below the jaw. The big man's head snapped up but he somehow managed to grab Kenan's shirt sleeve in a firm grip. Wren pulled him around in a throwing move.

Kenan rolled out of it and swept Wren's foot out from under him. Wren landed on his back with an audible thud.

The men supervising the dragon training were watching the fight. Kenan didn't care.

He stood over Wren and said through gritted teeth, "I don't know what this is, but I do know you're out of line. Friend."

Wren stared up at him. The big man's blood was up. He scrambled to his feet, landing in a grappling stance. He looked like he would happily tear Kenan apart.

Kenan shook his head. With effort, he shoved his aggression away. "I'm not here to fight you. I'm here because I was ordered. I obeyed. Now, I'm done with this place. I'm done with you." Kenan turned and walked away.

Wren didn't follow but called after him. "You're losing your way, Kenan!"

Kenan glared over his shoulder to see Wren wave dismissively at him before spinning to return to the dragon grounds. Tadd sat on a motionless Okay, staring wide-eyed at them.

KENAN walked alone back to the city, looming before and above him in the enormous trees. The view normally entranced him. Now, he didn't even look.

How dare Wren confront him like that? The man had no right. He had no say in Kenan's life. He shouldn't be telling him what to do. Who did he think he was?

Kenan didn't need them. He didn't want them. Wren turned on him. Lidai avoided him. Well, fine. He would make a new plan, without them.

He knew he could do this. Maybe he couldn't do it quickly, but he could do it slowly. He'd have to scout in Midreer. He smiled. Scouting was something he did well.

He might be recognized in Midreer. But Lamech had shown him a solution to the problem. He would darken his hair with something and get an eye patch. Or better yet, wind a cloth over his eye, like Char had in Blacktree. That would do the trick.

Disguised and in Midreer, he would search on his own. How many blond women could there be in Midreer? He would search them out and rescue them, one by one. He would put each on a ship back to Edeer, one at a time. It might take years, or even decades, but he could do it.

He would hunt the White Spiders. They walked around with the symbol on their shields and armor. They must be known in Midreer. He would find them, then he would hunt them. He'd kill them on the ground, in the trees, wherever they were, one at a time.

It might take centuries. It might be the effort of a lifetime. He couldn't think of a better way to spend it.

It was just the framework of a plan. But it could work.

His stompdragon could take him, but not fast enough. Besides, he expected the wilderness between the nations to be dangerous. Kenan wondered about shipping to and from Midreer. Did ships go there? They must. But directly? And how much would it cost? He needed more information.

Once back in the city, he walked towards the docks at the Waterbreach on the west side of the city.

This breach looked much like the Southbreach. A huge Flat sat just inside the gate covered in hundreds of vendor stalls. People sold everything, it seemed. One man called to him with grapes in his hands, "the sweetest you'll ever sample!" Another hawked brownnuts, "fresh from the southern reaches!" He glowered at them. One merchant fanned a variety of steel knives, the silver metal catching a stray sunbeam and flashing to him. Kenan would need a good knife. Bronze dulled quickly, but steel would hold an edge.

He had few coins. Most of his money, little that there was, sat in a small pouch under his hammock at the school. He'd come here for information, not to buy. His interest caught the vendor's attention, but one look at Kenan and the man turned away. It was just as well.

As he moved through the Flat towards the breach, he saw Lidai talking to a man. Why was the girl not in training? Her dark hair had been pulled back into a tail and tied with a green ribbon. It fell to the nape of her neck.

The man she talked with turned slightly. She spoke with Secretary Abram. Kenan thought about finding out what she was up to, and he also wanted to speak with the Secretary. After a heartfelt thanks, the man had been whisked away to the ziggurat after the day of barrels. Kenan hadn't seen him since.

But he didn't want to talk to his sister, so he skirted the nearby vendor stall selling bentwood furniture and took a different aisle towards the breach. He put Wren and Lidai out of his head. He needed to get to Midreer.

After traversing the long tunnel through the dragonwall, he came to a stone paved square lined on two sides by shipping buildings. Ugly warehouses sheathed in straight boards stood tall behind them. The west side of the square turned into a wide boardwalk, then docks. Ships and boats of all sizes and shapes tied up to the docks were swarming with men and women. They worked to load and unload cargo, perform commerce, and shout to one another from ship to dock and ship to ship. A man carried a wicker cage containing a pair of colorful birds past Kenan. One of the birds eyed him and said, "Ale! Ale!"

Beyond the harbor, other ships were moored to the edge of trees growing over the water. The enormous trees of Edeer grew out over the salty water on a mat of floating vegetation. No one knew how thick it grew, but it must be very thick to support the forest above. The great floating forest continued westward on the water for hundreds of miles. A channel cut through it, winding west and to the open sea. Kenan had never seen the sea. He pictured it like a big pond, water still, flat, and motionless. He knew villages dotted the channel. A small city, Archmouth, guarded the channel on the open end.

The shipping buildings identified their ships and owners with signs over their doors. He saw, "Three Pole Pretty," "Leviathan Runner," "A Tumble of Coins," and others. He had no idea where to start, so he went to the closest. The sign said, "Sweet Bilge Water." That seemed innocuous enough. He opened the door and stepped inside.

A dark-haired woman who looked to be three hundred years or more smiled at him. She was pretty despite the skin of her temples crinkling as her eyes sparkled at him. She wore a girdle over her dress and the top of her chest pushed out over it. "Hello, handsome. How are you, today?"

Kenan tried to return the smile. "Fine, thank you. Do you own a ship?"

"Oh, now, I don't own any ships. My old, decrepit husband does. Five, in fact. Looking to send something out of Edeer? Or looking for something coming in?" She shuffled several scrolls on her little desk. One, held open with a few exotic looking seashells, appeared to contain long lists of cargo and numbers.

Kenan tried to be nonchalant. The woman sat back in her chair, eyeing him up and down. She pursed her lips at him in appraisal. He shuffled his feet. He imagined this was how a slabdragon felt at market as a farmer checked the stiffness of its back plates. Kenan said, "I'm looking to book passage."

"And leave me already? Why, we just met!"

"Uh..."

"Oh, don't fret, handsome. It doesn't look good on you. Besides, one of my sons is due back at any moment. If he catches me looking at you, he might give you a drubbing. I'd hate to see one of those eyes blackened. My, you have brooding eyes. Very fetching."

"Perhaps I should..." Kenan moved towards the door.

"No, no, young man. Rest easy. I can't take another lover here, not after that last debacle. Seriously, the boy's probably still running. Passage, you say? Where're you going?"

"Midreer."

"No, no. You don't want to go there."

"I do."

"Really? Good trade in Midreer. But they have no idea how to treat a woman."

"So, can I..."

"Yes, if you insist. We can get you passage."

"When?"

"In a rush, are you? Well, the *Sloshing Bilge* runs out in three days. She's headed straight to Midreer, then the Yachoneer Isles. Where are you getting off?" Her eyes twinkled, though she'd unrolled another scroll and dabbed a reed pen in the inkwell.

"Uh, Midreer."

"We can do that. Hadn't planned to stop there, but we could for a little extra."

"I thought you said this route would take me to Midreer?"

She put the pen down. "Cute, but a fresh drop from the tree, I see."

Kenan bristled a little while she smiled at him with renewed interest.

She continued with an explanation. "Midreer has many cities, my sweet. Midreer is also a city unto itself, the capital of the country. We're going to Midreer the country, but not Midreer the capital. Still, it's a short detour. It wouldn't cost you much more for us to stop there.

Medahal had been correct about the size of Midreer. Still, he might as well start at the capital. "Midreer the city, please. How much will it cost?"

She gave him the price, which staggered him. He only had a tenth under his hammock.

"Um, how much to reserve my spot on the boat?"

"Oh, lovely man, that's not how it works. You pay it all up front. Unless you can make me a... better offer?" She leaned towards him.

He swallowed and took a step back. Steeling himself, he said, "Half up front, half when I get there."

She smiled at him and winked as she leaned back. "I can do that. Are you paying now?"

"No. I'll be back tomorrow."

"Come after midday. I'll be waiting for you." She smiled deeply. She was pretty, but Kenan somehow couldn't get the image of a hissdragon out of his head.

Kenan nodded and left. He could hear her tapping her reed pen on her desk as the door closed behind him. He didn't look back.

KENAN stood for a moment on the door stoop, his mind spinning with ideas. How would he get the coin? He had so little. He could sell Finch, which would net him another half of the fare, maybe more. And he'd need more than the cost of passage. He'd need coin when he got to Midreer. Would they let him work on the ship for wages?

He stood below the "Sweet Bilge Water" sign. He thought so furiously he didn't immediately notice the man approaching, trailing a dozen uniformed guards.

"Kenan, lad!"

Kenan made eye contact. "Secretary Abram!"

"I thought I saw you on the Flat. Please, let us talk."

"Oh, I need to be back at the school."

"Quite. As it happens, I'm headed in that direction as well. We can talk as we go."

Kenan nodded reluctantly and walked with Abram back through the breachgate. The soldiers split, with groups ahead and behind. Others flanked them, watching everyone. He spotted several more circling the square. Enosh was taking no chances with his secretary it seemed.

Lidai was nowhere to be seen.

"I just talked with your sister. She's in full blossom, the lovely child. You must be very pleased with her."

"Of course." Kenan tried to sound agreeable.

Abram quirked an eyebrow at him, but said, "And you and your big friend are progressing quite well. I owe you all my life."

"Oh, no, Master Secretary. We just stumbled upon you."

"I see. Please, call me Abram. You've seen me half naked, bloodied, and tied to a chair. The least you can do is call me by my name. Could you do that?"

"I suppose. The cut on your cheek is healing nicely. Abram."

Abram smiled at him. "See? That wasn't so hard. And thank you for saying so."

"What's happening with Tardain?"

"Oh, High Councilor Tardain is irascible as ever, I'm afraid."

"He's still a High Councilor?"

"Quite right. We could confront him directly, but one doesn't just accuse a High Councilor without a carefully laid plan, young Kenan. High Councilor Enosh is working on the problem."

"Which means, you're working on the problem."

"Quite." Abram's dark eyes sparkled. "Though don't dismiss the High Councilor Enosh. He's a very bright man. He's just, well, distracted by many concerns, including High Councilor Tardain."

"Tardain needs to pay."

"Quite right, again. And he will at the correct time." Abram's voice took on a hard edge. "The Almighty will judge. I hope to send the old man to that appointment someday soon."

Kenan nodded. He wished he could be here to help.

Abram's tone turned inquisitive. "So, young Kenan. What brings you to the docks today?"

Kenan almost tripped on a paving stone. "Um, an inquiry."

"Inquiry? How curious. I must ask, an inquiry into what?"

"I... I wanted to import something."

"Really? What do you want?"

Kenan said the first thing to come to mind. "I want a steel sword."

Abram laughed pleasantly. "The desires of young men. You know, I was young once, long ago. I dreamed of a steel sword, long and sharp on both edges. They're rare today. Back then, steel was, it seemed, impossible to acquire."

"Did you ever get one?"

"Why, yes, as it turns out. I did. I purchased it from a vendor right here in Edeer. Terrible balance, but beautiful none-the-less."

"I bet it worked fine in battle."

"I wouldn't know, Kenan. In my youth, I marched towards two battles and showed up too late to both."

"Oh. What happened to the sword?"

"I gave it to one of my third-sons. He bent it around something, quite by accident, so he said. It turns out the thing wasn't very well made, after all."

"Oh. I'm sorry."

"Don't be. I never used it. If I had, it would have failed me. It looked good on the wall, but it only proves a truth."

"What truth is that?"

"One of the oldest truths of all. Beauty is best at hiding flaws."

Kenan nodded again, contemplating.

Abram regarded him as they walked up a ramp to the first level. Stompdragons hauled carts around them, and the guardsmen glared at everyone. "So, tell me, Kenan, where are you going?"

"Going? I'm not..."

"Kenan, let me interrupt you, if I may. You see, I owe you my life. You came for me and faced many armed men for me. Indeed, you might have died for me. Therefore, you cannot anger me or disappoint me. I will always be here for you, and if I can help you, I always will. I cannot imagine what could happen to balance the scales between us. Despite all this, you can lose my trust. Please, tell me. Where are you going in a ship?"

Kenan walked for many paces before he said, "Midreer."

"Quite. Now, for the real question. Why are you going alone?"

Kenan frowned. "Lidai talks too much."

"Perhaps, but she tried hard not to reveal her concerns. I, well, I deduced. And I've been told I have some powers of persuasion."

Kenan looked at the man dressed in fine robes. "Yes, I suppose you do."

Abram smiled at him. "And you're not answering my question."

They walked in silence for some time, ascending another two levels on a lift. Finally, Kenan said, "I have to go."

"So, I gathered. Why? Why alone?"

Kenan thought about this question while Abram walked beside him in silence, waiting. Kenan grew irritated at Abram's intrusion. "Why is that important?"

"Because, Kenan, if you're going to do something big, knowing why will get you through. I'm trying to help. Why are you doing this alone?"

Kenan appreciated the Secretary's wisdom but couldn't come up with a believable answer. Finally, he said, "I don't know, Abram. I really don't. But I've always worked alone. I am alone. She's gone."

"Yes, I heard what they said. They confirmed our deepest fears. I'm very sorry, my boy. I'm sorry for your loss."

"Thank you."

"But you are not alone. I urge you to think on this, Kenan. Your Agliranna may be gone, but the White Spiders are your task, are they not? You don't want anyone else to lose their loved ones. You intend to stop the raids, correct?"

"Correct."

"Then, young Kenan, why are you leaving?"

Kenan didn't have an answer. They ascended another level on stairs and crossed a rope bridge.

At an intersecting boardwalk, Abram stopped and turned to him. "I am going that way, so here we part. Go to your school, Kenan. Please. Give Master Lamech my regards, and tell him something for me, would you?"

"Yes, of course. Anything."

"Quite good of you, my boy. Tell him that those who seek will find. Tell him that, in those words, if you would."

Kenan nodded his agreement. "If you wish it."

"I do." Abram pointed in the direction he planned to go, and several guards moved that way to scout ahead. Then, to Kenan he said, "Seek, Kenan. Seek in your school, not the shipyards. Great wisdom resides in that school. Seek and you will find."

Kenan grasped Abrams proffered forearm and the two parted.

Wisdom. Yes, Kenan needed some wisdom right now. But, if he wanted to leave, no one could stop him. Not Wren. Not Lidai. Not anyone. He was going.

He would go back to the school and train for a couple more days. Then he would rise early on the third day, pack his meager belongings, and head to see Gruntle about selling his stompdragon. He would be on the Sloshing Bilge when it departed Edeer.

# Chapter Thirty
# Grandmaster

KENAN sat alone finishing his very last breakfast in the dining room of the school. Wren and Lidai sat across the room, quietly conversing over their nutmash. They didn't look at Kenan. A few others nearby were finishing their breakfasts. Lamech sat with Belroon, scraping his bowl with a big, wooden spoon. Why was he not in his private dining room?

Kenan heard Lamech say, "I think this morning, Belroon. Can you fetch it?"

Belroon said, "Am I your fattest errand boy? Ha!"

Lamech shook his head at him. Did he smile, just a little? "It's not an item I trust to just anyone. Loosen your kilt just a little and see it done."

Belroon agreed with a simple, good natured, "Yah. I will." The massive man stood up and finished his big bowl as he moved to the table scattered with dirty dishes.

Lamech steepled his scarred fingers and watched Kenan. It made him uncomfortable, so he kept his eyes on his bowl and ate. When he finished, he checked and saw Lamech still watching him.

Kenan rose and brought his wood bowl and spoon over to the table, adding them to growing stacks of dirty dishes. When he turned to leave for class, Lamech stood at the door. Kenan nodded respectfully and made to pass the older man.

Lamech grunted. "Kenan, with me."

Kenan stopped mid step. "Master?"

"With me, boy." Lamech turned and left. Kenan's shoulders slumped a little. Had the old man somehow figured out what he planned?

He caught up to Lamech as he stomped down the short hall, past the kitchens, and through the battle hall. Finally, Lamech stopped at the temple door and pushed his way inside. Kenan frowned. Why the temple?

The room continued to make him feel uncomfortable. The walls gleamed in lacquer and bright wood grains. The altar stood solidly at the far end of the room, covered in big scrolls. Light streamed through windows stained with colors. Patterns of the light fell on the polished floor.

The oldest man Kenan had ever seen stood in front of the altar leaning on a thin staff. In his other hand he held a small scroll. He wore a heavy, white robe with a dark vest over it. He kept his little remaining hair and white beard short. Though at the school for many months, Kenan didn't remember seeing him before.

Lamech bowed deeply to the old man. Kenan hurried to do the same. Lamech turned to Kenan and said, "Kenan, meet the Grandmaster."

Kenan's mouth dropped open. He hurriedly bowed again, took a knee, and lowered his head in respect.

The old man's voice creaked as he said, "Enough of that, now. To your feet, boy."

Kenan rose, bowing once more.

Lamech joined him in the bow, turned, and left the room. The door shut behind him.

Kenan tried to surreptitiously observe the old man. How old was he? The Grandmaster smiled at him, showing one remaining front tooth.

Kenan cleared his throat. "How is it, Grandmaster, that we've never met? I've been here a long time."

"A long time? Well, I suppose you have, as most judge it. But we have met, after a fashion. I was here on your first day, boy."

Kenan didn't remember him, but he nodded anyway.

"Not boy. Man, should I say. You are how old, Kenan?"

"I'm 83, Grandmaster."

"Yes. 83. That seems right."

Kenan only nodded, his mind working to understand why he was meeting the Grandmaster.

"And what do you think of my temple, Kenan?"

"Your temple?"

"Yes. Mine. I built it, to the Almighty, quite some time ago."

"Well, it's, uh, beautiful."

"Thank you, lad. Kind of you to say. We haven't met because these days I only leave my little home for special occasions and to come to my temple, right here. I've not seen you here."

"No. Sorry."

"Sorry, you say. Why didn't you come?"

Kenan shrugged. "I'm not a... I don't..."

"Follower? Believe?"

Kenan ducked his head. "No, I don't. At least, I don't think so. Sorry."

"Don't be sorry, lad. Not yet. Why don't you believe?"

Kenan shook his head and stood straighter. He wasn't in the mood for a sermon, Grandmaster or no. Kenan answered with a challenging question. "Is God Almighty good?"

The Grandmaster smiled, showing his tooth and nodding his head. "He defines the very word, lad."

"With respect, Grandmaster, that is why I don't think I believe. There is true evil in this world. A good god would do something about it."

"Yes, you've seen true evil, have you not? Most have and most recognize it, but you've had a big serving of it. I know some of your story."

Kenan raised his eyebrows. "Oh?"

The Grandmaster continued, "Yes. Born and raised in Blacktree, the only son of a man who left you. You were raised with unkind siblings and a mother with a new husband. They loved your younger brothers well, I suppose? And then came the attack all those years ago. You were involved directly, I hear. Wounded, weren't you? You took to the trees and became a woodbender, working mostly alone, I'm sure. Let me guess, you prefer to be alone? Independent?"

Kenan gawked at the old man. "How could you possibly..."

The old man laughed an interruption. "Lad, when you've lived as long as I have, you can see a person's story in their eyes."

Right. Clearly, the Grandmaster had talked to Lamech. Though, what he said might still be true. A question slipped out before he could stop it. "How old are you?"

The Grandmaster flashed his tooth at him again. "I can hardly remember the last time someone worked up the nerve to ask me that."

Kenan looked at his feet. "I'm sorry. I shouldn't have..."

"I am 915, lad."

Kenan said, "Oh."

"Thought I'd be older?"

"Well, no. Maybe. I guess."

The Grandmaster's eyes sparkled under his white brows. "I've lived a full life, lad. It catches up with a man. Now, where was I? Yes, Blacktree. Raiders recently attacked your village again, didn't they? You and your little switch-sister sent them off with a black eye, all on your own. And you faced a Nephilim and lived to tell the tale. You spoke to him. Close?"

"Yes. Two, actually. One in Blacktree and one here. They glowed."

"Orange, and sometimes other colors. Yes, they do that when full of a spirit."

Kenan couldn't deny the supernatural when he'd seen it firsthand. "Spirit? Like, a spiritual being?"

"Very much so. An angel. A fallen angel."

"Angels can fall?"

The Grandmaster nodded. "Do you mind if we sit, lad? My knees don't work like they once did." Without waiting, the old man sank to the floor, gnarled hand sliding down his staff. He leaned back against the altar and toyed with the little scroll he held.

Kenan folded his legs under him to stay on the same level with the old man. It seemed somehow wrong to stand looking down on him.

The Grandmaster adjusted his robes. "Yes, angels were created with free will, just like you and I. They can be deceived and fall, just like you and I."

"Fall from heaven?"

"Well, yes, but also fall from God's presence. Actually, I'm not sure there's a difference between the two."

"The Almighty forced them out?"

"Perhaps. To understand this, you must begin to understand the character of God Himself. God is holy. We all know this, but we don't fully understand what it means. God is so holy that anything wrong in His presence will simply burn away. It's like saying fire is so hot that brown grass will burn in its presence. It's just the way He is. Out of His holiness flows the good you spoke of.

"Did He force out angels? Or, choosing to side with a powerful angel called the Great Deceiver, did the angels flee to avoid being burned away? I surely don't know. Perhaps one day, we will find out."

Kenan rubbed the cropped beard on his chin. "So, these fallen angels are now here, on earth?"

"Well, they're spiritual beings, not flesh like you and I. But they can take on flesh and walk the world. Some have."

"And these are Nephilim?"

"No, no. Angels are spiritual, not human. But fallen or not, they can take a human form and a human wife. Sometimes they produce a Nephilim offspring, a human being of power and renown."

"So, the orange glow was the Nephilim's power?"

"You know, I'm not entirely sure. Please understand, I'm no angel nor a Nephilim, though I have met both. As for the Nephilim, I'm not sure of their powers, but suspect they carry many spirits within them, age very slowly, and are fearsome in battle. Some can be carried away in the Spirit of God himself. The light they produce seems to be involved with the spiritual aspect of their being."

"You've met angels?"

"Yes. One. Or at least, so he said."

"Did he glow?"

"No. He looked like a normal man. It was quite the experience."

"I bet." Kenan should have thought this man completely insane with his talk of angels and spirits, but he could deny neither the man's lucidity nor what he'd seen during his encounters with the Nephilim Gharan and Rillain. "So, they're possessed by these spirits? Which are what, more fallen angels?"

"You've got it, lad. But you don't need to be a Nephilim to be possessed by a spirit. Many people are."

"What?" Okay, the old man was taking a deep dive.

"Yes, lad. Many people unwittingly open the door of their hearts to these fallen angels and end up with many troubles."

"Possessed people? You lost me."

"Lost as in you don't understand? Or as in you don't believe me?"

"I'm sorry, Grandmaster. I mean no disrespect. But I don't believe it. Nothing is possessing me. I choose my own path."

The Grandmaster eyed Kenan thoughtfully. "A path by boat to carry you to Midreer, alone."

Kenan's jaw fell open again, and he closed it with a click.

"Ah, to still have all one's teeth! I miss that. Don't be alarmed, lad. By now, you must know nothing happens in this school that Lamech doesn't know. And I know everything he knows. I am his father, after all."

Kenan's jaw fell open again.

The Grandmaster cackled a laugh. "You have the most wonderful expressions, did you know? That's right lad. I am Methuselah, son of the Enoch who was taken away by God."

Kenan breathed, "No wonder."

"No wonder what, lad?"

"No wonder you believe all of this."

"Ha! Yes, if you'd seen your father whisked into the heavens by God, you'd believe in Him, too."

"I don't remember my father."

"No? I'm sorry for you in this regard. But remember, God is sovereign and can use anything or anyone's action, good or evil, for His good plan."

Kenan nodded. "Thank you, but that doesn't explain how a good god could allow the rampant evil we have spilling blood and tears all over this world."

"Well said, lad. I agree. That's a different story, from the very beginning."

"Are you talking about Adam?"

"I am."

Kenan struggled to keep his eyes from rolling in front of the Grandmaster. "I've heard this story."

Methuselah nodded. "I'm sure you have. You've heard it so many times you think it just a story. But I believe it to be fact."

"Why?"

Methuselah grinned. "Because I knew Adam, personally. Yes, I'm that old, and so was he. Whether you believe it or not, Adam provides the explanation to your conundrum."

Kenan raised his eyebrows. "Because he took a bite of the forbidden fruit?"

"Yes, lad. This world, everything you see, and all the pain and suffering? It's not the way it was supposed to be."

Kenan shook his head, trying to wrap his mind around the Grandmaster's words.

Methuselah held up a bony finger, waving it in the air to emphasize his words. "Tell me, have you ever bent a gift for a child? Perhaps it took many years to bend just right. You presented it to the child with love, affection, and hope for their future. You have done this, no?"

"Yes, of course."

"Perhaps there was a time when the child treated the gift poorly?"

Kenan nodded. "All children are like that, sometimes." He thought about Tadd. "More than sometimes."

"I agree, the little rascals. Did you stop loving them?"

Kenan leaned his head forward. "What?"

"When the child ruined your gift, did you stop loving them? Did you take hold of their little bodies and force them to treat the gift right?"

"Of course not."

"If they broke your gift, and continued to break it, would you stop loving them? Would you abandon them? Would you turn your back? Perhaps you could punish them? You might simply end their little lives because a new child could be made, one that would treat your gift in the way it was intended?"

Kenan leaned back. "That's a little ridiculous, but I see where you're going with this."

"Yes, of course. God didn't stop loving us, just because we have evil thoughts and act on some of them. He may discipline us and wash away those who cannot accept Him from the earth. A time is coming, but not yet. He loves us and has hope for us still."

Kenan had him. "So, why doesn't He do something about it?"

Methuselah flashed his tooth again. "You mean come here and just fix it all? Snap his divine fingers and stop all the evil?"

Kenan nodded. "Yes. He's a god, isn't he? Isn't he supposed to be the one true God? Doesn't he have that power, that ability to make it good like it should be?"

"Oh, yes. He is the one and only true God. And He could do it. But if He came here to fix it, what do you think would happen to us all? You'd need to be perfectly holy and able to withstand His presence. You aren't holy, are you?"

Kenan chuckled. "No. No one is. And you're going to say if he came here in person to fix it, we'd all be burned to a crisp."

Methuselah smiled again. "Something like that. But don't think for a moment that God Almighty doesn't love us or have a plan for us and the world. He does, and He sends us help."

Kenan thought about this for a long moment. "Not all angels are fallen."

Methuselah laughed again. "Yes, lad. I like the way you think. The angel I met was not fallen, I would think. He spoke with God's authority and helped me immensely in a time of great danger."

"I have a hard time believing angels walk the world wreaking havoc or helping those in need."

"I understand. Then again, perhaps, lad, you've met one already and didn't know it."

Kenan shrugged. "I suppose anything's possible."

"Yes, lad. And I suppose God is real and actively helps His people."

Kenan became quiet, whispering, "He didn't help me in Blacktree."

Methuselah frowned and tapped the little scroll against his leg. "Perhaps He did. Perhaps He didn't. One way or the other, it's according to His plan."

"That sounds, if you'll forgive me, Grandmaster, trite and unhelpful."

The Grandmaster glowered at him. Kenan feared he'd taken it a step too far. The old man met his eyes and studied Kenan's face. Methuselah softened. "I think you're right, lad. I'm sorry I said it."

Kenan nearly choked at the words from a man of his age and authority.

Methuselah shrugged his bony shoulders. "I am not wisdom personified, lad. I am, like you, just a man. Whether or not you believe in God's plan, Kenan, believe this. There is a God. The evidence is all around you. The logic of His existence is unbreachable. He created you and loves you. He wants what's best for you."

Kenan looked the old man in the eyes. "Maybe. I'll think on it."

"You do that, lad. Now, what are you going to do?"

"About what?"

"The White Spiders? The entire nation of Midreer? Are you going to run away? Or should we start a little closer? What are you going to do about your friend and your spirited sister?"

Kenan's slouched over his knees, and he ran a hand through his brown hair. "First, I'm not running away. Second, what is there to do about Wren and Lidai?"

"Do you love them?"

Kenan sat up straight. "Of course, I do."

"Of course, you do. Do you still plan to leave without saying goodbye?"

Kenan thought for a moment before admitting, "That wasn't a good idea, was it? I can be a right fool, sometimes."

"Ha! Wisdom. There it is. Of course, you can be a fool. We all can. But to recognize it, ah, there's wisdom." Methuselah smiled. The tooth flashed at him again, and the old man's eyes held anticipation. "So?"

"I will talk with them."

"Good, lad. Good. Keep them close. Every man thinks he can survive on his own, and most can. But there's more to life than survival. No man can *thrive* on his own. No man."

Kenan nodded, unsure if he did so because he agreed or to mollify the old man. Perhaps. Perhaps both. He still planned to go to Midreer, but not before saying goodbye to his friends.

Methuselah grinned his tooth at him once more before he struggled to his feet. Kenan jumped up and offered a hand, but the old man waved him off. He stood with the help of his staff and held out the scroll. "Here, lad. Take this."

"What is it?"

Methuselah grinned at him. "Can't read?"

"Well, yes, I can. I just thought perhaps it would be impolite to open it here."

"Kind of you, but it's simply a promissory note. Give this to an Edeerian ship captain, and they will bill me for your passage to wherever you want to go."

"What? No, Grandmaster, I couldn't..."

"You can, and you will take it. Keep it with you. I hope you don't use it, lad. This mission of yours to Midreer is a fool's errand. You've got bravery, and it's a good thing, too, especially if you're to take on an entire nation by yourself."

Kenan shrugged and took the scroll. "Is being brave a bad thing?"

"Ha! I like you, lad. Bravery is a powerful thing. Bravery won't last long in a foolish person."

"Because a fool is a coward?"

"No," he laughed. "Because a brave fool is dead!"

Kenan bowed to the Grandmaster. Methuselah nodded back to him.

"Thank you, Grandmaster, for your wisdom."

"Yes, yes. Wisdom comes from God Almighty. I just have experience and plenty of it. Now, your friends have the morning off. You'll find them in the common room of your favorite inn."

Kenan turned to go.

"And Kenan? Would you do me a favor?"

"Of course, Grandmaster. Anything."

"Bring me some of good Master Gruntle's vegetable stew. It's the best in the city, simmered perfectly tender. Only got the one tooth, don't you know?"

KENAN entered the Goosedown Filler and was attacked in a bear hug.

"Young Master Kenan!" Gruntle boomed. He pinned Kenan's arms to his sides, lifting him off the floor.

By instinct and long training, Kenan slipped a toe under Gruntle's calf, which arrested the lift abruptly.

The older man dropped Kenan back to his feet. He bent over and grabbed his lower back. "Oh! That hurt!"

In a panic, Kenan helped Gruntle to stand straight. "I'm sorry, Master Gruntle. My training..."

Gruntle wheezed in pain. "I'm sorry, Master Kenan. I'm too old to be hefting the likes of you, it seems. And, I shouldn't have grabbed you like that. Terribly sorry, young master. My mistake."

"Master Gruntle, the apologies are mine! I'm sorry I hurt you."

"Oh, no fault of yours. I forget my age, sometimes, is all. I'm still a young man inside, you know. I think it's the age of my eternal soul."

Kenan raised his eyebrow at Gruntle, but the big man missed it as he rubbed his back.

"But how I've missed my young Blacktrian friends! And all three in one day!"

The common room stood empty, except for the boy named Grand, morosely wiping tables with a wet rag. The cold hearth had been fully set for a hardwood fire.

"Master Gruntle, where are they?"

"Ah, Master Kenan. They've become a lovely couple, haven't they? They walked in here holding hands, smiling at me with such warmth! Reminded me of my dear wife, may she rest peacefully."

"Let me guess. She was as amazing as her cooking?"

"Ha! Just right, Master Kenan. Taught me everything I know about the art of the kitchen. You know, when I was a lad, I never thought to be an innkeep. I was going to be a soldier, riding dragons into battle! Imagine me, on a crescentdragon with a dragonpike! Ha! But a good woman changes a man. At least, as long as she doesn't try. My wife, well, she never once tried to change me. She just lived right. You know, I followed her. I suppose it's meant to be the other way around, but when I look back on it, she knew the right way. I saw it through her."

Kenan smiled at him. "I'm sure she was wonderful. I'm sorry I never met her."

"Me, too, Master Kenan. You would've loved her, too. Now, you'll find Master Wren out in the stables with that giant beast of his. I suppose it's no larger than any other shielddragon, but it sure seems it. Eats like it, as well. That thing... well, you don't need to hear me go on about dragons. You know the way."

Kenan thanked him and left for the stables. He found Wren standing by Okay's stall gate. The big man held a spear and used the butt to scratch behind the dragon's shield frill.

Lidai stood leaning against the gate, looking up at Wren with a frown. "I don't think it's a good idea."

Wren responded without turning to her. "Why not?"

"Because he's..." She stopped when she saw Kenan.

Kenan shrugged at her as he approached. "I heard you. Say what you mean, Lidai. Because he's what?"

Lidai turned away to look up at Okay. She sniffed. "Because he's a dragonsphincter."

Wren pulled the spear out of the stall and stood it on the straw-covered stable floor, gripping it tightly with one hand. "What do you want?"

Kenan stopped out of stab range. "I've made a mess of things, haven't I?"

Lidai snorted loudly.

Wren said, "You think?"

Kenan nodded. "I have. I've been proud, more than a little. And arrogant, too."

Lidai continued to gaze at Okay and reached up to scratch around a horn. "Been?"

Okay snorted out his nostrils.

Kenan nodded again. "I am, still. I admit it. I'm sorry I endangered you in the city. I'm sorry I didn't wait for you. And I'm sorry I was a fool."

Wren nodded. "Good enough for me."

Lidai spun towards Kenan. She snatched up her bow and pointed one end at him. "Well, it's not good enough for me! You shut me out! You shut us out! After all we've been through, you went off on your own. You got in big trouble. You never even thanked us for saving your sorry hide! You're a real dragonscrape, Kenan. I'm ashamed for our mother."

Kenan's brows lowered. "Yes."

"Yes, what?"

"Yes, I did all that."

"And that's what you have to say for yourself? You did it? You're sorry? It's just air, Kenan."

"I am sorry. I didn't want it to end this way."

Wren stiffened. "End? Going somewhere?"

"Yes. I'm going to Midreer. I came to apologize and to say goodbye."

Lidai snorted again and somehow sneered at the same time. "It's true, then. Well, that's just dragonspitting great. So long. Brother."

Wren frowned at them both.

Lidai caught it. "Don't frown at me, you great tower of muscle. He's the one being a fool."

Fool. There it was again. And he'd earned it.

Wren said, "Easy, Lidai."

She huffed and leaned on her bow. She put a hand on her hip and glared at them both, kicking at her dress hem with one foot. The fabric fluttered violently.

Wren looked at Kenan. "Why are you going?"

"Anna's dead, but I will find your sisters and the other women of Blacktree. I'll send them back or die trying."

Wren quirked an eyebrow and looked down at Lidai. He looked back at Kenan, and the big man's face held resolve. "You've just shown us how well you'll do on your own. There's nothing for it then. I'm going, too."

Lidai exploded. "What? Dragonspit! Two brave fools!"

Kenan's frown deepened and, with supreme effort, he didn't glare at his sister. "You think I can't do it."

Lidai grew cold. She somehow folded her arms over her chest with the bow entwined. At least the weapon wasn't nocked. Quietly, she continued. "That's right. You can't. They're lost to us. You're just going to get yourself killed and my betrothed along with you."

Kenan pointed at them. "You're not betrothed. Not yet."

Wren's eyes darkened. "That's not her point."

"I can speak for myself," Lidai said softly. This coldness was much worse than her anger. "You two alone cannot invade a foreign nation, rescue our people, and live to bring them back. It's not possible. You'll die."

Kenan nodded. "Maybe I'll die. But not without trying. And you," Kenan pointed at Wren, "are not coming. You'll stay here and protect my sister."

Lidai corrected, "Switch-sister,"

At the same moment, Wren said, "No, I won't. She's safe here. My sisters are not. I'm coming with you."

Lidai cried, "Aaarrrrg!" She dropped her bow to the floor of the stable, turned, and threw her arms over the stall door. Okay's beak emerged to nuzzle the side of her face. She swatted at him, but he took no notice.

Kenan and Wren eyed each other. Kenan didn't want to endanger his friend, but Wren's sisters were in Midreer. He had as much right to go as Kenan. Perhaps Wren should come along. Perhaps alone was not best. He didn't want to just survive. He wanted this mission to thrive. Besides, if going alone was a fool's errand, then he'd be a dead brave fool. He wasn't going to help anyone by being dead.

Kenan nodded to Wren. Wren quirked a brief grin and nodded back. It was done.

Wren turned to Lidai. "Lidai, I..."

She turned to face him. "I want to say no. I want to say you can't go. But I have no right."

Wren shook his head.

Lidai smiled up at him. "Then let me try something else."

Kenan interrupted them. "We should go get our gear ready and prepare. The ship leaves early tomorrow morning. I need to sell my stompdragon.

We can..."

Lidai didn't acknowledge Kenan's words. She stared up at Wren. "Do you love me?"

Wren smiled down at her. "You know I do."

She nodded. "I know you do. I don't ask you to stay because of our love. I only ask you to listen to me because you love me."

Wren nodded. Kenan listened carefully. Some kind of female magic was at work here. He couldn't look away.

She took Wren's hand in hers and pulled it high on her chest, holding it just below her throat. "If you go, I want you to promise me something. I will never see you again because you'll be dead down in that God-forsaken place. Promise me something and mean it, as your final words to me."

Wren nodded again. "Our deaths are not a foregone conclusion, Lidai. I'll be back. But I will promise you anything, and I'll mean it. If it's in my power, it will be done."

She smiled at him. "I know it will. This is what I want." She took a breath, and softly said, "I want you to promise me you will kill every last White Spider in existence. Kill them alone. Kill them in groups. If you can, make them suffer. If you can't, end them swiftly. Spill their blood and crush their bones. Do it from the shadows. Do it in the open. However you do it, kill them all. Make them fear us. And, if you can, kill that Nephilim last."

Kenan's mouth fell open.

Wren smiled down at her, somehow not in the least surprised. "I promise it."

She released his hand and snatched up her bow. "Good. Thank you. While you're down there getting yourself killed, I'll be here, fulfilling your promise for you."

"What?"

"You heard me."

Wren grimaced at her. "I heard you, but I don't understand you."

She nodded, as if it were the most natural thing in the world. "Said every man to every woman."

He frowned. "Well, say it so I can understand."

"Fine. Let me lay it out for you. The White Spiders may come from Midreer, but they travel here to do their evil work. They'll be back soon, and this time we'll be ready for them. While you're down there getting your throat slit by some black-eyed bloodmother, whatever they're supposed to be, I'll be here. I'll meet them in battle. I'll put an arrow through each dragonspitter's eye. I will fulfill your promise for you, because the two of you can't possibly do it on your own down there. You can't, because they won't be there. They'll be here. And I'll be waiting for them."

Wren scratched at his short, blond beard. She watched him think.

Kenan said, "I think..."

Her arm whipped up, and she pointed at him without looking, her finger sketching a direct line to his chest. Kenan shut his mouth, thankful she hadn't instead hurled a knife at him.

Finally, Wren turned to Kenan. "You know, she's right."

Kenan had already decided he agreed. Grandmaster Methuselah had said he was running. Kenan realized running is exactly what he had planned. Midreer wasn't a mission, it was an escape away from the need to lean on others. He nodded once to Wren, and Wren nodded back.

Wren looked back down at Lidai. "Yes. You're right. I am staying with you. And I will fulfill my promise, not alone, but with you."

Lidai looked entirely too satisfied. She'd perhaps learned to handle a man – well, this man – but she hadn't learned to mask it yet. The magic wasn't fully formed. But oh, it would be. Kenan felt a little sorry for Wren.

Lidai turned to look at Kenan. "And you, dragonsphincter? What are you going to do?"

Kenan didn't answer. He just walked slowly up to her and put his arms around her in an embrace. She stiffened long enough he feared she would push him away. Finally, slowly, she returned the hug. She whispered into his collarbone, "I've missed you these last few weeks."

"Me too, little sister. I'm sorry, I mean it, and thank you for rescuing me. I hope never to have to return the favor to prove I'm more than air."

She snorted into his chest and pushed him away. "You'll never have to. I'm way better than you."

He smiled down into her wet eyes. "I believe it."

Wren smiled at them both. "Now what? We have the rest of the morning off. First, I'm staying here, then I'm traveling the world, then I'm staying here again. I'm tired and I haven't even done anything. I feel like I need a drink."

Kenan nodded back to the inn. "How about we go get an ale and talk about Secretary Abram? I ran into him the other day. I think he's up to something."

Lidai produced a small cloth and dabbed at her eyes. "Yes. I'm sure he is."

Kenan turned to lead them back to the inn, sniffing the air. "And maybe Gruntle's roasting a lamb today."

Wren rubbed his muscled stomach. "Almighty, I hope so."

# Chapter Thirty-One
# The Stick

ANNA awoke in her cell and stretched her limbs while lying on the thin cotton mattress. Her cell felt cool. Autumn must be approaching. It'd taken weeks, but finally the fevers and aches had left her. She wasn't sick any longer and was feeling back to her old self.

Someone wept a few cells down. Another woman cried, "Another red waterskin! Please! I ran out last night! Please! I need more water!"

Anna checked her own red skin of water. She still had half left. She couldn't imagine running out.

Her cell, it turned out, was large enough for the mattress, a bucket, and a few pegs that held several dresses and spare shifts. She got up and stretched again. Yarro would be by soon with breakfast and her morning seeds.

She peeled off the undershift she'd slept in and found a bucket of fresh water left just outside the stout wooden bars of her cell. That was new. She wondered what it meant. A rag was wrapped around a small chunk of soap floating in the bucket. She picked it out and used it to wash herself. The cold water felt wonderful on her filthy skin.

The woman across the hall wasn't from Blacktree, but she knew her name. Unarta's skin was an exotic shade of dark brown and her hair curled so tight it stood out in all directions. They'd talked now and again when she'd first been brought here. But now Unarta spent her days staring at the stone walls of her cell.

The woman down the hall again called for more water. "Please! I need it!"

Anna checked hers once more, uncorked it, and took a sip. It tasted metallic, but she'd come to appreciate the flavor. With her nose gone dead, everything else tasted like unbuttered nutmash.

After Anna finished washing, she found an undershift made of a silky material. She donned it and rubbed it against her skin. In Midreer, they had the most amazing fabrics. She donned a fine wool overshift before tugging a dress over her head. She loved the green color of the skirt, and the bodice shone bright blue. She imagined it brought out the color of her eyes.

Yarro strutted down the hall. He tossed a red waterskin to the crying woman who abruptly stopped her noises. Coming to Unarta's cell, he unlatched the door from the center where a prisoner couldn't reach it and pulled it open. "Come 'ere."

Unarta didn't look at him.

"If I 'ave to come in after you, you'll get a beating. Better, sweet, to come willingly."

Unarta stood and meekly left her cell. Was she blushing? Anna couldn't tell with that skin of hers.

Yarro turned and smiled at Anna. His cruel eyes studied her face, and he nodded. Taking Unarta by the upper arm, he marched her away.

Half an hour later, Yarro walked her back and put the woman in her cell. Anna watched as she grabbed her red waterskin and drank deeply, her full lips pressing against the opening. She brushed a tear away with a chaffed wrist, then she sank to the floor to sit gingerly.

Yarro unlatched Anna's door. "Your turn."

Anna didn't move. "Where are my seeds?"

"Out of your cell. Now."

Anna straightened her back and stepped from her cell. Her dress felt like armor. She would not let him see her fear. He clutched her upper arm just as he had Unarta's. Anna tried to shrug him off, but her arm felt like it was clamped in a vice. Well, she wore thin armor.

He marched her down the hallway lined with cells. Several of her sisters were still there. Two were showing pregnancies. They glanced at Anna but said nothing.

Yarro pushed her into a side room with a heavy door. Another guard stood by a strong, wood table adjusting a cord. The table had been drilled with four holes and a rope snaked up through the holes forming two loops.

The guard grabbed one of her arms and Yarro grabbed the other. She pulled back, but she might as well have been fighting the sway of a great tree in a heavy wind. They easily shoved her hands through the loops. The guard yanked a cord below the table and the heavy rope cinched tight about her wrists. She stood bent over with her forearms and stomach on the table. She struggled against the rope, her wrists burning from it. She looked around the room, wildly searching for a way out.

Yarro lifted her dress up over her back, then both her shifts. She felt the cool air. No. They couldn't. They wouldn't dare!

Yarro chuckled. The other guard whistled through his teeth.

"Don't you dare!" Anna screamed.

"And why not, sweet? Are you better than your friend across the 'all?"

"Yes! No! I don't know. Don't you dare!"

"I dare much. But no matter. I've been given special instruction, and I'm going to enjoy it."

Anna gritted her teeth as tears fell. "I'll tell Gharan! I will. I'll tell him what you did. I'm not to be touched. You heard him. I'm not to be touched!"

"And 'oo do you think gave me these instructions, sweet?"

"No! I'll tell the Most High! I'll tell him!"

Yarro barked a laugh and walked over to the side of the table. He adjusted his belt buckle and bent down to look at her. "Gharan is the Most 'igh's son. No one will say a word because I'm going to do exactly as ordered." He retrieved a palm length of balsawood from his belt with cords dangling from each end. He forced it between her teeth and tied it behind her head. He moved back behind her.

No! No! No! This couldn't be happening. It couldn't! She bit down on the wood, shaking her head and growling against what he would do to her.

She heard the unmistakable rasp of him drawing his bamboo stick from his belt. "I'd like to give you what your friend across the 'all got, but those weren't my orders for you, sweet."

Did he mean she wasn't going to be... She heard a whoosh in the air, and the bamboo stick struck her along the backs of her bare thighs. She gasped in pain and shock, and her eyes bulged as her ears registered the sharp slap of wood on flesh. New tears welled up and her nose plugged instantly. She breathed through her teeth buried in the wood bit.

Another whoosh through the air led to another inevitable sear of pain. Her knees buckled but the table held her up.

Another came. Then another. She screamed in agony, opening her mouth wider than the bit. It remained in place, secured by the cords tied behind her head. She tried to move her feet under the table, but there was an obstruction. She tried to roll to the side until hands grabbed her hips and righted her. The men laughed at her, but she barely heard them.

A higher strike brought hot pain up her back. Another stuck lower on her thighs and her legs jerked wildly.

"'Ey, can I give it a go?"

"Sure thing. Just be careful 'ere and 'ere. If you hit the tendons near the knees you can do permanent damage. If you 'it 'er tail bone, you could break it. Can't do that."

"I broke my tail bone once. It 'ealed up."

"Yeah, but it 'as something to do with birthing or something. I don't know, but I was told, and I follow orders. You'd better, too."

"Right, then." A lighter blow landed on her backside. It hurt, but almost seemed a relief compared to the burning on the backs of her thighs.

"Not like that. 'It 'er like this. See, side arm."

A stronger strike landed on her backside, and a cry escaped through her teeth. The guard got to work, landing several hard blows. Anna screamed through her bit.

"'Ere. Let me finish 'er up," Yarrow chuckled.

Another spot high on her thighs flared in pain as the stick struck again and again. Anna's world was the pain. Just when she thought the pain couldn't get worse, someone kicked her legs out from under her and beat the bottoms of her feet. The pain continued to burn even after the beating finally stopped. All she could do was concentrate on breathing through it. It consumed her thoughts. She needed some seeds, needed them desperately.

The cord around her head was untied and the bit pulled carefully from her teeth. Yarro cooed to her. "There. That wasn't so bad, was it?"

The rope loosened around her wrists, and her dress fell back down to cover her, but she didn't notice. Anna laid on the table, gasping between sobs.

Yarro stood her up with rough hands. Her head lolled on her neck. All her strength fled, and her knees buckled. Her feet were on fire. Would the pain ever end? Yarro caught her under the arms and straightened her. "Need to rest? No worries, sweet. First, 'ere, take your seeds."

Anna opened her mouth and looked at Yarro's dark, ugly face. The other guard popped two seeds in her mouth and watered her from a red waterskin.

Yarro tipped her head back to check her teeth. "You're alright, sweet. Nothing chipped or broken. Can you walk? No?"

Yarro picked her up and carried her to her cell in his arms. Her head hung weakly over his bracer, and she watched the cells go by, upside down. She saw one of her sisters standing at the bars, eyes wide as she watched.

He flopped Anna down on her mattress. Her bottom hit the rough stone wall and she cried out as new pain flared. She burned from low on her back all the way down to her toes. She'd had no idea what pain was until now.

She heard her door close and latch through the sounds of her own sobs.

THREE days later, Anna checked the backs of her thighs by carefully lying on her back, lifting one leg in the air and putting her foot on her knee. Her legs turned her stomach, mottled as they were with purple and yellow bruises. She couldn't touch them. She'd been sleeping on her stomach.

It was a good thing Kenan couldn't see her like this. He'd be repulsed by her now.

She wondered what he was doing. He might figure out she'd been taken to Midreer, but where in Midreer? He couldn't possibly know. Would he come anyway? Is he right now wandering the cities of this cursed country, searching for her? Or did he count her as lost. He wouldn't even know if she lived. When the women's pool had been raided, before she'd been born, no one went to Midreer to rescue anybody. The people of Blacktree survived and moved on with their lives.

Did she want him to come for her? Part of her desperately wanted him to come strolling down the hall, cut open her cell door with his axe, and carry her away from this place. She dreamed of it. But she knew, if he came here he'd die. She hoped he grieved a short time and found someone new. Though, he probably hadn't. He probably was up in a tree, bending branches. Alone.

Oh Kenan. Don't spend your life alone.

Since the beating, she'd been fed, watered, and applied with two seeds twice a day. Her bucket was carried away and brought back empty. Her shifts were replaced, but she didn't wear them. Anything on her thighs caused sharp pain. The seeds brought some relief, but not much.

With her wide, dark eyes, Unarta watched her cry until Yarro came and marched the woman down the hall, as she was every morning. Later, he brought her back. She never appeared to have been beaten. Anna felt oddly grateful. Better to be beaten.

Yarro turned to Anna. "Good morning, sweet. Got new orders for you. Get dressed or not, but you're coming with me."

Anna rose, glared at Yarro, then dressed as slowly as she could. Unarta watched her with sorrowful eyes. Anna appreciated the unspoken sympathy.

Yarro watched but didn't rush her. Finally, she had no choice but to turn to the cell door. "What are your new orders?"

"Come out of your cell, sweet. You'll find out soon enough."

He took her by the arm and brought her back into the room. The table and the rope loops were there, waiting for her. Anna stopped short just inside the door, panic building inside her. She couldn't stand another beating. She wasn't even healed from the last one.

"No! No! You said you have new orders!"

"That I do, sweet. Same orders but with something new for you. I'm to ask you a question, see?"

Anna didn't fight as she was forced into the ropes. She hoped the new orders would ease what was to come.

Yarro bent close to her ear. "'Oo do you love, sweet?"

Anna struggled against the ropes a moment. Without thinking, she blurted, "Kenan!"

"Wrong answer, sweet. Wrong answer." He forced the bit between her teeth and tied the cords around her head.

The pain came with each swing of the stick. She passed out before getting her seeds.

# Chapter Thirty-Two
# Uncut

LIDAI and Wren finished their morning run. Kenan was already in the conditioning room, sitting on a bench lifting weights and chatting with a girl from his bending class. She sat next to him, also lifting weights but managing to keep her eyes on him.

Lidai didn't like the look of her. Being pretty, she supposed, was the problem. She looked something of Anna, tall with a crown of short, blond hair growing back from her first trial. Her eyes were dark, almost black. That was bad. She might be different enough to hold his attention. Lidai had this girl in an archery class and knew she was trouble.

"Hey, there! How was the run?" Kenan dropped the weights and moved to the bar where he started doing his one-handed pull-ups.

"Fine." Wren sounded bored.

Lidai laughed and pointed at Wren. "He almost fell over a railing today."

"What?" Kenan looked over his muscled shoulder at them. The girl watched her brother, hungrily smiling.

Wren hung his head and grabbed one of Kenan's weights. He began pumping out curls with little effort. "I... I got distracted."

"By what? Did one of those children call you a bad name, again?"

The girl giggled and turned her smile on Wren.

Lidai looked at her – just looked – and the girl bolted from the room. It was really quite satisfying.

"Funny. No, it was your sister."

Lidai put on her best innocent expression.

Kenan laughed. "Did *she* call you a bad name? That's nothing new."

"Yes, but that wasn't it."

"Well, what was it?"

"She..."

"I patted his bottom as we ran. You should have seen him, Kenan! He looked like he got stung by a white-tailed wasp!"

"Uh, right,." Kenan eyed them. "Sounds like we should talk about bride price again?"

"Maybe," Lidai shot back, "you should just stop procrastinating and give him permission."

"Yeah, maybe."

She knew Kenan had approached Master Lamech about the situation. Their Master told him he'd not have the two betrothed as students. He wanted everyone to focus on their training. She didn't want to admit the old man was probably right, curse him. Dragonspit.

Kenan's face brightened. "Wren, perhaps you should talk to Master Lamech. We've had a dry spell, lately. I bet he has some big bats in the twin caves, if you know what I mean."

Wren glowered at him. "No, what do you mean?"

"You know. Corks in the wine jug. Plugs in the air vents ripe for picking."

Wren's brows furrowed deeper, and he shook his head.

What were they talking about? She hated inside jokes.

"Uh, Teachers?" Tadd stood in the doorway. He'd grown again, taller and skinnier. Lidai couldn't keep enough food in the boy. At least he was learning a little respect.

"Yes, Tadd," Lidai said. "What is it?"

"Master Lamech has called for you again."

Kenan dropped to the floor. "At the temple?"

"No. In the fight hall." The boy bowed to them each, one at a time. Bowed! Respect was one thing, but this was quite another. She wondered what had gotten into the boy.

"No time like the present," Wren said as he moved towards the door. Lidai wished he hadn't picked up the saying. It made him sound like a patriarch. She wasn't ready for that, yet.

They moved down the hall, Kenan leading with Wren following, bracketing her in as was their habit. She didn't like it. She couldn't see anything ahead or behind. But they always fell into this line. She stomped a little harder than was strictly necessary, just so the lunkheads would know she was irritated with them. They probably didn't even notice, which made her stomp harder.

As they entered the Hall through a doorway, every master in the school sat on the tiered benches. The wizened old Grandmaster Methuselah sat high on the top bench and smiled his one tooth at them. Maryleen sat on her cushion, looking at them implacably.

Lidai stared. She knew what this was. She wasn't ready. Was she? There was so much more to learn.

Lamech stood. "Shoes off. Stand at center. This is your Trial of Blood."

Well, that sounded ominous. But a thrill raced through Lidai's chest. Ready or not, it was finally time. The three quickly shed their boots and stood in a line in the center of the room.

Maryleen stepped carefully forward. "This is the Trial of Blood. None has ever left this trial without a scar to tell of it." The old woman pointed to a thin, white line on her hand. "This morning, you will show your skill by surviving. Or you will fail, and your family will be notified. Do you understand?"

This was a little more serious than she thought. She nodded her head along with the others.

"Very well. This is your last chance to survive uncut. You may leave now. Your name will be stricken from the rolls, but we will allow your departure."

Lidai didn't twitch.

"Indeed. I expected no less. Let the trials begin. Who will go first?"

They each stepped forward.

"Well, which is it?"

Before the men could speak, Lidai said, "Me, Mistress Maryleen. I will set the bar high for these two clods."

Maryleen smiled at her. "Indeed, young woman. Come forward. Clods may be seated over there." Kenan and Wren moved to where she pointed and sat on the front benches. Lidai stepped to face Maryleen.

The old woman looked at her with an imperious gaze. "Turn around."

Lidai did so. The woman fingered her ponytail. It dangled to the top of her back, thick and a rich, dark brown that shined in sunlight.

"Do you like your hair, young woman?"

"I like that another likes it, Mistress."

"An honest answer, though only in part. Do you want to keep it?"

Lidai stiffened. Would the old woman cut it off? "Very much so, Mistress." She tried to turn, but Maryleen had a grip in one tight, bony fist.

"Did you know hair won't grow back through a scar?"

"Yes, Mistress. I have seen it on some soldiers. I have a narrow scar of my own."

"Indeed. I saw it soon after you arrived here."

A large man, one of Belroon's students, thumped into the room. He was wearing full plate armor of freshly worked bronze and carried a shield the size of a tabletop. In his hand dangled a large hammer that reached the floor. His green tag hung from a cord around his thick neck and dangled on his breastplate. He stopped, smashed his hammer off his shield once, and

348

stood waiting.

"That man has been instructed to do one thing." Maryleen wiggled the ponytail before letting it go. "He is to cut off your hair. He is to take some of your scalp doing it. If he succeeds, you will always have a bald spot on your head, somewhere it will show, in a place where this hair someone likes so much will no longer grow. Do you understand, young woman?"

Lidai's face fell for a moment. "Yes, Mistress. And what am I to do?"

"Oh, nothing too difficult. Just survive and bring me his tag."

Lidai chest tightened with the challenge ahead. The man slammed his hammer against his chest armor. The sound echoed through the room. Some of the closer teachers flinched where they sat. The man let his weapon drop to the floor, freeing his hand. He reached up, took his tag, and showed it to her, smiling. He tucked the thing under his breastplate, took up his hammer, and advanced.

Lidai felt her stomach drop. This man was easily as large as Wren. She'd heard he was a blacksmith and had a new wife who fed him well. He looked it.

Lidai looked around for a weapon. The fight hall had many weapons ready for use. She wasn't near any of them. In the time it took her to scan the room, the man was on her.

The shield came at her first. She danced backwards. The hammer came next. She ducked and rolled to the side. The shield came again. She could see nothing but the shield! It struck her body from shoulder to hip, and she flew backwards and fell to the floor.

The man continued his advance as Lidai scrambled back. The hammer came down and she spread her legs. The mass of bronze shattered a board between her knees, filling her dress with splinters. As the hammer rose, she rolled away. As she moved, she felt another board shatter behind her.

Lidai tucked her legs high and tight against her chest and used the momentum to continue the roll backwards. She came to her feet easily. She quickly rolled back again as the hammer came around, nearly killing her on the spot.

Again, the man came in, stomping in his leather boots. Lidai had enough of being on the defensive. It was time to show this lout she was not easy prey. As the shield came forward, she spun around it and delivered a kick to the man's kidneys. Her foot struck metal armor and pain flared up her leg. He didn't seem to notice as the hammer came around again.

She back-flipped away and almost landed in Lamech's lap! He booted her bottom, and she rolled under the next hammer swing, coming up smoothly. She hiked up her dress and sprinted for the rack holding archery equipment. As she approached, she heard the blacksmith's boots thudding right behind her. There was no time to grab a weapon!

Lidai kicked off the sturdy base of the rack and jumped up on the highest bench, sprinting along it around the outer edge of the curved wall.

"Come back here, little chipmunk!" The man sounded like he was having fun.

Lidai reached the next rack and pulled off a short bronze sword. She was passing fair with a sword, but not great. She'd use what she had.

She couldn't return to the floor. The big man was right there. Instead, she leapt past a lattice window to the next high bench and continued her sprint along the curved wall.

The man hurled his hammer at her. It gave her a glancing blow on her thigh before bouncing off the plank wall and falling to the floor below.

Something guttural left her throat as she took the hit. The pain wracked her entire body. The strike to her thigh hurt with every step, but she ran onwards, limping slightly as she pushed the pain aside. She passed behind the seated teachers. This probably didn't look good. She was supposed to be showing her skill, not running from her opponent. But she grinned with determination. She had a plan.

She reached the Grandmaster, who sat with his hands in his lap, smiling up at her. She spun around and ran back along the high bench the way she'd just come. She would use speed and agility to defeat her opponent.

Her teachers all craned their necks to watch her. The big, armored man skidded to a halt. By the time he turned, she was off the benches. She hit the yellowwood floor in a roll and sprinted towards the knives. She limped a little but ignored the pain and kept going. A glance told her she'd have time. Probably.

She tossed her sword backwards at the man. She heard it clang off his shield and skitter across the floor. Someone shouted in alarm. She hoped she hadn't skewered anyone's foot.

She snagged a handful of throwing knives from the rack and turned to face the big man. He'd retrieved the hammer. He had it raised as he came at her.

With a quick flick of her wrist, she sent a blade at his eyes. He caught it on his shield. She flicked another and struck him in the bicep of his hammer arm. It didn't penetrate through his armor. The point was sharp, but the rest of the blade was blunted. The man roared with rage. If this didn't work, she was probably going to die right here. Or worse, get her hair cut again.

She threw another blade at his eyes. He lifted his shield and blocked it. He was almost on her.

He didn't see the fourth blade, but she was sure he felt it penetrate the arch of his foot through his leather boot.

The man took one more step and fell forward.

Lidai knew he would crush her under the weight of man, bronze, and wood. She stepped nimbly forward before falling back, twisting as she did so.

The man fell headfirst into the wall below the knife rack. His helm made a distinctive crack against the rack's base. He shuddered, then fell unconscious on top of her.

WREN couldn't believe what he was watching. His beloved woman fought against this beast of a man. He knew she could take care of herself, but he'd sparred with this man many times. He knew what he could do. It took every ounce of will to stay where he sat.

When the big man thudded into the rack base, knocking himself out, he watched in horror as Lidai simply disappeared beneath. The hammer was under there, somewhere. The massive shield was deadly when used properly and alone weighed nearly as much as she did. Almighty, the man himself was deadly completely unarmed.

The man groaned but didn't stir. He was alive. Wren could see his backplate heave with breath. How long were the teachers going to wait to see where Lidai had landed? Were they just going to sit and watch as she suffocated under the bulk and armor on top of her?

An arm shifted. Then a leg, but not under his own power. The man's head still hung to the floor.

Wren watched as a woman's arm curled out from around the man's shoulder. The man's body shifted slightly. Then a leg shifted. Finally, Lidai pulled herself out from under the big blacksmith. Her face was flushed red from the effort. She bled from scratches on her forearms, and she limped. But she stood up and faced the masters of the school.

Slowly and with a grim smile, she held her fist out. The green tag dangled beneath.

Wren leapt to his feet, arms raised in silent celebration. Yes! Yes!

Maryleen approached and stood in front of Lidai. "Good. How do you feel?"

"Exhausted."

Wren sat back down and clapped Kenan's shoulder. Exhausted sounded about right. He was exhausted just watching.

"Perfect," Maryleen said. "Fetch a bow and five arrows."

Lidai complied, limping to the rack of archery equipment. Wren frowned at the old woman. What more could she want of her? She'd shown her mettle. Wasn't she done?

When Lidai returned, Maryleen produced five green apples in a small basket. "To pass this test, none must reach the floor without a hole. But be warned, you'll need an arrow when you're done here, or you will fail this trial."

Lidai nodded and readied herself. She held four arrows in one hand and one between her teeth. Blood leaked out of one nostril from her battle with the blacksmith. The man rolled over against the wall, groaning. Two women in white robes tended to him. Wren longed to go to Lidai. He twitched and squirmed on the bench.

Without warning, Maryleen hurled the basket of apples into the air, flinging it high. The apples flew free.

Faster than Wren could count, arrows flew to the apples as Lidai darted around on the yellowwood floor. Apples burst into pieces and arrows thudded into the ceiling. Two apples were skewered with one arrow and quivered where it lodged in the ceiling. The basket fell and Lidai caught it on the end of the arrow she still had left.

Turning to Maryleen, she bowed. Maryleen looked up at the ceiling and smiled broadly. Wren had never seen the woman smile before.

Maryleen turned to the masters. "Master Lamech, please note that this Teacher must only replace one board from the ceiling."

Everyone looked up. Sure enough, all four arrows were stuck into a single short plank. An apple slid off an arrow and fell to the floor, rolling near Wren. He picked it up. They hadn't had breakfast, and he'd need his strength, so he gave it two big bites and gave the rest to Kenan.

The masters nodded to each other. Wren was pleased to see they seemed impressed.

Maryleen led Lidai to a window. "Do you see it, young woman?"

"Yes, Mistress."

"Can you hit it."

"Yes, Mistress."

"Be careful of the people."

"I will, Mistress." Lidai nocked her last arrow.

The masters all moved to other windows to watch. He might get kicked out of the school, but Wren wasn't missing this for all the stew in the world. He padded over to a window and Kenan joined him.

As they got there, the arrow flew. The black of the shaft stood out clear against the bright morning light.

The arrow arced up, leveled, then arced down. Everyone watched, and it seemed as if the room itself held its breath.

They heard nothing, but they watched the apple explode into green and white pieces.

"Yes!" Wren shouted with all his considerable volume. His was the only voice. Everyone turned and looked at him. Lamech glared. Lidai smiled.

Well, nothing to do but smile at them all. Wren and Kenan trotted back to their bench and took their seats.

Maryleen brought Lidai to the center of the floor. Whatever wound she'd taken on her thigh had grown worse. Blood stained her dress from mid-thigh to the hem, leaving a scarlet track of drops on the floor. Wren wanted this over for her. He yearned to go scoop her up and tend to her.

He couldn't sit and wait any longer. Standing, he took a step.

Lidai waved him off with a look and a gesture. Wren stepped back. He couldn't sit. He wasn't happy, but he would not damage her resolve. For her, he would stay put.

Maryleen looked at Lamech. "Master, I present to you and the Grandmaster a woman ready for you to test."

Lamech stood. He hooked a thumb through his belt as he approached her. He eyed the blood on her dress, then looked into her tired eyes. "Do you want a rest, girl?"

"No, Master. I am ready. Do your best."

Lamech laughed and it sounded like stone grinding. "I always liked your spunk, girl." And without warning, he hurled a knife at her.

Just ask quick, she caught it and returned it to him.

But he was already charging and dodged the blade. He produced a long knife from behind his back and lunged for her breast. Wren held his position, but barely.

She spun, elbowed Lamech in the nose, and danced away, limping.

Lamech backed off, holding his nose with one hand. Blood oozed through his fingers. "Do you have any idea, girl, how long it's been since someone bloodied my nose?"

Lidai smiled back. "Far too long, Old Patch Face." And Wren loved her all the more.

She circled the Master, keeping her eyes focused on him. Wren could see her favoring her wounded leg. Every moment of this last fight drained her. He could see it in the way she held herself.

Lamech smiled through his grisly beard. "Time to return the favor, girl." He lunged at her again, low, then punched high. This was a feint, but she fell for it. A hammer strike from the fist holding the long knife landed on her nose. The butt of the handle struck her just below the bone. Blood sprayed down across her chest as she fell backwards. But she rolled, thrusting with her hands and landing back on her feet, barely keeping her balance. Her thigh didn't seem to be working right. She didn't touch her nose. Lamech advanced.

She turned and looked right at Wren, who stood frozen next to Kenan. She screeched, "Wren, no! Stop!"

Lamech turned towards Wren, who smiled and gave him a little wave from across the room. Wren saw Lidai produce the dagger he knew she kept hidden on her thigh. Lamech swung back, quick but not quick enough.

Lidai darted out with the blade. Lamech got a hand up and was scored across the knuckles by the little knife.

Lamech backed off, holding Lidai at bay with the point of his long knife. "Good. Hold there."

Lidai slumped a bit but held where she was.

He dropped his knife to the floor and produced a small tube. He struggled with it, dripping blood all over. He finally uncapped the tube. He pulled off Lidai's green tag, taking her yellowwood city tag in one hand. He painted a wide, black stripe across the tag with the bristles sticking out of the open tube. He painted over her city information. Lidai wasn't a citizen any longer. Wren's beloved was now a black stripe of this school.

"Welcome, daughter. You have earned a place at my table."

Lidai smiled at him. Tears ran through the blood on her face.

"Now, go to Maryleen. She will take you to the healing room. Your leg has me worried."

"Thank you, Master."

Wren watched her go. The blacksmith was sitting up against the wall under the knife rack, testing his limbs. As she passed to leave, he said, "Good fight, little chipmunk."

Wren so badly wanted to run to her, but she warned him off with another look. She was so strong!

"She's so strong," Kenan said.

"Yes."

"I'll give you permission. As soon as this is over."

"I know you will." Wren stood and stepped forward. "Master Lamech. I am next."

"Hold there, boy. I have to wrap this cursed hand. You have a real viper with that one."

Wren beamed.

Maryleen looked back from the doorway. "I warned you she had a blade."

"Yes, yes." Lamech wound a strip of cloth around his knuckles. "So, you did. Now, boy, come here."

Wren approached the old Master, stopped, and stood smiling down at the man.

"What do you have to smile about, boy?"

"My woman bested you."

"Is that what you think happened?"

"How's your hand?"

Lamech regarded him. "You'll wish you faced me instead, before this is over, boy." Then he twitched a finger of his good hand at Trime.

The smaller man sauntered out on the floor. He wore no armor but carried a steel longsword at his waist. Steel. They had only practiced with

354

bronze. What could this man do with steel?

Lamech turned to Wren. "This is your last chance. Leave, if you wish. Your name will be stricken from the roll, but you will survive."

"I'd rather never eat again."

Lamech grunted, then looked at them both. "Master Trime, cut this man six times for me, if you please. Boy, you need only make Master Trime yield. Survive, boy, if you can." He sounded like he doubted it.

Wren watched Lamech stalk off and sit down. Wren turned back to Trime, eyeing the man. "A steel sword. What's the special occasion?"

"Your blood, lumberman."

"So sure?" Wren tried to sound unconcerned, but he heard a small break in his voice. In truth, he'd rather face three Belroons over this one small man.

Trime smiled at him, bowing.

Wren didn't hesitate. He threw an uppercut at the man, right in the nose. The blow knocked Trime over backwards. His sword hilt gouged the polished floor. Wren looked at it and raised an eyebrow at the man. "Your sword. You'll replace those boards."

Lying on the floor, Trime touched his nose and looked at the blood on his fingers. He made eye contact with Wren, and whispered, "You fool."

Wren gulped and bolted for the rack holding the shields. He had just enough time to snag a medium wood shield off the rack and thrust his arm through the straps. He never heard Trime rise or give chase, but he spun just in time to catch the tip of the steel on the shield.

"Ack!" Wren shouted, defending with the shield. He reached blindly towards the rack behind him, grabbed another shield, and threw it at the man.

Trime ducked the flying disk, stood back straight, and caught the next one in the chest just below his collarbones. He fell over backwards, again.

Wren didn't taunt the man this time. He left him on the floor and bolted for the rack with the axes. He glanced back to see Trime once more on his feet and coming on fast.

Wren ignored the big axes. He went right for a small axe with a long handle. He ripped it off the wall, turned, and charged back at Trime.

Trime saw the maneuver and feinted to the side. Wren didn't fall for it and barreled right over Trime, knocking him to the floor for the third time. He felt a tug on the back of his leg, however. He spun to face his opponent and felt warm blood trickle down his calf.

Trime got to his feet. "I'm impressed, lumberman. But that's one."

Wren snarled and advanced. It was a ruse. Wren hoped to make the man think he would attack wildly. As soon as he was in range, Trime exploded into motion. All pretenses gone in the face of the flashing steel longsword, Wren backed off, turning blade cuts with his shield and axe. He was nicked on the forearm holding the axe. He felt a cut along the ribs. And the tip of the steel sword flicked up against his arm.

Finally, Trime stepped back. Wren held his ground and eyed the steel blade. A little bead of red ran along both edges near the tip.

"Three, lumberman."

"Four. You got me under my arm, too."

"I see. Four it is."

"What are you waiting for? Come at me, rabbit."

Trime frowned. Wren wasn't breathing hard or favoring any of the wounds. Wren knew they could be worse, that Trime was minimizing the damage on purpose. Yet, Wren hoped he looked fresh to Trime.

Wren certainly felt fresh. Almighty, it was good to be here!

Trime hesitated.

Wren stepped forward and swung his axe.

Trime dodged the blow and darted in with the sword, tip first.

The move went exactly as Wren thought it would. He twisted away from Trime's blade and threw his shield at the man with all his strength.

Trime's eyes widened, and he fell back with a shout. It was the opening Wren needed. He leapt forward, grabbed the longsword high near the hilt, and wrenched it from Trime's hand. The blade flew across the room with a spray of blood from the cut on his hand.

Trime grabbed Wren with one hand and Wren felt a foot coil around an ankle. He knew what came next. So, he used it.

Sure enough, the wrist lock came, and pain flared up Wren's arm. At the same time, pressure on his knee caused his leg to lock straight. Wren fell backwards.

He pulled Trime down with him. "Welcome to the floor, rabbit."

Trime struggled. The man could roll but Wren thrived on the skill. Further, Wren was much stronger and much heavier. The match went on for a few more moments until Trime's arm was bent back at an awkward angle. He tapped out. Wren smiled down at him.

Then Wren felt a tap on his thigh. He looked down to see a small knife against his inner thigh.

Wren smiled broader as he eased off the smaller man. "Good match, Master."

"You think so?" Trime struggled to his feet. "If asked earlier, I would have said I could dodge shields better than anyone."

Lamech stomped up to them. "Agreed. What happened?"

"The lumberman simply outclassed me, Master. Clearly, I must have been overconfident."

Lamech nodded. "Perhaps. But Belroon has trained this boy well."

"Yah! He can crush the tiny rabbit!" Belroon roared laughter and pounded his feet on the floor in glee.

Wren felt troubled. "Master Lamech. Master Trime won this fight. These cuts are shallow. He held back."

Lamech nodded to him in approval. "Yes. He did. If this had been real, you would be dead, and he would have already found a horn of mead. Personally, I prefer red ale, but to each his own."

"But Master, I lost."

"No. I'm happy you can see the truth, boy. But you did well. None has bested Trime in over twenty years."

"Twenty-seven," Trime confirmed, then limped off to set his nose.

Wren nodded, bowing to them both.

"The initial strike was inspired, boy." Lamech nodded again to him.

"Thank you, Master. In truth, I feared him. I can deal with anyone, I think. But that man is scary good. I had to improvise and wait for an opportunity."

"And you found it."

"Yes, but only because I had time to think it through there, at the end. So, what's next?"

"You fight one more time."

"With you?"

"With me, boy. After all, you can handle anyone."

"That's not what I meant."

"It doesn't matter. You subdued one of my best. Time to pay the price."

"How do you suggest..."

Lamech's foot struck out, hitting Wren just above the left knee. Wren lost his balance and bent over. The following upper cut sent him hurtling through the air and thudding hard to the floor on his back. His breath left in a rush.

"How'd you like that, boy?"

Breath finally returned and Wren eyed him from the floor as he gasped. Wren reached up to his face, closed a nostril with a pinky finger, and blew blood out the other. It sprayed red mist into the air.

Lamech smiled down at him.

Wren climbed to his feet. He no longer felt fresh. His head spun a bit and his left knee swelled. His cuts stung with sweat. "I'm not done with you, Old Patch Face."

Lamech smiled grimly. "As good a name as any."

"Glad you like it. I have others."

"I bet you do, boy. Why don't you whisper them in my ear?"

Wren struck with a fist. He moved like it was a feint, but it wasn't.

Lamech blocked it almost lazily and poked Wren just below the breastbone with two stiff fingers. The breath whooshed out of Wren's mouth again, and he gaped at the older man. Lamech followed it with a swipe to Wren's eyes. The blow wasn't damaging, catching mostly eyebrow and ridge, but Wren's eyes watered.

Lamech stepped back. "You are growing slow as you..."

Wren spun and kicked. He might not be able to breathe but he could still fight.

Lamech saw it coming and moved, but too slowly this time. He took the kick in the stomach, and his air whooshed out as well. Both men stood, hand on knees, mouths gaping at each other.

Wren caught his breath first with a deep gasp. With air returned energy. He stepped forward and hooked a punch at Lamech's head.

Lamech breathed as he stood straight. The blow passed by harmlessly. He threw a ridgehand at Wren's temple. Wren saw it and blocked.

Punches continued to be thrown and blocked. The two men moved about the room. Neither had the grace of Trime, yet they danced with skill and attempted to land a blow on the other. Every attempt would, if successful, do lasting harm.

Lamech succeeded first, slamming a thrust punch into Wren's lower stomach. Wren collapsed downwards and used his momentum to strike Lamech in the thigh. Both men hit the wood floor.

Wren's eyes still teared from the eye swipe and the taste of blood filled his mouth. He gasped in ragged breaths through his open mouth. His nose had swelled to uselessness and throbbed in pain. But he reached out and found Lamech. He closed his fist around a wisp of white hair.

Wren rolled. He hooked a leg around Lamech and pulled him in close. Lamech produced a small blade. Wren knew it was there, caught the older man's wrist, and smashed his hand into the yellowwood floor. The knife skittered away as Lamech grunted.

Wren took an elbow to his forehead. Blood flowed and sprayed across them both.

Wren twisted Lamech's fingers and poked him in the throat as he rolled.

Lamech caught the thrust on withdrawal and twisted Wren's wrist back. All the while, Wren was unsure whether it was him or Lamech keeping the two together, wrestling for superiority.

Wren felt cold. This man could roll.

Wren's plan had been to get Lamech to the floor. He would finish the match quickly, as he had with Trime.

But Lamech was laughing.

KENAN watched the two large men roll on the floor. He knew rolling enough to fight from the ground. But this was something else. The two were expert rollers. One moment, Wren had an edge. He was younger and stronger. The next moment, Lamech had the edge. He was more compact and fought viciously. It was hard to tell who had more talent with the skill.

As they rolled, Kenan thought Wren was about to get caught in an elbow lock, until he maneuvered his body and nearly put Lamech in an arm bar. But Lamech squirmed out of it and put Wren in a choke. Yet, somehow, Wren got a hand inside the choke and saved himself.

And then Wren snaked a hand up around the top of Lamech's head. His fingers reached down over Lamech's face. He hooked two fingers up Lamech's nostrils and pulled him into a head lock. Lamech fought it for a moment, his nose pulled painfully up and around. The master gasped and finally tapped out.

With fingers still up Lamech's nose, both men looked at Kenan.

Kenan felt like he'd just been poleaxed. There it was, Wren picking Lamech's nose.

Lamech and Wren untangled themselves, stood, and bowed to each other. "Welcome, son. You have earned a place at my table."

Wren, breathing hard, smiled at the older man.

Lamech marked a stripe on Wren's yellow tag and Wren looked at it, smiling. He blew on the paint to dry it.

"Now, son, go and get your cuts tended. Some I see will need stitches and glue. Go."

"Thank you, Master Lamech." Wren turned and left the room, limping on a swollen knee.

All eyes turned to Kenan, who nodded. This had been a long time in coming. Kenan stood, squared his shoulders, and took a deep breath. He met Master Lamech at the center of the floor.

Lamech regarded him. "You will not stick any fingers up my nose. Got that, boy?"

Kenan grinned. "Yes, Master Lamech. No nose picking."

Lamech grunted at him. "You have a weakness boy. I hope one day to beat it out of you."

Kenan raised an eyebrow. "I have many, Master. To which do you refer?"

Lamech grunted again. "You think it's not a weakness. But you'll learn."

"As you say, Master Lamech."

"That sounded patronizing. Are you ready, boy?"

"Yes."

"You may leave. Your name will be stricken from the rolls, but you'll survive this day, Almighty willing."

"No."

"I figured. Belroon!"

The huge man, covered in steel plate and carrying a large wood shield, trotted into the center. "Here I am, Master."

"Pick two weapons, if you please."

Belroon trotted over and came back with two bronze axes. He handed one to Lamech. The weight jostled the older man despite his strong arm. Kenan stared at them both.

Lamech held out the axe. Kenan took it. Lamech gazed at Kenan with a steady eye. "That will be a tough choice for you, boy. He's an expert, and you haven't trained much with axes. To first blood, then. Have fun."

Belroon thumped his axe off his large belly, clanking bronze against steel.

Kenan swooped his axe back and forth. The weapon felt almost ridiculously large. Kenan eyed the huge man, who held up his shield as they circled. The wooden shield showed bronze rivets holding the planks together. Other rivets showed where the arm straps were attached.

Steel armor covered the man on the front and sides. It had few gaps. The tops of his booted feet were covered by plates of steel as well. A steel visor dropped down in front of Belroon's face, leaving a finger wide gap at the eyes.

The man looked impenetrable.

Kenan tested the huge axe some more. It weighed more than every other weapon he commonly used, combined.

"Boy!" Belroon bellowed. "What are you waiting for? Are you timid? You are also a rabbit, yah?"

Kenan circled.

Belroon stepped and swung. Kenan casually stepped back to let the blade swipe past. It seemed slow to him. Belroon looped the swing into an overhand cut. Kenan stepped to the side and the blade broke a board.

Belroon backed off a step. "You'll fix that, boy, yah?"

"You broke it, Master."

"Yah! Fight me, rabbit!" Belroon charged with the shield forward.

Kenan rolled forward and diagonally, avoiding the shield while ducking the axe. He saw an opening on the back of Belroon's leg and swiped with his axe.

Belroon danced out of the arc of the swing, unharmed. "Not bad, rabbit. You almost won. That would be too easy, yah?"

"Yah."

"You mock me, rabbit?"

"No, Master. I wouldn't dare." Kenan paused briefly, smiling with mischief. "Yah?"

Belroon stopped moving, resting the huge shield on the floor. He drew in breath to speak.

Before the master could utter a sound, Kenan struck, stepping and cutting with the axe horizontally. He gripped the axe low and high in both hands, putting his weight into the cut across the face of the shield.

Rivets popped free and clattered on the floor.

"What kind of stupid attack was..."

The big shield fell off Belroon's arm. He jerked and stared down at the small bracer on his forearm.

Kenan stepped back, choked up on the handle of the great axe, and swung it upwards. The tip scored Belroon's wrist just below the bracer.

"What?" Belroon roared.

Kenan dropped the heavy axe head to the floor and leaned on the handle. He grinned. "Yah."

Belroon looked from Kenan to his cut wrist and back again. Then again. Finally, the round man dropped his axe, ripped off his helmet, and boomed out laughter.

Kenan enjoyed the sound of it.

Wren, with a cloth tied around his waist and with needle and thread dangling down his bloodied arm, stepped out of a side room. "What's going on?"

Kenan glanced at him with a grin.

Belroon's laughter subsided. "Master Lamech, see here. I have been bloodied by this rabbit, yah? No, I shall call him a fishercat. He fights well, Master. I yield the floor."

Lamech came out to the center, shooing Wren back to the healing room as he came.

Belroon gathered his gear, Kenan's axe, and returned to his seat. He looked at Trime, who was wiping his nose. "Trime, I didn't even get to break a sweat, yah? You have done well, my friend."

Trime smiled from under a swollen, red nose at his robust friend.

Lamech stood before Kenan and glared at him. "Who taught you to break shield rivets?"

"No one, Master. It just seemed like the best way to get to something I could make bleed."

Lamech grunted at him. "Yes. And I should have remembered you're a woodbender and good with an axe. Are you ready for your next test?"

"Yes, Master Lamech. I'm ready."

Lamech eyed him. "I bet you are. Very well. Master Trime, if you please."

Trime looked eager to redeem himself. As the two passed each other on the floor, Lamech whispered something to him. When Lamech reached his bench, he turned and announced, "Again, to first blood."

Kenan didn't wait for Trime. He spun and bolted for the sword rack.

Reaching it, he yanked off a bronze sword. He spun to see Trime standing calmly in the middle, waiting and watching along with the rest of the masters. He felt embarrassed, but not much. So far, this trial had been ruthless. The only rule he'd been given was to first blood, and he wasn't going to wait while Trime attacked first.

Hiding the motion behind his back, Kenan snagged a bronze knife off the rack as well. He also grabbed a small shield and another knife which he held in his shield hand. If he was given time, he would use it.

"Are you quite ready, Woodbender?"

"I could run for some armor."

"I think not. Leave the room and you fail."

"Ah. Well, then. Would you wait while I run over there, grab a bow, and nock an arrow?"

Trime smiled wickedly. "You should have run there, first."

"I thought you'd be right behind me."

"I see. A wise assumption. Now, you'll have to bloody me the hard way."

"It won't be so hard."

"As you say, Woodbender."

The two closed. Trime's sword was steel and much longer. Kenan's sword was bronze, shorter, and heavier. But he had a shield and a couple of knives hidden and ready. Kenan knew Trime would have knives, too. He always did.

Trime held Kenan beyond reach with the tip of the longsword. The edge was not blunted. Kenan knew, if cut, he must rely on Trime's mercy to survive.

Trime glared at Kenan. He had a point to make to everyone in the room.

Right. Better not get cut. Kenan watched and waited for Trime to make the first move.

Trime jabbed with the sword. Kenan turned the point on his shield. Trime repeated the attack, testing and probing Kenan's defense. Kenan used his shield and held his sword at the ready.

Trime attacked low and high. Kenan defended, dodged, and turned attacks aside. He did not counter. He would be patient.

Trime grew bolder, attacking harder and more viciously. Kenan turned attacks, spun away, and deflected. He kept his sword ready.

Trime broke a sweat. Kenan did not and continued to keep a careful watch.

Trime unleashed a torrent of strikes. The sword flicked in from every direction. The man was quick! Kenan spun, stepped, and ducked. He blocked with his shield and parried with his sword, minimizing his movement and conserving energy.

Trime grunted with the effort. The attacks kept coming. Kenan knew one would get through. He knew his time was running short. Still, he parried and kept his shield up.

A sweaty shock of black hair flopped over Trime's eye. Finally.

Kenan deflected a blow with his shield and stepped to Trime's blind side. Trime turned his head to follow. Kenan feinted with the shield. Trime stepped back.

Behind the feint, Kenan dropped and swiped his sword at Trime's shin. It should have worked. Instead, Trime danced back out of range.

"Good, Woodbender. That would have worked."

"It should have worked."

"It would have, if I didn't know what you were going to do."

"Am I so transparent?"

"Not usually. But I saw the look in your eye. If I didn't know you, I would not have escaped."

"Well, next time, I'll close my eyes."

"I see. Seems dangerous."

"Come and find out."

Trime stood his ground. "I think I'll rest a moment."

"If you need to, rabbit."

"I see. Fishercat."

Kenan grinned at him. "You do know fishers eat rabbits, right?"

"In truth, Woodbender, I don't know what a fishercat is."

"It's sort of a vicious land otter. Fears nothing. I once saw a fisher chasing a big toedragon."

"Really? Show me."

"Okay, Master." And Kenan stepped forward. This would be fun.

Kenan used his shield. He pressed forward with every step, always at an angle, but forward. Trime used his sword to hold Kenan back. Off the tip of Trime's sword, Kenan couldn't reach Trime with his own blade.

He continued to press, conserving energy with short pushes and slides, holding his shield in front and close. Trime danced back in curves and angles, poking at Kenan with his longsword, trying to get around the defense.

Finally, Trime pushed too hard with the sword, and it skittered past on Kenan's shield. Kenan instantly turned and thrust at Trime's thigh with the bronze sword.

Trime saw the move. He dodged by rolling to the side. Kenan's thrust missed.

"Again, you almost had me."

"Tired?"

"Not tired enough, Woodbender."

Trime held his sword down, with the tip on the floor. Kenan knew it was bait, but knowing was useful. He could counter a baited trap.

Kenan moved in, bronze sword stabbing forward. Sure enough, at the last moment, the steel longsword flicked up in an attempt to cut Kenan's shin. Kenan cut down with his short sword to block Trime's cut, spun, and hit him high with the shield.

Trime fell to the floor, rolled backwards, and came back up to his feet. He felt at the side of his face, but there was no blood.

"That was good. Very good, Woodbender."

"Thank you, Master. Are you sure you're not cut there?"

Trime probed with his fingers again but came away clean. "I fear you must try again."

Kenan wasted no time, attacking in full. He attacked with shield and sword, both flying at Trime.

Trime parried, blocked with his free hand, and gave ground. He watched Kenan's attack carefully. Kenan watched him back with as much care. Kenan left a small opening. He covered it with his shield, but it was there. He waited for his master to take the bait.

Trime took it, darting in with the steel sword.

Kenan stepped back, feigning imbalance.

Trime pressed his attack. Kenan gave more ground.

Finally, Trime swung his blade down from above.

Kenan was ready. Instead of turning the attack on the face of the shield, he caught it on the edge. The blade split the shield down to the center cross member and stuck fast. Kenan used his body to turn shield and sword in Trime's hand, stepped, and kicked. The sword wrenched free of Trime's hand. Kenan hurled both sword and shield across the room.

Trime crouched, unarmed and wary of Kenan's sword.

Kenan smiled at his master. "I didn't have time to tighten the shield straps."

"I see."

"Give up?"

"I cannot start now."

"Right." Kenan lunged forward, sword tip stabbing low, shield knife in his other hand.

Trime deflected the blade with his leather boot, spun through the step, and brought two knuckles towards Kenan's temple. He moved with blinding speed. Kenan knew it would knock him unconscious instantly if he allowed it to connect.

Kenan ducked the blow he saw coming and cut Trime's arm with a light touch of the knife as it passed.

Trime jumped back, looked at his arm, and smiled. "Well done, Woodbender."

"Thank you, Master. For everything. I have appreciated your teaching."

"There's more to learn."

"I know, and I want it."

"I see. Let us learn together."

Lamech approached. "Are you cut, Trime?"

"Yes, Master. Kenan was kind and left me whole."

"Do you need stitches?"

"No, Master, just some glue, I think. But I'll wait until the trial is over." Lamech and Trime bowed to each other. Trime retrieved his sword from the shield and moved back to his seat.

Lamech eyed Kenan. "Good with axe and sword, I see. Knife, too."

"Thank you, Master Lamech."

"A woodbender of some skill. Very good with hands, feet, and at bending."

"If you say so, Master."

"I do. As you can see, I've had a rough morning. What would you like to do? How are you to prove yourself to me?"

"First blood?"

"Yes, I think..."

Kenan didn't wait. He dropped to his haunches without warning and slashed his hidden knife at Lamech's shin.

Lamech lifted his leg out of the way, casually, as if he expected the attack. Only, Kenan hadn't been aiming at Lamech's front leg.

The blade slashed Lamech's back shin just above his boot. He heard the man grunt.

Knowing there would be more, Kenan rolled to the side just in time. Lamech's long blade thumped point down into the yellowwood floor where Kenan had just been.

Kenan rolled to the balls of his feet and stood ready.

Lamech stood back erect, leaving his knife in his floor. "Boy, I just got these boots."

"Sorry, Master Lamech."

"No, you're not."

"No, I'm not, Master Lamech."

Lamech grunted at him, then smiled. It looked strange on his craggy old face. "I'm 645 years old. I have *never* promoted a student to black stripe without a mark on him. Dragonscrape, boy, you haven't even broken a sweat!"

"Yes, Master Lamech."

"Oh, that's enough of that. Welcome, son. You have earned a place at my table." And the old man hugged him.

Nothing could have shocked Kenan more.


AFTER all the cuts were balmed, stitched and glued, and after sore joints were pasted with strong-smelling ointment, the three ate their midday meal at their customary table.

Wren and Lidai ate slowly. Both were hurting in many places.

Lidai said, "It wasn't as bad as everyone thought. It's almost nothing. I'll have a massive bruise for a couple weeks or more. The hammer cut a line where the edge hit. Apparently, the bruise swelled faster than normal and made it bleed worse than it should have."

Kenan didn't eat slowly. He shoveled in food like his friend usually did. Wren eyed him balefully. Kenan grinned at him, winked, and turned to Lidai. "I saw you limp on the way in. It can't be nothing."

"It's the tube."

Wren turned to her. "Tube?"

"Yeah. The healer put in a small tube to drain the bruise."

"Why aren't you leaving bloody footprints everywhere?"

Lidai explained. "He ran the tube to a bladder, then bandaged the whole thing to the back of my leg."

Kenan stopped eating for a moment. His stomach tightened at the image. "Gross."

Lidai smiled carefully under her swollen nose. "Yep."

"I'm just glad he didn't break your leg. A finger or two closer, and he would have snapped your femur like a stick."

"Yep. I'm glad none of us have broken bones."

"Speak for yourself," Wren said, scowling. "My nose was broken."

Lidai smiled up at him. Love poured from her eyes. "I like it that way."

"What? It's all swollen and bloody. At least the healer set it straight."

"I think it makes you look even more dangerous."

Wren shook his head. Kenan resumed eating, trying unsuccessfully not to roll his eyes at the two. They all ate ravenously. They had missed breakfast before the difficult trial.

Lamech approached the table. "Congratulations, again. I'm proud of you all." The three started to stand, but Lamech waved them down into their seats.

Kenan looked up at him. "Thank you, Master Lamech."

"So," Lamech grunted, looking at all three. "Have you done it yet?"

"Done it?" Wren asked.

"The promise? Betrothal? Whatever you call it these days."

Kenan's eyes bulged. "Um, no Master. Not yet."

"What are you waiting for, boy? My wife would have the two of them married already."

The three gaped at him. Finally, Lidai said, "You're married?"

"Of course, I am, girl. I've been married 464 years. I've got 205 children. Or is it 206? Can't remember. Over a thousand secondchildren. Never counted the younger ones. There's a whole gaggle of them."

"I've never met your wife."

"Girl, she doesn't stay here. She's not pleased by all the blood and violence. Peaceful woman, my wife is."

Lidai smiled up at him. She seemed very happy.

Kenan said, "You're okay with a betrothal?"

"I am now."

"Okay." Kenan turned to his friend. "Uh, Wren, you have my permission."

Lidai rolled her eyes over her wide, happy smile.

Wren beamed back at Kenan. "Finally." And he turned and, careful to avoid touching noses, kissed his betrothed.

The room erupted in cheers. Students and masters alike stood for the couple.

# Chapter Thirty-Three
# Not So Gross

TWO weeks later, on a rest day, Kenan lay in his room alone. He swung a leg hanging from his hammock, which swayed with the movement. He should have fallen asleep. He often did after midday meal on rest days. But he couldn't sleep.

Wren and Lidai had gone for a walk together. It seemed wherever they were, they held hands since the betrothal. Kenan smiled at the thought, then frowned. They were out there, in a city full of inns, alone. Well, he trusted Wren to remain honorable with his sister. Lidai? Not so much.

Kenan glanced at his new ring. It glowed golden in the lamplight of his little room. The hardened gold, flat in one spot, showing a single stripe of onyx running through the gold field. He spun the metal around and around on his finger as he stared up at the ceiling, lost in thought.

The black stripe meant much to him. He taught at the school now, not as a student teacher but on staff. The accepted called him master. He knew he was not. They simply called everyone with a black stripe master.

It all might have gone to his head, but Lidai wouldn't let it. "Just because we have the black stripe doesn't make us experts. We still have a lot to learn, blockhead."

She'd been right, of course. Trime had taught him as much the very next day. "Not cut during your Trial of Blood. I'm both proud and ashamed. It will make you a legend, one day. Almighty, it already has. Better accelerate your learning, Woodbender, or some initiate will cut your throat before they're accepted." Kenan started to learn to use two swords at once.

Now, Kenan knew the truth. The black stripe only demonstrated a person was ready to start learning the good stuff. He soaked it up readily. He knew he would always continue to learn. There was no way to ever absorb it all.

Laying in his hammock, he needed to stop thinking about the past and start thinking about the future. He taught sword for the first time tomorrow. He needed to think through how to start with the young group of students.

A knock on his door interrupted him. A young voice called, "Master Kenan?"

Kenan rolled out of his hammock. "Come in, Tadd."

The boy stuck his head in the door first, then came all the way in and bowed. "Master Kenan."

Kenan glowered at him. "Tadd, don't call me master. You know I'm not. Not yet. And don't bow every time you run into me. Just when we're working. I know you're in sword class tomorrow. Bow to me then."

"Okay, Master Kenan."

Kenan sighed. "Did you want something?"

"Yes. Sorry, Master Kenan. Where's Wren? Lidai's not in our room. Are they out, again?"

Kenan laughed. "Yes, they are. Probably batting their eyes at each other and holding hands."

"Annoying, isn't it?"

"It is." Kenan gave him a mock frown.

"Master Lamech wanted to see you three."

"Oh? Well, let's not keep him waiting. Where is he?"

"He's in his dining room with that fancy man."

"Fancy? Which one?"

"The one with the gray hair and weird voice."

"High Councilor Enosh."

"I don't know."

"I've been expecting this. Let's go."

The two padded through the building, both barefoot. Black stripes, it turned out, got some leeway in how they did things. Kenan left his boots under his hammock and usually padded around barefoot all day. He found it easier, and his bare soles gripped better on the wood floors. His feet, already callused, were becoming even tougher.

They passed Jenn in the battle hall. She smiled at them both, her ponytail swaying as she walked. She tussled Tadd's hair as she passed and winked at Kenan.

Kenan took several more steps before he realized Tadd had stopped. He looked back at the boy.

Tadd stood, arms hanging at his sides, watching Jenn sway towards an exit in her form-fitting dress.

Kenan went back to stand next to him, watching as Jenn disappeared.

"What do you think, Tadd?"

Tadd's jaw clicked shut, and he shuffled under a red face. "Nothing."

"Uh huh. Are girls still gross?"

"Yes."

"Really?"

"Well, not that one."

Kenan laughed. "No. Not that one, Tadd. Let's go. And remind me later to talk to Mistress Maryleen. It's time you had your own room."

They reached the hallway to Master Lamech's dining room. A small table stood just outside the door with a pitcher of water, two pewter cups, and a bowl of plums. Kenan stole a plum and tossed it to Tadd with a smile. The boy smiled in return and ran off with his snack.

Kenan knocked quietly on the door. At a gruff, "Come," he entered and closed the door behind him. Master Lamech and High Councilor Enosh sat at a table with a map spread between them. Secretary Abram stood against the wall.

Enosh looked up at him. "Young Kenan! Congratulations on your black stripe. I'm so pleased to see it on you."

"Thank you, High Councilor. And nice to see you, Secretary Abram."

Abram smiled at him. "Master Kenan. Congratulations on your advancement. I had no doubts."

Kenan nodded in appreciation at his words. "Where is Assistant Secretary Eleenan?"

Enosh raised an eyebrow at the question, but said, "He's currently in Fallingwater."

Kenan nodded again. Of course. "Thank you, Councilor. Is there other news from Fallingwater?"

"Boy," Lamech growled. "Is a high councilor a messenger?"

Enosh waved Lamech down. "No, no, old friend. He's quite right. Yes, indeed, young Kenan. One of our scouts has found their camp. It was further downriver than they thought it would be. Young Eleenan thinks they plan to bring the boats up the river during the attack to bring captives back down the river after the raid."

"That makes sense. I understand they can bring their boats all the way to Fallingwater?"

"Yes. The village is quite well defended from the river. But it makes for a quick escape."

Kenan thought for a moment. "When do we leave?"

Lamech looked at them both. "Soon, lad. Yes, you're going. So are those other two, if we can keep them from swooning over each other. Many of us are going."

Enosh looked surprised. "You're mobilizing the school?"

"No. But myself and a few masters are going along. A few others. I'm leaving Maryleen and the rest of the red and green cards, but many of the senior leaders are coming."

Enosh grinned. "Most excellent. Thank you, good Master Lamech. We'll need your help. You're a legend the world over, even to the Midreerians."

Lamech grunted. "That was a long time ago."

"People live a long time. Anyone who's faced you and lived has the scars to remind them."

Kenan grinned at Lamech.

Lamech glowered back at Kenan. "Most of them. How many are you sending?"

"Me? None, old friend. We took losses with Abram's abduction, and I fear I'd be of no use on your hunt. But the king is sending an entire company, over a hundred strong. With the element of surprise and our superior numbers, you ought to make short work of them. Abram will join you."

Lamech nodded. "Good and agreed. Thank you for making that all happen. We'll send a few of the raiders back to spread the tale. Should be a long time before they send another raid our way. When do we leave?"

Enosh looked to Abram, who took a small step forward and said, "Is tomorrow morning too soon? The company is nearly ready."

Lamech nodded. "We'll meet them at the Trenchbreach Flat at first light."

Enosh rose. "Excellent. Now, young Kenan, we're going to the temple to pray to the Almighty for success against our enemy. Join us?"

"Oh, thank you, Councilor, but no. I must prepare."

"Don't care for the temple?"

"It's not that, Councilor. I just..."

"You're not a believer in the Almighty?"

"I'm not sure. Maybe."

"I see. It's all too common in today's young people. The evidence surrounds them, but they don't see it. Don't you think so, Lamech?"

Lamech grunted agreement. Abram smiled at Kenan, but his eyes looked a little sad.

Enosh said, "As you wish. No offense, Kenan. I was young once, too. I'll see you tomorrow to send you off."

Kenan said his goodbyes and thanks, then left the room. He couldn't wait to tell Wren and Lidai.

They were all going to Fallingwater.

# Chapter Thirty-Four
# Wisdom

THE next morning, Kenan awoke early and roused Wren from his hammock. After lighting a candle, the two gathered their belongings into packs and saddlebags. Wren opened the door to leave for the dining hall and breakfast. The big man tripped over something on the floor, falling against the far wall and sliding to the floor with a grunt.

Kenan looked down at the items. "What's this?"

Wren rolled over and sat up. "Tripping hazard."

Two bundles wrapped in dragon leather and tied neatly with a cord lay on the floor just outside the door. Kenan saw tags and lifted one into the candlelight to read it. "This big one's yours."

"Mine?"

"Well, it's got your name on it." He lifted the second bundle's tag. "This long one is for me."

They carried the two bundles back into their room, lit more candles, and opened the packages. Wren gasped. "Steel armor!"

Kenan just looked at his unwrapped gift where it lay on a clothes chest. A sword lay on the leather, longer than a normal bronze sword. The wood sheath was wrapped in dragon leather and stippled with tree branch patterns. Brass highlights decorated and protected the wood. The round guard separated the scabbard from a long hilt wrapped in leather and brass wire. It curved near the pommel which was capped in thick brass.

"Hey, Kenan! Look at this! Steel armor!"

Kenan stood motionless, staring at the sword.

"Kenan! Seriously, look, man. It's steel!" Wren flicked a piece with his fingernail, and it rang in the air. "Steel!"

Kenan mumbled, "Look at this."

Wren looked over his shoulder. "Wow. That's beautiful. Are you going to pick it up? Let's see it."

Kenan reverently picked up the sword. Holding the sheath in one hand and the long hilt with the other, he drew the blade. The single edged sword grew wider as he drew it. The edge curved up nearer the tip while the blunted back angled straight. It was decorated for half its length with tree branch scroll work. In the metal, some of the branches had been bent into the shapes of weapons, lattice, and spirals. Free of the sheath, the steel gleamed in the candlelight.

They both stared at it for a moment, awestruck. Wren finally said, "That's gorgeous."

"Yes. Yes, it is."

"Hey, there's writing on it, there, just below the scroll work."

Kenan read it aloud. "Belief in reality is wisdom."

"Those are solid words, Kenan."

"Yes. I think I'll call it Wisdom."

"Did you just name your sword?"

"Can't a sword have a name?"

Wren snorted. "Should I name my armor?"

"Go ahead."

"No, I don't think so. I plan to get a few dents in it. Wouldn't do to name it."

Kenan held the sword's tip and the hilt, bending the sword with his knee and a little grunt of effort. The blade curved a few fingers out of true, then sprang back into line when he released it.

Wren said, "Hey. Careful, you'll bend it."

"No. I think this one is without flaw."

Wren soon donned the armor, starting with an overshirt of heavy leather. The breastplate was etched with a woodcutter's axe. Large, round shoulder guards curled down over Wren's upper arms with overlapping plates of steel rimmed in brass. A skirt of steel splints hung from a wide belt buckled with brass. Forearm bracers, thigh guards, and shin guards that protected his feet completed the body armor. Finally, Wren donned a steel helm, open at the front but with nose and cheek guards angled menacingly. From the chin strap hung a throat guard.

Kenan nodded. "It needs polishing. You put fingerprints all over the steel."

Wren grinned at him. "Everyone's a critic. This suit is so light!" Wren hopped up and down a few times, shaking the room. Someone pounded on the wall from the next room.

They reached the dining room early, yet it was full of Masters, teachers, and students. None were armored and everyone stared at Wren, clad head to toe in steel.

Belroon looked up from his bowl. "Looks good boy. Yah. Going to wear it all the way to Fallingwater?"

Wren revealed his bright, red face as he removed the helm. "No, Master. Just wanted to impress you."

Lidai strode over to him and put a hand on his breastplate. "Well, my betrothed, you impress me. I think you look amazing. Very terrifying. I bet the White Spiders all just got a chill down their spine."

Wren beamed at her. "Thank you, sweet maple syrup."

She grimaced at him. "That's even worse. Try again, later. Come have some breakfast."

"We need to say thank you, first."

Kenan led Wren to the table of Masters. "Master Lamech. We don't know what to say except thank you for these wonderful gifts."

Wren agreed. "Yes, thank you."

Lamech looked up at him as he stirred the nutmash in his bowl. The mash was thick and nearly orange from egg yolks. "You're most welcome, lads. We all had a hand in the designs." He pointed to the other masters at the table. Trime grinned, glancing briefly at Kenan. Lamech continued, "However, we didn't pay for them. That came from elsewhere."

Kenan inquired, "Who? Who did this? Was it your father?"

Lamech arched an eyebrow. "The Grandmaster did not do this. He gave most of his coin to my son's project. No, this came from the palace."

Kenan and Wren looked at each with wide eyes.

Lamech grunted. "Yes. The king himself sent the coin with a note directing us to spend it on you both. You made an impression, boy."

Kenan said, "Well." He had to clear his throat. "I will thank him when I can. Until then, thank you all. This is most thoughtful."

At their table, after gathering their breakfast, Wren asked Lidai, "Did you get anything this morning?"

"Oh, the look on your face when you thumped into the room was gift enough. Dear." She grinned as she scooped up nutmash from her bowl.

They ate in the cacophonous room. Kenan smiled at the people around him, wondering where the thought that he should leave had come from. People laughed and cheered. They discussed plans and boasted about their upcoming parts in the battle coming to Fallingwater. He was glad to be going with them, but right now, he would rather be nowhere else.

WREN entered the Trenchbreach Flat with the other thirty or so from the Old Pine Tree school. Lidai held his hand and he gripped hers as tightly as he dared. Her hands were rough now with calluses on her fingers, but he didn't mind. Hers felt right in his own callused hand.

In his other hand, he held the lead rope for Okay. The laden shielddragon was one of two being brought on the trip. A bunch of crescentdragons milled about near the gate and a gaggle of stompdragons stood placidly to one side, waiting to pull carts or small wagons.

Kenan saluted his friends with two fingers and led Finch over to the other stompdragons. Wren could smell the fresh lamb he knew was in a box on Finch's back. Gruntle had met them in the stables with the treat, saying he'd heard about the march and wanted his friends to have some food for the journey. He'd said, "Be sure to save some for the Master Secretary, would you?"

Wren avoided the other shielddragon. Okay didn't like the other beast, who was also a younger male. A Flat was no place for a pair of sparring shielddragons. It'd take a week just to fill in all the ruts they'd make.

He saw High Councilor Enosh and Secretary Abram talking in the middle of the Flat, surrounded by nearly fifty armed guards scattered about. Though most of the guards were all talking with each other or with other citizens of the city up this early, they all watched every newcomer arriving to the Flat. Lamech, led by an energetic Tadd, walked towards Enosh and Abram.

Several men tried to make two clubdragons stand still. The beasts stood a bit shorter than Okay but made up for it in width. Their backs and edges were studded with spikes and bone armor. The long tails ended in massive bone clubs. The clubdragons both twisted to reach their harnesses with sharp beaks and with each reach of their necks their tails swung about, smashing anything in the way. Everyone stood clear and men finally used juicy leaves to distract them. Saddles and gear were strapped on top of the large dragons.

Jenn sauntered past, winking at Wren. His betrothal to Lidai only seemed to increase her flirting. She carried two short swords, one on each pleasant hip and a small shield on her arm. Her pack bulged with supplies. Her long hair had been tied close to her scalp and hung down over the pack, swaying as she walked. She kicked her feet up to show flashes of ankle. Lidai gripped his hand hard. His knuckles cracked from the pressure, but he just smiled down at her.

More people from the city trickled into the Flat in growing streams. They'd need to leave soon or the departure through the recessed gate would be a mess.

"Wren! Lidai! Hello!"

Wren turned towards the voice and saw a youth with one arm and a heavy pack helping an old man walk towards them. Medahal leaned on his staff, and he carried a large, leather satchel strapped over one shoulder.

The youth was Wren's brother, Johlick, who smiled at them. Lidai shook her hand free of Wren's.

Wren waved and moved to join them. "Master Medahal! How good to see you! And brother! You look well." Wren gave Johlick a hug. "Taller, I see. Tell me, is it hard to wipe?"

Johlick tried to grimace, but only accomplished a crooked smile. His left arm ended in a stump. "Not funny, Wren." The boy laughed with him. "Not funny."

Medahal chortled. "Good to see you too, my boy. And you, child, you're more lovely than I remember. Cut your hair shorter, I see." He smiled at them, showing the gaps in his teeth.

Lidai gave the old man a hug and stepped back to smile at him. "I think you know full well why my hair is shorter."

Medahal laughed and said, "Perhaps I do, young one. I'm so glad I caught you before you left. Only just arrived last night. The stompdragon I borrowed did not give me a smooth ride. Terrible animal."

Wren inquired, "But you had no difficulties on the road?"

"No. A dreadfully quiet trip, truly. I would have died from boredom, if it weren't for Johlick, here. Once I get back home, I doubt I'll leave Blacktree for the rest of my days."

Wren asked, "And everyone there is okay?"

Okay grunted loudly.

Medahal chuckled. "Indeed, my boy. We're fewer now, but there's an actual garrison of soldiers there patrolling the land around the village. We've gotten used to them. A few may even stay. One is likely to marry into the village soon." Medahal's large satchel squeaked and wiggled. "Speaking of home, I've brought you something."

He lifted the flap and a raccoon head emerged. It chittered at everyone and retreated back into the bag, deftly pulling the lid back down.

Wren yelled, "Quick!"

The raccoon emerged again. Seeing Wren, it lurched halfway out of the bag, pulling its fat body half over the edge of the satchel. It reached for him with its front paws. Wren scooped the creature up and set it on his shoulders. The raccoon shifted from shoulder to shoulder, playing with Wren's hair. Johlick's face split with a smile.

Medahal said, "Yes, yes, my boy. This rascal ended up at my house, though I'd like to know who released him there. My bird absolutely loathes him. I thought I should bring him to you. He's eaten me out of my own house."

Wren pulled out half a heel of bread he'd been saving for mid-morning and gave it to the raccoon. Quick took it greedily and Wren lowered the animal to the ground so it could go wash the meal in a nearby puddle. Lidai smiled at it.

Wren turned back to Medahal and Johlick. "And the children?"

"Your youngest brothers and sisters are all well, even the lad who took a knock on the head. They're with other families now, quieter than before perhaps, but growing. Even the babe is thriving. Young Marjie is raising the little lass. They're as well as can be."

Johlick said, "I've been staying in Warin's house, when I'm not training with Master Medahal."

Wren looked back and forth at the old man and the boy. "Training? Good! I bet it's not easy." Looking to Medahal, he added, "Please make sure it's not easy."

Medahal smiled and pressed his tongue against the gaps of his teeth. "There are plenty of one-armed forms to learn. Johlick here is a quick study."

Lidai asked, "And my family, Medahal?"

"Just fine. They've stepped up and basically support the entire village, I swear. Your mother still grieves your father, of course, but I've never met a stronger woman. They're all just fine. Oh, wait, is that young Kenan over there?"

Wren nodded and picked Quick back up. The raccoon noisily chewed the sopping bread and made a mess on Wren's shoulder.

Medahal gave Wren the empty satchel for the raccoon. "Oh, good. I have words for the boy. You two fare well, now. And, child, I'll talk to your mother for you. She'll beat an elder into announcing a betrothal. I saw the two of you holding hands. I assume a betrothal suits you both?"

Lidai nodded. "It does, Master Medahal. Only, Kenan already gave permission."

"Did he now? Well, that's right and proper, I suppose. I'm happy for the two of you. I see your rings. Black stripe or no, please do be careful on your journey, won't you? Johlick, come along, lad." The old man left them, shuffling off to Kenan.

Johlick gave a little wave with his one hand. "Good to see you, brother. Congratulations. I'm sure you two will be happy."

Wren clapped a big hand on Johlick's shoulder. "We will, brother. And we'll stop those animals from attacking us, ever again."

"I know you will. I'll see you soon, I hope."

Wren heard water flowing and soon the Trenchbreach Gate lifted from the bottom on long beams with clay counterweight tanks. The deep trench leading through the dragonwall lay open. Guards on top of the wall shouted down to people outside the city to wait until the force could exit the Flat.

At the shout, one of the clubdragons emitted a sharp bark, startling everyone.

Quick jumped from Wren's shoulder to Lidai's head. Both animal and its new mount squeaked on impact.

# Chapter Thirty-Five
# Breaking

ANNA awoke in her cell to pain. Pain was her constant companion. She lifted her head to look around. Unarta was already gone. It wouldn't be long, now.

It was the third day. Beating day. She closed her eyes and breathed. Her aching body shuddered, causing her to gasp through a painful muscle spasm. It knew what was coming.

In minutes, Yarro brought Unarta back to her cell. The woman looked healthy again, her skin flushed and eyes bright. She walked gingerly but looked somehow strong.

Yarro patted her back. "I'm pleased with you today."

Unarta nodded, her wild array of curly black hair waving in the air. "Thank you."

Yarro laughed. "Maybe you deserve some extra food, for the whelp. I see you've got one there, in your belly. A little Yarro spawn. You'll need more food to grow me a strong son. Well done."

Unarta carefully lowered herself to the stone floor and took up her red waterskin. She looked up at Yarro and gave him a little smile. Anna could see it in the woman's eyes. Unarta was lost to them.

Yarro closed and locked Unarta's door. Turning to Anna, he looked at her body. The bruises didn't seem to bother him. He finally made eye contact with her. "It's my favorite day, sweet. Do you know why?"

Anna didn't answer.

"It's beating day, sweet. Are you ready?"

Anna slowly and carefully got to her feet, her legs and back protesting.

Flashes of pain and muscle spasms wracked her, and she gasped, clutching the wall for support. She didn't bother with clothing. It wouldn't matter.

Yarro unlocked her door and Anna trudged out into the hallway, careful to walk with as little movement of her legs as possible. He took her arm in his strong hand, but she didn't fight him. She plodded down the hallway, moving gingerly on her bruised feet.

Atarra, her only sister left in the breedery now, watched her go. She showed a pregnancy now, holding her bulging stomach in one hand as she took a sip from a red waterskin. She wiped her mouth with the back of her hand.

In a back room somewhere, she listened to a woman giving birth. Her labor sounded normal but was interrupted by a man's angry voice.

Atarra rubbed her belly. "Why aren't you pregnant, sister? Is there something wrong with you?"

Anna stopped and stared at her. Yarro paused, snorting in amusement.

"Atarra, I..."

"Just let them do it. It's not bad."

Anna looked at her sister, or rather, this woman who had been her sister. She understood. There was no other option for them.

Atarra returned the look with a wild challenge in her eye. "If you just let them, they'll give you a child. Char has given me a child. See?"

Anna lowered her gaze to her own crusted toenails.

"Look at me! See? I'll have a boy. I'll have Char's son. He'll be a great warrior. Don't doubt it, my sister! A great warrior!"

As they resumed their slow walk to the side room, Atarra yelled after them, a note of hysteria in her voice. "Have their sons, Anna! Have their sons! They'll be great warriors, just like mine!"

Unarta was lost. Atarra was lost. Anna felt lost, too.

She wasn't sure how many times she'd endured Yarro's bamboo stick. Thirty? More? She'd lost track. Yarro's method was always the same. He bound her to the table and asked her who she loved. Then came the beating.

He never let up. Each strike was as hard as it had been on the first day. She tried to count the strikes, so she'd know when they'd end, but she always lost herself to the pain. All she knew was the pain.

Always he'd ask, "'Oo do you love, sweet?"

She remembered how she'd answered, "Kenan," the first five times. She was always beaten, new bruises darkening the old. After that, she tried to remain silent, but she was still beaten. She told Yarro she loved him. Yarro laughed and beat her. She said she loved Cols, Char, and even Himmons. Always the beatings came on the third day. Once, she'd tried saying she loved herself, to which he'd nodded appreciatively and still beat her. Most often, she said she loved the Most High, hoping that if she said it enough times, the beatings would stop. But they didn't. She was beaten every three days. She wasn't sure how long it'd been.

Her legs ached deeply. Though she was beaten on the backs of her thighs, the blotchy purple bruises wrapped around to the front. Walking hurt. Laying down hurt. The thought of sitting was enough to make her vomit. She could hardly bend her body from the ribs down.

They entered the room with the table. Her blood stained an area near the ropes where one day she had tried to smash her head against the tabletop. She had to end the pain. Now, they folded up a cloth to cushion any future attempts. It sat there, folded incongruously neat next to the ropes, waiting for her.

She didn't resist as Yarro walked her to the table. She didn't resist when he bent her over the surface, though her body was so stiff he had to force her down. Muscles screamed in protest, and she screamed a harmony.

She put her own hands through the ropes. Yarro nodded silently as he cinched them tight.

Pain. More was coming, but that was okay. Life was pain. The pain would never stop. Pain was constant. Wasn't it?

"Take the bit, sweet."

Anna opened her mouth wide for the balsawood bit.

Before he put it in, he asked her, "'Oo do you love, sweet?"

She knew what came next. And she knew the name they wanted. She'd resisted for as long as she could and could take no more. She had to do something. She had to do anything.

A thought came to her of the bright insects of the Edeerian forests. She imagined she was a butterfly. Bright and blue, she flew through the trees of Blacktree, free and beautiful. She paused at blossoms and drank the sweet nectar. She flapped her wings and curved up through the air over the Flat, watching the traders ply their wares below.

Kenan stood on his balcony, and she flew up to him. His house, with the addition still under construction, shone in the sun behind him. Butterflies don't smile, but Kenan did, and it showed in his broody eyes. His love for her flowed out of his eyes and filled her with warmth and safety. She and Kenan would live in that house and raise beautiful children, all smiling and dancing and...

She imagined a massive hand, like her father's, grabbing her as her blue wings fluttered over Kenan's balcony. Her heart sank as she realized she was going to say the word they wanted. She didn't want to say it, but she was going to say it anyway. The hand pulled her away from Kenan, and she shouted her love to him as she flapped her wings to escape.

The hand placed her in a small cage built from bamboo and lashed with cord. It had a balsawood door. The hand closed the door and locked it. She stayed in the cage, separate from her body, and watched what happened.

"Well, sweet? 'Oo do you love?" Yarro held the bit out to her, clearly eager to begin.

"Gharan." She supposed she should be crying, but she stared from her bamboo cage at the rough surface of the tabletop and the rope loops around her wrists. She had no tears left.

Yarro paused. "Say it again, sweet."

"Gharan."

"Say it all."

"I love Gharan."

Yarro sighed deeply. The stick stayed at his belt. The ropes slackened. He stood her back up and held her by the shoulders. "Very good, sweet. No more beatings. Here. Have a seed."

She was supposed to get two seeds. She needed her two seeds. She tipped her head back and opened her mouth, hoping he misspoke. He dropped one in.

She rolled it on her tongue to be sure. There was only one. She swallowed in case he decided to reach in and take it out. Only one seed. One was not enough. She tipped her head back again, opening her mouth.

"Of all things," Yarro said, "you look like a little bird in a nest waiting for 'er mother. I 'ave no more worms, 'atchling. No more worms for you," Yarro laughed. He took her arm and led her back to her cell. There was no second seed. She trudged silently in front of him.

That night, he kicked her cell door. Time for the evening meal. She looked forward to evening meal. Her food always tasted blandly fine, but she hardly noticed. She wanted her seeds.

She struggled to slowly rise from where she'd been lying on her stomach. She had chills again and felt terrible. She must be sick. She didn't really want her food tonight, but she desperately wanted her seeds. She finally gained her feet, wincing as muscles stretched and pain flared. Pain was fine. Yarro had seeds.

There was no food. She didn't care as she wiped a cold sweat from her brow. She didn't want food. Yarro held an arm through the bars, a seed sitting in his palm. She wanted two seeds, but she wouldn't turn down one. She reached for the seed.

Yarro closed his fist on the little dark seed with the silver stripe. He was toying with her. His smile showed white teeth against his dark face. She stood swaying in her cell. Her only option was patience.

He looked at her, glee in his eyes. "Say it."

Anna watched his fist from inside her bamboo cage. The balsawood door kept her safe. She didn't even hesitate. "I love Gharan."

His fist opened, and she snatched the seed out. She fumbled it and the seed bounced off her lip and fell to the filthy floor.

Anna dropped to her knees, franticly searching for her seed. Yarro laughed at her, kicked her cell door again, and moved away down the hall.

Over two hours later, she found it driven into the dirt between the floor stones. She must have kneeled on it. She didn't take the time to clean it off before popping it into her mouth and swallowing.

Her eyes remained dry as, from inside her bamboo cage, Anna wept.

# Chapter Thirty-Six
# A Barrel in Fallingwater

WREN sat on Okay's back, reigns in hand. He was happy to have his shielddragon back on the road. They traveled east to Fallingwater. He'd missed being on the road more than he'd anticipated. He'd missed having Lidai sitting behind him, arms wrapped around his middle, infinitely more. He patted her hands. He could hardly wait to marry the woman, if she didn't stab him first.

Wren shook his head. "I'm just saying. If you find yourself facing a charge, get behind me."

Lidai pinched the skin on his belly and huffed. "I'll do no such thing, and you know it. You know what I can do. I can save your life, blockhead."

"Yes. If there are twelve or less attackers. What if there's fifty? What if they have their own archers? Almighty, Lidai, you never know."

"I know."

"I just said you 'never' know."

Lidai rolled her eyes. He could tell just by the way she cocked her head against his shoulder. "I know that I'll never know. But don't think I'll just take cover behind you. You do make a good shield, of course, but I don't need..."

Wren smiled to himself. Sometimes he riled her up a little just to listen to her. He knew it was like poking at a mawdragon, but he just couldn't help himself.

When she paused for breath, he said, "I'm just saying I have a shield. A big one. See, right there." He pointed to the big wood shield where it hung on Okay, within reach. "If there's trouble, don't be afraid to use it."

She kissed his neck. It sent shivers all the way to his toes. Totally worth it.

Lidai reached down and checked her bow in its case hanging on Okay's side. A flap hung over the case mouth, protecting the weapon from the elements. Wren noticed but said nothing. She fretted over the thing. Two full quivers of black arrows hung next to the bow.

Wren smiled. "Go ahead. You know you want to."

Lidai kissed his shoulder, then reached down. In less than two heartbeats she had a quiver over her shoulder and bow drawn with arrow nocked. She put it all away, then did it again.

"I think you're getting quicker."

Quick, napping under Okay's shield frill, cracked an eye at him. Seeing no food, the creature fell asleep as quickly as its name, lulled by the motion of the shielddragon.

Lidai blew a strand of loose hair out of her eye, her hands full with bow and arrows. "Yes, but I need more practice. It's different from dragon back."

Wren smiled again. He smiled a lot around her, he noticed. He was under some kind of enchantment. He didn't mind though. Once again, he knew it was all worth it.

She put it all away a third time and wrapped her arms around him. She kissed his shoulder, again. It seemed to be her favorite shoulder.

Wren caught Kenan, leading Finch nearby, scowling at them. He tipped the man a two-finger salute. Kenan barked a laugh and shook his head at them. Wren kept right on smiling.

Wren and Lidai had a good view. Okay was nearly full grown, now twice the height of a man and able to pull many times his considerable weight. Master Gruntle had taken excellent care of the animals while they'd been training in the school.

He could see nearly fifty dragons in the force on the road to Fallingwater. Most were stompdragons, small in comparison to the other dragons, pulling carts. Both shielddragons, massive head shields ringed in spikes, pulled wagons. Riders scouted in all directions on crescentdragons and grinderdragons, their duckbills working against bronze bits. Somewhere behind them, someone had a pair of slabdragons who bugled back and forth to each other, annoying everyone. Master Lamech and some of the other masters rode the clubdragons. Everyone gave those armored dragons a wide birth.

Soldiers marched along the road ahead. Fifty strong men in bronze plate and shield strode in step carrying sword and spear. Their footsteps were in time, and the noise of it sent darterdragons scampering away and squirrels calling alarm. The sound of stomping boots comforted him. It sounded menacing, and they were on his side.

Nearby, a squad of archers walked casually, joking with one another. They didn't stomp a beat like the infantry, but their bows were strong. Each carried three quivers bristling with arrows on their backs. He'd seen them drill at night. Lidai wasn't impressed, but he was.

Other men and even women scouted, he knew. Fore and rear guards matched their pace out of sight.

The White Spiders would never know what hit them.

Okay pulled at the reins, so Wren dropped them. He used the shield spikes instead. Okay seemed to like it better. He idly reached down and scratched Quick's belly. The raccoon chittered at him in his sleep and drooled on Okay's neck.

During evenings of the trip, Wren worked with Okay. The animal performed well in battle formations. When training alone, he seemed to revert to domestic work, as if he were pulling a log back in Blacktree. Wren gave commands, guiding Okay with his knees and shield spikes. He wasn't a battle dragon yet, but he was making progress.

Okay wasn't the only one getting lessons in the evenings. Masters and black stripes gathered each evening to train. Several of the soldiers were also students from varying schools and joined in the exercise. They practiced Jempo in all its forms: rolling, bending, sword play, archery, heavy armor, and working singly or in groups. Lamech taught them tactics. Belroon taught the forming and breaking of shield walls. Trime and Kenan gave lessons in bending, knife work, and swords.

Tadd took part, which was a new development. The lad clearly already knew how to throw and use knives. His dexterity marveled everyone. Apparently, the lad had no difficulty plucking thrown knives out of the air, dodging repeated attacks, and was taking to bending in a way that had Master Trime and Kenan talking. His swordplay needed work, but the boy carried a bronze short sword on his back like a trophy and spent his time before bed sharpening the blade. If he kept it up, he'd sharpen the thing into a hilt and a pile of bronze shavings.

To Wren's relief, Jenn made friendly with one of the armored squad leaders. Wren caught her eye one evening as she rested her hand on the man's knee. She shrugged to him as if to say, "See what you're missing?" He lifted Lidai's hand in his and kissed her knuckles. Jenn scowled at him, but her eyes were smiling amusement.

Lidai led an archery class and some of the regular archers joined. She had a new bow, layered in blackwood, yellowwood, and dragon bone. The wood was stained so dark it looked almost black. Someone had painted a white spider on the upper branch, but it lay on its back with the legs curled up in death, pierced by an arrow.

At first, the other archers seemed amused at the archery training. A man named Jared said, behind his hand but loudly enough to be overheard,

"Been loosing shafts for over a hundred years. What's this scrap of a girl going to teach me? How to shoot in a dress?" By the flash in her eyes, Wren thought she might skewer the man where he stood, but she didn't. When it was the man's turn to shoot, he took aim and loosed. Lidai moved so fast it was hard to make it out. Her arrow knocked his out of the air. She arched an eyebrow at Jared. They all paid attention after that.

A small squad of men had brought a thumper, lashed to a cart pulled by one of the stompdragons. They didn't practice shooting it, but did practice lighting, snuffing, and relighting the wicks used to fire the weapon. They checked and rechecked jars of the dried and crumbled stickle sap they used in them and cast lead shot at night over the fires.

Wren taught rolling. Some of the regular soldiers joined. One asked, "What use is this, Master Wren. I mean no disrespect, but why would you do this in battle? While you're busy wrestling, his friend will just come over and put a spear in your back."

Wren looked at the man and nodded. "Good question. Why do you have a knife, sword, and a spear?"

"Different weapons for different situations."

"Thank you for answering your question."

The soldier blinked at him. He broke into a grin and nodded.

Wren smiled back at him and addressed everyone present. "Rolling Jempo won't help much in a pitched battle. But what if you're without a weapon? What if you must arrest a man without hurting him permanently? Or maybe you want to take a prisoner. And tell me, should rolling be any harder if the other man wears armor? Even steel armor?"

They all shook their heads. Wren nodded to them and smiled.

Wren also spent time practicing with his new equipment. He had a new axe along with the steel armor. The axe head was bronze and hardened on the edge. He'd worked with Kenan and the blacksmith student to produce a new design. The middle of the ax head was empty, making the weapon lighter and quicker. The blackwood handle stood long, straight, and strong. Wren could swing it at blinding speed and perform recovery or redirect nearly as fast. Steel would have been preferable, but it worked well for bronze. Master Belroon was impressed enough he was having one made for himself.

One evening, Wren looked over at Kenan as he grabbed Tadd by the wrist. The boy pulled, grabbed, and twisted. Kenan tossed himself into a roll and, when he rose smoothly to his feet, nodded to Tadd. They did it again and again, practicing Jempo bending and throwing.

Kenan wore his new steel sword on his back. He switched its position every day, trying a new place to carry the weapon. Wren wondered if it was too heavy for him. Steel or no, it had some heft to it. He thought Wisdom often did.

One day, only a few days out from Fallingwater, a scout rode his crescentdragon up to where the masters were on their clubdragons. The crescentdragon blew snot all over the ground as it gasped for breath, the curved crest behind its head reverberating as its ribs heaved. Three arrows sprouted from its back. The rider carried his bow, and arrows rattled in a half-empty quiver.

Wren heard talking but couldn't make out the words. He did hear the shout to halt the column. Soon Tadd ran by with an order from Lamech.

"There's hissdragon riders to the north! Hissdragons! Orders are to ready for battle." With that, the boy raced down the column, repeating the order as he ran.

Wren stood on Okay's back and donned his armor with Lidai's help. She kissed his thigh where his battle scar sometimes still pained him before strapping on the plate guard. His axe had been shoved under a strap with the gear on Okay's back. He retrieved it and hung it from a strap in reach of his saddle. He hung his large shield on the other side and held his spear vertically, the butt resting on his foot in a stirrup.

Lidai had her bow out. He wished she had her own armor.

As Tadd came running back by, Wren called to him. "Anyone hurt?"

"Yeah. One of the scouts didn't make it. Arrows. We lost a crescentdragon, too." Tadd ran back towards the clubdragons.

Wren shook his head. Lidai mumbled, "Dragonspit," under her breath.

Wren turned his head and quirked an eyebrow. "You know, butternut, if you keep swearing like that, Tadd will, too."

"Nope. Call me butternut at your own peril. Really, who uses a squash for an endearment? Oh, and he already does."

"He does? Tadd?"

"Yeah. But he mumbles it under his breath, like that somehow makes it better."

"I wonder where he got that?"

She grinned. "Must have been Kenan."

But Wren was frowning as the column moved forward again. The loss of a scout was terrible, but not strategically damaging. The real problem seemed to him that now the White Spiders knew they were coming.

As they entered Fallingwater, Kenan scanned the village with a critical eye. The sharpened wood stakes of the dragonring stood similar to Blacktree, only much closer to the village. Gardens grew everywhere inside the ring, breaking only for the village Flat, a couple barns, and two small mills along the river. The Fallingwater River flowed right through the village. Boys cleaned debris from the staked nets of a fish pen. Wheels turned in the water, powering a gristmill and a lumber mill. He regarded the lumbermill and thought Wren must be itching to get in there and see it.

The village boasted three levels yet was smaller in diameter than Blacktree. The lowest work level only supported half a dozen buildings. The upper two levels appeared to be homes. He saw no defensive platforms.

He heard the falls before he saw the mist rising from the river's horizon line. The village perched at the edge of a drop in the land. A waterfall roared down over stone crags to a large pool before flowing away to the east.

Kenan could see why they didn't fear an easterly attack from the river. Raiders in boats could not climb the falls. They would need to land, leave their boats, and circle the cliff to reach the village, all while thumpers and archers rained death down on them.

Kenan considered the layout, analyzing the village's strengths and weaknesses. No, he would not attack from the river. He would sack the village first and then retreat to the river. The Flat, a spiral staircase, and lifts were all to the south of the river. An attack would come through the forest from that direction.

Kenan felt for Wisdom on his back again, reassured by its presence. This time the blade stood up and the hilt hung down by his right hip. A clever spring kept the sword in its scabbard unless he purposefully drew it, and he used a leather binding cord common on knife sheaths. He'd been trying different positions and practicing his draw. He could draw and employ the blade quickly from this new position, but he started with a reverse grip. He liked the reverse grip for many initial strikes. He might keep the sword upside down on his back.

Even though the blade exceeded his expectations in size and reach, its light weight made it a joy to use. Steel felt so much lighter than bronze. He knew it wasn't so. Steel was stronger than bronze, so it took less steel to achieve the same strength and could be forged into longer blades. Still, the weapon swept graceful, silver arcs through the air when he worked his forms.

He'd also been given brass scale mail. The brass leaves, each less than a palm in size, were sown to a leather shirt, padded along shoulder, collarbones, and spine. A heavy, cloth, outer shirt covered the armor. A brass frame supported the mail across his shoulders, and guards curved down over his arms. The armor wasn't new. Several plates showed scores and dents. He also had brass guards strapped to his thighs and shins. He had thought it might hamper his movement, but the design of the light armor allowed him full flexibility.

His long knife and sheath were tucked in his boot and his hand knife hung ready on his belt, as usual. He had purchased a new pair of woodbender boots, and they were finally broken to his feet. His old woodsman's hand-axe hung from his left hip. He wouldn't go into the forest without it.

A small shield and a short bronze sword hung from Finch's saddle on one side, a bow and quiver on the other. The cart, now almost empty of food after the journey, bounced down the village road behind the stompdragon. Kenan patted him on his neck

He looked up to the south side of the village. Balconies and bridges hung from branches. He didn't see a single thumper up there. He saw railings but no parapets. Archers would be exposed.

Archers there were. Blond women patrolled the village above with long bows and quivers on their backs. Brass breastplates covered their torsos. These must be the Brookstone Brigade. They didn't exactly look like housewives. Eleenan was supposed to prepare the village and disguise the archers as locals. Something wasn't going to plan.

One woman stood at a railing leaning on her longbow and looked down on the force moving through the village. She made eye contact with Kenan and smiled. Her pretty face lit up and dimples showed on her cheeks. He could see all the way up to her knees from this angle! He blushed and watched his step. It wouldn't do to sprawl into the dirt in front of the beautiful soldier.

Most of the force moved onto the empty flat and immediately started to make camp. Kenan tied Finch off to a post before taking Okay's lead to help Wren and Lidai. They slid off the big shielddragon, easing their drop with the saddle rope. A boy brought buckets of water to freshen a drinking trough.

"Wren, your animal is getting big, even by shielddragon standards."

Wren patted Okay's shoulder. "Yeah, he's a big boy. Oh, and Kenan, look. There's a bucket for you."

Kenan punched towards his head, but Wren smiled as he dodged the blow. He moved well, even in all that shiny armor.

Lidai pointed. "There's Master Lamech and the rest, on the stairs. They're headed up. Think we should go?"

No had told them they couldn't go, so Kenan nodded and led the way. They caught up to their school masters before reaching the first level.

Eleenan met them on the boardwalk. He wore fancy robes but no gold except for a black striped ring on his finger. Kenan looked at Eleenan in a new light. This younger man was responsible for all the progress made against the White Spiders. If there was a chance to defeat the White Spiders, Eleenan had given them that chance.

Flanking Eleenan to one side stood a middle-aged blond woman in a dress, brass plate armor, and a fur mantle. To the other side stood an old man with a cane.

"Master Lamech." Eleenan posed a Jempo bow and held it. "It is very good see you."

"And you, Eleenan." Lamech returned the bow quickly. "Who do you have here?"

Eleenan straightened. "Ah. This is Captain Dinnane, captain of the Brookstone Brigade. They have been, ah, most accommodating, Master."

Dinnane laughed throatily. "Accommodating. Right."

Kenan started. Her voice graveled low for a woman. She sounded like Lamech.

She continued. "We were a thorn between this boy's toes for weeks, in truth. No one listened to him. Then, at training one day, he dumped three of us in the dirt without so much as a pat on the rump. I don't know which of us was more surprised! Almighty, we started taking him seriously after that. This boy is now in charge here."

"It's true," croaked the old man. "I'm Gentrol Fallingwater, chief elder here. We saw his wisdom right off. We saw no need to fall in the dirt."

Dinnane laughed again at the old man and smiled wide. Only, judging by her eyes, Kenan didn't think she was all that fond of him.

Eleenan nodded. "Now that you're here, Master, I'll gladly yield to you. If you want me to stay involved, I will..."

"Nonsense, lad. You're to stay in charge. I'll lead tactically, only."

"Master, it might be better if I returned to..."

"No, lad. My orders for you come from High Councilor Enosh himself. You are in charge. I take my orders from you."

Secretary Abram made it up the stairs in time to say, "It's true, my boy. You're to lead us."

Eleenan gasped and bowed deeply to Abram. Then, against all propriety, he rushed the man and embraced him.

Abram smiled and patted Eleenan's back. "Quite right, my boy. I'm here and alive. Thanks to our friends from Blacktree."

"Blacktree?" Dinnane asked? "Isn't that the little backwater that..."

Lamech said, "Yes. That attack spurred us into motion here."

Eleenan still didn't look comfortable with being put in charge. His already high voice ranged higher. "It initiated our plans here, yes. Others spurred us on. Master Lamech, I shouldn't lead. I don't..."

"You do. You have your instructions, lad. Follow them."

"Yes, Master. Perhaps we should meet in private for an update on our situation?"

"Find a big room, lad. Whatever you tell me I'll be telling everyone else from the school. They're all volunteers and risking their lives on this mission. They have a right to know. Unless there's something personally sensitive?"

"No. As you say, Master. We have a command post which should suit us all. Please, follow me."

Eleenan led them all down the boardwalk. Kenan followed with the group, hoisting Quick up in an arm. He didn't much care for the critter, but he didn't want him trampled underfoot, either.

A blond woman, younger than him, fell into step next to him. Her breastplate, he saw, was shaped for a woman. He tried not to look at the bright metal. "Hi," she said in a friendly tone.

He recognized the archer from the balcony. Her beauty up close took his breath away for a moment. He nearly tripped over his own feet. Finally, he stammered, "Hey there."

"I'm Olaine Brookstone."

"I'm Kenan Blacktree."

"I'm Lidai. I'm his sister." Lidai bent forward to peer around him. "He never introduces me."

Olaine quirked a pretty brow at him. "And why not?"

Kenan sighed. "Because she's as annoying as she is adorable."

Olaine smiled. "Mm hmm. Hello, Lidai. Nice to meet you both."

They didn't go far before turning into a building. It contained barrels and crates, benches and woodworking tools, rope making racks and metalworking tools, including a small forge and a cast iron anvil. Everything had been pushed up against the walls, clearing a space to meet.

Eleenan sat on a high stool and offered one to Lamech. The rest filed into the room and stood to listen. Lidai craned her neck in a vain attempt to see. Kenan gave her a look of commiseration. He could see, but barely, trying to find an angle through all the heads in front of him. Olaine stood next to him on her tiptoes and put a hand on his shoulder to steady herself. Kenan didn't object to the touch, wishing he could feel more than the pressure through his armor. Quick struggled to get away, and he was all too happy to let him go.

Eleenan gestured with a thin steel longsword to a map hanging on a wall. "We are here, at this spot. The road comes this direction, from the west. Another road fords the river and travels north. A small hamlet sits here, about a day's walk away.

"The White Spiders have made a camp here, along the river. They were clever about it, finding a small backwater off the river to hide three longboats. They're about two day's march from Fallingwater, much farther than our reports from the Blacktree attack.

"Our scouts count about ninety men and two hissdragons. They now have several stompdragons, presumably stolen. They've also taken three women who were out foraging without permission."

Belroon spoke. "What about their camp itself, yah? Is it well defended?"

Eleenan leaned his sword, the scabbard studded with silver, against a barrel filled with wooden staves. "It's hard to know the details. They put out sentries. The scouts can get around them easy enough, but it's dangerous. It's not a matter of safety but of secrecy. We don't want them to know we know they're here."

Trime said, "It's too late for that. They know. We ran into a scouting party on the road this morning."

Eleenan sighed. "I see, Master. We saw one of their scouts today as well and he got away. Well, this will make our work more difficult. We know they have a simple dragonring and have dug a trench behind it. They are well armed with dragonpike, spear, sword, and shield. These are not soft men. These are warriors, by their training and bearing. We should not discount them as rough brigands."

Lidai huffed. She jumped to see and huffed again. Tall men blocked her view. Kenan shushed her, and she glared back at him.

"What else?" Trime asked.

"We sent their front man to them at the correct signal. We had the man turned. I'm certain of it. But he didn't come back. We're not sure what it means. Did the man turn again? Did they figure it out and kill him? Or has he rejoined their ranks to lead them into our ambush? He was supposed to come back and tell us. We just don't know."

Belroon shook his head. "Yah. Wonderful."

Kenan made a grab at Lidai to make her stand still. He was having a hard time hearing. But he missed as she climbed up on a barrel.

Eleenan nodded. "I think we should execute our ambush but also be ready to be ambushed." He turned to a clatter. Quick had pulled down Eleenan's sword and was dragging the shiny object away. Eleenan jumped towards him.

Trime said, "We should increase defenses here. Where, do you think, would they be most likely to attack?"

Kenan didn't hesitate. "South."

Trime nodded, craning his neck to see who spoke. He smiled when he made eye contact with Kenan. "The woodbender is correct. They will attack from the south. There are no defenses to speak of in that direction."

Dinnane growled in her tenor voice. The effect was disconcerting coming from such a beautiful face. "We have archers watching there and set to respond to an attack."

Trime shook his head. "No offense, Master, um, Mistress? Captain Dinnane. I have seen good archers in action, and I have no doubts about your effectiveness. However, I saw no cover. I saw no thumpers. I saw no defenses on the ground or even a way to block off your stairs."

Wren cocked his head. "I could fix that." Everyone looked at him and his face turned bright red. "Well, I could. With the tools in this room, I could do it, maybe in half a day."

Kenan said, "And we should dig a trench across the southern gardens to protect a defensive line. And traps in the forest to the south."

Wren continued, "And I thought of a way to drain all the lift tanks with one pull of a cord. Empty lift tanks will stop the lifts and slow an attack."

Belroon nodded. "Yah. I will work with your people to build a log palisade wall around your Flat. It will stop the hissdragons in their tracks. They climb well, but not with riders, I think."

Lidai stomped her foot on her barrel and crossed her arms over her chest. Kenan tried to ignore her.

Lamech said, "A good start. But what are we to do about the White Spiders?" He turned to Eleenan.

Eleenan had retrieved his sword and sheathed it on his hip with a glare at the raccoon. "Right. If we make this a nut too hard to crack, they will simply leave and attack somewhere we are not. This is a game. The stones are on the board."

"Well said, lad," said Lamech. "But who's turn is it to move?"

Lidai put her hands on her hips and blurted out, "It's ours, of course!"

Kenan cringed at her outburst.

Lamech grunted and raised an eyebrow at her. The corner of his lips twitched.

Gentrol harrumphed through his few remaining teeth and thumped his cane on the wood floor. "Girl, answer when asked. Otherwise, be silent. Whose woman is this? Someone, get her in hand."

Wren scowled back at the old man.

Lidai was not done. "I don't think so. We're not going to just sit here on this apple tree waiting to be picked. Nor can we wait to see if our ambush plan will work with this level of uncertainty. We need to take the fight to them!"

Olaine put her face so close to his cheek he could feel her breath. It made his neck shiver most pleasantly. "I like your sister."

Dinnane stood near Lamech. She laughed and the golden curls of her ponytail bounced against her fur mantle. "Me, I like this girl! Who brought her? What is her name?"

"I am Lidai Blacktree and I'm going to kill every last man wearing the White Spider!"

Dinnane threw her head back and laughed again. "Ha! I like her even more!"

Belroon laughed along with Dinnane. "Yah! She reminds me of my fifth-daughter! Almost as dangerous, but not so round. Let her speak."

Lamech grinned as he watched her.

Lidai turned on her barrel to see everyone in the room. "We can't just sit here and let them attack. We'd just play into their hands. It's what they do. They figure out how to crack the nut and do so without mercy, taking what they value most.

"What are we waiting for? We know where they are. We have greater numbers. We have skilled warriors. We have offensive initiative. We have home ground. We even have a water barrier to use tactically. Let's go get them!"

A couple men raised a fist over their heads in answer to her cry. He saw Jenn nodding grudgingly at her, one eyebrow raised in thought. Olaine bounced beside him. She had slipped her hand down, taking Kenan's arm and squeezing his forearm muscles. He could feel her excitement through the contact. Almighty, this woman had just met him. And yet, his attention and his grin were for his sister.

Eleenan raised his hands to stop her. "And if, as we're marching to meet them, they pass us on the way upriver, what then? Do we leave Fallingwater defenseless?"

Gentrol pounded his cane a few times in approval.

Lidai raised an eyebrow and put her hands on her hips. "Who said anything about marching? You have a river. You're not out of boats, are you?"

Lamech gave Lidai a rare smile, nodding.

Jenn wasn't the only one eyeing Lidai in a new light. Kenan and Olaine both looked at Lidai, grinning. Wren, smiling so wide he might do damage, wiped a tear from his eye.

# Chapter Thirty-Seven
# Uncertain Opportunities

CHAR stalked through his encampment by the river, grumbling to himself. This mission was turning into dragonscrape. If it could go wrong, it did. First, they weren't close enough to the target. Then, Gharan discovered the dragonspitter front man had turned against them. Turned! All those blond women ripe for the plucking were actually soldiers, an expert archery unit brought in from the border with Ulneer. Now this.

The new scout commander had just returned on his hissdragon, reporting a significant force arriving at the little village above the falls. Almost immediately after, another scout watching the village confirmed the force's arrival. They had a small army of over a hundred soldiers, dragons, and a squad with a firepole. Well, they had what the Edeerians thought was a firepole. Still, it was dangerous enough.

Char wished Gharan had listened. They'd hit Edeer too often in too short a time. They should have targeted Ulneer, despite the difficulty. Maybe Kalenteer, though those slaves didn't bring the price these tall blonds did. He'd told Gharan. He'd urged him to give Edeer a break, that they would respond unpleasantly. What they lacked in military might they made up for in guile, tactical surprise, and elite units.

This was that slave's fault. Tall, blond, and blue eyed, she'd somehow beguiled the Nephilim. Oh, he'd said she was for the Most High, but Char knew Gharan better than that. Only Gharan had an ambition to match Char's own. Gharan wanted more like her, so he gave the order to come here.

Char stalked up to the traitorous front man. The man hung from a pole by his wrists. He was missing both legs below the knees now and barely lived. Char positioned himself right in front of the man, their eyes hardly a palm apart.

The man smiled insanely. "Cut me down, Commander. I can fight."

Char looked him over. The cuts at the knee were not bandaged but had been cauterized to stop the blood flow. "You'll lose a leg at the hip tomorrow."

"That'll make fighting more of a challenge."

Char shook his head. "Tell me about this force from Edeer."

The man grimaced as a wave of pain shook him. When he'd caught his breath, he asked, "What force is that, Commander?"

"We don't have to wait until tomorrow. We can take the leg now."

The man convulsed against the post, writhing and swaying by the cord around his wrists. His hands didn't move, the fat, purple fingers pointing to the trees above. The man cried, "I don't know about any force. 'Onestly, I don't. I don't know anything more. 'E knows. 'Ow does he know, commander? 'E knows everything."

Gharan. Yes, the Nephilim did know everything, it seemed. Usually.

Char left the traitor sobbing and moved to report the situation. When he reached Gharan's tent, the Nephilim stood outside. His prince rested one hand on the top of his helm which was perched on its customary pole. He talked with another man Char didn't know. Cols stood nearby at a respectful distance.

The unknown man stood tall in a shiny breastplate. He wore a neatly pointed beard and exuded lithe grace and danger. The long sword on his hip must be steel, so the man had wealth, perhaps prestige and power as well. The two spoke in such a way that suggested Gharan respected this man in some way.

Gharan was saying, "You didn't need to come all this way yourself, cousin. You must have messengers you trust."

"I do," said Gharan's cousin. "But the danger here seemed extreme. Your father would want me to handle it personally."

Gharan nodded. "As you say. What is this danger?"

Char joined the group and took a knee. "My Prince." He stood back up but stayed one respectful step back.

Gharan turned to him. "Ah, Commander Char. This is my cousin, Rillain. Rillain, Commander Char. If this danger is as extreme as you say, Commander Char will need to know."

Rillain eyed Char. A look of something passed through Rillain's eyes as he toyed with his red beard. Was that recognition? Char said, "Do you know me?"

Rillain shook his head. "I think not. You remind me of someone, that is all."

Behind, Cols studied the duff at his feet. Char wondered why he was even here near the command tent. After that debacle in Edeer, he'd been ordered to lay low around Gharan.

Gharan cleared his throat.

Rillain turned back. "Yes. The danger. The women in Fallingwater are not treewives, but rather archers from an elite Edeerian unit. They know you're coming."

Char said, "We know this."

Rillain raised an eyebrow. "As you say. There is more. Enosh sent a hundred of the King's Guard to Fallingwater to reinforce the village. Some are archers, a squad of men with a thumper, and dragon riders. Fifty heavy infantry. Some dragons, mostly crescentdragons. They may be there by now."

Gharan didn't look pleased. Char responded, "We know this, as well."

Gharan turned to regard Char. The motion was inquisitive and extremely dangerous. Gharan didn't like not knowing.

Rillain didn't look pleased, either. The man had come all this way only to give them redundant information.

Turning to Gharan, Char hastened to say, "My prince, I only just now received a report from the scout commander of this force from Edeer. His report was confirmed by another scout. They have reached the village. Master Rillain's report is accurate."

Gharan nodded, thinking.

Rillain said, "There is more."

Gharan and Char looked at him. Rillain continued, "Some of the Edeerian force are not from the King's Guard. Roughly thirty are from the Old Pine Tree school. Lamech is with them."

Gharan's eyes went wide. "Lamech!"

Char knew Lamech was a feared and hated enemy general. Wars now centuries past had been fought in eastern Midreer. Anywhere they faced Lamech, they lost. Stories said the man knew every battle tactic, every regional strategy, and every man's heart. Lamech fought with cunning and strength and could best twenty men on his own. He used magic, evil spirits, and even commanded the weather to overcome his foes. Char had always assumed the stories exaggerated. The look at Gharan's face made him rethink his doubts.

Rillain finally finished teasing his beard to a fresh point. "Gharan, is this a disaster or an opportunity?"

Gharan's blank face and searching eyes showed he was thinking furiously. Finally, he said, "Lamech is not to be underestimated. He will somehow turn one hundred men into three hundred. The three hundred will feel like a thousand to us. Commander Char, how many men do we have?"

Char knew Gharan already knew the number of men, but he promptly replied, "Ninety-seven."

Rillain nodded. "I brought thirty-five with me. We'll stay if there's battle or see you safely off if there's not."

Gharan reached out, and they shook each other's forearms. "Thank you, cousin."

Rillain asked, "So, what are you going to do?"

Gharan said, "Commander Char leads this expedition. He is quite a good tactician. Commander, what do you think we should do?"

Char deferred. "My Prince, thank you. This is a strategic decision. I leave strategy to you."

Gharan agreed. "Usually. In this case, I want your opinion."

Char watched both men as they looked at him expectantly. Go or stay? Much of their past tactics relied on surprise attacks and quick movement. They got in, killed, neutralized, took what they wanted, then retreated, covering their retreat with staggered defenses. The method had proved effective over the years. Yet now, they faced a relatively equal force who knew they were here and had come specifically to stop them. Plus, they were led by a great general.

And yet, retreat was not the Midreerian way. The culture, his culture, he reminded himself, was that of the warrior. War had been literally bred into the Midreerians. He made his decision.

"We need more information, my Prince. We know their numbers and their capabilities. But we do not yet know what they will do. These Edeerians are crafty. But they also decide things in council and committee. They will not act fast. They will sit and discuss the situation, strengthening their defenses in their precious little village. They will scout to assess their danger. They know we're here, but I doubt they know exactly where we are. We have far more men than in previous engagements, which will give them pause once they find out.

"I recommend we wait and do our own scouting. If they don't move, we'll have the initiative and can act. If they move on us, we'll still have the initiative and will attack them as they march. If we can neutralize their force on ground that favors us, the village will be ripe for the plucking. Those blond archers will bring the highest prices yet. If we cannot act in a favorable way, I recommend we pull out and strike something softer. I do not recommend returning to Mordeen empty handed. Regardless of what you choose to do, I am with you, my Prince."

Char glanced at Cols. It was obvious the shorter warrior wanted to say something but bit it back. Unfortunately for him, Gharan saw it, too. "And you, soldier? What would you do?"

Cols looked down. "It's not my place to say, my Prince."

Gharan's face hardened further. "I don't ask twice."

Cols rubbed at the scab on his shoulder. "My Prince, I agree with Char, uh, Commander Char. They will talk about their plans for days. I say we 'it them 'ard, right now. They won't be ready."

Gharan frowned at Cols. Char's second-in-command was too grizzled to wilt under the gaze, but Char could see Cols wanted to wilt. He wanted to sink into the duff and disappear.

Gharan turned to Rillain. "And you, cousin? What do you say we should do?"

Rillain rubbed at his trimmed beard again. "The longer we wait, the more likely additional reinforcements will arrive from Edeer or other villages. Still, High Councilor Tardain has maneuvered the king into a position where they're unlikely to send more. He need only activate a plan he has prepared in the High Council. The chance of a meaningful reinforcing party could be minimal."

Gharan eyed his cousin. "Ah, there it is. The real reason you came yourself. And what, exactly, does Tardain want for this service?"

"Another ten percent."

Char snorted before he could stop himself.

Gharan glanced at him then back at Rillain. "If we successfully raid this village and take a sufficient haul, I will pay him an additional five percent. If not, then no."

Rillain nodded. "Done. I agree with your commander. We scout and wait. My men and I are with you, cousin."

"Thank you, Rillain. Meanwhile, Commander Char, tell our new scout captain to send men to watch the road to this village. If new reinforcements arrive, I must know of it. This strategy relies heavily on our scouting squad. The captain had better be worth the pay he demanded. Also, double the sentries at all times. It's only a matter of time before they find us. We must know when they do."

"Yes, my prince. It will be done as you say."

"And commander?"

"Yes, my Prince?"

"Assume you have all the information and develop plans of attack on both the village and an attacking force. If they move quicker than anticipated, we must be ready to respond."

"Yes, my prince. I will be ready by tomorrow."

Gharan nodded, which was a dismissal. Gharan and Rillain entered the Nephilim's tent as Char collected Cols with his eyes and moved towards his own tent.

Cols ran to catch up. "Commander, we must assume Lamech will know every attack you can bring."

Char agreed. "Yes. But no man knows everything."

Cols nodded. "Unless 'e's a Nephilim."

"Nephilim are offspring of the Most High. I doubt Lam..." Two soldiers passed nearby. "I doubt their grand tactician is a cousin of Gharan. There aren't that many around."

"We 'ave two, right 'ere."

Char stopped in his tracks. "What?"

"Rillain. 'E's a Nephilim, too."

"Are you sure?"

"'E put on a light show back in Edeer. Gharan commanded me to say nothing."

Char frowned at Cols. "So, why are you telling me?"

Cols shrugged. "You're my commander. Plus, now you need to know."

Char continued towards his tent with Cols beside him. Yes, he needed to know. Nephilim fought like no others. Having two in camp seemed a strong asset he could use in the tactics to come.

"What if they get 'ere?"

Char glanced at Cols. "What do you mean?"

"What if the tree rats get all the way 'ere? They could be 'ere by tomorrow. Muck. If it were me, I'd attack tomorrow night."

"They probably won't attack at all, and if they do, certainly not that soon. They have to discuss everything to boredom before they'll do anything."

Cols protested. "When the scouts brought Rillain and 'is men in, I talked with 'im. 'E said those silty children from Blacktree are now Lamech's students. They took down that crew of dragon toes, or toenails, or whatever Rillain calls them. Anyway, those students cut their way through a pack of them like a browdragon through a 'erd of muddy sheep."

Char shrugged. "Toeclaws. And that can't be so hard. They're just a criminal gang."

"They're no warriors, for sure. But they're mucky 'ard men. And muddy mean. We 'ad six men plus me. There were only two of them, and one was a girl."

"I remember your report."

"Three to one, commander, and they looked like they was 'aving fun."

Char scratched at his beard. "This school sounds like something else."

"Yeah. Earlier, I saw what one of them did, all alone. Somehow 'e found us in a basement. I reported this already. Anyway, the tree rat took down three armed Toeclaws with a stick and joked about it. Silt. Gave Rillain a 'ard time, too. Nephilim or no. 'E cut 'im. The tree rat was good. Real muddy good. You know 'oo 'e is."

"Kenan."

"Yeah. That's 'is mucky name."

Char knew his name. Char knew more about him than most even

suspected. "You sound afraid. What's your point?"

Cols said, "Not afraid, just wary. My point is we can't afford to be surprised. We 'aven't treed a big sloth, 'ere. We've crawled into a silty badger's den and found the owner 'ome and ready for us. We've got to assume the worst and prepare for that first."

Char said, "I agree." Cols wasn't the brightest lamp in the room, but he had hundreds of years of battle experience. Char knew to listen.

Cols asked, "So, what if they get 'ere?"

"Undetected?"

"Well, I suppose that sounds unlikely, now that you say it."

"No, you're right, about all of it. Let's develop a plan for that, too. If you were to attack this place and were able to get here somehow undetected, what would you do?"

They reached Chars tent, and he held the flap open for Cols. Inside, Cols stood until Char invited him to sit on a small chest. Char sat in his hammock, absently adjusting his sword at his hip.

Cols said, "Well, I'd 'ave to take the scouts first, or at least cut off their return. Sentries would 'ave to go next. Our men are good, but these tree rats are sneaky good. Then I'd sit in the trees and rain arrows down on the encampment. We 'ave no defenses up to stop arrows or firepoles. Our men would be easy as fish flopping in the low tide mud."

Char agreed. "It's how I'd do it, too. What do we do to stop them?"

Cols rubbed his chin scars. "First, set up shield walls. Not with men, but on a frame, see? Someplace our men can take shelter from the silty arrows. Then, use firepoles loaded with small shot. We won't be able to see them in the trees, but we can spice up the muddy branches real good. Next, I'd send in the hissdragons. Riderless, they'll climb the trees and take out some of the archers. Maybe all of them."

Char nodded. "Do it. All of it. What else?"

"They 'ave riders, and 'eavy infantry, right?"

"Yes."

"They might pin us down with arrows until we 'ave to come out after them. That's when their force will strike."

"Yes. We can deal with that. That'll be your task. You know what needs to be done."

Cols grinned. "You bet, commander."

Char slapped his knees. "Good. Now, let's talk about something more likely. Say we'll attack the village, but let's assume they've had a couple weeks to fortify. What would you do to defend the village?"

They talked and planned late into the night, bringing in the squad leaders as needed.

THE next afternoon, Cols finished sharpening his swords. Five of the bronze beauties lay on a large piece of dragonhide, glowing a deep brown in the sunlight. Both leaf-shaped edges were already sharp, of course. He just touched them up. They liked the attention.

Cols nodded to himself, sheathed the blades, and pulled a leather pack out of his lean-to. He rummaged in the backpack, thinking of the commander.

Char did well as commander. He knew how to listen, which was the best trait of any commander. Cols had dealt with a lot of them. He knew. The man somehow always twisted Cols experience and advice into something far better. The plan to attack the village was simply... what was the muddy word? Enspited? Inspiled? Well, it was a good idea.

He finally pulled a small clay pot out of his pack. The thing had sunk to the bottom, of course. Whatever he wanted in his pack was never on top. Untying a cord, he lifted the lid and set it carefully aside. Then he dipped a finger in and pulled out a glob of bright red paste. He rubbed it on his arms, feeling the ridges of old scars against his fingers.

The plan to attack a force in the forest had been equally inspiled. The tactics were designed to force a defense, regardless of how good a tactician the enemy had. Knowing the defense in advance, Char could tear it apart systematically. Truly *inspiled.*

He carefully dabbed the red paste on his shoulder scab, cursing the silty girl who'd made it. He'd seen good archers, thousands of them over the many years of war. He'd never seen anyone as good as her. She'd killed two men with one arrow. She'd loosed arrows with deadly accuracy while climbing up to a balcony. Honestly, he had no idea how she did it. The flesh around the wound puckered and pain flared down his arm and up into his neck. The paste fiercely stung any open wound but also clotted up blood flow quickly and prevented infection.

None of the inspiled plans mattered. Good or not, Char's plans were useless. The tree rats weren't staying in their village. They weren't coming in a week or two. They were coming tonight, in just a few hours. He didn't know how he knew, but he did. Char wasn't the only one who could be inspiled.

He had a little extra red paste on his fingers, so he rubbed some of it over his brow, leaving a rough crescent of crimson. The mark would frown at the men preparing for the worst. They laughed and jeered among themselves like it wouldn't happen.

Cols knew better.

# Chapter Thirty-Eight
## Love Wins

THE morning after arriving in Fallingwater, Kenan enjoyed the cool air and walked away from the final tactical planning meeting with a bounce in his step. The day of reckoning had arrived. That night, he would kill White Spiders. Well, not exactly, but near enough.

On his way down the boardwalk, he found Olaine weaving a bowstring on a balcony near the top of the stairs. She saw him coming and tucked the material away. The beautiful woman didn't wear her breastplate. He couldn't help but notice her pretty blue dress.

He smiled as he approached. "Hey there."

She smiled back. "I wonder who taught you to do that."

"Do what?"

"Smile like that."

"Oh. Well. I'm not known for it."

She shook her head, her golden ponytail swaying behind her. "I doubt that."

"No, seriously. In fact, that's what I'm known for."

"Modesty?"

"Um, no. Seriousness."

"Uh huh. Don't see it."

"Get to know me more. You will."

She grinned. "Done."

"Done, what?"

"Cute. But we'll have to work on your listening skills."

Kenan started down the stairs, which were wide enough for two at a time.

He took the outside edge, which didn't have a railing. "What's cute is you already thinking you can change me."

"And why not?" The steps down the tree made her move in a way that distracted him. He almost tripped. With a wry smile she said, "Careful there, Woodbender. Watch where you're going. A fall from this height could kill a person, or at least dislocate something important."

Kenan chuckled and said, "You have no idea whether I can be changed. You don't know me. Yet."

She smiled, revealing a dazzling set of perfect white teeth. "Everyone changes. It's one of the truths of life."

"Got a lot of those, do you?"

"A few. Truths are self-evident."

Kenan shook his head. "Not always."

She nodded. Even that was pretty. "Okay. Not always. Sometimes you've got to dig down deep to find the truth. But when you find it, you know it."

"Okay. Got another of these truths of life?"

"Sure. Love wins."

They reached the bottom of the stairs as she said it and he stopped there, inadvertently blocking the way for a couple of soldiers going up. "Isn't it a little early to be talking about love? We just met yesterday."

She grabbed his arm and pulled him to the side to clear the stairs for the others. "Between you and I? Definitely. But in general? Never."

He nodded. "You're right."

She beamed at him, and he stopped breathing for a moment. She took his forearm in one hand. "I can't remember the last time someone told me that."

He grinned at her, putting his hand over hers. "Why is that? Are you usually wrong?"

She tossed her golden ponytail, took his hand, and led him into the Flat. Tents crowded the area so close the tent lines shared stakes. The King's men created neat, orderly rows. The school's masters and students arranged their tents in haphazard disarray. Yet he noticed the professionals stacked their weapons in piles and on central racks while the school had weapons close to hand at each tent. He judged the school able to respond quicker to a threat.

"I'm not usually wrong," Olaine said. "Well, sometimes. It's just, well, I'm young and female."

Kenan eyed her and smiled.

"Oh. You noticed, did you? Well, I'm not that young."

"I'm not that old. I don't think I'm more than twenty years older than you."

"More like thirty, I'd guess. Either way, we're close enough in age."

"Enough? I feel like you're checking off obstacles for your future."

She pushed him with her shoulder and adjusted her hair. "Is that a problem?"

"Depends on your goals, Olaine."

"Sure does." She crinkled her nose up at him and smiled hungrily.

"I feel like I'm being hunted."

"Don't like it?"

"Not sure yet."

"Well pay attention, Woodbender. You never know how I'll strike."

They strolled through the tent village hand-in-hand. Soldiers moved about working on a myriad of tasks. Men sharpened spears and knives. One man fixed the strap on a shield. Two others worked on fitting a breastplate. Others cooked, ate, and laughed in small groups. No one drank, but they moved with energy and purpose.

Kenan said, "They're not going to like the orders coming down."

"Orders?" Olaine asked, watching him out of the side of eye. "What orders?"

Kenan gave her a shocked look, though he couldn't help but grin a little. "Olaine Brookstone, you waited above for me specifically to pry the tactical plans out of me."

"There you're wrong. I waited for you for a bunch of reasons, only one of which was to pry the tactical plans out of you."

"A bunch?"

"You don't think women only think about one thing, do you? That's male territory."

Kenan laughed, and he saw the mirth in her light, brown eyes. She was right again. He was only thinking about one thing. Time to change that.

"So, about these truths of life. What do you do when you find one?"

"Oh, that's easy. You believe."

Kenan quirked an eyebrow at her. "Believe?"

"Yes. When you find the truth, believe it."

"Don't they go hand in hand? I mean, if you think it's the truth then don't you automatically believe it?"

"Semantically? You have a point. But we're messy human beings. We're really good at rationalizing ourselves away from the truth, even when it slaps us on the side of the head."

Kenan squeezed her hand. "That's wisdom. Quite a lot of it, actually, from one so young."

"I'm fifty-two, by the way. I'm not that young."

"And you're right again."

"Everyone knows their age."

"Yeah. But I mean, you're right about the age difference. Close to thirty years."

She smiled at him. "Let me tell you a secret."

"Please."

They stopped in front of the tent he shared with Wren. She leaned in close, took his other hand, looked him right in the eyes, and said, "Lidai told me."

Kenan tipped his head back and laughed. Olaine giggled in shared amusement.

"Hey. Do you two need a moment alone?" Wren ducked out of their tent and Lidai followed. Olaine sharply pulled her hands from Kenan's.

Kenan glanced at Olaine, looking at her hands. What was that about? Turning back to Wren, he retorted, "Speaking of alone, what were you doing in there with my sister?"

Wren grinned and winked. "Can't tell you."

Lidai butted Wren with her shoulder. To Kenan she said, "We weren't up to anything you weren't. Hi, Olaine."

Olaine smiled at her. "Hi, Lidai. He says he doesn't smile much, but I say he does. What do you think?"

Lidai tapped her chin with her finger. "I think we need to talk."

Kenan frowned, "Lidai..."

Lidai brightened. "See. There it is. The famous Kenan glower. Very serious."

Kenan turned to Olaine. "Told you." Then to Lidai, he said, "Behave yourself, sister. I won't have you gossiping about me behind my back."

Olaine nodded to Lidai. "I see it, now."

Lidai nodded once and gave Olaine a knowing look.

Wren turned to Kenan. "How do they do that?"

Kenan shrugged. "What? You mean making a man feel like he has a patedragon skull squeezing his brain?"

Wren smirked, and Lidai pushed him again with her shoulder. "It's not our fault you've got thick heads and small brains. Still, you're good for a few things."

Wren said, "I shouldn't ask, but I'm going to."

Kenan raised his hands to object. "No, please don't."

Wren asked, "What are we good for, Lidai?"

Lidai smiled as she looked at Kenan. "Spilling the nutmash about what's going to happen tonight."

Kenan frowned. He should have seen it coming.

Olaine pointed at him. "Oh, there it is again."

Lidai smiled at her but looked back at him expectantly.

Kenan stammered. He had planned to come here and tell Wren and Lidai everything about the plan for the evening attack. He wasn't supposed to, but he promised to be open with them. He obviously trusted them.

Yet, here he stood next to Olaine, whom he'd known for less than twenty-four hours. She made his heart flutter and apparently addled his brain, too. She'd been coming on strong, and he wasn't so naive to think it was all about him. He'd be a fool to reveal it all to someone he didn't really know.

Olaine could apparently already read him like an open scroll. "I see. Lidai, care for a walk?"

Lidai looked from Kenan to Olaine to Wren and back to Kenan. She huffed a little in resignation. "Sure. Let's go. Kenan, we're not done here."

"Wren and I will bring you up to speed. Promise."

The girls walked away, arm in arm. Olaine looked over her shoulder and smiled at him, her ponytail flashing in a sunbeam. His stomach flipped again.

He ducked into the tent he shared with Wren. Posts driven into the ground held up the tent and supported their hammocks. They sat in their hammocks, feet dangling to the ground. A napping raccoon scolded them with a chitter, then thought better of it. Quick scampered over and climbed into Wren's lap.

Wren stared at Kenan, running his hands through Quick's fur. The raccoon sighed and fell back asleep.

Kenan asked, "What?"

"What do you mean, what? Isn't it obvious?"

"I... she... I don't know, Wren. She is somehow reaching me in a way I wasn't sure was ever going to happen again."

Wren nodded. "I think I understand, Kenan."

"How does that happen in one day?"

"Only the Almighty knows."

"Wren, I'm really sorry."

"For what?"

"For my interest in this girl."

Wren looked surprised. "Why are you sorry? You have no reason to be sorry."

"I do. Your sister and I... well..."

Wren leaned forward and the posts creaked in protest. "Kenan, letting a woman reach you is not a betrayal of Anna. She's gone, lost forever. It's been a year. It's time for you open your heart again."

Kenan shook his head at Wren, smiling wryly. "How do you do that? How do you speak about feelings and all that? I swear, somewhere inside you is a teenage girl fighting to get out."

Wren laughed. "Explains why I eat so much. Look, if you're looking for my blessing because of Anna, you have it. I'm not mad at you. I'm surprised it took you so long. I had hoped you'd make a place for Jenn to put all her... affections. Seriously, that woman has a problem."

"Jenn?"

"Never mind."

A woman flipped the front tent flap up and stuck her head in. Jenn's hair draped down over the side of her pretty face. She smiled at them both. "I thought I heard my name."

Wren set his lips in a grim line. "Dragonspit, Jenn! What if we were changing? We could have been naked!"

"I could wish."

Kenan waved, friendly and courteous. "Hi, Jenn. We were just talking about fighting with two blades. You're the best."

She smiled at him. "I am the best. Oh, and Wren, you've got an animal right there, in your lap." Her eyes sparkled.

Wren grimaced at her but couldn't hold it. He sputtered a chortle and ran his fingers through Quick's fur.

"I'm spreading new orders. Eleenan says we're all to get some sleep. That does it, of course. We must be attacking tonight."

Kenan nodded. "Thanks, Jenn. Oh, and one more thing?" She turned back to him, eyebrows raised. "Keep an eye out for Lidai tonight, would you? I know you two haven't always gotten along, but I'd appreciate another set of eyes watching her back when the fighting starts."

The beautiful woman nodded. "Will do." She winked at Wren and left.

Wren blew air out his nose. "See what I mean?"

Kenan shrugged. "You have to set her straight."

Wren sighed. "You think I haven't tried? Almighty! Did you ever notice there's too many beautiful women around? Bah. Enough talk about women. I'm dying to know about the battle plan."

Kenan told him everything. It took a while. The individual parts for each person were quite simple. The way they interconnected and supported each other was not.

When he'd finished, Wren said, "So. You get to start it all. I think it's too dangerous for you. You'll be right there."

"It's not too dangerous. I'll be safe. You know I can handle myself in the trees."

"I know you attract arrows like toedragons to a stray goat."

"Did you just compare me to a goat?"

"Yeah. Apparently, I do that. Lidai didn't like it, either."

Kenan's eyebrows shot up. "What? How are you still alive?"

Wren shook his head, dismissing Kenan's question. "Kenan, it's too dangerous. You should take someone with you."

The back of the tent rustled as someone undid the ties holding the rear flap closed. A beautiful face poked through, light brown eyes alight with excitement. Olaine said, "I'll go."

Kenan gaped at her. "Were you spying on us?"

"Spying sounds bad. I was listening."

Wren frowned at her. "Spying."

Olaine finally undid enough ties to climb into the tent, trailing the hem of her dress. "Listening. Spying implies I'll tell someone."

Wren asked, "How do we know you won't?"

She clapped the big man on the shoulder then sat down next to Kenan in his hammock. He could feel her body heat. It felt good. "You don't. But," she said as she arranged her dress to cover her legs, "if that was my plan, I wouldn't have come in here and announced myself. I would have run off and told someone. That's spying. I didn't. So, therefore, I was listening."

Wren rolled his eyes and folded his arms. Muscles bulged.

Kenan grinned. "You know, she's right."

Olaine beamed at him. "Say it again."

"She's right. Besides, not much to do about it now."

Lidai burst through the front of the tent. "Olaine! You ditched me!"

Olaine's pretty face looked rather guilty. "I did. I'm sorry, Lidai. I wanted to show these patedragons I could be trusted."

Lidai's arms fell to her sides. "What? You heard them? Great. I'm always the last to know."

In Wren's lap, Quick snorted in his sleep.

# Chapter Thirty-Nine
# The Bamboo Cage

ANNA watched Unarta drumming her fingers on the bare bump of her belly, smiling to herself.

Anna watched her from where she sat on her overturned bucket. Her legs and back had healed, the last bruises fading as she gradually came out of her illness. This morning, she'd awoken to a wash bucket outside the bars of her cell. She'd used it and donned the shifts and the pale-yellow dress provided for her. Breakfast came with a single seed.

Unarta hummed to herself, drumming lightly on her belly bulge. Anna marveled at her. Despite everything she had endured, the woman looked happy.

"Why are you happy?"

"Because of the Almighty."

"The Almighty? What does he have to do with it?"

"He has to do with everything."

"No, he doesn't. Look at what we've been through, Unarta. Did he do this to us?"

Unarta glanced at her briefly. She kept drumming on her belly. "No. Yarro did this to us. They did this to us. But still, God provides."

Anna eyed the wood bars of her cell. "Why doesn't he provide an axe? I'd have us out of here in a few moments."

Unarta nodded, smiling down at herself.

Anna snorted lightly. "What would you do if you were free?"

"What is free?"

"What do you mean, 'what is free?' Free. Not here. Able to go where

411

you wished."

"I have never been able to do this."

"No? Did you grow up here?"

"No. Before we were attacked, I lived in the plains to the south. My people roam there, following the bison and the elephants."

"Bison? And what's an elephant?"

"A bison is like a shaggy horse with horns. An elephant is a big animal with gray skin and a long nose. Some have long teeth that poke out the front."

How very strange. She pictured a mawdragon with an overbite. "If you roamed, you were free."

"Not personally. I did what my mother told me. I went where my father said. He went where the elders directed. They went where the bison went. I was not free."

"You were free of Yarro."

"Yes. I was free of Yarro. Still, I thank the Almighty."

"Right. Because he's been so kind to you."

"He has. He has given me a great gift."

"Your child."

"Yes. He kicks. Here, see? I can feel him."

Anna didn't see anything move, but she'd seen it many times with her mothers and numerous aunts. But she didn't want to think about her family, especially not her mother. The grief still felt fresh.

Anna said, "You think God brought you here to give you that child?"

"I didn't understand. I still don't, but I know this."

"You know God gave you the baby."

Unarta smiled down. "Yes. I know this."

Anna stood and went to the bars. For what seemed like the seventy-seventh time, she pulled at them. Each stout bar was a palm in diameter and didn't so much as wiggle.

Unarta glanced at her again. "You are here for a reason, too."

"Really? What reason is that?"

"I don't know."

"You don't know."

Down the hall, a woman snored. Many of them slept inordinately long hours every day. By the sound, she knew it was Atarra. She recognized it from their many years sharing a bunkroom.

"Unarta, what do you miss about the plains?"

The woman looked up and stared at the wall, her eyes a little glassy from the water. "Tall grass and an open sky. The hills rising to the south. The men's drums beating out the call to break camp and move. The sound of children playing."

"That's... that's beautiful."

"Yes."

"And if you could leave, would you return?"

"I cannot."

"Yes, but if you could?"

"I cannot. I don't want to be here, Agliranna. But a woman alone cannot cross the plains. It takes weeks. There are dragons, cats, and wild dogs. Jackals hunt in packs. We must roam as a people or perish alone."

Cats? Dogs? Unarta spoke of such strange creatures. Perish. She remembered the Dragongrass. She understood. "But wouldn't you rather take that chance than stay here?"

"Before? Perhaps. But I cannot think of only my own body. I now carry another body that is not mine. I must think of him, too."

"But if you stay, he will be raised a slave, to serve them."

"Perhaps. You do not know this, and neither do I. The Almighty has a plan."

Right. Anna pulled at a bar again, just to express her frustration.

Unarta smiled at her. "Agliranna, what do you miss?"

"About home?"

"Yes, in your trees."

"I miss..." Kenan. She missed Kenan, but that's not what she said. "I miss green leaves and chipmunks. The sun dappling on a polished bentwood wall. I miss the fluttering of a butterfly's wings and the sound of children's bare feet pattering on the boardwalks."

Unarta looked at her as she changed the drumming on her stomach. It sounded like children's feet as they played. Her dark eyes smiled. "That is also beautiful. See?"

"I see it, yes."

"It is the beauty of the Almighty smiling on you."

Anna shuffled her feet. "I suppose you're right."

"I know this."

A door banged open on the other end of the hall, and Unarta stopped her drumming. A booted step echoed down the stone corridor. Yarro. He didn't usually come this time of the day.

Anna fled in her mind to her bamboo cage, pulling the balsawood door shut firmly behind her.

Yarro marched all the way down the hall and stopped in front of Anna's cell. He looked her up and down, nodding at her slumped posture. He unlocked her cell door. "Good. Come with me, Concubine."

When he pulled open her door, she stepped meekly out of her cell. She didn't look at Unarta.

Yarro took her by her upper arm and marched her down the hall. Atarra slept on her back in her cell, her stomach bulging up, striped with stretch marks.

At the end, they didn't turn to the room with the table, as she expected. They turned the other way and down another hall with cells. Some held women while some were empty.

They left the breedery and entered the castle courtyard. Drizzle fell from the sunless sky, but still she was blinded by the light. She shielded her eyes with her free hand, and Yarro laughed.

He marched her past men who eyed her. She didn't care. They walked up the courtyard and through the castle barbican.

Inside, they ascended two flights of stairs and through a room of women all at work. Some carded wool and others spun yarn. Some wove baskets of all sizes. Still others knitted, shucked peas, and worked on a myriad of other domestic tasks. What shocked her was the noise. They all chatted and laughed, as if this were a common room on a busy day in Blacktree.

Some stopped talking to watch her. Their eyes held no sympathy, only curiosity.

Yarro led her down a hallway lined with narrow doors that stood open. He pulled at her arm, stopping her next to one. "In."

Anna kept her head down as she entered a small room with a bed and a chest of clothes. An arrow slit in the thick stone wall let in light.

An older woman with dark skin like Unarta's stood in the center of the room. She held a thin reed in her crossed arms and frowned at her. Despite this, she held herself with a stately frame. At one time, this woman had been beautiful. "You're back, I see."

Anna curtseyed deeply. "Yes, Ideera."

"You remember me. Good. Yarro, I will take her from here, if it pleases you."

Yarro grunted before he left.

Ideera tapped a foot. "Will there be any more problems, Concubine?"

"No, Ideera."

"Will you have any more problems with the basement?"

"No, Ideera."

"Do you plan an escape?"

"No, Ideera."

"I see. You understand who you are now?"

"Yes, Ideera."

"Who are you?"

"I am the concubine of the Most High."

"Concubine. Yes. Will you answer my questions, now?"

"Yes, Ideera."

"Good. Sit on your bed."

Anna meekly walked to the bed and took a seat, careful to smooth her dress before she sat.

"Not like that, Concubine. Stand back up."

Anna stood.

"Reach back and pull the skirts forward. Cross your ankles as you sit. Hold your dress out, so I can see your ankles as you sit. Do it again."

Anna did as she was commanded. She wobbled a little, but not much.

"No. Stand."

Anna stood.

"Do it again."

Anna carefully sat.

The reed whistled through the air and caught Anna across the cheek and an ear. The sharp crack stung her, and she flinched.

"Did you like that?"

"No, Ideera."

"Good. Now, stand. When you stand, push out your chest as you push back with your hands. Do it."

Anna carefully stood.

"Better. Now sit."

Anna crossed her ankles and carefully sat down on the bed.

"You can be taught. That is good. But still, not good enough. Cross your wrists in your lap."

Anna did as she was bid. This time she flinched before the reed struck her across the backs of her hands.

"Not like that. Be graceful. Right over left. Try again."

Anna tried again.

"Better. Who do you love?"

"Gharan."

The reed whistled in and struck across her jaw. She didn't flinch this time.

Ideera frowned down on her. "Prince Gharan. We are not in the breedery, Concubine. Who do you love?"

"Prince Gharan."

"Good. Stand."

Anna stood up, careful to move as instructed.

"Good. Lift your chin. Pull your shoulders back. Straighten your spine, Concubine, if you have one."

Anna straightened as instructed.

"Good. What are you doing with your hands?"

Anna looked at her hands. "My hands..."

The reed slapped her across the wrist. "Your hands."

"I..."

The reed struck again, stinging the side of her hand. This one struck hard enough to cut her with the edge of the reed. Blood welled in the scratch but didn't drip.

"Yes, your hands. They hang there, on the ends of your arms. What are

415

you doing with them?"

"Whatever you tell me, Ideera."

"Good. Fold them in front of you. Yes, good. Now fold them behind you when you're interested in what your owner says. Good. Now, hold your elbow with one hand. See, it emphasizes your bodice. This is important."

"Yes, Ideera." Anna carefully kept her tone correct lest the woman think she mocked her.

Somehow Ideera still knew, and the reed whistled in to strike her chin.

"Keep your mind on what I am saying. Do you understand?"

"Yes, Ideera."

"Have you been with a man?"

"No, Ideera."

"Good. Widen your stance, and I will check to see if you tell the truth."

Anna suffered the indignity. What was this compared to the bamboo stick?

"Good. Sit."

Anna sat, careful to perform the actions as required.

"Good. Where do you live?"

"I live here, in Mordeen."

"Good. What do you eat?"

Anna frowned. "Nutmash, mostly, and fruit. And sometimes..."

The reed whistled in, striking her ear again. Her ear felt hot as blood rushed to the pain.

"Bad. What do you eat, Concubine?"

"Whatever I am fed, Ideera."

"Good. What is your name?"

"I..."

The reed whistled again, striking her neck this time. Anna thought furiously. Her name. But Anna was in her cage. She wasn't her any longer and she would not tell them what she called herself. Besides, a concubine has no name.

"What is your name?"

"I... I have no name, Ideera."

"Correct. You are a concubine. You are a vessel, to grow the child of your owner. You do not need a name."

Anna screamed against the bamboo bars of her cage. She kicked against the balsawood door, trying to knock it open. She could not.

She let a soft sound escape. "I do not need a name."

Ideera glared at her. "What are you?"

"I am a concubine."

"Who are you?"

"I am Concubine."

"And what will you do?"

"I will be a vessel for my owner."

"Good. You will need him to want you."

"Yes. To give me a child."

"Yes, and how will you make him want you?"

"I... I will..."

The reed struck her upper cheek and nose. Her sinuses clogged and a tear leaked out of her eye. She was not sad. She was not happy. The pain just was.

"How will you make him want you, Concubine?"

"I will make him happy."

"Perhaps. How will you make him want you?"

"I will please him, Ideera."

The older woman barked a laugh. "And how will you please him?"

"I do not know, Ideera."

"Good. Good. You do not know. You have never known. But I will teach you. I will teach you everything."

"Thank you, Ideera." Concubine meant it. She would learn all she could. Concubine understood now that she was woefully ignorant. She'd thought as a child for her entire life. It was time for Concubine to put aside childish ways and become what she was meant to be.

Anna imagined a beautiful butterfly flexing its wings and sunning itself on a branch as she sat with her back against the balsawood door and remained silent in her bamboo cage.

# Chapter Forty
# The Reluctant Edge

TRIME wished he were anywhere else than in a canoe on the Fallingwater River, silently paddling through the dark towards the camp of the White Spiders.

He wanted to help. He wanted to see justice for his people. He wanted to stop the evil. Yet he still wished he were anywhere else. A nice orchard on a sunny afternoon would do nicely, with a comfortable chair and a friendly, plump woman to keep him company.

He corrected his canoe's angle with a little twist of the paddle, careful to make no noise in the water. They were close.

The woman, perhaps, was his wife. Yes. Maybe it was time for a wife. Well past time, some would say. There could be little children wrestling in the grass and a shielddragon chewing leaves nearby. He could have a shielddragon, if he wanted. He liked Wren's shielddragon. The beast's intelligence startled all who worked with it. He could find one like that.

His children would be smart, too. He could have a little girl, perhaps, sitting on his wife's knee, learning her numbers. No, he would teach his daughter numbers, showing her the tables of nines himself. His wife, smarter than he, would teach her areas under curves, dynamic outcomes, and such. When hungry, he would reach up, pluck a ripe apple, and use his hand knife - his only blade - to cut it.

No, he would have no blade. His wife would cut it for him. He would have no tool with a sharp edge to cut things.

A man in the second canoe pointed over the water. Yes, a narrow beach glowed white in the moonlight on the river's south shore. They would land there. He gave the signal.

They'd paddled fast for most of the way down the river. The White Spiders probably had scouts along the banks. The trick wasn't avoiding the scouts. The trick was to get past the scouts quickly enough so they couldn't get back in time to give warning. There was also the hope the scouts would take no notice of two small canoes on the far side of the river, or if they did, wouldn't consider them a threat worth reporting immediately. Either way, the main Edeerian force rowed in larger boats far behind them but coming on fast. The scouts would report that many men and a couple of dragons to their commanders. Trime and his three students needed to work fast.

Paddling into the White Spider's backwater would get them all stuck with arrows. They assumed the White Spiders would post guards over the boats and their main avenue of retreat. Instead, Trime and his students would land here and start their approach on foot. They startled a little family of ducks who scuttled off through the shallow water, quacking softly. Fortunately, no guard raised an alarm in the night as they pulled their canoes into the brush above the beach. Trime untied the binding on his longsword.

He led his men through the forest just off the beach. One man, a bear hunter and absolute guru in the woods, took point. Nane claimed stalking men was easier than bear.

Trime had no idea the sentry at the mouth of the backwater had been killed until they caught up with Nane and found him standing next to a corpse. The sentry had a hand-axe buried in the back of his head. Trime quickly looked away and up to his student's eyes. The man looked for affirmation. Trime gave it to him with a nod and Nane smiled through his bushy beard. Nane was good but still had a lot to learn. Sometimes killing was necessary, but it was never to be enjoyed.

The group made their way along the backwater shore towards the enemy camp. Soon, they saw the boats. They crouched for a long moment scanning the water and the shoreline for dangerous animals. They saw none. Trime nodded to them, and the three students slipped silently into the water.

Trime didn't watch them slowly swim towards the nearby longboats. They knew what to do. Their task tonight was to cut the boats free and pull them to the river. They were to maneuver the boats downstream and tie them to the far bank. If they couldn't, they were to sink them.

Trime moved through the dark. No man could walk silently through the forest duff, but he could be quiet and invisible in the dark to prying eyes.

He looked carefully for those prying eyes and found two pairs before getting to the dragonring. Two men in dirty overshirts stood talking quietly as they watched over the boats. One smoked a pipe. They wore no armor, but each had a shield and a sword at their hips.

Trime approached from an angle behind and was soon close enough to hear. "I dunno. I think 'e's pretty tough."

"You think so?" The man took a drag on his pipe. It glowed hot and bright, probably ruining his night vision. "'E seems all 'iss and no teeth."

"'Ave you seen 'im with the sword? 'E practices all the time."

"Yeah, but so does everyone else."

"Everyone else don't carry five into combat."

"Five? 'Oo carries five swords into battle?"

"Someone 'oo bends them as 'e kills."

"'E should learn to use the sharp edge."

"'Eh. You think you're muddy smart. 'E bends them the long way, not the narrow. 'E 'its people so 'ard 'e bends the blades."

"You think? I 'it 'ard. I know 'ow to 'it with the sweet spot. It won't bend the blade."

"'E 'its with the sweet spot and still bends the muddy blades."

"Maybe." Another drag from the pipe back-lit the man's head, close now. Trime slowly pulled his longsword free of the leather scabbard as he took another careful step. The trick of walking quietly in the woods was one of placing your foot where you wanted and when you wanted. A slight rustle couldn't be helped, but it could be timed to happen when someone spoke.

Trime eyed an area of soft leaves free of sticks. Yes, there.

The pipe man continued, "Sounds like 'e swings too 'ard. It'll make 'im easier to avoid and easier to 'it back."

"You should spar with 'im. There ain't nothin' easy..."

Trime departed the man's head from his shoulders with a single slash.

The other man turned, eyes wide. The pipe fell from his open mouth. Once it passed his collarbone, Trime slashed his throat with a flick of the steel longsword.

The first man's body finally collapsed straight down. Trime kicked it in the hip and sent it into the soft leaves to muffle the thump.

The second man gurgled, clasping his throat with one hand. He started to pull his sword with the other. Trime knew he wouldn't make it. The man breathed a death rattle before the bronze sword came halfway out of the wood sheath. Trime slapped the pipe-man's sword pommel back into the scabbard. He reached up, took the man's hair in his hand, and pulled the body forward to land on top of his headless friend. No water splashed. No sticks broke.

Trime crouched down by the bodies and waited. He heard only the sigh of the breeze through the trees far above and a campfire crackling inside the nearby dragonring. Small ripples of water warped the mirror image on the backwater, caused by three heads, hand knives in teeth, swimming towards the two longboats.

Reports said there were three longboats. One was missing. Had some of them left? If so, they'd gone downriver. Trime and his three men hadn't passed anyone rowing upstream.

Trime stayed by the bodies and cleaned his sword on one man's overshirt. He watched and listened intently. No other guards or sentries approached. He waited there, not looking at the men he had killed. He didn't think about the orchard dream, the plump wife, or the smart children. He focused on the nearby camp. If a shift change came, he must be ready for new guards to appear.

No men came. His students cut the two longboats free and pulled them away along the backwater. Nane came up on shore by Trime and crouched next to him. He found the pipe on the ground, picked it up, and sniffed it. Apparently, he liked it because he popped the stem in his mouth and puffed to get the leaf burning again. The man's bushy beard twitched as he worked his lips on the pipe stem.

One student killed a swampdragon with a small splash, which got Trime's attention. When he looked, the man held the animal's upper body above the waterline. The dragon was only about six feet long. Still, where there was one, there would be more. Trime gave him the "danger close," sign and the man flashed a white grin in the dark.

Some of his students didn't yet understand the value of life and the pain of taking it. He hoped they didn't learn tonight.

Once the river caught the boats in its current, the students climbed in, disappearing downstream. Only then did Trime sheath his blade, motion to Nane, and move away. He would collect the canoes and then, as his part of the plan, move to and secure rally point two.

# Chapter Forty-One
# A Nest of Whitetail Wasps

KENAN and Olaine moved into position along the heavy branch. They kept a close eye on the White Spider's encampment as they moved, careful to avoid making any sound.

Kenan took lead. Olaine didn't need his help. Her father, she had told him, was a woodbender. She'd been climbing trees most of her life. He didn't doubt it. She moved with lithe grace and sure footing, totally comfortable in the trees. She didn't use her bow to balance even once.

Kenan's armor covered more of him. This was why he took lead. At least, that's what he told himself.

The branch extended almost over the edge of the dragonring around the White Spider encampment. But Kenan didn't dare get that close. Their weight and movement would surely cause the branch to move. Someone down there would notice. They stayed back where the branch hung wide and strong.

At a fork, they stopped where they had a clear view of the enemy encampment. Olaine wrapped a hand around his bicep, giving it a playful squeeze. "This looks like a great spot," she whispered directly into his ear. He enjoyed her touch and the warmth of her breath.

He turned to look at her face, only a palm away. He reached past with his head to whisper into her pretty little ear, exposed by her ponytail. "I agree. Can you take the smaller branch? I'll stay on this one."

She shivered at his breath and smiled. When he was done, she nodded.

His eyes lingered on hers.

Finally, she pulled her gaze away, looking uncharacteristically shy, and stepped onto the forked branch. She lifted her dress up above her ankles, which he knew wasn't strictly necessary. She was showing her leg to him. She had great legs, long with gentle curves. She settled into her position, deftly nocking an arrow and looking forward. Her brass breastplate reflected the camp's firelight.

With some effort, he turned from Olaine. He stepped forward on the main branch.

Rough lean-tos dotted the interior of the fresh dragonring. A tent stood in the center with a post driven into the ground outside the door flap. Some kind of helm rested on the top. Another tent, smaller, stood nearby. Several campfires burned around the encampment, maintained by a few guards. Several other guards stood watch inside the dragonring but facing out, their dragonpikes held vertical. Shields, most painted with the white spider, hung on racks. They formed a sort of shield wall stretching through the encampment. At one end of the camp, circular cooking pits sat cold. Near the other end, two hissdragons lay on the ground, eyes closed. Their saddles sat nearby. The animals were tethered to thick posts with heavy cords.

Kenan nocked an arrow on his bowstring, ready to start. He had first strike. When Kenan loosed his first arrow, the battle with the White Spiders would begin.

Kenan waited. A sentry stood not far away outside the dragonring.

The sentry suddenly dropped his bow and reached for his throat. A dark figure eased the body to the ground. As the sentry kicked his last, a stick broke and he could hear the leaves rustle faintly. The dark figure moved off into the trees. One of the guards in the encampment moved to the dragonring to investigate the noise, peering into the forest where the sentry's body lay hidden in the dark.

Now, Kenan could begin. He drew the bowstring back to his anchor. When his thumb found the back of his jaw, he aimed briefly and loosed. Olaine's arrow followed immediately after his.

The arrows arced ahead and down, finding their targets. His struck the side of the smaller hissdragon, breaking a rib and penetrating towards the lungs. Olaine's struck the neck of the larger animal and blood instantly spurted.

The animals rolled and kicked, hissing and shrieking. The guard shouted the alarm.

They launched two more arrows at the dragons. Kenan's stuck into the back of his target animal. He didn't dare aim for a smaller, more sensitive targets like the neck or eyes. Olaine's disappeared into the neck of the larger animal, not far from her first arrow. The woman knew how to send arrows down range.

One hissdragon broke its tether. The other pulled the post out of the ground. They both raced around the encampment, spreading chaos. They knocked over lean-tos and scattered racks of spears and pikes, spraying dragon blood everywhere. Men rolled out of their blankets and scattered, yelling. One man's leg was crushed under the big animal's foot.

The two launched arrow after arrow into the animals. Though they were at an awkward vertical angle and moving, the size of the creatures made them relatively easy targets. Soon Kenan's target sprouted half a dozen arrows along the length of its body. Olaine's target bristled arrows, at least twice as many as Kenan's, all at the neck. That one fountained blood in great gushes.

Kenan and Olaine watched the men scrambling out of their shelters, yelling to one another. They moved everywhere. It looked to Kenan like they'd swatted a whitetail wasp nest out of a tree.

Several men were trampled by the hissdragons before the big animals broke through the dragonring and disappeared into the dark forest to the east, away from anyone. Kenan couldn't tell for sure, but he suspected Olaine's target would perish from its neck wounds. Regardless, they ran off at speed. They wouldn't be back soon enough to make a difference tonight, whether they survived or not.

Several arrows ripped up through the night air. A few raiders set up behind the cover of the shield walls. But they couldn't see Kenan and Olaine in the darkness outside of camp. Their arrows flew blindly through the branches, none coming close.

A man in the camp strode through the chaos, bellowing orders and calmly strapping on brass armor. "H squad! Assemble! Squad E! Shield wall, over there! Himmons! Get your men over there. You're reserve! You! Yes, you! Bring me my shield!"

Kenan knew this man. He'd fought him on the boardwalk of Blacktree. Char was here.

Kenan's orders had been clear. Kill or drive off the hissdragons then take cover and retreat when clear. He was not to engage the men.

Char continued to issue orders. "C squad! Shields and bows! To the dragonwall, over there! Stand ready. Where are the firepoles?" A squad of men charged toward the gap in the dragonring. Those in front carried shields. Those in back brought bows. This was happening exactly to plan.

A squad of men arranged themselves behind the shields. They had long metal tubes, small enough to hold in their hands. Thumpers!

Kenan hissed at Olaine, "Get down!"

With a roar of flame, the leaves and branches around them snapped with the shot. The firepole squad ducked back down behind the shields to reload.

Char stood right there, in the open, shouting orders. He couldn't make out his face in the firelight and shadows, but he knew the armor and the size of the man.

Kenan made his decision. He jumped up, drew and loosed.

"Kenan!" Olaine whispered to him. "What are you doing?"

Kenan missed by half an arm length. He tried again.

"Kenan! Let's go!"

His next arrow missed again. The man never stopped moving, stalking around the camp issuing orders, ignoring the archery threat. Kenan watched him, hoping for a pause or an indication of where he'd move so he could try again.

The men with the thumpers rose behind the shields, pointing the weapons in their general direction, up into the trees. Kenan dropped again, and the vegetation around him once again snapped and cracked from the shots.

"Kenan!"

He jumped to his feet and turned to the beautiful archer, nodding for her to go without him. She scrambled to her feet as well but moved towards him.

An arrow ripped up from below. It hit Olaine on her breastplate, just below the right breast. If she were a man, the armor might have deflected the arrow. Because the metal curved for a woman, it struck square and penetrated. She jerked and stumbled backwards. Her back foot pawed the empty air, and her arms flew out, trying to regain her balance. She turned her head to look at him, eyes wide. She fell without a sound, backwards into the dark night.

Below, he heard the thump in the forest duff. He heard only silence after that.

Kenan looked for the enemy archer and saw a sentry had circled the camp and approached from the side. The man looked around in the trees. Kenan put an arrow through the man, piercing him from throat to lower back. The sentry crumpled to the ground with a loud wheeze, sobbing like a child before going quiet.

Another roar sounded from the encampment. Branches exploded around him. Something small, hard, and moving fast snapped a glancing blow against his scale armor and whistled away in the darkness.

Kenan dropped down on the branch and watched the White Spider's response unfold through hot, watery eyes.

Squad C filed out of the dragonring. Arrows launched into the men from somewhere behind Kenan. Most of the arrows struck the shields at the front, though one archer fell with a shaft through his forehead.

Squad C charged into the night after the Edeerian archers. Kenan knew the Brookstone Brigade had archers set up to draw any response force away from the encampment. The Edeerian heavy infantry waited at the flanks, ready in ambush.

Kenan didn't move from his position. The heavy branch provided cover as another volley of shot exploded up out of the encampment. All he had to do was wait. He didn't look straight down to Olaine. The silence below told him her fate.

In the camp, Char had donned his brass armor from the waist up and had five more squads organized into groups. He pointed and one squad moved off to the south and through the dragonring, away from the river. The other four lined up to move west, to follow Squad C towards the Edeerians.

Two other squads were deployed defensively around the camp interior.

Kenan saw movement at the tent. A man in steel armor stepped out of the tent and donned the helm on the post. Kenan recognized the armor and helm immediately. The Nephilim was here! Something stirred in his chest.

Kenan didn't move. He hardly breathed.

To the west, he could hear a pitched battle. Squad C was being attacked by the waiting Edeerians. Metal clanged off metal and men screamed in the dark. They weren't very far away.

The Nephilim talked with Char. They gestured, first to the east, then the south, and finally to the west towards Kenan and Squad C behind him. The Nephilim nodded and went to talk with a group of raiders standing ready.

Char turned to his men. "Move out! Double shield wall and spears. Tight crescent formation! Tight! Archers, nock and be ready!"

A column of men moved out of the camp through the dragonring, spreading into two double lines of shield men and spear men. Archers followed in a loose line behind, protected at the flanks by more shield men. Some of the archers had thumpers slung over their backs. They waited there until Char joined them. Char raised his shield and drew his steel sword. He commanded the force of about sixty men to move forward.

Kenan stayed on his branch. The force moved west, passing nearly under him. An arrow ripped in from the dark and thunked into the white spider painted on a shield, followed immediately by another. The White Spider archers returned several arrows without stopping. The archer battle began in earnest, with arrows flying in both directions. The White Spiders held their lines as they marched, protected by the shield wall.

In moments, the force moved past Kenan. The sounds of the battle with squad C dissipated, moving further west. The tromping boots of sixty White Spiders followed.

Darkness and silence descended. The camp grew still as the remaining men held their defensive positions in the camp and waited. One group worked to break down the tents and collect up tools. They were preparing in case they'd need to retreat.

Kenan lay on his branch, dropping tears onto Olaine's crumpled form below. He had done this, recklessly calling attention to their position after they were supposed to retreat and hide. Once again, this death was his fault.

"RIGHT flank! Half march!" Char issued orders to keep his force in a tight, defensive formation as they marched forward through the dark forest. Shields kept the arrows at bay. His archers followed the second shield and spear line closely. When they lagged back, one of them got stuck with an arrow. If they stayed close, they were covered by the shields.

His force burned no torches to limit their visual profile. Just enough moonlight leaked through the forest canopy above so he could see his men's movement and coordinate their formation. It was a blessing and a curse. If he could see his men, the enemy could see them, too.

Char hung back a few steps. He had his own shield which he held high at the ready.

"Right flank! Full march!" His lines were straight again.

They had passed a blond woman and her bow right outside of camp. She had an arrow in her and she wasn't moving. One of his men had gotten lucky.

Good thing, too. She had been a brilliant shooter with a bright mind. Those two hissdragons were more dangerous than half his men combined. One blond woman and a bow neutralized their advantage in less than a minute. He would put his mind to solving this problem after they'd driven the Edeerians off and retreated back down the river.

They'd lost two of their boats. Thank the Most High he'd relocated one of them to a secondary retreat point. Without hissdragons, the one boat would carry them all to safety. He just needed to force the enemy back far enough so they could retreat without further engagements.

They passed casualties from squad C. Two wounded men sprouted arrows. The other two were cut by sword. He'd been right. There was a sizable enemy force out here. He didn't stop to help the wounded. They pressed west, towards the enemy.

With the first arrows, he initially thought a random scout had stumbled on the encampment. A few arrows from an enemy scout would ruin everything. Their raid hinged on the element of surprise and initiative. So, he'd sent out a squad to kill the scout before they could flee.

Only, it wasn't just a single scout in a dress. There were more of the enemy. They'd cut down some of squad C. The rest were still ahead, to the west. He could hear them fighting still.

Char would press forward and gather up what remained of his wayward squad. If he could, he would attack the enemy. He would kill them all if he was blessed by the Most High. He'd be satisfied to drive them off.

Fallingwater was out of their reach for now, maybe even for a century. He'd lost the initiative, both strategic and tactical. They'd come back to Edeer too soon. And the enemy had moved on him too soon. Cols had been right about all of this. So, Char would push the enemy back, allowing them to retreat to camp and beyond to the remaining boat, unharried by these blond archers.

Good thing he was thinking of arrows. Another ripped in from ahead, over the shield walls. He caught it on his shield just in time. The arrowhead came through the shield and pointed at his head. That was close.

He broke the arrow shaft off and threw it to the ground. He didn't want to get cut by the sharp point. "Forward! We must reach our men! Forward at full march!"

He could hear a fight up ahead. He worried his force was being led into something ugly, but he had his own trick prepared. He'd sent Cols out to the south, as planned. By now, he and his squad would be circling back. Two ambushes would even the engagement.

He would rescue his men and throw back the enemy, making good their escape. "Forward full march!"

# Chapter Forty-Two
# All Armor Has Openings

ASHER'S shield dragged on a shrub, tipping the top over and nearly tripping up his feet. If he stepped on the shield, he would fall on it. He knew from bitter experience. He muscled the big slab of wood and bone back vertical in time to catch an arrow on it. Three arrowheads poked through the shield now. Splinters littered his shield arm. For the first time, he loved his shield.

Usually, the big thing felt like a chore. Its weight tired his arm. Its bulk caught on everything. He could partially sleep under its size but when he did, he always woke with sore shoulders. Better to sleep in the rain.

Another arrow thudded into the shield. Yes, he loved this shield.

Char shouted from behind. "Forward!"

Yes, yes. Forward. He might as well move forward. Any other direction would expose him to those dragonspitting arrows.

Asher used both hands to hold the shield. His bronze shortsword hung at his waist. If he could get close enough, he'd use it. He hoped he would. He was good with it.

The spearman behind him tripped on something in the dark. His spear haft thumped onto Asher's armored shoulder. Asher didn't much like the man, but he didn't say anything. Battle discipline was the strictest kind.

Up ahead, he saw a light. A torch? Yes, a torch. Who was stupid enough to light up a torch with archers everywhere?

"There!" Char shouted from behind. "Squad men, take a knee! Firepoles, ready...fire!"

Asher took a knee just before five men fired their firepoles towards the light. He heard a man scream and the light wobbled. It straightened and moved towards them.

"Reload!"

Asher thought it an unnecessary command. He could hear them already cursing and reloading. Commanders command. That's why they call them that.

The torch drew closer. Asher braced and the spear from behind him lurched forward over his shoulder. At the last moment, he recognized the man from squad C. He yelled to hold. The spear angled up to avoid hurting their own man.

An arrow ripped in from the night, piercing the man through the neck and splattering Asher's face with hot blood. As the man fell forward, he landed on Asher's shield, pulling it to the ground.

Asher yanked it back up. He noticed the torch had been lashed to the man's forearm and wrist.

A wave of at least a dozen arrows ripped in from the dark ahead. Most struck shields but one made it through. The spearman behind him gurgled and fell. Asher wouldn't miss him.

The command came from behind. "Forward!"

Asher moved forward, stepping carefully around the torch burning on the ground. He didn't want to get singed.

Another arrow came in at an angle and glanced off his shield. Then another wave of arrows fell on them from the front. Two men behind screamed in pain.

"Squad men, kneel! Firepoles, fire!"

Asher took a knee again as the firepoles erupted from behind. He liked the ripping noise the shot made as they cut through the vegetation.

"Forward!"

Asher stood and advanced grimly. Firepoles or no, he knew these tree rats and he knew their bows. He'd been at the business end of one. This wasn't going to end well.

"WHAT was that?" Lidai asked.

Wren shushed her. "Thumpers."

"Woah. They have better thumpers than we do."

"Yeah."

Lidai watched through the dark night. She could make out the movement of the White Spider force advancing through the forest. There were a lot of them, more than they'd been told.

When the enemy fired their thumpers, twin lines of shields and spears were outlined for the briefest moment. There must be fifty men or more.

Lamech was so stinking smart it irked her. He somehow knew they'd do this.

"I can skewer one right now."

"No, you can't."

"Of course, I can. Just because you can't see them doesn't mean I can't." She tried to jab him in the ribs but hurt her finger on the armor. She liked the way he looked in steel, but it had its drawbacks.

"Right. But we're under orders. We wait."

"I know."

"Then don't do it."

Lidai kicked the back of his calf with her toes. She didn't put too much force into it. She didn't want to bruise him there. "I won't."

The last remaining member of the doomed squad of White Spiders had been hit by the thumper volley from his own forces, but it didn't stop him. He raced towards his fellow dragonspitters. His torch trailed flame and smoke behind him. Lidai didn't look directly at it but appreciated the idea behind it.

Lidai watched him fall on the first shield wall. An arrow ripped in and hit the man's shield high. Those Brookstone women could shoot! She watched him stumble forward and drag down the shield he clutched.

Asher held that shield.

Lidai drew and loosed before Wren could stop her. The brass breastplate Olaine had given her didn't affect her movement or her aim. The arrow flew through the night and struck the shield as Asher raised it back up.

Wren hissed at her. "Lidai! Now they'll know we're over here!"

"Maybe. Look. They're still advancing."

Indeed, they came on in disciplined formation. The line of shields painted with the white spiders came inevitably forward. Now, with the torch burning on the ground, she could see the silhouettes of the oncoming raiders.

From this angle, she had a view of Asher's head. The torch burning on the ground gave her enough light to be sure. Again, she drew and loosed in an instant. She wasn't close to the enemy force, but it seemed almost too easy.

The arrow flew right through Asher's temples and struck the man next to him in the head as well. Both men dropped, opening a gap in the shield wall. Arrows from the Edeerians poured through.

She could hear the White Spider commander screaming, "Forward! Close ranks! Tighten up! Forward!"

Wren twisted to look back at her, favoring her with a frown. "Nice. Why can't you..."

"It was Asher."

"Really?"

"Yes."

"You get him?"

"Yep."

"Then, nice!" She could hear his approval. "You were right."

"Thank you. Um, about what?"

"He died before he knew you were here."

The ranks had tightened back up, closing the gap. Perfect.

Lidai kissed the back of Wren's plate armor. He probably didn't feel it, so she put some smooch into it, so he'd hear it. "I think it's time."

Wren's helm nodded. "I would give them five more paces, but it seems about right."

She waited. "It's been five paces."

"I'm sure it'll start soon."

"When?"

"I don't know. I'm not there. There's enough light. They can see enough..."

Thump! A gout of blue light flashed as the Edeerian thumper crew fired into the White Spiders.

Men screamed and fell. A gap in the shield wall appeared and the archer corps poured arrows through the opening.

Wren pumped a fist. "See? Told you."

Lidai rolled her eyes at his back and clenched the saddle between her knees, just as she'd practiced.

Wren did something with Okay's shield spikes. The big animal leapt forward towards the side of the shield wall. In three strides, he charged at full speed, nose down and shield up. Small branches and shrubs cracked as they broke. Snot flew with each of his snorts.

Okay tore through the men of the shield walls. He hit them on one end and swept them along the line. Some spears were turned in time, but to no avail. Okay's face and shield turned spears aside easily. Men were impaled, trampled, or scattered.

Lidai sat on the second saddle behind Wren. One quiver hung off her back. Another hung off each hip. She held arrows in her draw hand and loosed them at close targets. Armor was nothing; all armor had openings. She was close and every man turned to look up at the massive shielddragon and his riders. They looked right at her, exposing their unarmored faces. Each arrow flew into a face opening, more than three in a heartbeat. She didn't miss and each man dropped.

A second shield dragon charged the line from the opposite direction, plowing through the archers. Men screamed and scattered.

One man stood with a thumper and shot the other shielddragon in the face. Lidai put an arrow through the man's head.

Lidai twisted in her saddle to loose arrows behind her. A man tried to throw a spear at her, but her arrow caught him in the throat. He dropped his spear and fell backwards.

She killed nearly twenty men during the single pass. It felt good. These dragonspitters deserved every bronze arrowhead.

Wren turned Okay back to face the White Spiders. There was nothing much left to face.

Men lay in the forest, some groaning from their wounds. Others scattered and ran back towards their camp. Arrows rained down on them from the King's archers and the Brookstone Brigade.

Okay shook his head to dislodge a man impaled on a brow spike. He snorted out more snot when the man finally slid off.

CHAR stopped running. He took cover behind a tree root and peered back at the battleground. His men had scattered. He could hear them running through the forest all around, being followed by arrows ripping down from the trees above. His men ran back towards the camp. He didn't stop them.

This battle was over. What a complete disaster. And it was that woman's fault.

A man ran past Char's cover. An arrow ripped in and hit the man in the back of the helmet. He fell forward from the impact but regained his feet and ran on. Another arrow ripped by but missed. The man disappeared into the dark.

Char looked again at the battlefield. He had to be quick. He couldn't stay here. A force of men with tree-painted shields and swords ran through the clearing to give chase.

He could see the shielddragons. One was slumping to the ground, blood running down its snout. A firepole worked better than a dragonpike.

The other beast moved into the middle of the battlefield. The rider was probably trying to get it to step on the wounded, but the dragon tip-toed around the men, dead and crawling alike. Partially trained but still dangerous. The woman sat on its back, behind a big man in steel armor. Lamech?

He couldn't make out the woman's features. She was too far away and the night too dark. But he could still see her, bow in hand, arrow nocked, and scanning the forest for a target.

When had she learned to shoot like that? He'd *never* seen anything like it. She alone had killed nearly half his force, and on a single pass!

She saw him and they locked eyes. Her arrow ripped in and clanged off his brass helm. The force rocked his head back. He ducked down behind the root. It was time to leave.

This had been a major failure and an even bigger expense. The village was supposed to be ripe. Their inside man had given promising initial reports. The scout reports said the village brimmed with tall, blond women. They had a plan to deal with the hundred soldiers who showed up out of nowhere. A plan, he realized, that had been exceedingly similar to what had happened here.

And now he must return to camp and confess to the Nephilim. Char shivered, turned, and ran to climb a tree. He would take the limbs back to camp.

# Chapter Forty-Three
# Full Black

KENAN slipped the last distance down the massive tree trunk to the forest floor just outside the White Spider's encampment. From here, he could no longer see the camp. With concealing vegetation, he stalked closer. He wanted to say goodbye to Olaine.

He found her and approached her body slowly. She lay on her back, sprawled in the forest duff. The arrow jutted up from her brass breastplate. Her hair had broken free from its binding and was wrapped around her face. Dark red stained the locks on the back of her head.

Methuselah said that his god was real. Kenan wasn't certain yet, but here was more evidence he wasn't.

Kenan crouched down to her. Her dress had bunched and exposed one leg. He covered her, careful not to touch her. The promise of something good snatched away from him sat large and hard at the base of his throat. He paused to just gaze at her.

He noticed a cord around her neck and, careful not to touch her broken body, pulled a silver medallion from behind her breastplate. The stamp in the silver showed flowing water parting around a boulder. The metal was still warm in his fingers.

He pulled it over her head and settled it around his own neck.

"I'll want that back."

Kenan fell back and landed on his backside. Olaine reached up with her long fingers and pulled hair out of her face enough to look at him.

"You're alive!" Kenan gasped.

"Doesn't feel it," she mumbled.

"Are you in pain? What hurts? Is anything broken?"

Olaine waved him off. "Everything hurts. Something's wrong with my leg. Ooo, it's my hip. Dragonspit, that hurts! Give me a minute. Let me assess."

"Please, go slowly. If something's broken, you could do more damage."

She quirked a pretty eyebrow at him even as she grimaced and lifted herself onto one elbow. "Really? Didn't know that. Emergency medical care never comes up in soldier training."

He smiled down at her. "You can't be that hurt, though there's blood. Here let me help." He ripped a strip of cloth off the hem of her dress and wrapped it around her head.

She groaned. "How can you see in the dark?"

"I don't know. You can't?"

"No. I'm feeling my way through this."

"Well, be careful. Do you think you can stand?"

"I don't know. But we'd better find a way to move."

"Agreed. We're right outside their camp."

"Yes. You are," said a man's deep voice.

Kenan jumped to his feet. The fully armored Nephilim stood only twenty paces away, watching through the opening in his steel helm. His hands rested on the pommel of the sword at his hip. Four soldiers, partially armored, stood behind him, swords out. Their shields showed the white spider.

The Nephilim spoke. "So nice of you to come here. And look. You brought me a gift."

Kenan glanced down at Olaine. She pulled herself away by her elbows trailing a thin streak of blood on the forest duff. One of her legs lay at an unnatural angle. She grimaced against the pain.

Looking back at the Nephilim, Kenan said, "A gift?"

"Yes. For me or one of my men. Unless she's beautiful enough to be given to the Most High. Few are."

"The Most High? Another god. Right."

"You don't believe in gods?"

"Maybe. I'm told there's only one."

"Not true. I was sired by the Most High, a son of God. As such, he is also a god. I know his power. I have this power."

Kenan remembered. "I've seen it."

The Nephilim looked surprised. "You have?"

"Yes. The orange light in your eyes."

"You're from Blacktree. I hear it on your tongue."

"I am."

"Ah. Yes, I remember you. Pissoff, I believe you called yourself. Fun. You fought my commander. And we ... spoke. How do you feel?"

"Uh, fine. And you?"

Gharan ignored the question. "You came here alone, with only a woman to help you. You still like to fight independently, I see."

Kenan smiled at him. "I'm told I'm never alone."

"You were alone in Blacktree. Despite that, you fought well that day."

"Thanks."

"My commander has been looking for you."

"I bet."

"He has a special disdain for you. I didn't fully understand, but I do now, I think."

Kenan twisted his lip into a sneer. He had no idea what this monster meant. "Good for you."

"Your real name. You are?"

"Going to end you, here and now."

Gharan shrugged his shoulders as he turned to the soldiers. "Bring me his sword. If he resists, take his head."

Three soldiers charged Kenan directly. One followed behind.

Kenan leapt forward up high then rolled low. The center man slashed his sword. As Kenan finished the roll and heard the whistle of the blade over him, he drew his sword with a reverse grip and used it to slash the center man across both thighs. Wisdom cut to the bone. He blocked a blade from the man on the left, pivoted on his heel, parried the right man's diagonal attack, and took his arm off just above the elbow. Forearm and sword flew into the dark, followed by a spray of blood and a scream.

He stepped and avoided the left man's next strike, kicking him above the knee. Kenan spun and took his head cleanly off. A flourishing strike cut the throat of the one-armed man. The man with the cut legs lay on the ground, groaning. Kenan put the tip of Wisdom under his breastplate and pushed the blade through his heart. It was over in just a few seconds.

The fourth man settled himself into a solid back stance, sword at the ready, shield up. But he stiffened as an arrow took him in the ribs. Kenan might actually start loving the woman who, though broken and bleeding, had crawled to her bow. Kenan stepped forward at an angle and ended the man's pain. The head rolled a short distance before the body landed on it.

Gharan pulled a knife and hurled it at Olaine. He followed it smoothly with a second blade.

Kenan screamed, "No!"

Olaine deflected the first blade with her bow. She raised her other hand defensively and the second blade pierced her palm. With a loud snap, her bow, cut by the first knife, splintered and cracked. Olaine dropped it into the duff and leaned back against a root, grimacing in pain and exhaustion. She held her pierced hand before her, bisected by the hand knife. Blood ran down her forearm. She met Kenan's eyes. She had nothing left.

Gharan eyed her. When he saw she had no other weapons, he looked at Kenan. He pointed to the dead White Spiders on the ground. "I can see why Commander Char had a hard time with you, boy. You have a rare talent."

Kenan circled, spinning Wisdom to clear off the last of the blood. "I can whistle and juggle at the same time, too."

Gharan circled with him. "Care to try me? I'm here alone, now. My other men were instructed to stay in camp."

Kenan stepped forward and adjusted his grip in both hands. "Perfect."

Gharan drew his sword as his eyes flashed to light with an orange glow.

When Kenan was close enough, Gharan struck with a testing blow. Kenan deflected and reversed his grip again. He twisted and slashed down Gharan's arm. The blade caught in the unarmored gap at the elbow. The weight of the blade pushed through and slashed underneath. Blood etched Wisdom's edge.

Gharan leapt back, surprised. "You cut me."

Kenan held a guard stance, blade held high, again in both hands. "That's the idea."

"You've been training."

"A bit."

"Lamech." Gharan spat the name.

"He has that effect on everyone."

"Yes, he does."

"I'm going kill you. For Anna."

Gharan's orange eyes went wide, then narrowed. "Who?"

"Don't play games with me, creature. You took her. You know her name. Anna! Her death means your death!"

Gharan controlled his deep tones. "Agliranna. I didn't know she was called Anna. She kept that from me."

"Good. Tonight, I avenge her death."

Gharan pulsed orange. Glowing orange vapors rose off him. He laughed behind his helm. "This is almost too sweet."

Kenan quelled his emotions and calmed. His muscles relaxed. He heard something small rattling leaves as it ran nearby. He could hear Olaine's deep breaths. He heard a leaf crackle under Gharan's foot.

Kenan burst into motion. He attacked high and low, using both hands to quicken his blade.

Gharan used both hands on his steel longsword as well. He deflected each attack. The steel blades rang clearly, echoing off the branches above. The Nephilim knew his swordplay.

They danced. Gharan turned with the attacks. Kenan slid at angles and curves. But none of Kenan's attacks could penetrate Gharan's defense. The man moved to defend almost before Kenan could attack.

Gharan went on the offensive. His long steel blade pushed Kenan back and kept him out of range. Kenan angled as he parried and retreated. Gharan turned with him and kept the distance.

One attack from Gharan got through, slicing Kenan along the inside of a forearm near the elbow. A second attack sliced him on the side of his calf. Both were shallow but bled significantly.

Kenan knew he was outmatched. But he never lost focus, moving across the ground and keeping Gharan's blade at bay. He watched for an opportunity.

Opportunity came. The longsword blade pushed forward too far past Kenan's ear, leaving Gharan extended for just an instant.

Kenan spun in, knocking Gharan's blade aside with his forearm bracer. He slashed down at Gharan's thigh, but it was a feint. With his hand, he pointed with his first two fingers and shoved them into Gharan's helmet. He felt the Nephilim's right eye crush under his fingertips.

Gharan shouted and fell backwards. Kenan used the opportunity to slice at the man's shin, but his blade clanged off steel armor again.

Gharan rolled backwards and came back to his feet. He laughed and orange mist pulsed through the gaps in his armor about his head and shoulders. Except only one eye glowed from the depths of the helm.

Kenan glowered at him. "What's so funny, freak?"

"Look at your hand, boy."

Kenan changed his stance and immediately saw an orange glow creeping up his hand and wrist. "You did this before. What is that stuff?"

"An uncle."

"What?"

"A spirit. I spread them around as I'm led by my father. It furthers his mission."

"That's weird."

Gharan shrugged, the vapors off his shoulders glowing orange. "What's weird is that you haven't heard my men approaching."

Five more White Spiders ran into the clearing. They immediately formed a barrier between Kenan and Gharan.

Kenan backed off and shook his hand. The orange glow slowly faded, but it wouldn't come off no matter how hard he shook his arm.

The soldiers formed a line of shields and swords. Gharan stood solidly behind them, orange mist rising off him.

"What now, boy?" The deep voice beckoned him to attack.

Kenan looked down at his arm. The glow faded and was gone. And so was the initiative. He should have won. He was instead lost. He'd failed Anna. He'd failed Olaine.

He glanced at Olaine. His head snapped back to her. She held Gharan's hand knife, pulled from her palm. She didn't hold it for defense. She held

439

the tip to her own throat.

Kenan stared in horror. No. No, she would not. She could not. He would give her hope. He must.

Alone, he charged the line. He downed two more of them before something hit him in the head and the world went full black.

# Chapter Forty-Four
# Shielddragon on Guard

COLS leaned forward on the massive log covered in moss. Though he stood, only his head peered up over the top. The rest of his squad hunkered down behind the moist cover.

The battlefield was mostly deserted. Dragonscrape! He'd missed it all.

Men lay everywhere. None of the wounded lived. Whether they died in battle or were put out of their misery later he couldn't determine. Most had arrows in them.

A shielddragon lay motionless on the ground. It looked like the Spiders got one of them.

Another shielddragon stood nearby with three people standing near its head. Two large men wore steel armor. The shorter man held a torch up for light. The third person wore a dress under a brass breastplate and held a bow. He recognized her.

Cols thought this through. He didn't like planning. He wasn't good at it. But he wasn't stupid. He knew the value of tactics and he knew what sound tactics looked like.

What would he do? He knew he should turn his squad around and leave. The battle was lost. The village was lost. They would retreat.

But that woman put a hand on her hip as she cocked it to the side. Her body language spoke of spirit and strength. She'd be his while everyone else went back with nothing. He'd make her pay for the scab on his shoulder. She wouldn't like it, but he'd savor it.

One of his men peered up over the log even though they'd been told to stay down. "What're we going to do, Cols?"

"You want to go back empty 'anded?"

"No." Several other men quietly grunted their agreement.

"Me either. Most 'ave moved off. But there's an archer, a pretty one. I 'ave an idea."

OKAY'S face sported several new scratches from spears. None were dangerous, but one deeply scored the thin, tough flesh over the shield bone. The animal didn't bleed much. A few small streaks of blood dripped down his face. Wren wiped them away with a rag. "That score needs stitching."

Lidai stood next to him. "He's fine."

Okay nuzzled her with the edge of his shield. She almost fell. "Hey. Stop that!"

Belroon adjusted the torch and used his foot to scratch at an itch behind his knee. "No, it'll pull. Besides, I don't want to be around when you try to stitch him, yah? I'll show you how to use resin to fill the scratch. It'll heal. Don't worry about him, yah? This handsome beasty will have a great scar to strike fear into your enemies. He'll be back in Gruntle's stable in no time."

Wren stood tall and looked directly into one of the shielddragon's eyes. He had to pull Okay's head down a bit to do it. He'd gotten so big.

Okay looked back at him and blinked. Wren smiled. Okay would be just fine.

Wren released Okay's chin beak and turned to Belroon. "Thanks. I think you're right. It doesn't seem to bother him at all. He..."

Something buzzed through the air and struck Belroon behind his knee. The big man jumped and swatted behind him. "Aaah! Something stung me!" He danced for a moment, his armored kilt clanging as he collapsed to the ground.

Wren snatched his shield off Okay's harness and jumped forward to cover Belroon. Lidai had already scooted behind Okay's foreleg and had an arrow nocked.

Half a dozen men emerged from the forest. A big man in front held a shield with a white spider glowing from nearby torchlight. He wore some armor and held his head low behind the shield. Other men ran forward in line behind him, using the big man and his shield as cover.

Lidai loosed three arrows at the lead man in less than a second, all to no avail. Each arrow thunked into the shield.

Okay stood at an angle to the approaching men, which put him and Lidai at risk. Wren couldn't have that. "Okay, wheel right!"

The animal shifted its weight and turned to face the men head on. Lidai scrambled underneath as Okay moved.

Wren watched the approaching men. "Okay, shield up!"

Okay dropped his nose and lifted his shield up off his neck. He and Lidai were protected.

Belroon writhed on the ground. "Go, Wren, yah? Take her to safety! There's something wrong with my leg!"

Wren glanced back at the man. A small bolt stuck into his knee just below the joint. Blood spurted with every heartbeat. "Shut up, fat man. I'm thinking."

"Better do it faster! Here they come, yah?"

Lidai launched another two arrows. Both arrows streaked to the ground, hit a fallen shield, and bounced back up under the approaching men's shields. One man grunted in pain.

The front man dropped his shield lower to cover from this unexpected angle. Another arrow from Lidai struck him under his helm cap, right into an eye. Death and falling followed instantly.

The second man reacted slowly. He took an arrow through his helm opening and also fell.

An arrow ripped in from the darkness, passing near Wren. He tried to catch it on his shield, but it was too far. Lidai ducked back and the arrow bounced off Okay's shield frill. The shielddragon snorted but didn't move. Good boy.

From up in a tree somewhere in the dark, an arrow zipped down to the area behind the attacking line. A man shouted, then he returned an arrow back up to the trees. Lidai launched an arrow back at the enemy archer. Arrows flew around the battle ground from multiple directions, darts in the dark.

Wren stopped worrying about them. The White Spiders were on him.

Wren took their momentum away by charging back at them. He roared wordlessly, joyously. All his restraint fell away. He would kill them all.

Wren slammed the first man with his heavy shield. The man flew to the side with a sickening crunch. He wasn't small. Wren was simply big, strong, and heavy.

A simultaneous strike with his axe cleaved the next man's shield and arm in half. The man fell to the side clutching his bleeding stump.

Another man came, holding his shield high. The axe's new design made it float in his hands. Wren spun it with one hand to catch the man under the shield with an upper cut that opened him from crotch to sternum. The man lost his innards, grunting, "Oh." He sat down hard.

His momentum spent, Wren danced to the side. An arrow struck him in the chest, but his armor deflected the shaft. He heard Lidai's return arrow fly away, then another, all passing close to his head. They ripped through

443

the air. He ignored them all.

The last man in line stood shorter than the rest, a red streak showing across his forehead. He crouched and smiled at Wren. Cols looked just as he remembered. The well-muscled man had a shield in one hand and a sword in the other. Other swords hung at hips and over his shoulders. His arms reflected red in the torchlight.

Wren didn't hesitate as he attacked with his axe. Cols ducked under it and stabbed with his sword. Wren twisted and caught the blade on his shield easily.

Cols danced back out of range. "That was well done, big man. You gutted these dogs like they weren't even there. I thought I 'ad them better trained." The rasp in his voice focused Wren.

Wren circled Cols. "You did a great job with them."

"You mocking me, big man?"

"You have to ask?"

Cols frowned and moved forward. Wren let him, turning to expose a side.

Cols took the bait, striking with his sword tip like a viper at knee, elbow, and neck. Yet, Cols also left no opening. Wren defended, twisting and moving to catch the attacks on the blade of his axe. At the last moment, Wren spun to attack with his shield.

Cols saw it coming and slid back out of reach. Wren saw him move back and adjusted his spin to cover himself. Cols darted back in, but his sword only thumped into the edge of Wren's shield, sticking there.

Cols let go and jumped back. "Woah, big man. You think you can challenge me?"

"Why not?"

Lidai ran forward to stand over Belroon. "Wren!"

Cols raised his shield to protect himself from her angle.

Wren shouted back to her. "No! Don't, Lidai! He's mine! I want him alive."

Cols laughed. "You think so, do you?"

"Yep. The attacking line was a bad idea. Who taught you that? Only the man in front can see."

"Yeah. It seemed like a good idea. I was inspiled."

"Inspired."

"Oh, right. I thought your lady could shoot. Figured I'd give 'er only one target."

"I get you now. She can shoot."

"I saw. Would 'ave worked. Maybe. Planning's not my strength. Guess I should 'ave just made it up as I went."

"Improvisation."

"Yeah, I... wait." Cols voice rasped a higher pitch. "You?"

"Who else?"

"You survived?"

"What gave it away?"

"'Ah 'ah!" Cols' laugh sounded like someone stepped on a bullfrog. "I remember you! Glad I let you live, now, big man."

"You won't be, little man."

"Little? I'll cut you down to size."

"Your size? You didn't bring enough swords."

Cols opened his mouth, then shut it.

"You can't make me mad, short stuff. That man over there? He beat that out of me."

"Yah!" Belroon bellowed. "Make me proud, boy!" The man roared as Lidai wrapped another rag around the wound. Blood still spurted with every heartbeat.

Wren yelled back, "Okay! Cover!" The shielddragon had been trained to stand protectively over both Lidai and Belroon.

Wren turned his full attention back to Cols just in time. The quick man darted in with a swipe at Wren's foot. He felt the blade clink off his armor.

Wren stepped back and blocked the next cut with his shield. Cols came at him hard and fast. Wren twisted, turned, and stepped at angles. The cuts came but he turned them all, giving ground with each attack.

Another blade stuck into his shield. Cols left it there and drew another sword in an eye blink. The attacks never slowed.

Wren gave him openings. Cols either ignored them or took them carefully, not springing the trap.

Cols tried to slam him, shield to shield. Wren knew his stances, and the shorter man bounced off. Quick as a darterdragon, Cols dropped to a knee and slashed. Wren raised his foot to avoid the attack and snap kicked at Cols. But Cols wasn't there anymore.

They circled each other warily.

Cols rasped out a chuckle, but he didn't sound happy. "Don't know what you've been up to, big man, but it weren't chopping down trees."

"Nope."

Cols came in high, his blade cutting through the bone reinforcing the top of Wren's shield and splitting it two palms deep. The blade bent. The tip of the blade stopped at eye level. Cols slammed shields again, pushing them towards Wren. The tip of the stuck blade slashed down inside Wren's helmet.

Half the world went completely dark.

Wren screamed out at the pain in his face and danced back, but there was no time. Cols advanced, slashing and stabbing. The man had dropped his shield and attacked now with two swords, one in each hand. Wren twisted and turned, parrying to the sides, careful of the blades stuck in his

445

shield. It took all his skill and training to defend himself against the flurry of attacks. He pushed the pain to the back of his head, panting with the effort. He had to turn his head more to see them coming out of one eye. But he defended and waited.

There! An opening. Wren blocked to the left with his shield, parried to the right with his axe head, which leveled the axe handle at chest height. Wren thrust with the handle, catching Cols in the throat with the wood heel.

Cols dropped both swords and stumbled back, eyes wide and clutching his throat.

Wren was on him. He cut downward with the axe, taking the front half of Cols' foot off. He followed by slamming Cols' torso with his heavy shield.

Cols fell backwards to the ground with a gurgled shout.

Wren gave him no quarter. He dropped both axe and shield, as he fell on the man.

Despite his wound, Cols was ready. Wren heard a knife blade skitter across his lower breastplate. Wren caught the wrist holding the blade and twisted his body to protect himself, putting Cols in a wrist lock with the motion.

Cols fought back, twisting and pushing, but like a wrestler. Cols didn't know how to Jempo roll.

Wren smiled.

It was over in a few moments. Wren twisted again, sticking Cols in the hip with his own blade. Cols screamed. He spun around and pulled on an arm. Cols flopped over on his belly and the wind rushed from his lungs. Wren hooked him with a leg, lifted Cols arm, and pulled it easily from its socket with an audible pop. The dislocated arm went instantly limp.

Cols screamed again.

In a moment more, he had Cols' hands tied behind his back. Thinking of his mother and sisters, he looped a cord up and around Cols' neck. The man choked, gasped for breath, and choked again. Wren searched him for weapons and tossed two more knives to the side. He left the blade in the man's hip. There's no way Cols could reach it. Besides, taking it out might make him bleed out. Wren didn't want him dead.

Wren stood and glared down at Cols with his clear eye. "How does that feel?"

Cols rasped out two words between gasps of air. "Kill. Me."

"Oh, I don't think so. We have questions for you, little man."

Wren saw Cols' foot bleeding freely where it was amputated diagonally from the big toe up to near the heel. Wren pulled off the partial boot and tied a cord tight around Cols' leg just below the knee. The man screamed again, but Wren ignored him. The bleeding stopped. "Just saved your life. We're even."

Cols gasped and choked but would survive for now.

Wren turned back to the battleground. Okay still stood protectively over Lidai and Belroon. Though Lidai worked frantically on the big man, he lay on the ground unconscious. In the torchlight, his skin looked almost gray.

Wren ran over. He crouched down under Okay. "What can I do?"

Lidai looked up at him. Her eyes held no reassurance. "I put on a tourniquet. He's not bleeding as much, but he's already lost so much..."

Wren unbuckled the steel kilt around Belroon to free up some room to work. He saw she'd placed the tourniquet well. It should have worked.

He ripped off his gauntlets and put his hands on top of Lidai's, adding to the pressure.

Belroon weakly coughed. "That should hurt, boy. But I don't feel a thing."

"Sorry, master. We have to apply pressure."

"I know. I'm weak, yah? Cold."

Lidai looked to Wren. "Keep him talking. I thought I'd lost him. He needs to stay awake."

Wren nodded. "It's just a little bolt, master. Nothing to bother with. You'll be fine."

Belroon wheezed. "Didn't think it would be a little thing like this that would finally get me."

Wren tilted his head so his own blood wouldn't drip from his chin onto Belroon. "Yeah? What'd you figure it'd be?"

Belroon groaned, wheezing again. "Always figured it would be my wife, boy."

Lidai snorted as she tried to tie another bandage in place.

Someone approached. Okay spun over them faster than his bulk implied, facing the newcomer.

The figure stopped at Okay's snort of warning. A female voice called out. "Easy, big boy. It's me. Dinnane."

Wren loved Okay for this, but it was time to move him out of the way. "Okay. Side right." The shielddragon carefully stepped to the right. Wren continued, "Okay, guard." Okay turned to face away. Of course, he turned to the river, where a threat was unlikely. He was supposed to circle his position. Well, he needed more training.

Dinnane approached and growled, "How is he?"

Lidai looked at her. "Not great. We need to get him to a boat. We've slowed the bleeding but he's running low."

Dinnane smiled at Belroon with something like affection. "This man? Me, I think he has twice as much as normal men."

Belroon smiled up at her, then looked at Wren. "Boy, if anything important is exposed down there, I'll thump you good."

Wren smiled back at him and flipped his undershirt down over the tourniquet. "You're just fine, master."

Dinnane turned to Lidai. "Girl, what's your name? Liddon?"

"Lidai."

"Lidai. You're doing everything right. Stay here. I'll cut some poles. We'll get him to Rally Point Two. It's closer. Boy, keep him talking."

In minutes, Dinnane and a couple of her archers had poles cut. Soldiers and archers returned from chasing the White Spiders and rendered help. Soon, they had Belroon on a pole stretcher ready to be harnessed to Okay.

Lamech appeared. He wore heavy steel armor splattered in blood. He carried a cleaver-like sword, shiny steel and dripping blood, propped up on an armored shoulder. Tadd struggled to carry a big shield behind him.

Belroon smiled up at Lamech, but his words were weak. "Some coward stuck me with a splinter when I wasn't looking."

Lamech grinned down on him. "I bet he paid."

"Yah. He's right over there, trussed up for rest day dinner."

"We won the night, Belroon. We decimated at least half their force and drove off both hissdragons."

"Good. Yah, good." Belroon closed his eyes, falling unconscious again.

Lidai tied on yet another bandage, struggling to stop the blood. "Something's not right. It's not working. The blood keeps flowing."

Lamech sighed. "Something was on that bolt. Keep at it, girl. You're doing everything right." He moved off to coordinate the soldiers as more of them returned to the battle site.

Jenn stood by Wren, looking down on Lidai and Dinnane working on Belroon. She looked up at Wren. "What's wrong?"

"Apparently there was some kind of toxin on the bolt. The bleeding won't stop."

"No. With you. What's that on your nose?"

"Just a little blood."

"Let me see."

"No. It's just blood. You've got a bit on you, too, you know."

Jenn huffed, which looked out of place with blood all over her face and splattered all across her front. She glared at him. "Lidai. Your betrothed's been cut."

Lidai looked up. "What? Where? Jenn, I swear..." In the torchlight, Lidai's eyes widened. "Wren!"

Dinnane grabbed Wren by the arm. "Move over here. You, bring a torch. Jenn, was it? Take his other arm. Sit him on the ground."

Wren didn't want to leave Belroon, so he didn't.

Dinnane kicked him and pushed. It didn't do much good. "Fine, boy. Stand there, just turn this way." A man brought a torch. Wren squinted one eye at the light.

Reaching up, Jenn and Dinnane were just tall enough to pull off his helm. Lidai gasped over Belroon. She couldn't take her hands off the master's knee. "Wren!"

The slash from the sword embedded in his shield had parted his left eyebrow, sliced his eyeball, and left a gash down his cheek. He knew all this. He'd felt it happen.

"Easy, Lidai. It's not that bad."

Jenn slapped his hand out of the way. "Stand still, meathead." Her face was just inches from his.

Wren whispered, "If you kiss me again, woman, I swear I'll tie you up and leave you over there next to him." He hooked a thumb towards Cols.

Wren turned his head to look at Lidai. He had to know if she was horrified at his appearance. Would she be disgusted by him, now?

Dinnane snorted. She took his chin in a vice-like grip and twisted his head back around, eyeing the wound. "He's right. He's lost the eye, but it's otherwise not that bad. He needs stitches and a patch, but he'll be fine."

Lidai exhaled in relief.

Wren smiled through bloody teeth. "Hey, it could be fun. You'll never know if I'm winking or just blinking."

Jenn smiled at him. "I think it's fetching. Makes you look even more threatening."

Lidai growled as she tied yet another bandage around Belroon's knee. "I could use some help here..."

Most of the attack force had returned at this point. A line of men faced east, towards the enemy camp, and sentries were out, but otherwise most people gathered gear, helped the wounded, or ran errands for officers. Eleenan, his side covered in blood and his sword still in hand, pointed and issued orders. The thin scribe, it turned out, knew how to organize a fighting force. Abram knelt over a man who had a small, round hole in his breastplate, holding the man's hand as he struggled to breathe.

Wren took a knee. His eye at chest height, the women worked to wrap his head with a cloth. They stood close, too close. Both wore breastplates shaped for women, and he had nowhere else to look.

Lidai was suddenly there, elbowing both women out of the way. "Ahem. I'll finish this. Thank you, both. No, sorry. I mean it. Thank you." Dinnane smiled at Jenn as they moved away.

With her bloody hands, she unwound the cloth, carefully peeling it away from the wound. That stung and he winced. Her eyes widened slightly, then she studied the gash carefully.

"How does it look?"

"Open. You'll need stitches and glue. And we'll have to do something with what's left of the eye. You're not going to like that part, I'm betting. It's not bleeding much, now. Dragonscrape her, she's right. It'll be a fetching scar when it's healed."

"Seriously, Lidai. How bad is it? Am I ugly?"

She quirked her lip at him. "You've always been ugly."

"I have?"

"No, dear. Now you're handsome *and* menacing. That'll attract some, but it'll scare away others."

"Are you talking about other women?"

She kissed his good brow, which made his heart jump. She carefully re-wrapped the cloth around his head, covering the eye. He asked her to wind enough to pad over the top of his head, and she did so. "There. All set for now."

He wrapped his armored arms around her waist and pulled her in close, laying his bandaged head against her chest. She pulled his head in tight. "It'll be okay."

The ground thudded as the shielddragon moved over to them. He sniffed at Wren's head. Wren stood and patted Okay on the jaw. "You're a good boy. You did great today."

Okay snorted snot all over him, but he didn't mind a bit.

Men lined up to march to the rally point. It wasn't part of the plan for all of them to harry the enemy's retreat. The crescentdragon riders had that honor. Besides, they wanted some of the raiders to make it back, to spread the word that Edeer was no easy target.

Lidai said, "Hey. Where's Kenan?"

"I'm sure he's around here, somewhere. Look for Olaine. He'll be with her."

Lidai moved off to find them, muttering under her breath. "That woman moves fast."

Wren got Okay ready to travel, thankful the shielddragon hadn't been shot by one of those fiery thumpers. Belroon's litter now hung from Okay's harness, who would pull it to the rally point on the river. He checked the setup to make sure both Okay and Belroon would go smoothly.

The column of soldiers started moving north to the river. He saw Cols, still bound and now tied by the neck to one of the soldiers, who pulled him along roughly. Cols would walk, just like his sisters had, foot or no foot.

Lidai marched up. "Wren!"

"Yeah." He said it quietly. His wound made his whole head pound. He turned to her and had to keep turning until she came into view. He would need to get used to that.

Lidai towed a small man in dark clothing behind her. "Tell him what you told me."

The man looked shy, even though Wren knew him to be a deadly and cunning fighter. "Someone fell."

Wren asked, "What do you mean, 'someone fell'?"

The man twisted his arm free of Lidai's grip. "I was near the enemy camp, assigned to take out sentries. I saw someone fall off a branch."

"Kenan?"

"Not unless he wears a dress."

"Olaine."

Lidai pointed towards the enemy camp. "Wren, if she fell, Kenan would go after her. He's not here. I looked everywhere. He must still be there, by the camp."

Wren nodded in thought. "Or carrying her back here. It would take a while."

The small man nodded to Wren respectfully. He gave Lidai a wary look as he moved to join the departing force.

Dinnane approached. "We ready to go? I'll watch Belroon from the rear." The big man snored on his litter. The blood had finally stopped flowing, but Wren didn't like the darkness of his leg or the pale color of the rest of his skin.

Lidai snapped, "We're not going anywhere. Kenan's not here."

Dinnane frowned. "I'm sorry, both of you, for your loss. But we need to reach the boats. It's two days walk without it. And you, tall one, need to see that wound treated. We'll have to scoop out the eye. It'll fester if you don't. Can't have a head wound festering."

Wren said, "Captain Dinnane. Please take Okay and bring Belroon to the boats. See that he survives. Please. But we're going back for Kenan."

"Not alone, you're not." Jenn sauntered up into the torchlight. "I'm coming with you."

Lidai nodded. "Fine, but don't let me catch you playing with Wren's bandage, got it?" Lidai smiled wickedly and flourished a knife in her hand. Surely, she must be jesting.

Jenn smiled back and chuckled. "On my swords, archer. I promise. Let's go."

Dinnane nodded to them. "I'll let the others know what you're doing. Be careful. I'll also see to it the canoes are left at Rally Point Two so you can use the river to get back. Good luck."

Wren ripped the padded lining out of his helm and set the bare metal down over his bandage. It fit snugly over his head bandage. He didn't need luck. He needed his axe.

The three gathered up their weapons as well as a few waterskins. They walked east through the night, back to the White Spider's encampment.

# Chapter Forty-Five
## Vapor

KENAN dreamed of blond hair and a dazzling smile. He knew it wasn't real, but it didn't stop him from grinning in pleasure at the vision. The smile parted and a man's voice said, "Heave." Heave? Heave what? "Heave," it said again. No, that wasn't right. Who was smiling at him? Why was she smiling at him? What was wrong with her voice? And what was he supposed to heave?

He tried to reach out his hands to her to accept whatever he was to heave. His hands didn't appear. His wrists hurt. They felt like they were on fire. His head hurt with dull, pulsing throbs, sharper on his right side. Something stung his forearm. What was going on?

He finally cracked an eye to see a man squatting in front of him. The man grinned wickedly from under a dented helm, his thin, ugly face no more than a foot away.

Kenan jerked back, banging his head against a tree. His headache flared and a groan escaped his lips. He might have fallen from the pain except he was already sitting. His arms had been tied behind him and around a small tree. The wound on his forearm rubbed against the rough tree bark.

His armor and weapons were gone. They'd even taken his boots. He sat only in his undershirt.

"'Immons. 'E's awake."

Another man approached, bent over, and peered into Kenan's face. "Barely. But I'll report it." As Himmons walked away, Kenan saw Wisdom hanging across his back.

Kenan sat in a forested area adjacent to a clearing. In the early morning gloom, Kenan saw a pile of gear stacked nearby. A dozen men struggled to push a big boat with some kind of tower at the stern through the forest. One yelled, "Heave!" and the men responded with a shove. The boat moved less than a foot. They reset and did it again. And again, each time shouting "heave!" Three men stood watching, one in a steel breastplate, one in full steel plate armor, and one in brass armor. He couldn't see their faces.

Where was he? What had happened?

Kenan shook his head, which did nothing for the headache and made his vision swim. When his vision stabilized, he focused on the boat. It looked heavy. The keel dug into the ground below the thick duff layer. He snorted derisively. They should have cut and peeled some logs to use as rollers and skids. It would have been a lot less work.

A soft, feminine voice called his name. "Kenan."

He turned to look, but his head fell to his chest. With extreme effort, he picked it up and focused through the pain, squinting his eyes to identify the voice. A beautiful blond woman sat against her own tree, her arms extending back and tied at the wrist.

Kenan smiled at her, or he tried to. "Hey. You're pretty."

"Kenan..."

"Look. You're tied, just like me."

"Kenan, are you okay?"

"Nope. I'm human."

"What? Kenan, snap out of it."

A male voice said, "Give him in a minute, dear girl. He'll come around."

Kenan thought for a long moment, trying to clear his mind. He shook his head violently, but instead of clearing his head, he instantly lost consciousness.

When he came to again, he lifted his head and looked around. The boat was in the river, which flowed silently by their little patch of woods. Now he understood why the men had a boat in the forest. That made sense.

"Hey, look. He's awake again." The male voice sounded happy.

Kenan turned to look for the voice. It wasn't the ugly soldier or Himmons who'd said it. Tied to another tree and sitting on a root was a smiling, bright-eyed man with light brown hair and a trimmed dark beard. "Hey."

"Hello," said the man. "Nice to see you lucid."

Kenan blinked at him.

Olaine looked concerned. "Kenan, you took the back of an axe to the head. Are you okay?"

Kenan turned and blinked at her. He didn't feel okay. "Yeah."

"You know," said the smiling man, "You should really get a helm. It's a handy thing to have. It doesn't just protect your noggin, you know. You can scoop dirt, eat nutmash, and sit on it. I suppose there's even more uses. I bet we could come up with a hundred ways to use a helm."

Kenan turned back to him and blinked again. A helm?

"You could carry a clutch of eggs, collect up mushrooms, and even boil water in it."

Kenan peered closer at the man. "Boil wa... Hey, I know you."

"Not really. But it would be nice. I'm up for it if you are."

"You're that guy."

"Well, I have a man's body, if that's what you mean," said the man through his smile. "Is it hard to tell?"

"Yes. I mean, No. You're the dragonfly man."

The man laughed as if Kenan had told the world's best joke. "I like that. Can I use it? I'll tell everyone, 'I'm the dragonfly man.'"

"Sure. It's yours. What are you doing here?"

"Well, I haven't caught a dragonfly yet, if that's what you mean."

"No. I mean, what are doing *here*?"

The dragonfly man shrugged his shoulders. "I surrendered. It seemed like a good idea at the time. They shoved pointy sticks at my face."

Olaine said, "Kenan, what's going on?"

Kenan sighed. "I'm pretty sure they'll torture me for information, take you as a slave, and keep this one around for comic relief."

The dragonfly man shook his head and beamed at them both. "Oh, no. I'm not funny. Never really got the knack of it. But maybe they'll let me cook? I'd really like to try it."

Kenan shrugged. "Well, I have one piece of good news for you."

The dragonfly man brightened even more, light brown eyes widening in excitement. "Oh, good! Please, tell."

"If what I hear about the Dragongrass is half true, you're sure to find lots of dragonflies on our way to Midreer."

The man bounced in glee and clapped his hands behind his tree.

"Kenan," Olaine whispered. "I'm scared."

He could hear it in her voice. He was scared, too. "Be brave, Olaine. We'll make it through this, somehow. How's your leg?"

"Hurts bad, but they reset the bone into my hip. It took four of them. Never felt anything like it before."

"Anything broken?"

"Yeah. A whole bunch of ribs. Probably other things. My head aches something fierce."

"I'm so sorry, Olaine."

"Me too," she sighed.

The dragonfly man smiled at them both. "Look at the bright side!"

Kenan stared at him. "There's a bright side?"

"Of course, there is, lad! There's always a bright side."

Olaine sighed again. "Fine. What's the bright side?"

The dragonfly man smiled and shrugged his shoulders. "I have no idea. But you'll find it, I'm sure."

Kenan rolled his eyes as far as he could through his headache. "That's not helpful."

"Really? Hmmm. I thought it would be." The man didn't frown as he thought. He just smiled a little less.

"Enough talking. Time to go." Himmons strode up, kicking Kenan's leg. The blow struck brutally hard on his calf. His leg spasmed up to the hip, and he bit back a groan.

"Stop that!" Olaine hissed.

Himmons approached her. "You don't give orders around 'ere. You especially don't give orders to me. I own you, now. For taking 'im down alive, I got both the sword and the girl. I expect a promotion soon, too. This 'as been a disaster for us, but not for me.

"You 'ave lots of blood on your face. I can't tell how pretty you are. Sit still." Himmons wiped her face with a wet rag.

He couldn't tell? She was absolutely gorgeous, even with blood on her face. Kenan didn't argue with Himmons, though. He just tried not to throw up.

"Oh, you're a pretty one. I'm going to untie you and get you off that tree, pretty slave. Behave, or I'll give you pain."

The dragonfly man smiled up at Himmons. "There's worse things than pain, you know."

Kenan hissed, "You're crazy. Shut up."

Himmons kicked the dragonfly man, but he smiled through it as if it didn't hurt at all. "Is your foot okay? Next time, you should use a stick."

Himmons looked down at him, shook his head, and moved behind Olaine. Her arms fell free. She held them to the sides awkwardly, groaning as she tried to loosen her shoulders. Himmons moved to the side and rebound her hands behind her back. "Do I need to run a choker cord on you, pretty slave? You won't like it."

Olaine shook her head.

Himmons pulled her up to stand. She screeched in pain but found support on her good leg. She balanced precariously, so Himmons leaned her back against the tree. He pulled a hand knife from his belt.

Kenan struggled against his bindings. They'd been tied well. He tried to wiggle his fingers to see if he could find the knot. He couldn't even feel the cord. His fingers felt fat and numb.

Himmons smiled. "Now, pretty slave. Stand very still." He reached the knife up to her throat and she stiffened. With a tearing sound, he cut her dress down the front all the way to the hem, neatly parting the fabric.

The dragonfly man said, "I recommend putting a finger along the back of the knife. Wouldn't want to nick your prize, would you?"

Himmons looked over his shoulder and sneered at the dragonfly man. "I've done this once or twice, you know. Shut up, or I'll gut you like a fish."

Kenan fought against his bindings, his whole body straining against them. He pulled, stretched, and yanked. For the effort, he received burning pain on his wrists. His shoulders screamed at him. He stopped fighting, chest heaving to catch his breath.

Himmons cut the dress at each shoulder and down the sleeves to the wrists. The fabric fell away. He repeated the process with her overshift. It, too, fell away.

Kenan growled at Himmons, who ignored him.

Himmons talked to Olaine as he worked. "There's a stall vendor in Mordeen. 'E sells sugar candy. Some is minty, some is 'oney, some is fruity. Every morning 'e gives away a piece to any boy who comes along. Free, mind you. 'E charges them nothing, but they each only get the one piece, see. Later, they come back for more. You know what 'e does, pretty slave? 'E charges them twenty percent more than 'e would normal-like. See what 'e does? 'E lets them sample 'is wares, then 'e makes a big profit later. There you go, pretty slave. It's a bit chilly, so we'll leave you with your undershift, for now. I 'ave a wonderful evening planned for you on the boat. Don't worry. I won't keep you to myself. Everyone gets a free try. But just once. By the time we reach home, I'll have every coin on that boat in my pocket."

Kenan pulled at his bindings again, grunting from effort and pain. It didn't take long for his body to give out. He collapsed back against the tree, growling out his frustration.

Himmons chuckled at him.

The dragonfly man smiled at everyone.

Himmons picked Olaine up and carried her to the boat. She looked back at Kenan, eyes wide in terror. Kenan's eyes welled up as he watched her go. There was nothing he could do.

"What do you think, Kenan? Time to pray?"

Kenan gawked at the smiling dragonfly man. Pray? Kenan growled at him. "Shut up! You're mad! Do you know what they're going to do to her? Do you understand what's happening here?"

The dragonfly man finally stopped smiling and looked at Kenan squarely. Kenan recoiled from the man's serious expression. It looked somehow dangerous. "Kenan, it's always time to pray. God Almighty is listening, at every moment, no matter what is happening. He loves you and wants to help you. I know it to my core. Honor Him. Talk to Him. You'll see. You're never alone."

Kenan stared at him. Never alone.

Himmons returned. Without pausing, he trudged up and struck the dragonfly man across the jaw. The dragonfly man's head snapped to the side from the impact. When he turned back, the broad smile returned. "Good one, lad. You put your whole body into it. Nice form!"

Himmons took greater care with the bindings on the dragonfly man, tying his elbows, lashing them to his torso, and hobbling his legs before untying and retying his wrists. The dragonfly man gave advice on the knots the whole time.

Kenan rested his head back against the tree. The sky had turned a dull gray between the leaves of the great trees above him. A glidedragon wheeled up there, high above, turning in circles. Free. He watched it as the dragonfly man was marched to the boat. The madman smiled over his shoulder. "Never alone, lad. Never alone."

Men hauled the pile of gear to the boat. Gharan and Char stood nearby, talking quietly to Rillain. If Rillain was here, the Toeclaws were probably here, too. The three men watched the raiders prepare to leave by the river.

Two Nephilim: Gharan and Rillain. Kenan watched but didn't see any orange or red vapors rising off them.

Gharan glanced at Kenan as he spoke to Char. Char glanced back at Kenan as well. After nodding to Gharan, Char turned and moved towards Kenan. As he approached, Char removed his helm and rubbed a hand through his dark hair. Finally, as he got close, he lifted his head and looked at Kenan.

Kenan's heart leapt to his throat. "You!"

Char smiled grimly and said, "Yes. Me."

"Nehamane? But... what... I don't understand."

"Yes, it's me. But I don't use that name any longer. I am Char Roughrock, commander of the White Spiders." Nehamane squatted down to Kenan's level.

"But Nehamane, I... I..."

"Easy, switch-brother. I'll explain."

Kenan gaped at him.

Nehamane cleared his throat. "They took me, that night decades ago. They only take men when it's convenient or they're light on women. I woke up just as they were leaving, so they tied me up and made me walk with them. In Midreer, I was a slave, working in the battle yards. I learned to fight there and killed many other slaves. Life was... unpleasant, at the time. But that hard life also defined me, set me on the path."

Kenan listened, horrified and confused.

His brother raked his hair again. "Soon, I caught the notice of a certain man, and I joined his slaver party to make coin. Fierceness, ruthlessness, and a head for battle helped me. I made a lot of coin. I bought better weapons and took more slaves. I bought my own slave papers. Coin solves a lot of problems. After that, I had my own slaves. Some were valuable slaves. Soon, I joined the Spiders. They're the best in the trade, and my prince showed me the way."

"Nehamane, stop this," Kenan implored. "You don't have to do this."

"Oh, but I do. I want to. I have plans. Plans for wealth and power. This," Nehamane waved around at the men and the boat. "This is just the beginning."

"You attacked your own people!"

"No. I saved my family. No one was hurt, even when our mother tried to kill me."

"What?"

"When did she learn to use a bow like that?"

Kenan shook his head. "That wasn't..." Nehamane didn't know. He'd never met Lidai. She was born well after the raid at the women's bathing pool when Nehamane was taken. Kenan didn't want him to know her name. "That wasn't supposed to happen. She was supposed to stay in the house."

Nehamane nodded. "Yes. And she survived the conflict. I saw her again, tonight. She fought like an avenging spirit. I lost at least twenty men tonight to her bow alone."

"Well, she was never the kind of woman to anger."

Nehamane smiled at him. They shared memories: dodging their mother's grasp after stealing pie off the kitchen counter, being paddled for putting a dead snake in her bed, and hundreds of other childhood mishaps.

The scenes played out in Kenan's mind. This Char, this man, was still his brother. He said, "Nehamane, stop this. Please, let us go. We'll return to Blacktree and take care of our mother."

"We?" Nehamane paused and looked over at the boat. "Is that your wife?"

Kenan shook his head. It seemed unwise to let him know how important she'd become to him. "No. I just met her a couple of days ago."

Nehamane nodded. "I don't believe you. A wife will be strong motivation to push you along the way."

"What way?"

"The way of the Most High. The way of power. Kenan, these little villages you seem to find so important are completely inconsequential. They're sheep pens, raising ewes for profit. In Midreer, you'll see a real civilization. You'll see wealth, opportunity, and power. And you can have it, as much as you can seize."

Kenan shook his head. "No, Nehamane. This is evil. Slavery is evil!"

"And who defines evil? Good and evil are for temple priests to argue over while they grow fat on the sacrifices gifted them by the sheep. Kenan, the world is ours. We are here, and we can grasp it in our fists."

Kenan hung his head.

"The rewards are beyond your imagination."

"No."

Nehamane stood. "You don't yet know. You haven't seen, haven't tasted. But you will. This trip was, I thought, a complete loss. But with you, I see huge future profits, for us both. You'll see."

His brother turned and walked back to Gharan and Rillain. Kenan's spinning mind sank into darkness.

He heard a noise from the boat. Olaine screeched, and he heard someone get slapped. He heard her grunt, deep in her throat. Someone was beating her.

Desperation pulsed up in him, and he wrenched at the binding cord again. Either it would break, or he would. Pain flared as skin and muscle stretched and tore.

He broke. Not his wrist, but inside. He could not do this. He couldn't free himself. He couldn't save her. He couldn't stop any of this. His brother was lost. Anna was lost. And now Olaine was lost. He couldn't save anyone, not even himself. Hope dwindled and winked out.

He gave up. He felt completely alone.

"You're never alone," said a small, still voice.

Kenan looked around. He wasn't surprised to see no one nearby. Either he'd lost his mind, or God Almighty was talking to him.

He had nothing to lose. He had nowhere else to go. Without God, he was truly alone. He closed his eyes and whispered into the dawn. "God, I am so sorry for my disbelief. I am a prideful man. I think I'm capable, but really, I'm insufficient. I am not enough. I can't do this. I couldn't help Anna. I can't help my friends. I can't save Olaine. I can't do it. I need your help. Please. I give up. I give it to you. Help me or not, God, your will be done."

He distinctly felt three somethings, entities, he wasn't sure what they were, flee from him.

When he opened his eyes, he saw a white vapor rising off his chest.

# Chapter Forty-Six
# Let Them Come for Me

WHAT was that? Wren paused in his march eastward, spit on the ground again, and listened. Lidai must have been looking the other way because she thumped into his back, her bow clattering off his armor.

She rubbed her nose. "Ow."

Behind, Jenn chuckled through her nose.

His axe hung on his back. "Did you cut yourself?"

"No."

They could see now, and he extinguished the torch. The day had dawned, but without a sun. Overcast clouds hung low in the sky. To his right, he could hear something big moving through the forest.

Jenn said, "Hissdragon?" A moment later, a crescentdragon trumpeted through the forest, echoing off the giant tree trunks and heavy limbs. Another sounded, further off. Yes, the dragon riders were sweeping the area, looking for stragglers. They must have finished harrying the retreating White Spiders or lost them in the dark before dawn.

Wren quirked his lip. "Well, at least we don't have to worry about any dangerous dragons out here."

Jenn raised a perfectly curved eyebrow. "Really? I'd think all that noise would *attract* something hungry."

"I hate to agree with her," Lidai said, "but she has a point."

Wren nodded. "Probably. And, if you're a straggler, it'd make them easier to avoid, I'd think."

Jenn shrugged her shoulders. "I don't think they're trying to catch stragglers, though they will if they can. I think they're just trying to hurry them away."

Lidai looked at Jenn, and Wren smiled at the mix of irritation and agreement on her face. The smile pulled at the wound bisecting his eye and he tasted new blood in his mouth. Almighty, he had just finished clearing out the taste. He spit again.

Lidai looked at him with concern. "How is it?"

Wren growled, "Tastes just great."

"The wound, you oaf. Let me see."

"It's fine." He moved forward. The women followed after they both snorted in unison, then glared at each other. This mission was, he thought, a gnarly, old hornbeam tree with a broken top and heavy, dead limbs. It had to be chopped down, which was a lot of work, but it might kill him and those around him in the process.

He didn't think the crescentdragon riders had harried the White Spiders very far. After passing through the empty encampment, Wren had picked up the trail of the White Spider's retreat. The tracks of thirty men followed by several crescentdragons had been relatively easy to follow. At some point last night, the crescentdragons had lost the trail in the dark because now there were only signs of men.

From the back, Jenn asked, "Are you sure you know where you're going, woodcutter?"

Wren didn't answer. He kept his eye forward along the trail. In the light, it was easy to follow. He wasn't worried about losing them. He was worried about what was waiting for them. Before stopping for rest, the raiders would post a rear guard. Blundering into them could be fatal with only him and two women.

Lidai said, "Shhh. He knows what he's doing. You're the one who scoffed at fighting 'only thirty men.'"

Jenn said, "It's more than thirty, you know. If thirty left this trail, then there'll be another dozen or more as scouts and flanking forces."

Wren growled, "We're not fighting thirty men. We're not fighting forty. We're just trying to find them, and if possible, sneak Kenan and any other prisoners out to safety."

Jenn said, "His voice gets menacing when he's in pain."

Lidai shook her head, her brown ponytail swinging. "It's not the pain. He's angry."

"Oh."

Wren *was* angry. He wanted to kill them all. But he couldn't, not forty. Not thirty. That only happened in the stories told around the fire. He thought about Kenan and Olaine, if she even lived. They hadn't found the body. But he also had to think about those two women behind him. All of their lives were in his care. Therefore, he wasn't going to be able to kill all the White Spiders. His anger grew.

461

Ahead, a branch snapped, and not a small one. He crouched, his shield forward. His axe hung on his back in easy reach, and he carried a spear in his strong hand.

An arrow ripped in from an angle ahead. It wasn't aimed at him, but he shuffle-stepped and caught it on his shield anyway. A second arrow ripped in from another angle, too far for him to block.

Lidai coolly stepped to the side. The arrow missed. She returned an arrow, and a gurgling cry sent a small flock of darterdragons skittering and chirping as they ran away.

The trio moved to take shelter behind a tree. Wren said, "Nice shot, Lidai. Anyone see the other archer?"

Jenn said, "Nope. But I saw the hissdragon."

Lidai gulped. "I saw it, too."

Wren growled, "Where?"

Jenn said, "Where that branch broke."

"Did it have a rider?"

"I don't know."

Wren breathed out his nose. "Okay. Jenn, hide. You've got ambush duty. Lidai, head that way. See what you can do about the other archer. I've got the hissdragon."

Together, both women gaped at him. Lidai recovered first. "You what?"

"No time to argue. Do it." With that, Wren sprinted from behind the tree to stand facing the threat. Another arrow ripped in, but he saw it in time and caught it on his shield.

Before him, a patch of big ferns reached up more than three times his height. The fronds moved, swayed, and parted. Something big approached from concealment.

He heard light footsteps running through the duff to his side. That should be Jenn. Almighty, he hoped it was Jenn. He didn't take his eyes off the moving vegetation.

To the other side, he heard an arrow zip through the forest, then another. Someone groaned and coughed. It sounded male. It had better have been male.

The ferns parted further, and a hissdragon snout poked out, strong arms and claws pulling the fronds back. The beast's head and shoulders topped twice his height, gray skin rippling over strong muscles. Its snout bristled with teeth. Under sharp brow scales, yellow eyes with slitted pupils looked down on him in hunger. It hissed, long and loud, while a massive tail thrashed the ferns behind.

Wren's knees should be weak. He should be shaking in fear. Almighty, he should be soiling his armor. But he stood tall, shield forward, spear butted firmly on the ground, point up. He looked back up at the beast, hissing softly back through bloody teeth.

A man rode the hissdragon's back. He held a bow, arrow nocked. He drew and loosed at Wren.

Wren thought he could catch it on his shield, but the range was too short. He jerked up his arm, but not in time. The arrow snapped against the side of his helm, the metal ringing in his ear.

Another arrow came in from some distance away. He heard its long flight. The man on the hissdragon heard it too and turned to look just in time to take the arrow through his open mouth. The shaft went through and flew on, rattling through fern stems. The man slumped, fell forward, and slid down the hissdragon's neck to hang from a stirrup. The animal shook off the man, who landed with a thump in the duff.

Wren took a breath and hissed again.

The hissdragon took a step forward, watching Wren. It seemed hesitant. Or curious. Or maybe it was just toying with him.

Jenn appeared from the vegetation. In a single leap, she reached the side of the hissdragon, driving her sword all the way up to the hilt into its ribs.

The hissdragon screamed in agony, whipping its head around to bite at her.

Wren leapt forward and plunged his spear into the animal's neck. He let go and tried to jump back, but long talons grabbed his arm and lifted him off his feet. His shield fell away.

The animal ran, still holding Wren. The forest blurred past. His shoulder plate screeched as a claw scratched at the metal. He tried to reach his knife, but he swung too wildly, out of control. Pain flared in his shoulder.

The blur of the forest stopped as the hissdragon slowed. Wren suddenly fell free, thumping down on the duff. He opened his eye and looked up. The hissdragon towered over him, looking around. Blood flowed down its neck from Wren's spear attack. The animal coughed, and blood sprayed in the air. It was mortally wounded.

The dragon staggered and bumped into a small tree. One foot came down by Wren's head, and he flinched away from the massive toes and claws. Another foot kicked him in the stomach. His air left him as he slid away through the duff.

As he regained his breath, he heard the hissdragon scream again, cough, and thump away followed by its long, thrashing tail. Moments later, a massive thump lifted dead leaves all around him as the creature fell and thrashed in some underbrush.

Wren lay on his back, staring at the great tree limbs, leaves, and the gray sky beyond. His chest heaved with each breath. Something burned on his arm where he'd been gripped. He flexed the arm, testing for anything broken. Nothing was, but the back of his arm still burned. He removed a gauntlet and checked for blood. There was some, but not much.

Lidai ran up to him. "Wren! Are you okay?"

"Yep," he said, sitting up and hiding his wet fingertips. "Just went for a little ride."

"I saw! What is it with you and angry dragons?"

"Pretty sure I attract all kind of angry things." He smiled at her.

"Ew. Don't smile. You've got blood all over your lips and teeth."

He got to his feet, slipped on his gauntlet, and took Lidai's hand in his. She fit her fingers into his under his gauntlet armor. He let her squeeze his hand. "You got the other archer?"

"Easy."

"You're amazing."

"Yeah. I sure am."

Wren smiled again. More blood trickled down over his lip and into his mouth, but he didn't care.

They found Jenn struggling to remove her brass armor from around her torso. Her movements were careful, and her face grimaced in pain. The metal warped with dents and holes, front and back. They helped her out of it.

Jenn shook her head. "That dragonscraping thing bit me."

Wren laughed. "I see that. How'd you taste?"

"Well, good, of course. Did you expect anything different?"

Lidai blew air out her nose as she pulled at Jenn's clothing, fingers exploring the holes. "I need to see. You're bleeding on the chest and back, but I can't tell where or how bad. Wren, help me get these clothes off her."

Wren stood completely still.

Lidai rolled her eyes. "Listen, *dear*, help me lift everything off, but Almighty help you if you don't close your eyes."

"Only got the one, now." Wren closed his eye, lifting the fabric off and over Jenn's head. Jenn hissed in pain.

Lidai said, "Oh. This isn't that bad. You'll be okay. Jenn, what else hurts?"

"My chest. It bit hard. Something's not right. Ow! Stop prodding!"

"I have to. Quit complaining. Wren, I need bandages."

Wren hadn't brought any medical supplies. Almighty, what a stupid mistake. He turned his back so Lidai would know he wasn't peeking and started cutting Jenn's undershift into strips with his hand knife.

Jenn was soon bandaged and dressed. Wren tried to bend the breastplate back into shape so she could put it back on, but it was mangled beyond repair. It would need to be recast. He bent the back piece with his knee and hammered a few shards of brass into place with the back of his axe. He settled the contraption onto Jenn's back with leather straps reaching around her chest. They did most interesting things with her figure. "There. At least you have some protection from behind."

She smiled at him fondly. He didn't see it but heard Lidai's foot stomp into the duff.

The burning on his arm faded. He checked again for blood. What came away didn't seem fresh. He probed and found a ragged scrape where a claw had scratched him on the back of his arm. He ignored it and wiped away the blood before Lidai could see. He picked up his shield, using it to hide the evidence.

By the time they were ready to move, Jenn breathed easier. "I'm down a sword."

Wren said, "I know where it is. We can go get it." He heard another bout of thrashing in the underbrush from the direction of the dying hissdragon. "Nope. Never mind. You're good with one."

Jenn agreed. "We're down a sword, a spear, some armor, and a few arrows. Do we press on?"

Wren nodded. "That was just the rear guard."

Lidai mumbled, "Some rear guard."

Wren ignored her interruption. "Unless they sent a runner, we might still be far enough away for them to miss hearing the hissdragon. This is our chance to get close."

Lidai moved forward, but Wren stepped in front of her. He would take no chance with his betrothed. If arrows came, he thought, let them come for him.

# Chapter Forty-Seven
# The Masterplan

OLAINE tried to lift her leg. Too much pressure on her hip and knee made the joints ache fiercely. Himmons had given her splinters when he dumped her in the boat, and she shivered against the cold, rough hull. Her wrists burned behind her back where her binding chafed. At the other end of the boat, men loaded their gear onto the fore deck in the early morning gloom. One man organized the gear and kept an eye on her and the dragonfly man.

The smiling man lay on his side at her feet, on the narrow deck over the bilge. His hands, elbows, knees, and feet were tied with cords, which bit deep into his flesh. Another cord pulled his feet up to his elbows behind him. He didn't seem to mind any of it.

He smiled up at her. "I love a new day. Overcast or no, dawn brings the promise of something new. Unique. Dawn makes everything feel fresh with promise, don't you think? I might take a swim."

"Don't. Tied as well as you are, you'll drown."

Her hip throbbed and pain flashed through her ribs with every breath. She looked away and up at the tower. She had no idea why it was there and didn't much care. There were no planks or shields to protect an archer up there. It was just a place for her eyes, so she didn't have to look at the crazy dragonfly man.

He asked, "Thirsty? There's some waterskins, right there next to you."

She *was* thirsty, now that he mentioned it. Her dry throat croaked for water. Two red waterskins hung from a peg in the wale. She bent slightly, leaning on her good hip, and reached the waterskins with her teeth. She pulled the plug easily. Wrapping her mouth around the end of the skin, she sucked water into her mouth. She noticed it tasted slightly off, but she didn't care. She took a deep pull, then another, and then another.

"Not too much, now. One more pull, that's it."

She took two more, then defiantly looked at the dragonfly man.

He blinked at her over his smile. "Two is not one. Three is one, but that's not about water. Not *that* water." He kept smiling at her.

This man made absolutely no sense. But she was thankful for the drink. She left the plug dangling by its cord. "Why do you do it?"

His smile broadened. "Why do I do what, my dear girl?"

"Keep up this false pretense."

"Oh, and what pretense is that?"

"Your good cheer. You must be in pain. You're a slave, and you're being taken to only the Almighty knows where. Your fate can't be pleasant. Why smile?"

"That, my dear, is the best question I've been asked in a very long time."

She eyed him. "Well?"

"It's about foundations."

"Foundations? I don't know what that is."

"Foundations, you know. Basements. Stone walls holding up buildings."

"Branches hold up buildings."

"Yes, I suppose they do." He smiled and thought for a moment. "What holds up the branches?"

"Trees." Where was this going?

"What holds up the trees? What keeps them from toppling?"

"Roots." She got it now.

"Right. Roots are foundational for trees. Foundation."

"Foundation. Got it."

"What roots you, dear girl?"

"Uh, my feet?"

"I'm not asking about your body. I'm asking about your heart, your mind, and your soul. I'm asking about your very being. What is your foundation?"

She thought for a moment and smiled wistfully. "An arrow flying true."

He laughed. "Yes! I've never heard it put quite that way. Well said."

"Thank you."

"Now tell me. Is it the arrow? Are you basing your life on a stick with feathers and a bit of bronze?"

She frowned. "No. It's the true flight that's important."

He nodded, which looked funny as he was lying on his side. "Yes. Truth. It's all important and the best foundation."

She watched the men still working on the shore, thinking about the dragonfly man's words. Finally, she looked him in the eyes and asked,

"What truth makes you smile all the time?"

"Yes! I had so hoped you'd ask that question, dear girl. I'm excited! What a wonderful new day, indeed! My truth is so simple. Here it is. Are you ready?"

She nodded to him, not sure what she was going to get from the madman.

He cleared his throat. "God loves me and has a plan for me, a plan that fits into His masterplan for the ages. If I follow His plan, He is with me. If God is with me, none can stand against me."

She quirked an eyebrow. "That's it?"

"Why, yes, my dear. It's as simple as that."

"Uh huh. Is His plan really that great?"

"Of course. He is God, after all."

"Okay, I buy that. But how do I know His plan? I can't know Him. I can't know His plan."

"Have you asked Him?"

"What?"

"Have you *asked* Him? How would you know something about someone if you don't talk to them?"

She thought about it. "Do you talk to God?"

"Of course. All the time. Pretty much constantly."

"Really. And this is important now, so be serious. Does God talk back? Are you hearing ... voices?"

The dragonfly man roared in laughter. The soldier loading the gear looked back at him, hand on hilt, but went back to his work when he saw nothing amiss. It looked like most of the gear was loaded. They didn't have much time before hope fled.

Olaine quirked an eyebrow at him. "I wasn't being funny."

"Of course, you were. You think I'm mad."

"What gave it away?"

"Listen, lovely girl. You have ears to hear what I say. God is real. Do you agree?"

She nodded firmly. "Yes. I believe that."

"Good! Then you must ask yourself what kind of God He must be. If you don't know, you should ask Him. He will tell you when the time is right. I promise."

She thought about it. The pain in her hip, leg, and ribs seemed to ease. Her head still pounded, but it felt distant. Finally, she asked, "If God wanted to tell us, wouldn't He give us detailed information? Wouldn't He let us know about Him? I mean, couldn't He leave a pile of scrolls or something?"

He snorted out of his nose with mirth. "Oh, dear girl, He will, one day. Sixty-six of them. A long time from now."

"How could you possibly know that?"

"Well, I'm apparently mad. Maybe I made it up."

She eyed him again. "Why are you telling me all this? Once they take us away on this river, they'll do things neither one of us will like. None of this will be important, then."

"Have faith, dear girl. Believe in what you cannot see. Believe that God is real. Believe His way is the right way and follow Him. It will be enough, and you will be ready when God comes."

"He's coming?"

"Well, not right now."

"That's a relief."

"Well, I suppose to many it would be." He cocked his head and smiled deeper. "Have faith, dear girl. Talk to God and have faith in Him. Use that faith to build a strong, deep root in Him. Upon that strong foundation, you will stand tall and smile wide."

She closed her eyes. Talk to God? She hadn't done that since her family stopped going to temple when she'd only been a small child. On shore, she heard Himmons bark, "Last one. I'll call in the sentries."

A man out of sight asked, "What about the rear guard?"

Himmons said, "I'll verify with the Commander, but they should be 'ere soon."

She needed a strong root right now, something to hold her up in the wind. Because a storm was coming, a bad storm that would tear at her very being. Men were coming, with white spiders painted on their shields. They would not be gentle.

"What you need, dear girl, is something solid, something to cling to."

"I'll say. I was just thinking that. I'd take a bow and a quiver of those arrows. A knife wouldn't be amiss."

"No, no, dear one. Use your foot, there, and pull a stone out of the bilge."

"Why?"

"To cling to, of course."

"I need a rock to cling to?"

"Of course. And God provides."

Maybe she could hide the stone behind her knee. She could grab it with her hands, even bound as they were, and bash someone. A rock was better than nothing.

She felt with her foot. Immediately she felt a sizable stone under the deck which slid easily up the cold, damp planks.

"There, you have it."

She rolled her eyes. "Great."

The dragonfly man grew serious. "Cling to your rock, Olaine. God is your rock. He is there for you. He loves you and has a plan for you."

"Does His plan include what's going to happen tonight?"

"If you follow Him, He can use anything and anyone, no matter how evil, for His plan."

"Anything?"

"Anything. You need only believe. Talk to Him. You'll see."

She had nothing to lose and everything to gain. She silently prayed. "God Almighty. It's me, Olaine. But I suppose You knew that. It's been a really long time. I'm sorry. I'm in big trouble here. Bad things are going to happen. I'll need You to help me through it, to help me survive. I can't stop it. I don't suppose anyone can. Probably not even You can stop it."

Well, that didn't seem right. "Sorry. I guess You could. But I can't imagine why You would. Please, if You want to, save Kenan. Help him get away. Then, if You wouldn't mind, give me peace through what I'm to suffer. I don't know Your plan. But I have no plan, no way to escape what's coming, so I guess I'll just adopt Yours. Is that okay?" She smiled and tasted her own tears. "I guess that's it. If You want me to do something, or not do something, just tell me, okay? I'll do my best. For You."

She opened her eyes. The morning grew brighter, and she squinted for a moment.

The Dragonfly Man beamed at her. "Well? Did it help?"

"No. I don't..." But she did. She thought about it. She did feel better. Her problems hadn't disappeared, but God was with her. She somehow knew it.

"Yes. See?" The dragonfly man smiled broadly.

"Yes. But we're still going to Midreer."

"Well, I am. But you, dear girl, don't have to."

"Is God going to whisk me up out of this boat?"

The dragonfly man laughed. "I don't think so. But there's time yet for hope. Get that rock behind you and into your hands. Cling to the rock, Olaine. Cling to it."

# Chapter Forty-Eight
# Nephilim at War

MORE of the White Spider sentries came out of the forest. Kenan watched them come. He saw the sweat dripping down their temples, even from a hundred feet away.

He breathed in deeply, smelling the forest and the water. He could smell himself. He needed a bath. He could smell the men. They needed baths, too. He could smell Olaine and her fear. He could smell the blood from his wounds and raw wrists. He could smell rain coming. He breathed it in. Life surrounded him.

He heard a fat, black squirrel scamper past, rustling the duff. He watched it and realized he could smell it, too, musky and wild. It was pregnant and would have a big litter of little squirrels soon. It sat back on hind legs, standing over a foot tall. It sniffed, working its damp little nose. It scampered off, away from the men. He heard it, even as it disappeared into the forest.

Kenan still hurt, but he didn't mind it. He flexed his shoulders and the cords binding his wrists snapped clean. He smiled and picked the remnants away from his wounds.

He stood up, flexing his body and stretching cramped muscles. The white vapors rising from him like mist didn't obscure his vision. He saw clearly. He saw everything clearly now.

There, Gharan stood pointing to a group of sentries moving towards the boat. Over there, Nehamane picked up a spear. On the far side of the area, Rillain leaned against a massive tree root, arms crossed, chewing on a sprig of something as he watched the men. He looked bored. He was bored.

Kenan *knew* it.

Himmons approached him, looking down and stepping over a branch. He clutched a hand knife in one hand, his other swinging freely. He was coming to get him, to bring him to the boat.

Nope.

Himmons looked up, made eye contact, and stopped cold mid stride. His jaw fell open.

Kenan grinned at him.

Himmons grunted and charged forward. He fumbled to reach Wisdom but couldn't find the hilt. He charged instead with just the hand knife. Bravery and foolishness equal death. Kenan met the attack. The knife angled in with dangerous quickness. Himmons knew what he was about. But to Kenan, everything moved so slowly. He *knew* where the knife was and where it would go. He didn't have to see it. He *knew* it.

Kenan casually stepped to the side, the knife missing his chest by less than a finger span. He reached up and took Himmons by the throat in one hand. He squeezed, just a little. The man's throat crunched and crumpled under his fingers. The man's spine cracked, vertebrae dislocating. The body spasmed once and hung still on Kenan's outstretched arm. It felt light, like a child's doll.

"There! Hey!" A soldier pointed at him, and many heads turned to him. He dropped Himmon's lifeless body to the ground where it thudded solidly into the duff.

Half a dozen men drew swords and charged him. He smiled at them.

The first man to reach him held shield and sword. The blade swung down at him. Kenan deflected it by reaching forward, laying his hand on the other man's hilt, and guiding the blade to the side. With his other hand, Kenan punched the man in the face. Blood sprayed everywhere, the face collapsed inward, and the head fell backwards impossibly far. The soldier's neck broke, and the body fell backwards.

Another man threw a knife as he ran. Kenan was watching a closer man, but he *knew* the knife was coming. Without looking, he snatched the knife from the air by pinching the blade between forefinger and thumb, returning it to its owner with a flick of his wrist. The blade caught the man in the throat. He gurgled and clutched at the knife handle as blood filled his mouth and ran down into his beard.

The next man lunged at him with a sword. Kenan turned sideways and with an open palm, pushed on the man's shield. The man spent his momentum as Kenan slid back through the duff in a sideways saddle stance. The man lost his balance, spinning around his own shield. Kenan snatched his wrist, turned it, and heard joints pop. He took the sword and removed the man's head with a flick of the blade. The bronze bent, but it remained serviceable.

The next two came at once, both lunging swords first. Kenan parried both away with his sword and, with a reverse sweep, took off one man's arm. The man spun, clutching at the end where blood sprayed out onto the ground. He screamed his horror. Kenan angled forward with two steps, putting the wounded man between him and the other man. He *knew*. He somehow knew what was going to happen.

The other man shoved the one-armed man aside to attack Kenan but got sprayed in the face with hot blood. Kenan side stepped, extending his arm and putting the sword through the man's head. The man stiffened and fell on the wounded man, taking them both to the ground. Kenan let the sword go with him.

Another man roared as he charged, wielding an axe in both hands. Kenan stood his ground. The man swung the axe, but Kenan bent back at the waist. The blade whistled past. Kenan straightened, reached out, and snatched a couple of the man's fingers, breaking them instantly. The man screamed. The axe flew into the forest. The man wrenched his hand away, and Kenan let it go.

As the man's shoulders rotated, Kenan snatched up the man's uninjured hand, pinched the thumb, and twisted it ever so carefully. The man spun about. Kenan angled the thumb with a new twist, and the man dropped to one knee and rotated. An arrow ripped in. Kenan subtly rotated the thumb again, and the man twisted again in time to take the arrow in his back. He groaned, and Kenan let him fall away.

Char threw a spear. It arced in towards Kenan, on target for his heart. But it flew so incredibly slowly. Kenan twisted at the waist and snatched the weapon out of the air. He let the momentum of the spear spin him all the way around.

An arrow ripped at him. He didn't see it, but he heard it and *knew* where it was. He slapped it aside with an open palm. He hurled the spear at the archer. Now the spear ripped through the air with blinding speed. The spear went through the man's heart and most of the way through. The man fell backwards and pinned himself to the forest floor. He clutched at the haft for a moment before dying.

A deep, booming voice bellowed. "Hold!"

Most of the men stopped where they were. But one man, without the white spider, kept coming. Kenan *knew* where the blade would be before the man even swung it. Kenan spun on one leg and the blade passed by in the air. Kenan's spinning hook kick landed on the man's cheekbone. It crunched under his bare heel. The man spun and fell, his sword flying from his hand. Kenan snatched the bronze shortsword out of the air.

Gharan bellowed again. "Hold, you fools! Hold where you are!"

Kenan gave Gharan a little salute and strolled towards the soldiers who parted before him.

Gharan looked at him. "It cannot be." He still had both eyes. Kenan knew he'd crushed one, but somehow the Nephilim was healing himself. His right eye still looked red and swollen, but it was there, glaring at him.

"Sure, it can." Kenan smiled.

"No."

"Yes. I don't know how, but I *know* it."

"It's true then."

Char edged to one side. Rillain was nowhere to be seen. Gharan stood solidly in the middle of the soldiers, his helm in one hand and his other resting on his sword hilt. "I would have known. I should have known."

"We can't know everything, monster."

"But how?"

"How what?"

"You! A Nephilim!"

"Me? I'm no brother of yours."

Gharan nodded. "No, you're not. But you are Nephilim."

"I guess so. Your Most High must not be as singular as you thought."

Gharan tapped his helm against his leg, clinking the metal against his armor. "All of you, circle up. Don't attack him. I will handle this." The men all shuffled into a large circle, weapons and shields ready but making no move towards Kenan.

Gharan put his helm over his head and drew his sword, it's length long and shiny steel. With a puff of orange vapor, Gharan's eyes glowed orange. The Nephilim smiled with anticipation.

Kenan pointed at Gharan with his short bronze sword. The weapon was so old part of its length had turned green. The edge, at least, looked sharp. Kenan twirled it. He *knew* its balance, but it felt good to twirl the blade around in his hand.

Gharan circled his own blade once. The tip whistled as it cut the air. He lunged forward.

Kenan saw it but didn't *know* it. He parried and angled back.

Gharan smiled. "What's the matter, Woodbender?"

Kenan said, "Nothing. Still getting used to this." White vapor still rose from him.

"If you live long enough, you will. It takes decades to get into true form, to truly understand the depth of your powers. Too bad you only have a few minutes."

Kenan smiled back at him. "How's the eye?"

Gharan grimaced and attacked with a flurry of lunges and swipes. The longsword tip slashed in and out. Kenan could only parry each blow, angling back. He *knew* where the circle of men was and angled to avoid them without looking. But he kept his eyes on Gharan. The longsword stabbed forward again and again. Finally, Gharan scored a slash on the top of

Kenan's shoulder.

Kenan leapt back, too far. A shield smashed into his back. He *knew* the blow was coming but could do nothing about it. Men jeered and laughed at him. He was hurled forward, towards Gharan and the steel blade. The tip slashed in towards Kenan's throat. He desperately parried with his own sword.

Kenan suddenly threw himself, not to the side, not back again, but forward. Gharan's eyes widened, the orange glow bright, a moment before Kenan body-slammed him from knee to collarbone. It hurt. Gharan wore full steel plate. Kenan wore just his undershirt.

The attack didn't knock Gharan off his feet but did force him to step back. Kenan followed, inside the reach of the longsword, and stabbed downward. The blade skittered off metal. He angled a reverse cut up. Again, the blade scratched at armor. He angled the cut diagonally up and finally found cloth under Gharan's arm. He slashed it, and Gharan grunted.

Gharan hooked a punch at Kenan's head. Kenan didn't see it but could tell it was coming by the way Gharan set his back leg. Kenan ducked it, now outside his stance. Kenan stabbed in at Gharan's ribs. The armor there had a gap in the metal between front and back plates and he aimed for it. Gharan desperately swatted down with an open palm, deflecting the blade and earning a cut on his hand through the leather glove of his gauntlet.

Kenan had a foot hooked around Gharan's ankle, and now he used it. With a little tug, Gharan's foot slid in the duff. It should have caused him to fall, but Gharan threw himself back, rolled, and came back up to his feet. He still held his longsword in one hand. He squeezed the other and blood ran down his forearm bracer. Gharan looked at the blood. The orange vapor intensified.

The White Spiders fell silent, watching and waiting.

Kenan checked his sword, which was now notched, slightly bent, and the edge dulled. He *knew* where each of the soldiers were, what they held, and what they wanted to do. But he didn't *know* what Gharan was going to do. The Nephilim was a blind spot in these new senses.

Someone entered the ring behind Kenan. He didn't *know* it, but he heard it. Kenan feinted a lunge towards Gharan and reversed it into a spin to attack the man behind him. Rillain had his own thin, steel sword out and lunging for Kenan, so Kenan changed the slash into a parry. Rillain wore a steel breastplate and skirt, but his head and arms remained unarmored. His eyes shone orange and red.

He thought Gharan's sword moved quick, but he'd been wrong. Rillain whipped his nimble sword at Kenan in a fury of pokes and lunges, the tip darting in and around so fast it couldn't be seen. The blade warped and bent as Rillain worked it like a green reed. Kenan parried but, instead of retreating, he stepped into the attack. Gharan was right behind him so he couldn't give ground. Rillain shuffle-stepped back to keep Kenan at a dangerous range.

Kenan was going to lose this battle. He might win against Gharan or Rillain, but not both. He could not win.

To the side, Char hung his head.

Then Kenan sensed someone else nearby. Someone he knew. Someone he'd loved for decades.

Suddenly, one of the White Spiders gurgled and fell forward, an arrow through his neck. Then another. Then another. Arrows ripped in from the underbrush nearby, felling man after man. Kenan *knew* it but couldn't look. Rillain moved like a viper. It took all his concentration to keep the blade tip at bay.

Behind him, an arrow clanged off Gharan's throat guard. He bellowed, "Shield wall! Shield wall! Archers in the forest!"

The White Spiders leapt into action.

With Gharan occupied, Kenan could give ground to Rillain's flicking blade. The man's neat beard pointed forward as Rillain tipped his head back and watched through slitted eyes. Kenan struggled to avoid the flashing steel. He parried, again and again. The edge of his bronze sword earned more notches against the steel. He gave ground as White Spiders dashed past to deal with the new threat.

Men fell with arrows in their throats. Some raised their shields and fell to arrows in their stomachs or thighs. A shield wall formed, offering some protection. Kenan *knew* all of it. But he didn't *know* what Rillain's blade would do. He relied on his training, watching Rillain's arms, legs, and posture. He kept his eyes on Rillain's belt buckle, using his eyes to see the whole man, and parried for all he was worth.

Two other people approached from the side. He *knew* it was a man and a woman. He *knew* who they were, and he smiled. Truly, he was never alone. Almighty God is good!

A large man in steel charged the side of the of the shield wall. He carried a heavy shield painted with an Edeerian tree on one arm and a big axe in his free hand. A woman followed behind, a sword in one hand and Wisdom in the other. Her long ponytail trailed behind her as she ran.

He heard Jenn call his name, and *knew* she hurled the blade towards him. The shiny sword turned end over end across the battleground, arcing high into the air. It whooshed with each rotation, singing to him.

Rillain scored a shallow slash across Kenan's chest. Kenan threw the bronze sword at him and spun away, catching Wisdom by the hilt. His spin ended with a deep back stance, with Wisdom held level at his shoulder in both hands.

Rillain grimaced as his eyes flashed orange and red. "No matter, boy. It won't help you."

Kenan smiled back. "God Almighty is on my side. You lose."

Rillain slid forward, narrow sword flicking and slashing. Kenan spun Wisdom in his hands and became a whirlwind of cutting death.

Behind Kenan, Wren smashed into the shield wall. As men turned to face him, arrows passed through their ear holes or necks. Wren roared his rage at the men and flourished with his axe. He cut one man's leg off at the knee. He slammed his shield against another, knocking the man senseless. Another darted in with a sword, but Wren stepped around it and cleaved the man's head from his shoulders.

Arrows ripped in, one after another. It seemed a whole squad of archers attacked, but Kenan *knew* there was only one. He smiled as he parried and cut at Rillain. Wisdom whistled in the air. Now Rillain gave ground, eyes wide and flashing red. Wisdom cut at Rillain and Kenan slashed him across the thigh and again on an arm.

Gharan bellowed as an arrow hit his helm. He called out to his men. "Fall back! Fall back!"

The shield wall moved back. Some men turned to run only to find Jenn ready for them. She cut one down, then had two swords. She cut another one down, parrying and stabbing at the same time.

The shield wall broke. Men turned and ran for the boat. Some fell to arrows in their backs. Wren cut others down with his axe. Jenn danced this way and that, parrying attacks and cutting men down at the knees. She laughed as she fought. She killed her fifth, then her sixth White Spider.

Gharan's sword cleaved her pretty face from behind, from the crown of her head down to her throat. One eye blinked before she fell.

Kenan *knew* this but pressed against Rillain. He had to end this before he could help his friends, or they'd all die on Nephilim blades. Mourning would come later.

Wren roared and charged Gharan. Arrow after arrow hit Gharan. He didn't try to avoid them, but he moved so each arrow hit hard, steel armor. He did it without looking. He did it casually as he watched Wren charge him.

At the last moment, Gharan stepped to the side and swung his sword in low. Wren should have lost a limb. Instead, Wren leapt over the blade, rolled and came up in a crouch, shield ready and axe poised. Gharan moved in, the blade in both hands, the steel flashing as he worked it. Wren gave ground, angling and twisting, deflecting the blows with his shield.

More arrows slammed into Gharan, Kenan *knew*. Gharan slashed at Wren while twisting about. Every arrow clattered off his armor. Not one found an opening.

Rillain parried another slash from Wisdom then feinted low. Kenan stepped over it and slashed again. Rillain ducked under the attack and flicked up with the blade. Kenan stepped back to avoid it and Rillain pressed the attack again. The tip flicked in from all directions, the thin steel blade flexing as it moved. Kenan parried, now on the defense. Rillain drew a long, narrow dirk from his belt with his free hand, poised for use if Kenan gave him an opening. He had no such intention and continued to give ground to Rillain's sword.

Even as he fought, Kenan *knew* what was happening in the battle around him. Gharan attacked Wren with slash after slash. The shield broke under the onslaught, losing pieces. A plank cracked and the shield became unbalanced, exposing Wren.

Gharan arched back, sword high for one final strike.

Wren exploded from his crouch, the remains of his shield scattering across the battlefield, his axe arcing up at Gharan's exposed arms.

Gharan changed his death blow into a parry, slapping the big axe to the side. Wren never hesitated, whirling the blade in two hands and attacking with another uppercut to an arm. Gharan spun away, but Wren didn't let him go. He followed, the bronze axe whirling after the Nephilim.

At the boat, the remaining soldiers clambered over the wale. Char stood on the fore deck, untying the line holding the boat. He screamed, "My Prince! To the boat! To the boat!"

An arrow ripped in and took Char in the neck. It went clean through to splash into the water mid-river. Char sat down hard, holding his neck in one hand. The rope played out around the bow post and the boat started to drift.

Gharan gave ground to Wren's furious attack. His eyes flashed orange but he didn't look concerned. After another attack of the axe, he calmly stepped to the side and put his sword tip through Wren's shoulder, up under one of the overlapping plates.

Wren grunted.

Gharan twisted the blade and Wren fell to one knee, roaring in pain. Gharan pulled his sword out and flicked it downward, cutting Wren across the top of the knee where it was exposed. Wren gasped and twisted away, rolling, and coming to his other knee. He held his axe ready in one hand.

"You did well, Edeerian. We'll meet again, perhaps."

"In your nightmares, Nephilim."

Gharan spun and sprinted for the boat.

More arrows rained down on him, but each one hit armor and bounced away.

Kenan twisted away from another flick of Rillain's blade and parried the next with Wisdom. He tried to discern a pattern in the attack, but there was none. Rillain constantly attacked, changing his targets and technique from one heartbeat to the next. Kenan gave more ground.

The dirk flashed in, scoring Kenan across the back of his hand. His hand involuntarily spasmed and Wisdom fell to the ground. Rillain put the tip of his sword to Kenan's neck.

"A good fight," Rillain said. "But I need to be on that boat. Goodbye, Nephilim." He sneered the title.

An arrow ripped in from behind Kenan. He *knew* it would miss him, just as he *knew* it would hit Rillain in the face.

Rillain *knew* it, too. He bent to the side to let the arrow pass.

Kenan used his cut hand to push Rillain's sword away. At the same time, he reached up with his good hand, catching the arrow around the fletching. Rillain's eyes opened wide as Kenan pushed the bronze arrowhead into the man's throat.

Rillain dropped both sword and dirk to grasp the arrow shaft. His mouth opened wide. He wheezed as he gasped. Kenan could hear liquid running, like a pipe draining to a cistern during a rainstorm.

Kenan spun and kicked Rillain in the chest. The man stumbled backwards and fell. When he hit the duff, leaves roiled up at the impact. In a blink, Rillain vanished. Kenan stared at the patch of disturbed leaves. Rillain was gone. The arrow and a piece of a bush had gone with him.

Kenan heard a splash over at the boat. Men yelled as orders were given. Men pushed the boat away from shore with oars. Others held up shields. The boat moved out into the river.

Gharan raced to the water's edge and leapt at the last moment. He almost flew over the water, clearing more than thirty feet to land and skid across on the fore deck on booted feet.

Arrows arced down into the boat, but most only found shields or deck. The current took the boat, and it floated downstream.

Kenan gave Rillain's patch of ground one more look before turning away towards the shore.

Lidai slipped out of the underbrush, sprinting past both Wren and Kenan. She reached the shore and launched arrow after arrow into the boat.

Kenan ran over to join her, watching as the boat moved downstream. Rowers extended oars into the water. Men stood with shields to catch the arrows. Gharan stood tall on the fore deck, one hand on his sheathed sword hilt. He used the other hand to slap arrows away.

Wren limped over as Lidai worked her bow. He looked downstream. "How does he do that?"

"He knows," Kenan said. "He *knows* where they are, where they will be."

"How does he know?"

"He's Nephilim."

Kenan relaxed, and silently prayed, "Thank you, God Almighty, for your grace and protection." He didn't know where he got the words, but they seemed right. The vapor rising from his upper body faded out and drifted away. His eyes returned to their normal hazel.

He gasped and doubled over. His pains rushed back and hit him hard. His wrists screamed fire and his cuts felt sharp and stabbing. Bruises ached and his head exploded in throbbing pain. He felt every hair follicle where he'd been hit in the head with the back of Himmon's axe. Finally, he caught his breath and eased himself vertical. His friends had eyes for the boat and didn't seem to notice him.

The boat pulled further away, turning to put the bow downriver. Lidai finally stopped loosing arrows. "I could keep doing it. They're not too far. But these are all I have left." She fingered the few arrows remaining in her quiver.

They watched the boat round a bend and disappear.

# Chapter Forty-Nine
## Enough Have Died Today

LIDAI turned to Wren. Blood dripped down his face, his arm, and his shin. She needed to make sure he was safe. "You look terrible."

Wren nodded. "Thanks."

"Come on, let me patch you up."

"Okay."

They turned to leave, but Kenan didn't follow. She watched as he stepped right to the water's edge. He moved stiff and careful. His eyes squinted. Well, it made sense he had pains after being taken. She saw red matting his hair and blood staining his undershirt. He must have been beaten, perhaps multiple times. Still, he moved okay. She'd check him soon. Where was he going?

Kenan put a bare foot in the water and slapped the surface with it. "They're gone. You can come out now."

Olaine burst up out of the water. Lidai's heart lurched in surprise, and she watched as the woman shook her head free of river water. Her hair, dark from the water, slapped around her face. Olaine's hands were bound behind her back, and she held something. Was that a rock?

Olaine found Kenan with her eyes. She smiled broadly at him.

Kenan waded in and collected Olaine into his arms. "You escaped."

"Part of the Almighty's plan, I guess." She wouldn't let go of the rock as Kenan cut her ties and carried her up onto shore. He lifted her as if she weighed nothing. She wrapped one arm around his shoulder, looking up at him and smiling. Lidai tapped her foot. She had to get to know Olaine better, and quick.

Kenan set her down to lay on a tree root, careful of her injuries.

Olaine smiled at Kenan some more but started shivering, her chin trembling with the chill. Kenan said, "Stay here. I'll get you something. And I'll get a fire going. I'm sure someone here had a striker. I'll find it."

Olaine pointed. "My overshift is over there. You know where it is."

Lidai stalked up, towing a limping Wren. She said to her brother, "Find a helm, too. I need one that'll hold water. We need to boil some for bandages. Wren has injuries, too."

Kenan shared a look with Olaine, and they both laughed. He asked her, "Where's the Dragonfly Man?"

Lidai had no idea what he was talking about.

Wren asked, "Who?" as Lidai unbuckled a thigh guard from his leg.

Olaine, struggling to hold the rock tucked in one arm, answered Kenan's question. "He's on that boat. He said he wanted to go."

Kenan opened his mouth, then closed it.

Lidai had enough. "Would you two stop it? Seriously. Wounded man over here! Kenan, I need hot water, and plenty of it. Olaine, drop that rock. It'll pull away your remaining body heat."

Kenan left and limped off through the trees. Olaine clutched the rock closer.

Lidai finished with Wren's steel kilt before dropping to a knee to work on the shin guards. "I know you're cold, Olaine, but I could use some help over here."

"I'm sorry, Lidai. Of course." The woman finally put down her rock and rolled off the root. She dragged herself toward them.

Lidai stared. "What are you doing?"

"Crawling? I fell out of a tree."

"What? Right. Stay put! I'll be right there."

Wren started laughing, the big dragonscrape. "I think they have battle shock or something."

Lidai snorted. "They have something, alright."

Kenan limped back to Olaine. Was he limping less? He'd taken a soldier's overshirt and brought it to her. Kenan's sword hung in a sheath on his back. "Here, take that off, Olaine. No, stay on the duff. It's warmer. Here's your overshift. Lay on that. Put on this overshirt. Then wrap up in your dress like a blanket."

He held the dress up, creating a privacy screen for Olaine. The garment had been slashed into one big sheet.

Lidai remembered the scene at Babelwind Brook and shivered. At least the woman had a good reason to be half naked. Kenan turned his head away as Olaine struggled out of her wet shift behind the dress. Good man. Her brother wasn't all bad.

Lidai freed another piece of steel plate off Wren. "See. Watch Kenan. That's how it's done."

Wren laughed again, drat the man.

Kenan turned to Wren. "Jenn. How'd she end up with my sword?"

Wren quirked a grin. "Found it as we approached. Some dead dragonstool had it on his back. We figured you'd want it."

"Thank you, Wren. And thanks to Jenn, may she rest peacefully. I think I might not have made it, except for Wisdom."

Lidai raised her eyebrow as she continued to remove armor. "Glad you finally used some, brother."

Kenan laughed. She loved her brother's laugh. She'd missed it. He tailed off, however, as he gazed at Jenn's body.

Lidai finished freeing Wren's legs and scooted around to check his knee. The wound bled, but not bad. The cut ran deep, but not all the way to any tendons. Blood dripped on her head from his elbow. She looked up. "Kneel down, Wren. I need to see your shoulder."

"I can't kneel, Lidai."

Right. "Then sit, you big oaf. Here, I'll help you." Wren eased down to the ground. She pulled at the shoulder plates but couldn't see anything. She set to work removing the rest of his armor.

Olaine took her dress and wrapped herself in it. She still shivered.

Kenan turned to Lidai. "Is he going to be alright?"

Wren said, "I'm right here, you know."

"Okay. Are you going to be alright?"

"Yeah. I've had worse."

"I remember. Sorry about your eye. Even wrapped, it looks nasty. There's something seeping through, you know."

"Really? Gross. Doesn't exactly feel great, either."

"I bet." Kenan walked off, no longer limping. Lidai wondered how that was possible. He pulled a cloak off a nearby body and used it to cover Jenn's. Was he praying over her? It sure looked like it.

Soon, she saw him collecting up some branches. Good. She needed that boiling water.

Lidai called to him, "See if any of those dragonspitters have medical supplies. I need some antiseptic and glue. Needle and thread would be good, too."

As Kenan rummaged, one of the men lying near the shield wall pushed himself up to sit. The man held his head and swayed a moment. Lidai saw it and pulled a knife. Kenan glanced over at the man casually.

The White Spider soldier looked around at all the bodies, most sprouting arrows. He jumped to his feet and sprinted away. Kenan shrugged and turned back to rummaging. Lidai pulled her arm back to throw. It was a long throw, but worth a try. None of these dragonspitters deserved to live.

At the last moment, a big hand grabbed her wrist in an iron grip. "Stop. Let him go, Lidai," Wren said. "Enough have died today."

She nodded to her betrothed. My, that wound did make him look more threatening. Butterflies flew in her belly *and* her throat went dry. She sheathed the knife. She needed a better way to defend herself against his new appearance. If she couldn't figure it out, she'd be with child long before a wedding.

In short order, Kenan had a fire going. He carried Olaine to the flames, and she sat on her rock, wrapped in her dress and holding her bare arms out to the heat. Steam rose from her wet hair, reminding Lidai of Kenan's white vapor. Lidai shivered and eyed her brother. Kenan moved about collecting the White Spider shields. Mostly constructed of painted wood, they burned just fine.

Wren's shoulder wound looked far worse than his knee. "You'll have trouble with this. I'm going to have to clean it out. I'm sorry. I have to hurt you." She found a piece of wood in the duff, broke it to size, and gave it to him.

Wren winked at her. Or did he just blink? This was going to be a problem. "You're sweet, Lidai. And you only show your true self to me. Take care of me, my sweetness revealed."

Yes. Sweetness revealed. That would work just fine. She smiled at him and kissed him on his forehead. She grimaced. Uck. Sweat and blood. "Put that stick in your mouth."

Wren asked, "Did you see him?"

"Who him?"

"Kenan, of course. Did you see him?"

She paused. She knew what he was asking. She didn't want to think about it. "Yeah, I saw him."

"He's one of them."

"Yes."

"A Nephilim."

"That's what it looked like. Now be quiet and bite down." She pushed on the wound, and it bled more. She didn't like what she saw. Somehow dirt had gotten in there.

Wren mumbled around the stick. "Ow, Lidai, that hurts."

"Told you."

He spit the stick out onto the ground. "His eyes glowed white. White vapors and stuff came off him. I don't understand how, but he's one of them."

"No, he's not."

"You just said..."

"Just because he's Nephilim doesn't mean he's one of them. He's still Kenan. Look at him. He's broody and dangerous and besotted with that girl."

"She's older than you, Lidai."

"So? Can we talk about something else?"

He shrugged, wincing at the movement. "What do you want to talk about?"

"What kind of eye patch do you want?"

"Almighty. I hadn't given it a thought."

Kenan handed her not one but three glue packs he'd found on the soldiers, and some balm she thought might be good on wounds. He also gave her a couple of plant stems she knew were antiseptic.

"That was fast. How'd you find them?"

Kenan shrugged. "I could, uh, I smelled them."

"Smelled them?" Lidai sniffed at the plant pieces. "I can barely..."

Kenan rolled a sore arm. It turned out he had some cuts that needed stitching too, though his wrists and bruises didn't look too bad. Lidai spent most of the morning boiling bandages and gluing wounds.

Later, they found Rillain's sword and dirk, but no body. Kenan told them how the Nephilim had disappeared, as in, just vanished into thin air. Nephilim were creepy, Lidai thought, eyeing her brother. No two ways about it.

That afternoon, Kenan set out for one of the boats that were captured or, preferably, the canoes at rally point two, if they were there. He left instructions. "If Rillain comes back, flee. Swim the river if you must. Both of you." Lidai agreed for his sake, but if that rogue came back, she'd put an arrow through him. Or five.

While Kenan was gone, Lidai collected up a bunch of arrows, frowning if a shaft was a touch off center. Many were damaged, but she managed to fill a quiver with plenty of good arrows. She also gathered a bunch of spears, swords, and other weapons. They camped in the middle of a feast for any carnivorous or scavenging dragon who happened by. She needed to be ready. She built the fire higher, as well. Some dragons and most mammals didn't like fire. She did the best she could to prepare.

"I wish I could help more." Olaine sat wrapped in her dress and a blanket found in some discarded gear by the river. "I feel useless."

Lidai stirred yet more rags into the water boiling in the bronze helm. "You're not useless. You drove off that hissdragon, right?"

"Yeah, until I fell out of a tree."

"It happens, especially if you have an arrow in you. Here. Let me see that wound again." Olaine let Lidai inspect it. She poked and prodded around the wound. "You can still breathe okay?"

"Yes, except for the broken ribs."

"Uh huh. Have you coughed up any blood?"

"No. It's my head and hip that hurt."

Lidai checked her all over, keeping an eye on Wren, who politely turned around. "You're not bleeding anywhere outside. I think if you had a major bleed inside, you'd be gone already. Your biggest problems are that hip and infection."

"Thank you, Lidai."

"Sure. Now, what's the deal with that rock?"

Olaine laughed. "A symbol, I'd say. I pulled it out of the bilge. The Dragonfly Man told me to 'cling to the rock'. I think he meant the Almighty, but the stone held me underwater while the boat pulled away."

"How long were you under?"

"Not too long. Men rushed onto the boat at the end, but no one was watching me. I just stood up on my good leg and the weight of the rock helped pull me backwards over the wale. All I had to do was hold my breath for a couple minutes and cling to the rock."

"That was quick thinking."

"Thanks, but I think it was the Dragonfly Man's idea."

Lidai added more rags to the helm. "Who, exactly, is this Dragonfly Man?"

"I'm not really sure. You're going to have to ask Kenan. He seemed to know him."

Lidai raised her eyebrow at her, but didn't press her further about the rock or the Dragonfly Man. She'd press about Olaine's intentions with her brother later.

Wren, the big, handsome, frightening, loving, lunk of a man snored his way through a long nap.

Near dusk, Kenan returned by river with two canoes, saying the enemy boats had been taken. After discussing it, they all decided to wait the night. No one had the energy to paddle back upstream. Everyone would need sleep to recover for the return trip to Fallingwater.

Before the next day dawned, Eleenan and Trime arrived with a platoon of soldiers by riverboat.

# Chapter Fifty

# Alive

KENAN stretched out in a hammock along a balcony rail in Fallingwater. The air was chilly with approaching winter, but he didn't mind. He stared up at the dark leaves and sunlight streaking between them. Insects buzzed, butterflies fluttered, birds sang, and a squirrel squeaked at him. He smiled at them all.

Olaine lay in another hammock, on a balcony not far away. She had hobbled to it on a crutch, refusing help. Now she lay propped up with cushions, reading a scroll. She wore a little pair of spectacles to read. Spectacles! Strange for one so young and an archer as well. They looked good on her. He smiled at her. She somehow knew and looked up. She smiled back at him. Dazzling.

He laid his head back and looked up at the sky again. He relaxed on the third level. He could see quite a bit of the sky, here. A giant raven, so big Kenan could probably ride it, flapped past. It croaked noisily. He smiled as the squirrel darted into covering vegetation, squeaking in panic.

His wounds ached less and itched more. It'd been only two days since their return, yet his wounds were mostly healed already. Wren still bled. Apparently being a Nephilim helped him in ways more than just strength, speed and senses.

A Nephilim. He was a Nephilim. What did that mean? How did it happen? He didn't understand, but he thanked the Almighty for it. Without it, he'd be approaching the Dragongrass right now on his way to his death. He suspected both he and Olaine would wish they were already dead at this point.

He heard someone approaching, slapping their bare feet against the boardwalk harder than necessary. He listened to her sputtering under her breath, and he could make out every word. He inhaled and smelled the strong odors of medical alcohol and raccoon fur underlain by the light scent of his sister. Lidai stalked up, kicking her dress as she walked and trailing a small thunderstorm.

Kenan grinned up at her. "Got a darterdragon up your dress?"

"Shut up," she said. "It's time for Wren to get his eye socket scraped again. He said he won't do it."

"And you think I can make him?"

"Yes, he'll listen to you."

"Lidai, he won't listen to me. He only listens to you."

She huffed and crossed her arms across her chest. "I thought, well, maybe if..."

Kenan raised an eyebrow to her. "Yes?"

She lowered her voice for just the two of them. "Well, if you went all glowy, you could make him do it."

"Lidai. No. And don't talk about it. No one else knows, and I'd like to keep it that way."

"Why? Kenan, you've been given an amazing gift."

"Because I don't know what's going on. I need to be careful. So, please, shut up about it."

"Fine. What am I supposed to do with Wren?"

"Use your feminine wiles."

"What?"

"You know. Bat your eyelashes. Play with your hair. Touch his arm or something."

She frowned at him. "I don't think it works that way."

"Lidai. That's exactly how it works."

She regarded him for a moment, then sat down on the railing. "I have bad news."

Kenan sat up a little, hammock swaying. "What is it?"

"Master Belroon. He's going to lose the leg."

Kenan frowned. "How much?"

"From mid-thigh. The tourniquet was on too long."

"Oh." He wondered what this would do to the big man. For someone so large, he exuded energy and movement.

"And there will be a service for Jenn in two days. Lamech knows you two were close, like siblings. He asked if you'd say a few words."

Kenan nodded. He didn't like to speak in front of people, but he'd do it. She deserved it and more.

"Kenan, what are we going to do now?"

"Lay here. Rest. I was given strict orders."

"That's not what I meant."

"I know what you meant. I don't know. I never thought past killing White Spiders."

Lidai sighed. "I'm not sure I'm ready to go back to Blacktree. I think I want to go back to Edeer, to the school. I'm thinking about it."

Is that what he wanted to do? Go back to the school? Maybe. He liked his quiet life in Blacktree. He could go back to his trees and woodbend for a living. He glanced at Olaine. What was she going to do? Once healed, would she go back to the Brookstone Brigade? She was a soldier. Would he follow her? The idea of being a camp follower trailing behind an army made him feel sour.

A thought occurred to him. "I'll ask the Almighty. What I am, what I'm becoming, it's all from Him. He'll guide me, I think."

She shrugged at him and smiled at the boardwalk planks.

He thought about Lidai's efforts in all that'd happened. He thought about her standing on that barrel, passionately pulling everyone towards their eventual success. She had her own wisdom, of a sort. So he asked her, "What do you think I should do?"

"Me?"

"No. The darterdragon up your dress."

She frowned at him. "Why would you ask me? I'm not the Almighty."

"No. I'll ask the Almighty. But you always seem to know what to do. You think clearly. I value your words."

She smiled at him. "That's the nicest thing anyone's ever said to me."

"Wren had better step up his game."

She smiled. "Yes. But, Kenan, I'm just a woman. You should ask someone like Lamech."

"You're the best archer in Edeer. You're a battle leader in your own right. I heard you came up with the plan of attack beside the river. No, you're not fooling me. You killed more of them than any of us, maybe all of us put together. You kept your head under pressure, when others lost theirs. You're my sister, and you're you."

Lidai bent forward and kissed him at the top of his forehead. "Thank you, brother. I know what you should do."

"Yes?"

"Yes. Get up, go over there, and talk to that woman. Ask her to marry you."

Kenan jerked and nearly rolled out of his hammock to fall to his death on the Flat far below.

She clutched at him. "Careful, you clod! You'll get yourself killed!"

Kenan recovered himself. "Lidai, why would you say something like that?"

She got up and moved around to face him. She looked at Olaine for a moment, then looked directly into his eyes. "Because life is long, but opportunity is short."

Kenan sat up in his hammock and put his feet on the boardwalk. Marriage? But he was betrothed to... No. He was not betrothed. Anna was dead and gone forever. Olaine was here but might not be for long.

"Lidai, I think you're right."

She nodded in satisfaction. "I absolutely love it when people say that. Now, I guess I'd better get back to the other clod in my life. Really, I just needed a breath of fresh air. I didn't really want you to... you know."

"I know. Thank you, Lidai."

She patted his cheek and walked back the way she'd come with a spring in her step. He heard her say, under her breath, "Right. Feminine wiles."

Kenan rose to his feet, turned, and looked at Olaine. She still read her scroll in her hammock, which rocked gently. He prayed to the Almighty for guidance but didn't hear anything back. Still, he made his decision and felt good about it. He straightened his back, nodded to himself, and set off to talk to her.

HALFWAY to the other balcony, Tadd rose on a lift and looked around. He saw Kenan and dashed towards him. "Kenan! Kenan! I have a message!"

"Spill the nutmash, kid. What's going on?"

"Master Lamech wants to talk to you. It's something about that prisoner."

Kenan looked at Olaine. She was watching over the rim of her spectacles. She smiled and waved.

Tadd waved back, putting his whole body into it. "Wow. She sure is pretty."

"Yep. Sure is."

"You think maybe she needs some help, being wounded and all? You know, just someone to run errands, maybe to talk to?"

Kenan grinned down at the boy, but not as far down as he needed to just a few months ago. "You're growing up, Tadd. Now, take me to Master Lamech."

They found Lamech on the first level. He'd taken a potter's shop as his headquarters. The owner, a man named Shent, wasn't using it. His wife had been taken by the White Spiders but had escaped in the confusion of battle. Shent took care of her and left the idle shop to Lamech.

Lamech stood by a workbench with Eleenan and Abram. Dried clay stuck to the surfaces.

"No. Right here." Eleenan pointed at a scroll opened on the bench and held flat with trowels and other pottery tools. "I think that's it."

Tadd sat on a keg and pulled a knife to peel a violetfruit. Where'd the kid get the treat? He didn't have it when he first met Kenan. Tadd just ended up with stuff. He thought he'd have to have a talk with the boy about respect and filching what didn't belong to him.

Lamech said, "No. That's Achetai. It's a big city. I think it's that one."

Abram nodded. "Better that it's on the north side. Though I'm unsure if it's really that important. Can't we just ask him?"

Eleenan shrugged. "Maybe. I suspect he can't read a map or probably anything else."

Kenan cleared his throat.

The men turned to him. Lamech glowered at him, but he did that with everyone. "Kenan. Glad you're here. There's something you need to hear." Lamech turned and stomped to a door at the back of the shop. Kenan gave Abram and Eleenan a friendly wave as he followed. They returned the greeting, though neither man moved to join them.

They passed through the door, down a short hallway with an Edeerian guard, and through another door into a small storeroom. Inside, Cols sat tied to a chair. He looked haggard. Half of one foot was missing and he had bandages wrapped around his hips. Blood stained one side. The man was sweating profusely. The red paint on his arms and forehead had mostly dripped off, staining the chair and floor. His many scars shone white in the dim light of the storeroom.

Kenan crossed his arms and regarded the man. He wanted to hit him, but he held back.

Lamech grunted. "Want to hit him, don't you." It wasn't a question.

Kenan answered anyway. "Yes. Very much, Master Lamech, but I won't."

"Good. We haven't laid a finger on him, but we've gotten all sorts of information. Haven't we, Cols?"

Cols nodded, rasping, "Please? I've been good."

Lamech shook his head. "Sorry, no. Not yet."

Kenan asked, "What's wrong with him?"

"Nothing. He's just fine and healing from his wounds. You're fine, aren't you, Cols?"

Cols rasped again, "I'm fine."

Lamech grunted. "Cols, tell me again what you said about the prisoners from Blacktree."

"Yes, Master Lamech. Some of the 'aul didn't make it. But most did. Some were sold off across Midreer. By now, they've been sold and resold. I don't know where they are."

Lamech prompted, "And the others?"

"They're 'oled up in Blackstone Keep, property of my prince and his officers."

"And who's your prince?"

"Prince Gharan."

"Now, tell me again about his favorite. The one for his father."

"Oh, Agliranna. Yeah. She's being saved for the Most 'igh. She's to be 'is special concubine. None of us touched 'er. Not even my prince. She's to go to the Most 'igh unspoiled."

Kenan's jaw dropped open. He stared at Cols, shocked at his words. Finally, he growled, "You told me she was dead."

Cols leaked tears out of his beady eyes. "I did. Sorry about that. I won't do it again. Promise."

Lamech stood leaning on a shelf, arms crossed, watching the scene unfold.

Cols glanced at him and rasped out, "Please? Now?"

Lamech shook his head. "No, not yet. Tell him what it takes to prepare her to be a concubine."

"Well, each concubine needs to be broken first. Not in body. In spirit, you know? Then she 'as a year of training. Then a year of preparation, which is mostly pampering, so I 'ear. Last I 'eard, she ain't broke yet. Maybe she 'as been now, I don't know."

Kenan sank to the floor and started to cry.

Cols saw him and started to cry too. "I'm sorry for what I done. Really, I am."

Lamech gently took Kenan by the shoulders and firmly lifted him to his feet. "Come on, lad. Not in front of this idiot. Let's step out."

As they left, Cols cried out, "I'm sorry, I am! Please, I 'ave more! The concubine's sisters! They're alive, too! I know a 'Aley. And Atarra. I don't know the rest, but they're there. Please! Just a drop more!" The man sobbed as the door closed.

In the workroom, Abram and Eleenan were gone. Tadd sat on his keg, making progress on the violetfruit. Kenan sat on a crate of corks and wiped his eyes on his sleeve. "Sorry. Too many emotions."

"I understand, lad. But this is good, isn't it?"

"Yes! I... I'm just struggling to understand."

Lamech grunted. "I bet. Your world is turning over on you again."

"Yes. Do you think it's true? Is she really alive?"

"I think so. Cols could be lying, but I doubt it."

"What did you do to him?"

"Me? Nothing. No one has harmed him. Well, not since the battle. We've tended his wounds."

Kenan thought for a moment. "He was given something."

"Yes. Abram... well, he knows a lot of things. There's this sap from a plant out east. I don't remember its name. Doesn't matter. Between the sap and Eleenan's questioning technique, he broke in less than three days. Pretty impressive."

"Not for Cols."

"No. I meant Eleenan. He talked the man into circles. At this point, Cols will tell us whatever he knows, as long as I do the questioning. He completely shuts down if Eleenan's in the room. I think he's terrified of the lad. As long as we keep giving him doses of the sap, we keep getting information. We have enough sap for another few days."

"After that?"

"The withdrawal symptoms are as short as the addiction time, but most unpleasant, so I hear. He might not survive it."

Kenan grimaced. "Good."

"So, what do you want to do now, lad?"

Kenan didn't even hesitate. "I'm going after Anna. Her sisters, too, and any others I can find."

Lamech nodded. "Done. I'll talk to Trime and Abram. We'll see about who's going, what we'll need, and get us all outfitted. We'll need a boat, too. Those big river flatboats we used the other day won't work. We'll need something faster, something a little more seaworthy. The river gets wide down there."

"Master?"

"What, lad? You didn't think you were going alone, did you? You might be a Nephilim and all but going alone is no kind of plan."

"I completely agree." Kenan stopped. "Wait a minute. You know?"

"I suspected, but now I know."

Kenan eyed him. Lamech eyed him back.

Finally, Kenan asked, "What is it, exactly? A Nephilim. What am I?"

Lamech nodded and frowned at the floor. "I'm the wrong man to ask. My father knows so much more. But here's what I think I know. Nephilim are sons of sons of God. Angels take a human wife. Sometimes the offspring are Nephilim. Didn't know your father was an angel, lad?"

"I didn't know him at all."

"Ah. Well, congratulations, lad. Your father's an angel. Not many of us can say that, you know."

Kenan tried to grin. "Do you have any idea what a Nephilim can do? What their powers are?"

"Some. They're deadly quick and strong in battle. That I know firsthand, and so do you. They glow, but you knew that, too. It's weird, but as far as I can tell, not dangerous. And they carry evil spirits in them, sometimes. They can breathe them out onto people. I think it has to do with the person they're dealing with. Someone has a weakness the Nephilim wants to coax into full-blown sin against the Almighty? Well, they can help them along."

"Yes. It happened to me. I think it happened three times." He ticked them off on his fingers. "Once decades ago at Babelwind Brook, once at the battle of Blacktree, and once again the other night, when I was taken. I think they've been in me, working against me, all this time."

"I wondered about that. Should we go see my father? He might be able to help with it."

"I think the Almighty already did when I first knew I was Nephilim. I felt them go."

"Ah. Good then."

"Master Lamech, can Nephilim disappear?"

"Turn invisible? Not that I know of."

Kenan shook his head. "No. I mean, can they leave one place and go to another, but without walking there? Rillain just vanished. He took some leaves and a piece of bush with him."

"I heard your story. It sounds like you were killing him, and he was taken away by a spirit or something."

"Can that happen?"

Lamech looked out the window, gazing at the sun beams slanting in from the sky. He seemed to be remembering something long past. "Yes. I've heard of it. I don't know if it's a Nephilim thing or an angel thing. Men can be taken away by the Spirit of the Almighty, I know. My grandfather experienced it."

"Right. But I don't think the Almighty took Rillain away to spare him from me. I think it was a fallen angel, or maybe it's a Nephilim thing after all."

"Have you tried?"

"To disappear and reappear? Yeah. I got curious."

"And?"

"Nothing. I tried it as I usually am, and I tried it infused."

"Infused?"

Kenan nodded. "It feels like the right word. I ask the Almighty for his Spirit, and He gives Him to me. I think, because of my angelic lineage, this results in the glowing and an understanding of what's happening around me. I somehow *know*. I don't know how else to explain it."

"Interesting. Try harder to explain. What do you know?"

"When infused, I can count the flaps of a hummingbird's wings. I can smell a mouse under a log at fifty paces. I can hear the hungry rumble of a toedragon's belly. I caught an arrow approaching behind me without looking. I just *knew* where it would be."

"Handy, that."

"I guess. But I... I don't know who I am anymore."

Lamech squinted at him. "You're Kenan Blacktree, black-striped warrior and friend, woodbender and now Nephilim of the Almighty. Though I suppose you wish you had more answers."

"Of course. Don't you?"

Lamech grunted. "Sometimes. There are things we don't understand, things we may never understand. I think that's part of life. When I enter the

Almighty's presence, I'll ask."

Kenan quirked an eyebrow. "Right. Well, I do know one thing."

"What's that?"

"I'm finally going to Midreer. So, when do we leave?"

"Heh. Take it easy, lad. Not for a while yet. We've got wounded that need to heal. Plus, I suspect the boat we'll need isn't here. We may have to travel to get one or, if we must, build one here. Lastly, this won't be some skirmish in the forest. This will be a straight up rescue mission in an urban setting of a foreign nation where Nephilim rule and the Most High reigns. That's a whole new set of skills and planning. You've got time. You'll need it.

"Now, I suspect your big friend will want this news. She's his sister, right? I'd have him here with you, except he's getting that nasty hole in his face scraped out again. He could use some good news."

Kenan stood and bowed to his Master. Reaching, the men clasped forearms. "Thank you."

"Most welcome, lad. Off with you. And Tadd, where'd you get that fruit? Come here, boy."

KENAN found Wren back up on the third level in a small bunkroom that'd been serving as a surgery. He sat on a chest at the foot of a bed, of all things. The foolish contraption had another man lying in it, recovering from an arrow wound. In his arm, Wren held Quick around the middle like a fat, furry doll. The raccoon hung limp, resigned to its fate.

A woman leaned forward and worked a small metal tool inside the gaping hole where his eye should be. Wren bit down hard on a bit in his mouth, and his good eye watered. The rest of his body flinched as she worked, spasming slightly as she twisted the scraper. Quick wheezed with each squeeze. The wound above and below the eye had already been stitched and glued. It puffed up against the stitches, purple and yellow.

Lidai stalked back and forth in the small room. She only had space to take one step, but she used it like a champion.

The woman tugged and pulled a scrap of something gray out of his socket. "There, got it."

Kenan's stomach soured. He didn't want to see this. But neither did he move from the doorway, patiently waiting for the procedure to end.

Wren pulled out the bit. "Thank you."

Lidai scowled at him. "She missed it the first time. You shouldn't be thankful."

Wren said to the woman, "Don't mind her. She's just scared for me."

The woman smiled at him before turning her smile on Lidai. Kenan's sister didn't return it but nodded slightly. The woman said to Wren, "You'll be just fine. Come back in two days. I'll check on it." She turned to Lidai.

"You'll wrap his head?"

Lidai said, "Yes. And... sorry. Thank you."

"That's quite all right, child. This isn't an exact science. We do our best." She smiled politely and stepped past Kenan and out of the room.

Lidai glared at the back of the departing woman's head.

Kenan stepped all the way in and took Quick, who looked like he'd had enough squeezing. The little beast scrambled up his arm and onto one shoulder, balancing with ease. It chittered angrily at Wren.

Wren pointed. "Hey Kenan. Look over there, leaning in the corner. They found it in the enemy encampment."

Kenan turned. Wren's steel axe with the woodbent handle stood there. Kenan picked it up and ran his hand down the wood. "Well, it came home."

"Yeah. I guess Cols kept it. Someone found it in a lean-to."

"Very nice. I assume you're using it as a cane?"

"Yeah. I'm never going anywhere without an axe ever again."

Lidai arched an eyebrow. "Anywhere?"

"If you're there, I need it more than ever."

Lidai rolled her eyes and set to work bandaging Wren's head. His shoulder also had a bandage with a big red splotch on it. It still seeped blood and might need another surgery. The knee didn't have a bandage and had been stitched and glued closed. Sitting on the bed with his leg dangling, the stitches pulled against the skin.

Kenan grimaced. The sight of it all made his own wounds itch.

Wren looked at his friend. "Why are you here? Morbid curiosity?"

"Well, I've never seen an empty eye socket. It's ... fetching."

"I bet." He snorted. "Still, she seems to like it."

Lidai snorted in return.

Kenan shook his head. "That's gross."

Quick climbed down off Kenan's shoulder, landing on the floor with a solid thud. He ran over and rummaged around in a basket in the corner.

Kenan said, "I have news. Important news. Good news."

Lidai paused winding the roll of cloth around Wren's head. Both looked at him.

Kenan continued, "Some, maybe all, of your sisters... they're alive."

Wren stood up. Lidai lost the roll of bandages she was using to wrap Wren's head, and it rolled off the bed and across the floor. The man in the bed watched everyone with wide eyes.

Kenan smiled. "Anna. Haley. Atarra. More. They're alive. And we know exactly where they are."

Both of them smiled grimly and balled their fists. Wren smacked one into a meaty palm.

In the corner, Quick snacked on whatever was left of Wren's eye.

# Epilogue
# Influencing People

THE Most High sat in an opulent chair in his private chambers, reading a tedious scroll and contemplating his problem. The room featured fur carpets and whitewood walls with paintings, tapestries, and sculptures set on brass stands. Redwood beams supported a painted blue ceiling. Golden lampstands and iron braziers on marble pedestals stood to give light and heat in the evenings. The fireplace crackled with flame, but he didn't feel the heat. He just liked the way it sounded.

The scroll contained information about the corps strengths of his armies. Dull reading, but he needed to know. He had too many people in his nation's western reaches. They were pushing east fast, growing, and establishing new cities as they went.

Population growth, he knew, was an exponential curve. After over 1600 years, the curve steepened. He must prepare. New lands meant new conquests. New conquests meant armies. They must be well bred, well trained, well equipped, and highly motivated. He knew all of this and had set it all into motion long ago.

Armies were not the problem he contemplated.

He picked up another scroll. His people didn't rely on the provisions of the forests and plains any longer. They cultivated the land now, growing far more food than ever before. Getting it to the right places before it spoiled was sometimes an issue. Certain spices and salt helped. His people had finally come to enjoy the spice. Still, the report talked of food spoiling before reaching the furthest eastern reaches upriver. They needed more people there to cultivate the land and grow their own food.

He could get them there easily. The river was their road. But he knew expansion to the north and south was imminent. He made a note to talk to his civil planners this morning. One of his chemists had finally learned to make concrete. Real roads were coming to Midreer.

Food and roads weren't his problem either.

He thought of Gharan. This son had ambition and more than most. He'd come back from a raid to the north but had yet to report in, which was normal for the boy. Gharan didn't have to go on these raids. He had men to do such things. But he liked it, and he sometimes came back with the best additions to the palace harem.

The Most High knew Gharan only gifted these slaves to him to gain favor. The Most High had many sons and daughters, and some of them were Nephilim. His Nephilim sons all competed for his favor. The system worked, and the Most High smiled. Gharan had ambitions to one day supplant him. The boy didn't know it wasn't possible for a human, even a Nephilim like him.

Gharan wasn't his problem, either.

His problem was his own father. His father had told them all they would be allowed – within certain unfortunate limitations – to influence the people of this world. But he had not told them he would be free to influence them as well.

This was his problem. It had always been his problem. His father's influence countered his own in unexpected ways.

Well, he was the Most High of Midreer. He would use every tool at his disposal to influence as many people as possible, as he'd been commanded by his emperor. He had no choice, but it mattered little. He *wanted* to do it.

He set down the scroll. Food stuffs bored him. Roads bored him. He wanted a distraction, and a distraction was almost here. He took a breath.

His head scribe rang a chime on the other side of one the doors to the beautiful room. "Come," said the Most High.

The door opened to admit an aged man in long, many-colored robes and a golden belt. The man closed the door behind him, shuffled over and knelt. The man's knees pained him, but the Most High waited until he was on the floor before speaking.

"Rise, Willar. What do you have for me this morning, my son?"

The scribe struggled to his feet. "A scroll came this morning, my Most High. It had been delayed on the road, apparently delivered to your palace at Meer by mistake."

"From your brother, Gharan."

"Yes, my Most High."

"Was the mistake reprimanded?"

"Yes, my Most High. The messenger is in a cell, below."

He held out his hand. Willar placed the scroll in it, careful not to make skin contact. Willar had served well since birth from one of his concubines over eight hundred years ago. It would be a waste to kill him now. He still had another century of service to go before uselessness overtook him.

"You may go."

Willar bowed and shuffled out of the room, closing the door softly behind himself.

The Most High looked down on Gharan's wax seal. The signet mark looked correct, showing a stylized spider. The scroll was from Gharan. He *knew* it.

He broke the seal and unrolled the scroll.

> Father. The Most High of Midreer.
>
> Gharan, Prince, Nephilim of Mordeen, and faithful servant.
>
> All is well here, father, as you have commanded. My city grows and we reap to the north.
>
> I have recently obtained a significant supply of slaves from the village of Blacktree in Edeer. Some are normal slaves and bring income to your house. Many new bloodmothers were also obtained, broad of shoulder and hip. They have been sent to the war camps and are already brooding a new batch of warriors for you.
>
> We also obtained a dozen who are blond of hair and blue of eye. They stand tall and beautiful.
>
> One of these stood out from the others. She is most fair and strong willed. She has not been touched. We are breaking her now for you. She will make, if you wish it, an excellent addition to your harem. She seems ripe to produce Nephilim for you, father.
>
> We are ready, at your convenience, to receive your harem master. If she meets his satisfaction, we will proceed with initial training, then send her to you when she is ready. She is more beautiful than any other harem prospect I have seen.
>
> I hope you will accept this gift, father, as a token of my devotion to you.
>
> I return to the north. I have a report of another village with many valuable slaves. We go to retrieve them for you, father. I hope to find you yet another gift.

The Most High smiled and sank back into his cushions. Yes, this was exactly the distraction he needed. He could be in Mordeen, with her in her room, in an instant by taking the spirit road. His harem master, however, could not. The man would have to take a royal ship.

And yet, the Most High had work to do here. He decided not to go. Not yet. Beautiful or not, this new concubine would not be ready for some time. The harem master knew what to do. He would send him instead.

Besides, the Most High had been here since the beginning of time and would be here until the end of time. Patience was not a problem.

The End
of
*The Woodbender*

Book One
of
War of the Nephilim

If you enjoyed *The Woodbender*, please do this independent author the solid favor of leaving a review. The more reviews on the books, the more likely Amazon will be to put it in front of more potential readers like you.

If you stayed up late to finish this book, then go ahead and leave just the stars. The morning will come early. Got some time? Then feel free to say a few words. They really help.

Here's the link:

Thank you for believing.

Tripp<

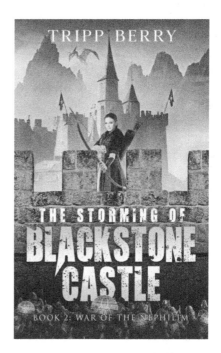

Will Kenan find Anna? Will Wren marry Lidai? Will someone finally feed Quick?

Find out. Read the next book, *The Storming of Blackstone Castle*, right now. QR code above.

# Glossary and Characters

**ABRAM Edeer.** [AY-bram eh-DEAR.] A man in his later years, fit and kindly. Master Secretary to the High Councilor Enosh in Edeer. Former student of Lamech. Known for strategic thinking, political machinations, and the love of roasted lamb.

**Age of People.** The people before the time of Noah lived much longer than today. They lived in a time genetically close to the original design created directly by God. Also, Noah's wife may possibly have introduced a genetic aging defect that she passed to her three sons and on to all the peoples of the modern world. In these books, puberty struck a person in their early teens, just like it does today. Cultural adulthood varied by nation and gender, with Edeerian men and women reaching adulthood at thirty years of age. Prime adulthood lasted until reaching several hundred years of age. The oldest man who ever lived was, as recorded, Methuselah, who reached an impressive 969 years of age, dying the same year the flood struck. Long lives could yield numerous practical, cultural, political, and technological implications. I hope the concept makes your mind spin.

**Agliranna, aka Anna, Blacktree.** [Agg-luh-RAHN-ah, AN-ah BLACK-tree.] A striking woman with blond hair and blue eyes from the Edeerian village of Blacktree. Mother: Alannoon. Father: Jaret. Betrothed to Kenan. Works as a gatherer in the forests around her village. Learning medicine from her mother.

**Alannoon Blacktree.** [AL-ah-noon.] A blond woman raising a large family in the Edeerian village of Blacktree. Wife to Jaret. Known to possess medical knowledge, both medicinal and surgical.

**Angel.** [ANE-gel.] A spiritual being, initially living in the presence of God. About a third of the angels bought into Lucifer's lies and fell with him. The remainder stayed loyal to God. Angels of both types have been known to possess people and animals, and/or take human form on the Earth. Angels commonly refer to the loyal angels, whereas fallen angels are commonly referred to as demons. The author has no idea if they really have wings, but he hopes so, because that'd be so cool.

# Glossary

**Asher.** [ASH-er.] A large man who immigrated to the Edeerian village of Blacktree. Known to many eligible young women who have varying opinions of him.

**Belroon Chimney.** [Bell-ROON (pronounced with a guttural 'R' if you can) CHIM-nee.] A strong, round man, teacher, and master at the Old Pine Tree School in Edeer. Master of armor, Jempo rolling (Brazilian Jiu Jitsu) and heavy weaponry, with knowledge of army tactics and calvary. Sometimes wears only a kilt because he knows it makes Trime uncomfortable.

**Blacktree.** The giant trees of Edeer (and many other places in the world) are extraordinarily large. At the trunk, they resemble the sequoias of California. Black trees (and many other species in Edeer, such as gopher or gray trees) have massive limbs, creating a heavy canopy over the forest. These limbs can support entire structures, keeping people off the ground for protection against aggressive dragons, other animals, and human invaders. The village of Blacktree is located in a large grove of black trees in the southern reaches of Edeer. Known to export fine bentwood products, wool, and bacon, the last of which is, of course, simply delicious.

**Bronze.** A yellowish-brown alloy of copper with a smaller part tin. Today, bronze is commonly used in sculptures for several reasons, including that bronze rust forms a weatherproof patina protecting the metal inside. By varying the makeup of the alloy, bronze can be relatively hard or soft. It could and has been used for armor, weapons, arrowheads, chains, nails, knives, cauldrons and bowls, bells, cymbals, and can be polished brightly enough to be used as a mirror. Bronze was old knowledge and in common use at the time this story takes place, with iron and, to a lesser extent, steel coming into popular use.

**Char Roughrock.** [CHAR RUFF-rock.] A dark-haired man and commander of the White Spider raiding party, known to wear brass armor and carry a steel sword. A skilled fighter, tactician, and leader of dangerous men. Has a thing for tall blonds.

**Clubdragon.** Dinosaur: Ankylosaurus and similar. Generally, an herbivore, though perhaps best described as opportunistic, the clubdragon can grow to 20 feet long and stand 10 feet tall at the back. Notable for back, limbs, and head armored in plates and spikes, and for a tail that ended in spikes or a bony club, the clubdragon was the tank of the dinosaur world, dangerous and difficult prey for any predator. Wanting mostly to be left

503

alone to find a mate, the clubdragon can be temperamental, something like the author's wife's cat.

**Cols.** [Coals.] A Midreerian raider of ill temper associated with the White Spiders. Short, heavily muscled, and overly scarred from many battles. Before battle, paints his arms with a red antibiotic and coagulating salve. His voice is relatively high pitched and raspy, which is fun.

**Crestdragon.** Dinosaur: Parasaurolophus and similar. A semi-biped herbivore with a length of 30 feet and about 12 feet tall at the hips, notable for a bony crest arcing back on its head with which it trumpets a loud call that travels miles, even in the forest. Often used by man as a mount capable of running for long periods.

**Darterdragon.** Dinosaur: Procompsognathus and similar. Not much larger than a big chicken, about 2 feet long and 1.5 feet tall, this omnivorous part-biped is considered a scavenger that can get into just about anything.

**Dragongrass, plant.** Dragongrass is a 6- to 10-foot-tall grass-like plant with somewhat sharp edges. Mature, the plant grows a stalk reaching higher than the blades to sprout a single, large, white flower. Areas dominated by dragongrass develop a thick mat of roots and mulch stretching to unknown depths below the surface.

**Dragongrass, place.** The Dragongrass is a large plain of, you guessed it, dragongrass, rumored to be dotted with smaller forests and swamps. The landform is roughly a thousand miles in diameter (about the size of Brazil) and drained by the Morderain River and many tributaries. The Dragongrass is a remote, wild place without settlements, rife with dragons of varied types and in large quantities. Would have no cell signal.

**Dragonpike.** A long spear is called a pike. Dragonpikes are regular pikes, but usually used to defend men against the larger dragons and angry wives.

**Dragonring.** Rural villages, settlements, and temporary encampments in remote, forested areas are susceptible to devastation from even a single large dragon, hungry or just ornery. Herds of dragons or other animals could wipe out a village in a single pass. A dragonring is a wooden palisade wall and/or a log/stick barrier made of sharpened stakes of varying sizes driven into the ground at an angle facing out, often with the larger logs forming the initial ring, backed by smaller posts and then even smaller stakes on the inner ring, in that order to prevent larger dragons from breaking off the smaller stakes. A ditch, wall, or traps may be incorporated into the dragonring. The barrier rings where people are sleeping and forms a deterrent to animals looking for an easy snack. If you love where you sleep, put a dragonring on it.

**Edeer.** [Eh-DEAR.] A forest nation on the western edge of a large landmass. The nation mostly exists along a low hump in the land that drains both westerly to the ocean and easterly into the Dragongrass. Most cities and villages are constructed in the trees to protect inhabitants from aggressive animals and potential invaders. A political oligarchy, Edeer has a king who presides over a high council, charged with the governance of the people. The king leads a police force called The King's Guard. The nation is defended by an army and a navy. The capital, also called Edeer, has access to the ocean via a narrow channel through the great floating forest along the shores of the land mass. The country is generally considered out of the way and inconsequential by most of the other nations, even though it's centrally located, sort of like Nebraska. Sorry, Nebraska. I love you.

**Eleenan Edeer.** [Ell-EEN-enn Eh-DEAR.] A thin, almost spindly man in his younger years. Assistant to Secretary Abram. Kind of nerdy and a little effeminate.

**Dinnane Brookstone.** [Dinn-ANE]. A tall, blond woman of middle years who leads the Brookstone Brigade, an Edeerian, all-female, archery unit. Has a gravelly, tenor voice some kilt-wearing men find alluring.

**Enoch Edeer.** [EEN-ock.] A high councilor of Edeer. Has a reedy voice that can carry.

**Fandragon.** Dinosaur: Dimetrodon and similar. (Experts argue on whether or not this is a true dinosaur. I'm not really into the debate.) A low-built quadruped carnivore, known to hunt near and in water sources. Notable for a tall fan growing on spines along its back, which it uses to moderate its temperature, to swim, and in mating displays. The animal commonly grows about 20 feet long and 10 feet tall to the top of the spine, though – like all dragons – is known to vary in size considerably.

**Flat.** The ground in forests is notoriously uneven in most areas, including Edeer. A Flat is an area cleared of undergrowth and worked flat. A Flat is used to gather military forces, as a marketplace, and as an open defensive area an enemy must cross to reach lifts, stairs, and ramps up into the branches of the villages.

**Gharan Mordeen.** [Gah-RAN (hard G) More-DEEN.] A dark-haired, blue-eyed man of average height and strong build who often accompanies the White Spider raiders. A prince of the Most High and ruler of the Midreerian city of Mordeen. Known to glow orange occasionally and supernaturally at the eyes and release a glowing orange vapor from his upper body, which is hard to explain in a spa.

**Glidedragon.** Dinosaur: Pteranodons, Pterodactyls, and similar. These creatures fly, with the front arms carrying wings somewhat similar to bats. The design of the body and head vary significantly, as does size. Larger specimens may be 25 feet long with a wingspan in excess of 30 feet. On the ground, they can stand 20 feet tall. Though found everywhere, they commonly roost in mountainous and cliff areas, especially near water sources and open landforms. They do not commonly hunt in heavily wooded areas because nothing ruins a glidedragon's day like a broken wing.

**Grinderdragon.** Dinosaur: Hadrosaurid and similar. Varying in size, the larger specimens could reach 40 feet in length and a height at the back of 20 feet. Herbivores, these "duck-billed" dinosaurs used bony jaw plates to grind their food, often noisily and messily. They make poor dinner guests.

**Gruntle Southbreach.** [GRUNT-l SOUTH-breach]. A rotund, affable man in his later years. Gruntle owns The Goosedown Filler, an inn and stable on the Southbreach Flat in Edeer, which, I assure you, makes the best lamb in the city.

**Himmons.** [HIM-ons.] A skilled soldier and lieutenant of the White Spiders. Has always been embarrassed his name starts with an H.

**Hissdragon.** Dinosaur: Allosaurus and similar. A bipedal carnivore with a length of approximately 30 feet and about 15 feet tall at the hips, it sported angry ridges over the eyes and rows of sharp teeth. Compared to the mawdragon and the browdragon, the hissdragon's arms are relatively long and strong, tipped with three sharp claws to grasp prey. Capable of climbing trees, hissdragons are commonly hunted by man to drive them away from dwellings. Some claim Midreerian use hissdragons as calvary mounts.

**Jaret Blacktree.** [JARE-ett.] A blond man and patriarch in the Edeerian village of Blacktree. Husband to Alannoon. A woodcarver by trade, though possesses a mind for engineering. Serves in the village's volunteer guard as a crescentdragon rider.

**Johlick Blacktree.** [JOE-lick.] A blond teenager living in the Edeerian village of Blacktree. Mother: Alannoon. Father: Jaret. Waves with one hand.

**Kenan Blacktree.** [KEEN-ahn.] A man with dark brown hair and hazel eyes from the Edeerian village of Blacktree who works as a woodbender and wood carver. Mother: Mardai. Father: unknown. Best friends with a man named Wren and betrothed to a woman named Anna. Has plot armor.

**Lamech Edeer.** [LAME-eck Eh-DEAR.] An old, grumpy warrior who heads the Old Pine Tree School in Edeer. Is renowned as a great general in previous wars. Lamech was an actual person, eight generations below Adam, and in the genealogical line of Jesus. He fathered Noah, of ark fame. I have no idea if my description is anything like the real Lamech. I'm old, but I'm not *that* old.

**Lidai Blacktree.** [Lid-EYE.] A young woman with dark brown hair and hazel eyes from the Edeerian village of Blacktree, just old enough to have lowered her dress hem. Mother: Mardai. Father: unnamed. A renowned archer who hates kitchen chores.

**Lift.** A rope with a loop or plank, or multiple ropes with a platform, used to raise or lower people and cargo, often to or from a Flat. Most lifts use water cisterns to generate hydro counterweights to lift or lower their loads. Wooden springs and cogs automatically fill and empty the hydro counterweights and brake the rope to control velocities. Lifts are operated by a simple wood lever connected to a controlling cord at each village level. This engineering is 100% plausible. Unintended heavier or lighter than normal loads could overwhelm the mechanisms, causing out-of-control lifts, which are super fun until they ruin your day.

**Mardai Blacktree.** [Mard-EYE.] A dark-haired and blue-eyed woman living in the Edeerian village of Blacktree. Mother to Nehamane, Kenan, and Lidai, as well as many others. May or may not be modeled after the author's own wife, depending on what she thinks of the character.

**Maryleen Archmouth.** [MARE-eh-lean ARCH-mouth.] A thin, willowy woman of advanced years, teaching as a master in the Old Pine Tree School of Edeer, primarily in archery, knife work, and for women and girls in the schools, who are outnumbered by men 20 to 1. Originated in the village of Archmouth, located where the Edeerian channel through the Great Floating Forest reaches the open sea. She could kick your butt.

**Mawdragon.** Dinosaur: Tyrannosaurus Rex and similar. A biped with a length of 50 feet and perhaps 20 feet tall at the hips, this large carnivore used massive jaws full of 6-inch teeth to eat whatever it wanted. Generally easy to identify from a distance, the mawdragon wasn't a common threat to man except when they were prodded. Has binocular vision, full depth perception, and can see you, even if you don't move.

**Medahal Blacktree.** [MED-ah-hall.] An older man living in the Edeerian village of Blacktree. Known as an expert and teacher in Jempo and a mentor of Kenan. Would slap each and every member of the village council if he could.

**Midreer.** [MIDD-rear.] A nation south of Edeer, along the western shore of a large landmass and extending easterly up the Morderain [Mord-uh-rain] River. The land is flat, sometimes hilly, and heavily cultivated. Peopled by dark-haired men, many of which are bred into the large army. All women in Midreer are slaves by law. The culture has nearly exterminated the family as a social unit. Procreation is instead a slavery business. The nation is led by a god-king known as the Most High. His sons, princes of the nation, rule cities along the river. Some raid other nations for women of prized coloring and physical features. Midreerians speak with a strong accent notable for chopping the H sound off the beginning of words, which is cool to hear but hard to write.

**Nehamane Blacktree.** [NEE-ah-mane.] A dark-haired man from the Edeerian village of Blacktree. Mother: Mardai. Father: unnamed. Switchbrother to Kenan and Lidai. Lost to a slaver's raid in 1546 AC. Nobody really misses him.

**Nephilim.** [NEFF-eye-limm, or NEFF-eh-limm, your choice.] The offspring of a fallen angel in human male form taking a human woman for procreation. These are real hybrid beings the bible says existed both before and after the flood. This means there could be actual Nephilim walking the earth even today. Stay tuned for future books. Biblical scholars do not agree what a Nephilim really is, what they look like, or what – if any – powers they might have. They were "men of renown," and may have been giants. The author has no interest in taking part in such arguments and makes no claims of biblical scholarship, so he just made it up. It's a writer thing.

**Okay.** An earnest and perpetually hungry shielddragon owned by Wren to haul logs. Likes to gross people out by blowing mucus out his nose at regular intervals.

**Olaine Brookstone.** [OH-lane BROOK-stone.] A tall, blond woman with light brown eyes serving as an archer in the Brookstone Brigade. Very good at making Kenan forget what he was about.

**Old Pine Tree School.** An informal educational organization headed by Lamech and three prime administrators: Trime, Belroon, and Maryleen. Teaches the art of Jempo, a way to manipulate conflict to favor the practitioner. In real life, the Old Pine Tree School is a real school headed by Hanshi Bruce Juchnik, teaching the martial arts of Kosho Kempo, Jiu Jitsu, and other styles in multiple countries. The author can be found from time to time sweating profusely in one of these dojos, trying not to get punched in the head. Again.

**Overshirt.** Most common men wear a heavy shirt hemmed at the knees and cinched with a leather belt at the waist. Sleeve length and pockets varies, depending on the season and activity. Under the overshirt, men wear, as you might have figured out, an undershirt, which was changed daily for a man to be considered presentable. Underwear was typically not worn for convenience in the woods and at the privy. Sandals or calf-covering boots were worn on the feet. Really, who needs pants?

**Patedragon.** Dinosaur: Pachycephalosaurus. A semi-quadruped of medium size, stretching to about 15 feet and 5 feet tall at the shoulder. Notable for a dome of bony skull trimmed with short spikes used for ramming. Wildly temperamental and the bane of the forest. Vocalize with an annoying croak.

**Quick.** A completely innocent and totally misunderstood raccoon, living in complete harmony with and to the unappreciated benefit of Jaret's household in Blacktree.

**Rillain.** [Rill-ANE.] A man over six feet tall with a well-groomed red beard. He's a Nephilim, with orange and red vapors, and fights with a rapier, which is a long, narrow steel sword of great dexterity and speed. He's also a Toeclaw, with the tattoo on his wrist. Everyone he meets wants to wipe the smirk off his face.

**Secondmother** (thirdmother, and similar.) A person's grandmother (and great grandmother, etc.). In a society where people commonly live many hundreds of years, you may grow into your prime while your great, great, great, great, grandmother is also still in her prime. With so many relatives, you would either number them or get great at saying the word great.

**Shielddragon.** Dinosaur: Triceratops and similar. A quadruped that could commonly grow about 30 feet long and 15 feet tall, notable for three prominent facial horns and a bony frill extending over their neck, though the number of horns varied. Domestically, often used to pull heavy loads and sometimes used in war. Capable of blowing out copious volumes of mucus, which is fun to describe in writing. Sorry. I stopped emotionally maturing at twelve.

**Slabdragon.** Dinosaur: Stegosaurus and similar. A quadruped, about 30 feet long, and notable for large, bony plates along its back and spikes on the tail. Some species had spikes in lieu of plates, and/or no spikes on the tail. Domestically used as a beast of burden by poorer workers due to a bugling cry that sounds similar to the irritating screech of an angry toddler combined with a Monday morning alarm clock.

**Spinedragon.** Dinosaur: Spinosaurus and similar. A semi-quadruped carnivore of large size, this creature could grow 60 feet long and reach 20 feet to the top of a distinctive, large, spine sail along its back. It was semi-aquatic, at home on shore or in the water, and ate a lot of fish and other aquatic species. Extremely aggressive near a nesting site or within its hunting grounds. Though dimensionally similar to or even larger than a mawdragon, it wasn't as heavy and was designed to be stronger in the water. Would totally not win against a T-rex. Period.

**Stalkdragon.** Dinosaur: Brachiosaurus and similar. A quadruped with a length that could exceed 120 feet and could reach 70 feet or more up, prominent for its large size, long neck, and whip-like tail. Intolerant of carnivores, small birds, and anyone trying to climb it for fun.

**Stemdragon.** Dinosaur: Brachytrachelopan and similar. A quadruped with a length of about 30 feet and a height of perhaps 15 feet. Similar to a stalkdragon but generally shorter and smaller. Stalkdragons consider them inferior cousins and turn their nose up at them, but no can tell because everyone sees them from below.

**Stompdragon.** Dinosaur: Scelidosaurus [good luck pronouncing that one] and similar. A quadruped with a length of about 12 feet and a height of around 3 or 4 feet. Skin often embedded along its back with bony plates shaped round, oval, or oblong, sometimes spiked. Can run gracefully but walks with a stomping gate. Often used as a beast of burden. Vocalizes by hooting. Loves to eat flowers and lick things.

**Swampdragon.** Crocodillian: Alligators, Crocodiles, and similar. Some species grew very long legs. Others grew much larger than their modern descendants. Hunts and feeds in and near water and will roll their body to thrash and injure their prey. Not known to shed real tears.

**Switchbrother** (switchsister, and similar). A partial relation. Half-brother or stepbrother, etc.

**Tadd Southbreach.** [TAD] An introverted orphan taken into the Old Pine Tree School of Jempo in Edeer. Eerily observant and quiet. If he likes you, good luck shutting him up.

**Tardain.** [TAR-dane.] An old man and high councilor of Edeer. He cackles, plays politics, and generally sounds friendlier than he is. He's high councilor Enosh's prime opponent. Invites people for drinks and is surprised when he gets stood up.

**Toedragon.** Dinosaur: Raptors, Velociraptors, and similar. Small, bipedal carnivores about 6 feet long and 2 feet tall at the hips, though larger species existed. Notable for one of their toes being retracted and the claw respectively longer, used to pierce larger prey deep enough to reach vital organs. Toedragons work together to harry prey into an ambush and to weaken and take larger prey. The females have been called clever.

**Trime Brookstone.** [TRIME BROOK-stone] A dark-haired teacher and master of Jempo and weaponry in the old Pine Tree School in Edeer. Though quiet and slight of build, he is one of the most dangerous men in Edeer during his time.

**Ulneer.** [ULL-near.] A nation north of Edeer along the western shore of a large land mass. Mostly mountainous, the nation thrives on the sea and along narrow fjords and river valleys protected by cliff-side fortresses. The people are tall and blond with blue eyes. Rumored to have exotic mammalian animals and glidedragon pets. Ulneerian metalwork is sought everywhere, and they have unlocked the secrets of steel, which they guard zealously.

**Whitetail Wasps.** Dolichovespula Maculata. A black hornet with a white face and white rings around its lower abdomen. Common across much of North America and the author's home state of Maine. They build gray paper nests commonly 12 inches in diameter and usually up in trees. They are the biggest jerks known to the insect world and the author hopes they all run into a giant can of Raid.

**Wren Blacktree**. [RENN.] A tall, well-muscled man with blond hair and blue eyes from the Edeerian village of Blacktree. Mother: Alannoon. Father: Jaret. Works as a lumberman, cutting trees and using his domestic shielddragon to haul logs to his village for cutting. Also works with his best friend Kenan carving wood. Sister of Anna and entangled with Kenan's sister, Lidai, perhaps against his will.

**Yarro Mordeen**. [YAH-roe.] Dark haired and skinned man working in Mordeen as the breeding master for Prince Gharan. See also: a man you want to stuff naked into a burlap bag with a roiled-up nest of whitetail wasps. Wow. That was dark. But still.

# Scriptural Apology

BUT, Tripp, this isn't at all what the world was like before Noah's flood. Yeah, I know. Sort of.

I've read the whole Bible, most of it many times. I'm not super smart or theological. I'm just getting old, love the Lord, and have been reading the Word daily for a long while. I repeatedly studied the early parts of Genesis before and as I wrote this book. I've been to the Creation Museum and the Ark Encounter in Kentucky, which, by the way, I highly recommend. They're worth the trip. For more information, go to www.answersingenesis.org.

But science is not my life's work. I'm an engineer by training, not an historical or biological scholar. Thankfully, I don't need to be. I just need to know enough to write a Christian Fiction book about a fantastical world that *might* be something like the world before the flood.

Could there have been floating forests over some of the ocean? Sure. Could Triceratops have been domesticated? Sure. Could Nephilim have burst into glowing vapors? Sure. Prove me wrong. But the world described in this book and the story contained therein aren't true. I made it all up. Other than the biblical principles presented in this book, it's not fact. It's fiction. Christian Fiction. It's right there in the name.

But, as I wrote, I tried to get it close based on my research and understanding. As an engineer, I use scientific discoveries. I don't make them and don't think I'm smart enough if I wanted. So, maybe I just don't know. If you think I got something wrong, I'm all ears and interested. Please help. Educate me by writing at www.facebook.com/TrippBerryAuthor.

If you do, please, don't be a troll. Be respectful. Cite your sources or your credentials. If you don't, I'll probably ignore you. I'm busy writing my next book.

# Acknowledgments

First, thank you to my childhood friend, Jeremy Rogers. In early 1990, he handed me the first book I ever read that hadn't been assigned by a teacher. The first edition, full sized paperback with a cover that screamed adventure was titled *The Eye of the World* by Robert Jordan. Thanks, Jeremy. You opened a whole new world to me way back then in wickedly rural Maine. The love of reading and adventure stuck with me for a lifetime.

In turn, thank you to the great writer Robert Jordan, may he rest in peace. Your work still entertains and inspires millions of people, including me. What a legacy!

Thank you to author Brandon Sanderson. We met once, at a book signing in nearby New Hampshire. You signed an Alcatraz book for my young son and told him he was, "Not Crapflapnasti." You inspired him to go on to a degree in creative writing. He still reads your books often and wears a T-shirt that says, "I am a stick!" At the time, I told you I also aspired to write someday, and I asked for a tip. You said, paraphrasing, "The number one tip I can give to an aspiring author is to just start writing." I hadn't planned to write this book until I retired from engineering, but I took your advice. I'm glad I did.

Thank you to Ken Ham and his team at Answers in Genesis. I'm a technical person and not a little nerdy. The history presented in Genesis was a real stumbling block to me when I was young. Your work helped deepen my faith and contributed significantly to my understanding of a pre-flood world. Please continue your important work, and may God bless you.

Thank you to my alpha readers. Kendall Bliss is wise beyond his demeanor and the best friend a man could have to trounce at cribbage up to camp. And, most of all, bar none, thank you to my darling bride and grammar guru Lisa-Anne Berry, aka author Evelyn Grace. Thank you. Every book I ever write will be for you. Always.

Thank you to all my beta readers. They are, in alphabetical order: Randy Bliss, Deelight Daniel, Tim Gallant, Rev. Doug Palmeter, Kimberly Smith, "Jumping" Jonah Sparling, Travis Tardif, and Carolyn Trevino. These friends spent their valuable time reading junk and helped me make it better. Thank you, all!

Even after all those drafts, edits and many re-writes, the book wasn't quite ready. I finished with gamma readers, and it's a good thing since I have no idea what comes after gamma. Thank you to Dave Ainaire and, once

## Acknowledgements

again, my bride Lisa-Anne Berry.

Thank you to Jamie at 100Covers.com, who drew the beautiful cover art that grabs your eye and makes you think, "Dragonscrape, I hate spiders." See their work at www.100covers.com.

Thank you to K&J Couture Designs for the awesome chapter and section graphics as well as the cover layout. See Kim's wonderful work at www.behance.net/kjcdesignsme.

Thank you to Edward Snyder who drew the map. Every adventure story simply must have a map, and I spent hours poring over this one. It's true magic. Contact him at www.fiverr.com/rogue451.

I thank my dad and mom for pushing me when I was young in the direction I should go. Now I'm old, and you still inspire me. Every good thing I've ever accomplished is because of you. The many bad things I've done are all because of me.

Most importantly, thank you to the one and only God of heaven and earth. Jesus, there is no one who loves me more than you. Thank you for dying so I might live. Thank you for your Word. Thank you for your church, and I pray she may be strong, generous, and full of love to glorify you. Come back soon. I can hardly wait.

# Exhortation

Not a Christian? Not sure? Well, it's important. Stick with me.

See, none of this is a cosmic accident. God made the world "very good," which is saying something from the perspective of a perfect being. But then we screwed it up by turning away from God. It wasn't just Adam. It was me, as well. And you. Think about it. We've all done bad things. Worse, compared to the holiness of God, all our sins are horrible, even the itty-bitty things. They're all disgusting, terrible, and wicked bad compared to God's perfect holiness.

God is also a perfect judge. Would it be right for a robed judge in a court of law to free a criminal because the judge is his father? It wouldn't be right for God to set us free either, not without paying the price for our crimes.

We all want into the kingdom of heaven instead of, you know, the other place. Heaven is in the presence of a perfectly holy God. He's so holy, His innate glory will destroy any impurity. To get to heaven, we need to be perfect and holy as well.

Have you felt perfect lately? How about holy? Yeah, me neither.

So, it makes sense. The price must be paid for justice to prevail and for us to enter heaven. What do we need to pay? Perfect justice has only one penalty for the worst crime. Our crime comes with the death penalty.

God knows our sins. He knows every little thing we've said, done, or even thought. God knows these things because He loves us perfectly as well. He pays attention to us. He knows we don't deserve to go to heaven, yet He loves us perfectly and wants us to be with Him.

God is perfectly holy, perfectly loving, and perfectly just. So, He did something awesome about our situation, something only He could do, something perfectly holy, perfectly loving, and perfectly just. He came down to earth, put on the body of a man, spent years living history's only perfect life, then paid the price for us through death on the cross. Only He could do it. And He did it because He loves us so much.

There's a catch. There's always a catch. Jesus died once and thereby forgave everyone for anything they have ever done or ever will do, which only a perfect person could do. But He will not let everyone through the gates into the kingdom of heaven. We must do our part.

Wait, what? Our part? You probably heard all this is free.

Yes, it's a gift, and what an amazing gift! But there is no such thing as free. We do have a part. Our part is simple. It's also very difficult.

We must accept and follow. This is no light decision.

Accepting means believing. God hasn't yet scrolled back the sky and peeked through so there would be no doubt. Believing means accepting God is real even though He is invisible to us. God really created the universe. God really created you and I. God really came here as a man and die for us. God really gave us a book about history and about Himself, so we could know what He wants from us. It's all true.

Accepting also means submitting to His way. We love to believe the illusion we are our own masters, but not so for a Christ follower. We belong to Jesus. We try to follow His way, not our way. In other words, we accept He is Lord of our lives. That's why we call Him that. We have a master and accepting means obeying.

Accepting also means being in a relationship with Him. We can believe. We can submit. But if we do not know one another, there is no relationship. This is where it gets fun. A relationship with God is awesome! He loves us, guides us, protects us, and calms us through the storms of this broken world. When I do wrong, which seems like all the time, He readily forgives when I ask, and we're friends again. Just for the asking! No one in your life can match it.

There is much to gain by acceptance and so little to lose. You get knowledge, guidance, character, and joy. You get eternal life in a place of love and wonder instead of a place of fire, tears, and anger. You get to know God and be in the most important relationship of all. But before you get any of it, you must accept.

Interested? Accept right now. There's no magic hand gesture. There's no televangelist's number to dial. There's no password. God is with you, right now as you read this. He's knocking at your door. If you haven't already accepted Jesus as your king, then He's hoping you'll do so right now. It doesn't matter what you've done. He loves you. He's crazy about you. He wants you to know Him. He wants a relationship with you.

Just talk to Him. Tell Him you're sorry you messed up so bad. Ask for His forgiveness; He'll deliver it. Tell Him you want to be part of His family, a child of God. Admit to Him you cannot get into the kingdom of heaven on your own. Tell Him you'll follow Him wherever He leads and mean it.

It takes faith in Him to take this step. It's a faith that He is real. It's a faith His way is better than your way. It's a faith His promises are true.

But it's not a blind faith. Read about His Way in the Bible. Try the book of John. Try the book of Romans. Try any of it because His love has been steady throughout history.

Want to know more? Go to www.fayettebaptistchurch.org . If you've just accepted, email them and ask for more information. Someone there will reach out to you and help you find someone in your area who will walk with you on your journey with God.

# About the Author

TRIPP Berry, aka Robert L. Berry III, P.E., Child of the One True God, is a country boy from the back woods of Maine. Whenever he can, he escapes to some quiet corner to the north, usually up to camp on Moosehead Lake, to fish poorly, chase woods critters with a bow and arrow, listen to loons, and write his heart out.

Tripp owns and runs Main-Land Development Consultants, Inc., a land consulting firm of engineers, surveyors, and environmental scientists helping people prosper on their property. Main-Landers are warriors in the battle for the American Dream.

Tripp serves on the board of directors for the Franklin County Chamber of Commerce, the Greater Franklin Development Council, and New England Bible College. Tripp helps on the committees for the annual Apple Pumpkin Festival in Livermore Falls, and the annual Spruce Mountain Sled-In Winter Festival in Jay, the latter of which he founded in a rash moment of over-exuberance.

Tripp also serves on the board of directors for Franklin Savings Bank, based in Farmington, Maine. You'll find no better community bank. Period.

Tripp wrangles middle schoolers in Sunday School at Fayette Baptist Church. Matthew 5:16. Shine on, you amazing kids. Never stop making noise!

Tripp lives in Maine, with his wife Lisa (aka author Evelyn Grace), three sons: Benjamin, Nathaniel, and Jackson, all of whom he is extremely proud, and his wife's nefarious, rotund cat named Maggie, but whom he calls, alternatively: Shai-tan, Odium, Sauron, or, when looking particularly fat, Maggie Meatloaf. Tripp's pretty sure it's plotting to kill him and take over his writing. If things take a particularly dark turn, then you know who to blame.

Made in the USA
Coppell, TX
13 February 2025